They're the
CALIFORNIA GENERATION

The golden spoiled youth in a sun-drenched land of dreams—where the stars come out at night to see and be seen, where money, beauty, and sex pave the way to success, and where everyone hopes to ride off into the sunset...

MICHELE, the young mother-to-be, is waiting for her happy ending.

STRYKER, the high school jock, is flirting with dangers beyond his dreams.

MARSHALL, the straight, is struggling with his own homosexuality.

LEIGH, the dream girl, has fallen into the arms of a most inappropriate lover.

KEN, the artist, is blinded by a mad passion for the movies.

YORK, the celebrity's son, just wants to be alone.

CALIFORNIA GENERATION
JACQUELINE BRISKIN

"A teasing and intelligent storyteller...
Jackie puts the creators of the trashy
Hollywood novels to shame."

—HOLLYWOOD REPORTER

"Fresh...marvelous!"

—LOUISVILLE COURIER-JOURNAL

CALIFORNIA GENERATION

JACQUELINE BRISKIN

BERKLEY BOOKS, NEW YORK

This is a work of fiction. The characters are born of my imagination and if they, by some chance, resemble any real person—living or dead—it is purely coincidental.

This Berkley book contains the complete
text of the original edition.
It has been completely reset in a typeface
designed for easy reading and was printed
from new film.

CALIFORNIA GENERATION

A Berkley Book/published by arrangement with
Warner Books

PRINTING HISTORY
Warner Books edition/July 1980
Berkley edition/October 1986

ISBN: 0-425-09537-1

A BERKLEY BOOK® TM 757,375
Berkley Books are published by The Berkley Publishing Group,
200 Madison Avenue, New York, NY 10016.
The name "BERKLEY" and the stylized "B" with design
are trademarks belonging to Berkley Publishing Corporation.

PRINTED IN THE UNITED STATES OF AMERICA

and helicopters from Helios
flew over us
            dropping free railway tickets
From Lost Angeles to Heaven

—Lawrence Ferlinghetti,
*A Coney Island of the
Mind*

As part of the twentieth reunion of the class of '60 a memorial was held in the red brick auditorium of California High. The alumni, after finding spaces in the school's new parking lot, glanced covertly through the hot, yellowish haze at one another, attempting to identify who hid under that beard (streaked with white, for God's sake!) or below that skillful make-up. All, inevitably, were trapped in an awareness of temporal corrosion. How could they be middle-aged, they who were so recently young comrades-in-arms at the disputed barricades of their decade?

Part One

1

California High draws its students from a district shaped roughly like a wedge of pie.

The narrowest point lies in the secret folds of the Santa Monica foothills. These peaked wrinkles are a wildly expensive geologic outcropping—in the midst of Los Angeles a crazy wilderness where mule deer forage and fox, raccoon, rabbit and the small gray field mice go their nocturnal way. Since this spring, 1960, has been wet, California poppies paint the chaparral-covered hills with giant brush strokes of molten gold; in another month tall white bursts of yucca will glow like man-high candles. Tortuously winding roads forbid sightseeing buses. Celluloid aristocracy, Baron York among them, are willing to pay a ransom for this rustic privacy.

Cross Sunset Boulevard and you come to gentler hills and less palatial, but still handsome, houses—tile-roof Mediterranean, Colonial and Tudor English—set back in accordance with zoning regulations a minimum of fifty feet from tree-lined sidewalks. This area, realtors will point out, is hot. Well-off business and professional men with young families compete to pay swollen asking prices for roomy houses on large lots, hopefully level, a bare thirty minutes from downtown, not during rush hours, of course.

Around California High families of Japanese and Mexican descent crowd in the small frame bungalows built forty years earlier by nostalgic Iowans who came west to retire with all-year sunshine and oranges-picked-right-from-your-own-tree.

Further south, in the flats between Olympic and National Boulevards, handsome new architect-designed factories mingle with shambled, crumbling motel courts.

The widest stretch, the crust of the school district pie, is formed by the vast stucco monotony of Parkdale. The tract was built on marshy ground after World War II with One and Three-Quarter Baths, 40-Gallon Water Heaters and Sidewalks, VETS NO DOWN. More than a third of all California High students come from Parkdale, and all of these are—in school board parlance—Anglos.

Before the morning's slow sun has burned through Pacific mist, California High's bastard sprawl of Gothic and Mission architecture, its long barracks of "temporary" wood classrooms erected at the same time as Parkdale to accommodate the influx of students, will echo, clatter, blare with a restless three thousand and twelve. Almost all are native Angelenos. They are inquiring of mind, tall, strong, straight of tooth and bone, tolerant, golden tanned and beautiful. Each one who is a day over sixteen carries a photo-imprinted driver's license, the State of California's official coming-of-age diploma. They seem mutants, a new race more akin to one another, despite the obvious economic and racial chasms, than to the war-weary ones who bred them. But then, as Dr. Schramm, the school's bald, gravel-voiced principal, rhetorizes, why shouldn't they be different? Aren't they the first generation to have transistorized music wherever they go, to be raised on smog and Dr. Spock, on parental permissiveness and paperback pornies, on televised puppetry and frozen TV dinners, on Charga-Plates, credit cards and chocolate-flavored cereal, on the black leather seating of orthodontists and child psychiatrists, on fallout-contaminated ice cream and Salk vaccine, on dual-control Driver's Ed and grammar school sex education?

The children of the angels. . . .

That one foggy morning in April it was all over California High. Dorot McHenry had it from the horse's mouth, and she spread the word to the other Rondelays.

"They're getting married Sunday!"

"So soon? Hmmmmm . . . ?"

"No fuss, no muss, no time to waste?"

"Is she?"

"You're undermining the institution of matrimony," said Dorot. "She claims she isn't."

"How d'you know?"

"The simplest way. I asked."

"Oh, Dorot!" The girls were thrilled. "You didn't have the nerve."

"Why not? We're friends. She said no, *no,* of course it wasn't *that.* But . . . she told me in gym. . . ."

"And?"

"Girls, believe me, she was having troubles zipping her shorts."

"I'm dying." Ruth Abby Heim fanned her face. "Michele Davy and Clay Gillies!"

"They're in love. That's why they're getting married."

"Leigh Sutherland, your problem is you think everybody's as unpolluted as you are."

"Hey. Where're they going to live?"

"With her parents."

"If you can't get away from that noise, why get married?"

"Ruth Abby, must you be so inane?" Dorot asked tartly. "I explained. Anyway, is there another reason?"

"I don't see why, with all that drugstore junk you can buy," Ruth Abby wailed.

"A girl can't buy any reliable form of contraceptive without a doctor's prescription."

"You've tried, Dorot?" someone asked cattily.

"Har de har har."

"Just think," sighed Leigh Sutherland. "Michele Davy married...."

"The first in our club."

"Doesn't it make you feel really ancient?"

A few minutes later, alone in a second-floor art room, Leigh Sutherland smudged green pastel onto inaccurate apples. Leigh was almost beautiful, but didn't quite make the grade; her mouth was too wide, the dreamy hazel eyes a shade too remote. Her most striking feature, the other Rondelays told her, was the dark red hair that had never been cut, only trimmed, and fell straight past her small waist. Males, however, noted her legs. On meeting Leigh guys would glance at those long, shapely legs, so fine-boned they appeared fracturable, and would mumble embarrassingly out-of-date words like *class* and *thoroughbred*. Through open windows came the raucous scherzo of California High enjoying midmorning nutrition. Leigh had foregone the free twenty minutes; her still life, scratched, erased and nowhere near finished, was due this afternoon and Leigh Sutherland wasn't the type to brazen out a late assignment, not even with an art teacher.

The front door swung open. A tall Japanese boy paused, gripping the knob, frowning at the board where alone, in the place of honor, was thumbtacked a sketch of the pseudo-Gothic auditorium. Leigh pasteled at one of the back tables, and the boy, not noticing her, moved slowly toward the sketch. There was something proud, arrogant even, about the way his neck rose from his square shoulders, about his ease of walk. He acted as if he owned this art room. Leigh didn't exactly know him, but she knew who he was. A friend of Clay Gillies. Ken Igawa.

Leigh coughed to let this Ken Igawa know he wasn't alone.

He didn't turn. Taking a yellow pencil from his jeans, with long, sure fingers, he corrected the pitch of the auditorium's roof.

Good manners were ingrained in Leigh. She coughed louder. Still no response. She cleared her throat and said, "Miss Verney's not around."

He penciled on.

All that noise! Could he have heard? Leigh was aware her voice was small—people, teachers especially, were forever saying, *Speak up, Leigh dear, we can't hear you.* She cleared her throat. Anxiously. Ever since Dorot McHenry—her friend!—had unearthed and displayed around California High the printed evidence that the Sutherlands, Leigh included, were listed in the Los Angeles Blue Book, Leigh worried she might get a reputation for being snobby.

This time she practically shouted. "You're a friend of Clay Gillies, aren't you?"

He turned. His flat-set eyes found her.

"Huh?"

"You're a friend of Clay Gillies, aren't you?"

He nodded.

"D'you know he and Michele're getting married?"

"Hey, no kidding?" He smiled. "When?"

"Sunday. Isn't that terrific?" Her enthusiasm, real as it was, had to be shouted over the din and across rows of tables and wooden easels. It rang phony. "I mean, seriously—"

"Seriously, it's Lee, isn't it?"

"L-E-I-G-H." As always, she spelled her name.

"Yeah yeah yeah. I knew it couldn't be plain, dull, ordinary L-E-E."

She felt heat rising from her collarbones to burn above the neck of her white sweater. Quickly she bent over her misbegotten green apples.

• • •

Stryker Halvorsen, six five and a natural athlete, paused on the raised mound of adobe dirt to fake a few slow curves; the muscles of his arms ridged easily. He continued across rank, pale grass to a bench where Ken Igawa rested.

Ken's rib cage, glued by sweat to a sleeveless gym shirt, expanded and contracted violently. "Ran the mile," he panted an explanation. "Five fifty-seven."

"Pretty good," Stryker said.

By now the sun had burned through fog and the sky was a hazed blue. The two boys watched the track. Runners strung out, chests thrust forward, reddish dust rising around their canvas shoes: to Ken they resembled figures on one of those old Greek friezes; to Stryker, a two-year letterman in track and basketball as well as baseball, they were a bunch of guys running the mile and not very well.

Ken, his breath coming easier now, asked, "Hear Michele and Gillies're getting married?"

Stryker turned his bright blue gaze on Ken. "How's that?"

"Joined in holy matrimony."

"Jeez—so he's been getting it," Stryker said good-naturedly. "A great-looking girl. How'd you like some of that?"

Ken gave Stryker Halvorsen a quick, uneasy glance. He was sweating. Maybe because he'd just run the mile in five fifty-seven, maybe because he was still shook from that L-E-I-G-H giving him the phony-snob treatment, or maybe because in moments like this Ken Igawa invariably sweated. *(Yeah yeah yeah, I know nowadays it's equality, fraternity and all that crap, but how'd you like me putting it to your sister?* This mental question he did not ask in a querulous chip-on-the-shoulder way; simply, he never quite knew how far any white guy felt general human conditions should prevail—he himself had a tremendous number of old-fashioned ambivalences and anxieties on the subject.) But Stryker's bold features, if lascivious, were relaxed.

Even so, Ken equivocated, despising himself for saying, "It's private now, just for Gillies."

"How'd you hear?"

"That snob redhead in Michele's club told me, the one who thinks she's so great."

Adam York strode clatterous halls the way all loners did, staring directly ahead. The intelligence of his pale wedge face was masked by oversize lenses of dark glasses. Short and thin, he kept his deformed hand thrust into a specially tailored pocket. There was no resemblance, none at all, between him and his famous father, and even though this meant York was neither handsome nor well-built nor tall the differences pleased him greatly. Who wanted to look like a phony-baloney, sexie-flexie movie smoothie?

Clay Gillies fell into step.

"Michele and I're getting married. Sunday," Gillies said without preamble.

York turned. The dingy yellow of bulbous overhead lighting fixtures bounced off his dark glasses.

"Christ! Gillies, you're a careless bastard."

They were passing the boys' head.

Clay Gillies, reddening furiously, pushed in.

York stared at the door as it swung in decreasing arcs. Although he prided himself on his cool, on not caring for others, his throat suddenly hurt and he wondered, *Why the shit did I say that?* Then he thought, *Maybe I can help.* He broke into a trot as if he were hurrying away from his own impulse to kindness. While he might be proud of his cool he also admitted that it never quite had penetrated his thin skin. He had acquired it years ago, age six, because he was sensitive and malformed and he'd seen even then that it's better to reject first than to take your chances at being rejected. This was the major reason he admired Clay Gillies. Gillies possessed the exact qualities that York dared not permit himself. Gillies was uncynical; he spoke with conviction about human goodness; his brown eyes could shine with enthusiasm. Gillies let himself become *involved.* As York jogged around the slower bodies that descended metal-edged stairs he couldn't help thinking of what this too-early marriage would do to Gillies. You might as well lock Gillies in a Leavenworth cell and throw away the key— he and Michele were that obviously mismated. York's thin eyebrows drew together. He'd seen at close range, in his own home as a matter of unfortunate fact, what happens in a rotten marriage. His well-polished boots moved slower. *Maybe I can help,* he thought again.

Third period Dorot McHenry, as eleventh-grade treasurer, took Student Government, which was required of all holding school office. She sat in her second-row desk not listening as Dr. Schramm, the principal, on an unscheduled class visit, lamented the perpetual litter on California High's campus. Dorot had more important matters to ponder. Michele Davy and Clay Gillies. Dorot's well-formed lips pulled together. She rubbed her retroussé nose where horn rims left a permanent dent—glasses were to Dorot, a straight-A student, the proud badge of the intellectual. But, far more than studies, people fascinated her. She accepted all things human without prejudice and a vast amount of interest. And now here hallelujah were her own friends getting teen-age married! Unconsciously she smiled.

Dr. Schramm, in his gravel tones, said directly to her, "I'm glad to see someone agrees with me."

Third period Marshall Mosgrove, student body president, also had Student Government. After Dr. Schramm departed, the class splintered into five policy groups to study the Keep Kampus Kleen Kampaign. Chairmen consulted with one another, then with Marshall. After a while Dorot came over. Her habit of forever asking personal questions and speaking more openly than most girls about sex were qualities that Marshall, for one, found alarming. They discussed painting trash cans yellow; then Dorot, in her loud voice, asked, "You've heard about Michele Davy and Clay Gillies?"

Marshall grunted noncommittally. It had been a low blow when Michele had broken up with him (the student body president!) to date Clay Gillies, a new senior, a nobody on campus.

"They're getting married," Dorot said. "Sunday."

It was as if she'd punched Marshall right below the buckle of his neat madras belt. His first thought was of the new-car smell of his grandmother's Buick sedan on that moonless night of the Thanksgiving Dance. He'd attempted to knead one of Michele's large, doughy breasts and she'd made such a fuss ("What kind of girl do you think I am!") that he'd spent the next half hour sweating through an apology. How she must have been laughing! The idiot he'd been! It was obvious now, wasn't it, that she'd been putting out for everyone but him?

Dorot, through her horn-rimmed glasses, examined his discomfort. "You used to date her, didn't you?"

"Oh, sure." Marshall gave Dorot a fine view of his orthodontia-straight teeth. "We're friends. Always have been. You're in the same club?"

"The Rondelays," Dorot agreed. "Everybody in school's talking about it."

• • •

   They were. Michele Davy, by virtue of dating almost every
worthwhile male around, was the best-known girl in the junior
class. At lunch the gossip exploded like water from a broken
dam, surging through the cafeteria, swelling over the hash lines,
washing across the Senior Patio and down ivied green slopes
to the paint-blistered tables of lesser mortals, rolling across the
straggly fields where raucous noon volleyball was played,
reaching behind the boys' gym, that favorite hiding place of
smokers. Whispers trickled through the dusty library where
lurked the sad lone wolves. Speculation whirlpooled in the
faculty dining room. Dr. Schramm let his rough voice rise as
he once again formulated the school board's stand on married
pupils: they cannot be denied an education—the girl, if pregnant (and what else?), may continue until three months prior
to delivery.
   Along with the talk went a lot of smirking, but as there is
no pollution in running water, so there was no condemnation—
except, of course, in the faculty dining room. Boys, in their
tight, pale Levi's, agreed that Michele Davy was great-looking
and Clay Gillies had been: (a) lucky, (b) careless and therefore
(c) unlucky.
   The consensus among the girls was that Michele Davy, at
sixteen years and seven months, had achieved her goal in life.
Love sweet love and its natural corollary, marriage.
   "My mother!" Ruth Abby Heim wailed at the Rondelay table
after Michele had departed hand in hand with Clay. "She's a
tiger about college."
   "Aren't they all?"
   "Yet *they* never use their educations," pointed out Dorot,
logical as always.
   "Michele did it right," Ruth Abby insisted, draining her
chocolate milk carton, not noticing the dribbly spill on her pink
sweater. Ruth Abby was a slob. A plump, rosy-cheeked girl
with thick, curly brown hair, thick ankles, thick unplucked
eyebrows and a clear, sweet singing voice. Even her best friends
(except Leigh Sutherland) admitted she wasn't real bright, but
they always brought up her voice as a countermeasure. She
carried her Martin guitar everywhere, from time to time removing it from its case and breaking into sweet, mindless song.
Ruth Abby continued, "Now she gets to drop out of school and
everything."
   "*Beaucoup* everything," said Dorot. "Imagine making love

with your parents in the next room?" Dorot, sociologically inclined, wondered what her idols, Drs. Kinsey and Terman, would make of this aspect of the increasing teen-age marriage scene. "Do you think—"

And then someone turned on her transistor.

The KRLA announcer: "—and now our fabulous, fantastic, phenomenal top five. . . . " A long pause. "'Theme from a Summer Place' by Percy Faith, 'Sixteen Reasons' by Connie Stevens, 'Puppy Love' by Paul Anka, 'Stuck on You' by Elvis Presley and 'Wild One' by Bobby Rydell."

"'Summer Place,' that's my favorite." Leigh sighed. "I hope they play it first."

"Michele's really lucky," Ruth Abby insisted.

"Time alone will tell," said Dorot. "Don't we all know the dismal statistics on teen-age marr—"

"Oh, Dorot!" the girls cried, disgusted.

Dorot, staring through her glasses in honest bewilderment, asked, "Well, don't we?"

"And now, the one, the only, the great Bobby Rydell and 'Wild One'!"

———————— 2 ————————

Michele Davy, in fifth-period study hall, saw two girls she didn't know lean acne-sprinkled cheeks together, whisper, then glance at her. They were talking about her. Let them talk! Naturally they were talking. Wasn't she Michele Davy?

Michele had carefully arranged, lustrous blonde hair, large round eyes of a sealike blue-green color and full lips that never quite seemed to meet. Yet when boys called her great-looking it wasn't her face they paid tribute to. Short and curvy, Michele gave tremendous care to the selection of well-engineered, lacy, D-cup brassieres. Her posture was such that she held her shapely breasts high and forward as if offering a tray of fruit. Today she wore a new sleeveless pink dress. New clothes were armor to Michele, and in this pink wool she was invulnerable.

The two whisperers glanced again at her. Michele caught

the eye of the fat one and coldly stared her down. *Drop dead*, Michele thought, *die now*.

She opened *A History of the American People* to the assigned chapter on World War I. Along the margin next to a photograph of Woodrow Wilson, twenty-eighth President of the United States, she wrote *Mrs. Claibourne Peter Gillies* and on the bottom of the page *Michele Davy Gillies*, curlicuing the final letters of each name and dotting her *i*'s with tiny daisies, smiling at her handiwork.

Michele liked the idea of being married.

Liked it a lot.

She didn't like the idea of a baby.

Not at all.

That was Clay's fault. It was up to the guy, wasn't it, to make sure *that* didn't happen? She stared at Woodrow Wilson's bony face and her full lips for once closed. She was unwilling to admit, even to herself, that if Clay had left her at any time, trotting into the slit of a bathroom in that dump he shared with his father to put on one of those thingums, or into the kitchenette to grab some Saran Wrap (everyone knew the nonkitchen uses of Saran Wrap, didn't they?), she would have been dirtied. It would have been an admission that they weren't carried away by passion. And in all the novels Michele had read—skimmed, actually, to get to the sexy parts—the lovers fell onto a convenient bed, soft fur rug, couch, shaking earth, sand (wet or dry), bathroom floor (wet or dry), car seat, mound of autumn-scented leaves, lovers borne away by great pulsing waves of ecstasy. Without a thought. Certainly not of precautions. Precautions were an open admission that this act was no tidal wave of passion. Using one of those rubber thingums or Saran Wrap admitted you knew exactly what you were about.

She slammed the book.

She told herself again that it was all Clay's fault.

Of course it wasn't.

Actually everything had started because Michele had a necrological crush on the late James Dean. Michele had been dating since she was a well-developed twelve. These boys, all well-known on campus, signified her popularity the way a bank passbook indicates wealth. But love? The trembling down there when she gazed at James Dean's broody photographs, that was love. The way she felt when she saw a rerun of *East of Eden*, that was love. Boy friends were simply entries in Michele Davy's personal bank balance.

"I want to meet this boy," Mrs. Davy would say at each first date.

"Of course, Mother."

"And I want you home by twelve."

"Aren't I always?" Michele would raise bored, tweezed eyebrows.

"And Michele. . . ."

"Yes, Mother?"

"You mustn't let . . . boys—take liberties."

Mrs. Davy, squat and massive bosomed, favored brown tones. Even her fixed Yorkie, Dozer, a snarling mop of hair, didn't have the black markings common to the breed but was totally brown. She had been forty-one when Michele, her only child, was born. This time gap overwhelmed her. Mrs. Davy, in the neat, brown, early American living room of her Parkdale home, would rest her thick, slippered feet on the ottoman to ease her varicose veins, brooding about the children of today . . . oh, the girls had no innocence, everything you read and saw nowadays was sex and smut and the boys wore indecent, satin-tight jeans. Mrs. Davy, taking a shaky breath, would wish fervently that she could fix Michele's dates the way she had fixed the tiny dog now nipping at her slippers.

Mrs. Davy needn't have worried.

Would a businessman gamble his hard-earned capital? Would Michele Davy allow more than a single open-lip kiss in the dull yellow glow of the light over her C-plan front door?

The fall semester of her junior year Michele noticed a new boy. A transfer from University High. A senior. He wasn't tall, but he was lean and tense and well built. Under thick brown hair his deep-set eyes were shadowed, giving him a vaguely haunted look, as if some tragedy were locked in his past. Michele asked Leigh Sutherland—they shared a second-floor locker in the Administration Building—whether Leigh thought this new boy resembled James Dean. Since the interior of their locker was papered with Michele's fan-magazine photographs of the dead actor, Leigh, murmuring a truthful "Yes," must have realized Michele's query was in the nature of a confession.

Clay Gillies was his name.

He proceeded to waste his time at those noon political rallies; he hung around with people like York—a nobody on campus even if his father was the movie star—and Ken Igawa, a Japanese. But there was something about Clay Gillies. . . . Michele started having these crazy dreams where James Dean blended into Clay Gillies, dreams from which she'd waken with her rounded thighs clenched and the funniest sort of empty pressure down there.

Michele plotted a campaign.

At the attendance office, using the pretext of finding an address for Miss Paton, her gym teacher, Michele committed to memory Clay Gillies' schedule. His classes were located as far from hers as geographically possible. Still, if she took the longest routes. . . . On the fourth morning she sighted him in the pergola. Shoving past a group of Mexican kids, she turned her head as if calling to a departing friend; she bumped into Clay Gillies full force with her breasts. "Oh, 'scuse," she said, placing a small hand on his firm arm to steady herself. He muttered, "S'O.K.," and continued on. Well, Michele's motto was if at first you don't succeed, try, try again. So she tried attending one of the weekly rallies on the lower patio, convincing Leigh Sutherland, who was the most humanitarianly inclined of the Rondelays, to go with her. Michele, liberally anointed with Jean Naté, maneuvered them through the crowd of nobodies until they stood next to Clay Gillies. The hot midday sun burned down. So much the better. Heat brings out perfume. Some Negro girl began to read a dull speech about restaurants in Alabama. Michele let her books thud onto cement. Clay Gillies hissed, "Shhh!" He didn't offer to help her pick up the books. Well, if at first you don't and et cetera. The next weeks she pushed behind him at the clattering fruit machine and in front of him at the library line; she paused to chat with friends near his locker; she yawned through every dull noon rally. Nothing.

Michele certainly didn't give up. But, in the meantime, she started dating Marshall Mosgrove, student body president-elect.

One Friday night Marshall took her to see a Natalie Wood movie at the Bruin in Westwood. Michele laughed, cried, enjoyed herself. Afterward Marshall and she went next door to Hamburger Hamlet. The red leather booths were jammed with people from California, Unihi and UCLA; at least seven groups waited ahead of them.

"We better try someplace else," Marshall said.

"Oh, look, look!" Michele cried. "Isn't that Ken Igawa? And the new boy, what's-'is-name? They've got a booth."

With that Michele shoved by the protesting hostess, through the almost palpable odors of barbecuing beef, around waitresses with laden trays.

"Ken!" she cried.

"Michele!" Ken cried in the same excited tone, then he gave her his easy, pleasant grin. From the corner of her left eye she could see Clay Gillies watching.

"Ken." She curved a hand to her firm stomach. "I'm dying of starvation."

"Yeah yeah yeah, can't have that, can we?" Ken, agreeably, squeezed onto the other side with Clay Gillies; Michele sat on just-vacated warm leather, Marshall crowding next to her.

After the introduction ("I think I've seen you at school," Clay Gillies said; "I don't remember," Michele dimpled) and the order giving, Marshall mentioned they'd just seen *Cash McCall*.

"It was excellent," Marshall added. Marshall believed in the power of positive thinking, and he had never, in Michele's hearing, made a negative remark.

"How could a movie with both James Garner and Natalie Wood be anything short of excellent?" drawled Ken in his easy, sarcastic way.

"It was quite thought-provoking," Marshall said.

"Hollywood has yet to make a thought-provoking film," Clay Gillies said. In his somewhat high-pitched voice lingered a softness, and Michele remembered hearing someone say he came from the South.

Marshall started, "They've certainly tried—"

And Clay interrupted, "Come off it! When you consider the field of civil rights alone, you must admit the failure. Has Hollywood ever shown Negroes except as chauffeurs? Or eye-rolling *Gone With the Wind* mammies?"

"I don't see the racial issue has any bearing on *Cash McCall*'s meaningfulness," Marshall said too slowly. Upset, he always spoke ponderously. Michele wondered if the tension between Clay and Marshall had anything to do with the anti-election rally Clay had organized last fall.

She opened her box-shaped purse which was in her lap, surreptitiously peeking in the mirrored lid to make sure her lipstick, Silver Apricot by Revlon, was still on. Politics of every kind bored her. Clay Gillies said something. Marshall Mosgrove stammered. Ken Igawa drawled. Marshall Mosgrove mumbled. Michele snapped shut her purse.

"Here we are," Clay Gillies was saying, "in the middle of the revolution of our century, and the movie industry pretends it's a snow-white world." Brown hair tangled at his wrists; a strong shadow of beard lay along his jaw. Michele decided she preferred hairy men. Clay probably had to shave before he went out on a date.

"I agree with Clay," she said. *"Cash McCall* was a waste of time." She heard Marshall's hurt little cough next to her. But Clay looked right at her and she stared boldly back. "Movies ought to change the way people think." She was speaking to Clay, only Clay. "I mean instead of the commercial junk they grind out—like *Cash McCall*—they should be right in there influencing people."

Clay Gillies, still watching her, put an ice cube in his mouth.

She went on. "TV, too. After all, do we ever see a colored person in a good role?" She broke the stare to glance at Ken Igawa, adding, "Or an Oriental?"

"Hey, don't mind us. We velly smarr minolity gloup."

They all laughed.

Except Marshall. He said to Clay, "Well, coming from the South, I shouldn't think you'd be such a liberal."

"Shouldn't you?" Clay replied, ice in his mouth and in his voice.

And Michele cried, "Oh, Marshall! What a tired old cliché. All Southerners aren't bigots!"

Marshall, betrayed, pressed his square fingers on the table until his neatly filed nails turned white. But evidently as they drove home his hurt anger faded. As they parted under the reproduction carriage lamp, Marshall asked her to go next Saturday night to the Cavalier. Michele, who'd been dying to get there, turned him down, saying she was grounded. It was a gamble. She won. Clay Gillies phoned about five on Saturday to ask if he could drop by.

Clay was very serious, all wrapped up in the civil rights movement; it was all he talked about, and the truth was Michele had to agree with Marshall Mosgrove that Clay's attitude was very unusual for a Southerner. Clay came from a little town in Virginia, Port Claibourne; Claibourne was Clay's full first name, and the place had been founded by his ancestors; although very poor, he was what novelists call "a gentleman born," descended from aristocratic slaveowners. While Michele cherished these romantic snips of information, she had to admit they in no way explained Clay's liberal notions.

From the first she'd known it was for real.

Before, when a boy kissed her and she felt that strange, coiled tightness growing in his pants, she'd been repelled. With Clay it was different. When it happened her own insides melted as if to engulf them both. They drove up to Mulholland, parked, spent hours and hours making out on the fraying front seat of his old Chevy coupe, the door open so they could stretch their legs out, the muscles of her pelvis submissively weak, his thighs hard and demanding, their armpits drenched with acrid sweat that, whatever TV commercials might say to the contrary, did not repel but acted as an aphrodisiac. She hated her parents, her mother, really, for the rule of twelve. Mrs. Davy, sensing something different about Clay Gillies, was invariably watching the late movie when Michele got home, calling out as Michele and Clay started their first tongue-thrusting good-night kiss, "Come in, dear, and bring Clay for a cup of hot chocolate. It's after twelve."

"What's going to happen after twelve?" Michele wailed. "Am I going to turn into a pumpkin?"

However on this particular subject Mrs. Davy, usually putty in Michele's small, exquisitely manicured hands, was surprisingly firm. "Twelve is late enough," Mrs. Davy said.

But. Anything you might do after twelve you can do before. Mr. Gillies went away for a weekend. Michele demanded to see where Clay lived, so he drove her two miles south of California High to a crummy court next to Mirano's salad dressing factory. When you opened a window the smells of vinegar, spices, garlic and heavy oil sickened you. But she loved him anyway. The dinky living room was jammed with gloomy, tall mahogany that had come from Port Claibourne, and over the sagging day bed where Clay slept hung a pair of swords crossed, points down, tassels like tarnished horses' tails drooping from worn gilt handles.

"The weapons of ole cuhnel Maxwell Gillies, CSA," Clay explained. "How do you undo this, Miche? He was hit by a Minié ball at Gettysburg."

"Never heard of it. Here, let me."

Time passed. Agreeably.

"We better stop," Clay said.

"Yes."

But she had no intentions of stopping. She tightened her arms around him, glorying in the wonder that her qualms (this *was* a big step) were minor compared to the pounding of her blood, the welcoming quivers between her open thighs. The cover of the day bed was coarse and smelled dusty and hurt her bare back and Clay's fuzzy hard chest was crushing her breasts and she had never, never in her whole life imagined something blunt could hurt so much and she began to despair; it would never happen, never, never, never, she was positive he couldn't manage it. She was almost screaming when he whispered, triumphant, *"Miche, Miche,"* and began to push, pull almost out, push, pull almost out, like the action of her mother's old Singer sewing machine, and this thought made her forget the pain—well, almost forget the pain—and give a small giggle that she quickly stifled. He was going faster now, sweaty and alien. She bled on dusty tweed.

In a couple of minutes he finished, jerkily and quickly, to sprawl panting on top of her. A strange, flat smell spread around them. She murmured, "Now I'm really yours." Months ago she'd thought up this remark for when Clay "took" her, but now the words didn't come out romantic and soft as planned. Clay's wet, inert body squashed her breasts so she could scarcely breathe, much less speak.

They did it a total of five times, three under the crossed swords of Colonel Maxwell Gillies, CSA, two jammed uncomfortably on the front seat of the Chevy coupe. To be honest, it was a disappointment. Nowhere near as passionate as making out. She had problems relaxing enough to let him put it in, and she disliked afterward, when he fell abruptly asleep on top of her. This made her feel, wrongly she knew, that she was only a body to him. Then, two weeks ago, it was raining, and Michele had just finished her routine nightly twining of blonde hair on huge purple aluminum rollers when she remembered a certain physiological fact. She swayed down the short hall, one small, balancing hand against brown patterned wallpaper. In the mirrored bathroom cabinet she found her mother's brown cascara. She swallowed five pills.

Violent diarrhea, nothing else.

A few days later the nausea started. Not only in the mornings like you read about, and never bad enough to make her throw up, but a constant dullness in the pit of her abdomen. Of course it was true. But . . . how could it be? How could such a niggling activity produce such disastrous results?

Her period was a subject she and Clay had avoided mentioning. She wondered if he, so mathematical, kept track. Two more days and she could no longer bear the wondering. As they emerged from the Bruin, in a very low, very grave tone she told him.

"You're positive?" he asked.

"I feel barfy all the time, too," she said.

He paled. The shadows under his brown eyes were like bruises.

"I love you, Miche," he said soberly, pausing in front of Coming Attractions to put a protective arm around her shoulder. "We'll get married. Right away."

In a funny way she'd been disappointed. Without actually thinking it through she'd hoped he would marry her *and* come up with a different solution for the other . . . still, she couldn't help being pleased that her Clay was so idealistic. Honorable.

Michele realized she was smiling. She also realized that the clock had just jumped noisily and under it the two acned girls were again peering at her and whispering. Well, a sad twosome like that, gossiping must be their only kicks. But not on little Michele's time! She gave each in turn a glare—if looks could kill!—and pimply faces reddened, hastily drooping over notebooks.

Michele reopened her *History of the American People*.

"—just the family," Michele shouted. School out, the clanging of lockers was deafening.

"So wonderful." Leigh, smiling her slow, dreamy smile, pushed back a strand of long red hair. "Think of it, Michele. Married. . . ."

"Clay doesn't want to put me through a bunch of old-fashioned ritual." Michele, giving an involuntary sigh of exasperation, peered in the round mirror glued to the door of their James-Dean-lined locker. "Only the family."

Clay Gillies always left his Chevy on Camino Road, three shabby blocks from school; parking time there was unlimited. The sea mist that had dampened the morning again drabbed the western sky. Clay carried his worn navy windbreaker, shivering yet not pausing to put it on. It was three twenty. At three thirty he was due at work, cleaning Dr. Feiner's pathology lab. He couldn't afford to be late, not now; he needed the job.

As Clay strode along he thought of Michele. Whenever he thought of her—like now—his whole body got in the act and he tightened and ached for her. The truth was, he was glad they were getting married. She was sweet and generous and he was crazy about her. His mother had died when he was born, he had no sisters, he'd never gone with another girl, and Michele's kookiness and softness, her giggling over Bobby Rydell or that dead actor, delighted him. Gender, definitely feminine. Yet they had long, serious discussions that proved to him they had everything in common. He was crazy about her. And married they wouldn't have to be sneaky. Clay loathed being sneaky. When she'd told him about the baby, her voice suddenly quaking, he easily had found the words to say they would get married. And once the words were spoken, his arm around her, his chest had filled with the same surge of power as when at noon rallies he emptied every last coin from his jeans pocket. He was doing the right thing. As far as Clay Gillies was concerned, the worst sin practiced by your older so-called liberals was the severing of their emotions from their actions. He, Clay Gillies, believed in the cause of the new abolitionists. He gave his all. He loved Michele. He would marry her. The same principle, really, if—

"Gillies," grated a masculine voice behind him.

Clay turned.

"York," he called.

He waited. He considered York a friend, but since this morning when York had made that crack about his coming marriage, Clay had ached to hit him. Again he felt his fists clenching. Then he reminded himself that York had a deformity and you don't go around clouting deformed friends. It wasn't an easy reminder. The slight, pale boy approaching, Clay decided, was your classic example of an obnoxious loner. Take, just for one example, the way York dressed. Not that Clay gave a damn about externals, but it *was* an indication. California High males, universally tanned, wore Levi's and unpolished black loafers. York ostentatiously differed. Untanned, he wore a houndstooth-check sport jacket, his crippled hand tucked, as always, in a pocket tailored high for the short arm, white shirt and striped silk tie, richly glinting brown calf boots, dark glasses. It was as if York wanted everyone to remember who was his father. Yet York, Clay knew—everyone knew—sneered at all phases of the motion picture industry, including that most illustrious phase, Baron York.

As York caught up, Clay again hurried toward his car.

York, keeping step, asked, "What's the rush?"

"I can't afford to get fired."

"You really *are* hooked?"

"York, listen, let's get this straight. It—is—my—business."

"I thought I heard you talk about college. I guess I heard wrong."

"I'll manage," Clay said. "It's being done."

"You've been reading Ripley." York's bony shoulders shrugged under checked cashmere. "An MA in Computer Science isn't the point. Tell me, Gillies, I know you're an idealist. The strong, honorable type. But every girl who lets you put it to her, you plan to marry?"

Clay's fists clenched again.

York continued, "There *is* a simple operation."

"Listen—"

"Why? I'm the one with something to say."

"Your father being a big movie star doesn't give—"

"You pious prick, *shut up!*" York hissed. The thin fingers of his good hand, the right one, gripped Clay's upper arm. For a furious moment they glared at one another; then York dropped his hand. "I'm trying to help," he said sourly.

Clay, furious as he was, realized this must be the truth. And York didn't go around helping people. As a matter of known fact, he went around rebuffing people. He said to their faces, *Either it's my brain* (York had an effortless four-point grade average) *or you want to kiss the sweet pimpled ass of a movie star's kid. In either case, forget it!* Clay himself had gotten acquainted with York only because of Ken Igawa. Igawa and York were friends, if you could use that term in connection with York's carbolic, strictly on-campus relationship with Igawa.

"Hasn't the idea," York was asking, "occurred to you?"

Clay shivered in the chill damp. Of course the idea had occurred to him! Dr. Feiner, the big-bellied, kindly pathologist, his employer, in trying to divert Clay from computers to medicine, let Clay use his library. Clay had committed to memory certain passages in the black-bound copies of *Diseases of Women*. He knew all about the steel bars to dilate the vaginal passage, the spoon-shaped curette to scrape unwanted material from the womb. A simple routine operation, a D & C. This new-found gynecological interest had nothing to do with the way he felt about Michele. She had bulbous pink nipples that drove him crazy. Blonde down grew soft on the inside of her thighs. He loved her. He loved her. He had made up his mind to marry her. This weekend. Still, wouldn't marriage be easier if they waited a while (preferably a long while) to start a baby? The truth was, the baby never had seemed real to Clay. Oh, he knew it *was* real, but . . . Without realizing it, he'd put on his jacket. He zipped it slowly.

"I'll call tonight," York said as if the matter were settled. "Give you the phone number."

Clay opened his mouth to say thanks.

Say it.

thanks, thanks. Thanks. THANKS. *THANKS!*

"Thanks," he heard himself say, "but no."

"No?"

"No," Clay repeated.

"If it's finance. . . ." York let his voice trail away.

"I don't have it," Clay said. "But that's not the point. The thing's wrong."

"What's wrong with a Stanford-trained Beverly Hills gynecologist? The guy's got an itch for the wrong horses and a letch for the right nurses, but so? Professionally, he's tops."

Clay's mind kept whirling around York's offer. The baby wasn't reality. At this moment, according to Clay's obstetrical reading, a blob the size of his little fingernail clung like a leech to the softness inside Michele. So why give a regular signed-in-blood *no* to York, York who not only offered the doctor's name but also his personal MediCal program? Why no? Clay was at his car. He gripped the rust-roughened door handle.

He said slowly, "I meant a moral wrong."

"Gillies, even *you* have to be kidding!"

"It's taking a life."

"You're a Catholic?"

"D'you have to be a Catholic to live by standards? You know I'm against killing—"

"Tell it to Pope John. This's a routine scraping."

"I mean it. Either you believe in something or you don't."

York's dark glasses fixed on Clay. Clay's head rotated almost imperceptibly. No.

"O.K." York shrugged. "We'll celebrate the ethical experiment Saturday. A stag at my place."

"York, I really appreciate the offer. And the party." Clay held out his hand.

York didn't take it. "Nine," he said. "My place." And without another word, he crossed the street to his bronze T-bird. Quick power hummed as he dug away.

Clay pumped gas until his coughing motor caught. Waiting

for it to warm, he relived the conversation. In the past he'd often wondered how he would react to a definite temptation to sever his beliefs from his course of action. He had worried. Up until now he hadn't been sure of himself in an acid test.

"I passed," he said to the old car. "I passed. What do you know? I passed." And as he shifted gears, his loud, true tenor sang out the words, "I passed, I passed, I passed. . . ."

3

Friday night
   on Hollywood Boulevard. At the wheel of his Thunderbird, York inched along, part of what he termed "the weekend pre-fucking parade." In front of him, in a low, open Mercedes, three pretty blondes jangled tambourines; trying to attract the blondes' attention a gang of guys in black letter sweaters loudly jostled one another off the curb. Sedate button-down college couples walked along eyeing the maneuver. Junior high kids raced, shrilly hurling Cracker Jacks at one another. York took in the excitement, his bulging, intelligent gray eyes automatically screening out Hollywood Boulevard's rare older pedestrians—sad, rouged old bags and unhappy fags, who in tight, bright slacks lurked near tawdry shops in an effort to evade the sharp glances of the Hollywood vice squad. York saw only the mindless, cheerful young. He felt a million light years from them.

He got out a cigarette. Unwilling, he thought of Gillies. In a grudging way he respected Gillies' decision. Yet, being York, he couldn't help seeking out the invisible worm that flies in the night. Why *had* Gillies said *no?* To make himself virtuous? Did he really believe his words? Did he fear for the boobed wonder's life? Was there some deep psychological connection with Gillies' own mother dying in childbirth? York couldn't figure it. He knew only that the *no* had hurt. A rebuff. In York's mind he had emerged from his safe, rejection-proof castle of privacy to aid a fellow human being. Even in this liberal, youth-oriented day there weren't many seventeen-year-old guys armed with access to a good abortionist, and he, York, had offered to share this precious weapon with someone who obviously needed it in the worst way. And for his pains had been rebuffed. A rebuff always reminded York what he was. A midget, skinny, with pimples on his back. Deformed. Gillies had reminded him that he was a sad creature to be pitied. York dropped his barely smoked cigarette on the car floor and with his narrow, well-polished boot viciously stubbed it out.

He was inching past the Egyptian. *The Lion Gates* was in its tenth road-show month. He gazed in the opposite direction. Above the Egyptian's glittering marquee jutted a floodlit, thirty-foot-high wooden cutout of Baron York in gold Greek armor displaying the fabulous musculature. Hollywood beefcake at its beefiest.

York made a sudden left, cutting around oncoming traffic, causing a wild jar of brakes, honking and obscenity. On the side street he fished a paper from above the dash. 9845 Poinsettia Calle was this week's address. Each week he sampled one of the numbers in his father's little black book. Actually the book was Gucci baby-brown alligator cornered with eighteen-carat gold, kept out in the open, in his father's mirrored dressing room, not hidden at all from the bewildered gaze of Linda Farnahan York.

The girl was a couple of years older than he, nineteen at most. She wore slacks, a V-necked powder-blue sweater, loose over tiny breasts. She used only pale pink lipstick and she smelled of lemon soap, as if she'd just showered. The addresses he copied from his father's little book were never call girls. They never mentioned cash. Generally, though, they would let slip a remark about a dress they'd seen in Magnin's; it cost forty-nine fifty. That way they kept their pride and you kept yours. *Never paid for it yet.* The money changed hands not for services rendered but as a thoughtful gesture, like tipping a *maître d'* because the meal had pleased.

She was staring at him, lines forming on smooth tan between her large green eyes.

"I called before," York said. "York's the name."

The girl swallowed. She had, of course, been expecting his father. Unconsciously—York could tell her action was pure reflex—she almost closed the bleached chestnut door of her apartment.

He said into the crack, "I'm not afflicted with rabies."

Tilting her long honey hair she continued to peer at him in perplexity. None of these girls quite knew how to gauge him, but so far—despite all obvious physical dissimilarities—each accepted him for what he wished he wasn't. His father's son. Therefore for a variety of reasons they all said, as she said now, "Come in, please?"

He did.

"Drink?" she asked. To make up for her recent uncertainty, she gave him a brilliant smile. "Mmmm . . . let's see. A bourbon man?"

His father preferred bourbon. "Beer'll do," York said.

While he downed Pabst Blue Ribbon she relaxed and relayed the news in *Variety* and *Reporter,* the trades, parenthetically mentioning a stunning sweater she'd seen in Saks' window which cost fifty-five dollars. York removed his dark glasses. Up until now there had been doubt. Now the odds were unbeatable. After ten minutes he shifted to the low white divan, cuddling the girl's shoulder with his left arm; it was child-short and only three fingers grew from the stubby palm. Her muscles tensed. Normally he kept the hand and arm hidden. But with these girls of his father's he felt a need to use it—let the *Psychoanalytic Quarterly* bunch make of this what they would. She reached for the lights. He said, "I prefer to see."

"So do I," she replied, pulling off her sweater. She wore no bra, her naked breasts were flat little cushions as tanned as the rest of her, the nipples large, flat, brown as maple syrup. She smiled, skinning slacks from her narrow, pantless hips. Her fine, neatly clipped pubic hair was the same color as the hair on her head. She sat naked and cross-legged on the white rug next to him, and from a certain angle she might've been a boy—almost. York was curious. He never called a girl unless in his father's large, uneven scrawl was written *Boffo!* above her name. What made this one superior to those tasty pneumatic actresses that normally his father nibbled? Why had this girl, gravely unbuttoning his shirt, earned Baron York's personal *Croix de guerre?*

She led York to the bedroom where she proved her skill; he didn't have to do a thing—*was old Stone Face getting lazy?*—she sighed satisfactorily and slithered her slim body at the appropriate moments, but as far as York was concerned she had no true vocation, none at all; the act was more lonely and impersonal than if he were masturbating while driving down

Hollywood Boulevard and she were in the next car doing the same. This was how it always was. He sighed. The fault, obviously, was his. As he dressed he dropped five tens and a five on the painted bedside table. "Send yourself a present," he said.

When he got home the hillside mansion had its nighttime air of being larger and more lonely than by day. But day, night, what difference? Lonely was the most descriptive adjective for the place, even though five servants, his two younger sisters and his mother were scattered in the twenty-odd rooms under the vast shingle roof.

In the den Mrs. York sat, feet up on the long, curving white couch, letting Jack Paar kid her not. As usual she nursed a drink. She wore a drapy, clinging, square-shouldered hostess gown that looked as if Adrian had designed it for an old Janet Gaynor movie. All York's mother's clothes were fitted and draped as though designed by A. for old J.G. movies. Maybe the style meant something to her, York had decided when he was on his Freud kick; maybe it was some sort of dream fulfillment from her hungry girlhood in the dusty flatlands around Bakersfield where Fox had been the lone, shadowy citadel of glamour and Adrian the magician who had spun wondrous garments for its princesses. Or, then again, maybe his mother simply had rotten taste. This particular gown was plum, a shade she unfortunately favored. It yellowed her skin and made her short-cropped black hair seem unnatural. Which it was. Its natural state was a premature pure white. Linda Farnahan York two days earlier had celebrated her forty-third birthday.

"Your father's not home," she greeted him brightly. "He had a business meeting with Carter." Carter Klein was his father's business manager and agent, a short, saurian-faced smiler subject to coronaries and therefore permanently condemned to a ten-o'clock bedtime. Yet Mrs. York, each evening her husband absented himself—and he absented himself every evening that he did not have on the following morring a six-thirty call at Makeup—delivered this same brightly spoken explanation to her children.

"Sit awhile?" she asked wistfully.

"If you like."

"I like."

"Jack Paar should package himself as an emetic."

His mother looked uncertain.

He added, "He makes me want to barf. Upchuck. Toss my cookies."

She giggled. "Honest, he works that way with me, too."

And she flicked at the remote control. Still smiling like a Cheshire cat, Jack faded. Mrs. York took a long swallow. York felt a sharp ache of pity. Life stunk. No matter how you sliced it, life stunk.

"Cheers," York said and sat on the end of the couch.

"Want something?"

"I already had my quota."

"How much?"

"Don't panic. I'm not your average teen-age alky."

She smiled.

"I like it when you do that," he said.

"Do what?"

"Smile."

"Honest, am I such a sourpuss?"

With two fingers of his right hand York pulled down the corners of his thin lips.

They both laughed.

"What was that?" she asked. "I've seen it before."

"The mask of tragedy."

"Ohhh."

"In Greece the actors wore them. Tragedy . . . the word derives from he-goat and—"

"Sometimes I wonder where it comes from—your mind, I mean," she said. "I'm not really what you call bright—"

"Don't underestimate."

"And your father's talented. He is, Adam. But he quit school in tenth grade. Where *does* your mind come from?"

"The stars, dear Mother; the fault lies not in ourselves, but in our stars."

"Fault? Honest, most people would jump for joy if they had an IQ like yours. One hundred and seventy-one they told me at school."

"Those tests're notoriously inaccurate."

"You're brilliant."

"This cross-my-palm-with silver character reading, it's not the real you."

"I was being sort of philosophical tonight." She sighed. "Some day you'll hit forty-three and you'll understand. You want to see what it all adds up to."

"Found the sum?"

She shrugged helplessly.

"My guess," York said, "is that everybody's adds up to the same."

"Well, I have three nice, bright children. A good husband." As she spoke her lips trembled.

For Christ's sweet sake, York ordered himself, *don't argue either point.*

Outside, one of the huskies howled, waking the others to chorus mournfully into darkness.

Mrs. York asked in a purposefully brisk tone, "Where were you?"

"Hollywood. The lights are bright." And abruptly he added, "Tomorrow I'm having company."

Mrs. York sat slowly upright, purple crepe flowing around her. The dogs quieted.

York, in his seventeen years, had been neither a guest nor a host. Even in kindergarten he never had invited anyone home, not so much as a girl. As he grew older no pals came to the sprawling house bearing chamois bags of marbles; no buddies for a game of pickle—and the Yorks' side lawn was larger than a regulation baseball field; no chums to watch movies in this long room—a screen was concealed by the (supposed) Monet water lilies over the fireplace. About his friendlessness his mother had kept her silence, either out of sorrow, pity, empathy, guilt or helplessness, whatever the combination of emotions that a mother must feel for a lonely, imperfectly formed child. Or why not call it by its rightful name? Love. *Love.* Just as from love of her, York never brought up the unpleasant subject of his father's behavior.

She recovered. "That's nice," she said.

"Guy I know's getting married."

"Isn't he in school?"

"Ahhh, but he knocked up this girl and marriage's the way *that* cookie crumbles."

"A stag?" she asked.

"A stag," he agreed.

"When we got married, one of the assistant directors threw one on the sound stage. Even though your father was only a bit player then, honest, everybody came. Glenn, Harry—"

"I'm sure it was a clubby get-together." York cut his mother short. Give her a chance and she'd extol the Great Granite Face until he appeared better beloved than George Washington, St.

Paul, Odin Allfather, Agamemnon and King Arthur rolled into one—he'd played them all.

"Should I order cheese or—"

"Pretzels. Beer. That's all."

"I should stay away...?"

"Girls wishing to attend a stag should always dress in drag."

She smiled. Suddenly York could no longer take the hopeful pleasure shining in his mother's somewhat bloodshot gaze.

Yawning elaborately, he said, "It's been a long night." He stood, rotating his narrow shoulders as if the muscles ached with weariness.

She inclined her cheek. He bent, touching lips to paper-dry soft skin. She smelled of twelve-year-old Scotch and that queen bee jelly she imported from Paris in black jars at forty bucks an ounce to keep herself young. He kissed her good night. He loved her with a love, he'd decided, in which there was nothing Oedipal. It was simply a case of to the victims belong the other victims. To the victor belong the spoils.

York's father, who was called Leroy York in those days, had come to Hollywood out of the Ojai oil fields, not a victor but a six-five, broad-shouldered tool dresser of nineteen. He could sit a horse well and was possessed of a nerveless kind of raw physical courage. He became a stunt man. He drifted, content with the attentions of pretty extras, enjoying poker games with grips and fellow stunt men. Strictly small time. Small time he would have remained if it hadn't been for two accidents.

York, undressing in his high-ceilinged, book-lined room, thought about those two accidents. He was the second.

The first...

One blazing dusty August afternoon at the Columbia ranch in Burbank the stallion Leroy was riding threw him as planned, then kicked his head as not planned. Silver replaced missing bone.

During World War II, Hollywood lost the able-bodied men it needed to fight its celluloid battles and Leroy York, 4F by virtue of silver in his skull, was promoted. He was Cary Grant's cowboy shipmate, the one who died so valiantly in the first reel; he was Van Johnson's kid brother getting his legs blown off ("Don't tell Mom yet...promise, Buzz?"); he was Rita Hayworth's first love being knifed by sneaky Japs at the jungle beginnings of the movie, before poor Rita became a tramp. Leroy York's diction was stilted, there was a sameness of expression, a stoniness to his handsome, rugged features, but he moved across the screen as lithely as an Indian brave on the prowl.

After the horse kicked Leroy, a goodhearted script girl—he'd been boffing her pretty steady; she had a plain Irish face but a fabulous figure that she displayed with flashy clothes—invited him to convalesce at her place. After about ten and a half months she told him of the second accident.

York, getting into his nicely turned-down bed, imagined the scene.

She'd always been a good sport, so she doubtless added, "There's a doctor over in Van Nuys."

"What the hell, honey, why do that?" Leroy probably replied. He, too, liked to think of himself as a good sport.

And so they were married.

It was Linda Farnahan York who got her new husband a top-notch agent, that black-suited renegade from MCA, Carter Klein. It was she who suggested that Leroy York didn't ring quite true and anyway Baron sounded more like a big, masculine sort of guy. She was the one who constantly telephoned, badgering and badgering Carter Klein—"Honest, you haven't made the arrangements *yet*, Curt, doll?"—until finally he arranged a test for the newly dubbed Baron, never dreaming a bit player had the smallest chance at the year's shiniest plum, St. Paul.

Baron got the part.

Since the script dealt with that rugged playboy of the Roman world, Saul, before he hit the road to Damascus, Baron's sex appeal, hitherto submerged by treacly, eunuchoid roles, came across larger than life. As Carter Klein said reverently during the wild applause that broke out from time to time during the sneak preview, "Jesus! He grabs 'em by the crotch, doesn't he?" After that, Carter saw to it that Baron York roles were tailored: Baron played himself. Sexy, uncomplicated, sexy, strong, sexy, brave, sexy, untamable. And the Great Carved Head remained, along with Gable, Wayne, Lancaster, Douglas and Heston, in heavy demand. Masculinity personified. Is that a talent, York wondered, turning out the light? Does he, in suggesting the Sower of Life, the Godfucker every girl yearns for, possess real talent? The affirmative answer might be painful, but York admitted its validity.

After Adam, Mrs. York gave birth in rapid succession to two bodily perfect little girls, then busied herself with her family and hard drinking. Baron made widescreen epics. As perennial president of the Screen Actors Guild he battled those damn commies in the union. And he fooled around.

His girls Baron kept no secret. His wife chose to ignore them. When he showed up at home roaring drunk and accompanied by pretty little things she would explain, bright-voiced, to the servants and children that "he's testing for bits in the new movie."

The Yorks' retouched photographs were generally captioned "Hollywood's Happiest Couple."

The marriage might or might not be Hollywood's happiest, but the cynical, brilliant first child of the union had to admit it among the most stable. Like a marblecake, loneliness and misery and needs, love, drives, old debts to be paid, vast properties, images both public (his) and private (hers) were so intricately baked together that neither seriously considered divorce. And on the rare occasions that Baron York sought his wife's king-size bed, she was happy for weeks after. Gladly she forgave everything.

His son, however, could never forgive.

There was the matter of his mother. She was, York admitted at moments like this, alone in the darkness, the only person who made any difference, any difference at all.

There was the matter of personal wounds. Sad, deep psychic wounds. And actual physical wounds.

"Forget it," York muttered. He closed his eyes.

Sometime during the night he woke. His father's heavy baritone, raised in toneless song, "Oh, give me a ho-o-ome where the buffalo r-o-o-oam," moved closer up the curving marble staircase. York heard, or thought he heard, soft feminine titters. He squeezed his hands over his ears. He would have prayed, had he believed there could be anyone running this fucked universe, that his mother slept. Or was too stoned to hear.

To the stag York invited the mixed bag who ate lunch with Gillies at the trestle table on the lower patio.

Only Igawa hesitated. "Saturday? Hey, I promised Mosgrove I'd take in *Moulin Rouge* with him."

York, barely knowing Marshall Mosgrove, despised him. Marshall Mosgrove was student body president, and all California High knew how *that* had come about. Last fall the two candidates for office had been disqualified after leading a noisy protest of the "inedible garbage" served in the cafeteria, and as a matter of honor every likely senior had refused candidacy. Marshall Mosgrove had tossed his hat in the unopposed ring. Which was the only way Marshall Mosgrove could have won. York had no intention of spending an evening with such a guy. Still, on the other hand, didn't Ken Igawa come closest to York's *verboten* word, friend?

So, after a moment, York grunted, "Bring him along."

York led his rubbernecking guests across the vast marble entry, through long, thick-carpeted rooms and out a sliding glass door. Below, in three directions, Los Angeles glittered like treasure tossed onto black velvet.

"Jeez." Stryker Halvorsen whistled. "Some layout."

"Give the American public what it wants," said York acidly, "and you, too, can live on Mount Olympus."

"That's what you call this place?" Stryker asked.

Laughter. Good-natured.

"Mount Olympus," Marshall Mosgrove explained in the tone he used addressing assemblies, "was the home of the Greek gods."

They moved between shadowy avocado trees down shallow steps. Four terraces fecund with odors of well-tended soil and expensive shrubbery, then flat chlorine, as they circled brightly lit water to the pool house, an airy building considerably larger than the Davys' C-plan Parkdale home. At this time of the year nobody went near the pool house. Except York, to smoke a secret joint or two. Now he broke out the Olympia, and as beer lubricated the guys they got over their awed nervousness and acted as easy as if they were lunching on the sunlit lower patio at school.

Marshall Mosgrove, Ken Igawa, Stryker Halvorsen and Clay Gillies gathered around glowing logs on the raised hearth.

York hunched apart. In his pallid face only his gray eyes were alive, and dark glasses hid this animation.

Slightly boozed, the others discussed what they would do once their sentence at California High was served. York listened.

Stryker Halvorsen, still in eleventh grade, the youngest

present and All City in baseball, stretched his long legs. "I'd sure like to get into pro ball."

"The Dodgers give bonuses to guys like you."

"I'm not that great. There's terrific players from all over the country. Most of them never make the majors." Stryker's face creased into a frown unnatural on his large, handsome features. "I guess I'll have to figure on college."

Someone snorted. Stryker was notoriously the worst student around—it wasn't stupidity, everyone agreed, just that Stryker was interested solely in athletics.

He said, "Oh, I know it'll be on a baseball scholarship. But jeez, man, you *need* a college education today."

"Absolutely," agreed Marshall Mosgrove. He sat on the couch, somewhat flabby in Levi's that made him, York decided, look as if his testicles were undescended. "And to compete for a decent job, you ought to try for a really good school." Marshall smiled.

Typically Mosgrove! The others—Clay Gillies, Ken Igawa and York himself—already had mentioned they were going to nearby nongood UCLA. Fire crackled and orange sparks flew up. Marshall's smile began to look as if it had been injected with Novocain.

Then Stryker, because that was the sort of good-hearted guy he was, said, "I guess you're right. Might as well aim high. Hey, Mosgrove, where're *you* going?"

"Stanford," Marshall replied with low modesty.

Clay Gillies, certainly no Mosgrove fan, snapped, "That Wasp hive!"

And Stryker put in hastily, "Stanford! Jeez, you've been accepted?"

Marshall beamed. "Last January."

"Class. Pure class." Stryker grinned over his beer can. "Know what you're going to major in?"

"Law."

"I'd like to paint," Ken Igawa said. "But who can paint and make a living?"

"A living!" the others cried. A living—that was an obscenity uttered only by drab nine-to-fivers.

"Hey, you affluent society! My father's a gardener. I've *got* to think about hacking it," Ken responded, a little too loud.

"My mother's a nurse," good-hearted Stryker reassured Ken.

"What will you major in?" Clay leaned toward Ken.

"Writing fortunes in a Japanese cookie factory. A whole

new field. Hey, how should I know? I don't know anything. Except painting. My mother says landscape architecture's good. You?"

"Computer Sciences. But"—Clay's voice slowed—"I don't want it to be my whole life."

"No chance of that," Stryker cracked. "Not with Michele around."

Everyone guffawed. Lasciviously.

"I want to alter history," Clay said.

His beard-shadowed face was so intent that even though he was a couple of months short of his eighteenth birthday, the crazy words *I want to alter history* rang true. York, examining Gillies, reflected on the mystery of people. Some guys their age couldn't give their own phone number and sound reliable; others, by virtue of voice, expression, personality, could formulate grandiose, nuthouse schemes and make them sound plausible. Well, hadn't Alexander set out, a teener, to conquer the world?

"Buddy"—York leaned forward, speaking for the first time in almost an hour—"history is a picture of human crime and misfortune."

"Who said it first?" asked Ken Igawa.

"Me. Then Voltaire."

"I don't see what's wrong with changing that." Clay turned to face York. "Do you?"

"There is no changing it," York replied. He was pretty high; around four that afternoon he'd regretted the stag and so he'd stayed down here a long time, smoking grass to unloose regret. Since, he'd been hitting it pretty hard with Pabst. "Humans, by nature, buddy, are a rotten bunch. Even a power like *you* can't change that fact."

"Some're rotten," Clay agreed. "But if I believed we all are, I wouldn't want to live."

"Die then," York said.

This Gillies ignored, saying, "Everyone here knows if there isn't an improvement in the racial situation soon, this country's going down the pipes."

"You bet your ass." Stryker Halvorsen nodded.

"It's about time the South ratified the thirteenth, fourteenth and fifteenth amendments," Clay said.

York smirked. "One hundred years between passing the amendments and the consideration of putting them into action. Let's hear it again: we are not rotten."

"That was other generations," Clay said. "We'll do better."

"I won't hold my breath."

"Of course we'll do better."

"Can't fail."

"Look at the sit-ins in the South."

"All people our age."

"What've any of the older people done?"

"Will they hire Negroes?"

"Or work with them?"

"Do they have Negro friends?"

Newest profession for an enterprising young colored guy,
York thought: *hiring out as "Negro friend."*

"All they do is foam at the mouth, red-hot liberal."

"The good ones."

"The good ones! Balls!" Anger etched Ken Igawa's normal,
easy sarcasm. "Those old farts! They're in love with their own
words. They're worse than your Ku Kluxer because they believe the same as Ku Kluxers but they aren't honest enough to
put on the white sheets!"

York, protected by dark glasses, stared at his guests in turn.
Mosgrove's square indignation. Igawa's usually pleasant bony
face hard. Stryker Halvorsen angrily running his fingers through
his bright hair. Gillies' brown eyes those of a furious god. Of
course each thought he was sincere as all hell. But York knew
this year, the first year of the sixties, people their age were
using civil rights as a put-down on their parents. *You failed,
you failed;* that was the rallying cry. Failed. York thought of
his own mother. She was closer to Mrs. James and Mrs. Igawa
than with any of the other PTA ladies who were her only friends.
He doubted she noticed their respective races. But then his
mother was a part-time lush.

Up ivied terraces Mrs. York sat in her white silken bedroom.
One thin, ringed hand rested on maroon satin over her stomach.
The lump on her left side was definite now. She pressed. No
pain, but the lump, the walnut-size lump, moved. It didn't
frighten her. She had told no one, and the secrecy reminded
her of those early months when, slumbering in her womb,
known only to herself, curled another of her claims on her
husband. The memory of that joy was the reason she had told
no one, for she didn't kid herself. She pressed again, breathing
deeply; only Adam would care.

· 4 ·

They planned only a brief service in Dr. Roberts' study—the Davys belonged to his red-brick Lutheran church over on National. Mr. and Mrs. Davy for once were united with Clay. "Private," the three of them kept repeating. "Only us," they kept saying. The Davys worried about future embarrassment resulting from a date that everyone could count back to. Neither would admit it, not to Michele or Clay or even to one another, but not for a minute did they believe Michele's denials of pregnancy.

Clay, on the other hand, already felt married. "Michele, you know the wedding's just a formality."

"I want one!" Michele said and burst into tears.

They compromised. The wedding would be private as planned, but Mrs. Davy promised a reception afterward.

Sunday, following the brief ceremony, the five of them, Mr. and Mrs. Davy, the new Mr. and Mrs. Gillies and Mr. Gillies senior, who smelled of bourbon, drove through soft drizzle to greet their guests. Aside from relatives there were two neighboring families and Mrs. Mallory from Altar Guild. Leigh Sutherland, Dorot McHenry and Ruth Abby Heim. Michele had ached to invite all the Rondelays, but Mrs. Davy had pointed out the small living room couldn't hold that many. Of Clay's guests only his father and Stryker Halvorsen showed. Clay also had invited Ken Igawa, but thank heavens Ken had to go with Miss Verney to an art contest in Barnsdall Park; Michele's family weren't very up to date about that sort of thing and they kept eyeing poor Ruth Abby Heim as if she should have some visible sign of Jewishness. York, too, had been invited. He'd refused. Typical. Mrs. Davy, though, at every opportunity, raised the ghost of his presence. "Baron York's son gave Clay a party . . . you know, the movie star's son."

Each time she repeated the famous name the shadows under Clay's eyes darkened.

Michele, in a new white lace suit hastily bought for the occasion, went around talking to guests, displaying the soft little hand with the shiny gold ring, clutching Clay with the other. She was very proud and happy. But when Aunt Ethel started dabbing her handkerchief at the liver-spotted bags under her eyes and crying over Michele—"I don't know why you girls want to get married so young nowadays"—a shiver went through Michele. She leaned against Clay. It was all he could do not to enfold her comfortingly in front of everyone . . . his heart expanded with aching warmth.

Mrs. Davy had refused to serve champagne—"So many children," she'd said—but she had provided coffee and Hawaiian Punch and Mr. Davy had brought home a sheet cake frosted with white goo and topped with a plastic bride and groom from Pixwood Market, where he was manager. Everyone stood around the dining table and Ruth Abby played "Here Comes the Bride" on her guitar while Michele cut the cake. As Michele slid the first slice on a plate, for no good reason everyone started shouting "Congratulations!" hugging, shaking hands, embracing, kissing. Dozer, upset by all the excitement, had an accident on the dinette hooked rug.

Leigh Sutherland disappeared for a minute, returning with a big box of Uncle Ben's rice. Michele and Clay weren't going anyplace. Tonight they would be sleeping in Michele's room. Tomorrow was a school day. Anyway, who could afford a honeymoon? They were staying here. Rice, Clay decided, was more old-fashioned froo froo. Stupid. But Michele gazed up at him, her big blue-green eyes full of happy tears, and he heard himself saying, "Let's go outside," so they ran laughing through the front door into sweet spring rain, Uncle Ben's rice pelting around them.

"Oh, be happy." Leigh Sutherland's light voice followed them. "Be happy forever and ever."

"The honeymoon's over," Dorot McHenry announced to the Rondelays.

"Ohhhh?"

"You should have heard them!"

"What was it about?"

"I wasn't close enough to catch the exact wordage."

"Sex, you think?"

"What else?"

• • •

It was about Michele buying a pair of red patent Capezios which had cost sixteen ninety-five and Michele, as usual, asking her mother for the money.

Here was how Clay felt: "We're married. I'll buy your clothes."

"But you only make twenty a week!"

"Then you can't afford many seventeen-dollar shoes, can you?"

And that started a hot one.

Clay went directly from school to Dr. Feiner's lab, so Michele continued to take the blue bus home. Usually she got off a block from her house, but today, needing unlined notebook paper, she got off at the shopping center at Athens and Monrose. She bought paper with the small change Clay had doled out, then browsed around Sally's, trying on a skirt or two, a pair of slacks—if she sucked in her breath six junior petite still fit—finally starting home around four thirty. The neighborhood north of Parkdale was in transition. Old frame bungalows, small lots used as nurseries, smelly, dark little Japanese markets and Mexican delis were being replaced by sharp new apartments.

Michele stopped to admire a glittering white stucco building with a gilded sunburst ornamenting the windowless front. In the tiny strip of fertilizer-odored new grass, a sign:

APARTMENT FOR LEASE
SEE MANAGER
APT. 1B

and, on impulse, with no other interest than curiosity, Michele stashed her books under a convenient rubber plant.

The apartment was gorgeous. It smelled of fresh beige paint. There was beige loop wall-to-wall carpet and a breakfast bar. Michele mentally furnished the bedroom, adding an Indian screen to hide the corner with the baby crib.

It's perfect, Michele thought. *It's perfect!*

"We-e-e-e-e-ell . . ." she said. "We *had* decided on a nicer area."

"If you're really interested I'll talk to the owner. He's been known to give the first and last month's rent."

This being far more important than red Capezios, Michele decided as she retrieved her books and paper, she would have to handle it more cleverly, a lot more cleverly.

• • •

That night, after Clay switched out the light and crowded into her twin bed, Michele lay rigid.

"Mother's still awake," she whispered.

Clay licked her ear, which generally excited her, and kissed her nipples. He'd noticed the breasts were fuller now, and there was a different scent to them, a warm, milky odor.

"Clay," she whispered warningly.

And, as if on cue, Mrs. Davy sneezed loudly. The builders of Parkdale economically had used thin plasterboard for interior walls; the sneeze echoed as loudly as if Mrs. Davy lay in Clay's bed. Clay sighed, resting his cheek on Michele's full breasts. He might be ready to climb the plasterboard walls, but he had to admit she was right. How could you make love when your mother-in-law was in bed right next to you?

The morning after that—a Sunday—Clay moved to Michele's bed. Michele murmured, "Clay, I'm dying to, just dying. But I'll bet Mother's going to knock on the door and tell us breakfast's ready."

She probably was, decided Clay, who had grown to dislike his mother-in-law thoroughly. Several times in the four weeks that Michele and he'd been married, they would begin embracing and all at once there would be a knock on the door. Just like that. Not a preliminary footfall. "Children," Mrs. Davy would call. "What're you doing? If you like, I'll fix some hot chocolate." Clay decided that under his mother-in-law's shelf-like bosom lay an antisex thermostat that rose to a boiling point just as they were about to ball. Now, as he kissed Michele's ear, sure enough, "I'm starting the pancakes," said Mrs. Davy right outside their door.

Five celibate days and celibate nights passed.

On the sixth night Michele made elaborate preparations for bed. Normally she showered. Tonight she filled the tub, pouring in the rest of her good bath oil, lying in steaming, scented water, listening to her transistor, humming along with Connie, shaving her legs and armpits, pausing to admire her glistening body. Her nipples, no longer bright pink, were the pale brown of angel food crusts, her breasts rounder. Otherwise, she noted with a smile, there were no ugly changes. She dried herself briskly, lavishing Jean Naté *friction pour le bain* on her breasts, thighs and the kinky blonde curls down there. She sprayed Arrid, which stung her freshly shaven skin. Instead of rolling her hair on purple aluminum cylinders she brushed it hard.

Then, slipping on her new short white peignoir set, she padded on bare, rosy little feet into the living room to kiss her mother good night.

Clay stopped his Math Analysis homework, pulling Michele into his lap, burying his scratchy face in the curve of her neck, his fingertips tracing the blonde down of her thighs, moving up to crisp, perfumed hair—

"Hop right under the covers, dear," Mrs. Davy called softly.

"Yes, Mother." Michele giggled.

"Good night, children."

Ten minutes later. Michele whispered, "Claypoo, you know Mother's still up."

At eleven thirty Michele whispered, "I thought I heard . . ."

At ten of twelve Clay groaned, "What we need is a place of our own."

(A happy marriage, Michele decided, comes when both sides see the same things as necessity.)

"We'll have to borrow from my folks," she said.

"No," he said, very serious. The following morning, they were dressing for school.

"But how else?" she asked. *"Your* father doesn't even have—"

"I won't borrow."

"In two months you'll graduate. This summer you'll be working full time. You'll pay them back."

"We'll need the money for other things."

"You said we needed our own place."

"Miche, I hate asking for favors." *Especially from people I despise.*

"Oh, pooh, Serious-head. We're living with them. That's a favor, isn't it?"

"Borrowing's different."

"I don't see how."

"We have to have our own place!" Clay said angrily.

"I'd like to be able to give you the money." Mr. Davy gave a cough, the thin sound of dry leaves rattling. He was a small, frail man with heart trouble and the dried-out, caved-in look so many angina cases get. "I wish circumstances were different. But soon I'll be retired and—"

"I wouldn't accept anything but a straight loan." Clay flushed.

Talking of money embarrassed him. "I'll repay you this summer."

Mr. Davy nodded. "Have you ever considered a better job? Checking pays well."

"I enjoy my work!" Clay burst out. It was true. And more, while he'd never admitted it out loud, though he merely cleaned a pathology lab, he felt a sense of dedication, as if in his own small way he were aiding humanity. To Clay this was primary. He knew he couldn't work long at a job he didn't consider worthwhile, and taking in money at a market came low on his list of importance.

His father-in-law was questioning him with pale blue eyes, hurt evident. "I didn't mean to interfere," Mr. Davy said. "But Mrs. Davy—Mother—and I are concerned about you and Michele. You see, she came to us late in life, and she's still our little girl."

Clay moved a step closer to the older man. Under Clay's shirt (ironed by Mrs. Davy) he felt a rare warmth. After all, he, too, would soon be a father—even if Michele *did* insist on keeping this fact a state secret.

Mr. Davy said, "We only want what's best for her." He coughed. "The two of you." He smiled anxiously.

"This job'll lead to more." Clay attempted an explanation his father-in-law might understand. "Dr. Feiner's been teaching me a little pathology. Some day soon, he says, they'll use computers for diagnosis."

"Sounds like a very rewarding field, financially speaking."

"But that's not what's important." Clay, in this moment of peculiar closeness, wanted absolute understanding between them. "It's the *work* that interests me."

"Oh, but if you get in with this Dr. Feiner, you'll get rich. Jews're shrewd." Mr. Davy spoke with envy, but his smile invited Clay to share indulgent superiority.

Clay's brief but wholehearted yearning for intimacy evaporated. How could he have forgotten his father-in-law was a walking encyclopedia of bigotry? Taking a step back, he said, "I'll have every cent paid by August."

Of course Clay argued the apartment was too expensive. He'd had in mind one of those awful green barracks that were rented to married UCLA students. Even when Michele showed that with the first and last months' rent free, the apartment would cost only around eighty, stove, garbage disposal, drapes and carpeting included, he remained stubborn.

But Mrs. Davy was on Michele's side. Mrs. Davy said although the place was in a bad neighborhood ("all those Japs and Mexicans") it was close to home, and the Davys had a right to say where their loan went. Clay must understand.

Clay not only understood.

He agreed.

His sense of honor said that if you borrowed five hundred dollars, your soul was collateral and you did exactly what your creditor ordered. But Michele couldn't convince him to buy furniture. Not a stick. She used all her wiles, but he wouldn't budge. They used her old bedroom suite. In the living room, on looped beige carpet, stood a battered bridge table, three Samsonite chairs—the fourth had been broken beyond repair—and an ancient couch (a large coffee stain marked the worn gray tweed of the middle pillow) that the Sutherlands had been about to donate to Goodwill. Every afternoon when Michele got home from school and saw her beautiful new home with its miserable furnishings she didn't know whether to laugh or cry.

Once the Gillieses moved in their friends dropped by on weekend nights. It was a much-needed gathering spot for the dateless—and unless you happened to be half of a current couple, you were dateless. California High students frowned on casual dating; they either did what disapproving parents called "going steady" or on weekends they took in a movie with others of the same sex. Now there was a third choice. The Gillieses'.

Clay Gillies made it clear that, while everyone was certainly welcome, he and Michele could not afford to supply refreshments. The Friday after they moved in, as Michele started to cut a lemon-filled angel pie—baked by her mother—he said, "Look, Miche, we can't afford to put on a spread. Let's get that straight from the beginning." And host and hostess retired to the bedroom for a discussion. Only her shrill side was audible. The remainder of the pie, as Dorot McHenry whispered loudly, was *hors de combat*, stuffed down the brand-new garbage disposal. After that, Dorot, Leigh Sutherland and Ruth Abby Heim took turns bringing the food, generally pizzas fixed with tomato paste and English muffins from a *Seventeen* recipe. Sometimes, though, the three of them would splurge, stopping either for a genuine pizza or for a big greaseproof cardboard tub from one of the new take-out chicken places. Even Dorot— and Michele certainly never would label Dorot generous— admitted she was glad to bring food, for, as Dorot put it, they were for the first time citizens in their own country. At the Gillieses' they were subject to their own laws, which were very different from the laws of their parents.

------------ **5** ------------

"My mother, she calls a J a reefer." Ruth Abby giggled. "She's sure the first puff's a slimy slide to"—Ruth Abby let the narrow, hand-rolled, wheat-straw cylinder dangle expertly from her lips (she was a heavy away-from-home cigarette smoker) as her stubby hand slid a downward glissando on her omnipresent Martin—"blindness, madness, ruin and"—she sang out of the corner of her mouth, bringing from deep in her chest the last tones—"de-eath."

Everyone laughed. It was well after nine on a Saturday night. In the Gillieses' living room heavy autumnal smoke hung in subtle layers and a rosy warmth lit cheeks. Some of the guests sprawled on the floor, others on the couch; none used the upright bridge chairs. Ruth Abby's occasional guitar blended with voices that were easy and slow. That is, until Dorot McHenry wondered out loud, "How many've tried it by the time they graduate?" Behind Dorot's horn rims her pupils were enlarged. "I mean at a school like California. Sociologically speaking"—and she often spoke sociologically—"a mixture of lower, middle and upper class."

"Fifty percent," York said. "No. Make it sixty."

"Ten percent, no more than that," was Marshall Mosgrove's opinion.

"Buddy," York sneered, "when even you—"

"Now—hold—on—just—one—minute," Marshall said ponderously. "Tonight I tried a couple of puffs, so—"

"The compleat man." York took a long drag. It was he who had supplied the grass gratis, he who showed the novices (Ruth Abby Heim and Leigh Sutherland) how to hold a joint between thumb and forefinger; it was he who had insisted Mosgrove, the group's only holdout, smoke. "Dorot said *tried*. Who knows about other schools? But I say sixty percent's a modest minimum at California when even the very rectangular president of—"

"Now look here—"

"—the student body's tried it!"

"Marshall, must be forty, fifty percent at least," Stryker mediated. He generally came between York's sneers and Marshall's square indignation. "If it's around at a party, you turn on. Jeez, every day more and more're following the yellow brick road."

Marshall frowned. "It's like drinking to our parents' generation?"

Stryker grinned, nodding.

"It ought to be legal," stated Clay Gillies. He squinted at Marshall. Clay neither warmed nor cooled toward Marshall— it was on principle alone he'd fought Marshall's student body presidency. He did, however, consider Marshall a pawn of the older generation. For this reason he would've preferred Marshall not be his guest. However, Marshall had been Michele's steady when he had started going with her; therefore Clay, somewhat shamed by his larceny, feeling he had an obligation of sorts to repay, welcomed Marshall into his home. "We'll make it legal," Clay said firmly.

"Think how shook the advertising industry'll be," Ken Igawa said. "Can't you see it? A distinguished white-haired old party puffing against his baronial fireplace, quoting, 'My brand's Pale Yellow. It turns me on....'"

Laughter floated in heavy-odored air, and eager voices chimed in how life would be on that joyous, ever-nearing day when they came to power.

"Instead of cocktail parties we'll give joint parties."

"And get legally stoned New Year's Eve."

"And offer our m-m-mother an after-d-d-d-d—" Ruth Abby was overtaken with a fit of laughter. "Oh, I'm st-st-st-ston-ed."

"Very few get high their first time," Dorot asserted.

"Many are called but few are chosen," said Ken Igawa.

"I'm ch-ch-chos...." Ruth Abby collapsed into more giggles, laughing until tears shone on her pink cheeks. Someone banged on her back. She bit her lips, forced herself to calm.

"I'm starved," someone said.

Others agreed. So Leigh set out the savory-smelling fried chicken she'd bought.

Ruth Abby chewed on a drumstick. A calm she'd never before experienced settled over her. She smiled, ate a crunchy wing, smiled again and leaned back on the couch, voices around dwindling, smoke buoying her until she weighed less than a swan feather; she was all loose and flying, oh, she was high in a blue, blue sky, she floated far above her woes. Very educational. For the first time in her life she was able to look dispassionately at herself.

Usually Ruth Abby hated everything about herself.

There were so many things wrong with her. She had an unfortunate tendency to giggle. Her tear ducts worked overtime, and to prevent others from seeing this weakness she blinked away water with a hasty motion of nose and eyes. This was interpreted, she knew, as a habitual twitch. She wasn't very smart, and in class her brain completely absented itself. As for her looks! Her too-curly brown hair would have been the bane of her existence if it hadn't been for her even more unfortunate ankles. Her heavy brows Mother didn't permit her to pluck. So was it any wonder that up until this March she'd never had a date? The sad truth was, no boy had even phoned. She found herself praying at odd moments, at dinner or in class or just as she fell asleep on her orthopedic mattress, *Please, God, please let some boy like me. Please, God....*

God didn't see fit to answer her prayer until three months after her sixteenth birthday. Then He presented her with Kevin Palmer.

Serene and soothed by pot, Ruth Abby for the first time could remember Kevin without wanting to cry.

He sat in front of her in History, a dark-haired boy with a brown mole near his mouth and a shy, warm smile. There was a small gap between his two front teeth. Ruth Abby liked him. This fact she kept secret—which meant she told only Leigh Sutherland, who could keep a secret. Then on the fifth of March Kevin Palmer turned around and blurted, "You going to Assembly?"

Speechless, Ruth Abby nodded.

"I'll sit next to you," Kevin said, turning crimson.

He did. And the next two days Kevin—plus a friend—kept passing and repassing the Rondelays' lunch table on the lower patio.

"He really likes you," whispered Leigh.

Delighted, Ruth Abby prodded, "What makes you think that?"

"Oh, you know. The way he looks at you."

And sure enough, Friday, March eighth, when Ruth Abby met Kevin outside History, he blurted, "Saturday a bunch of us're going to the Bruin. Wanna come?"

"Yes. Oh, yes."

"Pick you up at eight." Kevin started to shove open the door. Turned. "I forgot," he mumbled. "What's your address?"

His ears burned red all during class.

"Who is he?" asked Mrs. Heim.

"I told you!" Ruth Abby said impatiently. "Kevin Palmer. He sits in front of me in History. Third row from the windows. There!"

"I don't like that tone."

"Oh, *Mo*ther!"

"And I don't care for you driving with someone I don't know."

"He's got a license."

"How long has he had it?"

"How should I know? Oh, Mother. . . . A real boy, a real genuwine boy has asked me to a movie. Me! And he's really nice and I like him and he likes me. A date! Aren't you glad?"

Mrs. Heim, not answering, poured herself another cup of coffee. Saturday morning, they were alone in the sunny breakfast nook, Dr. Heim—a bald, humorless, conscientious internist—having departed five minutes earlier to make his hospital rounds.

Mrs. Heim sipped her coffee. "Is he Jewish?" she asked.

"Yes," Ruth Abby replied promptly. She wasn't sure. Although open and honest by nature, experience had taught her truthfulness generally failed in her dealings with her mother. She lied when she had to.

"Palmer . . . it could be. . . ." Mrs. Heim mused. "You're sure?"

"Oh, *Mo*ther!"

"And don't keep 'Oh, *Mo*ther'ing me!" snapped Mrs. Heim. Not for nothing did the Rondelays call her Tiger. She was small, pointy-tongued, sleek of build with a bad complexion. She lost and found her temper a minimum of ten times a day. Like a tigress she was totally dedicated to her only cub. She chauffeured Ruth Abby to innumerable lessons, she supervised

Ruth Abby's diet and elimination, and if it were possible she would have liked to have Ruth Abby's interior processes as visible to her as one of those educational clear plastic dolls that show brain, heart, uterus, vagina and other organs. She shopped at Bullock's Westwood for Ruth Abby's clothes and assiduously sewed on buttons and repaired bra straps in a vain effort to lick Ruth Abby into neatness. Mrs. Heim's voice rose. "I am sick of it!"

"So don't keep bugging me," Ruth Abby replied sullenly.

"Keep this up," Mrs. Heim shouted, "and I'll send you to a private school! *They*'ll put the clamps on you!"

She often threatened this. Ruth Abby, blinking and twitching, bent to butter another slice of wheat-germ toast. Strangers petrified her. To be exiled amid unknown but doubtless snobby private-school girls was her particular idea of hell.

"Your father and I are going out," said Mrs. Heim in kinder tones. "But naturally we'll wait home to meet him."

Kevin showed up in jeans and a maroon windbreaker. Dr. and Mrs. Heim were dressed for a dinner party. Mrs. Heim, minked and made up, insisted the four of them converse in the living room. Kevin stared down at his scuffed shoes. His embarrassment was so evident that Ruth Abby saw him not as a knight in shining armor come to rescue her from the swamps of datelessness but as a sixteen-year-old who didn't yet have his full height, who shaved the down on his upper lip and who was very shy.

Mrs. Heim interrogated. "Do you live around here?" The Heims' red-brick English lay on the proper sides of UCLA and Wilshire Boulevard.

Kevin shook his head.

"Oh?" Mrs. Heim inquired.

"On Glenway."

Mrs. Heim nodded. The address, though on the wrong side of UCLA, was on the right side of Wilshire. The querying went on. How long had he had his license? Three months, since his birthday. What sort of car was it? His mom's new Olds. Maybe she'd met his mother, Mrs. Heim said. Was she in PTA? She was, but she didn't go much. Any other organizations? She did something or other at University Synagogue; they belonged there. Smiling, Mrs. Heim released them. "Drive carefully, Kevin. And Ruth Abby, be home by eleven thirty. No later. We'll be back by then."

Kevin phoned every night. When he could borrow his mother's car he dropped over. Ruth Abby was, he told her awkwardly, the first girl he'd ever gone with. Ruth Abby's thick ankles seemed slimmer. She sang all the time.

The romance didn't have the same euphoric effect on Mrs. Heim.

She became a regular Jewish Gestapo. She listened on the extension to Kevin's phone calls; she scavenged through Ruth Abby's bureau on the pretext of straightening messy drawers, but in reality she sneaked looks at Ruth Abby's diary. She poked and prodded and pried into what they did and where they went. Sometimes she reduced Ruth Abby to a twitching mass of misery.

Mrs. Heim didn't mean to be cruel.

It was true, as she often told a tearful Ruth Abby, that she loved her and wanted only the best for her. Mrs. Heim honestly believed that "you have to give firm, adequate supervision" in order to "bring up a girl properly" in this difficult era. And wasn't it up to her? Though Dr. Heim had adopted Ruth Abby, her real father lay someplace in the icy North Sea amid the wreckage of his B17, so Mrs. Heim felt doubly obligated, both to herself and to that brown-eyed, jitterbugging boy she'd married when she was twenty, to raise their daughter right.

At the Gillieses', Ruth Abby understood her mother's logic without bitterness. Someone had turned on the radio and brassy, rocking beat ascended into the thickened air; the tub of chicken had disappeared; Marshall Mosgrove was no longer around. Ruth Abby rested her cheek in her palm. Since she had remembered this much without weeping, cautiously, as if tongue-testing a raw-nerved tooth, she let her mind wander back to the worst time, that foggy April Saturday night. Safe, serene and stoned, she discovered the memory brought surprisingly little pain.

That night Mrs. Heim had a heavy cold. Since she would be home, she permitted Kevin to come over—it was a firm rule that he and Ruth Abby not remain in the house one unchaperoned minute.

Mrs. Heim said, "You'll leave by eleven thirty, Kevin?"

"Sure, Mrs. Heim," he replied.

At the foot of the stairs she blew her nose, turned. "No later."

"No later," Ruth Abby and Kevin chorused.

"Good night, children."

Ruth Abby went back to her guitar. Although Mrs. Heim

normally banned "that junky new music" as she called Ruth
Abby's folk rock, Kevin enjoyed it, so Mrs. Heim had lifted
her ban, evidently feeling hands that were strumming a Martin
could not be employed elsewhere.

Upstairs a door closed. Kevin shifted from his chair to the
couch. He put his arm around Ruth Abby.

"We better wait," she whispered. She shrank from physical
contact on her own home ground—their limited making out
had been done in his mother's Olds.

Reddening furiously, Kevin slid to the far end of the quilted
couch.

Ruth Abby sang "Man, Man" and "Forever," songs she'd
written herself. Kevin moved closer. Again his arm snaked
around her. By now her own fears were lulled and she felt all
eager. She set the guitar down, turning to kiss him. His big
teeth pressed hard against her lips and she felt the tip of his
tongue. A hot quiver went through her full body.

She managed to pull away. "Maybe they're still awake,"
she whispered. "I better keep playing."

Kevin pulled away awkwardly. Their noses hit. "Sorry," he
mumbled.

"Listen, I'll turn on TV. That ought to hold 'em."

She tuned in an ancient movie with Loretta Young and some
old English actor. Ruth Abby and Kevin settled on the couch,
kissing long wet kisses. In the foggy, windless dark, crickets
sounded. They stretched out, pressing closer and closer. Ruth
Abby wished Kevin didn't always take so long to hold her
breasts. She loved him to. She wished and wished he would.
She wondered if the girl ought to tell the boy what she liked
him to do. Or should she simply place his hands on them? She
wished she'd dated more so she'd know how to behave. His
hands inched up her sweater and she held her breath until finally
he cupped them. She kissed his neck with gratitude. Once she'd
heard Michele assert boys like you to rub the back of their
necks. Ruth Abby tried that. It must be true for after a long,
breathless while he reached under her pink sweater, stroking
her. Under her embroidered cotton bra her nipples ached for
his naked touch.

All at once he moved away, reaching for the lamp switch.

"Kevin," she warned.

"What?"

"You know . . . Mother."

"S'been over an hour. She's asleep." Kevin gave her his

warm, shy smile and Ruth Abby, despite warning bells ringing inside her head, let him reach behind to turn out the big brass lamp. In the flickering dimness of the TV he was less timid, far less timid, fumbling with her bra snap. *Should she help?* Finally elastic relaxed. Kevin pushed up her sweater and bra.

While her breasts did not puff out like Michele's, neither were they tiny, like Dorot's. The nipples were brownish, the veined mounds firm and wide across her sturdy rib cage.

"They're beautiful," Kevin breathed.

"Thank you," she murmured.

And she pressed his hot face between them. He nuzzled there. English voices spoke crisply, commercial followed commercial, more English voices backed up by sad music. Ruth Abby didn't hear a thing except their loud breathing. She forgot Mother. This pleasure was peculiarly her own and Kevin's, it had no part in her Mother-dominated life, and now Kevin was lying on top of her, not really, his legs rested on one side but his pelvis covered hers and his upper body was raised while he kissed her breasts alternately; strong tongue action would flick one erect nipple, then his hand would cover the dampness and he would give his attention to the other. Her eyes squeezed shut. There was only the pounding inside her, the heat, the sound of their panting, and fierce, intense joy—

Suddenly

light

Mrs. Heim, wearing her robe and blue slippers, stood in the doorway. A fine net covered her upswept hair. Her face shone with night cream and fury.

Kevin scrambled up.

Ruth Abby, sitting, yanked down her sweater. The loose bra ridged. This worried Ruth Abby, even though she knew her mother needed no further evidence. Who knew how long she'd watched in the flickering grayness?

"So this is how you behave," said Mrs. Heim in a low, terrible voice.

"We were . . . we . . ." Ruth Abby quavered.

"The minute I let you out of my sight!"

"Mother—"

"You ungrateful slut!"

"It's not what you think—"

"I don't think! I *saw*."

Kevin, paint white, hands thrust into his jeans pockets, watched helplessly.

"Mother, I know we were being bad. Listen, though, we were just making out, only—"

There was no dealing with Mrs. Heim; her distress and her active temper had briefly driven her over the bridge of reason. She screamed, "The first boy who comes along, you throw yourself under him! Anything to keep him! You'd sleep with—"

"No!"

Mrs. Heim showed her teeth. *"I saw. I saw."*

"Please, Mrs. Heim, listen to her," Kevin managed to get out. "It's not what you—"

"You!" Mrs. Heim whirled so fast that her white gown showed under her long robe. She pointed at the door in an age-old gesture of dismissal that would have been funny if any of the three had been in the condition to think of it. *"Out,"* she cried. *"OUT!"*

"Please, Mother, please."

"And stay out! I'll call your parents in the morning!"

Kevin, his lower lip almost disappearing beneath the upper, slunk by Mrs. Heim. Not looking at Ruth Abby, he left so hastily that he didn't quite close the front door. Wisps of chill fog seeped through the crack.

"Go to your room," Mrs. Heim ordered. After slamming the front door she followed the shaking Ruth Abby upstairs.

"Get undressed," she ordered. "Put on your nightgown. No pants. Then we'll see, we'll see." And she watched from the doorway while Ruth Abby barged about doing as she was told.

Mrs. Heim summoned her husband. She told him what he must do. He tugged at his bathrobe lapel, demurring. "No, Shirl, don't."

"She's my daughter. I want to *know*. I have to!" And so, while Mrs. Heim watched from the foot of the bed, Dr. Heim made an examination between Ruth Abby's full, shuddering thighs.

Ruth Abby passed. But it was the worst time in her life. If she lived five hundred years she would never forget that awful, gentle prying accompanied by the sound of her mother's sniffles.

The following Monday Kevin wasn't in History.

Two days later Dorot McHenry reported he'd been transferred to Mr. Bowers' class. "What happened there?" Dorot demanded. "I thought you two were all hot and heavy."

"S'all over," Ruth Abby sighed.

Of course it was all over. When they passed in the hall he
reddened and quickly turned the other way. *And this was the
worst thing:* the avoidance pleased Ruth Abby. Why? She
couldn't understand why. For she liked him still; she would
never, she was positive, like anyone half so much even if (and
it was a big if) anyone did ever ask her out again. She cried
herself to sleep over the loss of him.

So why didn't she want to see him?

She couldn't understand it. At least, she couldn't until this
moment. Ruth Abby swung her short wide feet onto the Gillieses' couch. Now, still high above herself, very calm, the
explanation seemed perfectly simple. Maybe old people would
say all they'd had was puppy love, but Ruth Abby—and Kevin,
too, she was sure—had felt deeply. And now it was all mud-
died. Dirty. You can't go back. Her mother's frenzied accu-
sations had humiliated her to the depths of her simple soul,
just as Dr. Heim's test had humiliated her thick, firm girl's
body. A beautiful thing had been bulldozed and gouged into
ugliness. You can't go back. . . .

"Care for another?" It was York, sitting next to her.

Ruth Abby returned to the land of the living. "Thank you,
but no," she said. "I've got to go home."

"A good little girl."

"But it's bitchin'. Makes everything seem O.K., you know
what I mean. Thank you."

"Now my day's complete," he said. "I've corrupted you."

Normally his sarcastic tone would have set Ruth Abby
twitching. But she was still lit with Tijuana warmth. "Where
can I get some?" she asked.

"It's a turned-on city."

"Where?" she persisted.

"Know the Pearre twins?"

"They're in my gym class."

"There's convenience for you." York gave her another sour
little smile and turned away.

The Pearre twins, Di and Vi, were long, thin and black-
haired. They charged fifty cents a joint. But since Mrs. Heim
gave Ruth Abby no allowance, doling out cash for approved
purposes only, how was she to afford even fifty cents? The
answer came two days later, also in gym. And unexpectedly.
As she was changing, Karen Henigman walked up.

"Listen, Ruth Abby, can you sing at my Sweet Sixteen?"

Ruth Abby had never sung for money. Now her white tennis shoes shuffled. "How much?" she stammered.

"My mom, she said she'd give up to ten dollars— Hey, Ruth Abby! What're you doing?"

What was she doing? She was waltzing around assorted girls in various stages of undressing, singing at the top of her most adequate lungs, "Oh, I've got plenty of something, twenty plenty of something. . . ."

There was a demand for entertainment at parties. Teen combos and singers accompanying themselves on a guitar were nonunion, cheap and in. Ruth Abby's loud, clear enthusiasm went over big at Karen Henigman's catered luncheon. That led to another job and another. Naturally she didn't tell Mrs. Heim. Leigh Sutherland covered for her—in a city the size of Los Angeles even the most zealous mother can't find out everything.

At least not right away she can't.

Ruth Abby watched the red tail lights disappear over the hill, then she lowered her thumb. Sighed. This time of night very few cars traveled on Santa Monica Boulevard. Alone, she wore a wilting purple cymbidium lei over her pea coat. Tonight at Karen Henigman's aunt's luau she'd sung moony Polynesian songs. Her cover was a fictitious Rondelay all-night get-together at Leigh Sutherland's. Leigh was meant to pick her up, but Leigh had phoned, all shook, to say she had a dead battery. The luau cateress had given Ruth Abby a ride as far as Santa Monica Boulevard and Beverly Glen, and here Ruth Abby decided to break one of her mother's prime commandments: Thou shalt not hitch.

So far no luck.

Headlights again flooded the empty street. Ruth Abby raised her thumb, smiling.

A black and white squad car pulled up. "You'd better come along with us," said the tanned policeman.

"Got you a customer," said the tanned policeman.

A red-faced sergeant with thick gray hair put on rimless glasses, picked up a pad and pen and walked past the rows of empty desks to the counter.

"Name?" he asked.

Ruth Abby, blinking, shook her head. How could she say her name? Ever? If Mother found out about the jobs, the hitching—Ruth Abby shivered, unable to pursue the thought.

His ball point hovering over the thick pad, the policeman repeated, "Name?"

Again she shook her head, blinking harder.

Through rimless bifocals he examined her. "All right," he said finally. "We'll come back to that. Give me your guitar, sis."

She did, watching him wire a label around the handle.

"Ring and bracelet," he said.

Ruth Abby dropped her pearl ring and gold name bracelet into the manila envelope he extended.

"Purse?"

Ruth Abby handed him the small white clutch. Instead of stowing this, he opened it. As she heard the faint metallic opening click she remembered the contents: two lipsticks, a Tampax, three quarters plus the ten-dollar bill that was her pay for the luau, the flattened penny Kevin Palmer had given her.

And two joints wrapped in a wax-paper sandwich bag!

Ruth Abby begged, "May I have the purse. Please . . . just a moment, please?"

Retarded, she was retarded.

Wax paper rattled. The policeman turned to the empty desks. In the last row sat a plump, gray-haired woman packed into a tight gray knit.

"Marge," he called. "Here."

Whispering, the two examined Ruth Abby. Her face stiffened with terror, her neck hairs prickled as if they were standing up. Was she fainting? She hoped she would faint.

"Your name?" the desk sergeant asked in a new, unpleasant tone. "Your name. Come on!"

Ruth Abby dropped her face between her palms, started to sob, sobbed, sobbed harder. After a few minutes the Marge woman put a soft arm over her shoulders, "Come on," she said, leading her down a corridor.

"Shhhh, dear," Marge murmured. "Shhhh. Nobody's going to hurt you." They passed under naked bulbs. Marge took a long key chain from her pocket. "It's not the worst crime in the world," she said. "As a police officer I shouldn't say this. But God knows, dear, it's not the worst crime. As a matter of fact, a first offense, if we see the person's genuinely sorry, the way you are, dear, we generally call the parents down, then we release the person to their custody—you *are* under eighteen, aren't you?"

Ruth Abby nodded.

"And what's your name?"

At this repetition Ruth Abby sobbed harder.

"All right," the woman said, unlocking an ordinary door. "We'll talk about it later."

The door might appear ordinary, white painted and all, but behind it was a jail cell, a regular jail cell with high, wire-netted windows, an open, seatless john, a mattressless cot, smells of strong disinfectant. "Now have a nice rest," the woman said, gently shoving Ruth Abby.

A click.

She was alone, locked in a jail cell.

Naked springs creaked as she sank down. She tore the petals from her orchid lei and threw them into the yellowish bowl. Purple stained her fingertips. In her confusion she snatched at stray ideas. How could she have been such a dumb clod? Oh, she barged and banged into life like a puppy with unopened eyes. She was marooned weaponless in a world where everyone was either hip or armed with intellect. Disinfectant odors, she decided, burned your nostrils. She thought of that last night with Kevin . . . Mother yelling. You could get no lower than a jail cell, that's what Mother would say. Mother. *Mother*. MOTHER. Her thoughts were being swept together as relentlessly as small animals fleeing a circle of fire. WHAT WOULD MOTHER DO TO HER? Ruth Abby's arms and legs went numb and tingly. Suddenly she understood there was no point in keeping her name a secret. Tomorrow morning her mother would make her routine checking call to Leigh (who'd be plenty worried) and, not finding Ruth Abby, would call each Rondelay alphabetically down the list tacked to Ruth Abby's bulletin board, maybe call Kevin's mother, certainly call hospitals, then the police station. Thinking of her mother's short panicked fingers dialing, Ruth Abby felt her terror mingle with pity. She wiped her eyes. She flushed the john, watching petals whirl slowly.

She banged on the door, surrendering.

Mrs. Heim, no make-up covering old acne scars, nylon gown showing under her tweed coat, stood silently at the desk. The effort of silence showed in her tensely twined, short fingers. Ruth Abby was silent also, but silence was no effort—her vocal chords were too painfully knotted to function. Dr. Heim, usually the wordless one, kept saying over and over,

"But she's a good girl. Never hitchhikes, never. And she was at a club slumber party." Under his suit jacket his rumpled red plaid flannel pajamas showed. The desk officer read the typed report of how Ruth Abby was picked up on Santa Monica Boulevard, the illegal contents of her clutch purse. "Oh, my God! Drugs!" Dr. Heim exclaimed. His wife and stepdaughter watched while he conferred in grave tones with police officers, male and female, then signed the release for Ruth Abby and her property, minus, of course, the Js.

They had walked maybe ten steps in the chill night air, along the well-lit path to Athens Avenue, when Mrs. Heim stopped, turning on Ruth Abby. Her face mottled. A curious red tinge lit her eyes. "Where did I fail?" she shouted.

"Shirl—" Dr. Heim took his wife's arm.

"Where?"

"Shirl, don't."

Mrs. Heim's sudden color receded. Her fleshy nostrils moved. Suddenly she ripped the guitar case from Ruth Abby's limp hand, hurling the expensive Martin to the cement, stamping on it, kicking it along the path and into the water-filled gutter.

"There's one trouble!"

"Shirl—"

"Don't try to stop me! Didn't I always tell you where this rock 'n' roll garbage leads?"

"It's not so terrible. Her name isn't on the records."

"Drugs! Dope! Sex!" Almost incoherent, Mrs. Heim ran along the path repeating *drugs, dope, sex, drugs, dope, sex* over and over.

Once in the car, Mrs. Heim turned to the back seat where Ruth Abby cowered. "Jail!" she exploded. "*No*body in my family ever went to jail. And we were poor!"

As they turned under the shadowy acacias lining Concord, their street, Mrs. Heim's voice broke. "Where have I gone wrong?"

Ruth Abby shuddered. The broken sadness in her mother's voice frightened her more than the previous, familiar yelling.

And in the same low, sad voice, Mrs. Heim went on, "I've been investigating a Green Harbor School in Arizona. They give plenty of supervision. They'll cut out your garbagy singing."

"Please, Mother, I'll be good," Ruth Abby babbled. Her worst nightmares were coming true. Exile amid strangers. "I'll be good, I promise."

They were parked in the garage now, but none of them moved.

"Shirl," Dr. Heim said, "we're all tired. Upset. There's no reason to make a decision tonight."

"Why not?" Mrs. Heim sighed wearily. "I admit it. I've failed. I don't understand how. But I have." Another sigh. "Ruth Abby, I've given you love. I've made it my business to know where you went and what you did. I've never neglected you. I've chauffeured you. Lessons. Sunday school—because of you we joined the temple. We've tried to be good parents. Subscriptions to *American Girl*. *Seventeen*. A lovely home, a room and bath of your own. Nice clothes. And you—you run wild. Sex and dope." She was silent a moment. "I've tried so hard. But somewhere along the line I've failed—"

"I don't want those things," Ruth Abby murmured. "Magazines and lessons and stuff. I want to be *me*."

"I HAVE BEEN A GOOD MOTHER!" Mrs. Heim burst out.

"Shirl—"

Mrs. Heim took a deep, calming breath. She said, "Maybe it's just the times. This Green Harbor'll be best."

"Once I'm eighteen," Ruth Abby said, gathering her poor tattered shreds of courage around her, "you'll never see me again."

"Once you're eighteen you'll have the sense to appreciate what I'm doing." Mrs. Heim opened her car door, then added, "One day you'll have children of your own."

----------------- **6** -----------------

Summer vacation

and everyone at California High, or almost everyone, turns into a beach bum.

Even on days when a gray sky reflects a sullen ocean, they are drawn west, hitching, riding the big Wilshire buses, driving their own or their mothers' cars to Santa Monica; like lemmings they race down tall, eroding brown cliffs. They jam the broad yellow beaches, preferring lifeguard stations 14 and 15, smearing Coppertone into each other's tanned backs, playing football and Frisbeeing on wet sand, dragging into the surf screeching girls, the stacked or pretty ones who often shout for any and all to hear, "Let me down, let me down! I've got my period!" swimming, belly surfing. They get wiped out by huge green breakers. On days when there's a strong rip tide lifeguards drag them out by the dozens. They get salt water up their noses and sand in their crotches; they relish warm Cokes and cold grease-pervaded French fries; they gossip about who's doing what to whom. Stryker Halvorsen and his cohorts grade tits: watermelons, cantaloupes, grapefruits, oranges, lemons, limes and Thompson seedless—tall, skinny Dorot McHenry, they decide, has those under her padded swim top. They discuss the convention, the Democratic one, which is taking place right here, now, in the new Los Angeles Sports Arena, and Leigh Sutherland hopes they will nominate John F. Kennedy, who is handsome, brave and the shining hope of young people everywhere. Sometimes they stretch out on hot sand, drowsing to the rhythmic surf and Station KRLA's Top Hundred—the Top Five currently are "Itsy Bitsy Teenie Weenie Yellow Polka Dot Bikini," "I'm Sorry," "Tell Laura I Love Her," "Because They're Young" and "Twist" by good ole Chubby. They endure family trips, teen tours of the United States, Mexico and Europe, necessary jobs, visits to grandparents in Fresno. For there is this one thought to sustain them.

Soon they'll be back on the beach.

For Marshall Mosgrove this particular summer was limbo between California High and Stanford. Generally he spent summers in self-improvement: working out at Bruce Conner's gym in Westwood (Marshall, alas, was inclined to flab), a UCLA extension course in public speaking, or regular summer school. But right now, a high school graduate, he wasn't sure which tools would be important in college, so he wasted his days at the beach—at least when he got to Stanford he'd have the asset of a good tan—and his nights he squandered at the Gillieses'.

There was a change in the group, a certain cohesion and relaxation with one another that Marshall, who had never before experienced the phenomenon, could only assume was friendship.

With Stryker Halvorsen he felt particularly at ease. Stryker was younger than the other guys—like the girls he had a full year left to graduate. This spring Stryker had taken up surfing. He developed knobs on his knees and on the front of his ankles; his chest muscles expanded; sun and salt further bleached his blond hair, which he'd let grow the way all surfers did. With his tallness, bright blue eyes and bold nose Stryker reminded Marshall of a colored illustration in the old brown mythology book of his grandmother's: Baldur, the Norse god—Marshall as a small boy had read that book, wishing someone larger than life, like Baldur (Superman would've done in a pinch), would champion him, coming to earth to put a few of his tormentors out of action. While Stryker certainly never championed him, Marshall was amazed to see how often this big, good-natured, not-so-brilliant athlete's viewpoint coincided with his own. He liked and admired Stryker. Stryker was a really nice guy. Everyone said so.

Stryker, in faded denim Bermudas, would sit on the couch, his long legs propped over the arm, his tan feet, with strong bleached hairs sprouting from arches and toes, swaying easily. Sometimes in his smiling, inarticulate way, he would talk surfing.

"What sort of board d'you use?" Marshall asked.

"Hobie."

"Wood?"

Stryker threw back his head and laughed.

"What's so hilarious?" Marshall asked.

"Jeez, a wood board?"

"So?"

"Fiberglass, man."

"If I took it up, I sure wouldn't trust myself on plastic," Marshall said.

"You couldn't lift wood."

"No?"

"Weighs a ton," Stryker said.

That night when Marshall got back to Grandmother's place— that was how he thought of his home, a low-slung, tile-roof Mediterranean—he went directly to his room, stripping in front of his mirrored closet door. He examined himself, wondering for maybe the thousandth time why people didn't like him, why they invariably tried to put him down. He'd acquired a good tan. His face, under the crew cut, was sort of square,

and although he had a faint case of acne on his forehead, the
beach was curing it; his nose, straight, his chin manly—well,
maybe the chin receded a fraction, but not enough to disfigure.
Taking the good with the bad, Marshall decided, his face was
all right. Left shoulder lower than right. His belly—he gripped
a handful of flesh. Soft. He was well hung, he thought parenthetically; he'd observed the guys stripping for gym and he
knew in that area he was more than adequate. His thighs were
meaty. *You couldn't lift wood.* He was out of shape. That was
his problem. Why Stryker had put him down. Who likes a
sloppy, out-of-shape type?

Still naked, Marshall opened the closet. Smell of camphor
mothballs hit him. From behind three pairs of neatly aligned
shoes, he took a weight bar, putting fifteen pounds of black
disks on either end, fastening both with red end pieces. In front
of the mirror he raised the weight until his elbows cracked over
his head. Grunted. Lowered the bar behind his neck. Up again.
Elbows lock. Lower to chest. Ten times. He watched his naked,
quivering muscles. He doubled the weight to thirty pounds and
lay on the green carpet, grunting and sweating as he raised the
bar over his chest. Torture. He then managed seven pushups
and collapsed gasping on the rug.

After a few minutes he put the weights back in his closet,
pulled on his shorts, from the lowest bookshelf selected the
Saracen and lay on his green and black bedspread thumbing
through, looking for the California High athletic teams. In the
house was only the sound of pages rattling. His grandmother
and his sister Lois were visiting Aunt Myra in Seattle. Varsity
track and basketball featured Stryker Halvorsen, and there was
a full double-page layout of Stryker Halvorsen as captain of
the baseball team and All City second baseman.

Three nights later.

"How much do those wood boards weigh?" Marshall asked.

"I don't know, Mosgrove. Fifty pounds."

"I use more on my weights."

"Jeez, maybe sixty. Why?"

"I'm thinking of surfing this summer. I told you. I like the
idea of wood."

"Then you'll have to find yourself a board in an antique
shop." Stryker laughed good-naturedly. "Man, nobody uses
wood!"

"Nobody?"

"Maybe some old guy who still drives a horse." Stryker laughed again.

Marshall laughed, too.

The next day, Friday, Marshall left the beach early, around three, driving up the incline, turning on Santa Monica Boulevard, parking his grandmother's Buick in front of the public library. He headed directly for the stacks marked 796—last summer he'd learned the Dewey Decimal by heart, quite a feat!—squatting to get two books. He hefted his selections. Far too light. Marshall distrusted light books; he felt they couldn't contain real knowledge. The third volume weighed in satisfactorily. The three books under aching arm muscles, he headed for an empty table. Read. Took copious notes. His grandmother and Lois being in Seattle, he wasn't forced to stop for dinner. Marshall preferred to absorb knowledge in great, grinding doses.

Sunday night Stryker showed up at the Gillieses' with a large bruise above his left eyebrow.

"What happened?" asked Marshall.

Stryker grinned, sheepishly. "My board hit me."

"Where were you?"

"Rincon."

"Were they humping?"

"Pretty good." Grinning, Stryker touched a tanned finger to his raised bruise. "That's how I got this."

Later, after grass—courtesy of York—had loosened one and all, Marshall said, "I hear Doheny's great."

"The greatest."

"Ever camped down there?"

"Only been for the day."

"Like to?"

"Camp?"

"Uh huh," Marshall grunted.

"Sure," Stryker said. "Sure."

"Listen, I've got a tent and all the—"

And that was the moment Clay Gillies chose to interrupt, shoving a crudely mimeoed newsletter under Marshall's nose—*The Student Voice*, it was called—and there was something on the first page about a new student civil rights group, SNCC, being formed. Who cared? Certainly not Marshall Mosgrove.

• • •

Two nights later. Tuesday.

"Been thinking about Doheny?" Marshall asked.

"What about it?"

"You know. We were discussing"—was he talking too slow? speed it up—"camping down there."

"We were?"

"The other night."

"Jeez, Marshall, I'm sorry. I didn't mean it. I couldn't've. I'm pretty low on funds."

"All we need is groceries and gas."

"I mean, I'm broke. Flat."

"My grandmother's in Seattle. She left me loaded with credit cards and food money." Marshall could hear his own slow, ponderous conviviality. Why did he always have to plead for friendship? *Think positively,* he ordered himself. *You and Stryker Halvorsen are friends.* "Heard they're really humping this week."

Stryker sighed. Regretfully.

"Listen, the truth is," Marshall said, "I'd like a good surfer to teach me."

"No kidding."

"It's doing me a favor."

Seventy miles south of Los Angeles lies Doheny State Park. Set in a green cove with wind-shaped pines sheltering the campsites, waves break far out in the natural bay and surf rolls up to the beach in great, creaming lines. A surfer's haven. Heaven.

Luck was with them. They found a free campsite facing the beach. Together they unloaded the Buick, Stryker helped Marshall raise the mended pup tent Marshall had used in Boy Scouts, then Stryker took off to ride a few before it got too dark. Marshall worked. The familiar masculine routine of camping satisfied him; he whistled as he leveled off two sandy rectangles inside the tent for their sleeping bags and muttered aloud, "This is the life," as he sliced hot dogs into Campbell's beans for their dinner.

Stryker pushed away his sectioned dish. "That was great, Marshall, really great."

The stars were huge and glittery; dark waves grumbled; invisible below the incline and from a distance came the smell of meat roasting, laughter, a guitar playing "Bluetail Fly." Marshall lost his nagging, constant worry that the world and everyone in it disliked him.

"Sure is great." He relaxed, arms crossed on the table. "Getting away from it all."

Stryker agreed.

"Does a guy good to get away. You know, from women."

"Marshall, jeez, who needs to get away from the stuff?"

"I didn't mean women-women. I meant family-women. Listen, my parents died when I was three, killed in an airplane crash near Chicago."

Stryker mumbled embarrassed sounds of consolation.

Marshall said, "I don't really remember them, so it's not that. But since, I've lived with my grandmother. And my sister Lois." Marshall raised his voice to falsetto. "That's all I hear. My sister Lois, all she does is whine. My grandmother, well, she's old and she repeats herself. She says she likes to get everything straight, which means she repeats over and over and over. And over."

"Old people get like that."

"And she and Lois're always together. Shopping, going to lunch. The movies."

"At least they're out of your hair."

"Oh, they're home plenty. Watching *their* shows on TV, rearranging the house—they're forever getting me to move furniture."

"Rough," Stryker sympathized.

"You get used to it. Still, it's a relief not to have it around." Marshall coughed. "You live with your mother, don't you?"

Stryker agreed he did. "My folks're divorced. Jeez, though, Mom's O.K. Quiet."

"Rare in a woman. She's a nurse?"

"Obstetrics at St. John's."

Iodine damp of the sea settled on the table and into their clothes, but it wasn't cold. Marshall could barely see Stryker. Their small fire flamed occasionally, glowing on bright hair, touching tooth or eyeball. Stryker Halvorsen, Marshall's friend.

"Women-women," Marshall said. "Stuff, it's fine with me."

"Hey, Marshall, you ever?"

Marshall's spine straightened. Ease left. The massive, eternally ready defensive forces under his crew cut pulled to the front. Stryker had attacked a weak bastion.

Marshall grunted. Noncommittal.

"Have you?" Stryker persisted.

Marshall thought of his sole sexual experience, if you could call it that; the time after the Thanksgiving Dance when he slid a hand down Michele's formal, curving around warm, squashy flesh, and Michele had made such an outcry that he'd itched through a half-hour apology. And then—hadn't it turned out she'd been wholesaling it?

"I used," Marshall said slowly, "to date Michele Davy—Gillies."

Stryker gave a short, excited laugh. "Hey?"

"Last fall," Marshall added.

"Did you?"

"Stryker—"

"Just say yes or no."

"Michele happens," Marshall said, "to be married to one of my best friends."

"You're right," Stryker said.

A wave crashed.

"But jeez, Marshall, you did?"

"There's things that—"

"You're right, you're right." Stryker's teeth glinted as he smiled. "Jeez, you're lucky. That's one great-looking girl."

Marshall thought, *I never said it.* He tried to change the subject. "Tomorrow—"

"She sure is," Stryker said. Then, in a lower tone, "I never."

"I've heard about that."

"About me?"

"Of course not," Marshall said hastily. "Athletes aren't meant to."

"Training, you mean?"

"Uh huh."

"That's what Coach Reo says. But he's a teacher. Anyway, over forty. Guys that old don't remember what it's for."

"I read in a medical book that athletes shouldn't." Marshall *had* read this, but he couldn't remember where.

Stryker gave an impressed whistle.

"The semen goes back into your blood stream," Marshall explained. "Makes you stronger. Every time you do it, you lose something. Get weaker."

"Sounds like typical bullshit propaganda put out by old uptights."

"It was a regular medical book used by doctors."

"Still bullshit. Anyway, it's not the reason. . . . Jeez, Marshall, I'm really hot to. Listen, there's this girl, she goes to Uni. Last week I took her up on Mulholland. I've scouted this parking place where nobody can see. No fuzz. Nobody. I got her all hot and bothered. We touched . . . you know, each other . . ."

"Oh?"

"I know it's nothing to a guy with experience—jeez! Michele!—but this one had big tits and her hair was all dark and snarky and she let me, you know, with my tongue. Man, I really got her hot. But . . ." Stryker sighed. "Nothing."

"Most of 'em're teases."

"And there was this other girl I dated last fall, before I was sixteen and got my license. I had to hitch over to her place. On Bellagio. A huge place. Sometimes her folks'd go out. She let me play stinkfinger." Stryker groaned. "Sometimes I think I'll *never* get laid."

"A guy like you shouldn't have any problems."

"I ought to push it more?"

"You have to."

"Did you push Mi—"

"Look, Stry—"

"O.K., O.K.! Keep a cool tool, man. I didn't mean to mention her. Hey, Marshall, you still hung up on her?"

"She's a friend." Marshall, thoroughly sick of the pretense, wondered, could he get out of it without admitting his semi-lie? "The wife of a friend."

"You're right. You shouldn't blabber if a girl lets you," Stryker said. "Maybe some stuff'll show up here."

"Wouldn't that be cool."

"Hey, maybe it's here already?"

"Maybe."

"Think we could sniff it out?"

"Tomorrow." Marshall yawned. "I'm tired."

"Me, too. Easy stuff. That's what we—*I*—need."

Stryker rose, stretching. Marshall admired the unconscious grace of the movement.

After they undressed and sacked in Marshall's sleeping bags, Stryker said, "Some old gal of twenty-two, twenty-three, one who's really horny, she'll come along and push me over and try to rape me. Don't, please don't. Don't, don't, don't." Stryker pretended to pant. "Stop, no, don't stop, don't, don't don't don't—"

"G'night," Marshall said. "Sweet dreams."

• • •

Marshall woke early. As he took the rutted path to the long cabin of toilets, shivering a little in the chill early morning sun, he realized that practically all the campers were male. Surfers, waxing boards, grinned up at him. From an eleven-year-old gremmie to two bald guys (Marshall later learned they were Los Angeles County Hospital interns) vacationing in a brand-new white Open Road camper, there was a uniform sense of camaraderie, an all-masculine society bound by a common interest. Marshall, carrying under his right arm the secondhand board Stryker had found him, decided all he had to do was to get the hang of surfing. Which looked easy, a small matter of balance, like riding a bike. Marshall said so.

"It's harder'n it looks," Stryker said. "Let's head up the beach." He paused. "They break easy and it's sort of private."

Stryker taught Marshall to paddle through soapy surf. He gave Marshall a push so Marshall would catch each wavelet at the right moment and the right angle. "Now," he would say. "Go, man." He tried to teach Marshall to stand on his board.

"Like this." He demonstrated, pushing easily to an erect position.

Marshall fell every time.

Salt water clogged every passage in his head; he made *chhh-chhh* noises deep in his throat to stop the salt itching behind his ears. By noon his shoulders ached fiercely from paddling—working out hadn't done much good, had it? A dark continent bruised his meaty left thigh where his board had hit. The problem, Marshall realized, was this crummy secondhand board Stryker'd found him. Small waves would turn into roaring mountains as they reached him, and through his mind, as a drowning man is said to review his life, flashed every story he'd ever heard of surfing deaths; each time he either escaped behind the wave or fell into churning water rather than entrust himself to twenty-five pounds of secondhand white plastic.

"Today I'm pretty uncoordinated," he said, rising from sucking foam.

But Stryker, catching Marshall's board, saw the truth and, being a straightforward type, said it aloud. "You gotta have confidence. When I began I was sorta scared, too."

"It must've been a natural for *you!*" Marshall snapped.

"Jeez, man, I forced myself not to chicken out."

Chicken out! As the next wavelet approached, Marshall gritted his teeth, a habit with him when he was trying especially hard. Terrified, he gripped the rails, forcing himself up to a wide-legged ape crouch.

"You made it! Man, you made it." Stryker's cry held respect.

Marshall's squatting hams shuddered with fear. But he managed a sickly smile of triumph. His friend's respect meant everything.

On the way back for lunch, Marshall brought up the subject of his student body presidency.

"I ought to have plenty of confidence," he said. "An office of that type gives it to you."

"Uh huh," Stryker agreed.

"Also, it looked good on my record when I applied to Stanford." Marshall shifted the board so it didn't weigh on his sore hip. "I get a sense of . . . well, it sounds old-fashioned, but it's true. Of dedication. I feel dedicated every time I get up in front of assemblies."

"Leadership?" questioned Stryker, jogging around a coil of seaweed. Water had dried on his long, tanned jaw, leaving a powder of white salt. He gave off a clean, salty odor. "S'that what you mean?"

"Not exactly. I feel like I'm doing some good—"

"And it's doing you good—"

"A guy in student government doesn't get back half—"

"Clam yourself, man, clam yourself. I meant being president helped you get in Stanford. You just said so. And my grades!" With his free palm Stryker slapped his forehead. "Jeez, maybe *I* ought to run for office so my record'll have a little class."

That night the surfers gathered around a communal driftwood blaze. Stryker expressed ideas in his diffident manner and the others listened; when Marshall spoke invariably someone either belched loudly or chunked more driftwood into the fire. A crew cut who routinely was wiped out by the smallest ripple! Marshall was less than the eleven-year-old gremmie and the others let him know it.

It was routine for him to be snubbed.

He ate his charred, juicy hot dog thinking about it. From the beginning he'd been snubbed. Well, maybe not the beginning. At first there were soft breasts, warmth, a soft voice. A hard chest and deep voice. Love. But when Marshall was three, after that plane crash near Chicago, he and his baby sister came out to Los Angeles to live with their grandmother. Marshall loved Grandmother. She smelled spicy and salty and her kiss prickled. He wanted her to love him. But right off the bat she preferred Lois. Spoiled her. Bought her crisp organdy dresses, took her places. "Shopping is for girls, Marshall dear." "But I need some new jeans." "Little men don't go to luncheon fashion shows." So Marshall trotted out in the jungly back yard and pretended he was Tarzan. "Marshall, why can't you play quietly, like Sister?"

School, too, started out on the wrong foot. The first morning in kindergarten with everyone cross-legged on mats listening to a wondrous tale of a faraway land, Marshall raised his hand, waved it, waved it frantically, then—oh, shame—before he could get the pretty blonde teacher to look up from her illustrated book, scalding water, humiliating water, ran down his legs, darkening his new brown corduroys. From that first day he was known as Wetpants Mosgrove. Even new kids picked it up. However hard he tried with a new boy, and Marshall tried hard all the time, before the new kid's first day ended he was calling Marshall Wetpants. Marshall was forced to hang around with the lowest of the low, those lacking the skills of four square, sockball, kickball, pickle, one bounce and tetherball. Even this bunch of retards picked on him. *Hey, Wetpants, catch!*

He hated and feared school.

He ached with loneliness at home.

It wasn't until he started California High that he gained companionship. He read on the bulletin board about Forensics Club. After a great deal of worry he signed the attached sheet. Tuesday afternoon, at three thirty, using all the courage imparted by a giant Hershey, he entered the Forensics sanctum, Room 120. The Forensics president, a tall twelfth grader much admired by Marshall, stood at the lectern. As Marshall paused at the door, the tall president consulted his list, smiled at Marshall. "This must be our new member, Marshall Nasgrove. To welcome Marshall, let's have a big hand." People clapped and smiled at Marshall. After that he was a joiner. He joined Philately, Future Legal Eagles, the Lapidarians. *Quo Vadis*, the Latin club. The Camping, Hiking and Drama clubs. Many of the three thousand and twelve students at California High might recognize him, but Marshall understood this didn't make him Mr. Popularity. He knew the world. His memberships meant nothing beyond a casual *Hey, Mosgrove* in the halls. Still, whatever you said, wasn't this a giant step up from *Hey, Wetpants?*

Then, that hot afternoon last November, during fifth period, his craziest, wildest, furthest-out dream came true. Dr. Schramm asked him to run, unopposed, for student body prexy! Marshall hesitated, though. *How many had turned Dr. Schramm down already?* Three days ago the two guys running had been temporarily suspended and therefore disqualified. After the suspensions Clay Gillies (then a new transfer from University High) organized a monster rally on the football field, and there everyone vowed, in one air-shaking cry, not to run for that office. Marshall's hesitation lasted less than a moment. Whatever that rabble-rousing Clay Gillies said about the complete irrelevance of school office, a student body president was respected. Wetpants would be forever dried up. Marshall had said in his sincerest tone, "Dr. Schramm, sir, I appreciate the trust you've placed in me. I'll do my utmost to live up to it."

Two days later into a nearby front site drove a Ford station wagonful of girls. They set up sloppy camp, waggling their tightly shorted backsides and making a shrill racket. Marshall, a secret snob, thought they must be waitresses. He resented their intrusion into this masculine paradise.

But Stryker felt otherwise. He said, grinning, "Time to make us some connections."

"With those old hags?"

"They're stuff, man. I can sniff it this far away."

Marshall made a grunt of disgust.

"Jeez, why so fussy?"

"We can do better."

"Not down here we can't," Stryker said. "C'mon, let's get there before the crowd."

It was late afternoon and salt wind rattled sea-stunted pines. Marshall shivered. Not cold from sea damp, but cold with fear. The women did look easy. What if he and Stryker did connect? Then what would happen? Either Stryker would find out he'd lied or he'd have to go through with it. What if he couldn't? After all, it would be a first time. Marshall dreaded any type of first time. He glanced through lengthening shadows at the women. Bundled in their cheap, bright coats, they drank beer from cans. Six of them, one less attractive than the next.

"I'm used to better fare," he said.

"I'm not! Jeez, I am sick of letting my meat loaf!" Stryker burst out with rare anger.

"With girls like that"—Marshall gave a single hand clap—"is pretty sure. You eager for the old penicillin treatment?"

Stryker glared.

"Listen, don't you think I'm as red hot for it as you are?" Marshall demanded. He could hear his own voice, too loud and somehow hollow.

Suddenly Stryker grinned. "Jeez, Marshall, they are horny-looking old bags, aren't they? We'll wait for some better-looking, younger stuff to show up."

"Now you're talking."

Stryker forgot the female sex.

A couple of days ago over the car radio had come reports that a hurricane had lashed Baja California. A hurricane in Mexico means large southerly swells a couple of days later in California. And Stryker had been complaining that the waves, which seemed monstrous to Marshall, weren't worth taking. Stryker spent that evening waxing his board and happily listening to small-craft warnings.

During the night waves roared, wind shuddered against canvas and salt odors intensified.

Thin morning light showed the beach: great brown snakes of kelp coiled around driftwood and dead fish. Far out on the horizon, monsters reared. As Marshall shivered one rose higher, higher, displaying a curved green underbelly in which were undigested logs and great colons of seaweed. With a deafening shriek the monster collapsed. Turbulent white bones raced shoreward. A ranger, passing in his jeep, cupped both hands, bawling at them that nobody should go out today.

"He thinks we're insane?" Marshall asked, goose bumps forming under his fleece-lined jacket.

Stryker took out his wax.

"Stryker, you heard him!"

Wind hurled Marshall's words back in his face. He tried again.

"You'll get yourself killed, you know that, don't you?"

Stryker began to wax the top of his board.

"Killed!"

Stryker moved the square of paraffin.

"It's suicide!"

Stryker squinted up at Marshall. "That's why it's the test."

"Test?"

"To show what you are."

"Talk sense," Marshall shouted.

"Everyone's got his own test."

"Tests're in school."

"I've gotta."

"Why?"

"Jeez—oh, hell, you know I'm no good at explaining."

"Stryker—"

Stryker rose, balancing his board under his arm.

Marshall trotted after him. He wanted to grab Stryker the way wind grabbed at stunted pines; he wanted to shake and rattle Stryker; he wanted to shriek the logical reasons Stryker should stay on land. Stryker was his friend, his only friend after all these lonely years. *Can I be held in any way responsible if Stryker goes and gets himself killed?*

Only Stryker and the two bald interns, encased in tight black rubber suits, went out. Marshall, shivering on wet sand, watched the three boards cleave over, then disappear behind a huge wave glittering with dangerous cracks of surf.

"They're crazy, those guys," Marshall shouted over the incessant roar of wind and sea. "Sick sick sick."

Stryker

straddling his board, gripping the rails with his total strength, arms aching, hands bent like metal hinges around fiberglass, fingers blue, water roaring under his board until the anger of the sea filled his body. Iodine wind, salt, cold. A mysterious thread of blood appeared on his shoulder. He licked the salt wetness, feeling raised bumps of skin with his tongue, feeling on numbed skin scalding heat of his own saliva. The other two huddled well behind the surf line. They hadn't taken any, they were terrified, this Stryker knew because of echoing terror in his own body. He'd taken three of the smallest. Now, under him, a set formed, waves hurling themselves at the shore, hillocks of water that bucked him like a rodeo horse. He strained to weld his body to floatable fiberglass. He breathed in shuddering gasps.

Suddenly a sort of calm. A stillness as if the storm had ended.

Stryker glanced over his shoulder.

A line of water hid the horizon.

Water rising, rising, sucking sound and water into itself. Huge, deafening, growing. Yet somehow calm. The eye of the hurricane, he thought. The rubber-suited interns paddled wildly; this monster would break well behind the surf line, and they needed to make outside before it smashed over them. Stryker had a couple of moments when he could have turned and tried to catch up; everything was being sucked that way, and his mind ordered his arms to paddle, paddle with all the strength left in them so he, too, would be behind the point that this wave would break. *Escape,* his mind ordered, *escape.* He was terrified. Terrified? There was a weakness in him that turned his stomach to jelly. Was that why they called it gutless? Your guts dissolved on you? All at once Stryker understood quite clearly what he'd tried to explain to Marshall. Of course a guy like that never could understand. This *was* a test, but not the way Stryker had thought, between him and the sea. The test was a showdown between Stryker Keith Halvorsen and a goddam pansy chicken who lived inside his guts. If Stryker couldn't conquer that jellifying pansy, jeez, what had he tested today? He knelt, paddling in the opposite direction of the pull. Forward. To the point where the monster would break. He stroked hard as he could. Water sucked him back, yet in the uneven battle he managed to hold his own, moving neither forward nor backward. The wave reached him. It curled over him. For what seemed an hour he was sheltered by a translucent green cathedral arch embedded and ornate with strange patterns of seaweed and rocks. The wave caught him; thrust forward as if by God's great hand, he fought to maneuver the board into position. Under him churned sand and huge rocks. If he landed in the trough he'd never make it to shore, not alive. Dead. Dead. Dead. Salt spray cut on his skin. He'd die before he'd had his first piece, die a virgin, die before he hit a grand slammer. Die before he'd eaten juicy pig roasted in a luau pit or drank champagne or seen the silver grunion spawn on the beach under a full moon. O.K. So he'd die. It was more important, wasn't it, to conquer that pansy chicken?

"Now," he grunted.

Wildly, frantically, he maneuvered the board.

"It's the tall blond guy," somebody shouted. "He's standing up."

"Jesus! That crazy nut. Doesn't he know you can't ride *that*."

Marshall, his square-cut face distorted by fear, raced down

the incline, thrashed into surf that sucked at his feet; he spread thick legs to keep his balance.

Stryker made it almost to shore. His board jarred, shooting high out of raging water. Marshall, wearing his good jacket, dived into the dangerous undertow. But Stryker staggered in by himself, his rib cage expanding and contracting like an accordion. A streak of red grew in his long wet hair. He was smiling.

It was dark now, the storm had died, and the tent was silent except for the humming of the Coleman lantern. A smell of wet sheep came from Marshall's jacket, drying on a nail driven into the tent pole. The interns recently had cupped gentle hands around Stryker's skull, probing for cracks. "Looks fine to me," said the balder of the two, and he'd knotted seven stitches to close Stryker's wound; they'd departed.

Marshall untied a wet Ked. "What was it like out there?"

"Best ride ever."

"I mean, weren't you afraid?"

Stryker shrugged inside the khaki sleeping bag.

"You heard the others," Marshall said. "They both admitted it was the most terrifying experience of their lives—and one of them'd been in Korea."

"I figured I'd had it."

"But you just said the ride was the greatest?"

"Unless you're afraid, what does it mean? Jeez, Marshall, you gotta be scared, otherwise what've you overcome? How can anything be great if you aren't afraid? If it's easy? Know what I mean?"

"Uh huh," Marshall lied. He unknotted his other Ked, asking, "You feel O.K., Stryker?"

"Tired."

"Remember, if you feel nauseous—"

"Calling Dr. Kildare, calling Dr. Kildare." Stryker grinned. "Heaving, it's a bad sign."

"You don't have to look so pleased with yourself. Honest to God, Stryker, I sweated blood while you were out there."

"Hey, there. I never knew you cared."

"I mean it."

"Thank you, Marshall." Stryker yawned. "Jeez, am I tired!"

After a while Stryker slept. The interns had cautioned Marshall to listen for changes in Stryker's breathing, so he moved his sleeping bag closer. He folded damp Bermudas and sweat shirt over a tent rope to dry. He closed the valve of the lantern. He zipped himself into his bag.

It was, Marshall knew all along, a dream.

But being a dream didn't make it any less frustrating. He was on a crowded beach when Michele Davy—no; in the dream Marshall corrected himself: Michele Gillies—sat next to him, baring her breasts, placing his hands on them. In front of everyone she loudly explained that nobody liked him. "You weren't given a standing ovation at the last assembly," she said, "and everybody knows it's California High tradition to give the outgoing prexy a standing ovation." Then, taking her bare breasts with her, she left the beach. Marshall realized everyone was leaving. He saw people moving like a chain of spears up the brown cliffs; his grandmother, Lois, Michele, Gillies, York, Dr. Schramm, the two bald interns, all of them moving up the cliff leaving him. He tried to follow, but he couldn't move. Afraid. So afraid. He squeezed his eyes shut, hardly daring to breathe, for he knew somehow he was a sacrificial tethered goat. A victim. But staked out for whom? Or what? From far away came an awesome rumble. A great tidal wave rolled toward him. *Where have I seen one like it?* He struggled to get up, he tried to crawl, anything to escape, but his muscles were paralyzed. *Help,* he cried, and no sound came. But what difference would sound make? Who would come back to rescue Wetpants Mosgrove? His heart a pounding captive in the nightmare, he watched the Everest of water move closer. Closer. Just as it was about to engulf him, long, strong arms reached out, clasping him to safety.

Marshall, with all his strength, grabbed his rescuer.

And in this overwhelming dream embrace, he forgot the nightmare.

Now he was conscious only of a tall, lean body. He touched firm flesh, running his fingertips along hard biceps, tracing the central line of flat, hairless chest, journeying downward to caress the taut belly; crisp hairs grew in the indentation of navel, and Marshall's dreaming hand delayed, making trembling, voluptuous circles of discovery. In Marshall's sleeping brain a censor ordered the body to change, grow breasts, soften, become female. The body remained hard, firm, breastless. And infinitely exciting. A terrible grief overcame Marshall. He felt tears on his cheeks, for now the censor informed him that this much-needed love was wrong, even in sleep it was wrong; his dream was criminal, wicked. Yet the error of his way only increased the pleasure. The muscles at the base of his body tightened.

And at last his sleeping brain admitted the evidence.

In his dream he caressed and desired not just a male body, firm flesh, as he had in other dreams, but a person, a living person with a name. He murmured that name: "Stryker."

He dreamed Stryker and he lay together.

Excitement in Marshall swelled, growing, growing until the pressure became unendurable; the dream took its course. He moaned aloud. Twisted. Groaned.

"Stryker," he cried. Asleep, he yanked at the long, heavy zipper. "Stryker!"

He woke.

He was clasped, ejaculating, around Stryker's sleeping bag.

Abruptly Marshall let go and rolled away, pulling his own bag around himself. He ordered his spasmodic panting to cease. But in the darkness he could hear his muffled gasps. The noise was a terrible indictment. For his doomed dream, Marshall felt sure, could not possibly be understood by anyone normal. Marshall, encased in damp, kapok-filled fabric, crawled yet further from Stryker, telling himself the unspeakable desire that so obviously had lurked underground in his subconscious, to emerge in his dream, could never be imagined by a heroic type like Stryker. Much less shared!

Stryker's breathing was slow and regular, the sound of sleep. Yet Marshall was aware (don't ask him how) that Stryker feigned sleep.

Had he called Stryker's name aloud?

Marshall's spent body knotted with tension. Pain, acute physical pain, tore at his chest. If Stryker had heard, then he knew the full, perverse extent of Marshall's dream. Some animal rattled a nearby trash can. Did Stryker know? Did he? If Stryker knew, *if Stryker told,* then Marshall Mosgrove (Hey, Wetpants!) was doomed to a far worse section of that desolate country, rejection, than he'd ever before inhabited. Marshall lay awake the night, his stomach icy yet his skin burning as if he were in the last throes of diphtheria.

The following morning was overcast.

They'd planned to leave the next day, which was Sunday.

But Stryker, refusing to meet Marshall's eyes, said, "I can't surf with this." He touched white gauze that turbaned his head. "Let's hit the road."

Stryker knew. *He knew!*

For three days Marshall lived with terror.

Then he heard from Michele Gillies that Stryker had gone to visit his father in San Diego. Stryker would stay until school started, she said, her voice free of innuendo. Marshall's body relaxed. Safe. He was home free. Free. Yet as Michele jabbered on, a funny thought came. This wondrous relief, how did it weigh on the scales with his loss, the loss of first friendship?

7

Leigh Sutherland had love on the brain.

A romantic, she always focused much attention on the subject; that summer she turned seventeen love went public:

Princess Margaret marrying her photographer,

and the Democratic candidate with his glowing Jackie, smiling, chic and pregnant,

and Marilyn Monroe and Arthur Miller, beauty and the brain, TV announcers called them,

as well as Brenda Starr weeping over her black orchid.

James Dean might be dead, but after Leigh and Michele drove to a dusty theater down on Western Avenue to take in a revival of *East of Eden* and *Rebel Without a Cause*, Michele admitted to Leigh that spiritual love forgets death.

York's father was pictured on the cover of *Confidential;* the article hinted Baron took three girls to a hotel room and kept them happy for a grand total of sixty-one hours. Leigh wondered, how often and how long could a man? And she felt terribly sorry for Mrs. York—but. Did people who'd been married that long still do it with one another?

Those girls were so terribly scarred it took plastic surgeons these many years to remodel them. Now they were ready for love. The Hiroshima maidens, people called them.

Leigh was vulnerable to novels, poems, movies and television programs about love, songs of love.

She had invented a fantasy of love.

Almost every night she would stare into darkness, polishing details. This, she knew, not only was ludicrous but also completely immature and possibly sick. Yet she couldn't shake the habit. . . .

Her parents and younger brother Stevie are away for the weekend someplace, maybe at her grandmother's sprawling summer cottage at Malibu—anyplace. She's alone in the two-story house. She has never yet figured out a convincing reason why Maria, the Sutherlands' Mexican housekeeper, isn't around, or why her parents, so loving and solicitous, would have left her alone like this; they never had. But no matter. Alone.

She lies by the pool in her new blue flowered bikini, sun beating hot on her. Drowsily she inhales the richness of sun-warm rose bushes, hears bees buzzing. Then the heavy gate that leads to the alley creaks. Standing there is a stranger in madras shorts. He's tanned, with the easy, long-muscled grace of a basketball player. Leigh, barely five five, doesn't need a tall boy, yet for some reason she's never yet figured supple height remains his constant, unchanging characteristic—his features fluctuate: sometimes he's Steve McQueen, Paul Newman or Dr. Richard Chamberlain, never a boy she's actually gone out with. They stare at one another and he lets the gate close behind him, moving on bare feet around the pool. She doesn't protest—how can she? All dizzy and limp, she can scarcely breathe. Without a word he pulls her to her feet, leading her to the pool house. Why don't they use the big white Colonial, so carefully emptied of inhabitants? Because to Leigh the chlorine-scented pool house seems more languorously suitable for love, an aqueous, submarine cave. In this underwater dimness he unsnaps blue fabric and as her top rustles to the cement floor he gazes down at her naked breasts and she floats at the bottom of a waiting sea, waiting until at long last he cups both hands gently around her breasts. She trembles and goes damp in her place at this thought; her nipples are unusually sensitive—she takes much care when buying a bra that there's no undue pressure—and his imagined kiss, lips and tongue on each tender pink point is almost too exquisite to bear. . . .

Oh, one hot summer day love would come, she knew it, and in the meantime she went to the beach and heard music spool from transistors:

> *Come on, baby, let's do the twist,*
> *Come on, baby, let's do the twist.*
> *Yeah . . . just like this.*
> *Come on, Daddy's sleepin'*
> *and Mamma ain't around,*
> *   —come on and twist.*

At the beach Cindy Cameron admitted to the Rondelays that she was doing it; her parents both worked, and afternoons they had the apartment to themselves, she and Bob.

Leigh drove Dorot home.

Dorot said, "That makes nine out of twenty-two Rondelays. Pretty soon we'll be a minority group."

"Cindy says it's real traumatic." Leigh flushed. "*I*'m waiting until I fall really in love."

"He makes her do all sorts of things. One time he got her to put Wesson oil all over them; then they balled in the bathtub."

"She shouldn't tell," Leigh said. "If she loved him, she wouldn't."

At the end of July, Ruth Abby saw an article in the *Times* about an Obon Festival in west Los Angeles. She suggested to Leigh, the only friend Mrs. Heim permitted her (and this friendship under strict maternal supervision), that they go. Ruth Abby didn't have to push it. Leigh said, "Yes, let's," right away.

Mrs. Heim, shrilling a command that they meet her here, right here, in an hour and a half exactly, dropped them off near the beige stucco Buddhist church. The jammed block had been roped off and over the street, like an excess of moons, hovered Japanese lanterns printed with the words *Kikkoman Soy Sauce;* their multicolored lights illuminated the haze, so the scene glowed with soft colors like an old block print. In the center of the road, on a dais, a muscular Oriental in a black *hapi* coat sweated and banged a heavy drumstick on a huge drum while to his slow, hypnotic beat circled maybe two hundred brightly kimona-ed dancers, three mincing steps forward, swish of bright fan, two steps back. The dancers were every age from gray-haired grandmothers wearing magnificent brocade *obis* to plum-

eyed baby girls who look "exactly like Japanese dolls," as Ruth
Abby whispered to Leigh.

After two interminable dances Ruth Abby said, *"She'*ll be
back before you know it. Let's eat." So the two made their
slow way to the courtyard. Their noses led them to the savory-
scented *teriyaki* stall but Leigh, glancing at skewered meat
sizzling on huge *hibachis*, said, "Let's look around a minute;
maybe there's stuff we've never tried, you know, something
sort of exotic," so they wandered; in the end Ruth Abby headed
back to the *teriyaki*, but Leigh discovered a bowl of thin noodles
topped with a strange sauce. They bore their meal into the
church. Gold chandeliers blazed. Gold Buddhas gazed on vo-
tive offerings of plastic fruit, plastic flowers. Long trestle tables
had been set up; they were pretty crowded but Leigh and Ruth
Abby found places. No silverware, so Leigh unwrapped dis-
posable chopsticks and, after pulling apart bamboo, she ex-
perimented—a noodle slithered onto her yellow cotton dress.
She napkined the spot clean, tried again. She managed to lip
a sliver of something so hot it burned her nostrils like Coleman's
mustard. She fanned her face, breathing heavily.

Ruth Abby giggled with a trace of her old mindless cheer.
"You'll be all night."

Leigh lost another noodle. "Probably."

"Try something else?" Ruth Abby suggested.

Leigh shook her head.

"O.K., be stubborn," Ruth Abby said, rising. "Me, I'm for
some of those puffy fried things."

Leigh watched Ruth Abby's navy slacks disappear in the
crowd, thinking sympathetically that since the trouble she might
be somebody else. Minus her guitar, plus twenty pounds, seldom laughing, she was a stranger. Leigh pitied Ruth Abby but
at the same time tremendously admired her—each Rondelay
agreed that *she* never would have had the nerve to buck Tiger.
Leigh, struggling with narrow noodles, tried to think up ways
to gladden Ruth Abby. She didn't notice Ken Igawa until he
stood over her.

"Hey, look who's here. It's L-E-I-G-H Sutherland," he said
to a round-headed Japanese boy that Leigh recognized from
California High.

"How'd you pronounce it?" the short boy asked.

Leigh swallowed her mouthful so she could tell him.

Before she had a chance to, though, Ken Igawa said, "Beats

me," and swung his long legs over the bench to sit next to her.
The short boy leaned against the table.

"Have you two eaten?" Leigh asked politely.

"Later," Ken said. "You go right ahead."

Leigh hesitated.

"Don't you dig *soba?*" Ken asked.

"What?"

"The noodles."

"It's delicious."

"Then why aren't you eating?"

Lifting the bowl to her mouth as she'd noticed the Oriental
diners doing, Leigh maneuvered her chopsticks. Noodles slithered down her chin and back into the bowl. Ken Igawa laughed.
He was very good-looking when he laughed. She wished him
dead. She tried another noodle, this time capturing it partially,
sucking it between her lips with a loud embarrassing noise.
Both boys grinned. The calf of Ken Igawa's leg touched hers.
Accidentally she assumed. She moved. His leg followed. A
set little smile creased her mouth as she fought slippery noodles
with unfamiliar weapons, at the same time trying to escape the
pressure of his calf.

"L-E-I-G-H," Ken said. "You *might* pronounce it Lee—"

"Yes," she said.

"But Lee's pretty ordinary and common—"

"It's how you say it."

"—and on the other hand there's W-E-I-G-H."

Both boys guffawed one brief time.

Leigh felt her face get hot. She said, as politely as possible—
after all, what were manners for, if not to help you through
these awful moments?—"Why make a federal case out of my
name?"

Ken Igawa shrugged. His calf, warm and assertive, pressed
closer. To Leigh's horror, her leg started to tremble. Ken Igawa
gave her a brief, thorough glance, raising one eyebrow. He did
not move his leg.

"Finish," he ordered. "You want Nakamura to think you
don't like Japanese food?"

Leigh tried to laugh. "I am pretty clumsy," she said.

"Yeah yeah yeah."

"I am," she insisted.

"Wasn't arguing."

"And chopsticks aren't the easiest."

"Hashi are quaint, aren't they?" His sarcasm bit. His calf

shoved hers, which quivered harder.

He was forever chopping her down. Why? The sole reason she could figure: in the past, unwittingly and in an unknown manner, she had offended him and he was repaying her. Yet why behave like a spiteful seventh grader? Or was this childish? Managing to swallow a noodle, Leigh conceded that he wasn't being childish. Were it time of war, Ken Igawa would be raping her.

"Well," he said suddenly, "got to be going." The pressure of his leg withdrew as he pushed up easily. "Have a good time at the festival, L-E-I-G-H."

"Lay! That's a great name for a girl who . . ." Nakamura's snort faded. He followed Ken Igawa to three pretty Japanese girls who chattered by the entry.

The following week was very hot. Leigh walked miles along Santa Monica sand. She would never, she decided, never go to the Gillieses', not ever again; she never wanted to see Ken Igawa again. Never. She belly surfed the waves more recklessly than usual, thinking as she raced shoreward, *I will not go to the Gillieses'; I never want to see Ken Igawa again.* To staunch the hot embarrassment that welled inside her each time she thought of the incident, she repeated over and over, *I won't go to the Gillieses'; I never want to see Ken Igawa, never, never, never again.* But Friday afternoon when Michele phoned and asked in her roundabout way if Leigh was coming and if she was would she bring along pizzas, Leigh heard herself reply, "Sure. Be glad to, Michele."

She arrived late. Ken sprawled on the stained gray couch. He didn't make any cracks. As a matter of fact he didn't say a word to her, not even hello, but from time to time she caught him examining her, and under his narrow-eyed gaze she felt as if she were wearing a Saran Wrap dress and she was positive he saw this nakedness.

She escaped into the kitchen.

There she fumbled with the string of a flat white pizza box. Ken followed her.

"Let me," he said.

She shook her head.

"Why don't you cut it with a knife?" he suggested.

She continued to fumble. Pulling strings buckled the slim box.

"You *are* clumsy," he said.

"We've already agreed on that," she muttered. Bending her head she whispered, "Leave me alone. Just leave me the hell alone!"

"Tsk, tsk. Obscenity from the perfect lady."

"What d'you expect after the other night?"

"A good-conduct medal?"

"Oh!"

"O.K., I let my true immature sadism creep through. Listen, it bothered me seeing you there."

"But why?"

"The pukka sahib white lady come to view the colorful natives."

"That's not true!"

"Why else?"

"A lot of people were there! The *Times* said *every*one was welcome! Ruth Abby was there! Was it your private party?" Her low, furious words spat out. Leigh rarely lost her temper, but Ken had jabbed once too often. "Did Ruth Abby or the others upset you?"

"So you haven't noticed."

"Oh, shut up!"

"In the shining words of somebody or other, only you upset me."

Still caught in her fury, she opened and slammed drawers until she found Michele's serrated knife; then the words he'd just spoken hit her. *Only you upset me*. That was an admission of sorts, wasn't it? Why hadn't she acknowledged that he upset her, too? Upset her plenty.

She didn't pause to consider.

"And you me," she said. Still holding the knife, with her left hand she touched two fingers first to her own lips, then to his warm mouth. He grinned and raised an eyebrow. His eyebrows peaked at the center. She dropped her hand quickly. It was, she realized too late, a gesture left over from babyhood and probably hilarious to him, especially since he, even more probably, hadn't meant a single thing beyond his routine sarcasm. Why had she let herself in on another thrilling game of Sadist's Delight?

"Hey Leigh—"

"If you make a single crack I'll—"

"I was only going to mention that when I was little, my mother taught me to kiss long distance, too. Germs, you think?"

The sarcasm was muted but still evident. Tears sprang to her eyes.

"Hey," he breathed, "hey, listen, listen. When you were going someplace and your face got dirty, did your mother make you spit on her handkerchief to wipe you clean?"

She tried to say yes, instead swallowed twice. Nodded.

"A very distinctive odor, a face washed with saliva, right? And when I didn't clean my plate, mine'd tell me they were starving in Asia. Yours?"

Europe. And it hadn't been her mother but both her grandmothers who'd said *They're starving in Europe*, but it was too complicated to explain so she nodded once more.

"Yeah yeah yeah. I should shut up, I guess. But I came out here to say it, so I gotta say it." Ken took a small step closer, staring down at her. His eyelids were flat and complex at the corners. His eyes didn't slant—why did people say Japanese had slanty eyes? Using the same two fingers she had, he touched first his own lips, then hers. His hand smelled of clean soap and turpentine. "I'm apologizing." He tarantara-ed a whispered bugle call. "A first, with me."

Her mouth opened a little.

"You'll forget the other night?"

She nodded.

"Not to carp, but it's O.K.?"

She nodded.

"Yes?" he asked. "Is it?"

She coughed to clear her throat, then murmured, "I'm sorry I lost my temper."

"Lose it if you must," he said. "Otherwise ulcers."

She nodded gravely.

"Friends, then?" he asked.

"Friends."

"Smile?"

She managed a smile.

He smiled back at her.

In the other room laughter peaked raucously, a rich aroma of herbs and tomato and mozzarella rose from the open cardboard box, upstairs a toilet flushed, and over the sink nylon curtains ballooned with summer wind; a Santa Ana blowing off the desert, it flicked a straight, very black strand over Ken's right eyebrow. Her hand ached to push back the hair. His eyebrows went up, then down. He moved closer, not close enough to touch, but her nipples, always very sensitive, responded to his body temperature and it was the same as if they were touching. His smile faded; his eyes almost closed. "Hey Leigh," he whispered. "Why did I act that way? Why?" The reply must be as obvious to him as it was to her, so she didn't answer but kept gazing up at him, taking this moment—naked and separate—refusing to think about the mountains of time piled up before it. And after it.

Part Two

——————————• **1** •——————————

She could hear the shower running as she snugged deeper into the blankets. He cold showered every morning, and every morning, as now, she shivered a little under the covers, listening to the icy water. He hot showered when he got home from the market—he couldn't work two jobs and also manage college, so he'd quit Dr. Feiner. The watery rush stopped.

She'd better get up.

For breakfast he mopped up eggs over easy with three slices of whole wheat toast. She preferred white, and she got a really warm feeling each time she picked up a brown cellophane-wrapped loaf rather than a white one. It came to Michele, still curled in bed, that the sense of giving to another person was the major satisfaction in marriage. Sex? Michele had known since that first time under crossed Confederate swords sex wasn't the main bit for the girl. (Now she was so large Dr. Johansen had advised her and Clay to use the posterior position and she didn't like it, not at all, but she never once let on to Clay.)

She pushed herself out of bed.

As Clay came into the kitchen he switched on the ivory clock radio that had been in her room at home.

"D'you have enough money for gas?" she asked.

"Shhh," Clay hissed. The announcer spouted away about some school integration going on in New Orleans. So far away. Michele wondered how Clay could be so wound up in what happened so far away. The commentator began an unconfirmed report that Princess Margaret was pregnant, which interested Michele, but Clay—trust him—chose that exact moment to turn down the volume and answer her question.

"Two dollars," he said. "That's plenty."

"You had three fifty-four yesterday." She set the eggs in front of him. Last night, while he showered, she'd counted coins and crumpled bills on the dresser—she'd plan to coo from him what was left over from gas. She needed it as part of a down on this gorgeous lamp she'd seen at Broadway, a big orange ceramic base with hot pink shade piped with the same color orange. Mrs. Sutherland owned a lamp in these very colors, and Michele admired everything about Leigh's chic, style-conscious mother. Clay was so unreasonable about buying things. Once the lamp was all paid for, she'd surprise him.

Clay ate. She poured hot chocolate into one of the bright orange mugs that had been the Rondelays' wedding gift.

"Did you need a book?" she inquired.

"I spent the money."

"You spent it!"

He wiped up yolk with toast.

"You mean you gave it away," she accused.

"So?" he asked. "Wasn't it mine?"

He was staring at her with those big, bruised-looking eyes. Even in her anger Michele felt an upsurge of love aching in her swollen breasts. When he was upset Clay looked exactly like James Dean. Would Clay die young, too? She crossed her fingers at this unlucky thought and continued to do battle.

"But Clay, giving! When we don't even have enough to buy chewing gum—"

"I seem to remember it was your idea that we should each have something to spend privately."

Just like him! Making it sound as if she was in the wrong. It had been her idea. She'd read in Ann Landers that there was less pressure on a young marriage when each partner received a small sum to be spent exactly as they wished. Accordingly, each took a pitiful dollar fifty from Clay's every-other-week pay check—this money, though, Michele had assumed, was to be spent on gifts for each other or teensy luxuries. Not thrown away. She started to tell him that in her opinion those civil rights workers should get out and earn their own fare south. But she stopped. Remarks of that type invariably got them into a big hassle, and if they hassled he'd be sure to find out about the lamp. She'd never get it.

Grabbing his books, Clay started for the door.

"Kiss?" she asked.

"Kiss," he agreed.

Both were smiling as he hurried out.

She left the dishes. Her mother would drop by around eleven, and while Dozer yipped at the end of his leash tied outside to the front doorknob, Mother would whip through housework, fix lunch and a dinner casserole. This they kept a secret from Clay.

Michele smeared peanut butter and jelly on toast, carrying it into the living room, switching channels on the twenty-one-inch portable that her parents had bought, on time, as a wedding gift. Wasn't it glorious not to have to race off to school? She found a givaway on 2. Michele adored givaways—*Tic Tac Toe, Do Re Mi, Seven Keys* and the other daytimes—but this, *You Name the Price*, was her favorite. The baby kicked down, toward her vagina. Michele winced.

They loved one another so it wasn't a question of love, but they *did* react differently: take, for example, the simple matter of generosity. They were both generous, but Clay donated to faraway, impersonal causes while she gave on a practical, personal level, like eating this brown bread when she really preferred white.

The TV audience gave a shrill squawk. Don White was about to give away a gorgeous ten-foot sectional. Michele's tousled blonde head moved forward. Wouldn't it look terrific in this room? She wished Clay had worked at the market all along, instead of at that Jewish doctor's; if Clay had been at the market all the time, already he would be getting the routine union raise and they could afford to buy, on time of course, a couch like this.

Clay should have started at the Pixwood.

For Clay, Pixwood Market was death.

That evening, just before six when Mr. Davy went home, he called Clay into his office. As always punctilious about not showing "favoritism" to his son-in-law, he asked in the dry, flat voice he reserved for subordinates if Clay had cashed a check a week ago for one Ellamae Smith.

Clay had.

"Without an initial?"

Without an initial.

Mr. Davy's pale, spatulate fingers extended a white counter check stamped *No Account*.

"You know the rule," Mr. Davy said. "Always call me or Bob." Bob Dewing was the night manager.

"It was such a small amount."

"The rule is, *every* check must be initialed."

"Bob was having coffee."

"Then you should have asked the customer to wait."

"She had three tired little kids."

Mr. Davy re-examined the bad check. "The address is cross town. Was she colored?"

Clay's fists tightened. "She was."

"You have to be especially careful then." Mr. Davy gave a series of dry, hacking coughs.

"I can see no reason to differentiate between customers," Clay said.

"Three children with her, you say. . . . No wonder none of them grow up with decent respect for honesty." Mr. Davy coughed again.

"Take it out of my next pay check," Clay said.

"It's the principle. We haven't had a check bounce in a month."

Clay's fingernails dug into his palms. *O.K. I'm sorry I made you look bad with the big alligator-shoe boss,* he thought.

Mr. Davy said, "Clay, while you're working here, you'll have to obey our rules. Bob or I initial every check."

The market had emptied of customers. Clay leaned on the damp recently wiped counter of number two, the sole check line open. He had never hated anything in his life as much as he hated this place. It looked immaculate to the eye (the customer's eye) but Clay knew that gray mice could not be discouraged from raising their fuzzy broods in the bread gondola over there; at night rats scurried between the storage room and the row of tall garbage cans in the alley. Everything in the place smelled of chickens rotating slowly over the electric spit.

Worst of all, as far as Clay was concerned, his job seemed completely useless. What could be more futile than to stand every day ringing up pennies on this NCR machine under the beady, Special-oriented eyes of middle-aged, middle-class white housewives? "That oleo's twenty today, not twenty-two!" they would bark, as if the two cents were a matter of their lives. What more futile than counting the money he'd taken in on his shift and handing it over to his father-in-law to recount? Clay pressed on the no-sale key, the register rang and the drawer slid open. He stared down at neatly segregated change and bills, stacks of ones, five, tens—twenties and larger went underneath into a hidden compartment. The money's ultimate destination was Mr. Tapley, bald and fat with a taste for alligator shoes. Not that Clay had communist leanings, but what could be more futile than spending your life jangling a cash register to enable some fat market-chain owner to indulge a taste for reptile?

Clay slammed the cash drawer.

Clay, on the UCLA campus, was alive.

He was arguing that sit-ins, stand-ins, pray-ins, buy-ins, these were the only way. Nonviolence, that was the key. RG Richards, at the other end of the table, bawled in his slight stammer that those New Orleans mobs d-deserved something better; say, if you gave those dumb crackers a beating, maybe chopped off some balls, they'd respond better to the laws of the land.

Clay banged on the table, reiterating furiously, *nonviolence!* It took a good deal of nerve to shout this, for RG Richards was a Negro and certainly more entitled to opinions on the matter than Clay Gillies. Clay's forehead shone with light sweat. *Nonviolence,* he repeated. His high-pitched shout penetrated. Momentarily he was the center of the noisy group that ate lunch together at one of the long green tables at the Snack Shack near the old student union; in the background, from the rising new student union building, rang a clatterous hammering. You had to shout to be heard, but this bunch would have shouted anyway; they were thinking, vocal, full of ideas about changing old ways, not a fraternity pin among them.

Later, as the carillon played the hourly chimes, some tune vaguely Mozartian, Clay hurried around the bustling quad.

"Hey, wait up!" RG Richards shouted behind him.

Clay hurried on, shouting over his shoulder, "Can't. I'm late."

"Wait!" RG commanded.

RG Richards and Clay Gillies had met while registering in the dusty, crowded men's gym. Trestle barricades, students waiting docile under crude paper signs, the absence of human guidance—UCLA's registration of new students had all the welcoming qualities of a Chicago slaughterhouse, and Clay had voiced this opinion to a fellow freshman in front of him. The tall, slight boy with dark freckles splotching soft brown skin gave him a quick, warm, agreeing smile. They began to talk. RG Richards had an alert eagerness that gave him a tendency to stammer. They took to one another and from that day on Clay Gillies and RG (for Roosevelt Grosvenor) Richards were friends in the manner of students on a large commuter campus like UCLA. Close at school, never seeing one another away from it.

RG's father, killed during a Korean sub battle, now lay in the Veterans' Cemetery in Westwood; near her dead husband, in the big, ramshackle Wadsworth Veterans' Hospital, RG's mother worked. His mother, RG said, chewing his nails, was willing to sacrifice anything so that he, RG, could make the giant step up the educational ladder, become an engineer or even a doctor or a lawyer. RG, bright enough, had no trouble with his classes. Still, he told Clay, with every quiz he felt burdened and very fearful, as if he were about to flunk out. The reason for this, he told Clay, was he carried a heavy figurative flag blazoned with the motto *The Richardses Are Middle-class Negroes* that on his graduation day he must plant, victorious for his family, on the red-brick towers of UCLA.

"Slow down," RG panted, close now.

"I'm *late*."

"Philosophy 1A, Dr. Larker, right?"

"You make it a habit to memorize everyone's schedule?"

"I looked it up," RG said, trotting a step behind Clay. "We've got someone there who'll take n-notes for you."

"We?"

"Give me time to explain."

The brick paths of the quad were almost empty now, carillon chimes dying, dying, into warm, smoggy air, then, from all directions, an abrasive electric bell. One o'clocks had started.

"You're l-late already." RG spilled sunflower seeds into his palm. "Why not l-listen?"

So Clay, frankly curious by now, followed RG along red-brick paths to a concrete patio shaded by the humanities building.

Was Clay, RG asked, spitting fragile gray shells onto ragged grass, really interested in what they'd been talking about?

"Talking about what?"

"For example, what's g-going on at William Frantz School in New Orleans?"

Clay thought of the news; four tall United States marshals guarding a petticoated, hair-ribboned colored six-year-old through a schoolyard while all around an ugly mob jeered. Pictured the last three nights on TV. The dead-dead show.

"Who wouldn't be?" Clay asked.

"There's a meeting tonight. A d-discussion group."

"NAACP or CORE?" Neither of these organizations was

allowed to recruit on campus.

"A group of our own. A younger bunch."

"I work nights."

"We d-don't invite everybody, man."

"RG, you know I'm married. She's pregnant." Clay wanted to add they needed every penny he'd earn tonight, but about personal finances he could never be blunt. From an open second-story window came a chorus of words in a Slavic language.

"We like your views," RG said.

"Who's we?"

"My discussion group."

"Listen, if it's for the bite"—Clay flushed—"I've already given all I can."

"Money! Man, you d-don't think we want a few lousy bucks? Tell her you have to work overtime."

"I don't lie."

RG groaned with disgust.

Clay shrugged. "I don't. Anyway, in this case, there'd be no point. She'd know. I wouldn't have the cash. And her father's my boss."

More Slavic floated down on them. Clay watched a pair of good-looking sorority types saunter into the red-brick entry of Royce Hall.

RG leaned toward him. Freckles stood out on light brown skin. "You big white liberals," he growled. "Always spouting off to make yourself sound g-good. But when it comes right down to the nitty gritty, man, you're always too f-fucking busy!"

————— **2** —————

The old shingle bungalow was jammed.

Cigarette smoke wreathed the harsh light of two unshaded bulbs; there was the ripe smell of many bodies in a small area. About twenty-five people sat on window ledges; they leaned back on a pair of sagging, chenille-covered beds; they sat on the bare linoleum. Most of them were under twenty, maybe three quarters were Negro. Clay immediately recognized two good-looking girls, honey and coffee colored, who were among the five hundred plus in his Philosophy 1A lecture; one of them must've made the neat notes RG had handed him this afternoon. On the floor sat an ugly white threesome; Clay never had seen *them* before; they wore thick brown oxfords and didn't shave their legs. There was a blonde with spectacular breasts displayed in a low-cut sweater holding hands with a short, bespectacled man. And, in the shadows beyond a narrow archway, York

slumped in a wicker chair, posed characteristically, arm tucked in at his side, pale face with inevitable dark glasses hunched into black sport jacket. A turtle withdrawing into its shell. Clay nodded. York gave no answering sign.

Clay found space on a window ledge and sat. Everyone listened to RG Richards.

"I still say it would be better if we chartered a b-bus. That way we'd get our publicity."

"We don't want publicity, not now," said one of the uglies on the floor. "We're not ready."

"B-baby, speak for yourself," RG said. "I am ready."

"Then you say we charter?"

"With what?" asked the ugliest girl.

"Yeah, what with?"

"Anyway, the company finds out what we want with their bus—no can do."

"Cars—"

"—cheaper anyway."

As the discussion progressed, Clay realized they were planning (hopefully) a trip to New Orleans. Clay leaned back against the uncurtained window visualizing Clay Gillies, one arm protecting a little girl, guiding her through a jeering mob into the brick entry of William Frantz School. . . . He felt a sudden anxious draining in the pit of his firm belly. School integration down south would be beaten and all he would have done was talk. Talk is cheap. The older generation talks. If only . . . for the first time he repented, truly repented, his decision. Not that he didn't love Michele and wouldn't love their child, of course he would, but if he'd accepted York's offer (Clay glanced at York's indrawn, pale face) he would be less encumbered; Michele could work. What was one unformed embryo stacked against this struggle?

A woman with glowing white beads around her firm brown

neck came through a door. She carried a platter of sandwiches. She wore her hair naturally, frizzed and springy, it wasn't black but a very dark brown, and Clay, who never remembered meeting a well-dressed Negro woman with unprocessed hair, admired the effect. She looked proud. Free. Everyone seemed to know her. A chorus of greetings broke: "Hello, Odessa." "Odessa!" and "Hey, Odetta." Sometimes the name sounded like Odetta, sometimes Odessa. Clay couldn't tell which. She *did* remind him of album jackets of Odetta, though she wasn't as large or heavy as the singer, who—come to think of it— wore her hair the same way. Odessa (Odetta?) smiled and called back greetings. Clay stared at her until her gaze met his; then for some reason instead of smiling back he looked away. The discussion broke up into noisy conversations. Cigarettes were lit; someone opened a window. Clay moved around vocal seated bodies to York.

"Didn't expect to see you here," Clay said.

"RG taught me the grip and gave me the code word."

"Your first time?" Clay squatted next to the wicker chair.

"My first."

"Well?" Clay asked.

"Well what?"

"What d'you think?"

"That they'll never make it to New Orleans."

"I think—" Clay started.

But at that moment a platter of sandwiches was thrust under Clay's nose.

"Have one?" asked the dark woman with the glowing white beads and frizzed hair. With a smile she added, "I'm Odessa Norris, your hostess."

"Mrs. Norris"—Clay rose—"I'm Clay Gillies, and this is York. Adam York."

"He and I met before." She smiled. "Listen, I'll feel like I was around before the sack of Rome if you don't call me Odessa."

"Like the singer?"

"Ode*ss*a. With two esses. I was named after Russia's only warm-water port. Make of it what you want."

They laughed.

Odessa said, "I guess I ought to mention it. I asked RG to invite you tonight."

"But—"

"Sit back down. Please," she said. When he did, she continued, "I've been wanting and wanting to meet you. RG's always talking about this friend of his who speaks so well."

"Can't be me."

"Clay Gillies, he said."

"I never spoke anyplace."

"RG says you speak." She chuckled. "A lot. He says you dominate the lunch table; you have something—his word, if I remember it right, was *hypnotizing.*"

York snickered.

Clay rarely got embarrassed, but he sure was sweating now. He hadn't realized he talked so much—yet at the same time, he couldn't deny a small sense of pleasure.... Dominating, hypnotizing ... he?

Odessa Norris again offered the platter. "Please have one," she said.

He was still full from the lamb casserole Michele'd fixed for dinner, but he couldn't refuse Odessa. "Thanks," he said, adding, "Odessa."

"You're very welcome," she said, giving him another smile.

Her eyes were unusual, large and very luminous, as if a flame glowed behind them, narrowing when she smiled into two wonderful dark glitters. Although Clay permitted himself little curiosity about people—he considered such personal curiosity petty, along the same lines as gossip—he couldn't help wondering how old she was. She was built like a woman, full-breasted and full hipped, not fat, but also definitely not girlish, and the way she moved, with confidence and large grace, was not girlish either, yet under the cap of hair her face was young and completely unlined. Too, he wondered where she came from. Her ripe contralto was educated, completely devoid of southern slurring, yet at the same time she had none of those too-precise, almost British mannerisms that older, college-educated Negroes often fall into. Odessa....

Someone in the other room bawled, "Hey Ooodesssah! Need you!"

"Right away," she called back. She turned to Clay. "Can you stay awhile?"

"Well—"

"We haven't had much of a talk."

Michele would kill him—no. She'd hold out on him, which was almost as bad. But he said, "Sure."

"Later, then." Odessa smiled, proceeding with her sandwiches into the jammed little living room.

"Buddy," York said, "she certainly is impressed with hypnotic you."

Clay's jaw tightened. "Will you quit with the buddy-buddy routine?"

"She's giving you a secret Ovaltine decoding ring, so why shouldn't I be jealous?"

"They want you here, too."

"Ahhh, but with me there's an ulterior motive."

"You believe in what they're doing, that's why you're here. Why they want you."

"Bullshit," York said, "on both counts."

"Then why'd you come?"

"Would you have missed them planning the Reichstag fire?"

Voices rose in the other room. Clay controlled his fury. "Sometimes, believe it or not, York, you're funny as a crutch."

"What an original phrase; did you coin—"

"Why do *you* think they want you?"

"For *der tag,* buddy, *der tag,* when they're ready for that publicity."

RG, chewing a sandwich, had wandered over to lean against the rough plaster wall.

York glanced up. "I can see the headlines: BARON YORK'S SON ARRESTED IN CIVIL RIGHTS DISORDERS WITH NEW ABOLITIONISTS." He shrugged. "Or whatever the hell you call yourselves."

"Use only f-fictitious names, m-man, to protect the guilty," RG said.

"I'm right."

"Never righter." RG grinned.

York sank back into the wicker chair, his pale cheeks drawing in as if he sucked on a lemon. If Clay hadn't known York better he would have sworn York was hurt at this rejection of his personal self—but he knew York better.

RG said, "A bunch of us're ready, waiting to go south and help. We're committed. Man, we're going to show those old phonies, b-black and white both, what it means, one nation under God, with liberty and justice for *all.*"

"And Mrs. Norris?" York asked. "What's she got to do with all this?" He turned his head in the direction of Odessa Norris. "She doesn't look exactly under the age of consent to me."

"Odessa?" RG poured sunflower seeds into his palm—he'd finished his sandwich. "This is her place. We always meet here. She lets us. You don't know our old people! Yassuh, nossuh, that's all they got in m-mind to say. All Uncle Toms and—"

York interrupted, "But why does Mrs. Norris lack the Harriet Beecher Stowe syndrome?"

"Why don't you shut up?" Clay defended Odessa Norris against York's vinegar wit.

And at the same moment, RG, biting open a sunflower seed, replied, "She's Odessa, that's why!"

"Tell me about yourself," Odessa said to Clay.

It was an hour later, a few minutes past eleven, and the others had left, except for RG, who sprawled across one che-nille-covered bed, and Clay, who sat on the other. Odessa drank black coffee next to him.

"I told you the details," RG said. "Born in a fungy, mungy Virginia town, Port Claibourne, birthplace and ancestral home of uncounted generations of C-Clays and Gillies and their as-sorted darkies. But Clay split when he was ten, so he's un-contaminated."

"RG's a gold mine of information." Odessa smiled.

"S' true," Clay said.

"But there's more to you than that," she said, touching one of the nacreous beads at her throat, smiling quizzically at Clay.

"What would you like to know?" he asked.

"For example, what do you think of what newspapers love to call the current Negro revolt?"

"It's about time."

"RG mentioned you don't believe in violence?"

"No," Clay said, "I don't."

"Not even when the Mississippi police sic their dogs?"

"No," Clay repeated.

"Let's face it. Wouldn't a beating with a tire chain be con-sidered reasonable provocation?"

"Would you come down to their level?"

She smiled. "I agree with you. But me, I'm a good deal closer in age to Mahatma Gandhi."

"You *are* for nonviolent change?"

"Of course I am," she said. "But you—Clay, I only met you tonight, so stop me if I'm wrong; I often am—you aren't an observer, like your friend, York. You aren't a talker. Ba-sically you're an activist—oh, Lord! How I hate these *terms*. You're a fighter."

Was he? Clay didn't really understand himself or his motives.

"And there's a good deal of anger in you," she said.

"Aren't we all angry? Otherwise, why'd we be here?"

Odessa gazed thoughtfully into her coffee mug. "Yours is pretty strong stuff," she said.

He couldn't figure if this pleased her or not. Suddenly he wanted very much to please this enigmatic woman.

He said slowly, "Maybe you're right. . . . Listen, the other night . . ." His voice faded. The story he wanted to tell was true, but he was very aware he never would tell it if he didn't crave to look good in Odessa's luminous eyes.

"Tell me?" she said.

"I work part time," he started. "Well, it's almost full time, as a checker in Pixwood."

"She knows, she knows," RG interpolated.

"It's part of the story," Clay explained. "A few days ago this woman, she was colored, came in the market. She had three little kids, two boys and a girl baby. The baby wore a white knit cap pulled over half her face. It was around six thirty, that's a very slow time, so we were alone, the woman, the kids, me . . ." Clay paused. His intense desire to please Odessa hurt his normal self-assurance.

"Go on," Odessa prompted gently.

He took a breath. "I watched her. She was poor. Her heels were worn down; her dress didn't button properly. The two little boys stayed very close to her. They never begged for stuff the way most kids do in the market. I watched her go up and down the empty aisles, picking out the cheapest. She pushed the basket over to me, and after I rang up the order and bagged it she said, 'Please, sir, you gotta counter check? I'm flat out of cash.' I knew from the way she spoke there was no account behind any check she would write, and I knew from the way she was looking at me, pleading and anxious, she *knew* I knew. The baby started to whimper. Odessa, I swear it, that baby was hungry. *Hungry.* I gave her the counter check."

"And cashed it?" Odessa asked.

"Without identification," Clay agreed.

"Then?" she asked.

"Last night my father-in-law, he manages the market, got back the check. He chewed me out. He's a real bigot, that man, and right off he figured she was colored. I clenched my fists, getting angrier and angrier. Sometimes I get that angry."

"Violent?" she asked.

Clay shook his head. "Violence's wrong." He extended his palms. Four slim, bluish lines marked each palm. "*I*'d rather bleed."

RG and Odessa looked at his hands. Odessa's mouth twitched with a repressed smile. Instantly Clay dropped his hands. His face got hot. How transparent his desire to please must be to her! What a self-righteous ass he must sound! *How young!*

Her expression was serious again. She sucked in her lower lip thoughtfully. "Tell me something. Would you have helped her if she'd been white?"

"She wouldn't have been so desperate."

"There are, believe it or not, some desperately poor white women in this country."

"If she was," Clay said, "yes."

"I don't believe you," Odessa said. And Clay saw sadness— disappointment?—in the dark, beautiful eyes.

He shifted on the bed so he faced her. "I would," he said earnestly. "I would."

She finished her coffee. "Don't you see, Clay? It's not the woman you helped. It was . . . well, she was a symbol. You helped an abstract idea."

"Of justice," Clay agreed. A passing car washed yellow light into the room. Clay held his breath.

Odessa smiled. This time her smile was infinitely sad, yet somehow, Clay decided with joy, accepting of him. Approving.

After that, Clay, over Michele's hot arguments and cold denials of her body, spent Wednesday nights at the lively meetings held at Odessa's old shingle place. The bunch never got to New Orleans. But there were other, nearer plans.

"A picket," Clay suggested.

"Where?" Odessa asked.

"The Woolworth's near UCLA," Clay said. "You know, in sympathy with the sit-ins."

She nodded.

"We'll hit 'em where it really hurts. The national pocket-book," Clay said.

Hot November sun blazed down on Clay, RG, six other guys and four girls in bright, pretty dresses as they paced a slow oval outside the Woolworth's on Westwood Boulevard.

RG, wearing his good dark slacks and an ironed white shirt, balanced his handmade placard in the crook of one elbow while holding a paperback *Faust* with his other hand; he had a German quiz at two. Clay glared furiously at the middle-age housewives who eagerly rushed in the open doors of the five and ten, departing with brown paper sacks clutched in their fat fingers.

" 'We shall overcome,' " read a legless pencil vendor from his little wagon. "What does it mean?"

"That colored people will be able to eat at any Woolworth lunch counter anywhere in the country," Clay answered.

"Who the hell'd want to?" the legless one shot back.

RG, momentarily leaving Goethe, glanced down. "Anyone who c-can't," he said.

"But everyone saw you!" Michele cried. "Mother and Mrs. Mallory saw you! You were picketing!"

"It was my lunch hour." Clay forked tuna noodle casserole. "And nobody, excepting evidently your mother and Mrs. Mallory, noticed us."

"Everyone stared, Mother said."

"Why didn't she come over and say hi?"

"Mother thinks—" Michele started furiously, then stopped midsentence. Mother had arrived about three with this tuna noodle and the information that she'd seen Clay picketing, the only white boy in with a big group of Negroes—Mother had flushed puce with memory—after all, as she kept pointing out, she'd been with Mrs. Mallory! As she had cleaned the apartment she'd had quite a few words to say, oh, not about Clay, Mother wasn't like that, but about the crowd poor Clay had fallen in with at college.

"Well, what does your mother think?" Clay prodded.

Quoting Mother wouldn't accomplish a thing. And little Michele had made up her mind to accomplish. A lot. So she said mildly, "*I*'m not sure it's the right way."

"Is that what your mother said?"

"Listen, Clay, you know I'm as much for civil rights as you are. But I think you—and they—have to be dignified."

Clay gave her one of his cold looks.

Suddenly Michele slumped in her chair. She placed a small, soft hand on the pink piqué bulge. She gave a low moan.

"Miche, what's wrong?"

She moaned again, louder this time, biting her lip. "Nothing."

"Does it hurt?"

"No."

"It does."

"S'nothing," she murmured. "Sometimes it happens."

"But you're in pain!"

"No," she denied again, letting her glazed eyes admit he spoke the truth.

Clay rose from the card chair, coming around to pull her gently to her feet, leading her to the gray couch, helping her lie down. He sat on the looped carpet next to her, taking her hand. She moved their clasped hands to her stomach, sighing. "That's better."

The baby moved, a knobby shifting. It seemed almost alien that there was a person inside.

Michele sighed. "I'm so fat."

"Not to me."

"And ugly."

"Your skin's like velvet."

"I'm a mess."

"You're beautiful," he said. "Miche, you really feel better?"

She nodded.

"Rest awhile. I'll do the dishes."

"I guess I was upset."

"Miche, look, I don't mean to upset you. But try to see it my way. This is something I really believe in. It's happening. Now. Look, how could I face myself the rest of my life if I didn't do something to help?"

"Clay, you're so good."

"How can I stand by and do nothing?"

"Unselfish."

"I've *got* to do it."

"I want you to be happy, that's all."

"I am."

"Mother thought you looked mad. Angry. That's the only reason I got upset."

"I *was* angry," Clay admitted. "We were picketing. And the stupid old housewives went in and out and never cared *why*."

"But Clay, I don't understand. The Woolworth's in Westwood doesn't even have a lunch counter. And if it did, colored people could eat there as much as they wanted. They can eat anyplace in Los Angeles. You know that."

"Woolworth's is a chain. We want to hurt them economically; then the branches in the southern cities'll have to give in. Understand?"

She nodded.

"So in a small way, even though I don't go south, I will be helping."

"And I promise to do my bit, too. Never shop there. Never again!" She held up two joined fingers. "Brownie's honor."

"Nut."

"Serious-head." She wrinkled her cute little nose at him.

"You feel better?" he asked.

"Clay," she whispered, "come up here wif me?"

Clay Gillies organized no more picketings. But nothing Michele did, threatened, or pleaded or said could stop him from heading every Wednesday night to the lively, noisy meetings. By December Clay decided they ought to have a name.

"Students Nonviolent but Active Participants," he suggested.

Everyone applauded.

SNAP.

· 3 ·

The nurse led her down a brilliantly lit corridor. It was dawn, but doctors and nurses popped in and out of doors as busily as if it were high noon. On her wrist she wore a strip of green plastic with a typed insert:

GILLIES, MICHELE DAVY
f   9   17   1943

The nurse ushered her into a small room, telling her to undress. Just then another pain gripped; her stomach was being compressed as if into a small round brick, and everything blurred, the green walls, the metal furniture, the white washbowl dripping slow water, and she stood there, trembling, her polished fingernails (Shining Pearl, applied last night in anticipation) digging into the fabric of her shift. The nurse bustled around getting out a coarse green linen hospital gown, a clean towel to lay on a high leather bed, and Michele wanted to scream at the plump, gray-haired old woman, *Stop it, stop, stop, stop, I'm dying, help me, help me, damn it....* The pain relaxed. Michele took off her shift and started to put on the back-fastening gown. "Your bra and panties, too, dear," the big old nurse said. While Michele turned away, removing her underwear, the nurse asked questions. Was this her first pregnancy, was she a prima—that meant was this her first baby—how old was she? "Seventeen? My, my, we get a lot of youngsters today. Seems like nowadays nobody over twenty has a baby any more." Laugh, laugh. And she asked had the bag of waters broken yet? "Bag of what?" Michele asked, and the nurse replied, "I guess it hasn't. How long have you been in labor?" Michele told, adding a couple of hours. The nurse used a prehistoric rusty blade to shave her down there. Michele could hear scraping and feel pulling, but she couldn't see over the swollen ugly mound of her belly, stretched and shiny, navel popping out. A pain began and she thought, groaning loudly, that popping belly button once had connected her to her mother just as the interior baby was still attached umbilically to her. If it was a girl (and Michele really wanted a girl) someday it would be attached to another baby girl, and she thought of a million million umbilicuses stretching back into time and forward into time, women connected to one another by a big pulsing cord and she was part of them all, a link between her ancestresses and her descendants. The pain relaxed. It was really awe-inspiring; she, Michele Davy Gillies, was a link in the eternal chain of womanhood. So what if she was a high school dropout? This was the real meaning of life, not any of that junk that'd been crammed into her at California High. She was glad she'd insisted Clay call her mother. Once she'd thought she wanted to be free of Mother, but now she knew she didn't. Mother and she were part of each other, just as this baby was still part of her. Poor Clay, he'd really glared. It was true, all those jokes about men hating their mother-in-law. Maybe men sensed this linklike closeness, mother linked to daughter, daughter linked to mother, daughter, mother, daughter, mother, daughter stretching back through time, forward through time, linked on a single pulsing cord from one end of eternity to the other.

"Upsy-daisy," said the nurse.

She led Michele down the hall to a cubicle with three empty hospital beds. "Relax. With the first it can take hours." Michele gave a pitiful smile and said how about a shot? The pain was killing her. "Your doctor hasn't ordered medication yet," the nurse replied.

After a while Clay and Mother came in. When the pains caught her, Michele let loose, screaming and clutching Clay's hand. Her mother glared at Clay and fussed at the interns. "She needs some ether."

"Nothing yet," the intern said, moving the stethoscope from his ears and raising his head from Michele's stomach. He smiled, winking at Michele even though she must look a sight.

"But the poor child's in agony!" Mother cried. Clay gave Mother a look of loathing. Michele felt centuries older than her husband. Poor Clay, people said he was cold, but the truth was he just didn't understand how to get close to other people, which doubtless was why he got all wound up in idealistic, impersonal stuff. Suddenly she felt as if her rectum were being torn apart, but babies didn't come through there. . . . *Ooooooooooowwww!* She really screamed. *Oooooooowwwwwww!* Sweat poured out of her, her eyelids stung with salt and she could taste the salt in her mouth. Her throat ached with the prolonged *Oooooooooooowwws*. A nurse and an intern came running. They ordered Clay and Mother to leave. Just as Clay stepped into the hall, the pain diminished and she called him back. As he bent over her she whispered, "I love you." At the moment it certainly wasn't true. Wasn't this all his fault? But Michele'd read a novel where the heroine dying in childbed says this and she'd decided to say it, too, when she gave birth.

The nurse hypoed something into her butt.

Finally.

She was beginning to worry they were still hung up on that natural childbirth kick of the fifties. She drifted away from herself and it was if she were watching everything happen to someone else. Who was that poor girl? Why torture her? Why rip her apart? Why humiliate her by letting strangers peer between her legs and poke fingers up her rear end? Where were they taking her?

Numbness . . .

Nothingness . . .

From a great white cloud above her she heard a majestic voice roll, "It's a girl. Michele, you have a daughter. A little girl."

"Thank you," she whispered. "Thank you, God."

"Easy delivery..."

"...little doll..."

She floated away again to the great clouds that held her gently, softly.... A mother.... A link in that great chain.... After what seemed like hours she awoke to hear a nearby masculine voice, not the majestic one who'd announced her daughter's birth, cry out, "Oh, Jesus! Dr. Johansen, look! She's hemorrhaging!"

Although it was the twenty-ninth of December, a sterile-looking, too-small aluminum tree still parodied Christmas cheer in the living room. Expectant fathers paced, rattled through old *Look*s and *Reader's Digest*s, filled the big orange ceramic ashtrays with stubbed-out cigarettes, told one another nervous jokes, catalogued details of the deliveries of their other children and— after a summons from a nurse, "Mr. Levoy, oh Mr. Lee-ee-voo-ooy!"—hurried off to the plastic-shielded telephones on the other side of the corridor where they could be heard relaying the glad tidings with hoarse, embarrassed joviality.

Mrs. Davy and Clay waited for three hours, five, six.

Not a word passed between them.

Clay, jackknifed on modern green plastic, his face white and expressionless, unmoving except for a taut muscle at his jaw, thought of Michele twisting and contorting in pain, gripping his hand. He thought of his mother dying when he was born. *Anything, I'll do anything, only let Miche be all right.* There was pressure on his bladder, but he couldn't force himself to journey up the hall to the men's head. *Anything, I'll do anything, only let her be all right.* Each time a nurse appeared at the entry he wanted to jump up and shake her until she told him the truth about Michele, but each time his mother-in-law beat him to it, heavy-footing over to demand, her wrinkled underchins shaking, "What about my daughter? How's my daughter? Gillies is the name."

The nurses repeated the same formula: "Her doctor will send word."

And Mrs. Davy would throw her son-in-law a slit glance as if to say, *It's all your fault.* No words, only these poisonous glances, passed between them. Once Mrs. Davy deserted her post. She phoned, asking someone—probably that gossipy neighbor who'd been at the wedding party—to give Dozer his noon kibbles. She did not, Clay noticed, phone Mr. Davy.

Clay had been at the hospital since six in the morning.

It was seven past four when Dr. Johansen finally stood in the broad corridor outside the waiting room. He wore a black business suit, an unknotted blue tie. He looked completely done in. Why was he here? Why not a nurse like with the other fathers? *Anything, I'll do anything, only let her be all right.* Stiffly, Clay pushed himself to his feet. Mrs. Davy beat him to the doctor's side.

"How's my daughter?" she demanded.

"She's fine. Now."

"Now?" Clay's voice cracked.

"She hemorrhaged."

"Oh, God!"—Clay.

"How is my daughter?" Mrs. Davy's needle was stuck in the groove.

"Fine." The doctor sighed. "But right after the baby—"

"Baby?" Clay echoed. He was taken by surprise that a baby was involved in this awful purgatory.

"Didn't the nurse tell you? A girl." Dr. Johansen managed a weary smile. "A little doll."

"How's my daughter?"—Mrs. Davy.

"We did all we could. She's out of the woods, and thank God for that." He took a deep breath. "In order to stop the hemorrhaging we had to remove her uterus."

Mrs. Davy tried to control a sneeze. Failed. Long quiet hospital corridors echoed with the sound of Mrs. Davy's deviated septum.

"God bless you," said the doctor. "She can't have other children, of course, but otherwise she's fine. We had to do it. She would have bled to death."

So, Clay thought. *Dead....*

"Bled to death!" Mrs. Davy turned on Clay. In her old brown coat she was a squat, malevolent fury. "Bled to death!" she cried, slapping at Clay's face. "See what you've done to her? You! You!"

He didn't move.

She hit away with meaty palms. "What can you do to make it up, how can you ever make it up to her?"

Clay, unanswering, unresistant, completely numb, remained motionless while she swung, aiming at his deep-set, shadowed eyes, his well-formed mouth, his nose, as if she wished to destroy his good looks as these good looks had destroyed sweet young female organs. Dr. Johansen and a passing nurse, fortunately a husky one, managed to pull her away. Dr. Johansen led the shuddering woman toward the service elevators.

Clay got to see Michele as they wheeled her from the recovery room. A thin beige blanket was strapped above her breasts and at her knees, outlining her flat abdomen. Her face was the dead waxen shade of tallow. He walked alongside the stretcher, and when the attendant stopped at the elevator Clay bent to kiss her cold forehead. "Michele, oh, Miche..." he whispered.

"Mmmmm..." she mumbled.

"Whatever you want, whatever, I'll do it. I'll make it up to you."

The elevator closed.

At the far end of the hall, a door marked DO NOT ENTER swung open. Out came a skinny nurse in a rumply green uniform, hair and lower face veiled with the same unironed green. She held a small bundle under her crooked elbow.

"Are you Mr. Gillies?" she called.

"Uh huh."

"Don't you want to meet your daughter?"

Slowly he walked down the corridor.

A pink head the size of an apple, throbbing membrane of open skull, scraggly patches of damp hair, unfocusing eyes of a color that might be blue. Toothless, yawning mouth. The nurse showed him wrist beads. "G-I-L-L-I-E-S F-E-M-A-L-E," she spelled out. She folded back the blanket. "See? A girl?"

Between skinny kicking legs, a great red gash, raised and prominent. From his daughter rose a smell of sweet oil and something very faint yet infinitely more primal. Hot and salty. Like semen. Or blood.

Strange. Standing in front of a being you had created—and at so great a cost—that you should feel no more than weariness and this overpowering need to urinate.

"Isn't her a doll?" demanded the nurse, rewrapping.

Clay, too numb to think, said the first words that came. "She's pretty red, isn't she?"

"You young fathers! Always have to play it cool, don't you?" snapped the nurse. Holding up the baby, crooning through green cotton. "Her's a little doll, a little doll," she shouldered open one of the swinging doors. The draft hit Clay like another slap in the face.

Clay used the head, strong yellow arc foaming. He tried to force himself to think. Wasn't this meant to be one of life's big moments? This *was* life's big moment. His first born. His only child. He flushed the toilet. So why were his feet cold, his head numb, his muscles heavy as if he were in chains? Clay wandered up the hall. Was this another fake, like New Year's Eve, when people pumped excitement and sentimentality into themselves with liquor?

Suddenly he thought of Odessa Norris's dark, glowing eyes. Instinctively Clay distrusted older people, but Odessa, to him, was apart from the generations; she was free of the dishonest mud that Clay saw smearing the skin of older people. She would understand, and help him understand, why he felt so little when he should feel so much. He fished out two nickels.

"A daughter!" Odessa exclaimed. "Oh, Clay, how wonderful."

"Michele almost died."

Odessa gasped. "Terrible, terrible. For you, too."

"For me? Yes, for me. Odessa, I swear I never thought this rationally before, but the truth is, up until now I felt as if once Michele had the baby, I'd be . . . well, sort of exonerated. I'd have done the right thing. The gates would swing open. I'd be free." He closed his eyes. "I don't mean I'd planned to run away or anything low. But subconsciously I figured once the baby was born . . . if we both wanted, we'd be free. Before today I never really felt marriage was a life sentence. Does that sound cruddy? Dishonorable?"

"Young. And very human."

"But she almost died. She can't have any more babies. It's like she's been fixed." A green-uniformed male attendant pushing an empty stretcher glanced at Clay. Clay was silent until the man passed. He said, "Listen, her parents are narrow-minded. They're bigots. She refuses to get upset about it. But also she stays up until the middle of the night to fix me hot chocolate. Her body's soft and warm and she works me with it." Clay didn't understand how he could be saying any of this out loud, not even to Odessa. "Sometimes I never want to see her again. Yet I love her. How can that be?"

"Clay, there's no such thing as pure love."

"It *has* to be pure."

"Emotions're always mixed up."

"I can't accept that."

"But that's how it is."

"Never." Clay spoke fiercely. "Odessa, listen, I've never told you how Michele feels about SNAP. It's not that she doesn't believe the same as I do. Everyone our age believes. But she also thinks I've taken on more than I can handle. A wife. The baby. College. My job at the market. She's always thought I was doing too much for SNAP."

"Oh?"

"I'm not spending the time with her, understand?"

"Yes."

"Anyway"—Clay took a deep breath—"from here on in, I'm *going* to spend my time with her."

Clay hadn't planned the words, but as he said them, he knew they were right.

Biblical justice.

Old Testament, of course. He'd promised to do anything, hadn't he, if she lived? Well, she was alive. An eye for an eye, a tooth for a tooth, Clay's balls for Michele's uterus. He straightened, standing erect (nearer my God to Thee) in front of the black phone. "So I guess I won't be around."

"Oh, Clay!"

"I told you—"

"How can you—"

"—she almost died."

"—believe this was your fault?"

His cheeks ached with Mrs. Davy's scratches. The pain pleased.

"It wasn't anyone's fault," Odessa went on. "Anyway, how will serving out the rest of your life on a penitential platter cancel what happened? Clay—"

"I'm too tired to explain."

"I *know* you feel your obligations strongly. That's what's so great about you. But I don't intend to let you forget you also have an obligation to yourself." Her voice deepened, and she managed the difficult words with no trace of phoniness. "Clay, you're strong and fearless and utterly committed. You have it in you to be a very great man."

"I have to show Michele how much she means to me."

"Clay." Odessa's voice now came thin, as if she were much further away. "Whenever you're ready to work with SNAP again, the door's open. Remember that."

Clay hung up. Swift California night had fallen. He closed his eyes and in that minute—or was it a shorter time, a couple of seconds only?—he drowsed on his feet. . . . His little girl running in a field of unbelievable green strewn with daisy, daffodil and yellow buttercup, his little blonde girl laughing, whirling in a great, happy, hand-in-hand circle with the vari-colored children of every race of man. . . . Clay's head jerked forward and he woke.

"Michele, listen, I've been doing a lot of thinking. With you being . . . sick. And the baby. I won't be able to make it to SNAP meetings."

Michele raised her bright head from tough hospital pillows to stare at her husband.

"There'll be more time together, for the three of us."

"More time together," she repeated. She sounded pleased.

"Yes. So something's got to give."

"You *were* letting those people walk all—"

"I handed out pamphlets!"

"I notice they didn't get York or any of the others to do it."

"Miche, what's the difference? I'm going to be with you more."

"Good." She smiled.

"Miche—"

"My stitches are killing me." Michele, using both hands, braced herself gingerly to shift her pelvis. "Ouch," she moaned. "My tummy's all blown up."

During Michele's pregnancy, she had decided to call her baby, if she was lucky enough to have a girl, after Mrs. Kennedy: Jacqueline Bouvier Gillies, Jackie for short. But the night-shift nurse told Michele that in the nursery were three little girls named Jackie. So Jackie was altogether too ordinary, Michele announced to the three mothers who shared her room; after all, she added somberly, this would be her only child. The others nodded. They knew every grim detail of her delivery just as she knew the all-too-ordinary details of theirs. What did they think of Johna, after JFK? Clay, who was being sweet and considerate—he'd even promised from now on not to waste so much time with *that* bunch—sat in the straightback chair next to her bed, listening to her change her mind. The only thing he suggested was that Claibourne be the second, or third, name. Michele absolutely agreed. She'd always adored the aristocratic ring of *Claibourne*.

On the back of her hospital menu Michele would write names: Tami Claibourne Gillies, Wendi Sue Claibourne Gillies. Kimi Claibourne Gillies, Robyn Claibourne Gillies, Claibourne Stacy Gillies. Traci Claibourne Gillies, dotting her *i*'s with cute little daisies.

Michele was staying seven days instead of the routine three, and on the fourth Leigh Sutherland visited. Leigh brought an adorable gift from Saks (!), a teensy white dacron dress with smocking, handmade in the Philippines. It was she who gave Michele the name.

"I've always thought when I have a little girl. . . ." Leigh's soft voice trailed away. Flushing, she wound pink satin ribbon around one slim finger, and during this brief pause Michele remembered that last summer she and Dorot had been pretty sure there was something between Leigh Sutherland and Ken Igawa. However, since the middle of August Ken had been going with some Japanese girl, also from California High and also at UCLA, going so hot and heavy that they never saw him at the apartment, and for the past two months Leigh had been dating Daws Huntington, one of *the* Huntingtons, so obviously Leigh had more sense than she and Dorot had given her credit for. Leigh finished, "I like the name Lissa."

"Lissa?"

"L-I-S-S-A."

"Short for Elizabeth?"

Leigh shook her head. Long silky red hair swayed. "Just Lissa."

On back of the embossed white Saks box Michele wrote *Lissa Claibourne Gillies*.

"Pretty," Leigh murmured.

Michele wrinkled her cute little nose at her friend, Leigh Sutherland, to show appreciation. "Lissa Claibourne Gillies she is."

4

A baby means you're a slave.

Although most of the time Michele adored and loved to play with her Lissa, she didn't bother denying it, not to Mother, or Clay, or anyone, that with a baby you never have one free minute for yourself. Right now five-month-old Lissa had awakened from her morning nap and in her crib in the bedroom was whimpering and jouncing, ruining Michele's lunch, a meager peanut butter sandwich eaten in front of TV. Michele got up to slam the door. *Today,* she thought, *her royal highness'll just have to wait. This is important—current events. I'm going to watch.*

On screen, a grainy still of a dark-haired, stocky man with broad Slavic cheekbones. Offscreen a deep-voiced announcer: "... and on April twelfth in the year of our Lord nineteen hundred and sixty-one, the first man to leave this island earth returned to tell us of his historic voyage. Our planet, Yuri Gagarin told us, is divided into black and light, these separated by a ribbon of delicate blue. He saw, Major Gagarin told us, the sun and stars at the same time, vast continents of clouds. And now our own astronaut"—brief cuts of American flags blowing in front of a gantried spacecraft—"has returned from the far voyage. In his own words, our man in space tells us what it's like 'out there.' " Joyous music burst forth, "Everybody's Talking bout the Shepard Man," while onscreen a handsome man, not young, but virile and magnificent in shining space armor, his helmet under one arm, moved laughing across the screen. Under Michele's full breasts surged pride, patriotic pride. *However much Clay puts down the space program,* she thought, *however much he says we ought to spend the money integrating the South,* she thought, *I'm proud to be part of it. ... Our generation's fabulous! Able from our own living room couches, however stained and humble, to watch history being made.*

"Our man in space, Alan B. Shep—"

Lissa was really shrieking.

Michele, running her tongue around her teeth to get rid of peanut butter, thought of Lissa's lunch, a jar of strained liver warming in hot water. A job Michele loathed, forcing meat into her baby. Lissa spat out every kind of meat. Michele, carrying her plate and milk-cloudy glass, couldn't help noticing the mess around the breaky bar. A year ago this beige shag had been the best part of the apartment. And now look at it! Matted. Spotted. Ugly with meat. Michele grabbed the luke-warm jar. Paper slid off. In her irritation she felt the sodden label on the floor.

Fitting her red-faced, panting child in the low chair, she said in a firm tone, "Now. You're good and hungry. You'll eat."

But Lissa, at five months, already had a firm mind. At the first mouthful she spat gummy gray-brown liver all over Michele's good piqué shift, recently ironed by Mrs. Davy.

Michele, furious, started to the sink for the sponge.

On the waterlogged label she slipped. Instinctively she put back a hand to save herself. She fell. Her right index finger bent back.

She heard the bone snap.

Before Clay unlocked his front door that afternoon he heard the phone ringing. He knew without answering that it was his wife; often in the morning Michele would put the baby in her stroller and walk south to spend the day at her mother's, and around the time he was due home from UCLA she would call for a ride, letting the phone ring and ring until he answered. He opened the door. He fixed his angry gaze on the noisy black instrument. Michele visiting her parents was, in Clay's mind, a scaling of his personal Berlin Wall. He disliked both of the narrow minds, and he'd barely spoken to his mother-in-law since that terrible afternoon Lissa was born. Michele knew it. She also knew he had sacrificed what meant most to him on the barbed wire of their marriage—why was she so damn intent on defecting back to the other side?

Slamming the door so Michele's hideous orange and pink lamp rattled, he stalked across the room. It was one thing to say in a moment of high emotion, *Here, take my balls.* Another to live without them. Without SNAP meetings and activities, Clay felt useless. Futile. Futility always angered him. He grabbed the phone.

He could hear *Things go better with Coca-Cola, things go better—*

"Clay?" Michele said.

"Well?" he demanded.

"Its me."

"Who else?"

"I'm at my folks."

"Where else?"

"Do you have to growl." She inhaled audibly. "I broke my finger."

"How?"

"I slipped feeding Lissa and—"

"She O.K.?"

"She's fine."

"Good."

"Aren't you going to ask about me?"

"Is it a bad break?" Clay forced sympathy into his tone.

"Awful. I really was in agony. Daddy had to drive me to the doctor. It's a double fracture, and I've got this huge splint that comes way past my wrist. My right hand. I can't do a thing."

"A thing?"

"Not a thing," Michele said cheerfully. "I guess I'll have to stay here. Clay, will you pack Lissa's and my junk and bring it over? My pink slacks, my yellow shift—"

Clay took his pen from his shirt pocket and tore a lined sheet from his Philosophy 1B notebook. As he wrote his anger increased. It occurred to him, and not for the first time either, that Michele's sole aim in life was to return to Parkdale where she could be petted, spoiled, enslaved and desexed like that miserable brown snaggle, Dozer. Breaking her finger, he decided as he wrote, crossed out, rewrote each time she changed her mind, was a subconscious means to this end.

He was still fuming when he got off work, yet he told himself it wasn't anger that steered his car. Still, did motive matter? What mattered was he headed through the routine sea fog that on May nights veils west Los Angeles. He drove past hazy clumps of small shops along Pico, turning left onto a shabby side street, making a right, then another left to Odessa's narrow bungalow.

Cigarette smoke, light and heat spilled from the bare living room. On the two day beds were stacked yellow mimeographed sheets. About thirty people sat in a semicircle on the gray linoleum rug, listening intently to a short Negro with pitted cheeks and a bald pate that glinted with sweat.

" . . . to avoid disfigurement of the face," the short black man, ignoring Clay's entrance, continued, "bring your elbows together, like this, in front of the eyes." He dropped his bald head into the protective V of white shirt sleeves. "And girls, to prevent internal injuries—and they do love to kick, you know—lie on your side and bring your knees to your chest." Surprisingly agile, he fell folded in the fetal position onto worn linoleum.

Watching, Clay shut the door.

RG, brown, freckled and gnawing on a thumbnail, nodded up at him. York, long pale Hapsburg chin cupped in good hand, turned to fix dark glasses momentarily on Clay—typically York, Clay thought, to sit apart and above everyone in the room's only chair. Then Odessa, twin lights glowing in her dark eyes, picked her way around seated bodies to him.

"I'm so glad you're here, Clay," she whispered, taking his icy hand in her warm one, leading him to a free space near the dinette. "We're finally moving. We're going on the Freedom Ride."

The Freedom Ride. . . .

Clay sat on the floor, unconscious of the chill seeping through his faded denim pants. Freedom Riders, as every involved UCLA student had known since March, were college people from all over the country out to expose the deep South's illegal segregation of interstate travel by the simplest possible means— sitting together, black and white, on southern buses and in southern waiting rooms. Every noon RG, Clay and the others, over waxed milk cartons and sandwiches, hashed and rehashed brief accounts hidden in back of newspapers, repeated stories told by friends and friends of friends. They burned to go. *Listen, isn't it time some of us stopped talking and started acting?* they said, and *The old farts never do a thing, so it's up to us,* and *Who c-cares about a degree if you're not f-free?*

"Count me in," Clay whispered to Odessa, surprised that the words came with such guiltless ease. Were promises made for the wrong reasons always so simple to break?

Odessa, sitting next to him, smiled. He caught odors of hair, dry and sweet like fresh hay. He clasped hands around his raised knees, listening to the short lecturer. He forgot about Michele and Lissa, he pushed from his mind the jangling cash register, his constant worries whether his pay check would last out the two weeks. And would the old Chevy need new brakes soon? And did he have enough to pay the pediatrician? He relaxed, listening to the speaker detail techniques of nonviolence.

Home. He was home.

This is where he belonged.

Nowhere else had he ever felt this same sense of completeness, of companionship. Away from here, among other people, he felt like some science-fiction alien jabbering words others could not understand. And he couldn't understand them. Clay narrowed his eyes, thinking of Michele's favorite phrases: "making a living," "buying on time," "getting ahead," "we need a new couch," "I want a new dress," "I want," "we want," "money, money, money, that's what we need." *We?* Could he ever make himself care about material crap? He faced one fact squarely: Michele was with the majority. He was the outsider. But he couldn't change other facts: what they (Michele) hungered after meant nothing to him, and they (Michele) never could dig him.

But here . . .

So good to see them again. Odessa, RG, Scott, Jeni, Ralph, Mons, Arthur, Lynette, Caton and York—white and black, male and female, rich and poor, they were interested in the same things as he. They were alive. They weren't imprisoned by "I want." The game they played—no irresponsible play, no ordinary adolescent identity crises—was not for personal ends. They shelved educations, families, romances, they put their lives on the line. Everything must change. The old ways and usages, master-slave, they're-happy-riding-the-back-of-the-bus, the separate-but-unequal facilities, the easy acceptance of such wrongs in your own country just so it's a long way away, all the cruel centuries that had passed since the slimy, foul holds of slaving vessels had rocked their cargo of human misery across the Atlantic Ocean, all must be wiped clean. The people in this room burned as brightly as the two bare incandescent bulbs dangling above them. Their game was for the highest stake of all. The future. . . . Clay leaned his back against the wall. His thoughts were grandiloquent. But—facing it again— he liked grandiloquent thoughts.

He gazed around the small room.

And he was overtaken by love. Group love. Could he experience the solo kind? he wondered, then pushed the thought away. He loved these people. Acned Jeni leaning her pimply cheek against stucco, the bushy-haired boy—Rom Levi, Clay remembered, was his name—tall dark Caton with his loafers kicked off to show yellow, matted sweat socks. The sad-faced white guy holding hands self-consciously with honey-beige Lynette. York and his pale-lipped sneer. RG, chewing what must be the shortest nails in the state of California. Clay loved them all. He loved them all. Never in his life had he felt so close to any single person as he felt to these people at this moment, not to Michele in the hot, wet marital spasms, not to Lissa, flesh of his flesh. These seated, earnest UCLA people were him. He was them. They were joined not by ordinary bonds of church or law or blood or race or family but something far more propitious. They were joined by the overwhelming meaning of their own time: all men, whatever color, must become brothers or perish.

Inside Clay the strange tenderness grew, the love grew, until he felt he must burst. Love ached under his rib cage and the unspoken words reverberated along his vocal chords: I LOVE YOU AND TOGETHER WE SHALL SIT ON BUSES AND IN DINGY WAITING ROOMS THROUGH ETERNITY.

"I've missed you," Odessa said.

"Me, you."

"We've all missed you. Clay, you don't know how you sparked us."

"Me?"

"You. Clay Gillies," she said with a smile.

"Always the wry wit."

"You really don't know the effect you have on people?"

"None."

"Take my word for it. Plenty."

"Around here we work on one another. I was thinking that before," Clay said. "S'because we believe in the same thing."

Clay and Odessa were alone. The others had left fifteen minutes earlier, taking with them the string-tied bundles of yellow mimeographed sheets that they would distribute on Westwood Boulevard as close to UCLA's red-brick entry as the campus police would permit. Odessa drank black coffee on the bed nearest the fake fireplace; Clay sprawled on the other bed nursing a mug of watery cocoa she'd fixed him in lieu of coffee—Clay, almost nineteen, hadn't yet gotten around to acquiring a taste for coffee.

The warmth he always felt when he and Odessa were alone brought a sound of contentment from deep in Clay's throat, and he said, "God, I missed this." He glanced around the ashfull saucers, the Scotch-taped window blinds, the rumpled day beds. "Listen, Odessa, I've missed it more than you possibly could've missed me. I was thinking that before."

"You *were* being pensive." She smiled.

"I just went through the motions, that's all. You know, getting up, going to bed, shaving, eating, checking out those damn groceries. But all the time I was frustrated. Itchy—no. Dead."

"You felt you weren't building anything?"

"That's it!" Clay exclaimed. "How'd you know?"

"I've been there myself."

"Oh?"

Odessa rose to get more coffee. The percolator was almost empty, and she concentrated on pouring what little there was. As usual she had veered from personal revelation. Nobody knew her past, and various conflicting rumors drifted through SNAP's membership. Clay ignored them. Which was just as well, since none were remotely tied to truth. The truth was Odessa had been born and raised in San Francisco's North Beach area. Her parents were Party members and writers. Their apartment was always open to those of similar interests. In the cultural and intellectual ferment of radical bohemia, in one of the rare places where black and white met as equals, Odessa grew up. She joined the Party. Briefly. Her balance—her sense of humor, if you will—told her that ideals can't slide neatly along Party lines, so her elders' rigid ideology, rather than inspiring or disillusioning her, hit her in the funny bone. She left without the normal recanting acrimony. She married another ex-comrade, a young Jewish writer (unpublished) with a resonant voice and curly blond hair. After a year of marriage and no sales he lost the creative urge and went into the family plumbing supply business. The bourgeois world was too much with them. The marriage floundered painfully. They parted. For two chill years Odessa was lost. Then, with contributions from various old friends, she began to spend more and more of her time as a rallying point for the enthusiastic, undoctrinated young.

Odessa sat back down. She sipped her coffee. "I've heard tell, though," she said, "that some men consider it enough to have a wife, a child, earn a living and an education."

He shrugged.

She put the mug on the floor, raising her arms, stretching. Her breasts were clearly outlined under navy wool. During those few stretching moments Clay was acutely conscious of their shape, oval yet round, like ripe summer pears.

"Lordie, lordie." She smiled. "But Clay Gillies, he needs a cause, too."

Clay didn't like Odessa's tone; he never had cared for humor about that which he categorized *serious*. Yet he was solaced by the shape of Odessa's company. The shape of her company? Her breasts were shaped, not her company. And from the depth of his mind, from the fringes of time before memory, he dredged the solace of huge, dark breasts soft under his drowsy cheek. . . . Diddie, his nurse, had pillow-size breasts and sometimes on cold Virginia nights he wet his pajamas and she let him in her bed and he snuggled against the huge warmth; she had strange, rubbery nipples as long as his middle finger. . . . Mama, he'd called Diddie. Were Odessa's pear breasts long-nippled? Why did this idea hurt?

What mattered the shape of Odessa's breasts?

Wasn't she old? And he married? Wasn't their relationship, his and Odessa's, friendship of the highest order?

Odessa was watching him through lowered lashes. Her smooth eyelids were several shades darker brown than the rest of her face. "How'll your wife feel about your going?"

"Michele's broken her finger so she can't look after the baby so she's staying with her mother so we won't be together anyway," he hastened to explain. "Why should she care?"

"She might."

"She won't!" he burst out. *Why should she?* he insisted to himself. *What's it to her?*

"You're sure?"

"I told you! She's at her damn mother's!"

"Why so worked up? Clay, you yourself told me she's jealous of SNAP—"

"THIS IS RIGHT. THIS IS RIGHT!"

He was halfway up from blue chenille when Odessa, on the other day bed, said, very softly, "Clay," and hearing her voice somehow soothed his anger, her voice and the understanding in her eyes.

"She will care," he admitted, slumping down. "Of course she'll care, but she's with her parents and they'll look after her and Lissa. For these few days I'm free. If I don't take my chance this time I may never have another; you see that, don't you? This might be my only chance to do something. The rest of my life . . . these few days are all I've got."

"I know how it is." She sighed.

Clay shook his head. "No, you don't. You're not tied like I am."

"Maybe once I was."

"Not the same way. Never this same way. What happened to Michele was my fault—"

"No! Listen, Clay—"

"It was. And I have to make it up to her." Clay dragged his knuckles across his thickly stubbed cheek. "This is time out and I can use the days how I want." Odessa was smiling at him, so he asked, "Do I sound like a little kid ditching school?" Again he rubbed his cheeks. *"I have to go."*

"It's so important to you, the Freedom Ride?"

"Isn't it to you?"

She nodded.

"Then why shouldn't it be for me?"

"It's my own people. It's really for *me,"* Odessa said. "But you—Clay, I'm serious. Do you understand your own motives?"

"Yes," Clay muttered.

"Tell me?"

Clay mumbled.

"What?"

More mumbling.

"I can't hear you."

"I WANT TO SIT NEXT TO YOU ON THAT BUS. OTHERWISE I'M DEAD!" he shouted, his neck tendons standing out.

Michele, naturally, couldn't see it.

In the three days before his departure she made every effort to bring him around to her point of view.

She brought up his promise to foresake all SNAP activity. She flopped on the bed—the twin beds were now in their apartment and his mother-in-law, pointedly, had replaced them with a crib and the narrowest single available—and from this supine position reminded him that the promise, since it was made practically on her deathbed, should be considered in the nature of a sacred vow. She waved her right hand with its plastic splint. She wept. Sniffled. Referred, obliquely to be sure, but so he couldn't miss her meaning, to her absent uterus. She coaxed, showing her pretty, slightly protruding front teeth. She turned sober and explained in earnest tones that this trip could be "terribly dangerous. Clay, I really mean it. You could get hurt." Here emotion got the better of her; this was the third time she cried and her sobs were the loudest, the longest and the most difficult to bring under control. She pointed out his obligations to his daughter. She paraded around her old pink room wearing only lace bikini underpants, and when he wanted to make her nakedness uniform, she went back to her old tricks. "I want to, you know I do, but Mother's in the next room," she whispered in his arms. "Claypoo, let's go home." She predicted that during his absence he would miss so many classes he would flunk out. In other words, she went all out to make Clay see the Freedom Ride her way.

She didn't alter his vision one iota.

"What's a few days out of our whole lives?" he asked. "I'm going," he said.

York, too, was heading for Alabama.

Why?

Clay knew that since the end of August—and now it was the beginning of May—Baron York had been on location in the windy, arid plains south of Madrid; he was starring in *Episode in Corinth,* a long-overdue sequel, or so press agentry decided, to his first great starring role of St. Paul. In December, January and February a highly salacious and much discussed series of articles had come out in *Confidential:* HOW BARON SATISFIES HIS FIERY YOUNG SPANISH MISTRESS. This Easter vacation Mrs. York and the two York girls had flown to Spain for a *gemütlich* family reunion—after all, the movie, of religious content, was for a family audience—much pictured in *Look* and *Life.* Clay figured York's decision, his father's publicity and his mother's trip were closely related. Yet Clay shied from connecting these whys and wherefores. A Pavlov reflex. Clay considered speculation about other people an ugly waste of time.

He did, however, congratulate York on his decision.

"It's great to see you've finally cut the noninvolvement act," Clay said.

"Oh, Jesus."

"You're on the right track."

"Truth, justice and the American way?"

"If you want to put it like that."

"As the fine old Biblical quotation goes, there ain't no justice."

"Soon there will be."

York pushed his dark glasses up, staring at Clay.

"Come off it," Clay said. "That's why we're going."

"Have you, Gillies, ever considered the salient fact that what might look, feel and smell like justice to you, looks, feels and smells like a man-eating shark to some other guy?"

"Meaning?"

"I'm obscure?"

"You generally are."

"Those rednecks might, just possibly, think you're fucking with their States' Rights."

"But you don't believe that."

"I don't?"

"Nope." Clay's shadowed, serious face was transformed by one of his rare smiles. "Or you wouldn't be coming."

"Me? I'm along for the kicks. I want to see you redhot activists rousing the mungy, fuggy Southern Negro. 'Lift that barge, tote that bale to the front of the bus': 'Yas-suh, mass—' "

"Odessa shouldn't," Clay interrupted furiously, "let a bummer like you come. You might foul up—"

"Foul up! Listen, Mr. Wonderful, you really think *you* can make one quick trip and alter the fear patterns of centuries in those poor black peons?"

"Bummer!"

"That's the way the cookie crumbles," York said. "We bummers foot the bills for you red-hot idealists."

---------- **5** ----------

It was almost two in the afternoon, May eighteenth; Clay, RG and York, flying home, were due to land in fifteen minutes. They had not taken part in the Freedom Ride. And this, Clay admitted as he pressed the recline button of his seat, was his life's biggest disappointment. He'd been on his way to Jerusalem's holy Battle and he'd stumbled over his own socks.

"We'll be landing at Los Angeles International in a few minutes," said the strawberry blonde stewardess as she bent over York. Her pale hair, teased and colored and lacquered, resembled a scoop of strawberry ice cream. "Right now, Mr. York, we're over California."

"Home sweet home," York said.

Clay, on the window side, stared out. The amber flecks in his brown eyes shone as he gazed past wingborne jets onto fields of sunstruck clouds. Shining. Beautiful. Clean as snow. Below those clouds, however, if you chose to think, and Clay chose, lay ugliness. The shits. He leaned his aching head against cool glass.

"I brought you a paper," the girl was saying to York.

York shook it open with his good hand. The other was bandaged and therefore, for once, he could not tuck it in his pocket.

"BARON YORK'S SON HURT IN CIVIL RIGHTS DEMONSTRATIONS." Clay read the headlines aloud. "We didn't even make it to Birmingham, yet they write it up like you led all the rest."

"Abou ben Adam." York laid the newspaper across his bony knees. "So I did my bit and got publicity without sitting in the back of the bus. So what?"

The stewardess inhaled. "I think what you're doing is wonderful. Helping all those poor people down there in the South." Another breathe-in, this time expanding her trimly uniformed breasts to graze York's narrow shoulder. "I'm a real fan of your father's," she said.

"I'll just bet you are," York said. "Now, fan, how about some water?" He jiggled a phial of yellow painkillers. "I need one of these."

Swaying slightly, the girl hastened up the aisle.

Clay's head ached. This pain he'd had in varying degrees for three days, since that weathered Louisville Slugger had descended on him. His ears commenced to make those strange, interior echoes, *queel, queel, queel,* against the membrane of his eardrums. He put his hands over his ears. The sound didn't stop.

He thought of the long trip under those clouds: three days and three nights they had sped toward Birmingham in York's

Thunderbird, tied to reality, if you wanted to call it that, only by the radio.

Mississippi's governor had said, "The Negro is different because God made him different to punish him."

And Alabama's governor said of the Freedom Riders, "The people of Alabama are so enraged that I cannot guarantee protection for this bunch of rabble rousers."

If this were the case, retorted the President of the United States, it was the federal government's responsibility to guarantee safe passage in interstate travel. If necessary, United States marshals would be dispatched to Birmingham, Alabama.

Clay, RG, Odessa and York never made it to Birmingham. Fifty miles and two hours short of their goal, in a dusty little town, Collierville, they had been stopped for speeding (fourteen miles per hour; Clay had checked the speedometer as the cop ordered them to the side of the road) and held in the homey Collierville jail until Monday noon.

Monday, after a large fine and a larger lecture, they emerged from the red-brick courthouse to discover in the square a small mob that seemed larger because its members held old guns, steel pipes or baseball bats. It was possible that they could have walked around the square to the Thunderbird and nobody would have moved, but Clay, deprived of the Freedom Ride, stared at the gathering under dusty magnolias and decided he would not back away. He would not! Fixing his gaze on a single enemy, a hulking man with a baseball bat and a face the same intense red of Lissa's when she moved her bowels, Clay stepped, nonviolent, into battle. He crossed the street. The other three followed.

From the beginning he'd been out cold. The others had told him of the melee, a gray-haired grandmotherly type aiming her sturdy Red Cross shoe at York's crippled arm after he was shoved into the gutter, a skinny bald guy punching RG in the genitals, men beating Odessa about the head, and the slow walk of the grinning cop as he arrived to break up the fun. Mrs. York, from the Castellana Hilton, dispatched a sizable money order to pay doctors' fees and buy plane tickets. Odessa, since she didn't have to get back to school, had promised York she would drive his car cross country after a stay in Montgomery where she now was with the Freedom Riders.

Clay opened his eyes. He felt an overpowering impulse to say to York, *You and I were blooded in the same battle and*

now we're brothers. But how could you say a thing like that?
Especially to York. So instead Clay remarked, "You'll have to
admit that the white Southerner is rotten."

"It's in all of us," York replied. "Get out your Crayolas and
color us all rotten."

"I don't see it that way."

"You wouldn't," York said. "But then you're afflicted with
myopia."

"Come off it!"

York turned, taking off dark glasses so his bulging, intelligent gray eyes were visible.

Clay started, "The South—"

"Will rise again," York interrupted. "And it's no worse than
any other place, including our destination point, the city of the
angels. People are places, places are people. Black, white,
southern, northern, you, me, Governor Wallace. Some might
be worse than others, but none wins the virtue blue ribbon in
every division."

"Listen—"

"No. You listen to me. For what it's worth, Gillies, to you
alone I bare my pimple-back soul. On this trip I have discovered
the Big Truth."

"Truth?"

"To the Big Question that's supposedly gnawing all our
generation: Is He or isn't He? And to you alone I pass on the
Big Answer. God is alive. Very. A thousand years in His sight
is but as yesterday when it is past, and a watch in the night.
Nice ring to it, eh? He lives, the God of that first irrevocable
animal-thigh weapon, the God who blessed the obsidian knife
to carve out the living heart, the God of the Appian Way
decorated with thousands of crucifixions in working order, the
God of the Inquisition, the God of Belsen gas showers and the
God of Hiroshima. He is alive. He is both sides of the same
coin, and each generation we reissue Him in our own image.
I am He. You are He. He is all of us. We are He."

"Then we have to change."

"You, too?"

"All of us."

"Gillies—"

"Especially the South."

"I saw you egging that poor cretin to lower the boom."

"What?"

"You marched up to him and—"

"Should I have fallen down, cringing?"

"What words?"

"Words?" Clay frowned. Had he spoken? The baseball bat had canceled memory.

"I saw you. . . . Ahhh, what the hell does it matter?" York sank into the high-backed airplane seat. "So with our generation it's all *mea culpa*. But the question remains. Both sides of the same coin, remember? Did they attack us? Or we them?"

"They had clubs and guns—"

"Maybe only to frighten us. They were ignorant, illiterate, undernourished sharecroppers. What did you say to that cretinous son of a Kallikak?"

"York, this is what happened. This." Clay, leaning his elbow on the chair arm between them, spoke patiently. "They were outside the courthouse waiting for us because we were Freedom Riders. A mob, with guns and clubs to beat us. Look at your arm. Look at me." Clay glanced across the aisle. "And RG. Now. You explain. How are *we* guilty?"

"They were ignorant slobs, living in an ignorant past. We stepped into their all-white park with our offensive color scheme."

"Offensive!"

The flaps went down. The plane seemed to stand still as it lost altitude. York winced, tensing.

"The other side," he asked, "is always, without question, the bad guys?"

"Otherwise I wouldn't be against them," Clay agreed.

"Christ, I envy your easy answers." York replaced his dark glasses.

The NO SMOKING/FASTEN YOUR SEAT BELT sign reddened.

"I sat there glued to the TV," Michele said. She unzipped Clay's borrowed duffel bag—she could manage well enough with her right hand, the broken index finger now being braced only by a sliver of plastic. "I got so scared I was shaking."

"I told you. If I could've phoned from the jail, I would've."

She shook out his good pair of A-1 Peggers. "Filthy," she said, dropping them on the pink rug. "They kept showing that awful mob. Men with crowbars. And that fat sheriff—"

"Bull Connor."

"—he told the announcers he couldn't stop it. It was Mother's Day, he said, and he didn't have enough men. And I kept thinking, 'I see Clay,' and 'Oh, no! That's Clay,' and 'Oh, my God, somebody's hitting Clay.' " Michele pulled out a stained tee shirt. The smell of harsh sweat came from it. "Ugh," she dropped it next to the pants. "What did you do? Sleep in your clothes?"

"I told you. We drove straight through. Listen, Miche—"

"I couldn't do one thing. I just sat all day glued to the TV. Finally Leigh came over to be with me. We were both crying."

"You really put in a rough time!"

"What does *that* mean?"

"You watched on TV, so you were more involved than me!"

"You were in jail."

"Yes. Jail," he said defiantly. "From here on in it's going to be different. People are going to be proud of going to jail!"

"Shhhh . . ."

He paced to the closed room, shouting, "I AM PROUD OF GOING TO JAIL!"

"Lissa, if you'll remember, is napping." Michele gave a sobbing sigh. "On Mother's Day."

"So?"

"Mother's Day," she repeated.

"It's not a religious holiday."

"My *first* Mother's Day." She unpacked another tee shirt. Stiff rust splotched like a map of the Hawaiian Islands. "Clay, what's this?" she cried.

"Tee shirt."

"Looks like blood."

"Is."

"Blood?"

"Yes."

Michele clutched the bloodstained tee shirt to her full breasts. "Why didn't you tell me you were hurt?"

"I've been trying to."

"What happened?"

"Listen—"

"I begged and begged you not to go," she cried. "Did the police—"

"This is important," he snapped. "Will you shut up and listen!"

He was tired, he'd been hurt, so she said in her most understanding tones, "Tell me about it, dear, while I finish unpacking."

Now that he had her attention, Clay paced up and down. Silent.

"Well?" she asked gently.

"I don't know where to begin. Listen, there's so much, so much. I lived there and I never noticed. They—RG and Odessa—couldn't use the heads in the gas stations. Other places, the toilets were *White Ladies*, *White Gentlemen* and *Colored*. Miche, they were denied the dignity of being men and women. They couldn't drink from filthy, rusted drinking fountains that said *White*. Listen, we never got to eat a proper meal. They wouldn't let us in the same cruddy places, so York and I took hamburgers to the car. Cold and greasy. Everything so greasy. Christ, I never ate so much rancid grease in my life. So that morning—"

"What morning?"

"Sunday."

"Oh. *Mo*ther's Day."

"We stopped at this farmhouse, colored, and we offered the woman money for breakfast. She fixed us food. Scrambled eggs. Hot corn bread and other stuff. The best meal I ever ate. And she kept putting more and more on the table. But her husband . . ." Clay got a funny, almost embarrassed expression. He paused at the vanity, fiddling with one of her perfumes.

"What about her husband?"

"A skinny little guy," Clay said. "He was afraid."

"What of?"

"Us."

"You?"

"In a way. If the white people saw us in his place, they'd hurt him. Or his kids. He has eight or nine kids." The shadows under Clay's eyes were very dark. "Think of it, Michele; he couldn't have people in his own house without being afraid. *Afraid.*"

Michele pulled out the last of the clothes: two pairs of jockey shorts, more filthy socks. Clay's toothbrush and shaving stuff wrapped in a Baggie. She deposited this on the bedside table. She turned the duffel inside out. "To air," she said. "The farmer was afraid, so he beat you up?"

"You crazy?" Clay frowned at her. "No black man in the South beats up a white man."

"How *did* you get hurt?"

"Not there. We ate breakfast, that's all."

"Did anyone hurt him?"

"Nobody saw us at his place. He wasn't hurt."

She bent to pick up the smelly heap of clothes, depositing it in the pink clothes hamper. "Then?"

Clay walked the ten-foot width of the room from the door to the window. "Then?" he asked. "Then we headed for Birmingham. But in this little dump, Collierville, we were picked up. Speeding, the cop said. I was driving. *I* never went through those one-horse towns faster'n fifteen. There must've been some sort of order out to arrest anyone who looked like a Freedom Rider. In jail we were segregated. Me and York with eighteen other whites. Drunks. Degenerates. When York and I tried to sing 'We Shall Overcome' they stuffed rags soaked with piss in our mouths."

"Uhghh!" Michele gagged.

"The next day we were fined two hundred and they let us—"

"Two hundred dollars!"

"York paid," Clay said with lordly impatience, as if a sum like two hundred dollars mattered not at all. "We went outside. There they were, waiting for us. A mob. They had guns and bats and steel bars. They came at us. A big slob hit me with a baseball bat."

"Oh, Clay. . . . Did you fight back?"

"I was out cold. Anyways, nonviolence."

"I begged you—"

He went to her, gripping her shoulders until she winced. "Michele, people have to know what it's like down there." His eyes blazed.

"It was on TV."

"Odessa has an idea," he said slowly. "I ought to give some speeches about our experience."

"You?"

"To different groups."

"Speak?"

"To get people's interest," he said. "We have to get people aware of what SNAP's out to accomplish."

Michele was proud, yes, proud, of what Clay had done. But once was enough. He'd been hurt!

"It won't be every night, of course," he said.

Michele was silent.

His fingers, clutching through cotton, hurt her shoulders. "We'll raise money," he said. "We'll go south again."

Never, never.

"I was so afraid," she said, putting her hand on his cheek. "So afraid...."

"Here I am. Safe and sound."

"You just don't understand how I felt."

"I do—"

"No. You're never scared like me." She ran her fingers down his cheek, dallying on the way with rough stubble, gliding down to his Adam's apple.

For a moment he accepted her caress. "This isn't a whim, Michele," he said. "I've thought a lot about it. It's something I must do."

"You already have."

"People our age have to fight. The older generation never will."

Gently she tugged on crisp chest hairs rising above his tee shirt. "You said yourself," she murmured, "the colored people are afraid to have you down there."

"We have to destroy the cause of their fear."

"You're making troubles for them."

"No."

"Then why was that farmer afraid?"

"Don't you understand?" he said angrily. "You have to begin someplace."

She tried another tack. "Clay, it's dangerous," she whispered. "The tee shirt... blood."

He pressed three fingers into his rough brown hair, massaging gingerly as if something pained. "I want to let as many people know as I can," he said.

Her caressing hand dropped. She'd hoped she wouldn't have to bring up the promise, but didn't one of them have to be sensible? *Michele Davy Gillies*, she thought sternly, *you can't let him wreck both your lives, maybe get himself killed.*

"When I was in the hospital—" she started.

"It won't work," he said. "Not this time."

She struggled to keep anger from her voice. "Of your own accord you promised to quit SNAP."

"I can't. And that's that."

"Later, you'll have time for it." She got her voice back on its own sweet, even keel. "We'll both have time. But right now I've got Lissa. And you've got work and school. Clay, we've been so happy these last few months."

"What's happy got to do with it?"

He was staring down at her with the strangest expression. His brown eyes . . . not cold, not angry, but gauging as if she were a stone trapping him in some tunnel and he was wondering if he could shift her. Then, for no apparent reason, he began to kiss her, roughly, bruising her lips, forcing them open, invading her with his tongue. She managed to break away.

"Stop that!" she whispered.

"It's what you were trying to get me to do, wasn't it?"

"Clay!"

"C'mere," he muttered.

And pulling her against him, he braced his hard thighs against hers, forcing her to step back. Back. She couldn't argue. Mother might hear. He smelled of harsh, masculine sweat. On the narrow bed, ignoring the weak protest of her hands, poor broken hands, he pulled at her clothes until she heard the loud rip of cotton panties—fortunately she was wearing everyday ones—hitting her sharply on her left hand when she tried to stop him, forcing her thighs apart, pushing, overpowering, forcing. Rape. That's what it was, doing it without even giving them time to brush their teeth. Rape. She with a splinted finger, Mother sneezing as she watched in the living room, baby napping, Dozer yapping, aluminum Venetian blinds open and the radio next door blasting:

> *Let's twist again,*
> *Twisting time is here*

and his fingers, too, fighting the same battle down there, pulling, tugging, cruel . . . and, wonder of wonders, she was losing herself in movements of her bare hips and suddenly it was not rape but something quite different, certainly different, something she had never before experienced and—

he stopped.

She could hear her own loud breathing. "Don't stop, don't stop, oh, Clay, please don't stop," came out on that harsh, eager breath.

"Michele," he said against her ear. "Michele, I have to do it."

"Clay—"

"I'm going to. Hear?"

"Don't stop," her breathing said. "Don't stop."

"Understand?"

"Ride more, Clay, please."

"I'm going to live my life my way."

"Please."

"My way?"

She pushed up, an ineffectual movement since he lay full weight on her, pressing down so she couldn't move.

"That's the way it's going to be."

"No," she said.

Suddenly he gave her a thrust and her willing—no, pleading—pelvis rose to meet him. He rolled off her.

She turned, reaching for him. How could her own body that she tended with such faithful care be betraying her?

"Take it or leave it," he said.

She took it.

Later, she thought, later she could argue, later, later later later later later oh later

Later Michele wondered how she had given in. Later it seemed inexplicable. And how had Clay known that one particular time, the first actually, he could take advantage of her good nature? Not that what she wanted mattered any more to Clay Gillies. The trip had changed him beyond all belief. He didn't seem to care how she felt. It was annoying, yet oddly exciting. He ordered her, "Get your stuff packed. We're going home."

And that evening over Mrs. Davy's vehement protests ("She can't manage the baby with one hand, Clay. You know she can't!") the Gillies family returned home.

Part Three

That rainy January day Leigh had fixed egg sandwiches for lunch. Now the smell of eggs scrambled in butter almost drowned out the more pungent odors of turps and Grumbacher oil paint that filled the circular room.

Ken Igawa lived four short blocks south and two long blocks west of the University of California's Berkeley campus, in the windowed turret of one of the elaborate turn-of-the-century places that have been divided into student housing. Stacks of old canvases leaned under windows, sketches were thumbtacked to cracked paneling, the battered kneehole desk and two tables were confused with sheets of half-finished sketches, open boxes of pastels, cigar boxes filled with squeezed paint tubes, pencils, nub ends of charcoal, a large white marble square that Ken used as a palette. Only one surface was cleared, the end of the long table where they'd just eaten lunch. Ken sat on the floor reading. In the makeshift kitchen area—sink, double hot plate, a few open shelves and a leaky icebox, the antique kind you had to buy ice for—Leigh washed dishes. She pulled out the rubber sink stop, and while slow water gurgled down rusty pipes she dried plastic dishes and stainless steel, then rubbed Jergens lotion into her hands. Leaving on the radio, she sat on the thin maroon rug next to Ken.

"I have to have this committed to memory by three," he said.

"I'll tell you what happens. This sweet old guy retires—"

"Abdicates," he said. "Your hands smell nice."

"Thank you. And divides his estate—"

"Kingdom."

"—between his three daughters."

"Two."

"That's right. One's called Gonorrhea."

"So *that's* how it's pronounced."

"And then he visits between them. He's a very family minded lawyer—"

"Hey Leigh, king."

"But he doesn't visit his youngest daughter, the red-headed one."

"Why?"

"She's away at college, going with an NJB."

"In this version Cordelia's married to France, the king of."

"The author goofed."

"Maybe poetic license?"

"One day he flips."

"Who?"

"You *know*. The sweet old guy. Right before the NJB visits."

"Why?"

"Because he discovers his older daughters are bad."

"Not Cordelia, though?"

"See? You know it all."

"Yeah yeah yeah. Except the last ten pages."

"Oh, they all die. There's a rule for you to remember. Beethoven and his final coda. Shakespeare's tragedies and the cast dying onstage."

Ken held the paperback to his face. Leigh, with a strand of long red hair, tickled his neck.

"That's the sort of thing that's going to get me flunked out," he said.

"I just told you the plot."

"A lawyer divides his estate between his two older daughters, one's called Syphilis—"

"Gonorrhea."

"—and then his youngest daughter's boy friend, a nice Japanese boy, visits, and everybody gets the death urge."

"Exactly."

"My own Willemina Shakespeare." He grinned. "Hey Leigh, how do you do it?"

"Oh, when I had on my body cast, I read all the time. It seemed more real when I substituted people I knew for the characters." Again she tickled him with her hair. "You're taking it pass-fail."

"Fail-fail," he said. "Sharper than a serpent's tooth."

"You're pretty."

"Who said it?"

"Say thank you."

"Boys're handsome. Who?"

"Kent, I think," she said, kissing his left eyelid.

He dropped the book, putting both arms around her, pulling

her so she lay across his lap. "Now you've done it. Now you've gone and done it," he said, kissing her. Thoroughly.

In the semester they'd been up at Berkeley, there had been an awful lot of making out. Not the whole way. Nor messy stuff that keeps a girl a technical virgin—almost nobody on the Berkeley campus practiced *that*, the hypocrisy of their parents' generation. But whenever they were alone they did a lot of making out. Like now. At the circle of windows, rain, a noisy curtain separating them from the world, music coming from a silver-horned transistor, Beethoven, Mozart, Mendelssohn, the lovely old squares, pulsing strings, faraway bugles, drum rolls reaching into their very flesh in some mysteriously tender manner, arms around one another, kissing, hardly daring to move lest moving they lose the wonder of it.

A very refined torture.

The truth was, for Ken their whole ambivalent relationship was torture.

He'd known it would be.

And he'd fought it. At the Obon Festival a year and a half ago the childish fury of his attack on Leigh Sutherland had bewildered him. Oh, certainly he'd understood why he'd attacked her. It was in the nature of necessary revenge for the cool, snob way she spoke to him; this vengeful twist of his nature Ken loathed, and that was putting it mildly. However, from his occasional cruelties he extracted a powerful magic that momentarily changed him into one of *them*. What he hadn't understood was the force of his attack on Leigh Sutherland. It was like a bludgeoning. Or a rape. He wasn't a very bright Japanese boy. The following week, in the Gillieses' kitchen, when he had almost drowned in wide-set hazel eyes, he understood. He actually felt as if his lungs were filling with water. *He was in too deep.* A mistake of the first order. "Only Japanese girls," his mother had repeated over and over, brainwashing Ken and his older brother from their respective puberties on— the two Igawa girls never would have dared be seen with a non-Japanese. This redhead with the rich phony name and the high round breasts was off limits, he thought, as his legs shook in a physical remembrance of her calf trembling against his.

Ken fled.

The following morning he phoned Shigeme Futaba. Shigeme, sweet, humorless and thick ankled, kept him safely clear of the Gillieses' place and Leigh Sutherland.

He hadn't known Leigh was coming to Berkeley.

As a matter of fact, he himself hadn't planned to come. The only way he could afford a college education was to live at home, commuting to nearby UCLA. He would still be at good old nearby UCLA if it weren't for Professor Little.

Oliver Little, as Ken and other West Coast art buffs knew, before marrying oil money had been an accepted if minor Bay Area artist. After his marriage he devoted his time to teaching Master Classes. A small, slight man as his name suggested, he was also excitable, intense and considerably more talented at teaching than he was at his own easel; he soon became the Rosina Lhevinne of art students. From all over they traveled to study under him. He was on what you might call a talent scouting expedition to UCLA when Standish showed him the tall Japanese kid's work. Professor Little squinted, stepped back, silently examined the nine canvases. "Yes. . . ." He nodded. "Yes. . . . Student awkwardness . . . but there's considerable emotional impact here." He turned to Ken. "Ever considered Berkeley?"

The criticism, *student awkwardness,* hurt. Criticism always hurt. The offer pained more. Even living at home, money was pretty tight. . . . Oliver Little asking him, Ken Igawa, to come to Berkeley!

"The local branch," Ken said slowly, "is fine with me."

"I could teach you a lot."

"Art can be taught?"

"Oh, spare me the shit. I mean, save you time. Show you techniques you'd eventually figure out for yourself. Look, if you put viridian here." Little made a brushing motion at the left corner of the small landscape. "See?"

"If I wanted to ape Renoir."

"You think of someone better?"

"Also I could paint by the numbers."

"Would you calm down if I said I prefer a do-it-yourself approach? There are, however, techniques to be communicated."

Ken shrugged. Put both hands in his pockets.

"You don't believe me?" Little asked.

"I like it here."

Little, who was squinting at the monochrome abstract, turned his sharp gaze on Ken. "So that's it. The humiliating fact you've got no money. Right?"

Ken looked away.

"Don't you think I remember the beginnings?" Little asked. "There's money around."

"Who needs favors?"

"Who said favors? Igawa, maybe you're my Van Cliburn."

"With all the student awkwardness?"

Little laughed. "We'll get along," he said. "We'll get along, you independent young bastard." He walked back to the landscape. "You're not awkward. You're good. Too damn good! I'll see about a living scholarship. And don't argue! A *scholarship!*"

The second day of the fall semester of '61 was gaudy; the wind came off the Bay to sweep every cloud, every trace of haze, so that unobscured sunlight rimmed each building, each bush and tree, each blade of grass in gold, like a holy Byzantine mosaic. Ken paused at Sather Gate to take it in. He noticed someone in the crowded plaza, a slender, well-put-together female with a mane of red hair, at this moment gold-aureoled like it belonged to one of those gentle Byzantine madonnas. At the sight of Leigh Sutherland his skin prickled with pleasure. Involuntary reaction. He smiled. His first rational thought was *Run, run, it's a mistake!* Then, in the bright clear Berkeley air, his reservations (his? didn't they come directly from his parents?) seemed as out of date as a Norman Rockwell painting.

"Leigh!" he called.

She stopped, turning, blinking uncertainly in the strong light. Again reservations had flashed through his brain. *Get out, get out you dumb Jap while the getting's good.*

"Hey *Leigh!*" he'd shouted.

This time she'd found him. Had smiled and waved.

He had broken track records running to her.

The rain stopped before Ken left for his three o'clock. Leigh walked with him, a sedate eighteen-inch separation, as far as the dorm complex, four new tall beige cubes surrounding a landscaped court and low-slung commons building. Leigh shared her fifth-floor box in Cunningham with Dorot McHenry.

Dorot was exercising. Still underweight, she had decided to gain curves with those new isometrics. Crosslegged on Leigh's white sheepskin rug, she made werewolf faces at the ceiling.

"Did I get any mail?" Leigh asked.

"Your parents're flying up," replied Dorot through clenched teeth. "Friday."

"There's federal laws against tampering—"

"You always let me read Miss Arthur's masterpieces."

Leigh sighed. Dorot was right. Dorot was always right. Methodical. As Dorot kept a filing card in each of her drawers listing its contents, so for each friend or acquaintance she had a mental card listing that person's family background, sexual habits, approximate IQ and permissions granted. There never was any arguing with Dorot. Miss Arthur's letters were a gas and Leigh *did* share them with her friend. Mr. Sutherland, a busy lawyer, would tell family news to Miss Arthur, his colored secretary, who then translated lively family gossip into the language of last will and testament.

Leigh picked up the neatly slit envelope. Dorot stretched on the lambskin, slowly raising her thin left calf until her long white thigh formed a right angle with her body.

Leigh glanced up from impeccable typing. "My father has business."

"So I read."

"Important business."

"Oh, sure."

"What does that mean?"

"Hasn't it struck you he businesses up here most often?"

"He has clients in San Francisco."

"Your parents're possessive."

"They are not!"

"No? You haven't been here the last three times they phoned."

"Well?"

"Tell me why parents fly up?"

"Huh?"

"Come off it! To see what big bad wolf's been monopolizing little red riding head's time."

Leigh took off her coat.

Dorot persisted. "When are you going to tell them about Ken?"

Leigh put her new camel-hair in the closet. Two wrinkled shirts of Ken's hung there waiting to be ironed.

"Ken's very presentable," Dorot said. "Talented, high IQ, not long in the torso and short in the leg like so many of your Ori—"

"Oh, Dorot!"

"I'm only pointing out that he's perfectly *présentable*." Dorot gave it the French pronunciation. "Why should they mind?"

"Guess."

"Well, aren't you the girl who's forever telling of her parents' lack of bigotry? A Negro secretary and friends of every stripe and color. All the time and money your father gives to ACLU."

Dorot had herself another unarguable point. Whenever people spoke of the antiquated attitudes of their own parents, Leigh, in her quiet way, would brag about her father; Sidney Sutherland was an outspoken advocate of racial equality, and—as Leigh would say, her fine-boned, freckle-dusted nose crinkling in a smile—he put his money where his mouth was. Money to CORE and NAACP, money to bus colored kids into all-white districts, and—despite his busy practice—he would always take a deserving case without any fee. He had a scar in his right shoulder from the winter he'd fought with the Abraham Lincoln Brigade in Spain, and he limped slightly from an ankle shattered while rescuing a Negro shipmate in the Coral Sea during World War II. Leigh was wild about her father. She sat on the edge of her bed staring at the clearing clouds. One was shaped like a giant lobster claw.

"Well?" Dorot asked.

"How would *your* parents feel if you sprang a Japanese boy on them?"

"Funnee." Dorot sat upright. "Droll. *You* know my parents belong in the eighteenth century. *You* know they're charter members of the John Birch Society. They consider Goldwater to the left of center and Eisenhower an out-and-out communist dupe. They have joint fits of apoplexy whenever they think of me rooming in a dorm with all sorts." A typical Dorot remark; she never meant to be unkind; it simply never entered her rational brain that she might hurt an Oriental, Jewish or Negro girl by calling her what she was to her face. Leigh was forever defending her tactless roommate. "If they heard I was dating a Japanese, faster than you can say Tokyo-Nagasaki Express I'd be attending dullsville UCLA and living in the bosom of my family."

"They're all the same." Leigh sighed. "It's their hot button."

"With your parents, though, there's a good chance that they'd accept the situation."

Leigh shook her head.

Dorot, pushing to her feet, grunted, "Bet?"

"Impossible." Leigh sighed with stubborn melancholy. She had given the matter well over a thousand hours of sad, disillusioning thought to come to this conclusion. "Impossible."

"But your father—"

"It's got nothing to do with his beliefs."

"That's contradictory."

"He wouldn't think it's smart."

"Why?"

"There's so many problems involved."

"Do you believe that?"

"Of course not!"

"But your father does?"

"Don't they all?"

"Do they?"

"Dorot, you know—"

"Noooooow I understand. Comes the dawn. You're afraid to put your father to the acid test."

Leigh went back to staring out the window. The lobster-claw cloud had merged with a towering cumulus. Dorot, with her yen for pure reason, enjoyed this sort of analysis. She thought she was helpful, using her skills as a sociology major, psychology minor, to aid people; she was forever taking a friend's emotions to scrub clean, iron wrinkle free and return in order, but in doing so she, alas, faded all human passion.

"Are you?" Dorot persisted.

Leigh, reaching for towel and washcloth, escaped. A couple of minutes later she returned, moisturizing cream in one slender hand. Dorot still exercised, her elbows knobbing as she strained them backward.

"How?" Leigh asked, creaming her forehead and her chin. "How could I get them to . . . you know . . . Ken?"

"Accept him as your boy friend, you mean," Dorot said.

"Uh huh."

"Slooo-ooow. Work on them slooo-ooow." In time with the *slows* Dorot's bent, raised arms moved back. "Remember 'Mithridates, he died old'?"

"Wha'?"

"The king who immunized himself to poison by taking it in small doses. Finally no amount could hurt him. Dig?"

"Yes," Leigh said. "No. Go on."

"It's obvious. To start out, they've already taken quite a lot of poison. All these years they've talked liberal—"

"They are. My father *is*."

"All to the better," Dorot said. "Now what you've got to do is introduce Ken Igawa's name in small doses. After a while they'll take the name for granted. He'll be a person. A friend.

Then you'll introduce him in the flesh and—"

"It won't work."

"It *will*. It *has* to," Dorot said. "After all, they—your father—is such a big liberal. How could he break the old image?"

"It's not him. It's me."

"You?"

Leigh flushed. "I don't have any reason to talk about Ken."

"That shouldn't be difficult."

"Like what?"

"Anything'll do."

"Like what?" Leigh repeated.

"Leigh Sutherland! You mean to tell me you don't have a
single *legitimate* interest in common with Ken Igawa?"

What did they have in common?

Leigh herself had never quite figured it. She often counted
the reasons she loved him. His sarcasm, bitter without casting
gloom. She loved him for the proud way he carried his head.
The wonder that he could create a world on a blank square of
canvas. The fact he was superior to her in all ways. She loved
him for the way his heavy black hair flopped over his forehead.
The warmth, sweetness (sweetness sure wasn't an appropriate
word for a masculine male like Ken, but she'd never yet thought
up a better one) and generosity that he tried to hide but that
everyone, even that ultrarealist, Dorot McHenry, saw right
away. The only thing they had in common was a high regard
for classical music, Beethoven's in particular. But their regard,
high as it was, could hardly be construed as a bond. So what
was the tie? Leigh knew only that with everyone else, except
her family, she felt herself tighten into polite knots. She knew
she was called stuck up. This hurt. But she couldn't hang loose.
Except with Ken. With him she could be a toilet-going, belch-
ing, wanton female who could overeat, laugh at a dirty joke,
his or hers, until her hazel eyes streamed; she could get furious
enough to punch his firm stomach, and when they made out,
as he pressed his tongue into her mouth, she felt she might
faint, she was so passionate.

But sharing? Why, he'd never even told her how he felt
about her!

Well, who said you had to match, like sweater and skirt, to
be in love?

• • •

"Films, everybody's making them."

That's what Leigh said to Ken later that week. The idea came to her as he tried to sketch the tumult around leaflets being hawked, people clotting around a card table where five pretty AE Phis sold inedible, unkosher pickles to raise money for Calcamp, four wandering dogs, three playing pups, two lovers kissing and one bearded evangelist pacing in long robes across the crowded bridge. Ken tore another sheet from his sketch pad, muttering that he could *not* get it, not the swirl, not the excitement, not the *movement*. So she said, "Films. Everybody's making them," and he crushed heavy paper, hurling it at a trash can, missing.

"Yeah yeah yeah," he said. Sour.

"Films move," she pointed out.

"Cecil B. Igawa."

"I mean, experimental," she said in her soft voice. "To me it's the new art form."

"Not to me! And if you don't mind, I'm trying to concentrate on an old one."

"And Dorot and I're working on this film," Leigh said. "Ken Igawa, he went to California High, too, he's in on it with us."

"Sounds terrific, babe." Mr. Sutherland patted her hand enthusiastically. A successful, outward man, full of energy and action, he was delighted when his dreamy girl gave him a concrete interest for which he could show enthusiasm.

"Ken Igawa?" Mrs. Sutherland's smooth forehead crinkled. She raised her left hand with a big pear-shaped diamond that had been her twentieth anniversary gift, pressing her temple as if the effort of thought pained. "Isn't Igawa a Japanese name?" She looked at Leigh.

Mr. Sutherland, too, glanced at his daughter, his shrewd brown eyes piercing the dimness inside the cab that sped them down a steep San Francisco hill toward Ernie's.

"Oh, sure. He's here on an art scholarship."

"Dorot and I're going to write the script," Leigh said. They were in another cab traveling through drizzle from Ernie's to the hungry i.

"It sounds fun," Mrs. Sutherland said. "Real fun. When I was in Beverly High I took a class, Radio Speech. We put on a fifteen-minute radio program every Saturday."

"Ken Igawa's going to direct. Photograph it, too."

•   •   •

"Ken's a terrific artist, so Dorot says we can't miss," Leigh said Saturday.

"If you need film, babe, I can get it for you."

"Thanks, Daddy." Leigh put her slender, gloved hand in her father's broad one and they climbed Geary swinging clasped hands. A crowded cable car clanged by, trailing incense smell of brakes. "Sixteen millimeter. Ken says thirty-five costs too much to develop."

"—and Ken Igawa thinks I ought to photograph well, so maybe I'll have a part."

"Oh, and Ken Igawa says—"

Leigh hated it. For two reasons. First, she seemed to be the only person alive who still loved her parents. Second, she had firm ideas about fair play. Working people, especially those you love, through devious means, was to Leigh the worst kind of dirty pool. Especially she hated being devious with her father. His name was Sidney and as a little girl she had sometimes confused his youthful fighting in Spain with the probably apocryphal story of that perfect Elizabethan gentleman, Sir Philip Sidney, also battling Spaniards, dying yet refusing a cup of water in favor of a wounded soldier: *"Thy necessity is yet greater than mine."* How could you work a parent like that?

Sunday, just before her parents departed, Mrs. Sutherland went to use the dorm john and Mr. Sutherland said, quietly— there was an intense bridge game at a nearby table—"I hope this movie hasn't stopped your having fun." They were standing. Mr. Sutherland, only a couple of inches taller than Leigh, although much broader, stared gravely into her eyes.

"But it *is* fun."

"Still dating?"

"Sure."

"Mmmm?"

Praying she wouldn't blush—why was she such a rotten liar?—she said, "Last week I went to this big dance at the SAE house." Dorot had. "And Thursday I went to San Francisco with Artie Curtis to hear Rubinstein." Leigh had heard Rubinstein, but with Ken. Artie Curtis was Dorot's current and choice.

"Good. Good. Take your old man's advice, babe. Play the field while you can."

· 2 ·

Around ten the following night, Monday, Ken jogged downhill on Haste: he'd just walked Leigh from her English Lit seminar across the dark, windswept campus to the dorm. Monday nights he always walked her home. Usually he enjoyed it. But tonight all she'd done was yatter, yatter, yatter about some home movie. Her voice was very soft, almost a whisper, and for five days now she'd kept at him in her quiet, stubborn way about a home movie. Finally, tonight, as they'd reached Cunningham, he'd told her to get off it. They had not kissed good night. Although there was nothing unusual in this—they never kissed or even held hands except in the privacy of his place—still, the unresolved curtness of his remark had left him plenty shook. Conscience stricken. He'd rather battle the strong than the weak. Ken unlocked his building, slamming the door, shivering stained-glass insets. It was warm inside. He trotted up uncarpeted stairs, along the hall with its alternating odors of bacon, fish sticks, frankfurters and baked beans: student dinners that could be cooked on a hot plate. Up the second flight of stairs, some of which creaked. More hall smells. More stairs. He flung open his own door—he never locked it; what did he own worth locking? Closing the door, he leaned against wood. He had left bullet lights on and he blinked rapidly as his pupils adjusted; loudly breathing in the familiar odors of turps and paint, he told himself, *We didn't argue. I simply told her where to get off, and then I walked away. That's not an argument, is it?*

On the bed lay a pink sweater. Leigh was one of those rare redheads with enough light in her skin to look great in pink. He walked slowly to the bed and stood staring down. A bewildered expression grew on his long, bony face as if he'd never seen a girl's sweater before. He held it up, then crushed soft cashmere between both hands. He could detect—faintly—

her light odors mingled with the scent of Cashmere Bouquet soap.

He stood in front of the wooden easel staring at the canvas he'd roughed in with turps-laden umber: Leigh bending over a book. He gauged his work, trying not to think. But evaluations kept roughing up his consciousness: the composition was fine, the tonal values, now only a wash, also. Enough was down so that Ken already knew when he finished everyone would say, "Nice job, Igawa, nice work." Maybe the subject and style were somewhat sentimental—Berthe Morisot Igawa—still, all in all, not too hackneyed. The planes were O.K., musculature correct.

Stinks, shouted the raucous, unsympathetic critic inside. *Stinks.*

True, true. The lack, though, had nothing to do with technique. Little, as promised, had imparted technique. Ken moved back a pace. The technique was sound. Leigh's portrait stunk because—

Because—

"Why?" he muttered aloud.

She wasn't down. Could anyone aside from another painter understand this? He had not penetrated the innermost places of Leigh Sutherland. A taut smile of lust pulled the corners of Ken's wide mouth. Certainly not in the sexual sense, but so what? Screwing the model wasn't a necessary adjunct to portraiture, was it? No . . . he hadn't shown what people in an earlier age might have called her "soul." She on the canvas was an elegant redhead, nothing more. A painter must reveal a redhead, a landscape, a bouquet of flowers, or even abstract patterns as no one else has ever before seen them. Was it Oscar Wilde, poor faggy Oscar, who'd said of Turner, "Before him there was no London fog"? A painter must see his subject through eyes unsmeared by the accumulated vision of others. New. Fresh. Unique. *Yes, yes, that's it!* says the man in front of a Turner, and thereafter he always sees fog lying on the Thames through Turner's eyes.

And this was the only justification for trying to paint; to make people see through your unique eyes.

Ken began to squirm. He always squirmed when contemplating one of his flops—nobody else called them flops, but Ken was a vicious critic of his own work. He put the sweater over his face, shutting out the canvas.

"Why'm I such a mess?" he muttered. "Why keep trying?"

As always, when he asked this particular question, his mother's advice came to mind. Paint as a hobby; settle down (his mother's favorite phrase) and study something useful (her favorite concept) like landscape architecture (her fondest hope). Go back to poor, dull, thick-ankled Shigeme Futaba who had been sincerely, if dully, in love with him. The smells of the sweater mocked the thought of poor Shigeme. The smells of Leigh. . . . Ken thought how he felt when he held her; full of lust, yes, but also high as if he were listening to the last glorious chords of *Tristan*.

"What the hell is the matter with me?" Again out loud.

Sick.

He was sick.

I am sick so comfort me with apples. This made him think of the way Leigh's eyes filled with slow tears when he cupped his hands around them apples. They'd never discussed it, but she was, he knew, as ready for him as he was for her. Yet, typically, he hadn't done a thing. Why? The answer was as obvious as the difference in their faces. Ken Igawa's sterling Lutheran heart rebelled against screwing a virgin he was hung up on and couldn't marry.

Priggish?

Old-fashioned?

Galahad Igawa. That was him, through and through.

Yeah yeah yeah. *I can't paint but I won't give it up*, he thought. *I refuse to ball my girl, but I keep on making out with her and giving myself the stone ache*. Sick. He was sick. The truth was, if you really wanted to know, sometimes he wanted to tear his damn cock out, toss away his paint brushes and follow his sensible mother's sensible advice. Again he stared at the pink sweater.

He hurried from the room, racing down the first flight of stairs fishing change from his pocket. He dropped a dime in the phone, dialed. Said, "Five twelve Cunningham." Said, "Hey Leigh you left your sweater here—yeah yeah yeah, I *know* you know. It so happens I want to talk to you. Listen, how're we going to make a film if I don't know the first damn thing about it? Film-making's not exactly the easiest. You have to know *some*thing."

Leigh discovered the hole-in-the-wall art theater. It was a long way out on Shattuck so they had to take the bus, but the theater offered a monthly pass that made the effort worthwhile.

They took in a flickering Festival of French Film Classics: Cocteau's *Beauty and the Beast* (Leigh was repelled by the human caryatids and the candelabrum formed by human arms, but Ken admired these macabre touches), Vigo's *Zero for Conduct*, and *The Crimes of M. Lange*, produced by Jean Renoir— the son, Ken said, of *the* Renoir—as well as other, newer, French films. Ken sprawled back in an itchy velour seat, watching through almost closed lids. Leigh stared at the screen through round, wire-rimmed reading glasses that she had come to wear unselfconsciously with him. They soon made friends with the theater owner, a sweet old man with a thick German accent, bad breath and a red bulbous nose like W. C. Fields. He called them *kleine Kinder*. He had been, he told them in his hoarse gutturals, a *Kinematographer* with the great Josef von Sternberg, and after they explained they planned to make an experimental film, he would leave his post at the box office to breathe sourly down their necks, pointing out camera angles, cuts, fades, clever bits of business that not even Ken would have noticed on his own. Ken began to understand why nowadays people who might've been writing novels, painting, sculpting were making films. He wanted to see images *he* had captured up there on the screen.

A couple of weeks later Mr. Sutherland flew up, this time only for the day, strictly on business, and therefore without his wife. What would Leigh like to do that night? Leigh would like to see *Hiroshima, Mon Amour*. So, after dinner at Charles', lamb with bearnaise sauce still rich in their mouths, father and daughter drove back across the Oakland Bay Bridge in a Hertz Fairlane.

Dorot and Ken were leaning on the box office counter chatting with the sweet old German. Dorot embraced Mr. Sutherland, whom she'd known since she and Leigh were in kindergarten.

Leigh introduced Ken.

"Hi, Ken," said Mr. Sutherland, offering his hand.

As Ken shook the warm hand, icy apprehension jabbed his belly. This was his girl's father; however hopeless the situation, this was his girl's father. *Like me*, he thought, *please like me*.

Leigh's father was almost a head shorter than he, about the same height, Ken decided, as his own father. Equal height, though, isn't the common denominator in the human male. Leigh's father was younger, broader, infinitely more substantial than his own father; Leigh's father smelled of Havana cigars, Scotch, and—sweetly—of success. In fact, you might say Mr. Sutherland stunk of success. His coarse brown hair, receding in an uneven widow's peak and graying about the ears, had been skillfully clipped; his dark mohair suit had been tailored with golden shears; his shining black shoes had been hand sewn by a golden needle. His loosened tie said here was a man who could, despite his sartorial care, wear whatever he pleased, wherever and whenever he pleased.

"I've heard a lot about you and the movie." Mr. Sutherland, smiling, returned Ken's examination.

Under his gray pullover Ken shivered. Suddenly he was conscious that he hadn't had a haircut in several months—who at Cal bothered the barbers?—that his loafers needed a rub, heels too. That his ears stuck out. He was aware of everything wrong about himself, even hidden things like the ripped tee shirt beneath his sweater.

Most important, of course, he was conscious of being Japanese.

Mr. Sutherland's pupils glazed. Ken's quick eye caught the almost imperceptible blanking; it was as if he, Ken Igawa, were no longer in focus. The invisible man? No. Send Ken Igawa's apologies to Ralph Ellison, but it was the classified man. Full classification rendering further examination or interest unnecessary. *Shit,* Ken thought, *oh, shit.* When he was little he'd used fists on much larger white guys to change his classification from *nothing* to *feisty Jap bastard.*

Mr. Sutherland, pulling bills from a pregnant gold money clip to toss in front of the old German, said, "So you're the photographer?"

"Not yet," Ken replied.

"We haven't started a script even," Leigh put in quickly.

And Mr. Sutherland said, "Oh?" Obviously amused. "After all the talk I figured you were ready to shoot *War and Peace.*"

"We want to understand what we're doing," Leigh said. "We don't want commercial junk."

"God forbid. Nothing commercial." Mr. Sutherland took Leigh's hand. "Come on, babe, it's freezing."

Hiroshima, Mon Amour was, of course, a rotten choice. A love affair between a Japanese and a Frenchwoman could only awaken ideas better left dormant in Mr. Sutherland's well-barbered skull. As far as Ken could tell, though, no ideas of any sort occurred to Mr. Sutherland. He shifted his weight, whispered to Leigh, who sat between him and Ken, held his cleft chin thoughtfully, watched, closed his eyes, yawned. After about twenty minutes he rose, returning juggling three cartons of popcorn. He handed one each to Dorot, Ken and Leigh, then sat down to share Leigh's.

The popcorn tasted like soap, the rancid butter nauseated; Ken stuck his carton on the seat next to him. When the people behind left, popcorn scattered, rolling down the slanting floorboards.

Mr. Sutherland whispered, "Want another?"

"No thank you, sir."

"I'll get it," Mr. Sutherland said aloud, as if Ken were deaf.

"No thank you."

"No trouble—"

"Thanks, but—"

"No trouble at all."

"Daddy, *please!*"

As they left the theater, Mr. Sutherland invited them to Pizza Haven. Dorot bowed out regretfully; she adored pizza, she sighed, but she had a Soch quiz at eight the next morning, her major!

They dropped her off at the dorm. At Pizza Haven Mr. Sutherland consulted the menu tacked to the wall and without questioning tastes ordered the one with meatballs, green pepper, mushrooms, pepperoni, anchovy and bacon, the most expensive, then he began to talk about a goldfish-swallowing contest he'd put on back at Stanford Law to raise money to buy planes for the Spanish Republicans. There must be a smell around a campus, Ken decided viciously, a catnip odor that roused rahrah instincts in the old and made them recount their fusty cutups—or had the word been capers?

Mr. Sutherland chuckled. "I'd forgotten about that." He patted Leigh's bare forearm. "I've got to hand it to you kids," he said. "Nowadays you're much more creative. It takes guts to tackle a movie." Turning to Ken he said, "If you're short any equipment, have babe here write me. I'll get it."

"We don't need—"

"Won't be any problem."

"We're not ready to start," Ken said.

"I know people in the industry."

"Ken, didn't you mention some kind of light meter?"

"York'll get it."

"Baron York's son?"

"Uh huh."

Mr. Sutherland turned to Leigh. "You saw a lot of him at Michele's, didn't you, babe?"

Leigh flushed. "Ken and York and Clay—Michele's husband—are friends."

A fat weeping girl hurried down the long noisy restaurant to disappear into the toilet.

"You kids have a plot figured?"

"S'unnecessary in the type of thing we're planning," Ken said.

"Well, then you know what you're going to do."

"We don't."

"That's what I mean." Mr. Sutherland smiled affably. "You don't have a plot yet. We saw *El Cid* last week. Good story there." The tone remained disgustingly good humored.

There was just so much flesh and blood could bear.

"That Spanish turkey," Ken said.

He saw Leigh swallow convulsively. Any form of social unpleasantness, he knew, was the rack for her. So what? Who gave a shit? You bet your sweet ass not Ken Igawa. Adrenaline raced. Sweat poured under his arms. He clenched his fists under the table.

"We can't compete with big commercial spectaculars." Leigh's soft voice held a plea. "That's what Ken means."

"Hey Leigh, I can get my ideas across without an interpreter."

Their aging waitress set the aluminum platter down. Spicy odors rose on visible wisps of steam. The waitress tottered away between crowded tables. Mr. Sutherland asked, "Why did they have to walk and walk like that?"

"Technique. Resnais wanted to stretch the amount of time. Make it more important," Ken said, coldly professional. "The way a novelist does."

"Let's face it." Mr. Sutherland redefined the slices of pizza, sawing through hunks of pepperoni, mushroom, bacon in his path; then he gestured they should help themselves. "A plot holds your interest."

Leigh murmured inaudibly.

"I like a plot." Mr. Sutherland smiled. "Most people do."

"We aren't making this film for most people, sir."

"Who, then?"

"Us."

"Well, I don't know a thing about movie making." Mr.

Sutherland was totally unharmed by Ken's barrages—a class-ified man's fire cannot wound? "And you're the artist—"

"Painter."

Mr. Sutherland bit into pizza. A blob of tomato paste dripped into the cleft of his chin. He wiped it away. "But it's a big effort. So you ought to make it as interesting as possible, hey what, babe?"

"Leigh thinks films're the new art form, sir."

"They are," she whispered miserably, "they are."

Ken's paint-smeared fingers pressed on the table. "You really think that?"

"Yes."

"Then what's wrong with trying it on that level?" Ken asked. "What's the sense of making a commercial, plotty pile of junk? In this sort of thing you have to go by intuition. Risk failure."

"Ken's here on an art scholarship."

"And I have to keep up a three-point. Or out." Ken stood. "There's an English paper I didn't finish. Thank you for the movie and the food." He hadn't taken a bite. He added, "Sir."

The next day, as usual, Ken met Leigh after her ten o'clock in Dwinelle. She hurried out of the classroom and was almost up the stairs before he caught her.

"Hey Leigh."

She refused to look at him.

"So it's hostilities?" he inquired.

Wordless, she hurried to her eleven o'clock on the second floor of Wheeler. Outside the closed door he waited for fifty minutes. As she emerged he fell in step with her. "I feel pretty hostile myself," he said.

She refused to look at him.

He followed two paces behind her through Sather Gate, along the crowded plaza, past Ludwig's fountain where several assorted mutts were taking unseasonal dips, up Bancroft, along Bowditch. Ignoring three separate greetings of "Igawa," he stayed precisely two steps behind her until she got to the nougat-colored dorm complex. In front of the dining commons he swiveled to face her.

She stepped to the left. He stepped to the left. She stepped to the right. He stepped to the right. Three girls in trenchcoats stared curiously at them, and the short ugly one said, "Leigh, Dorot's saving us places."

"Thanks, Margie."

"You're eating here?" Ken inquired.

"It's paid for," Leigh said. "Room and board."

"You never let that influence you before."

"Excuse me." Again she tried to get around him. Again he stepped in front of her.

"Hey Leigh, I'm just as eager to throw the first stone as anyone."

"I'm eating with Dorot."

"But I'd rather it was in private."

Leigh tried once more to evade him. "She's waiting. Excuse me."

"You really are polite, aren't you?"

"Hungry."

"Hey Leigh." He took a deep breath. "You can go after I explain how stupid I am. It took me until this morning to figure something. Leigh, why're you so hot to make a film? A great yearning after the new art form? A sudden creative urge? Tell me, Leigh."

"I . . . I wanted to . . ." Leigh faltered.

"Let me tell you how *I* have it figured. You needed an excuse to see old slant-eyed me."

Her lips parted as if he'd slid a sharp dagger between fine-boned ribs, and he felt a tremendous, if painful, surge of satisfaction in knowing he was right. Her large hazel eyes filled with tears. Oh, excellent, excellent.

"Well?" he asked.

"That's not the only—"

"Oh, it's enough for inferior me. I mean, my sort goes on a real ego trip just knowing his girl spends her free time thinking up reasons to introduce him to her Daddy-O."

She gave up the idea of lunch: Clutching her books she started for the entry of Cunningham. Again he stepped in front of her. This time, trying to dodge him, she tripped, falling to rough, exposed aggregate. People on their way to the dining commons stopped and one, a pink-cheeked boy who appeared far too young to be in college, extended a large, chapped, helping hand.

"Go!" Ken snapped.

The boy hunched into his sheepskin collar, jogging hastily into commons. Leigh pushed herself to her feet.

"Hey Leigh, there's blood—"

"It must come as a surprise to you that I *can* bleed."

"Let me wash it off?"

"Leave me alone." She was crying, but she said the words clearly, passionately. "Leave me alone!" For the first time he realized her chin had the same cleft as her father's.

"With pleasure. I leave you alone with pleasure! Hey Leigh. I knew all along it was a mistake!" He was shouting. "Take my advice. Go out and get yourself a rich white guy, babe, one Daddy'll like!"

"Ken, shhh—"

"A polite, rich white guy who digs movies with a plot. As far as I'm concerned, I have had it!"

She dropped her spiral notebook; not pausing to retrieve it. "I HAVE HAD IT!"

She disappeared into the dorm. Let her go, let her go. Let her go. He felt fine about her going. He was a painter, wasn't he? Weren't painters meant to have girls all over the place? So toss this one back in the sea, it was fine with him, very fine. His eyes itched. As he jogged home, they began to water.

Dorot, rotating her upper arms, tightened her meager pectoral muscles. Leigh, who didn't smoke, lit one of Dorot's Pall Malls, pacing up and down their small room. She puffed hard. Choked. Puffed again. Choked again. Stubbed out the cigarette.

"If you're going to waste them, buy your own."

"Lay off, Dorot, please?"

It was three miserable days and three miserable nights after the battle.

"It's ridiculous the way you refuse to talk about it. Everybody knows talking helps," Dorot said. "Listen, Ken and you, statistically and sociologically speaking, never stood a chance."

"Who said anything about Ken?"

"Who hasn't been?"

Leigh, with rare meanness, snapped, "I figured gossip was sort of passé, but it's all anyone on this great modern campus ever does."

"Then why pick commons at high noon for your arguments?"

"We didn't argue."

"Of course *you* didn't. You're much too introverted. Too polite. *He* did."

"We simply decided we'd be happier not seeing each other."

"S'not the way I heard it."

"And I am."

"I heard he pushed you down."

"He did not! I *fell*," Leigh snapped. "Anyway we're better off apart."

"Is that why you've cried through the last three nights?"

"I slept soundly."

"Must be the nightmare season, then. What made you decide you'd be better off minus him?"

"You can tell the others he's immature. He really is. I told you how he kept arguing with my father, trying to chop him down. All Daddy was trying to do was show interest. Ken was repulsive." Leigh sat on the bed and said quickly, as if she'd been hoarding the words, "Oh, Dorot. He figured out what I was doing." She paused, adding, "It certainly isn't your fault, any of this."

"If you're better off without him, why should I get debits?" asked Dorot, always rational. "And naturally I assumed you'd discuss the plan first with him."

"How could I? I mean, Dorot, what would you have said?"

"The truth. I needed a legitimate reason to be seeing him."

She would've, too, Leigh thought, closing her eyes. "Well, he figured it out for himself. So it's over. Over." Eyes still closed, she said, "It's best. We're both better off."

"I agree."

"And if he asks about me, tell him—"

The phone rang.

Dorot's snicker following her, Leigh broad-jumped across the small room, getting it before the end of the first ring.

"Leigh?"

"Yes?"

"I've got to talk to you."

"You're talking."

"See you, I mean. Hey Leigh, don't make me crawl."

— **3** —

"What've you got against him?" Leigh asked. They were walking up and down in front of the dorm.

"For openers, the way he paws you."

"O.K. It bothers you we've got a good relationship. What else?"

"He's narrow minded."

"He is not!"

"Why else did you need a reason to introduce me?"

"Ken, I said I was sorry about that."

"Didn't you notice how he talked to me? Like loud. Did you tell him I was deaf? Or a foreigner?"

"That's how all older people talk to us. He was only trying to be nice. Interested in what we're interested in." She paused. "Ken, you've got him all wrong. He's liberal."

"You mean he didn't ask me to sit in back of the theater?"

"Not my father."

"Oh, never him!"

"He isn't like that."

"Everyone his age is. Face it. A fact of life."

"Not my father. To him people are people. He's very liberal."

Liberal! How Ken loathed the word. Why did she keep saying it? Icy wind came off the Bay, skidding along dark, empty streets. They passed the Chinese-looking Christian Science church that had been designed by Frank Lloyd Wright; wind shivered blanketing vines. Out of the shadows slunk a gray cat, eyes lit as if by electricity. It bolted across the street. Without discussion Leigh and Ken were following their well-trodden path to his place.

"Listen, Leigh, they all are. Remember when that business with Eichmann was in all the papers and TV?"

"What's that got to do with—?"

"And you were weeping all the time about concentration camps. Remember? Well, you're with someone born in one."

"A concentration camp?"

"A concentration camp."

"But—"

"Forty-eight dash three dash F. That means block forty-eight, barracks three, compartment F."

"I didn't know," she whispered.

"I have my own little secrets."

"Where?"

"Utah."

"But *how?*"

"Head first and—"

"I meant, how in a concentration camp?"

"Quite simple. During World War Two on the West Coast every Japanese and every American of Japanese descent—I think up to one-eighth part Japanese descent—was hauled off to a concentration camp. The motto of the day: a Jap is a Jap is a Jap and so what if he's an American?" Ken pushed back thick hair. "Haven't you heard about it?"

"I guess I have." She walked slower, not looking at him.

"I wouldn't be surprised if you hadn't. It's not exactly our country's moment to remember. People prefer the Alamo. Or the *Maine*."

"Why? Why did they do it?"

"Self-protection. When they looked at us, they didn't see American citizens, they didn't see little American kids like George—he was six—or my sisters, they're younger. They saw sneaky yerrow devirs who bomb Pearu Halbo." Ken made a whistling, explosive sound between his teeth, flung his hand up, down, up. "So what else *could* they do? They put us behind barb wire where we couldn't do it again. Oh, not me. I wasn't born. But when I arrived, you know damn well they had to keep me behind barb wire so I couldn't commit any acts of infant espionage. I can't remember the place, but George can. There was a huge, tall tower, George says, with a machine gun facing our barracks. Hey Leigh, how's that for memoirs of an American boyhood?"

"It's unconstitutional!"

"Yeah yeah yeah. But that's not always the name of the game."

"Anyway, my father was in the navy. He had nothing to do with it. He wouldn't have let it happen. He's in ACLU—"

"Civil Liberties did nothing to stop the deportation."

"But my father—"

"I know. He's very liberal. Bullshit! Your liberal father was brought up like the rest of California. They called us the Yellow Peril. They didn't let Japanese immigrate here; only the ones brought to work on the railroads and stuff could stay, and they couldn't become citizens. People who'd been born over there but lived here most of their lives couldn't become citizens. They couldn't buy a home or land—that's your Oriental Exclusion Act. They couldn't practice a profession, or even raise goldfish. I mean, like how could you trust the sneaky Yellow Peril to breed innocent goldfish? So when the war came *your* father could have done only one thing. Lock up my father and mother even though they were born right here, in California.

And my brother and sisters—Posy, she was eight months old at the time. How could your father have gone off and fought when the home front was unprotected from Posy? Believe me, if he'd been here, he would've shipped my family off to the camps before he joined the navy!"

Passing headlights flooded white on her face, and he saw the horror in her eyes. The fury that had burned in him for three days and three nights, the fury that her father had roused, evaporated. Wind cut through his old gray sweater. What was he doing? What? Committing the worst sin of all, that's what. Shifting the bitterness of one generation onto the next. Visiting the sins of her father on her.

They were outside his place.

"Come upstairs, Leigh?" he asked in a quiet voice. "I'll fix us hot chocolate."

While he heated milk in the chipping enamel saucepan, she watched.

"If we'd been really close," she said, "we would've talked about that place."

"I guess we would've," he agreed wearily. "Sometimes it sticks in my gut and I want to vomit it up. But I've always hated talking about it. Ashamed, you think? Anyway, I don't remember the camp, so it's sort of an acquired bitterness, like olives. My parents really were bitter. Especially my father. He gave me a regular Japanese name. Meet Kenji Igawa." He held out his right hand as if for her to shake, then let it fall to his side. "They changed it legally after the war. Even now, though, the deportation's the only thing my father'll talk about. Yak yak yak. When he left he had to sell out for like five cents on the dollar. He lost a lot of property. The southeast corner of Parkdale was his celery field."

"It's a long time ago."

Ken stared down. The milk was beginning to foam at the perimeter. He lowered the heat. "And yet," he said, "and yet, it could happen again tomorrow. They could nail the evacuation notices to the telephone poles again, and we'd all go quietly."

"*You* wouldn't."

"I'd get my gun, you think?" He was half questioning, half sarcastic. "Look, we're a small group. There's maybe a half million of us in a population of two hundred million. We look different, so we couldn't mow down the guards and escape." He swung an imaginary machine gun, making *kch kch kch* noises. "Maybe the Jews in Germany could've tried to mingle.

But we couldn't. Not then. Not now."

"It just doesn't sound like the Ken Igawa I know, going quietly."

"I'd *kamikaze* a few of them . . . who'm I kidding? I'd worry they'd hurt the others. No! I'd fight!" More imaginary machine gunning. "I'd show 'em. They didn't use gas chambers, did they? Of course, nobody knew that the first time, but now we know. So why not?" He flung his head back to get hair out of his eyes. "Sure I'd fight. They'd have to come and get me." He was snarling in his Cagney voice. "Come and get me, ya crummy cops. I'm not going! Y'hear? Not going. You'll have to take me dead. *Kch kch kch kch!*"

From the set of shoulders under camel hair he realized Leigh was making an effort not to cry. Turning out the gas, he went to her, whispering, "Hey Leigh, I'm not going to psych out on you." Putting one hand under her coat, flat between the fragile, quaking shoulder blades, with the other he stroked long, cool hair. "Shhhh. . . ."

After a while she stopped crying and rubbed her face against his old sweater to dry her cheeks.

"I'm glad you told me about it," she said.

"Friends?"

"Friends."

"No more plans? No more home movies?"

"With us none of that old-fashioned junk matters."

"It matters."

"Not to me, Ken. Never."

"It gnaws me," he said. "It's like a cancer."

"You mustn't let—"

"Don't talk about it." He kissed the top of her head. "Hey Leigh, I missed you."

"If you hadn't called"—her narrow, soft hand lay briefly against his cheek—"I'd have died."

Downstairs a hi-fi, or maybe a radio, started to spin Beethoven notes.

"Emperor?" he asked.

"Yes," she said. "The milk's getting cold."

"You care?"

"Terribly."

They lay on the bed. He pressed his tongue into her mouth, exploring the softness of her inner cheeks. He ran his long hands up and down her body. She did the same to his. *Hey,* he thought, *I'm gonna drown, yeah yeah yeah. I am drowning.*

But at the same time a part of his mind (his conscience maybe?) remained clear and he wondered about love. What did the word mean? What were its properties? For example, was love stronger than death, more powerful than the grave, as his mother's Bible explicitly stated? Was love more powerful than those forty-six infinitely small particles that mastered every cell of Kenneth, né Kenji, Igawa's body, the forty-six that mastered Leigh Sutherland's? Or was it forty-eight? What did that matter? What mattered was can love be stronger than genetics? Her clothes were in his way and he started to pull, unbutton, unzip. She helped him.

It was the first time they'd been together naked. He half knelt by the side of the bed, gazing at her. He'd seen many girls nude, mostly models; some were hags, some good looking, but none this beautiful. For example, her skin tones. There were no two ways about it, he could spend the rest of his life studying the texture and luminous quality of her skin and still not figure how to paint it. Where the sun had hit her, a faint powdering of translucent freckles; the narrow strips hidden by bikini, a rich, velvety white. Skin so tender it retained light pressure of bra and cotton underpants. Her full white breasts, fleshed out at the side because she lay on her back, were veined with purest blue, and more blue veins lay in the hollow between her delicate carved pelvic bones. Soft hair curling on the raised mound, he noted, was much paler than the hair on her head.

"Hey Leigh, you're beautiful, all over so beautiful."

"So're you," she whispered. But her eyes were tight shut and glossy brown lashes shadowed her flushed cheeks.

"You haven't looked," he said. This, he perceived as he spoke, was terribly important. She must look at him. See what she was about to get herself into. No. Who was about to get into her. "Please, please, Leigh. Look?"

Could she ever refuse a *please?* Emerald raying into brown and he wished for once he could see himself through those wide-apart hazel eyes.

"You're very beautiful."

"Boys're handsome."

"Don't laugh. Not now."

"I'm not laughing," he whispered. He kissed her pink nipples in turn; they tasted of strawberries—some kind of body lotion? Her?

"I love it when you do that," she whispered shakily.

He tugged at her hand. As she realized what he had in mind,

she pulled away, unwilling. Their hands struggled, but he held tight and said, "Please?" so she let him place it. Her eyes shut, she blushed all over, then her fingers circled the hardness.

"Ken, I never asked. Have you ever?"

"Yes."

"Ohhh."

"Doesn't count."

"I hate her."

"It was just bodies."

"Them."

"This is the first real time."

Her fingers tightened and she caressed the veins in back.

"I love it when you do that," he whispered. "Leigh?"

"Yes?"

"Just Leigh." He kissed her neck and shoulders, touched his lips to her forehead, which was moist, and her closed eyelids, which were strangely cool.

"If you don't want, we don't have to," he said.

"I do."

"It's sort of irrevocable for the girl."

"I want to."

"I'm really hung up on you either way."

"Ken . . ."

"Hey, you're shaking."

"So're you."

"I want you so much I'm high with it."

She put both arms around his neck. "Now," she whispered in his ear.

He raised up, turning off the lamp, lowering himself onto her, spreading her knees gently with his knee, and as he caressed the moisture between her thighs he was filled with an aching tenderness too great to be borne. "I love you, I love you," he whispered. "I never said that before, Leigh, not to anyone."

"I love you," she said and her words were almost a scream. Then her body seemed to melt. He was her. She was him. He could feel her heart pounding—or was it *his* heart? They lay, mouths open, breathing the same air with the same long, trembling gasps. He began to move. Her fingers dug in at his waist and she turned her head, moaning deep in her throat. He was hurting her. He knew he was hurting her, yet he couldn't stop; the tenderness remained, but now he wanted to hurt her, to mark her so she would be his no matter who they were or what they were and she, seeming to understand his need, or maybe needing it, too, let her thighs fall loose to give him the freedom he demanded. "Leigh, love me, love me..." and her body began answering his, tentatively; then they were moving together, pulling back at the same moment, joining close, back again, and he knew he'd penetrated whatever mysteries existed, dark caves, shadowy seas, jungle rivers and all that phallic jazz you read about was for real and he must go further, further, further, her breathing in his ear the only guide in this unexplored world, and all at once she started to move wildly, gasping, *Ken, Ken Ken Ken... Oh*—and he felt a tremor as if something had broken in the fragile body under his and answering her name he moved as fast as he could, triumphant, like a winning sprinter, until deep inside him all the dammed-up love, goodness, hopes, what you might call his unique soul began to trickle, faster, faster, faster, into her, exploding inside her.

A long time later he heard the rattle of branches, the faraway, round, droplike notes of Beethoven. He moved to her side, pulling the blanket around their damp bodies, and still entwined they fell asleep. The wind died. Faraway notes drifted into the circular room, then faded forever. The full moon rose, its nacreous light painting their bare shoulders, hers gently freckled, his umber, with the same pale, impartial sheen. In the middle of the night he felt her curled around him and, imagining himself in the familiar dream, he stroked the soft warmth of a naked breast. She reached for him. He remembered.

This time it was even better.

"Sweet Leigh rhymes with sweetpea," he said against her ear. "We're naturals."

"I love you. Don't leave me."

And he still inside her they went back to sleep.

"I'm only trying to help," Dorot repeated.

"And I don't want to talk about it," Leigh repeated for the third time in her soft yet intractable way. Two months after Leigh had begun spending her weekends at Ken's place, late on a Friday afternoon, she poised tiptoe on a chair reaching for the smallest of the matching white Samsonite cases on the top shelf of her closet.

"It's mid-Victorian to be so prudish," Dorot said.

"I'm not."

"What else would you call it?"

"Private between Ken and me."

"I've read a lot, kept up with the subject, and you just admitted you aren't exactly majoring in Contraceptive Devices." Dorot took a last puff, then crushed out her cigarette. "I'm your friend. I want to help."

"The last time you helped we almost broke up."

"This is much more concrete. No theory involved. Simple biological fact. Do you do *anything*?"

"Sometimes he . . ." Leigh blushed crimson. "He—well, he—you know . . ."

"You're trying to tell me you use *coitus interruptus?*"

Holding the small case by the handle with three slender fingers, Leigh turned on the chair seat to stare blankly down at Dorot.

"The male withdraws before ejaculation," Dorot explained in loud, uninflected tones.

Leigh's blankness turned to unbelief. Then horror. She stepped down.

Dorot said, "It's the oldest method."

"And the worst!"

"A lot of people do it. You've never come across it in your reading?"

"I wouldn't let him! It's inhuman!"

"And unreliable."

"I mean, I feel terrible for him when he has to use a thing."

"A condom?" Dorot asked, and quickly, before she had a chance to draw another blank look, added, "He wears a rubber?"

"Sometimes."

"Sometimes?"

"We use the rhythm system."

"You've taken temperature charts?"

Leigh shook her head.

"What then?"

"It's—oh, Dorot. You make it all so cold and practical."

"Go ahead. Have your romance with a capital R. Get preg."

"Around my period we . . . well, we just do."

Dorot clapped a prominently boned hand to her forehead. "That's no rhythm system!"

"I heard you can't get pregnant then."

"Either you heard wrong or someone talked wrong," Dorot asserted. "A matter of known fact, it's the most fertile time for certain women."

"I'd rather not talk about it." Leigh moved her chair back to her desk and clicked open the case.

"It'd be disaster, total disaster. You can't marry him." Dorot stopped. "Don't look at me that way, Leigh Sutherland. I'm only saying what everyone else whispers behind your back."

"Thanks."

"You know you can't. Ken does too. I'll bet he hasn't brought up the subject." Dorot peered at Leigh.

He hadn't. Leigh busied herself with a Baggie of nylons, testing with an open hand for runs. She selected two pairs of runless, matching stockings.

Dorot said, "Listen, haven't we been friends since kindergarten?" They had. "I never knew a more naïve soul—you bring out all my protective instincts, and that's God's honest truth." It was. "You need help in the worst way." Leigh did.

Leigh pulled unfolded lingerie—neatness wasn't her forte— from her top drawer.

Dorot went on, "If it's any comfort, I think you're doing absolutely the right thing, getting it out of your system. These little marriages you see on campus are the best thing that can happen to a mixed. Look at Poppy Carver and Loop James. You know if they'd had this sort of opportunity they never would've raced down to Tijuana to get married, then have *both* families toss them out. Poor Poppy, she ends up with a divorce and a *café au lait* infant. Now who'll want her—them?"

At the far end of the hall a girl shouted, "Fourth for bridge, fourth for bridge," through the open window came the smell of macaroni and cheese dinner, and Leigh gazed toward the last golden light flooding the green Berkeley hills.

"Leigh Sutherland, I loathe and despise that mental vanishing act you do when something displeases you," Dorot said without rancor, continuing in the same breath, "There's vaginal foam. You don't need a prescription."

Leigh turned, gazing at Dorot.

"It's only about ninety percent reliable, though," Dorot said. "Lately they're trying a permanent loop in the uterus, but that can set up a serious infection. Anyway, you need a doctor. And—of course—there's the good old standby. The diaphragm."

"Don't they always make you think of flabby-thighed, middle-aged women?"

Dorot agreed they did. "Anyway, you have to be fitted by a doctor."

They both wrinkled up their noses and shrugged hopelessly.

"You can douche after," Leigh offered shyly. She pronounced the word *dawsh*.

"Douches're practically useless." Dorot tactfully emphasized the correct pronunciation.

Leigh reddened. "Anyway, I couldn't leave that hideous rubber bag thing hanging in Ken's bathroom—he shares it."

"As far as I'm concerned there's only one safe, esthetic contraceptive."

Leigh, a white net brassiere dangling in her hand, gave full attention.

"The Pill," Dorot said in professional tones. "It's been thoroughly tested for two years now. It's the method of the future. It sets up a hormonal change that infertilizes. It isn't taken precoitally, but daily, like vitamins; therefore it has no connection to the act and cannot act as an anaphrodisiac. . . ." Dorot stopped. "It takes a doctor's prescription." She sighed. "What doctor's going to give the Pill to a girl unless she's married or about to be?"

Leigh, also sighing, shook her head.

"There's the older generation for you!" Dorot lit another cigarette. "Discover a method of birth control, then deny it to the group who needs it most."

Leigh, shaking her head, sighed, "True, true."

"I've been hearing," Dorot mused, "about this new doctor in Student Health—"

"Student Health!" Leigh uncharacteristically burst out. "Remember when I needed penicillin? They wouldn't give it without the signed consent of my parents! By the time I got that, who needed a shot?" She shrugged, compressing her lips. "Never in a million *years* would they give me the Pill!"

"This new one's a woman. She worked with Planned Parenthood in Kansas City, so doubtless she's sympatico. Naturally, though, she's bound by the outdated faculty code around here. So we'll have to help her out a little. I'll sign any forms she wants for you. You can sign for me."

"You?"

"Who knows the day and hour"—Dorot gestured casually with one hand—"when I may succumb?"

Any other girl alive would have demanded to know more. But Leigh, being Leigh, fastened her overnight case, then stood in front of her mirror brushing shining red hair twenty strokes;

she considered it a breach of etiquette to question a friend's sex life.

"It's A-O.K. with you?" Dorot asked.

"The word is go." Leigh smiled and pulled on her pale blue coat. "Dorot, I'm sorry I chopped you. I know you're trying to help and I do appreciate it."

"What're friends for?"

"Will you make the appointment?" Leigh paused at the door and, flushing, said, "I'm checking out."

"Have a good time," Dorot shouted bawdily after her.

Leigh fled to the elevators.

Dorot waited a full five minutes. She locked the door, moved quickly to her bureau. From under the half slips she took a small leather-bound book with a lock. She fished out a narrow gold chain on which dangled a tiny key, still warm from the warmth of her meager bosom. This locked book contained a secret survey of Cunningham girls' sex lives. Dorot did not record for prurient interests; her cool inductive mind cut through the mysteries surrounding human reproduction, which she felt should be treated unemotionally and scientifically. To this end the book contained research for a projected doctoral thesis, a survey following the lines of Dr. Kinsey: The Sexual Habits of the Berkeley Female Undergraduate. She riffled through pages until she came to *LEIGH V. SUTHERLAND,* writing under her last entry, *Contraceptive method—irregular uses of condoms.* Dorot had decided terseness was one key to honest research. She flipped through more partially filled pages. On the first blank she wrote *DOROTHY E. McHENRY.* For there was no truer handmaiden of science than Dorot. She intended to use her own experiences as detachedly as she'd used those of other girls and, as she'd told Leigh, she had made up her mind to divest herself of virginity as soon as a suitable moment arrived. She had not an intention of falling into the same trap as poor Leigh.

Dorot, staring at her own neatly printed name, in all honesty couldn't fathom Leigh.

Not that Dorot went along with the girls who proclaimed Leigh looked just like Audrey Hepburn. As Dorot pointed out to them, the resemblance rested solely on long dark red hair, wide-set eyes, fine bones draped in a fabulous college wardrobe painstakingly selected by Mrs. Sutherland. Still, on the other hand, Dorot was the first to admit Leigh had fragile charm and a nice sense of humor, even if she did tend to murmur so you sometimes missed her best lines. Certainly Leigh could have attracted tons of eligible males. So why choose the impossible one? Yet oddly enough Dorot found this flaw of irrationality very appealing. Her friend Leigh was a unique. And Dorot, while she didn't hesitate to point out the problems involved, stood squarely behind the star-crossed lovers.

However. She herself was not interested in battling the establishment by risking either pregnancy or involvement with an unsuitable male. The dates she accepted were eligible types. And Dorot dated a lot. At Berkeley she had become what her mother archly called, "Quite a college belle." Fortunately college men found Dorot's lanky good looks appealing and—being intelligent—they realized the relative unimportance of secondary mammaries. Dorot had not pledged a sorority despite the fact Mrs. McHenry had fully expected her to follow maternal footsteps into the Chi O House. As far as Dorot was concerned sororities were archaic fossils of another age. But this prejudice against female Greeks in no way prevented her from being attracted to and attracting fraternity men. Blue-eyed Artie Curtis in particular. Artie Curtis, an SAE psych major, kissed skillfully and spoke of matters sexual in a well-informed manner that fascinated Dorot. Letting the leather binder fall closed, Dorot pensively gnawed the eraser end of her ball point, asking herself if her emotions for Artie Curtis were love. As she locked the notebook she felt a pleasant, most unscientific twinge of pelvic anticipation. The next entry might be her own.

Leigh drew the first appointment.

Diogenes could shine his lamp on her. She was a cripple of a liar. Leigh, like all introverts, imagined her thoughts as visible as the freckle-dusted nose on her face and, safely back in their fifth-floor room, she reported to Dorot that the tall, gray-haired lady doctor's eyes had probed right through her. The doctor had dark, pleated skin under those all-seeing eyes; she sat on the business side of her desk, her wrinkled hands forming a-church-and-steeple-and-here's-the-people, while Leigh fumbled through a tale of being engaged and needing a contraceptive before her marriage next month. The doctor's gray eyes never seemed to blink. Leigh broke down and admitted she wasn't engaged at all, simply in love, really in love with another student. The doctor leaned forward to offer Kleenex. Leigh mopped her tears. The woman told Leigh for any such coun-

seling she must see her own family physician; then she sat back
to deliver herself of an Ann Landers' desist-and-resist philosophy.

"You ask for help. She gives you a stone." Dorot snorted.
"What did she say?"

Leigh deepened her soft voice. " 'I know you girls today
think it is perfectly moral to engage in premarital coitus. Believe
me, though, Leigh dear, there's still a mighty strong case for
chastity. Our cultural, moral and ethical mores are still set up
on the side of virtue. Premarital chastity requires will power
and discipline which, I'll admit, aren't always easy. Yet, on
the other hand a great deal of permanent damage may be done
by engaging in premarital sex. Tremendous psychological guilt
often ensues. The relationship suffers. And. I am sure you will
consider this old-fashioned, but believe me you will be cheating
your most intimate relationship with your future husband. There's
still, unfortunately, a double standard, and no man in his heart
of hearts can respect a girl who succumbs before her wedding
night, even if *he's* the one. Unfair, I know, but that's how it
is. And as a physician I ought to point out that physiologically
the sex act simply isn't gratifying at first for females. Your
generation of girls have been sandbagged by mass media into
believing the pleasures are free and immediate. Believe me,
Leigh dear, and I've worked with literally thousands of young
married women—I was with Planned Parenthood—at the
beginning it often takes months of patience on the part of a
young husband to bring his wife to climax. And, whether you
girls will admit it or not, biology is against you. An important
part of the act for the female is anticipation of motherhoo-hoo-
hoo . . . ' " Leigh broke down in giggles.

Dorot joined in with her surprisingly deep peals of laughter.

Leigh's giggles faded. Sighing, she said, "It was hopeless
from the beginning."

"The wrong technique, that's all."

"What d'you mean?"

"Don't you know by now it's impossible to tell *them* a story
remotely tied to truth and expect more than a lecture?"

"But you don't lie!" Leigh exclaimed. "I never once heard
you lie."

"With them I do. I learned the lesson at my mother's knee.
Or rather, over it. It—is—absolutely—necessary—to—lie—
to—anyone—over—thirty."

"What'll you tell her?"

"I've been researching that. *AMA Journal. Lancet.* It seems the Pill corrects menstrual irregularity. I think I'll tell her about"—Dorot clutched her flat pelvic area and gave a bawling groan that might've been wrenched from a cow in the last stages of labor—"my terrible, nauseating, unpredictable, devastating, death-urge periods."

Dorot, after a long, skillful lying session, was handed the prescription for the pancake-sized plastic compack containing twenty-one tiny pentagonal white pills. She got Artie Curtis, too, for all that was worth. After the big cool talk he turned out to be a virgin. A one-minute egg.

Leigh kept on with her rhythm system. It had worked so far, hadn't it?

4

"Igawa!" shouted someone on the first floor. "Hey, Igawa! Visitors."

Hiding behind a short, curly brown beard was Clay Gillies. With him, a tall colored guy Ken had known last year at UCLA. RG Richards. Rain dripped down RG's freckled brown face and from Gillies' new beard. The boys explained they had hitched up from Los Angeles.

"Need a place to sack?" Ken asked. The offer was wrenched from him in muttered tones. This was one of the rare weekends that Leigh's phony parents weren't flying up and on the agenda had been love sweet love.

"Thanks," RG said with his warm, nervous smile.

"There's some people we need to talk to," Gillies said. "Can we use the place?"

"Feel free."

Ken lent them dry clothes, fed them steaming Campbell's vegetable soup and sandwiches thick with bologna; he borrowed sleeping bags for them, gave RG his mattress and Gillies his box springs, sacking down himself on the thin napped rug.

Saturday it was still raining. How word had gotten around

the bogged-down campus that Gillies and RG Richards were at his place Ken never discovered, but the word had. In twos and threes so many people banged on the front door with its stained-glass insets that Mrs. Gauthier, the fat, good-natured landlady, said to leave it unlocked. The smoke-filled circular room smelled of damp wool, damp hair, the heat of too many bodies, and Leigh kept struggling to raise heavy old window sashes, but rain would slash in and right away someone would shove down the window.

They all came. The Snick bunch. The SDS guys who shouted speeches from Sproul Steps. The SNAP workers (one, Dick IoPorto, actually had gone south), the bright pretty girls who would soon drop out to marry IBM men but who right now were storing up a lifetime of social significance, the sad ugly girls who delighted in any cause that filled lonely time, the boys and girls who tutored over in Oakland, the intellectuals who read Camus and Sartre and accused themselves. They came, the active, involved ten percent of Berkeley, the ones who were out to change their decade, their country, their world. Ken sat by his wooden easel, knees to his chest, his long fingers itching to capture the eagerness tightening their faces.

Five times Gillies gave the same speech. Each time the room filled he would start, drawing and keeping attention as if twin magnets were embedded in his brown eyes. In the midst of his new beard his firmly carved lips tensed.

"I wish," he would start, "I wish I could describe the beauty of that morning, that Sunday morning almost a year ago. Mother's Day. We were on our way to Birmingham, Alabama. . . ." Here Gillies would pause while the significance of place and day reached every person in the circular, smoky room. "The sun shone. Birds sang. Honeysuckle grew over the small cabin, and we stopped to beg hot water for shaving. Mr. Redfern, the owner—no . . . not the owner; he was a tenant farmer, a sharecropper—insisted we stay for breakfast. I wish I could describe the warmth and friendship in his crowded two-room cabin, the friendship that comes only to people who aim for a common cause. More, I wish I could repeat to you the phrases that Mr. Redfern used when he spoke of the better world he hoped for his nine beautiful kids—four girls, five boys. But we hadn't had a hot meal in days—where can white and black eat together in our southern states? I'm ashamed to admit it, but I was hungry and mostly interested in the scrambled eggs and steaming corn bread that Mr. Redfern kept bringing us from his wife's wood stove. But I remember that he spoke of his hopes that his children would be able to get an education, able to earn a decent living in this so-called democracy."

"As f-free human beings," RG would interpolate.

"He was a good father, Mr. Redfern."

"A good man," RG would echo.

"Our memories're sadly incomplete. . . ." Gillies would pause. "But they're all we have of Mr. Redfern. He gave us scrambled eggs, he gave four hungry Freedom Riders breakfast. . . ."

Silence.

Rain pattered at windows, people shifted uneasily on bare boards while Gillies would fix his laser-beam glance first on one person then another.

"RG and the others and I went to jail."

"S-speeding, that was the charge."

"Segregated jail cells."

"Black and white s-separated."

Ken would think of revival meetings.

"And Mr. Redfern?" a female voice would query. Never in those five times, Ken noted, had a guy asked.

"The local papers reported it. Two lines on the back page. A Negro hunting accident, they called it. . . ." Clay's somewhat high-pitched voice at this point always stopped. And as the listeners drew breath and conclusions there would come splatters of anger.

"Bastards!"

"Makes you ashamed to be white!"

"To be an American."

"The rest of my life," Gillies would continue quietly, "the rest of my life I'll live with the knowledge that because a man fed me eggs and corn bread, his brain was exploded with a shotgun shell."

More voiced anger.

Gillies would go on. "Now there's nine kids can't go to school."

"There's no money f-for shoes."

"No firewood."

"No flour."

"There's practically no food."

"N-none."

"It's cold now in Alabama, but there's no firewood to warm those nine beautiful kids."

Everyone would fish in purses or pockets. RG would move around the room, not noting amounts, shoving coins and bills indiscriminately into a manila envelope, blue-crayoned *Contributions for the Redfern Family*.

By ten thirty everyone had left. Leigh was gone—not even a good-night kiss was possible—and RG, too, had departed to see a cousin who lived in San Francisco, a lawyer in the DA's office. RG had promised his mother this visit. She was praying some of the cousin's middle class would rub off on him, RG had jested, so he'd quit this fooling around.

Ken opened a can of Heinz spaghetti, asking Clay, "How'd you find out he'd been killed?"

Gillies, in the midst of stacking dimes, frowned.

Ken persisted, "You subscribe to the funky Alabama papers?"

"S'far as I know"—dimes jangled into the envelope—"he's still alive—and sharecropping."

"Then why the violins?"

"You think they'd give if I just asked?"

Ken stirred red spaghetti and thought thoughts that he preferred not to think.

"So you've crapped out," he said finally.

Gillies turned angry, dark-shadowed eyes on Ken.

"Well?" Ken asked. "What do *you* call it?"

"Ever hear of Camellia in Ward County?"

"Miss.?"

"Yep."

"One third white," Ken quoted, "two thirds Negro. Ninety-five percent of whites of voting age registered. Only two percent of the Negroes."

"Exactly right."

"Even to this outpost," Ken said, "believe it or not, Snick and CORE come."

"It's virtually impossible for a Negro farmer in Ward County to figure the registration rules. We had to get a lawyer to explain them to us."

"Why go to that sort of trouble?"

"We're starting something new. A voter registration school." Clay raised the envelope. "With this."

Ken felt small, petty, rotten, lousy, guilty about his suspicions, yet as he stirred the pot he couldn't for the life of him resist asking, "Why lie about Mr. Redfern?"

"That's not his name. I don't know his name. We paid his wife for a good breakfast, and all the time he worried local whites would find out and make things tough on him. And on his family. That's all I know about him."

"But—"

"When I told the story straight not even Michele paid attention," Clay said. "Not even my own wife."

"Why don't you explain about the school?"

"Christ, Igawa, you ever try to raise money with facts and percentages? I dropped two classes, gave four or five speeches a week. The facts, I gave them only the facts. A quarter here. Thirty cents there. Never any folding money."

"Emotions do pay better."

"It's not for me." Gillies sounded tired, and—Ken couldn't figure why—he looked at least four inches shorter and thirty pounds lighter than when he had orated to the crowd. "I don't keep a cent."

"Time was when you wouldn't have stooped."

"Yes." Gillies, surprisingly, agreed. "But that was before I was hit over the head with the South. Christ, Igawa, if you could see how those people're treated! In our own great, free country, like they're animals!" Gillies played with the envelope flap. "It's *my* conscience. If I knew a better way to get the money, you think I'd go through that circus?"

You enjoyed every revival-meeting second of it, Ken thought. Immediately he reneged. Clay Gillies might have changed, but he was sincere, totally, honestly sincere. Tomato steam rose. "It's ready," Ken said. "Let's eat."

He divvied the spaghetti in unequal portions, his guilt giving almost all to Gillies. Gillies didn't notice. His white teeth bit into French bread sopped with thick red sauce.

"At the school," he said, swallowing, "we need volunteers."

"I've got a scholarship," Ken said. It sounded weak, he knew, but the bigger truth, that he had race problems of his own, sounded weaker. "Leigh's been talking a lot about the Peace Corps."

"Lee?"

"Leigh Sutherland."

"I thought I saw her here."

Ken, tearing bread from the long loaf, found himself saying with a hint of shyness, "My girl. S'hopeless."

Gillies shrugged. Obviously to him personal matters were

totally unimportant. "How about you?" Gillies asked. "What do you think of the Peace Corps?"

"S'O.K.—"

"It is bullshit! Pure, meaningless bullshit! Set up by bureaucrats!" Gillies' beard jerked. A crumb fell. "Snarled with another generation's red tape!"

"Kennedy—"

"The great young white father of us all!" Gillies' bearded face twisted with fury that seemed out of all proportion to a discussion of the Peace Corps. "It's one more of his political ploys; he wants to divert us from the fact he's not getting through any civil rights legislation."

Gillles' blazing, angry eyes sapped Ken's will power. Was that why Clay Gillies seemed larger in a crowd? Those eyes *were* magnets, attracting the steel filings of others' wills to enlarge Clay Gillies.

But Ken Igawa, while weak willed, never was one to retreat from battle. "And you think that"—he nodded at the full manila envelope—"will do more than the President can?"

"You know what's wrong with you, Igawa?" Clay Gillies exploded. "You're a skeptic! This is the history of our times, being written by us! But you—you're so damn busy questioning details that you can't identify with it. Or anything else! Skeptics never do one damn thing, Igawa, except poke holes in other people's beliefs!"

A motorcycle revved noisily. For a full minute Ken Igawa and Clay Gillies glared at one another, fists clenching unconsciously. Then Ken decided Gillies was right. He, Ken Igawa, was a selfish, sarcastic SOB.

At the same moment both raised sheepish eyebrows.

"The little old Swiss cheese maker, that's me," Ken said.

"Essentially you're on the right side," Gillies admitted. "Otherwise you wouldn't be my friend. But you have to work on it." Gillies shoved his plate away. "I mean it, Igawa, we can use you in Mississippi."

Ken shrugged negatively. He said, "Want something else?"

"No, thanks."

But anyway Ken found two Delicious in the back of the icebox. He felt impelled to offer Clay Gillies something—anything—in lieu of himself. Were two red apples that smelled on the cidery edge of spoilage an adequate exchange?

• • •

Later, when Leigh asked if Clay had said how Michele and Lissa were, Ken couldn't remember that Gillies had. As a matter of fact he was positive that Gillies had mentioned Michele only once, tangentially with his Freedom Ride.

------------------ **5** ------------------

Death had come to woo at the York place.

In the long bedroom with the genuine Modigliani over the marble fireplace he sweet-talked Linda Farnahan York as she'd never been sweet-talked before, not even when she was a script girl with a pair of firm knockers and a sweet ass to counterbalance the plain, honest, pug-nosed Irish face. She lay feverish, restless with drug-numb pain. Death whispered: come with me, no more enemas, no more needles, no more taut sheets to press aching nerve ends, no twisting pain, no helplessness, no crab to eat soft flesh, come . . . come . . . come. . . . She would lean toward him. Her pale lips would move, making no words; her head would toss from side to side as in the lusts of adultery. All at once death would step back. Fever dropping, she would fall into peaceful sleep.

When she wakened, Miss Rodman, the efficient, heavy-jowled registered nurse, would draw silk drapes and open windows. Miss Rodman would wash and perfume and assist her patient into a draped satin bed jacket, hand her the make-up tray and mirror.

Beautified, comforted by Miss Rodman's needle, Mrs. York received visitors. Through open windows came a raucous, head-over-heels ode to life—a tribe of misplaced mockingbirds nested in the avocados, and their continuous song filled warm summer air. The PTA ladies, Mrs. York's only friends, would tell in soft voices of fund-raising carnivals, teas, lecture meetings, Phoebe Apperson Hearst awards. The ladies lied magnificently, vowing Linda never, never looked better. Why, she should be up and helping them right now, they chided. They saved their handkerchiefs until her door had closed behind them.

After school the girls would drop by. They were embarrassed by death and therefore angry with their mother—oh, the adultery she considered! She would discuss with them their friends, dates, new dresses, new hairdos, new sports car. On low-slung white silk furniture, the two girls would squirm, eyeing the door.

At six thirty on a good day, Miss Rodman would carry up a silver cocktail tray laden with twelve-year-old Scotch, Steuben crystal, sterling bar equipment, setting this by the bed, discreetly rustling away. Baron York and his wife would have a drink; then he would say, as he'd said so often before, "Some important business, Lin. See you later."

Soon enough, though, cruel crab chelae would again rattle. Close. A new infection. The invisible presence again would hover around the king-size electric hospital bed which had been purchased for this last liaison, and Mrs. York would sigh, groan, mutter aloud that she'd had enough of this farting around, take her, take her, take her.

All this was observed from behind dark glasses by intelligent, protruding gray eyes.

On the far side of the long room, in front of the sleek marble fireplace, on one of the paired white silk easy chairs, York cupped his long chin in his good hand, watching. He'd dropped out of UCLA over a year ago, when he had returned from Alabama. Since, he'd educated himself with Nietzsche, Bergson and Buber and Berkeley, Kant and Camus and Kierkegaard, Hegel and Hume, James, Sartre and Spengler and Spinoza and Socrates, de Chardin, Abelard, Mach and Marx, Plato and the other heavy boys. Completely disregarding chronological or philosophical order, York had devoured and digested over five hundred books. He had found no answers, but a hell of a lot more questions. Two months ago, when his mother took to her bed, he gave up reading to stay with her. He stayed fourteen, sixteen hours a day, all day, every day, never moving from the room, not even when doctors and nurses insisted. "Have to go now. It's time for our enema." Or, "We're going to have our examination now. I'll call when we're finished." York didn't answer or argue. Or budge. They couldn't carry him out, could they? Miss Rodman ordered a light hospital screen, using it when necessary, and she and the others soon came to accept his presence as they accepted the watchfulness of the uneven-eyed Modigliani. All York's meals he ate in the sickroom. Bad days Rosann, the maid, set his tray on the low marble table between silk chairs. Good days she pulled the brass teacart to his mother's bed.

These times when Mrs. York felt better, they would talk by the hour. As she neared the truncated end of her life, a need possessed her to bestow on him her memories: she told him of her depression girlhood in hot, dusty Bakersfield, how she and her friends used to sneak into the air-conditioned delights of Fox West Coast and how they used to swipe from the Good Humor man's tricycle and eat in the park "Ladies" where he couldn't follow. "Even today when I eat an ice cream bar I always smell pee," she said. She told him about the Kresge's fountain; she was only a kid then, but she was really stacked and fellas would make passes until they learned, via a kindly senior waitress, that they ought to "leave the kid alone, she's only thirteen, and don't tell the manager or she'll get canned."

They rarely discussed York, he preferred it that way, but once his mother said, "You ought to go back to college."

"Why?"

"You wouldn't ask if you'd had to drop out of junior high," his mother replied. "Honest, you're brilliant."

"Then they can't teach me much."

"It's a rounding off."

"I prefer the jaggeds."

"Me, I only got to ninth grade."

"You're sorry?"

She turned, winced, lay back on the raised hospital mattress.

"Sorry?" he prodded.

"I hated school all the way." She managed a smile. "Still, for a man it's different. He has a living to earn."

A meaningless remark in this case. Baron York's tax structure was extremely complicated and his agent manager, Carter Klein, assisted by Eliot Goldsober, a genius of a tax attorney, had set up trust funds with what the government would have grabbed anyway. To none of Baron York's three children would money ever be a problem.

"Adam, honest, what're you going to do?"

"Eat what Miss Rodman's ordered for lunch. So are you."

"I meant with your life."

"Live it."

"How?"

He shrugged his thin shoulders.

"Alone?" his mother asked.

"How do most people live?"

"With other people."

"I'm buying a high marble pillar. I can become a stylite."

"Huh?"

"A pious hermit who lives high atop a pillar. Or a post."

"That's not living," she said. "I know nowadays it's all blamed on the parents, but honest, your father—"

"What say we try a little telly?"

"—is no ogre."

York opened the *TV Guide*. "A Zorina-Phil Baker movie."

"He's—"

"He's one of my favorites, too, Phil Baker. Along with Charles Drake, Warren William, Arthur Lake, Louis Hayward and Zachary Scott. How do you feel about Phil?"

"Once I worked with him. Your father is—"

"Maybe this. *Goldwyn Follies?*"

"Not that one." She gave up on trying to heal breaches between him and his father. "Adam, what'll you do after?"

They never tried to avoid the fact soon death would win his suit.

"Maybe travel," York said. "The isles of Greece, the isles of Greece, eternal summer lives there yet."

"I want you to live." She raised up on her thin arm. Without protection of flesh, her bones ached. She grimaced. She'd lost so much weight that she resembled those terrible snapshots taken by GIs touring Auschwitz and Dachau. "Live," she murmured.

And because she was so close to the other choice, he promised, "I will."

"Accept your father," she said. "Otherwise, honest, you'll eat yourself away."

Accept his father.

During the bad times, when he could do nothing, when others were in constant attendance behind the hospital screen, York would slump in the silk chair, turning over the phrase. Accept his father, accept his father. What did the words mean? Wasn't it like saying black is white? A paradox. Linda Farnahan York, whom Adam York loved greatly in his non-Oedipal fashion, knew the two major reasons he, her son, could never accept his father.

First, for her sake.

Second, for his own. In that order. The second reason lay buried in the year of the horse.

Six was the year of the horse.

Before that there had been a broad-backed, lethargic Shetland pony, Eeyore, and Adam loved Eeyore; he had a velvet nose that gobbled sugar cubes, he smelled like hay and clean horse-do, his broad back carried reassuringly low and slow. Eeyore was Adam's friend. When nobody else was close Adam would lean forward cautiously—he worried about heights—and do a sissy thing, kiss the rough, shaggy fur. The pony would flick his hairy ears.

Then one hot morning after fourth of July fireworks, Adam and his father, just the two of them, drove to the ranch in Chatsworth. Adam was in heaven. Miraculous, wasn't it a miracle to have all to himself this strong, wondrous being who smelled of whiskey, cigars, sweat and hair tonic, the way a god should smell? His father, humming, rested his left elbow on the rolled-down window, easing the station wagon through Valley traffic as if motor and wheels were extensions of his big, tanned right hand. Adam pretended he was driving one-handed, like his father. He, too, hummed. But his father's deep *hmmmm* was mysterious, as if he had a secret.

His father did have a secret.

Stabled next to the big black American-bred stallion was a small brown mare, sunlight coming through the open top of the barn door to prink her long neck.

"What d'you think?" His father grinned.

"She's pretty."

His father was still grinning. "She's yours."

Adam peered around the long, dim stable. "Where's Eeyore?"

"Shetland ponies're for babies."

"I like him."

"Girl babies," his father said.

"Where is he?"

"There's nothing to be afraid of, son. This here is a real gentle piece of horseflesh."

"I want my Eeyore!"

"And I figured I had me a boy."

"You do! I am!"

His father winked at Jackson, the stableman. "I guess I got me three girls."

So Adam permitted himself to be lifted onto the brown mare. His hands, the good and the bad, grabbed at reins and hump of western saddle.

"Should I fix the lead rein?" Jackson asked as he adjusted the stirrups.

Adam's father winked again. "Us saddlepardners don't need it," he said.

The brown mare swayed dangerously under Adam. He clung to the pommel. His father trotted ahead, big and easy and part of the beautiful black stallion the way he'd been part of the station wagon. He faded in a distant cloud of beige dust. The brown mare chewed on golden mustard growing at the side of the trail. Orange smells drifted from a citrus orchard, part of the ranch. His father returned.

"Come on, saddlepardner, let's have us a race."

Adam wanted more than anything in the world to race with his big strong father, but he was almost up with the two mashed-potato clouds and the mare swayed so frighteningly when she moved that he worried his hands, specially the three-fingered one, might lose the reins.

"I like it here," he said.

"What's the use of having a horse if you stand around like you did on that damn pony?" His father's face, glowing and sun-red, twisted with anger. "Your mother's turning you into a regular sissy, you know that? Well, I'll be God damned if I'll let her."

And he gave the mare's shining brown flank a sudden slap.

She took off, racing along the trail fast, so fast there blew a gritty gale, reins hung loose in Adam's small nerveless hands. He flew up to the lumpy clouds, he flopped down, up. "Sto-oo-o-o-o-o-o-o-op, sto-o-o-o-o-op!" he yelled. "Sto-o-o-o-o-o-o-o-o-op!" And the sound acted as a spur to the mare. Wind tore at Adam as he tossed between sky and hard saddle, helpless and weightless as a ping-pong ball. "YIIIIII-IIIIYIIIIIIIIYIIIII . . ." Adam shrieked wordlessly. "YIIIIIIIIIII-YIIIIIIIIIIIIIIIIIIIIII . . ." Terror wrote on his brain, terror pumped his heart and after he couldn't remember if terror had willed the fall or if the brown mare had thrown the screeching from her back. But there he was falling, falling through dusty heat, spinning through the air, crashing into hard, scabby, hurting earth, rolling over and over into cutting mustard grasses. He tried to protect his hand, but it was bent under him, and he was screaming now not with terror but with agony.

So there was another operation. He'd already had four, but this one hurt most and his mother stayed with him all the time. Except once. He fell asleep and woke to find her gone. He heard talking outside his hospital room.

"—certain the arm can't ever grow." A lot of pacing foot-steps and a man's voice, not so deep. "It'll always be this size."

"Oh, sweet Christ!"—his mother.

"We did all we possibly could"—another man's voice, deeper.

"Oh, Lee! How could you?" Adam's mother cried. Adam knew she was upset; she never called his father Lee unless she was upset.

"I swear to you, Lin, he wasn't even trotting. Just a fast walk. He froze."

"But he's only six—"

"You overprotect him!"

"Never—"

"He let himself get thrown."

"Lee, he'd never been on a real horse, and with his hand—"

"My luck! I have to get a goddam cripple coward for my only son!"

And Adam—no, now he thought of himself as York—felt something click in his head, which rested on a soft pillow. Click. Just like that. He was sensitive, the words cut deep, very deep, but also he was a very intelligent six-year-old. And in that instant he understood that his father's action had no real reference, not to him, not to anyone in the world. Other people, as far as his father was concerned, existed only as mirrors. He admired himself in their eyes. Manly companionship *(old sad-dlepardner)*, gifts, affectionate words and friendly pats were not directed at his son but were intended to reflect in York's round gray eyes a larger-than-life man, a pal-to-his-son-though-a-famous-movie-star. And in that same odd click the boy knew that however large his father appeared on screen and off, he was in reality petty, vain, stupid. He saw his father, as all children eventually must, for what he was. A human being. A god came crashing down.

In York's brain the lifelong mourning began.

For three days Mrs. York tossed, rolled, thrashed, moaned in her drugged pain. Miss Rodman, other nurses, the doctors did what could be done with tubes, needles, ice bags, bottles, syringes. York remained in the low-slung chair, barely eating, occasionally dozing to waken with an afghan over him.

On the third night Mrs. York sat up, calling, "Lee! Lee!!"

Before his mother had called often for her husband, but by the name she had given him. Understandably, Miss Rodman gave York a confused glance. But York didn't stop to explain. There was something different in that cry. He hastened through connecting bathrooms and dressing rooms to consult his father's alligator address book, a new one started last year, and on the *N* page he found today's date, crudely inked with the name Noreen and an address.

A girl opened the door a crack. She was younger than he, with straight blonde-white hair. Her he hadn't sampled. Since his mother's illness for York the coldest place on earth was between the thighs of one of his father's girls, or between the thighs of any woman, for that matter.

She blinked sleepily.

"Baron York?" he demanded.

"Who you?" she asked, rubbing her eyes.

"He's here."

"No." She was more alert.

He pushed her out of the way, flinging open doors. A kitchen with dirty glasses on all counters. A bathroom, sheer blue nylon hazing the floor. A bedroom with his father and another girl entangled on a huge round bed, flowered blankets crumpled back where the blonde had rested.

"Get your hairy ass out of here," York said. "She's dying."

And without another word York drove a steady hundred across the sleeping city and up dangerous dark hill roads to his home.

As he bent over his mother's bed she opened her eyes. Huge, blurred, bewildered eyes. Touching his short arm she made the only reference to his deformity that she'd ever made in his presence.

"Addie, I'm sorry," she whispered. Then, as if someone were crushing her wrists, her fingers fluttered weakly and collapsed limp on the sheets.

"Don't be, Mother."

"Sorry, Addie, sorry."

"It's not your fault," he said, "Mother."

"Your father..." Her voice faded. Adam bent yet closer. "...not his fault...." The tenuous whisper disappeared in gasping, struggling breath.

Miss Rodman, impersonal as ever, tears brimming behind her rimless glasses, lifted a wristbone. Said, "Dr. Martin's on his way." Took the pulse. Said, "I'll phone for the ambulance."

"No," York grated.

"The hospital has the proper equipment."

"God himself doesn't have the proper equipment and you know it."

"She ought to be—"

"Let her go. For Christ's suffering sake, let her go!"

"Lee?" Mrs. York muttered.

"He's coming."

"Lee?"

"I had to get him off the set."

"Lee?"

"It's Adam."

"Lee?"

"Mother, I love you," he whispered.

"Lee?"

"It's Adam. *Please know me.*"

She gasped harshly.

Miss Rodman took her pulse again. Miss Rodman turned to York, her face impassive but tears flowing. She shook her head, wiped her cheeks and set about changing linen in the hospital-approved manner.

Baron York arrived within ten minutes. He was too late. The skeletal body gasped—uneven, unmeasurable pauses at inhalation and exhalation—for two and a half hours while five doctors performed obscene last rites that earned their fat fees. But Linda Farnahan York already had eloped into the cool, starry California night. Even if the doctors would not admit it, somehow the mockingbirds in the avocado trees knew. York, at seven, had believed in Poe's tales, in the Lovecraft stories of Arkham; he had scared himself out of sleep with this belief. Of course there was no more belief in him . . . but didn't those damn mockingbirds sing every other dawn?

Suddenly he held his breath. His bad hand clenched inside its pocket in a paroxysm that denied release.

Silence.

Total silence.

After a while the doctors left, the nurses and, last, Miss Rodman. In the gay early morning light, by his dead wife's bed, Baron York sat, expensively massaged actor's shoulders slumped. York, who had not stirred in the last three hours, rose to kiss his mother's dry cheek as he'd done every night of his life. The cheek was still warm.

"Good night," he said aloud. "Good night, Mother."

And he wished he knew who to beg to be gentle with the

little black-haired girl who once had swiped Good Humors in a hot Bakersfield park.

Baron York, not raising his head, said, "I'm nothing without her."

"Balls."

"No child can understand what was between us."

"You gave that a lot more of the old pizzazz in *Round Table*."

Baron dropped his rugged, handsome face in his big hands. A car crunched over the gravel drive; somewhere in the house Moira, the youngest, shouted hysterically. Baron remained in the same position.

York said, "No reason to give an academy-award-winning performance. It's just me."

Baron looked up. "It's not my fault she died of cancer, is it? She was my wife. I loved her, whatever happened to separate us."

"King Mark, isn't it? *Immortal Isolde*."

"Can't you cry decently for your own mother?"

"Episode in Corinth."

"You miserable, inhuman little cripple!"

"The first original line. That's really what you hate, isn't it? I can't play Andy Hardy to your Judge?" York removed his jacket, rolling up the left sleeve, exposing pale, scarred flesh. "This is nothing to the way you're crippled. You can't speak, move, mourn your wife or hate your son unless some hack's written out the lines for you. And even then you can't give a credible performance unless someone's out there applauding. Listen, why don't I call up those cunts of yours. They could come over and watch you play the bereaved husband. They'd enjoy it. They weren't born when you made *Round Table*, were they?"

Baron, breathing heavily, rose. With considerable force he slapped the pale face. Dark glasses fell and, as the boy staggered, with big hands the actor shoved his son to the thick white carpet next to the dead woman's bed. Kneeling astride his son, Baron York shook the boy with all the ferocity and strength he'd possessed as a young man in the Ojai oil fields.

"You goddam cripple, it wasn't my fault she died." Baron swung at his son's pale cheek. "It wasn't, damn you."

"She wanted you here," York panted.

"Not my fault."

"She loved you."

"Cancer's a disease."

"She suffered—"

"God damn you!"

"—because she loved you."

"SAY IT WASN'T MY FAULT!"

And finally York understood. This was the Big Trial Scene. He, the dead woman's son, played prosecuting attorney, and the actor in his father sought absolution. But it wasn't up to the attorney to absolve, was it? Only the Judge could do that. And neither of them believed in any Judge other than good old Lewis Stone, so there was no Judge present. For the first time in his life, York pitied his father.

Baron, sobbing, aimed at his son's mouth.

York, short, hairless arm stretched out, naked and fully visible, didn't fight back or try to escape. He lay on his back, tears streaming down pale cheeks. He didn't notice the beating, not hardly at all, for he was realizing that not one of the books written by the learned men of every century and every place had warned by so much as a single word that the emptiness would be as icy as this.

6

HOLLYWOOD TO JOIN BARON
IN MOURNING WIFE

Leigh, down from Berkeley, sat in the breakfast room drinking fresh orange juice and reading the morning edition of the *Times*. Sunlight squeezed through shutters, drawing bright yellow lines across newsprint: photographs and columns of Mrs. York's life. *Death separates Hollywood's closest couple . . . beside her husband she leaves a son, Adam, and two daughters, Tara and Moira.* There were pictures of Mrs. York with her husband, with the two girls and with York as an infant.

Should she, Leigh wondered, find some mutual friend of hers and York's to go to the funeral with? For example, Ken

Igawa. Especially Ken Igawa. She hadn't seen Ken for two weeks and three days, since they'd left the Oakland Airport, she on Western, he on PSA. They had decided in the drafty PSA waiting room that it would be easiest if they met only at the Gillieses' place. While they talked their embarrassment, though veiled, had been evident; already they were part of their families. Leigh's eyes were attracted by a posed portrait. Despite glamorous black pageboy, penciled eyebrows and curve of dark lipstick, Mrs. York looked so sad . . . what sort of necrological phony would she be to use death as an excuse to call her boy friend?

She saw Ken on the far side of the Forest Lawn parking lot. He was opening the car door for a lady wearing a black straw hat; Mrs. Kunoshi Igawa, Leigh remembered, had been active in the California High PTA, as had Mrs. Baron York. Mrs. Igawa—short, moon-faced, plump in sleeveless black— lifted a hand to brush back heavy hair that flopped on Ken's forehead. Maybe it was the intimacy of the gesture. . . . As Leigh stood by her own mother's Jaguar, it came to her with a force that made her gasp.

He was an Oriental! The fact had never really gotten through to her before, not that time at the Obon Festival, surrounded by gaudy cultural reminders, not that windy night Ken'd been so explicit about his birth in a Japanese relocation center, not with his repeated demands that she *face it, this is crazy, you and me.* . . . No no no. She never had accepted their differences. He was Ken, she was Leigh. That was all. Period. But here he was, unfamiliar in a black suit and tie. With a Japanese mother.

A Japanese guy.

Did it matter?

Well, did it?

Ken saw her. They stared at one another. A bronze Rolls-Royce slowly backed into the parking stall next to her and still she and Ken stared. Leigh felt her face grow hot. Turning, she almost tripped on the parking divider.

Did it matter? Did it? Suddenly Leigh's thighs trembled. She was remembering the last time they'd made love, quickly, so they wouldn't miss the airport limo that left the Durant Hotel at four ten, no time to undress, he'd sat on the straight chair, she straddling his lap, his hands at her hips fitting her to him faster and faster. Would realizing their differences lessen love? Shouldn't love conquer every contingency? Why had she thought immediately of sex? A sliver of headache started above her left eye.

"Wait," Ken called. "Leigh, wait!"

She waited. Her breathing calmed.

"Mother, this is Leigh Sutherland. Leigh, my mother, Mrs. Igawa."

Black eyes examined Leigh.

"Ken tells me you're going to Berkeley, too," Mrs. Igawa said in a brisk, matter-of-fact California accent.

"Mother never trusts me. She likes to check."

"He tells me you were working on that movie?"

It was all Leigh could do not to give Ken an inquiring glance.

"I hope you didn't waste as much time on it as he did. I just don't understand Ken. My other children concentrated on their studies. But not Ken. He fools around. Drawing. Painting. Oh, art's fine, but in its place." Mrs. Igawa spoke with throaty fondness, but the words spelled annoyance.

Shaded by navy silk flowers of a hat borrowed from her mother for the occasion, Leigh smiled politely.

Mrs. Igawa said, "Well, he has to work, so he won't be able to waste *too* much time."

In the crowded chapel coolness, the rich scent of a million flowers and a Unitarian minister in plain dark suit making a pleasant speech, dwelling not on Mrs. York's untimely end but on the cheerful aspects of her life. He recited her favorite poem:

"How do I love thee? Let me count the ways.
 I love thee to the depth and breadth and height
 My soul can reach, when feeling out of sight
 For the ends of Being and ideal Grace.
 I love thee to the level of every day's
 Most quiet need, by sun and candle light.
 I love thee freely, as men strive for Right;
 I love thee purely, as they turn from Praise.
 I love thee with the passion put to use
 In my old griefs, and with my childhood's faith.
 I love thee with a love I seemed to lose
 With my lost saints—I love thee with the breath,
 Smiles, tears, of all my life! and, if God choose,
 I shall but love thee better after death."

Leigh, who had always adored Elizabeth and Robert and Flush, sobbed, then felt guilty that her tears were mere old-fashioned sentiment and not grief for Mrs. York. *I really am a phony, a big fat phony*, she thought, dabbing gloved fingers at her cheeks. Ken fished out his handkerchief, and Leigh, without thinking, reached. His mother! she thought, pulling back to rummage through her good navy purse for Kleenex. As soon as the brief service ended, she hurried out of the chapel.

In the dappled green shade of giant chestnut trees, reporters, TV cameramen, soberly dressed mourners clustered around the bereaved widower and his two sobbing daughters. Alone, apart, stood York, a pinched sneer on his pale lips.

"I met her only once"—Ken offered awkward condolences—"but she was a nice lady, your mother."

"Thanks."

"Hey, this is a rough time to ask, but we're making a film. We don't know the first thing. We need *help*."

"Sure thing, sure thing," York replied loudly. His father and several others turned reproachful dark glasses in their direction. "Isn't that what the world needs? Another York cranking out the old garbage?"

Ken leaned against the hot metal of Mrs. Sutherland's Jaguar. Leigh was trapped in the cars clotting the exit.

"The film's the only way," he said. "The rapid capitulation of Honest Abe Igawa." There was more than a hint of self-anger in his tone. "What're you doing tonight?"

"Nothing."

"Good. Like to talk to you."

Leigh gazed past stalled cars toward the Chevy. Mrs. Igawa, chatting with another lady, watched Ken and her.

"I see," Ken said softly, following her gaze.

"Eight?"

She opened the door. A two-story hall, acres of shining dark wood that gave off the lemon smell of fresh polish, emerald excesses of Boston fern in three wicker planters. From the top of the curving staircase floated music—*In the jungle, the mighty jungle, the lion sleeps tonight. . . . Awhimaway, awhimaway. . . .* Leigh, several steps ahead, moved past entries to dark rooms, leading Ken into a brightly lit sort of den. There was a wet bar, shelves with metal glint of golf trophies interspersed with best sellers' bright jackets, armchairs, a tremendous semicircular couch, two slab coffee tables that looked as if they were meant to have feet put on them. It was a pleasant, comfortable room furnished for use, not effect, and Ken couldn't deny it. The trouble was, the fly in the comfortable ointment was, the room contained more footage than his whole house. Somewhere nearby dishes clattered.

Ken nodded toward the sound. "Your mother?" he asked.

"No."

She perched on a chair, pulling her dress around narrow, shield-shaped knees. The modesty, even as it annoyed him, reminded him of the times when she had forgotten that modesty. *Down, boy, down,* he told that much-denied part of himself. He sat on the couch a good distance from her.

"Very nice," he said. "The room."

"Thank you."

"Relax, Leigh, your parents won't come in to find you in my foul clutches."

"They aren't home."

"Oh?"

"They go out a lot."

"Nice for them," he said. "Listen, I came here to impart the distilled poetry of much concentration. We call it a *haiku.* Mine isn't the seventeen syllables it ought to be, but it *does* refer to a season." He took in the room again. "As a matter of fact, I never realized it would be this nice."

"Thank you."

"The point is, such surroundings make it difficult to recite my *haiku.*" He banged his fists together as if playing cymbals. "The yellow plum ripens in the summer and hey Leigh, we ought to let our parents in on it. Us."

She burned crimson.

"I want to *see* you." He emphasized the word. "See, that's all."

"Did your mother say something?"

"About you?"

She nodded.

"Nope. She was too busy talking about the beautiful daughter of Mrs. Ushiyama, the lady she met at the funeral."

"Is she beautiful?"

"A fashion model."

Leigh sighed. "You think your mother guessed anything?"

"She's not a moron. The way you bolted! She'd have to suspect *some*thing."

"I'm sorry."

"Don't be. Hey Leigh, without you I just about psyched out."

She did a funny, nervous thing with her eyebrows and the tip of her nose.

"You?" he asked.

"The same."

"Hey . . . relax."

"I am."

"Yeah yeah yeah."

"I am."

"Listen, if it's strictly on campus, say so."

She shook her head, staring down at her dress. She had a great many clothes, and this dress he'd never seen before, a loose shift thing the heavy color of yellow ocher right from the tube. She pleated the brilliant fabric between slim, nervous fingers. In the kitchen, clattering stopped. The dishwasher started.

"Look, as my mother pointed out, I don't even have a major yet, for Christ's sake."

She nodded.

"And I've never been in a place like this before. Except York's." He leaned forward. "The truth is, even if I were crass and loaded, it would never be easy for us. I know you don't like to admit it, but hey Leigh, even Luther Burbank didn't try to mix oranges and apples."

She swallowed. He could see the saliva travel down her long, creamy throat.

"It won't be easy," he repeated.

She shook her head again. Again. Infuriatingly again.

"If you keep doing that," he snapped, "you'll unscrew your damned neck. Listen, you've taken the vow of silence, write me a letter and I'll forget the whole idea and—"

"Yes," she interrupted.

"Yes?"

"Yes."

"Yes, what? You've taken the vow of—"

"Yes, I'll marry you."

Grinning he sat back on the couch. He wiped his sweating palms along his cords. "Married?" He tilted his head. Though he'd considered little else for the last couple of weeks, he wasn't, God knows, ready for marriage yet. The words seemed pressed from him rather than spoken. "I'll have to consult my number one and number two wives about your proposal."

"Do that," she murmured.

"If they agree, I'll take you on immediately after graduation."

She nodded.

They listened to the watery song of the dishwasher. Again he stared around the room. It seemed to have stretched ten yards in all directions.

"Of course I've had a while to get used to your little suggestion," he said, "but before we tell our parents anything too specific, we ought to let them see us together. The film?"

She nodded.

"Hey Leigh, I know I made a big noise when you tried the devious route. You might say I went sorta King Kong?" He glanced questioningly at her. She shrugged. He said furiously, "Who needs the We-Kiss-in-the-Shadows act?"

"S'different."

"How?"

She cleared her throat. "You're letting me in on it."

"Bully for me!" He put his hands over his ears and shook his head. "I kill myself, you know that?"

"Ken—"

"But with Clay down south and Michele at her folks, how else can we hack it?"

She sighed.

He sighed.

"With the general conditions that prevail," he said, "I guess we play it cool."

She came across the room slowly, standing in front of him, but when he tried to put his arms around her waist she evaded him.

"What's the matter?"

"Come," she said.

"All day you've been acting like I need Listerine."

"My brother's home. And Maria." She pushed open the sliding screen. "There's two steps down."

They crossed the patio; then his Keds sank into spongy, damp grass. He could see an unlit oval swimming pool shining black as tar, a cabana. She opened the cabana door, closed it soundlessly behind them. Heavy cold odors of chlorine laced with sweetness of suntan lotions. It took his pupils a while to adjust to the dim blue reflection of house lights that slanted down through a clerestory window. He heard a thump as she pulled a chaise pad from a shelf.

"I've been thinking, that's what's the matter," she said in a hoarse, anxious whisper that filled the blue-shadowed dark. "Ken, you looked different. Do I look different to you? Have I always?"

"We are different, we are. Listen, maybe you ought to think more about—"

"No."

"Yes—"

"No! I don't want to think about it again. *Never.*"

"But—"

"I love you, I love you."

"We ought to discuss—"

"I *won't* discuss and dissect. Ken, I love you. Always and forever." As she spoke, she reached to the back of her dress and he heard the screech of a long zipper, rustling as her loose dress fell to the floor. She wasn't wearing underwear. In the darkness her slight, pale body shimmered—chiaroscuro, he could see nothing else, that was how chiaroscuro worked... full high breasts, shadowed triangle.... She unsnapped her barrette, finger-combing long, shampoo-scented hair over shoulders and breasts the way he always did, *Hey Lady Godiva,* before they made love.

"That's not the only ans—" he started.

"Shhhh..."

He, too, despised words and reason. *More than two weeks it had been.* Light, sharp female scents. Feel of velvet, thermal skin. Curved waist. Globed butt. They were both shaking.

"Our parents love us," she whispered. "We won't hurt them, will we? Oh. I've been crazy without you. Crazy...."

He whispered a disjointed stream of involuntary and most obscene endearments.

"Yes, do that," she breathed. "And that, oh please. Wait, darling." She sank to her knees, unzipping and pulling. Her lips encircled, her teeth felt like sharp white dabs of paint, her tongue fluttered. "I love it. I love all of you. Don't ever leave me, never, never." They sank to the chaise pad. "Hurry, Ken, I...oh, love."

It was after twelve when the Sutherlands arrived home. Ken Igawa and their daughter were playing cards, a large slab of coffee table decorously between them.

Mr. Sutherland strode across the hall. "Hi, babe." At the entrance of the family room he stopped, surprised.

"Why, Ken," he said.

Ken got to his feet. "Sir."

An awkward silence.

Mr. Sutherland said, "I thought . . . I mean. . . . Well, Leigh told me you kids had given up on the movie."

"We're back on it again," Leigh said.

"S'better now." Mr. Sutherland sat and so did Ken. "Summer. You won't have to take time off from studying—does that sound stuffy and paternal? Frankly, it's best if I don't discuss it. The last time, up in Berkeley, I felt like a regular Philistine."

"Anyway, right now"—Leigh glanced at the cards—"we're playing rummy."

Mrs. Sutherland came in. Ken stood and Leigh introduced him.

"They're making the movie again," Mr. Sutherland explained.

"How nice," said Mrs. Sutherland, pulling off a white kid glove. "With Dorot?"

"York, too," Leigh said. "Maybe Michele."

"Sounds like wonderful fun." Mrs. Sutherland smiled her bright, pretty smile. "A whole group of you."

At breakfast the following morning only Mr. Sutherland and Leigh were up.

Mr. Sutherland said, "I know you kids're pretty involved."

"But?"

"Well, do you think you ought to . . . "

"Would you want your daughter playing gin with one?"

"That's not fair!"

"Isn't it?"

"You know I'm pretty much the same toward everyone."

"Regardless of race, color or creed?"

"Sarcasm isn't like you."

"And you aren't being like you."

Mr. Sutherland laughed. Uneasily. "O.K., babe. I trust your judgment."

Every day Dorot and Leigh stretched out by the Sutherlands' pool drinking iced coffee and wrestling with a script outline. They brainstormed idea after idea, blending, melding, discarding—the creative process, said Dorot, who delighted in labeling, is very wasteful. After ten full days of work they emerged with a Romeo-and-Juliet. A shy heiress, eighteen years old, is disinherited when she marries her impecunious young tutor. A baby is born to them, and when this infant falls ill they cannot, alas, afford proper medical attention. Their child dies. The grief-stricken young parents die, too, in a terrible freeway crash that might (or might not be) an accident—the girls purposely left this ending ambiguous in the current fashion.

Dorot typed it, making three extra copies with fresh black carbon.

Ken winced as he read. He was surprised at Dorot. He had always considered her bright. But Leigh! Leigh had betrayed him. Ken was outraged that she could be so devoid of artistic sensitivity. He might have started this film as an excuse to see, and be seen with, Leigh Sutherland, but once working he could not be dishonest. On canvas he instinctively treated the world with respect, all the candor he possessed, and with much love. This—he crushed his onionskin copy—treated the world with marshmallow contempt. This was crap, pure crap. Under the circumstances, he decided, he better keep script discussions on an impersonal level. To this end he suggested the four of them meet.

"At my place?" Leigh asked.

"According to Plan One-A," he agreed.

But of course her parents were out.

Ken didn't have to say a derogatory word. In a few choicely obscene sentences York demolished the six-page outline.

"Thank you, James Agee!" Dorot snapped.

"De nada," York said.

"Since you have such a way with words," Dorot said, "let's hear your suggestions."

"Listen," Ken said before York had a chance. Ken had given the matter much thought and had gotten the germ of an idea from the sad, treacly outline. "Listen, why don't we try it like this? Cut the melodrama but keep the couple. Show one day in their lives, an ordinary happy day they spend with the baby."

"So you're keeping the kid? Oh, those regulations on child actors are dan-dee!"

"Lissa Gillies," Dorot said in a saccharine voice, "will not demand we keep to the letter of the child labor law."

"And who for the guy?" Ken asked.

Leigh forgot her hurt. Dorot forgot anger. York forgot cynicism. They leaned forward, all talking at once. Who? Who? Who? It was York who remembered Stryker Halvorsen.

"He's got that dumb, athletic magnetism," York said, "that just might, if we're lucky, come across."

Stryker!

They agreed, the four of them. Stryker Halvorsen. Tall, great build, with bold Viking features. Perfect.

"What's he doing now?"

"USC. Baseball scholarship," Ken said. "I'll try him on the phone." As he crossed the room he said, "Pray he's home this summer."

Stryker held the receiver between his ear and muscular, peeling left shoulder. Ken Igawa was talking about a film he was making with York, Leigh Sutherland and Dorot McHenry. The old California High crowd. Stryker had avoided them since two summers ago. His conscious mind also avoided thought of the Marshall Mosgrove episode. Yet often he would dream of Marshall waking him, Marshall close, pulsating, gasping. *And in the dream Stryker, too, shared the excitement.* It was a thick, dark, compelling dream that Stryker fought to escape.

"And we need a leading man with looks, talent, sex appeal," Ken finished.

Stryker was silent.

"Like you," Ken added.

Stryker hesitated before he asked, "Anyone else involved?"

"Maybe Michele Gillies," Ken said. "Steve McQueen wanted a go at it."

"Jeez, Ken, you ought to take up ole Steve."

"Yeah yeah yeah. But you're the type."

"I'm pretty busy." But as Stryker spoke he remembered that Ken had wet-nursed him through geometry, the second time round.

"Hey, Stryker, it's important." Ken's voice lost its cool.

In Stryker Halvorsen's good-natured, easily balanced books, a guy did you a favor, you owed him one back. "Sure," he said. "Call when you're ready to roll."

York, inhaling deeply on a roach, led Ken through the pool house. He opened double doors, flicked a waist-high switch. Three recessed fixtures blazed, revealing a closet maybe twelve feet long and lined with cedar-odored shelves; these shelves were crowded with photographic equipment.

Ken whistled reverently. "Your father's hobby?"

York's handmade Italian boots echoed to the end of the

closet. Carefully he stubbed out the minute butt. "Once he said aloud he was interested."

"And he bought all this?"

"It was given," York said, "by grateful producers, agents and et cetera."

Ken followed slowly, staring as he went. "I didn't realize you needed all this."

"You don't," York said. "But did you think making a film was free, like painting?"

"No, but—"

"A Brownie and loads of vision?"

Ken scratched his nose.

"Well, to work," York said. "Sixteen millimeter?"

"You're the expert."

"TV and most of your experimental stuff is shot in sixteen."

"Sixteen, then."

With his good hand York removed a small black metal trunk from the shelf, setting it carefully on the floor boards. Ken squatted, opening the metal catches. Wrapped in sheer plastic lay a large black camera.

"Arriflex Sixteen," Ken read aloud.

"Arri for short."

"Looks brand new."

"Probably is."

"Maybe I shouldn't—"

"Sure you shouldn't. Let it rot here." York, using one hand, began removing equipment, setting it on the floor beside the trunk, cataloguing. "Triangle base. Tripod. Magazine. Battery box. Cord." He unwound a thick black cord. "Matte box." He accordioned out the matte box. "Keeps the sun off the lens."

"Lenses . . ." Ken frowned, trying to remember what the old German *Kinematographer* had told them.

"Ten, twenty-five, fifty. There's others if you need them." York tossed a small, leather-bound book. "When in doubt, consult the bible."

"ASC Manual," Ken read.

York dropped a large, oddly shaped black velvet hood over the unfolded tripod.

"Is that," Ken asked, "for wearing when you lynch white people?"

"*Chacun à son goût.*" York shrugged into the holes and hood so his arms, head and torso were completely covered. "You can also use it to crawl into when you need to change four-hundred-foot rolls in daylight." His voice came muffled through heavy velvet. "A portable darkroom." He emerged.

"You know this, don't you?" Ken said.

York didn't reply.

"Hey York, thanks. Listen, I guess I ought to let you in on why I'm so hot on doing this—"

"Let's see if I'm bright enough to figure it by myself." York squinted at him. "You need an opportunity to see a certain beauteous white maiden."

Ken's muscles tightened with anger. Then he remembered. York was stoned. Lately York generally was stoned. Well, circumstances warranted, didn't they?

Ken said, "Anyway, thank you." He lifted the camera, pressing his left eye into the gray rubber view finder. "Hey, I can't see a damn thing!"

Leigh and Ken searched for locations.

After Ken's six-to-two shift at the Texaco at Olympic and Bundy, he would drive home, scrub his oil-black hands with Ajax, splash in the shower, then head for Leigh's. In his mother's old car they explored the city. Yellow summer sun blazed on them. They zipped up Stadium Way to the flagged, castlelike new Dodger ball park. They cruised the Santa Monica mountain range that divides the city proper from the Valley, gazing from narrow, sun-baked adobe ledges ("view lots") down on the San Fernando Valley—tract developers' Elysian Fields. In Beverly Hills they inched past iron-spear-fenced old mansions that had belonged to pucker-lipped silent movie stars like Vilma Banky. They zoomed on freeways to East Los Angeles, stopping to buy tamales at a rundown *tortilleria* that might have been transported from old Me-hico. They stared up at those strange, soaring, blue china towers, the Watts Towers, the life work, Ken said in an envious tone, of one man, Simon Rodia. They pushed their way through the savory odors and tourist bustle of the Farmers' Market; they strolled the prim stucco miles of Parkdale. They walked the wide beaches.

They examined their city.

Their city returned the compliment.

Unsympathetically.

Ken had not, on the liberated Berkeley campus, considered the power of the world to hurt and destroy; he had assumed their families were the only dragons to overcome. Now, in the disapproving city that was their home, he saw how naïve he'd been.

As he walked the hostile streets with Leigh Sutherland, Ken realized there wasn't a question about it. None. No man is an island, not until he's with a woman of another race, surrounded by that race. He grew angry. Frightened. Could he and Leigh be torn apart by cold, round, unsympathetic eyes?

Late-afternoon sun would be slanting down in strong golden rays when Leigh and Ken arrived back at the big Colonial house. He would park under the shady sycamores, forcing himself to wait in the car when every nerve ending cried out he should get the hell away before six when her father would pull his big white Imperial into the circular drive and come over and talk to them in too hearty, too colloquial terms. *He couldn't take it*. The truth was Ken ached for Mr. Sutherland to like him, but each time he heard that hearty voice he heard his own voice answering in sarcastic monosyllables.

At the Farmers' Market while Dorot and Michele whispered next to a scarlet pyramid of strawberries, Ken, in a rented wheel chair that York pushed (and insisted on calling a dolly) rolled beside Lissa and Leigh, filming them as they moved toward the patio. The camera whirred. Middle-aged, middle-west tourists, *their* cameras dangling over plump, flowered bellies, from time to time obscured the slight redhead and rotund blonde baby. Leigh seated Lissa at a round table. Stryker came over. He held a paper plate with an eclair. Leigh smiled up at him; a breeze fluttered, shifting overhead green awnings so that sunlight slanted first on his face, then on hers. Lissa's plump hand reached for the plate.

Ken let the heavy camera on his shoulder keep rolling; it was going well, he was afraid to consider how well. Keeping his eye to the view finder, he clicked off the Arri—if you took away your eye too soon, he'd learned from the rushes, the footage faded. He looked up. Seeing this, Dorot and Michele picked their way through a crowd of giggling Campfire Girls to the table.

Lissa, sighting her mother, cried, "Me gotta go."

Public sanitation facilities delighted Lissa, and every ten minutes she insisted on inspection.

"Me gotta go . . ." she wailed.

Michele raised a plucked eyebrow. "And Mother had to go

toilet train her! Later, Lissa doll, later."

But Leigh, who was wild about Lissa—after all, she'd named her—took the damp little hand, saying, "Hit the road, Missa Lissa." And the two of them started toward the green door marked "Ladies."

Ken aimed the camera after them.

Sun baked the beach. The three girls clustered around Lissa, helping her dunkie-dunkie in the gentle surf. Stryker knelt on sand, his good-looking face unnaturally sober as he fitted wood tripod into metal base. York, wearing inevitable long-sleeved shirt with immaculate white ducks, talked to two fat giggling girls. Ken wanted them in a shot and therefore York, most professional as producer, insisted on getting the gigglers to sign release papers.

Ken squatted on hot sand, searching through his khaki camera kit. If films were indeed an art form, then of all the arts this one demanded the most of you in the way of patience. Getting set up took hours. He squinted at the blinding sun, extracted a cardboard-covered lens filter.

"Well?" Dorot sat on the towel next to him. "What today?"

"We're going to try a long shot," Ken said, "with a three hundred lens. Leigh and Stryker'll run along the sand toward us, but they won't seem to get any closer."

"Spatial distortion?" wondered Dorot, who preferred her explanations complicated.

"Yeah yeah yeah," Ken agreed. "And maybe we'll try a close up of *them*"—he jerked his chin at York and the gigglers—"with Lissa."

"You're going at it too hard, babe."

"We want to finish."

"Is he so busy, Ken, that he can't get to a barber?"

"His hair's short as Stevie's. Daddy, you really are *changing*."

"Because I say he should get a haircut?"

"If you really want to study technique," said York, "watch the commercials. That's where the talent and the money's at."

"I want a psychedelic blinking effect here," Ken said. They were in York's pool house, watching the rushes. "How?"

"Two frames of exposed film, two of still," York replied.

• • •

Michele was enjoying herself more than she had in an age. The movie might not be serious, but it was fun. She might not have pretty clothes like Leigh, but she *was* married. Part of the old crowd, yet more than the rest. Being a wife and mother set her ahead. Even though she disapproved of Clay's current activities in Mississippi, at the same time a lot of people *did* approve. However much her parents might knock Clay, to the young people (and who else counted?) he was a celebrity. People she had known back in California High would stop her on the streets of Westwood, saying, "You really must be terrifically proud of the fabulous work Clay's doing." People would say, "Clay's fantastic!" and "Clay's got real charisma" and "Clay's really showing those old phonies down there." Most important to Michele, Clay had been interviewed two Sundays ago by Channel 5, a full hour in-depth interview on student protest in the South, taped to be shown this Sunday at four thirty. So even though she wasn't rich she was by marriage famous. From her superior stance, Michele felt it her duty to warn her old friend.

She said, "Dorot's just egging you on to satisfy her own curiosity. You know she is. But Leigh, if you're really serious about Ken, you're making a big mistake, both of you. Certainly you know I'm not prejudiced, nobody's doing more for racial equality than Clay and me, but the truth is, even a normal couple like us, we have our little adjustments to make."

Ken parked next to three tall garbage cans in the dark alley south of the Sutherlands'. Barefoot, careful, he padded on hard-packed earth to quietly unlatch the gate. Leigh waited in the cabana.

"I'm sick of this skulking," Ken said.

"Me, too."

"I feel like Lady Chatterley's lover—"

"That dirty old man!"

"Let's go someplace where we can"—he raised his voice to a hoarse whisper—"shout."

"Like?"

"Mmmm . . . the beach."

"KKKKKKKKKKKKKEEEEEEEEEEEEENNNN-NNNNNNNN. . . ."

• • •

"LLLLLLLLLLLLLLEEEEEEEEEEEIIIIIGGGGG-
GGGHHHHHHHH. . . ."

Hand in hand they shouted at the sea. Surf roared, covering their shouts.

"KKKKEEEEEENNNNNNN AND LLLLLEEEIIIIGGG-
GGHHHHH. . . ."

"LLLLLLLLEEEEEHIIGGGGGHHHH AND KKKKKK-
EEEEEEENNNNN. . . ."

There were no beach parties in Santa Monica, there never were because you couldn't have a fire, and if the dimly seen mounds were couples making out or sand castles built during the day by little kids, what did it matter?

"Race?" Ken asked.

"Where?"

"Station thirteen."

Along dark wet sand she ran, awkwardly as girls do, from the knees. He gave her a good start, but he passed her up before Station 12 and not long after that she collapsed on chilly dry sand. She was still gasping when Ken trotted back, panting and laughing. He belly-flopped near her.

"You win," he said.

"No, you."

"What's the prize?"

"Lascivious me."

He laughed.

"In B films—"

"Movies," he interrupted. "By now you should know if they're Bs they're movies."

"In B *movies* the sea always symbolizes—"

"Passion."

"Mad desire."

"Sex," he said. "The salt wet beginnings of life."

"Sea and sperm and lonely tide and thin gull's crying."

"The sea is calm tonight, the moon lies fair on the Catalina Straits."

"Break break break."

"That's death," he said.

"The start or the end. Same thing."

He rolled over so he lay on one side, curled up facing her.

"So you think it hackneyed?" he asked. "Here?"

"Don't joke."

"My future wife takes her sex seriously."

"Say it again."

"Takes her sex seriously."

"The first and you know it!"

He squirmed closer. He put his face next to hers. Her cheeks were still hot from the running but her nose was cold, a sign of health. He said in her ear, "Hey wife, is it all right, you know, plain?" He was stinking on dates and times of the month.

"Yes," she whispered. He knew she was the same as he was, careless. But. . . . Sand gritted a little, making it almost unbearably exciting. The sea, the corny, hackneyed sea, scalloped bubbles over their bare toes like with Burt Lancaster and Debby Kerr in *From Here to Eternity*.

By the middle of August in York's pool house closet lay eight large, flat, silvery cans of the type that normally held 35mm film. Four were haphazardly crowded with varying size rolls of 16mm negative, four jammed full of working print.

Ken's loosely outlined script was on film.

Before this Ken and York had seen it, but in bits and pieces. York, the producer, after each shooting day, had hurried the exposed film to Consolidated in Hollywood. When the lab had returned the rushes he and Ken had pored over them vociferously and at great length. Now, though, the two of them were going to view all the exposed film for the first time.

As York set up the projector Ken could feel his nervousness growing. *Maybe it stunk?* The film was silent (sound would be dubbed later) and so they could have discussed the Los Angeles odyssey if they chose. But Ken couldn't talk. He stared at the rectangular screen, noting flaw after flaw in the camera work that he'd previously somehow overlooked. A chill gripped him. Twice York made his blood run even colder with the remark, "You held on that shot too long." Otherwise York was silent. Finally each roll was run.

York switched off the projector and turned on the light. Dark glasses made his expression unreadable.

"Well?" Ken asked, his voice a shade too high.

"Well what?"

"What do you think?"

"You're a blooming, uncontaminated genius, that's what."

Ken's breath loosened shakily. *It was good*. He smiled. "Stryker really carried it off, didn't he?"

"To the manner born," York agreed.

"And Lissa—"

"Jesus, I'll admit it. I was plenty nervous about using her.

Most kid actors are to vomit over."

"I thought Leigh was pretty fair."

York snickered. "She was fantastic and you know it."

"They seemed to belong together, the three of them. So alive—"

York interrupted. "You know what? While I was watching I was jealous. Me! Jealous! You know that, you son of a bitch? To instinctively grasp all the techniques—"

"I told you. An old guy in Berkeley showed me."

"It's one helluva sensation—pardon the expression—film."

"S'half yours." Ken grinned. If the film had flopped he would have felt the entire crushing weight. Success, he shared. "You're the producer."

"You did it all. And I *was* the producer." York spoke casually. "I'm leaving tomorrow for Athens."

"Leaving! Athens!" Ken, without thinking, was on his feet clutching York's collar. York stared at Ken's hands and Ken let go. "Athens . . ." Ken repeated. "Why?"

"Why not?"

"You never mentioned you were going."

"Close mouthed, that's me."

"Listen, there's the editing—"

"I'll lend you the Moviola, a splicing block. I presume you own a pair of scissors, a razor blade and a grease pencil."

"York, I don't know one damn thing about editing!"

"You talented idiot, *you* don't need to. Just take the film home and run it over and over and over and cut, cut, cut the working print. I'm banking on a masterpiece."

"Banking." Gratefully Ken took up the word. "Listen, York, you put up the cash. You've gotta help."

"I've got to get away!" York's thin mouth formed a crooked curve. And Ken thought about the late Mrs. York, York and his phony famous father. Ken's ready sympathies stirred. He said no more. York taped the final roll of film closed. "Editing, you'll find, is a lengthy procedure. There's large opportunity for you and your redheaded pal to get together."

"You sleeping?"

"Not yet, Daddy." She raised up on her elbow. "How was the party?"

"Same as all the others." He closed the door and in darkness came to sit on the edge of her canopied bed. The mattress creaked. "We haven't had a chance, you and I, to get together much this summer."

She said, "Remember when I was little? Before you went out, while Mother was dressing, you'd read to me. Mostly fairy stories."

"I figured you liked those best."

"I did, I did. But you always deleted the ogre."

"You were the sensitive one, babe." He chuckled. Then sighed. "Lately I've been having this ogre image of myself. I was about to delete me."

"Never."

"Some people I know push their children, mold them. I've tried never to."

"I appreciate it."

"S'no virtue. S'done because I want you to think I'm the best father around."

"After taking seven impartial polls, you are."

"I say I, but I mean your mother and me—Oh, who the hell am I trying to kid? I say I, I mean I."

"I know you love me."

"That's the truth," he said. "More than anyone."

"And I love you."

"More than anyone?"

This was an ancient liturgy evolved before Leigh's third birthday. She was meant to reply, *That's the truth*. Of course in liturgy repetition is what counts, not truth. But Leigh never could lie smoothly, not even in ritual matters.

"What I have to say. . . ." He coughed. "It isn't easy. About your mother and me. . . ."

Leigh, who had been dreading an open question and answer period, relaxed a little.

". . . and certainly I've never regretted marrying her. . . ." Mr. Sutherland's voice came out of the darkness. "Never. She's a beautiful woman now, but when she was a girl, she was a miracle. Strangers on the streets stared after her. Men and women both. Naturally there were squadrons of eligible bachelors. Much wealthier, better looking ones than me. I'm short and even then I was losing my hair. I hadn't passed the bar yet, and it was right after I got back from Spain, so my shoulder had a meaty look. You can bet I wasn't too great around the beach club. Maybe there were fifty who rated better. But you know me. Competitive."

"You shouldn't be telling me this."

"I have to, so you'll understand. There was the excitement of the chase—" His voice grew low, almost inaudible, but Leigh knew he intended her to hear. "More important, the pull of sex. I forgot what it was I intended doing with my life. You know I've never cared for the country club bit, the society business?"

"I sometimes wondered—Daddy, I used to think you wore silver armor in the wars."

She could tell he was smiling.

"Tarnished from the word go," he said, then fell silent. When he continued his voice was a low rumble in the night. "We've lived a compromise, the two of us. I think I've made her happy, but that's not what I mean to tell you." Her father leaned closer and Leigh was inundated with odors so primal they might be part of her cellular make-up, of whiskey, stale cigar smoke, bay rum shaving lotion, starchy ironed white shirts. "The truth is, I *do* love you more than I love anyone. You mean more to me than anyone else on this whole God-forsaken ball of mud."

Half sitting, she hugged him. Through sheer cotton, against her breasts and sensitive nipples, her old love felt oddly thick, heavy, soft. After the hardness of Ken, strange and forbidden.

"I love you," she whispered.

"Babe, I want only the good for you." His voice was barely a whisper. "Always remember that. Only the good."

And he pulled her closer, pressing her to him until the buttons of his dinner jacket dug into her breasts. Her father's heart beat fast and strong near her own, heat poured from his body and he pressed his rough cheek to hers. "Only the good, babe," he repeated. And in a flicker of insight, a flicker so brief it lasted only the time it took her to draw breath, she understood this was the logical maturing of the love they'd shared since her babyhood . . . long-ago memories of quick California dusks and lights burning warm in her soap-fragranced bathroom, her father sitting on the edge of the tub, white shirt sleeves rolled up, coarse-haired hand disappearing between her small thighs as he washed her innocent cleft with bubbly washcloth, his hands rough-toweling her dry while she giggled, his hands gently patting Johnson's baby powder on her small body. "Now to bed," he would say, and she would curl pressing through blankets around the satisfying heat of his rump, listening to his deep voice telling a story, inhaling the odors that were him while his hand smoothed her hair. They, her father and she, could never love distantly, feebly, with only the spirit, and now her father's hot, forbidden flesh strained through layers of tailored cloth. It was a terrible moment. Understanding, sharp, naked. God help us. She prayed her father didn't understand the reason for his quickened heartbeat, the warmth his body was generating, why his arms tightened their circle around her, why his fingers on her back edged trembling under the sleeveless, loose armholes of her nightgown.

She exhaled.

"Daddy," she said sharply. "I'm smothering."

Abruptly he released her. He sat back. She retreated under the covers, pulling rosebud sheets and pink blankets to her chin. Crazy. She was crazy. *A nut,* she told herself. Her father was her father and he'd had too much Scotch, that was all. And it was her fault, wasn't it, that he was drinking so much this summer?

"I know you only want what's good for me," she whispered. "I'll always remember it." *And this I'll forget,* she thought, *this momentary surrender of innocence. I love you.*

A breeze rattled hibiscus vines on the porch that ran the length of the second story. The grandfather clock in the downstairs hall sounded two faint silvery notes.

"Getting late," her father said, rising. "G'night, babe."

--------------- · **7** · ---------------

One week after they had waved York into his Pan Am plane, toward the end of that hot August, Mr. Igawa suddenly became ill. While clipping eugenia hedges around the ornamental pool at one of his Brentwood accounts, he fainted, luckily falling neither on his recently sharpened shears nor in the murky water. He came to shivering despite the heat.

Hospitalized, Mr. Igawa silently suffered drugs, electrocardiograms, antibiotic injections, X-rays, electroencephalograms, blood tests, bone marrow tests, catheterization. It was five days before Dr. Nakamura felt equipped to meet with Mrs. Igawa and Ken in the third-floor consultation room, a windowless cubicle stuffy with memories of announced malignancies.

"We've discovered the problem," Dr. Nakamura said. "An

improperly functioning kidney."

"Is it cancer?" Mrs. Igawa never minced words.

Neither did Dr. Nakamura, at least not when he dealt with Mrs. Igawa. "Not as far as we can tell," he replied. "But it is diseased. And we're unable to treat it."

"Can you live without a kidney?" asked Mrs. Igawa.

Her tone was matter of fact, her sole betrayal of emotion, plump, black-gloved fingers tightening on plastic handles of her purse. Ken took tremendous pride in his mother's even tones. He himself couldn't speak.

Dr. Nakamura replied, "George will confirm this: Yes. Very comfortably." George, Ken's older brother, was a resident at St. Joseph's in Seattle.

"Then it must come out," said Mrs. Igawa firmly.

"We have every reason to believe the operation will be successful."

After Mrs. Igawa had cleared off the dinner dishes, stacking them with quick competence on the drainboard, she returned to the Formica breakfast table with pen and scratch pad. She came right to the heart of the matter.

"There'll be the hospital for ten days at least." She wrote as she said, "Thirty-five a day."

"Drugs," Ken said.

"I'll put down ten a day."

"Should cover it," Ken said. "Surgeon's fees."

"How much?"

Ken shrugged.

She kept staring at him.

He said, "Four hundred?"

"That much?"

"Probably. And there's Dr. Nakamura."

"Do they charge for operating rooms?" his mother asked.

"Yes."

Mrs. Igawa wrote fifty dollars.

"I guess George'll have to clue us in, but there'll be other expenses. An anesthetist and a pathologist. An ambulance home."

"We can manage with the car. But he'll need a nurse when he does get home."

They stared at one another.

Money.

Or rather, lack of money.

There was no health insurance. No social security. The savings account had melted into five days of hospital care, drugs, lab tests. No money available. Ken's sisters could not help, for they had babies and struggling young husbands; his brother George a resident's pittance. Mrs. Igawa worked as a bookkeeper in Donald's drug store in Santa Monica—she'd put her three older children through college with her salary, but now that money would be needed to keep the house going. For Ken no money had been a permanent fact of life. And it had never mattered—of course it would've been great to zip around in a bronze T-bird like York or to shower presents on Leigh. Still, he'd never felt deprived. Inferior, yes. And talentless. Impoverished, no. Money was not what made Ken Igawa run. But then again, had he ever before been in a position where money could buy life?

Mrs. Igawa's lips tightened.

"We'll have to borrow," she said.

The words were wrung from her. His mother, Ken knew only too well, was out of date enough to consider *borrow* a dirty word and its four-letter corollary *debt* obscene. Debt meant any bill unpaid by the fifth of the month; debt meant buying on time. How often had he heard his mother's brisk voice state unequivocally that debt meant you were slovenly like the Chinese? Debt was not for the Igawas. The Igawas were decent people; they never borrowed, not to buy the stripped-down six-year-old Chevy, or his father's pickup, or any appliance. There was only the mortgage on this small, elderly frame bungalow with a narrow front porch.

"How about the house?" Ken asked.

"Today I looked into refinancing," Mrs. Igawa said. "A thousand at most."

"It'll help," he said.

"But it's not nearly enough." She sighed.

Ken pushed open the screen door and stood on the back steps in cool night air, fingering tiny prickles of a *bon-sai* pine. The art of dwarfing trees in shallow dishes is ancient, and this miniature pine (*ippon-dachi,* Ken remembered, was the name for a single trunk) although barely two feet tall, hinted at great age and greater loneliness. *Bon-sai* currently was in. Japanese aristocrats did it for a hobby. Ken's Californian father did it for needed cash. Money . . .

"We'll manage without nurses at home," Ken said. He spoke quietly. "I'll work my shifts around your hours at the drug store."

"No!" Mrs. Igawa cried vehemently.

"Yes."

"College starts in two weeks!" Mrs. Igawa's tone was yet more vehement. As she loathed debt, so she loved education. Under the living room window stood a low bookshelf filled with blue and gold UCLA yearbooks collected by her children.

"My salary'll help with the bills."

"Ken, your scholarship—"

"It'll keep. Little can fix it."

"If you stop now, you'll never get back. *Never*. I know you."

"One semester, Mother?"

"Not that you're doing so much up there as far as I can see. But it's important you finish."

"A year at most?"

"Is it the only way?"

"Yeah yeah yeah," he said. "And even so it'll be an epic struggle."

She sighed, capitulation in a single breath.

So it's settled, Ken thought. *Didn't it get settled very quick?*

After a minute he heard her running water for the dishes. He sat on the top step. *So it's settled*. He yearned to be casual. Shrug with the right amount of cool. Clouds coming off the Pacific blotted out certain western stars. Ken didn't feel cool. As a matter of fact his stomach lurched as if he were parachuting into unknown enemy-held territory. He was alone in the dark, confused and questioning. Typical. He'd acted in the only feasible way, hadn't he? So why question? *Hey Leigh, what've I done?*

Why was he always so skeptical of his own actions? Why couldn't he give answers loud and clear and definite like, for example, Clay Gillies?

"Well?" he muttered to himself. "What else could I've done?"

Let his father die? He thought of his father hunched over these Lilliputian trees, a short, spare man in khaki work clothes and a pith helmet like Jungle Jim's, cigarette dangling from chapped brown lips. A silent man. The rare times Ken heard his father speak beyond monosyllables came when Mr. Igawa would relate the sad tale of his truck farm. In the prewar days only an American-born Japanese like himself was permitted to

buy land. He had sweated to save enough, then sweated to earn
a reputation as grower of the largest, lushest strawberries; during the 1942 deportation his land had been stolen—or bought
for five cents on the dollar, which (Mr. Igawa would state,
coughing) was worse than theft for it added humiliation. And
now it formed one corner of Parkdale! Mr. Igawa told the story
often. Ken rubbed his finger along sandpaper bark. Whatever
his father's faults, Ken loved him, loved him with the fierce,
inverted, convoluting love that a child feels for a parent who
is a loser.

The phone rang.

His mother answered. She came to the screen door. "Ken,
it's for you," she said. Her tone was puzzled. He wondered if
it were Leigh as he pushed to his feet. But Leigh never called
here. But then again he hadn't had a chance to phone her in
three days.

"Ken?"

"Yes?"

"This is Sidney Sutherland."

"Sir?"

"I'd like to talk to you. Would tomorrow at three be all
right?"

"Yes, but—"

"Two four five South Hill."

"Sir—"

The phone had gone dead.

The following morning at breakfast Mr. Sutherland asked
Leigh to drop by his office. Around three, he said, "A jeweler's
bringing over some bracelets. I want you to help me pick one
for Mother's birthday."

Ken was leafing through the latest *Saturday Review* in Mr.
Sutherland's outer office when Leigh arrived. Miss Arthur
glanced at Leigh, at Ken, then turned on the IBM electric and
started to type at breakneck speed.

"What're you doing here?" Leigh murmured, her voice lower
than ever.

"Beats me." Ken, too, lowered his voice. "Your father phoned
last night. It must've been around nine. He said he'd like to
talk. Hey Leigh, I've got to tell you—"

At that moment Mr. Sutherland flung open a carved door.
"Leigh, Ken," he greeted. "No phone calls, please, Miss Ar-

thur," he said. "Come in, both of you," he said.

First making sure the heavy door was properly closed, Mr. Sutherland sat behind a massive desk, gesturing to a pair of mahogany chairs. Ken remained standing. Leigh sat. She fiddled with the broad gold bar holding back her hair. Nobody spoke. The office was air conditioned; with its shelves of leather-bound books, intricate blue Persian rugs, gleam of polished old mahogany and heavy antique silver this room might have been hermetically sealed not only from the city's noisy heat but from time, too. Mr. Sutherland leaned back in his chair, watching Ken. The expensive hush made Ken most conscious of his poverty (and race) and of his girl's privilege (and race). Desperately he searched for something, anything, to feel superior about. Leigh glanced up at him questioningly, her lips parted. Ken thought of the pleasure when those lips sought out various parts of his body—*Hey Mr. Sutherland, your daughter gladly gives me a blow job, so doesn't that make me just a little superior?* Instantly he repented the thought.

Leigh cleared her throat, asking, "It's not about bracelets, is it, Daddy?"

"No." Mr. Sutherland leaned his elbows on the silver-cornered blotter. "Ken, sit." Ken sat. "I don't know how to begin. I've never done anything like this before. It's not easy, believe me. Leigh says I'm not cut out for the heavy father routine." He glanced questioningly at Ken.

"Sir?"

"Leigh's right." Mr. Sutherland rubbed the back of his head. "But every time I try to talk to her, she sluffs me off. Ken, you tell me something. You've gone to a lot of trouble to make sure I see you with her—"

"We've been making a film," Leigh interrupted.

"I'm not stupid, babe, and I'm talking to Ken."

"Sir?"

"If you simply wanted to see her, I'm well aware you kids could've met someplace. Therefore. This openness means you want me and her mother to realize you are . . . well . . . fond of one another?"

Ken glanced at Leigh. She gave an almost imperceptible nod.

"I want to marry her," he said.

"We're going to be married," she said.

Mr. Sutherland paled. Ken experienced one of his numerous

flashes of sympathy—in this case, he decided, completely unreasoning.

"Ken, what do you do?" Mr. Sutherland asked.

I want you to like me, Ken thought. "Go to Berkeley," he said.

"And work in a gas station?"

"Summers."

"I'm a little unnerved. I'm sorry. I meant what do you want to do?"

"I don't know yet." Ken shifted in the wide-seated chair. His long, pleasant face had assumed an unyielding arrogance. "Paint," he said. But as he spoke he asked himself if maybe he didn't also want to make films or sculpt neon or weld metal or engage in any of the other activities that could only be lumped together as an occupation under that despised term *artist.* Ken had always felt those who called themselves "artists" were old types who never worked seriously but instead sat around drinking Gallo red and spouting off. So it was with a strong note of defiance that he added, "Be an artist!"

"That's not a very certain pro—"

"Money," Leigh interrupted, "it's not as important to our generation as it is to yours."

Her father managed a tolerant smile. "Because you people've always had enough."

"I'll work—"

"Babe, be quiet. Listen, Ken. Do you think your parents approve of the . . . marriage?"

"I haven't discussed it with them yet."

"Do you think they approve of Leigh?"

"My mother only met her once, at Mrs. York's funeral. She knows we've been making the film together. But that's all. She hasn't said anything."

"To me she has. She phoned maybe a month ago to ask if I knew what was going on. She said in her opinion there was entirely too much togetherness. I said I trusted my Leigh. And she said she trusted you. But. Wouldn't it be best if we put a stop to—well, whatever it was that was going on?"

"Why didn't you tell me?" Leigh cried.

"Why should I? As I pointed out to Mrs. Igawa, since the two of you were only working on a movie in collaboration with quite a few others there was no point in making an issue. She sounds like a very practical woman, Ken, but as far as you're

concerned, she's got a blind spot. She implied the movie was
Leigh's way of chasing you. Girls, she said, have chased you
ever since you started junior high. She said it was up to Leigh's
mother and me to curb our daughter. If it were her girl—"

"Only Japanese boys," Ken said sourly. His heart pounded
with his mother's betrayal. How could she have gone to Leigh's
father behind his back? Didn't any of that generation have
scruples when it came to manipulating their children?

"Her very words." Mr. Sutherland gave Ken his frank, open
smile. "To be honest, her tone annoyed me, although I certainly
admired her straightforwardness." He paused. "Ken, you don't
like me, do you?"

Leigh put in too quickly, "Daddy, I don't see where this is
getting us."

"Keep quiet, babe. You're only here to see I'm not making
any shady deals." He extended his hands. "See. No hidden
aces. Cards all out in the open. Ken's decision will be his own.
Now. When do you plan to get married?"

"We haven't thought about dates," Ken said.

"But not for a year?"

"Why a year?" Leigh asked.

"Because in this state, babe, you're over the legal age of
consent. Nineteen. But it's different for a boy. Until he's twenty-
one his parents have to sign the wedding license. Mrs. Igawa
didn't sound as if she'd sign." He glanced at Ken.

Ken shrugged.

"So you have a year?" Mr. Sutherland persisted.

"There's forty-nine other states and Mexico." Ken despised
his mumbled equivocation.

Mr. Sutherland ignored it. He said, "Now your father's
going to have an operation. A kidney removed."

Leigh exclaimed, "So they figured out what's wrong."

And at the same moment Ken asked, "How'd you know?"

"I'm a lawyer."

"And?"

"And you haven't been watching your Perry Masons." Mr.
Sutherland loosened his tie. "I'm going to say this very quickly
because I don't like to hear myself saying it. Things are rough
at your place, Ken, and I'm going to take advantage. I'll pay
the medical bills. I'll pay your tuition if you choose to go away
to college. In return I want your promise that you won't see
or talk or otherwise communicate with my daughter until you're
twenty-one."

"Oh, Daddy!" Leigh cried. In the fragile spareness of her face, lines of sorrow appeared and it was easy to see, if you had a painter's eye, how she would look when she doubled her age, a sweet, faintly mournful, loving wife and mother.

"If you're both of the same mind then, it's fine with me. I'll give you a big wedding. The works. I'll be on your side. The family'll slaughter me and so will my wife. But I'll be on your side."

"And if we don't agree?" Leigh asked.

"It's not up to you. I'm talking to Ken. *He's* got the sick father. Unless I'm mistaken he's already decided to help foot the bills, which will mean he's not going back to Berkeley anyway."

Leigh turned to Ken.

He nodded.

Mr. Sutherland went on, "There won't be enough, though, even if he does drop out. Medical care's fantastically high nowadays. And Ken's talented. Very. I've talked to Professor Little up at Berkeley—I am thorough, you see. Professor Little's most impressed with Ken. Certainly a year in, say, Paris, would be better for him than a year working in a gas station."

"Oh, Daddy . . . " Leigh whispered. "You sound like Faust."

"I don't see why. You won't be together for that time anyway."

"Hey Leigh, Mephistopheles!" Ken burst out. "Sir, it must be groovy to have all the loot in the world. You can buy anything you want! Hey Leigh, have a diamond bigger'n the Ritz! Hey Leigh, I'll buy off your Jap—"

"Stop it!" Mr. Sutherland was on his feet, leaning across the desk, shouting. "Stop it!"

Ken, standing too, stared down the older man and kept right on. "I'll buy you a white boy. No, I've never liked you, sir, and I'll tell you why. Whatever you tell yourself, you're prejudiced as all hell. At least my mother's honest about it. She doesn't puff herself up she's a big fat modern liberal. You're a bigot from the word go and you won't admit it, not to yourself, certainly never to Leigh!" Ken often had lost his temper, but never before had he taken such total satisfaction from it. Anger obliterating all else. Release. Glands he'd never known existed poured hot secretions into his blood. His armpits sweated. "You're a bigot!" he shouted. "That's why you don't want Leigh to—"

"*KEN!*" Leigh shouted.

She shouted so rarely that the yell caught him.

He turned, blinked at her, blinked again, turned away.

Mr. Sutherland paced, limping slightly from an ankle wound that, Leigh once had told Ken proudly, he'd acquired in World War II. As he got to the fireplace, he stopped, facing them across the long office.

"Listen, try to understand," he said in a low tone. "You're me. You're not quite thirty, just out of prison camp, really in rotten shape, all eighty pounds of you. Nobody understands you any more." His fingers tapped on the carved mantel. "Everyone else has their own business. Even your wife. But there's this smiling baby. And she's yours. She pulls at your hair, what's left of it, she stares up at you as if you glitter and she calls you Daddy, but really she means God." Mr. Sutherland yanked again at his tie. "I'm not the nicest guy around—I don't think I'm petty enough to dislike another man because of his race. But otherwise—I admit it—there've been occasions when I've cheated on my income tax, traffic tickets. My wife. But to this little kid, I was the best man in the whole damn world." He paced to a window, staring through shutters as three fat city pigeons rose on purple wings to Los Angeles' smoggy heaven. "The truth is, Ken, she's got this crazy, freak talent. It's much rarer than being able to paint, or write a novel, or win a Supreme Court case. I've never met anyone else with this particular talent. And I've been around a while." He paused. "She can love another person completely."

"I know, sir," Ken said.

At this Mr. Sutherland wiped his forehead with a folded handkerchief. "Well, I'm willing to spend money, to do anything, even look like a heel in front of her. I do now. Because I want her to have a chance." He undid his collar button as if it cut unbearably. "And what you've got to offer, frankly, isn't what I had in mind for her. A twenty-year-old kid, no money, no prospects of earning a living. No particular ambition. Disapproving parents. A very large racial chip on your shoulder. She's barely nineteen. And shy. Shy. It wouldn't matter if you were black, white or maroon. I'd want her to have a chance to consider. I love her. It's too damn easy to make a mistake—" His face contorted. He gripped his forehead, hiding his eyes. "I'm sorry," he muttered. "I didn't mean to say any of this."

Leigh went to him.

Blindly he put his arms around her and buried his face in her shoulder.

"Please don't, Daddy, please...."

For a long moment Ken approved the perfection of the pose. His eyes were able to view impersonally, as if old Vincent Van Igawa were about to put paint to canvas; he could see details, rich blue twists of hand-knotted fiber where sunlight striped the rug, glint of gold lettering that had almost worn from dark lawbook bindings, many shades of gold and brown and auburn combined in Leigh's silky ponytail, strong brown and white hairs springing from Mr. Sutherland's bowed skull. Ken saw each detail. On Leigh's back Mr. Sutherland's broad hands tightened, the tendons standing out in tanned flesh, mortal skeleton visible ... beautiful, sad and short-lived, we humans, yearning, impossible, hopped-up mankind.

Ken blinked away his impartial view. Anger returned. He strode to the door as far from Mr. Sutherland and Leigh as he could get.

"Ken—" Leigh looked at him.

"Pay the doctor's bills," Ken shouted. "Pay what you decided with my mother—"

"She had nothing to do with—"

"Whatever she needs, pay. Nothing else!"

"Ken," Leigh pleaded.

She still embraced his enemy!

More fury shot through Ken's blood. There was only one antidote, wasn't there? "It's what you want, isn't it, *babe?*" He flung her father's pet name at her. "Whatever he says, shy little you does! Go ahead and hug him!" Ken's ears hammered so he could barely hear his own strangled, high-pitched shouts. "Don't kid yourself about his motives, though. Black, white or maroon—balls! Hey Leigh, if you thought he was so damn color blind, how come *you* didn't tell him about us right away?" Ken flung open the door. Miss Arthur and a pair of startled businessmen stared at him. He rubbed his knuckles across his eyes. "Now you've got a whole year to figure out what's wrong with you that you love a sweating, impoverished, slant-eyed shit like me!"

He slammed the door behind him. Pencils rattled in a jar on Miss Arthur's desk.

He trotted past the gauntlet of three pairs of eyes in Mr. Sutherland's waiting room, other eyes in the law office's common waiting room. Reaching the hall he started to run. Ignoring the old-fashioned glass-doored elevators, he ran down emergency stairs, taking metal-edged cement two, three, four at a time, and on the third flight his feet danced a little shuffle, his body slipped, he dropped, thumping down.

At the bottom he curled, welcoming pain. A *minute* passed. Supporting himself on scraped palms and aching knees, he peered up the stair well. Hoping for what? Hoping she was coming, that's what. She could console him, together they could figure out a way to avert separation. *How?* Thick light filtered through dirty windows. Nobody came. *So she was staying with the other side.* For that, God, damn her to hell for all eternity. Throwing back his head to get hair out of his eyes, he wiped blood from his scraped palms onto his handkerchief. Straightening his shirt, stepping back into the hall, with aching, shaking fingers he pressed the elevator button. His eyes burned. He tasted salt on his tongue. *Odi et amo.* Nothing like a Berkeley education. If he hadn't had two years of college how would he have understood at this moment he was experiencing old Catullus' *odi et amo?* Hate and love for the same person combining into unbearable pain.

September 11

Hey Leigh,

Your father carried out his side of the bargain. Me, I'm cheating. But I can't leave the continent without telling you, can I?

First of all, I had to sell some paintings, and the only ones Little could find a buyer for were the nudes of you. Obviously it's not the painter but the subject matter. I think he put in some cash, but he, of course, denies it. I have loot for plane fare and the rest, well, I'll be one of the current crop of carefree American college wanderers that Time*'s always slavering about.*

I'm off to Japan first. Maybe I can kipe ideas from Utamaro the way the Impressionists did. I'll come by old U more honestly. Also, maybe I'll be able to do what they call find myself. Here the writing changed and skipped a long way down the page. *Hey Leigh, remember me? Not one to write a logical, coherent letter. I'm thinking about that rainy night in April. A Friday, so you were sleeping over, but you'd just gotten your period so you couldn't wear me out. Remember? We just lay there all night, talking about all sorts of things. Love. Life. Where are we all going? What does it all mean? Typical college bull session. I remember thinking in my inimical confused*

*way that you were obsolete, like a fairy-tale princess
with your long red hair, Rapunzel, and your storybook
belief in quaint ideas like honesty, loyalty and living
happily forever after. I also remember feeling very lucky
to have trapped me such a rare, obsolescent creature.
I'm erotic, hot, horny. God knows there's other things,
"our things" you always call them, to think about. But
it's strange. I think most of that night, listening to rain,
holding one another, talking until it got light. Remember?*

I love you
Ken

————— **8** —————

Four Steps Down is one of those small, impermanent shops
that lately have sprung up around college campuses; their lack
of neon and fittings is a direct reproach to the glittering, in-
terchangeable squadrons of chain supermarkets, drugstores, gas
stations and department stores that stand over every American
community. Four Steps Down catered, more or less, to Berkeley
students, all of whom were in revolt, more or less, against the
slick, sick society. The customers went down four sagging,
unsure wood steps to buy their *Berkeley Barb*, their *Oracle*,
their *Ramparts*, their *Summerhills*, their *Tibetan Book of the
Dead*, Tolkien and *Siddhartha* and *I Ching*. The place was
owned by a happily unmarried couple who stocked grass, acid
and diverse pills for people they knew; customers could also
pick up accoutrements of marijuana smoking as well as candles,
posters, buttons, bumper stickers, unsentimental greeting cards
and inexpensive decorative items made in the far East.

Leigh had taken to shopping there.

Since the semester had started she'd bought a pair of thick
orange altar candles gnawed by the small gray mice who dwelled
in the stockroom, a *kakemono* of two courtesans by the great
Utamaro, a brass teapot, a slender Imari vase and a woven
basket like those intended to cage singing crickets.

On that particular rainy Friday afternoon in late October she was shopping for wind chimes. She touched a crystal drop, listening to its tinkly music. *The heart of man,* says Tsurayuki, *can never be understood, but in my native village the flowers give off their perfume as before.* How was she going to live the rest of this icy year even if she did buy every bit of merchandise imported from Japan? How could she cut her growing doubts that at the end of the year he would come back? She touched another wind chime.

By the cash register stood a girl in a sopping handwoven poncho. Her back was to Leigh. Very fat; her stained, too-tight jeans clung in a horizontal crease where her large round buttocks met massive thighs. Ankles, thick. Feet, sandaled, mudsplatted and blue. Drenched curly brown ponytail tied carelessly with a shoelace. She carried a guitar wrapped in dry cleaner's plastic.

As the girl turned Leigh was still staring at her.

Pink-cheeked, with several new chins squaring her round face, Ruth Abby smiled.

Ruth Abby had seen Leigh first. Regulation college girl paisley scarf tied over regulation long straight hair (red in this case), zitless, even features, camel-hair coat—doubtless under that damp real camel-hair, a sorority pin, which wasn't regulation for Berkeley but was regulation for Blue Book girls like Leigh Sutherland. Ruth Abby decided to split. After all, what did they have in common beyond membership in a California High version of a sorority? Friends? Had they been friends? It seemed to Ruth Abby that in those ancient days she hadn't known the meaning of the word *friend*. The Rondelays had simply permitted her to hang around. Leigh, though, Ruth Abby remembered, had never made remarks about bad grades or cracked a single of those awful Jewish jokes and, too, Leigh had covered during her brief encounter with professional singing. Leigh touched a wind chime. Crystal rang. She had a sad look around her gentle mouth, and Ruth Abby almost called out. Then she thought the better of it. What was the point? Leigh would insist on knowing why and how she was here and then she would have to describe the painful struggle that had slowly risen to today's free-flying happiness and of course Leigh Sutherland, square in camel hair, would decide the struggle had led downward. No. Ruth Abby had no interest in being forced into explanations. None. But edging toward the door she caught Leigh's eye. She smiled. What else could she do? And as she turned her big toe stubbed the uneven bottom step, nearly tripping her. She put her free hand out to save herself.

"Ruth Abby!" Leigh cried, running to her. "Are you all right?"

Ruth Abby wiggled her toe experimentally. "Fine," she said. She had to answer, didn't she? "You going to Berkeley?"

Leigh nodded, taking the guitar case so Ruth Abby could make sure there were no splinters up her toenail.

"I'm hanging around up here, too," Ruth Abby volunteered. Leigh nodded.

"You live in a sorority?" Ruth Abby asked.

"A dorm," Leigh replied.

One of Ruth Abby's remarks led to another and soon they sat at a tiny round marble table at Ranio's, sipping gritty espresso paid for by Leigh.

Leigh didn't ask questions. Ruth Abby should've remembered Leigh Sutherland never snooped, but anyway Ruth Abby, always inclined to blurt, poured out the story of her recent life.

"First Green Harbor School. Sometimes I think I hallucinated that place! You'd never believe it, Leigh. We were meant to call one another Miss Heim, Miss So-and-so." Ruth Abby held up a limp hand as if for a la-de-da shake. Leigh smiled. "They put saltpeter in the food, but it didn't do any good. Everybody snuck out anyway to meet guys from the University of Arizona. There were classes in posture, make-up, hair styles, which fork to use when and what to say at an art show. No kidding. And the girls soaked it all up. Wall-to-wall snobs. I mean, it was the worst torture chamber in the history of the world. I was so glad to get out that when I got home I made a real effort to get along with my mother. I said I'd go to college, even. Me! But I was balling and Mother found out."

"How?"

"Like I said, I tried to get along. But I didn't keep secrets. When I was a little kid I lied all the time to keep her happy. But at Green Harbor I'd had it up to here"—Ruth Abby drew a line across her full throat—"with the phony route. I was spending a night with this guy, and instead of making up an excuse, I told her."

Leigh nodded admiringly.

"It was at dinner. Mother dropped her fork. Then she went into the routine speech, you know, everything she'd ever done she'd done for me. How could I do *this* to her? 'Nice Jewish girls don't,' she said. And I said maybe in her day they didn't. Now they did."

"You said that?" Leigh laughed over the chipped rim of her small cup.

"S'true. Anyway, she turned purple. My stepfather, he joined forces with her. The message came through loud and clear. Until you stop this open shacking up never darken our doors again."

"Oh, Ruth Abby!"

"No, Leigh, they were right. I was wrong. It was dirty to live off them if they hated what I did. What I was. The next morning I moved out."

"You're strong."

"Not really. I felt like I needed iron. But. They were *right*."

"How did you manage?"

"Sometimes I sang at the Purple Hippo on Sunset. And I moved in with this old guy of thirty-five, he had all sorts of hang-ups and believe me, life was one big hassle." Ruth Abby smiled. "Then came the biggest day in my life. I met Gilgamesh—"

"Gil Who-mesh?"

"Gilgamesh. All one word. It's not his real name. Gilgamesh's a Babylonian myth. He called himself that after he dropped out from being some sort of priest or minister—he graduated from Princeton Theological Seminary! But he came to see big organized religion has to be phony. Leigh, he's the only person I ever met who understands what it's all about. He sees the important things big. He sees the little crap as little. And I moved up here to be near him. We live several blocks away, a whole bunch of us, in Gilgamesh's place. We share everything. Food. Clothes. Whenever anyone gets money there's this big jar on the sink and nobody knows who put in what or how much. Like Gilgamesh says, what's money? Only a small inch of the whole yard. Right? When there's none, pretty soon one of us goes out and works."

Leigh's eyes shone. She shook her head with admiration.

Ruth Abby said, "This's the first time I've been me. *Me*." She paused. "What've you been doing?"

Leigh said in her quiet, reserved way, "I'm engaged to Ken Igawa."

Ruth Abby leaned across the small round table, her shallow-lidded brown eyes opening wide with surprise. She remembered

Ken Igawa from California High; he'd come to the Gillieses'. A Japanese artist type. Sarcastic. Ruth Abby didn't dig sarcasm, especially directed at herself, but Ken, maybe sensing this, never had chopped her down. Still, Ruth Abby, gazing at Leigh, slim and elegant, would have expected something— someone—different, and thinking this she had trouble following Leigh's story of how Mr. Sutherland, in a complicated wheel and deal, had separated them for a year. "Nine and a half months, really," Leigh finished.

"But why?" Ruth Abby cried.

"He wants us to be sure it's the real thing."

"And you *let* him?"

"Ken had to have the money for his father's operation," Leigh whispered. "Ruth Abby, I explained. What else could we do?"

Ruth Abby stated one of her firmest beliefs. "Give 'em a chance and they'll melt you down and make soap out of you. Tight little squares, just like them." Impulsively she added, "Come along, we'll talk about it at the place."

It was raining hard, slanting lines of cold gray, and Ruth Abby couldn't repress a grateful thought that at the house a rain-drenched Leigh Sutherland would look less out of it than a dry Leigh Sutherland. Gulls circled in the leaden sky. As they walked Ruth Abby thought of the world Leigh was still part of. Rules. She never had been able to dig that bewildering jumble of rules. Clutching her guitar case she jumped across a swollen gutter stream. Orange peels darted like goldfish in racing water. During her childhood her mother had run her life; Ruth Abby had been a passenger driving along a narrow road without any understanding of the whys and wherefores of the motor. Singing was the only thing she understood. And Mother had stamped on her good Martin guitar. Yet Leigh, whom she admired, clung to the rules. This disturbed her—didn't it prove that maybe she was wrong? She glanced at Leigh's wet face. Raindrops ran like tears down her cheeks. Ruth Abby, kind and softhearted, dropped an arm around slim shoulders, letting the wet poncho cover them both; since she'd been up here she had learned that touch is good and you don't have to show human affection only to the guy you happen to be currently balling.

The place was almost empty. As Leigh glanced around, Ruth Abby tried to see it as her old friend must: a big bare room furnished only with a few tatamis and torn pillows, on the far wall a framed scroll and on the low table in front of the scroll a browning bunch of bananas, a jelly jar with a single jagged Oriental-looking fir branch, a saucer with incense burning, its heavy scent filling the room.

Donolly and Todd knelt in front of the scroll, bending forward and leaning back on their knees, shaking the beads in their hands as they chanted, loud as they could and not in unison:

"Nam myo ho renge kyo, nam myo ho renge kyo, nam myo ho renge kyo, nam myo ho renge kyo, nam myo ho renge kyo . . ."

Todd, glancing up, greeted, "Ruth Abby."

And Donolly, not pausing, smiled his slow bearded happiness at seeing her. Ruth Abby dropped the guitar, peeled off her soaking poncho, kicked away her sodden sandals, gesturing Leigh to do the same.

Ruth Abby got a new pack of chocolate Oreos from the kitchen, then led her friend to the back room, which was free. They sat on the mattress, leaning against wallpaper patterned with huge, hideous orchids. Ruth Abby set the Oreos between them. She ate. Leigh did not.

"Other guys while you're waiting?" Ruth Abby asked.

Leigh shook her head. "But I've been busy. Tutoring two fourth graders over in Oakland." She gave a small smile. "Joella and Willamine. Also I help at the Headstart Nursery School."

"And Ken?"

Leigh's hazel eyes filled with tears. She struggled to control herself. Ruth Abby shifted closer and with a stubby, grubby hand she patted Leigh's shaking shoulders. Touch, though, rather than soothing, unlocked more tears.

"I don't know," Leigh finally sobbed.

"Know what?"

"Whether he's with . . . other girls. I don't know. . . ." Leigh's slender hands covered her face. "Yes. He is. He couldn't go that long without. . . . Ruth Abby, what if he likes one better? What! Maybe he won't come back."

"He will," Ruth Abby said, but without certainty. A year was a long time.

"He wouldn't if he knew what I've done." Rain pattered at the windows. Dark shadows quilted corners. Leigh turned, her big eyes all blurry in the dim light. "Ruth Abby, I've got to tell someone, otherwise I'll go crazy." She paused. "Promise you won't tell?"

"Tell what?"

"Just promise."

"I promise."

"I've done a terrible thing. Awful. Ken would hate me if he knew. He'd never come back."

"That's crazy."

"Promise you won't tell anyone?"

"I already did."

"I hate myself."

"Never do that," Ruth Abby said. She'd learned this bit of wisdom the hard way. "Never hate anyone."

"I do. Me."

"Nothing you did could be *that* bad."

"I had an abortion."

Laughter bubbled inside Ruth Abby's round throat. That was why Leigh was so shook? That was all? Ruth Abby repressed her giggle, rising to switch on the light, a single unshaded bulb in the triple wall fixture. To soothe poor, messed-up Leigh, she also decided to shed a little light on the subject, and so as she sat down again she said, "Only screwed old people think abortion's wrong. It isn't. Listen, I've had three."

"You didn't feel terrible after?"

"A little sore."

"And guilty?"

"Why should I?"

"Ruth Abby, a baby!"

"No," Ruth Abby denied. "Not yet."

"A baby is a person."

"Not inside your stomach."

"It would be one," Leigh insisted.

"No. An accident. So wasn't it better to stop it? Leigh, it's the old perverts who make girls have unwanted babies. They don't care about those poor, sad babies. In their dirty little minds it's punishment for balling. And by them balling's the worst crime. That's why they're so hot and heavy against abortion."

"But we made it, Ken and me...."

"Why didn't you have it, then?"

"My father—"

Ruth Abby's full, red-cheeked face hardened.

"—explained," Leigh hurried on, "it wouldn't be fair to the baby. I wouldn't be married."

"But Ken wants to marry—"

"I *told* you. That's part of the bargain. This year I'm not to know where he is. His mother doesn't either. Maybe Japan still. Maybe he's found someone there—" Leigh shivered.

"Shhhh," Ruth Abby lulled. "Go on."

"And nobody wants to adopt mixed babies, my father said. Anyway, how could I've given it up? But would it be fair to a baby to make it illegitimate? What could I do? Daddy agreed with you. The abortion laws're antiquated, he said, and it was the only answer. I flew down last Friday and a friend of his, an OB, did it in his office with his nurse. I didn't even miss school." The idea of a safe, sane abortion without missing a class further upset Leigh. Tears started again.

Ruth Abby leaned back too baffled to comfort Leigh. Who could understand? Here was Leigh telling her that her father had helped with an abortion which Ruth Abby agreed was the only answer. Yet there was something wrong, terribly, terribly wrong, and Ruth Abby, listening to her friend's politely muffled sobs, frowned, for she couldn't quite figure that wrong.

Leigh wiped her eyes. Her pretty, embroidered handkerchief was sodden. "How could he still love me?"

"You're the one who's so shook. I'll bet Ken wouldn't be."

"Yes," Leigh insisted. "He would be. He'd think I did it because we're . . . different. You know, because he's Japanese."

"But your father arranged—"

Leigh stood. "It wasn't Daddy's fault," she said coldly. "Not at all."

"But you told me he sent Ken away," Ruth Abby said. "Doesn't that jar you a little?"

"He paid for Ken's father's operation. We wouldn't've been together anyway." Abruptly Leigh sat back down. "My father felt awful. He said he never would've sent Ken away if he'd realized we were . . . you know. . . ."

"He thought you were playing Jacks together?"

"He didn't think I—"

Ruth Abby snorted.

"Anyway," Leigh sighed, "he admits it's all his fault. He does, Ruth Abby. I feel so sorry for him. He stayed with me all that day, just sitting in the bedroom on the pink ottoman, his shoulders slumped, his hands dangling between his knees. He looked so old, wrinkled in the face. Defeated. He kept saying, 'Blame me, babe, not yourself.' He was trying to do the best thing. And it turned out so badly."

"Badly," Ruth Abby echoed, completely bewildered by Leigh's attitude.

"Daddy, the nurse and the doctor. And now you. The only ones who know."

"Yes."

"Ken can't ever know. *He can't!* But Ruth Abby, I had to tell someone." She was shaking.

Ruth Abby wondered about nervous breakdowns. "I won't say a word, ever. I promise." She pushed away the cookies. "Listen, come over later. Gilgamesh'll be here."

When Leigh told Dorot about meeting Ruth Abby, Dorot, naturally, was fascinated.

"You say her religion is free love?" she demanded.

"Not at all. They live in this big old house, sharing food and clothes and money and—"

"Love."

"—responsibility. They practice a form of Buddhism. Not Zen. Nichiren. They chant."

"Hippies."

"Why always label?"

"The scholar in me." Dorot, at her desk, sank into meditation, cupping her chin in her hand. "Well, in Ruth Abby's case it's to be expected. Most of them're dropouts from upper-income families, especially upper-income Jewish families."

"You would see it that way." Leigh lit a Pall Mall in that campy Bette Davis way that seemed to come naturally since Ken's banishment. Dorot did all she could to help her friend, but obviously her type of help meant little—didn't everyone know the havoc sexual deprivation can wreak? Don't certain European monastic orders scourge themselves tri-weekly? Leigh held the cigarette in front of her mouth, puffing rapidly. "Ruth Abby was unhappy before."

"She was forever giggling."

"Searching."

"Twitching."

"She never had her own father so she felt all alone. Now she's found a place where she belongs."

"Face the facts. She lacked confidence in her own socio-economic level, so she's blowing her mind."

Leigh turned away with that dogged expression of sadness.

Dorot had made a solemn inner vow not to argue with Leigh. It wasn't an easy vow to keep. Still, Dorot managed to ask pleasantly, "You're going tonight?"

Leigh, head averted, nodded.

Around torn blinds seeped a light so dim it did no more than fade the blackness. Leigh's tentative knock was answered by Ruth Abby, who emanated a strange excitement. Two candles barely lit the large front room and Leigh, peering, saw that about fifteen people were sprawled on the floor. Incense filled the gloom. A chill touched Leigh's spine. It was crazy— but had she stumbled into some alien rite to an unknown god? Or devil? Her anxiety was intensified by the bearded, long-haired man who walked up behind Ruth Abby; without being told Leigh knew this was the lapsed Princeton theologian. Gilgamesh. Ruth Abby introduced them.

"Thank you for letting me come," Leigh said politely.

"The place's community property," Gilgamesh replied. Under his heavy sweater he was bulky of shoulder and barrel-chested like a wrestler. Yet his voice held surprising gentleness.

"C'min," Ruth Abby said impatiently.

As Leigh started to take off her coat, Gilgamesh said, "Ruth Abby's told me a little about your problems, the way your father separated you and your boy friend."

Leigh's awkwardness grew. Her hand caught in her sleeve.

He helped her extricate herself. "You're embarrassed?" he asked.

Leigh nodded.

"Didn't she mention anything about me?" he asked. "My wicked orthodox past?"

Leigh nodded again.

"So we're even." He smiled. He hung her coat on a convenient nailhead. "Leigh, we've got some acid. Care to join us?"

So that was what it was all about!

The offer surprised her. First of all, Gilgamesh must be at least forty, and she never thought in terms of old people dropping acid. Secondly, although legal, you heard all sorts of stories about it, pro and con. Mostly con. As a matter of fact, now she thought about it, the idea sort of scared her. Yet . . . with Ken's absence—and now the abortion—she felt trapped in the bottom of a numb gray sea and when she tried to swim upward she found herself in such misery that she gladly sank back into chill waters. *Why not?*

"Yes," she said. "Please."

"We think of it as a door. You understand? To see what we can't see, to know what we can't know." Gilgamesh handed her a capsule, poured water into a glass. As she downed the cap he said, "I'll stick around with you."

"Me, too," Ruth Abby said.

On a *tatami* by the window wall they sat, Leigh in the middle.

After fifteen minutes Leigh announced, "I don't feel a thing."

"You won't, not for a while," Gilgamesh said.

"I'm hoping it'll . . . you know, give me a lift."

"You're cold all the time?" Gilgamesh asked.

"Yes."

"And empty?"

"Yes."

"And lost some place very, very deep?"

"How'd you know?"

"It happens, it happens. To all of us," he said. "I promise you that. We aren't group creatures, we're not ants or bees. So we're trapped inside ourselves. Loneliness, it's a place. Like New York. Everyone visits. A lot of people live there permanently."

"You can get away," Leigh insisted. "If you're with someone you love." Tears came. She knuckled them away.

"There's other routes, too." Candle flames shone in his sympathetic eyes. "Some're sad, like drinking, or drugs. Or too much of this. But there's positive ways. As you put it, love. Finding joy in the world and everything in it. God. Listen, stop me when I begin to sound like a tape of the Sermon on the Mount."

She gave him a watery smile.

He went on. "You can put your whole heart into benevolence, right thinking, and speaking, and action—"

"That's Buddhism, isn't it?"

"It is," Gilgamesh agreed. "But I hate like hell to pin down a way of life. Words distort. And dogma kills dead."

"But I've been trying to figure out Buddhism," she said. The lines around his eyes were deep. All at once she felt completely at ease with him, which she seldom was with strangers, especially older strangers. "Can you explain it? A little?"

So Gilgamesh told more of the Eightfold Plan. His words were of peace, but more important, his voice held peace. Leigh listened. Some of it got pretty complicated, and to absorb his meanings she found her mind growing. And reaching. She'd never before experienced this indescribable intense stretching. It was as if her brain cells were actually becoming porous to soak up Gilgamesh's concepts. Now her eyes began to view the room differently. No walls met each other or the floor or the ceiling at right angles; it was as if she and the others rested in an immense hollow tree trunk with yellow candle fire touching the darkness. Gilgamesh's tranquil voice flowed, part of the glowing arcs. When he fell silent she barely noticed. Ruth Abby held out a daffodil. Leigh's slender hand rested on Ruth Abby's thicker one and the two of them stared. The color shone so pure there could be no name for it. The flower's significance was sex, for Leigh perceived the frilled trumpet as a golden vulva, and with a gentle finger she explored the incredible softness. Was this what Ken felt inside her? The thought of Ken roused no immediate sorrow, only the meanings they made together.

Leigh willed her mind to stretch further. She must understand all meaning and all being.

People shifted. Gilgamesh rose infinitely slowly. And Ruth Abby, leaving Leigh the flower, floated to sit by the brown boy called Donolly. The voice that was Ruth Abby's unique gift rose in multicolored strands that formed a rainbow bridge between one person and the next. How long did she sing? Leigh couldn't tell, for time carried her lightly.

Suddenly—

No warning!

A tawny-maned lion opened its vast, cruel-toothed jaws.

Leigh cowered. Her body shook.

The lion gave a vast, silent roar. She must escape. She must! Yet her body was separated from her mind. She went rigid, gripping the terrible lion. She was evil, evil, evil. She had done a fearful wrong. And the beast knew it, and she and it were alone on an endless landscape, and soon it would happen again, soon the monstrous thing would happen again, soon the cruel knife-tongue would flick out, would curve into her body, into the innermost recesses of her womb, and devour the soft, helpless, boneless creature. She cried aloud, "Ken!" But he wasn't here. She was evil. Evil. She began to squirm. A dread sound arose, a wailing that wasn't sound at all but the awful red light that surrounds a dying sun. She was evil and her horror was greater than she could bear. The sound grew.

"Take it easy." A man's arms held her. "Leigh, take it easy."

She screamed.

"Shhhh," he soothed. "It's all right."

She struggled to escape the beast, but thick arms pinioned her.

She screamed again and again. Until finally a word came out. *"Lion."*

And a hairy hand removed the lion.

"See? A daffodil. Leigh, Leigh, Leigh. You're safe. Safe."

"HELP ME."

"I will."

And with both hands she grasped his hand. His other arm he put around her shoulders, pulling her close to warmth. Then Ruth Abby was there. She and Gilgamesh sat with their arms around Leigh, talking to her and talking and talking, and eventually their bodily warmth and their words sank into her, reaching, easing, soothing, until even the loneliness that once more wrapped her seemed bearable.

She could again contemplate the daffodil. Now it was simply a flower. But what a flower! Had there been one like it since the Garden of Eden? The incandescent glow of the ruffled bell a deeper gold than six wondrous curved petals, the stamen and corona (somewhat bruised by her own finger) graceful and life-giving. In this flower lay the mysteries of existence, the paradox of life and death, the perpetual perishing and rebirth in all existence. *And she understood.* She inhaled the scent and curled up on the *tatami*.

Sun slanting through dirty windows awoke Leigh.

"Morning." Ruth Abby smiled. She sat next to her. "I thought you'd never wake up."

"G'morning." Leigh yawned and stretched stiff arms. "Were you here all night?"

"Uh huh."

"Ruth Abby, thank you. But why?"

"Why else? You had a real bummer."

"I did?"

"You did. Screaming and thrashing around."

Leigh's brain flashed knowledge that didn't quite make sense. "I do sort of remember," she admitted. She glanced at the daffodil which lay crushed where she'd slept on it. "It was a live lion, then a flower. And I understood everything in the whole universe."

"That's acid for you."

"I don't think I'll try it again. Ever."

"We don't, not often," Ruth Abby admitted. "I've only had three trips. All good. But anyway, who needs to be a head." She pushed her rounded bulk to standing position. "C'mon. There's oatmeal cooking."

Leigh got up, straightening her sweater and finger-pressing the pleats of her rumpled skirt. "Thanks, Ruth Abby," she said, adding shyly, "I feel good around here. And Gilgamesh—he's something else again."

"I told you." Ruth Abby smiled. "Whenever you want, come. No fancy invitations're necessary."

That semester in her Oriental Language class Leigh sat next to a Mr. Marx. He was tall, thin, his coarse beige hair was clipped into a crew cut. He wore horn rims and when he succumbed to one of his constant sneezing spells these slipped down on his broad nose. He looked very young; once a week lightly with his razor must do him. He was very bright (Leigh had glimpsed a ninety-eight and a ninety-nine on his returned quizzes) and very shy. Leigh empathized. She spoke to him. They got acquainted and after a couple of weeks she learned he was a freshman from Beverly Hills and knew no girls on campus. Impulsively she said, "Listen, tonight I'm visiting a friend. Why don't you come along?"

She felt a twinge of embarrassment as she led Larry Marx into Ruth Abby's place. Everything here seemed half done. Nothing was finished. Someone had started to repaint the green walls but had left off after smearing one black; on the uncertain new darkness was whitewashed *LET'S WEED OUT THE SNAKE IN THE GR* and *MINE EYES HAVE SE*. On dusty floor boards in front of the scroll and makeshift altar someone had dropped a string of tasseled amber prayer beads. You had the feeling that most inhabitants had left at noon today, immigrating to Middle Earth.

"Ruth Abby," Leigh called. "I'm here."

Ruth Abby hugged Leigh (Leigh had noticed since Ruth Abby'd been up here she'd become addicted to hugging, patting and touching) and Leigh introduced her to Larry Marx.

They glared at one another.

Two days later in class Larry Marx said, "What an infestation of cockroaches. How can they live like that?"

"Ruth Abby's my friend."

"I didn't mean it as a reflection on you." He sneezed and Leigh said *gesundheit*. "Has she ever considered Metrecal?" Another sneeze. Another *gesundheit*. "Or a bath?"

"He's up too tight to pee!" Ruth Abby sneered, and she was not one given to scorn. "With his crew cut and phony egghead talk. Yech! Just what Mother had in mind!"

"What do your parents say about you living up here?" asked Larry Marx.

"Who cares?" Ruth Abby replied.

"We're all conditioned to care."

"Not me, not any more. I've blocked it out. It's like I was living someone's else's nightmare," Ruth Abby said. "Look, there was only one thing I could do. Sing. And she took that away."

This was Larry Marx's fourth visit. Their initial dislike had dissolved and now they were friends. Tonight the two of them were rooftopping, smoking, their backs flat on sagging tarpaper, the starless night draped like a blanket around them.

Larry Marx said, "You sing now."

"I'm hanging around up here," she said. "And so are you."

They puffed companionably into the dark.

"You mustn't be up tight," she said.

"I can't help it. It's like—Ruth Abby, in old legends sorcerers would draw a pentacle on the floor, cook up a brew of lizard's hair and toad's eyes, then mutter loud incantations to summon up the devil. The devil was forced to appear to do their bidding. But he couldn't step out of the magic pentacle that contained him. That's how I am. My parents're ambitious and materialistic. My father owns a cabinet shop, or rather, it owns him. Kitchen cabinets. And my mother's avid for my-son-the-Phi-Beta-Kappa. They're both too typical to be true, you know what I mean? One minute they're drowning me in schmaltz and the next they're shouting after all they've *done* for me the least I can do is get As and date swingin' Jewish girls. And the worst part is, I'm trapped in their pentacle."

"You gotta hang loose."

"Impossible."

"You can do anything you want."

"I'm improving—I *am* engaged in the illegal use of marijuana, aren't I?"

*"Every*one turns on."

"Blessed art Thou oh Lord God of the Universe who createst the marijuana plant."

"Amen," Ruth Abby said and they both laughed.

A car drove by, headlights casting a dim yellow glow up to the roof; someplace nearby a radio played Bobby Vee's *The Night Has a Thousand Eyes*.

"You want to?" Ruth Abby asked.

"Want to what?"

"Ball?"

"I—"

"Grass makes it groovier."

"I—well, I don't feel like it."

"O.K.," Ruth Abby said agreeably.

"Not tonight."

"Just put your arm around me, then. That's friendly, too."

He didn't move. "I'm like that," he said. "Either I want to, or I don't. Right now it's no go. So I'd ejaculate prematurely."

"If you don't want, we won't."

"It's a form of temporary impotence."

"Put your arm around me," Ruth Abby repeated, and when he didn't she rested her curly brown head on his narrow shoulder. "I like you, Larry."

"It's not I'm not attracted to you."

"I know you dig me."

"I do."

"I know."

"And generally I'm very potent. I've been with quite a few older women. My French teacher at Uni; two of my mother's friends. They complimented me. Of course they're used to older men and it's common knowledge that the male reaches his full sexual powers in the late teens while a woman doesn't mature until she's middle-aged, in her thirties."

The dark clouds parted. A few stars showed.

Larry began to sneeze.

"The hay fever again?" Ruth Abby murmured sympathetically.

"I'm lying." Larry snuffled and wiped his nose.

"What about?"

"I never did."

"Ball, you mean?"

"Uh huh."

"That's a bummer," Ruth Abby said. "But why lie?"

"I'd like to. In fact, up until now, that's been my main problem. Am I ever going to—that's all I think about."

"Why not now?"

"I'm afraid I won't be able to at all, much less be adequate."

"It's the most natural."

"Not for me. I'm so tense."

"But we're friends."

"I can't even speak to girls."

"You're speaking to me."

"Yes. That makes it worse."

"Why?"

"We're friends."

"Whatever happens, Larry, I'll still be your friend." She lifted herself on one elbow. "It'll be right, you'll see."

And lowering her lips to his, she brushed back and forth, sometimes licking him lightly, sometimes not. He put both arms around her. *I've got a right,* he thought, as softness of unbrassiered breasts closed against his chest. Yet he panicked as her hand reached between their bodies for his fly. Her hand held him. She pressed her round face to his, whispering, "Feel mine, Larry." She was asking no sacrifices, no late-night studying, no overcoming of self to talk to bright-eyed, too-witty Beverly Hills girls, no being the swinger when he was a mud clinger. She asked only that he curve fingers around this soft moist woolly part of herself. His panic eased as he rubbed fingers along the complicated wet flesh. The night was chill, his narrow, long feet icy, but their locked torsos (clothes pushed up or down) burned. He kept stroking. So did she.

It was natural, Larry Marx decided, the most natural, like sinking into thick leaf mulch, girl flesh with girl mouth, girl with leafy autumnal odors, full-mounded girl, steamy heat rising to surround him, to lead him on, the murmuring rich voice gasping from soft warmth to encourage him. Then he needed no more encouraging for he was free, riding home free.

Part Four

---·— 1 —·---

Under a two-column photograph in the *Los Angeles Times:*

> *Betrothal of Miss Leigh Van Vliet Sutherland to Mr.*
> *Kenneth Gordon Igawa, son of Mr. and Mrs. Kunoshi*
> *Igawa of Sawtelle, has been announced by her parents,*
> *Mr. and Mrs. Sidney L. Sutherland of Holmby Hills.*
> *They both attend the University of California at Berkeley.*
> *Miss Sutherland, a fourth-generation Californian, was*
> *presented as a Las Palomas debutante and is the grand-*
> *daughter of Mrs. Dormin Van Vliet and the late Mr. Van*
> *Vliet, and of Mrs. Sidney L. Sutherland and the late Mr.*
> *Sutherland. A June wedding is planned.*

The Gillieses, of course, were invited.

But how can you go to a wedding if you have to wear a three-year-old suit? The same ratty white lace you yourself had been married in? Wearing that lace how could Michele enjoy one moment of the wedding?

Clay, of course, never took one moment to consider how she might feel. On the evening he came home to find Michele, rich cream envelope in hand, bubbling excitedly about her biggest party ever and how she must have the right clothes, he'd demanded, "What's wrong with that lace outfit? You look nice. And you've only worn it half a dozen times."

"Whose fault is that?" Michele, knowing she had a battle on her little hands, made a valiant effort to keep her voice under control. "Clay, you know you won't ever go anyplace dressy."

"This month we can't afford one more thing."

"The lace is ready to fall apart!"

He was silent.

"It really is."

More silence.

"You know how old it is."

"Then wear your new dress," he said.

A pink polished cotton, pretty enough, she'd shopped devotedly to find something decent she could afford, but how could she wear an everyday cotton to any wedding, much less one this big?

Clay added, "We're just going to Ken and Leigh's wedding—"

"That's what I'm trying to tell—"

"They're our old friends and—"

"—you. We have to look our best!"

"—I don't see how it matters what *you* wear!"

Their voices had risen.

Clay's eyebrows beetled furiously. Michele, determined to stay cool and equally determined to get a new dress, sat on the gray couch and taking a deep breath again remarked that this was a *big* wedding, there were five hundred of these (she shook the invitation) mailed out. It was a real social event. Therefore clothes did matter. It wouldn't show proper respect to the bride and groom to wear an everyday dress. With tremendous difficulty she kept her voice reasonable. "So you see I absolutely can't go in the pink cotton."

"And your lace is no good?" he asked.

"Falling apart," she agreed, holding her breath, hoping, praying.

And he said in his coldest, most infuriating tone, "I guess we can't go then, can we?"

He went into the bathroom, using it without closing the door, which he knew bothered her.

Michele retired to the bedroom. Closing the door she thought, and not for the first time, that her marriage was a big nothing.

Zero.

No matter how you added it. Zero.

An ache formed under her full breasts. It wasn't that she pitied herself—what good would that do?—but lately she'd begun to fear that she, like her marriage, was turning into an ugly round nothing. She wished she could turn on the light to reassure herself in the mirror that she was still alive and pretty. But she couldn't. Lissa was in the room, breathing inaudibly in her crib, Clay having refused to buy a youth bed for his own daughter even though she was two and a half! Oh, Michele tried to forge something out of her marriage. She really believed in marriage. She scrimped, scrubbed, stewed cheap cuts of meat, slaved, she never mentioned—well, hardly ever—the chances that she, even at a mere sixteen, had turned down. And when her husband gloated, "Miche, we registered forty-two more this time," or, "Miche, we raised a thousand, easy," or, "A sure thing, we're going to get Willie Lou Martin on the ballot," she managed a loyal smile. She went to interminable dull SNAP meetings instead of parties. In short, she honestly did her best.

On his side, Clay did nothing.

Take, for only one example, the matter of their personal finances. Clay, eager to talk about impersonal fund raisings, refused to discuss their own problems; he acted as though money was beneath him, yet after an argument such as this he was fully capable of wordlessly handing her a budget drawn up on lined notebook paper in his small neat figures proving that three people could live comfortably on three hundred a month. Comfortable on three hundred! Naturally Michele would fight *that*. Invariably he would reply, if not the exact words, the chill spirit: *"You're my wife. I don't see why you can't help instead of hinder. Don't you understand by now how crucial SNAP is?"* Michele flopped across her twin bed wondering how he expected himself and her and Lissa could manage on less than those colored people on relief. The few times she'd exceeded this meager amount, he turned to ice. He was totally unmovable. This was what was killing Michele. Didn't people who love one another compromise? And her husband refused to see any point of view but his own. He'd quit Pixwood after arguing with her father, and now, at Ralph's on Wilshire, he checked exactly enough hours to earn three hundred after taxes. The rest of his time he devoted, or wasted, whichever way you chose to look at it, with SNAP. How could Clay be so unreasonable about one single dress?

Wasn't it proof he didn't love her?

The ache in her chest grew too vast to bear.

There was only one thing to do. Tell her mother.

When her mother heard the problem, she agreed that definitely Michele needed a new dress for the wedding and she would pay.

At St. Albans, the pretty gray stone church opposite UCLA, Michele kept her coat buttoned. No problem. Even though outside at five thirty it was hot and sunny, inside dull gray light slanted into cold stone. Seated in a pew toward the front, Michele listened to the organ drag through "I Love You Truly"

and tried to forget her annoyance with Clay. The music changed
to the Wedding March and bridesmaids in lemon organza paced
slowly. Then Leigh, veiled, cloudy white, arms full of tiny
yellow orchids, came down the aisle. Mr. Sutherland, pale and
haggard, moved more deliberately than the bridesmaids, even,
gripping Leigh's slender arm as if he wanted to slow her down.
Michele shifted uneasily. Yet where was the tragedy? Leigh
and Ken were ecstatic.

Men in gold uniform jackets parked cars at the Sutherlands'
house. Michele and Clay moved inside. The moment had come.
She must give up her coat.

Clay darted one furious glance at the new shell-pink dress.

"Where did that come from?" he demanded.

"Shhh . . ." Michele cautioned. Guests politely averted their
eyes from her and Clay.

"Where?"

"Let's enjoy the party," she pleaded softly.

"Where?"

"I'll explain later."

"You bought it on time!"

"Clay—"

"You're forever getting us in debt for meaningless crap!"

"I didn't—"

"And I'm wasting my life bailing us out!"

"My mother paid," Michele said, managing to sound chill
and at the same time to smile warmly.

"Your mother! You're always begging from her!"

"She didn't want me to wear rags to Leigh's wedding."
Michele managed another smile, this time to the maid who
took her coat.

"I told you not to—"

"I am not your slave!" Michele whispered, taking a ticket
from the maid. "Now! Let me enjoy the party!"

Clay glared at her, his lips tightening in his beard, the gold
flecks in his brown eyes seeming to catch fire. Abruptly he
turned, marching through the family room where the receiving
line stood, leaving Michele stranded, holding her own coat tag.

But.

She was not going to let a scene, even a humiliating public
scene like this, ruin a party. Not when she wore a pretty new
dress with dyed-to-match shoes!

A butler held out a silver tray laden with wide-mouthed
champagne glasses. Sipping, holding the frosty glass with a

folded white cocktail napkin, Michele made her way along the receiving line, smiling and gracious to the expressionless Iga-was, kissing the numb-smiling Sutherlands, hugging Leigh and Ken, joking with those bridesmaids she knew.

The back yard tenting was magnificent. High green canvas was chandeliered with crystal, looped with great chains of white and yellow shasta daisies. Potted fern and other greenery filled the corners. The florist's bill alone, Dorot said, came to over four thousand dollars! A dance floor covered the pool, the pool house served as backing for the bar.

Michele danced with Daws Huntington, who was one of *the* Huntingtons and an old boy friend, and with Marshall Mosgrove, former president of California High and also an old boy friend. Who was Clay Gillies? She paused for another champagne. Let him worry about her for a change.

She and Stryker Halvorsen danced a wild watusi. People gathered, clapping them on. Michele soaked up the applause. Finally, panting and laughing, she stopped, saying, "Whew! I'm pooped." She wasn't. She was beginning to worry about sweating through her Arrid onto new pink silk.

Michele sank down at one of the small tables circling the dance floor. She glanced around. The little tables were crowded with older guests. There were very few Japanese, maybe seven couples who looked, she decided, like impoverished sparrows trapped in an aviary of gaudy parakeets. French champagne had done good work. Diamonded ladies smiled and chattered amiably while their well-tailored husbands eyed the young girls, including Michele. The orchestra blared. A half-dozen barten-ders briskly dispensed hard liquor; waiters pressed champagne; waitresses kept hot hors d'oeuvres coming.

This was magnificence.

For a moment Michele couldn't help herself from comparing this with her own poor, sad excuse of a wedding—Hawaiian punch, a market cake and Dozer peeing on the hooked rug. Why hadn't she been born right? *She* would have known what to do with Mother Nature's gifts. She never would have thrown everything away like Leigh was doing. A Japanese gardener's son! And after a year abroad more determined than ever to paint. Michele might not have a high school diploma, but she knew practical arithmetic; painting plus gardeners' sons adds up to poverty. Michele, alas, knew that sum only too well.

Dorot, arranging her long lemon bridesmaid's skirt, sat next to Michele.

"It really is a sign of the times there is such a wedding." Dorot's voice could be heard over the six-piece combo blaring "Walk Right In." "Did you know that up until nineteen forty-eight this wouldn't have been legal, not here in California? Orientals and Caucasians were forbidden by law to marry."

Michele, who was surprised, nodded. Shadowed by one of the potted palms stood Clay and his dark echo, RG Richards— even RG wore a black suit. Clay was the only man here not wearing one. And he'd expected *her* to be equally conspicuous. Michele averted her gaze. She asked, "Do you think Leigh minds what her father did? Separating them?"

"Leigh resent her father! As far as I'm concerned there's always been something a mite clinical about *that* relationship."

"Then you wouldn't of thought if her father was against it she'd have married—"

"Oh, that doesn't mean to say she's not wild for Ken." Dorot blew a smoke ring. "But I've been thinking. This marriage will have more than its expected problems, which are many."

Michele leaned forward, hoping for more.

Dorot said, "It still isn't in sixteen states."

"Isn't what?"

"Legal."

Michele gave a disappointed sigh.

"I researched it," Dorot said. "To this day sixteen states consider interracial marriage a criminal offense."

And at that moment Mr. Sutherland put one broad hand on the back of Dorot's yellow organza, the other on Michele's pink silk. Michele gave a small prayer that he hadn't overheard Dorot. The heat of his palm soaked through her dress.

"Girls, how goes it?" he boomed, exhaling the ripeness of Scotch. Obviously he was under the influence. Very.

"A beautiful wedding," they chorused politely.

And as if by command, the three of them turned to watch the dancers, *I'm going to walk right in,* and at that moment Leigh reached up to push Ken's hair back. He took the hand, the one with the new broad gold ring, pressing it to the side of his forehead. They stopped moving. They stared at one another, seeming to hold their breath, his mouth stretching, her clear eyelids fluttering, and very slowly he drew her narrow wrist to his lips; the kiss for some reason seemed to Michele more meaningful, more strikingly sexy, than if another couple had begun going at it right on the dance floor. It occurred to her that before today, Ken and Leigh's wedding day, she'd never even seen them touch. A photographer's blossom of white exploded. Ken blinked, letting go of Leigh's hand. They started to dance again, slowly and languidly, still staring at one another. The dance leader must have noticed, for he slowed his beat to "I Left My Heart in San Francisco." Their romance having climaxed there, no pun intended, Leigh and Ken considered this "their" song. Several older couples rose. Draggy numbers like this revived the box step.

A tall, stoutish man, he looked at least thirty, with thinning, neatly combed brown hair and a clipped red mustache, stood by the table. On the pinkie of his large, hairless right hand he wore a star sapphire.

"Uncle Sidney," he shouted over loud, syrupy horns. "Fabulous wedding."

"Thank you, Everett." Mr. Sutherland took his hand off Michele's back. She prayed that no mark remained on delicate silk. "Do you know these pretty girls?" Mr. Sutherland asked.

"I know Dorot," he said, but it was little Michele he was staring at. Mother had protested the low cut of the neckline, but Michele's arguments—*there's nothing else* and *you know I've looked and looked*—had carried the day.

"Michele, Everett Sutherland. Everett, this is Leigh's friend, Michele Davy—Michele Gillies, I mean."

"Hello there," he said.

Michele smiled up at him, fluttering her carefully mascaraed lashes.

He kept staring at her.

"Why don't you join us?" she asked.

"Thank you." He sat. "Fabulous wedding," he repeated.

"Really wonderful," Michele murmured.

And Mr. Sutherland repeated his thanks, turning to Dorot. "Isn't it about time for the father of the bride to ask her maid of honor for a dance?"

"I wondered how long I'd have to wait." Dorot smiled.

"Why don't we?" Everett Sutherland leaned forward. "Dance, I mean."

Michele rose.

Everett Sutherland danced as old men do, holding on. They passed the bar where Clay, the-only-man-here-not-in-a-suit, orated furiously to York. York now lived in Athens, Greece, he'd jetted specifically to attend the wedding, but being York he was acting as if he didn't care to be here, dark glasses blank, one side of his thin mouth up, the other down in a twisty smile. Everett Sutherland held Michele gingerly as if she were fragile pink meringue. His shoulder, where her hand rested, felt soft and solid at the same time. In the three hours they'd been here Clay hadn't come near her. Typical. When angry he turned to ice, staying silent for an entire day—longer, lately.

"I noticed you before," Everett Sutherland said.

Michele smiled up at him.

His large, flat cheeks wobbled a little as he danced. "You were doing the watusi with a tall boy."

"Stryker Halvorsen."

"You're the best dancer here."

Michele dimpled modestly.

"You deserve better than me."

"Silly!" Michele smiled. "You're really light on your feet."

As if to prove her point he whirled her around twice. "I asked Leigh who you were."

"You didn't!"

"I did. And I asked her if you'd always been so pretty—"

"You!"

"—and she said you had been as long as she'd known you."

Michele smiled.

"She said you were in the same club at California High."

"She's a darling girl."

"She said you were the most popular girl there."

"Friendship overtook honesty."

He shook his head. "Leigh said it." His already deep voice deepened. "I told her I could see why."

"Aren't you kind?" Michele gave him the wink that she'd spent a full week of her fifteenth summer perfecting in front of a mirror.

"So I know all about you."

Michele threw another wink.

"And then I saw Uncle Sidney with you. So I came over."

He whirled her another circle, she dipped, and he kept staring at her. Heavy lids folded over outer edges of his gray eyes, giving him a faithful-hound expression.

"You know about me," Michele said. "It's only fair I know about you."

"USC," he said. "And I just got out of the service."

"Army?"

"Air Force."

"A flier?"

"I was with supply in Germany."

"Europe! Lucky you!"

"I prefer good old California."

"And now?"

"I'm training as a stockbroker."

"You like it?"

"The market's fabulous."

"I've heard," Michele said. "What else do you do?"

"Else?"

"You know, hobbies. Girl watching, say?"

"Only like now, when the girl's worth watching," he said, smiling. "I play golf. Chart stocks. And of course I have to give some time to Mother."

"Oh?"

"I'm all she's got," he said. "My father's dead."

"Oh, I am sorry," little Michele consoled.

"It happened quite a few years ago."

"Was he Mr. Sutherland's brother?"

"Cousin, actually. But we're a close-knit family."

"I'm family minded, too," Michele said, speaking from the heart. That zero wasn't. He never spoke to his own father, even, not that she blamed him there, Mr. Gillies being the pickled-in-bourbon remnants of a Virginia gentleman. "I love close families."

"You and me both," said Everett Sutherland. "Anyway, I always call him Uncle Sidney."

"He's terrific."

"A warm person."

"Very."

"He's forever doing all sorts of thing that he never lets on about. For example, after my dad died, Uncle Sidney stepped right in. We never could have managed without his help."

Help? That didn't sound good, did it? Did you ever hear of the rich being helped? Poor relatives, they got helped.

Everett went on, "I was only sixteen at the time."

"How terrible."

"And it was quite unexpected. Things were in a mess. Uncle Sidney was fabulous. He arranged the funeral, put everything in order. He took off weeks from his practice—and I guess you know he's very successful—then wouldn't even accept the minimum fee, which in this case would have been pretty substantial."

Michele, sliding her pink silk shoes to three bars of cha-

cha beat that were splintered into "I Left My Heart in San
Francisco," shook her head admiringly.

"A very warm person," Everett said. "Of course now I look
after Mother's portfolio."

"Portfolio?"

"Her stock market investments."

"So that's what you meant, help her!" Michele smiled, letting her charming, slightly buck, very white front teeth rest
for a moment on her full lower lip.

"I told you I charted stocks."

"Ohhh. . . ."

"How did you think I helped, you little nut? Held her knitting
wool while she wound it?"

"Oh, Everett!" Michele giggled. "You're too much."

Everett Sutherland's fleshy face took on a pleased grin.

She wondered if he knew she was married. Hadn't Leigh
told him? Could he have missed the plain gold ring glinting
on the soft hand resting on his white dinner jacket? *She* had
noticed *he* wasn't wearing a wedding ring. But of course ring-
lessness wasn't proof positive in a man, was it? Still, Michele's
every feminine instinct told her this was a bachelor. For some
reason the delightful vision of a mile-long rack of new dresses,
all hers, drifted into her mind, and Michele let the inner smile
it brought reach her lips. For the first time she stopped worrying
about keeping her shell pink in perfect condition. What was a
mere forty-nine fifty when you owned a mile of new dresses?
She didn't realize she'd moved closer to Everett Sutherland,
her breasts resting against his dinner jacket, until she felt the
large, hairless hand tense on her back.

"What does it mean?" she asked. "Charting stocks, Everett?"

"It's technical."

"I want to know." She smiled. "The stock market fascinates
me."

The group who'd met at the Gillieses was present and accounted for, Dorot thought, as she and Mr. Sutherland fox-
trotted past York, leaning against a tent pole listening to Clay.
All, that is, with the exception of Ruth Abby Heim. Leigh had
gotten very close with Ruth Abby this past year (friends who
drop acid together stay friends together?) and had asked Ruth
Abby to be a bridesmaid, but Ruth Abby had said no thank
you, religious ritual turned her off, and she hadn't even come

down for the wedding, staying in that Berkeley hippie kibbutz of hers.

Dorot, attempting to keep time with Mr. Sutherland's old-fashioned dancing, peered around. She didn't see Marshall Mosgrove. Marshall was her date. And he'd disappeared. So had Stryker, but Stryker doubtless was someplace with *his* date, a vacuous blonde from that idiot farm, Pasadena Junior College. Where could Marshall be?

It wasn't like him to neglect a social obligation.

2

The Sutherlands' back yard was cool, fragrant with the night scents of damp earth and growing plants. Marshall Mosgrove and Stryker Halvorsen stood a full ten feet apart. They were as far from the blaring tent as possible, in the tree-surgeon-tended grove that hid the back wall.

Stryker caught Marshall's cigarettes.

"Thanks," he said.

"Matches?" Marshall asked.

"Please."

Marshall tossed.

"Thanks," Stryker said again.

"You're welcome."

Stryker, gauging Marshall with the slit-eyed, nervous respect a National League pitcher might give Maury Wills on first base, lit his cigarette. Although both were ushers and there had been much prenuptial festivity, this was the first time Stryker had permitted himself to be alone with Marshall. He had not spoken to him. Stryker had never talked about (or even admitted) Marshall's behavior at Doheny, but obviously the memory had stuck.

Marshall smoked his own cigarette. Enough time had elapsed so he could accept in a rational manner what had happened; in each and every one of us is born an inclination toward both sexes, and that storm-ridden day he and Stryker had shared a terrible tension that had demanded release, so during the night

Marshall's fag had found a subconscious escape hatch.

It was a dream that every man, deny it as he may, experiences at some time or other.

Marshall's perspective hadn't always been this cool. Especially since that wet dream starring Stryker Halvorsen had nightly reruns. Marshall, to put it mildly, had been plenty shook. And with all of today's relaxations on old tabus, he knew a million snickering jokes but amazingly few facts.

So the month before he started Stanford he gave over to intensive study, going at it in his usual grinding way, buying books, a volume here, a paperback there, at bookstores in distant parts of the city. No use courting trouble. He noted how much paperback literature there was. Obviously the homosexual was a subject of widespread current interest. He hid his purchases in his new leather suitcase, a graduation gift, locking it from his grandmother and the prying green eyes of Lois. From his reading he learned about the universal tendency to homosexuality; the latent queer's always there and it's only a matter of how big he grows. Some civilizations foster the growth. Greeks routinely took lovers from comrades at arms and so did patrician Romans—the noblest of them all was nicknamed the Queen of Bithynia long before he crossed the Rubicon. Arabs, Florentines, the fierce Samurai preferred men to women. Warriors all, brave fighters. So thinking of the Doheny episode in the context of battle fatigue—and after the storm and Stryker's danger was there any other way to think of it?—nothing abnormal emerged. As a matter of interest, in the aforementioned civilizations most men would have considered Marshall queer to be so obsessed with worry.

True.

But

not in ours.

Kinsey might aver that fifty percent of American males have engaged in some sort of homosexual activity, and this may (or may not) be true, but this percentage keeps its activity well hidden. It has to. Marshall knew, as did every Los Angeles boy over the age of seven, that the LAPD spends tremendous effort, time and monies in its attempt to box fruitcake. In this current age of supposed sexual freedom, Los Angeles fags are repressed, suppressed and more harassed than Negroes, Mexicans, Indians, juveys and junkies put together.

Marshall, struggling to return his heavy suitcase to the closet shelf, reflected that even if he had discovered in himself definite homosexual tendencies, he would have fought these tendencies with every ounce of his strength. Hadn't he served his time as Wetpants?

The night before he left for Stanford he drove to the top of the Sepulveda Pass and threw the books, one at a time, down toward the San Fernando Valley, then drove home singing "Itsy Bitsy Teenie Weenie Yellow Polka Dot Bikini" as loud as he could, breaking into laughter twice as he thought of a hiker or a surveyor coming across the moldering remains of his specialized library.

Stryker rubbed out his cigarette on the curving jacaranda trunk, and Marshall again tossed him cigarettes and matches.

"How's the baseball?" Marshall asked.

"O.K."

"Any offers?"

"Angels."

"Interesting?"

"Bonus."

"What's holding you back?"

"School."

"New breed of ballplayers. College men." Marshall was sweating under his white usher's dinner jacket. They'd been friends, hadn't they? Nothing had "happened," had it? Why was Stryker playing it so rough? "Great-looking girl you're with."

"Patty. Yeah. Great in the sack, too." Stryker spoke aggressively.

"Why not marry her?"

"Patty?"

"Uh huh."

"What the hell for?"

"Draft exemption."

"Exemption?"

"Then you could quit college," Marshall explained. "Join the Angels."

"I *want* to finish. Jeez, I want a crack at the astronaut program."

"Zoom. *Ffffttttt*. Blast off. The new frontier and all that jazz?"

A few of Stryker's muscles relaxed and he jumped to attention and with the large hand holding his lighted cigarette whipped a mock salute. "Flash Halvorsen at your service!"

They both laughed.

"Hey, Mosgrove. You lavaliered to Dorot?"

"Planning it, planning it," Marshall lied. The payment for his lie: Stryker relaxed completely. The truth was Dorot frightened Marshall: she was too sure of herself; her well-shaped mouth clattered like a computer as she chewed out facts. Studying demanded his time, but if he'd had leisure for women, he would've selected a gentler sort, like the bride. He went on, "Not lavaliered. I'm a fraternity man. She'll get my pin—you know how it is."

Stryker gave a small lascivious chuckle that said, *You do?*

And Marshall's answering chuckle prevaricated, *Sure.*

Stryker's grin of relief shone in the darkness. "And Ken and Leigh're getting legal. Hey, Mosgrove, you for or against?"

"Me? Why?"

"Patty's against. On principle, she says." Stryker sounded worried.

"Anything that doesn't hurt another person is fine with me." The basic tenet, the Allah is One God, of his age popped easily into Marshall's mouth.

Music stopped. Voices roared over them.

Marshall asked, "How's your chance of getting in the space program?"

"Pretty slim."

"I'll keep a good thought."

"Jeez, keep a headful while you're at it."

And laughing companionably, they started across damp grass to the kitchen door where a uniformed caterers' helper in stockinged feet smoked.

"Listen, after this is over," Marshall said, not looking at Stryker, "what say you and me and Dorot go to Hamburger Hamlet and—"

"Patty mightn't want—"

"Sure she will. She can sit and look gorgeous while we three California alums reminisce."

In the long ensuing pause Marshall thought, *Damn Doheny,* over and over. *Damn Doheny.*

At last Stryker said, "Fine."

Marshall's smile was total reflex, pure and genuine. He held out his hand.

They had reached the back door and the cateress blew a smoke ring, pretending not to watch. Marshall's hand felt cold and strange as if he'd thrust it into a vacuum. Stryker shifted his weight uncertainly. In his twenty years, Marshall guessed,

Stryker Halvorsen never yet had ignored an outstretched hand. Stryker's mouth moved uncertainly; then he took Marshall's hand. Stryker's palm was calloused, his grip firm. And very brief.

"Better get back." Marshall smiled. "Maybe the groom needs his men's assistance."

"Didn't look like it."

They both laughed.

At Hamburger Hamlet the three fellow alums reminded one another about the good old days at good old California while Patty maintained her spectacular smile. As they exited laughing, Marshall said, "I haven't had such fun in years. Listen, why don't the four of us take in a Dodger game tomorrow night? Koufax is pitching."

Koufax fanned sixteen, winning one to nothing.

A couple of nights later they saw Drysdale lose one to nothing on an error, a heartbreaker. Saturday night, Ladies' Night, mighty mouse Maury Wills stole three, but the home town lost again, two to five. The Dodgers departed in their jet for a road trip. Marshall suggested they take in the Angels. After all, hadn't the Angels offered old Stryker a bonus? Patty vetoed: "It's bad enough having to sit through the Dodgers. Nobody goes to the Angels," was the way she put it. Patty might be gorgeous, but she never let you forget she'd been a Rose Parade Princess and she wore contacts which gave her blue eyes a strange, inhuman glitter. Marshall smiled down at her and suggested the four of them have a beach party at Playa del Rey.

"You can have a fire there," he said.

"You can anyplace"—Stryker.

"Not legally"—Marshall.

"Aren't you the law-abiding one!" Patty cried.

Marshall set about planning ways to be with his friend Stryker minus Patty.

Stryker's athletic scholarship paid his tuition at USC and that was all. To save money he slept on a rollaway in the stuffy living room of his mother's small Westwood apartment, commuting to school on his Honda. So he certainly needed the money he earned at various summer jobs. Yet last August and this August again he had signed up to counsel gratis at Happy

Valley, a pine-shaded camp run with funds from Vista. Catering to underprivileged boys between the ages of eight and fourteen, Happy Valley was situated at the six-thousand-foot level in the San Bernardino Mountains a mile or so north of Lake Arrowhead. Marshall knew that Stryker worked there in JFK's spirit of doing for his country, although Stryker, whenever the subject came up, always grinned and said easily, "How else can I swing a free vacation?"

"What's the best way to get into the program?" asked Marshall.

"You, personally?" Stryker asked.

"I'd like to help out if I can."

Stryker was silent.

"I'm a pretty fair camper." Marshall gave an apprehensive laugh.

Stryker said, "I'll ask old Edwards if he needs anyone."

Dr. Edwards did need someone. So the following week Marshall sat in a drab second-floor office near UCLA pondering which multiple-choice answer would best prove him adequate to give an August of his life for his country.

3

The Arrowhead air was so clear and fragrant that it almost hurt your lungs to breathe. The air was sweetly warm except in the shade of the pines; there it was fresh and sharp like the first bite of an astrakhan apple. The air was so enervating that at first all you wanted to do was lie on your narrow cot gasping purity into your smog-frayed lungs, but the air, after a couple of days, began to exhilarate and then you wanted to race on slick pine needles and act like a fool; you wanted to dive into icy blue water and climb tall trees; you ate the hotcakes and oatmeal and creamed chipped beef on your divided metal plate, then went back for seconds.

Marshall was in charge of a group of eleven-year-olds called the Bearcats because of the cartoon of a bearcat etched over their cabin door. After vomiting along every curve of Rim of the World Highway, the ten Bearcats cried until they fell asleep. Each wet his bed. Two rows of five cots to be changed, ten thin mattress pads to be draped over rough-hewn porch railings. Then, under the effect of salubrious air they came to life. Enuresis ended. They swore lustily, lied mightily, cheated and happily stole from Camp Happy Valley, from one another and from Marshall.

Never in Marshall's protected cocoon of middle-class life had he come across those the current government labeled underprivileged. What a revelation! There wasn't one of his ten boys who didn't have a social worker, a car, a television set. There wasn't one of them who could remember meeting the man who fathered him. To make up for this lack there was a superfluity of grannies and aunties and, in most cases, a mama: These ladies were Supreme Authorities: "My granny, she say it good for you to stay up till two," and, "My mama, she rub lard and chili pepper in my chest when I get a balls-on cold like this'n," and, "Sure they's hants. My Granny, she die sitting on the stool and she stay there for three days until she stink worser'n shit. Mama say now she's a hant."

Marshall's ten boys used more outright obscenity than Marshall, liberated and tolerant member of the Pepsi generation, had believed possible. Marshall always thought of his boys the same way his government did, en masse, not as individuals. Only one, Henry Lee Ward, stuck out like a sore brown thumb. Henry Lee started ninety percent of the fights, for he was the proud ungenerous owner of a transistor that he kept blaring all the time, jamming clear mountain air with static-laden Motown.

Henry Lee refused to listen to Marshall's orders. "I got my radio on, so I didn't hear you, you ofay mother, you," Henry Lee would state. He disliked Marshall. So did all of the Bearcats.

Marshall returned the compliment heartily.

This mutual ill will didn't prevent Marshall from performing a conscientious job. He always had enjoyed the atmosphere of Spartan masculine living, and his knowledge of mountain lore was complete from Eagle Scout days. Marshall kept his Bearcats busy all day. They slept long before Lights Out.

At the first week's Counselor's Confab, Dr. Edwards said, "Congrats to Mosgrove. He runs the tightest cabin in Happy Valley. Don't be surprised if the Bearcats win the Best Tepee Award."

Dr. Edwards paced in front of the stone hearth, repeating his rules over and over.

"Again I remind you," he said, "never, never rely on what a boy tells you. Check for yourself. I'll be checking you to make sure that you check."

Someone groaned.

Dr. Edwards saw who it was. "Raskin," he snapped. "You, I'll check with especial care. These boys, you have to remember, have been raised to survive against authority. We represent authority. Therefore it is only natural that they will try to evade us. And consider my—*our*—position. If something should happen to a single boy the entire program will be jeopardized. The responsibility for President Kennedy's program rests on us."

"Jeez, it's really flying," Stryker whispered to Marshall. They sat side by side on the sagging couch.

Dr. Edwards ignored the whisper. He squared his plump shoulders under red plaid. "I insist that you know where each of your boys is at every minute."

"But Edwards," said the counselor called Raskin, a careless, hirsute, brilliant and very typical Berkeley student, "it's impossible."

"Is it?"

"Flatly impossible."

"Mosgrove runs a tight cabin. Tell us, Mosgrove, do you find it impossible to know where each of the Bearcats is?"

"No, sir." Marshall rose from the couch.

"How do you manage?"

"Every night I work out a schedule for the following day. The boys are busy the entire time. With me."

"Brown nose," someone whispered.

Dr. Edwards maintained professorial deafness to dissent. He gave one of his rare smiles. "You see, Raskin? Your problem is a simple lack of organization." He paused in the precise center of the knotty pine room. "Keep your boys busy. Check, check, check. Know where every boy is at every moment. He might be at the lake and I don't have to remind you of the temptation provided by expensive boats. At Arrowhead there have been several cases of children drowning. Do I make myself clear?"

Every morning between ten and twelve was free time; the boys could choose their activity. Marshall Mosgrove's assignment was lifeguarding the long unheated pool. He would sit on the high wooden platform, a red cap blazoned *Camp Happy Valley* protecting his crew cut from the intense mountain sun. Below, in the pool, churning, splashing, ducking, farting, peeing and cursing boys.

It was boring as all hell.

His sole relief came from the fact that the platform gave him a vantage point over the baseball diamond. Stryker, wearing his Happy Valley cap, would squat on the mound, making himself approximately the same height as a small brown boy. "See, Carlos?" Stryker would say—it never ceased to amaze Marshall that Stryker, the world's worst student, could keep clear the name of each of the one hundred and six boys at the camp. "Take the ball between your thumb and first two fingers. Good. Very good. Now get that weight back on the left foot: Pause. Now . . . throw!"

Carlos would gaze fiercely, throw weakly, and the ball would dribble off toward third—the field slanted sharply in that direction. The catcher, cursing loudly, would shag it and Carlos would whine, "One more time, Stryker man, show me one more time?"

Stryker, in graceful slow motion, would hurl.

One of the counselors smuggled in a couple of cases of Lucky Lager. After Dr. Edwards checked Lights Out, the smuggler threw a beer bust behind the Mountain Lions' cabin. A moonless night, huge stars seemed tethered to shadowy pine branches and in the dark it was impossible to see who was talking. Voices came, disembodied, out of chill, piny air, and by the time you had one placed someone else was speaking. After a couple of bottles of beer apiece, the subject of the swimming pool came up.

"Think a guy could dive from the observation tower?"

"Hell no!"

"Water's too shallow."

"It's maybe four feet from the edge of the pool," Marshall pointed out. "Impossible."

"Bet?"

"How much?" rumbled a deep voice.

"Five says it can't be done."

"And five says it can."

"Who'll prove the bet?"

"Yeah, who's going to try?"

An owl hooted: *Whoooo* . . . and laughter rose easily from beer-lubricated throats.

"One more damn good bet gone to waste."

"What a bunch of chickenshits."

"I can dive pretty good," a voice said. Immediately Marshall recognized Stryker.

"Like hell you can!"

"Who says?"

"Me. Marshall Mosgrove."

"Show me the way to the poo-ool," Stryker sang. "I'm tight and I want to get wet."

"You can't!" Marshall sobered completely. "Jesus, Stryker, you can't."

"Hey, Mosgrove, you Halvorsen's keeper?"

"He needs one. That water's too damn shallow!" said a resonant voice. Raskin? Yes, Raskin. Oh, that wonderful, sensible, hairy Jew Raskin on Marshall's side.

But of course there was no stopping Stryker. In his veins ran the blood of berserk Norsemen and also a quart or more of Lucky Lager. Marshall argued earnestly as they stumbled in slippery pine needles down to the pool area; he argued while, along with everyone else, he scaled the wire fence. He grabbed hold of someone he thought was Stryker. "You can't!" he cried. But it turned out to be Flynn. "Hey, Mosgrove, I never knew you cared," falsettoed Flynn.

By the time they crowded around the observation tower, several more disembodied voices lost their slurring good humor. "Forget it, Halvorsen." "Bet's off." "You'll crack open your damn skull, for God's sake!"

"No lights," Stryker said, starting up the ladder. "Edwards'll see."

"You goddam drunken *goyische koppe!*" Raskin hissed. "You schmuck. You haven't even taken off your clothes. For the love of God, Halvorsen, forget it!"

The sluff of Stryker's bare feet on wood slats faded upward. He called softly, "Someone light a match. I need to see the edge of the pool."

"Please, Stryker, please come back down." Marshall flung himself against the rough wooden framing. *"Come down."*

And at the same moment someone called drunkenly, "Dive, you son of a bitch, dive."

A match flared.

There was silence. Utter, complete silence. In the darkness Marshall saw a shadow arc, hang for a long eternity, then, almost without a splash, enter the water.

Stryker surfaced. "Jeez, it's cold."

Marshall's pent-up breath escaped with a sob. They had to hurry back to their cabins; Dr. Edwards checked at midnight.

Marshall lay on the beach, warmed by the sun, content. Soon, though, cold air chilled his flesh. His heart slowed. In his familiar nightmare everyone had deserted him, everyone was escaping up the brown palisades while a tidal wave, implacable and awesome, rolled forward to destroy him. He couldn't move; he sprawled on icy sand utterly deserted, utterly helpless, utterly alone. Was there nobody to save him from the engulfing waters? *Don't look for brave saviors, don't.* . . . But the nightmare changed to the dream, moving to its predestined conclusion that crushed him with guilt yet raised him to moist ecstasy.

"Stryker!" he cried, welcoming the ultimate moment.

Well, he thought, rolling over on the bed to a dry spot, punching the hard pillow supplied by Camp Happy Valley, it was another of those dreams brought on by stress. Of course sometimes the dreams weren't brought on by stress, they simply occurred, and those times Marshall grew desperate. This time, though, God was in His heaven, there was excellent reason for stress and all was straight in Marshall's world. Stryker Halvorsen was his friend, a friend, nothing more.

"Henry Lee still giving you a rough time?" Stryker asked.

"He's too damn smart," Marshall replied, "that's his problem."

Marshall had invited Stryker over for a pre-sack smoke, and together they sat on the sagging wood steps of the Bearcats' cabin. Two orange circles glowed in the dark.

"Kids here are all smart," Marshall added.

"It's rough for them. Jeez, never having a chance!"

Inwardly Marshall disagreed. He had a strong aversion to poor people. Poverty he considered to be on the same level with alcoholism; maybe both *were* a disease, but, it seemed to Marshall, ones that could be cured by personal effort. He knew, of course, that as a true bleeding heart of his decade he should pity pop-eyed Henry Lee for being black, for living with his black mama and auntie in a rented Watts shack. Therefore, slowly zipping his nylon quilted jacket, he said, "The courts ought to do more about providing equal education. Those kids ought to be bused out of their district. Henry Lee, he's a talent. You know his radio?"

"Do I know his radio? Man, he never puts the damn thing down." Stryker chuckled. "First kid I ever saw shag balls like Snoopy, with his mouth."

"He's afraid it'll get stolen."

"He's damn right."

"He can imitate every deejay on KRLA," stated Marshall Mosgrove, the world's foremost authority on Henry Lee Ward.

"No kidding?"

"You never heard him?"

"Nope."

"You should."

"Jeez, Marshall, he's really a nice little kid."

"Really nice," Marshall lied and lit a fresh cigarette. Match light gilded Stryker's face. Stryker stared up at the starry sky and nail-paring new moon. Marshall stared at Stryker.

"Someday . . ." Stryker sighed and fell silent.

"Someday what?"

"I'll really live."

"Live?"

"Free."

"Where free?"

Stryker nodded upward.

"Not so free in those space capsules," Marshall said.

"Oh, I know I'll be canned Spam. But jeez, it's never been explored."

"Free because you'll be first?" Marshall puzzled.

"Right."

Marshall thought as he inhaled. "Cortez and Columbus you mean, they were free in a new world?"

Stryker nodded.

And the two of them stared up at the cold, glittering sky. On the rim of a medium-size galaxy, on one of the smaller planets of an unimportant solar system, sat two minute beings, one dreaming of conquering the infinite, the other experiencing that rare and peculiar wonder, human friendship. Marshall tried to capture the warmth aching under his quilted nylon jacket.

• • •

Henry Lee Ward, his transistor blaring static, chunked stones down the embankment, aiming at the weedy water around a derelict dock.

"Stryker, man"—he turned to pine shade where Stryker and Marshall relaxed after a noon cookout—"how much you think that big fucker out there cost?" He pointed at a tremendous Chris Craft carving a white line across the blue lake.

A squirrel paused on a high branch, staring gravely down. Stryker gave the matter his full consideration. "A hundred thou," he said.

"It the Herk-you-leese," Henry Lee said.

"How'd you know?" Stryker asked.

"Dock's over there."

Across from them out of the steep mountainside jutted a huge stone summer place with seven chimneys. The house belonged to an ancient Greek, and rumor said he'd come to California at the turn of the century with fifty cents in his pocket and gone into oil and now was worth so many millions nobody could count them. Henry Lee pointed to the dock. A sailboat and a smaller motorboat were tied up. In front of a smart blue canvas cabana two black-haired, bikinied girls were sunbathing. The first girls they'd seen in over two weeks.

Glancing meaningfully at Marshall, Stryker said, "Tend the Cougars for me."

"S'against the rules."

"Tend."

"Dr. Edwards'll be sure to drop in and—"

But Stryker had already skinned easily down the almost perpendicular embankment, pulling off his torn sweat shirt on the way, slowing on the rotted dock to kick aside his Keds. He took a magnificent running dive and cleared the underwater weeds.

Soon a faraway dripping Stryker hauled himself up the steps of the luxurious dock. Both girls sat up and Marshall watched as Stryker pointed toward the Bearcats and Cougars.

Soon Stryker was borne back across the lake in the smaller Chris Craft. Carrying his Keds and sweat shirt up the incline, he stretched out on pine needles to let his Bermudas dry. "They'll pick us up here at eleven," he said quietly so the boys couldn't hear.

"We can't."

"Why the hell not?"

"Dr. Edwards checks the cabins and—"

"You've got to be kidding!"

"There's too much risk," Marshall said. "He could kick us out for leaving the boys alone. We'd have black marks."

"Great-looking girls throwing it at us and, jeez, you worry about black marks!" Stryker turned abruptly away.

Marshall lied earnestly. "Dorot and I're serious."

"Hell, two serious weeks and cold showers've quit doing me any good." Stryker rolled over. "Come, don't come."

At ten fifty they were at the half-sinking dock. A cloudy night, the half moon showed as a ghostly white semicircle, then was gone. The *Hercules*, lights blazing, sped across still water.

"Helen, Leda." Stryker broad-jumped into the boat. "This is my old buddy, Marshall Mosgrove."

The roar of expensive motor drowned out replies.

At the dock one girl pulled chaise pads from a coffin-shaped trunk, another opened a low refrigerator. *"Fix,"* she said. "Around here even the beer's Greek." She filled four icy tankards.

In dim yellow dock lights the girls talked. Helen and Leda were cousins staying with their Midas-touch grandfather and all the rumors about him, good and bad, the girls said, were true. Beer tankards emptied. "Want another?" asked one of the girls.

Stryker shook his head, "Thanks, no. But how's about showing me around?"

They departed to another finger of the dock. Which girl Stryker took Marshall didn't know. At least not at the time— it would take him three years to sort out Helen from Leda. But whichever, she and Stryker reclined, Stryker with his back to Marshall, her hands showing white against Stryker's dark sweat shirt, pale hands traveling up and down Stryker's torso. Marshall, wincing, looked away.

He and his girl, whichever she was, drank another beer. She told him more of her grandfather, who owned three lobbyists in Sacramento and one in Washington.

Dock lights painted gold reflection on dark ripples, drifts of music, "Days of Wine and Roses," floated across the water, and Marshall shifted in his neat stay-press Ivy Leagues, more frantic with every minute. Soon he would be called on. Many are called, many are chosen. Few fail. Marshall Mosgrove would fail; he knew he would fail. For some reason he remembered those cruddy girls who'd camped at Doheny. Other crazy thoughts crashed through his round skull. He wouldn't be able to get a hard on. A guy he'd heard of at Stanford had been so nervous he'd gotten it in the wrong hole and the girl'd needed stitches. What if he got a hard on but couldn't perform? How could he perform? When this girl disregarded every masculine prerogative to initiate the proceedings? The girl—no, she was a woman, a moment ago she'd admitted to being twenty-four—touched his arm to make a point. He flinched. Talking on, she clasped her hands around her raised thighs. She smelled, or so it seemed to Marshall, of antiseptic birth-control lubricants.

"Well?" she asked.

He realized she'd stopped talking.

"Well what?" he asked.

"For a beginning, how goes it with the underprivileged?"

"It's a good cause," he said defensively.

"I'm not a believer in good causes."

"Neither am I," Marshall blurted. Despite his fear, speaking the truth relieved him. And it came to him that safety lay in conversation. "And to be absolutely candid," he went on, "I think most of us're up here because it's the sort of thing mass media tells us everyone our age is doing."

"The social conscience of the sixties?"

"Exactly. No more dropping out into easy executive jobs and outer suburbia for us. We're dues-paying members." He paused, watching a boat streak lights across the lake. "Except Stryker. He's a really nice guy. Honest. Straightforward. He does it . . . well, because he really believes in it." Marshall coughed. "He's involved."

She rose, moving to sit cross-legged near Marshall. She traced her fingertips down his lower arm. The hair rose, but this time he managed not to flinch. Her touch was light, not unpleasant, not pleasant. The caress of her fingertips meant no more to him than cool mountain air. What she wanted . . . impossible. . . . Impossible.

"I have a girl," he burst out.

"Oh?"

"We're engaged."

She moved closer, still smiling, letting her legs dangle over the dock. Her beer-scented breath warmed his cheek, her bare leg warmed his leg. He clutched his tankard in front of his chest, then, realizing the humor of his gesture, laughed too loudly.

"I don't want—I can't be . . . I—disloyal to her."

"Stop worrying," she whispered. "I know all about you."

She did? What was there to know? Dark water lapped under the expensive dock and Marshall's poor brain whirled like a terrified Arrowhead squirrel trapped in a cage. What did she know? Certainly nothing concrete. But could she somehow divine his strange, unnatural, guilt-invoking dreams? Or how he felt about Stryker? Or his fears? Could she, whispering sybil she, read his mind?

Half rising, with a swift motion as if shedding a second skin under her loose dress, she wriggled out of her pants, throwing aside the black lace wisp. She slithered down beside him, putting her arms around him. She hadn't taken off her broad-strapped sandals.

She murmured. Words his brain refused to understand.

He shut his eyes, succumbing. In God and her skill he trusted.

It was her show all the way. She manipulated him to erection; she sank down on him, rising and descending as if she were posting on an English saddle, and once when she rose too high and they were momentarily separated her hands were wildly busy. He, acquiescent, breathed more and more heavily. Yet when it was over and he lay depleted, she kissing his neck, Marshall admitted it had been nothing more than flesh rubbing flesh. Nothing to be afraid of—he could do it again. Easily. That is, if he wanted to. But why would he? A man and a woman together. Flesh rubbing flesh.

This was what all the shouting was about?

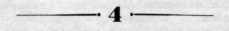

Two nights later a storm broke. Menacing white lightning zipped around peaks; there was an awesomely short pause; thunder cracked. For ten minutes lightning and thunder alternated wildly, a storm so monumental it seemed the black sky was being torn apart to let some monstrous creature be born of the night. Several huge mountain raindrops splashed on cabin roofs, increasing until a torrent pelted.

Marshall slammed into the Cougars' cabin. He ran between double rows of cots to the bed where Stryker slept.

"Stryker!" Marshall whispered, urgent, shaking a bare, hard shoulder. *"Stryker."*

Stryker mumbled wordlessly.

"Wake up!"

"Mosgrove?"

"Henry Lee, he's missing!"

Lightning blazed in the cabin and Stryker blinked. "Jeez, what a storm—what'd you say?"

"Henry Lee, he's gone!"

"Gone?"

"Not in his bed."

"In someone else's? The storm—"

"No! I *checked*." Desperation rose in Marshall's voice.

Stryker threw back his blanket and in almost the same motion pulled jeans over his jockey shorts.

"He's probably in the head," Stryker said through his torn sweat shirt.

"The head?"

"Storm caught him in there and he's scared crapless."

They raced through the downpour to search the long cabin. Urine-odored stalls were empty.

"The commissary?" Marshall wavered.

They ran again. They shone flashlights through streaming windows of the locked commissary. Empty.

"Where the hell can he be?" Stryker asked. Rain plastered his hair like pale ribbons to his dripping forehead.

"The lake?" Marshall asked.

"On a night like this?"

"We've looked every place else."

"The lake then."

"But he's afraid of hants," Marshall said, "I mean ghosts."

"Not the lake."

"Oh, God! Must be the lake. Oh, God! Stryker, what if the little bastard's gone and drowned himself?" Marshall sobbed.

"If you don't keep a cool tool, man"—Stryker bent his wet face to Marshall—"we'll never find him."

"The lake."

They left the cluster of cabins that was Camp Happy Valley. Smells of electricity and rain-drenched trees filled the air. The watery blackness was immense, huge, lonely, terrifying. Yet, far more terrifying, the lightning that blazed so close Marshall was positive tall pines must split to fall blazing on him. Every nerve in him ached to turn back; he wanted to bury himself in his bed. Yet, following Stryker, he forced himself into the storm, slipping and falling in rain-slick pine needles and mud. His poor overworked heart would surely burst. As they raced down the last lap, Stryker's flash beam caught a huddled shape on the dock.

"Henry Lee!" Marshall shouted at the top of his lungs. *"Henry Lee!"*

The child, drenched pajamas clinging, head cradled in thin arms, crouched on the edge of the dock.

As they reached him, Henry Lee managed to gasp between shivering, terrified sobs that he was looking for his transistor; it hadn't been in the cabin, it hadn't been no fucking place 'round, so he figured he must of left it here, but it wasn't here, wasn't here. Stryker raised the hysterical boy astride his shoulders and started back to camp, Marshall trotting behind. From time to time Marshall's throat emitted small animal whimpers.

In the cabin, behind the louvered screen that was meant to give Marshall all the privacy he, a counselor, needed, Stryker undressed Henry Lee. The boy's penis was shriveled to a dark pimple; great goose bumps rose on black skin. He submitted to Stryker's rough-gentle toweling—like all the campers, Henry Lee idolized Stryker Halvorsen. Marshall changed his mud-thick clothes. Stryker carried Henry Lee to his cot, which happened to be first on the other side of the screen. Marshall moved the screen and the two of them sat side by side on Marshall's bed watching like anxious parents until the boy's teeth stopped chattering. He slept.

"Jesus." Marshall dropped his face in his hands. "What if something'd happened?"

"He's fine," Stryker reassured.

"It would've been my fault."

"I better get back to the Cougars."

"What if he's got pneumonia?"

"Calm yourself, man."

"What if he wakes up?"

"Jeez, Marsh—"

"What if he wakes up and finds only me here?"

"He'll go back to sleep."

"He'll start bawling. Stryker, you know he doesn't like me."

"You're crazy!"

"Listen, I'll sit on his bed, you sleep on mine." Marshall sobbed. "He hates me! *Stay.*"

"O.K., O.K." Stryker capitulated. "Soon as I've changed into dry stuff."

"Borrow mine. Listen, you sack down. Sleep. I'm going to sit up and watch. Make sure he's not sick or something."

Stryker stripped down to his shorts, which he insisted were dry, immediately diving under Marshall's blankets. Marshall sat on the end of Henry Lee's cot watching the boy sleep. What a close call! If anything had happened to Henry Lee, wouldn't it have been a black mark that could've never been erased? A black mark that would have stopped him from getting into Stanford Law, stopped his future cold? How close he'd come to disaster. He, of all people, who must do everything correctly. Yet, oddly enough, despite these thoughts, no retroactive panic churned in him. With his friend Stryker so near, Marshall was completely calm, as his friend Stryker would say.

Stryker slept, one hand covering his forehead, the other buried under blankets. His bold features were relaxed, making him look like a child despite the crisp yellow chest hairs curling over the top of khaki blankets. Here was Stryker sleeping, long, lean, magnificent and very close. Yet Marshall felt no desire. How strange. No desire at all. Only a great, over-whelming sense of gratitude. Stryker had saved him. And now in the feeble light of a single naked low-wattage bulb hanging over the bed, Stryker slept while Marshall kept watch. They were two soldiers, two battle-scarred comrades.

Rain fell lightly now. Clean scents of rain-washed mountain came through open screening. One of the boys moaned, tossing. Moaned again. Marshall clipped a sheet of notebook paper over the bulb, dimming the light. The boy quieted.

Marshall resumed his watch, this time sitting on his own bed. He yawned, rubbing his eyes, resting his weary crew-cut head on the bed. It was uncomfortable doubled up, and he stretched on the hard mattress, taking great care not to touch Stryker, staring at the slow breathing of Henry Lee until he, too, drowsed.

He woke with a start.

He didn't know what time it was or where he was. Maybe in a dream. It took him several seconds to realize this was no dream. He was awake.

Stryker was stroking his back. Marshall, thinking Stryker asleep, pulled away. Stryker, groaning wordlessly, again pulled him close, clasping him spoon style to his strong body. Marshall was intensely aware of Stryker's odors, of Stryker's male leanness, of Stryker's hand now tracing the line of Marshall's chest. Marshall began to tremble. He didn't dare question the miracle that Stryker wanted him. Yet at the same time he wanted to cry out *stop, stop,* for he greatly feared the implications. It was one thing to use books and statistics to rationalize that everyone shared your most secret desire. Quite another to act it out. Would this be proof positive he was a homosexual? But Stryker held and caressed him. And he was helpless to prevent his body from reacting, his need was too vast, he'd loved (yes, loved, he admitted it now) Stryker for too long. Marshall pushed aside thin, coarse camp blankets. Stryker, curving one thigh over Marshall, with a movement so slow that it drove Marshall wild, let his strong, calloused hand explore under Marshall's clothes.

Neither spoke.

Marshall rolled over and Stryker's breath trembled on his face. They embraced, entangled, hands caressing the other's unfamiliar yet far too familiar sex, and Marshall briefly questioned what had brought them to this primitive act of love. He shoved the question away, for Stryker's hand had grown more demanding. Clothes were pushed aside. The excitement in Marshall swelled to unbearable proportions. So different, this, from the mechanical Helen-Leda episode. With a sudden rough movement Stryker turned him onto his stomach and Marshall forgot the sounds of ten sleeping boys, forgot the mountain rain, the world, forgot everything in his wild, pulsing joy.

Four, at the most five minutes from his waking to this final, triumphant spasm. Natural. This was natural. Didn't the silence between them, the ease, the simplicity, the brevity make it natural?

He fell back listening to his own ragged breath coming from a long distance. He was utterly at peace. Stryker got out of bed, but Marshall kept his eyes shut, for he wished to retain the dreamlike perfection. With warm, glowing ears Marshall listened as Stryker left the cabin; then he fell into a sleep so profound that it seemed as if the clock jumped into morning.

• • •

After breakfast Henry Lee found his transistor under Snake Estrada's mattress. He punched Snake in the nose. Marshall was holding a chunk of ice to a bleeding brown nostril when he received the message that Dr. Edwards had invited him to lunch. It was the Head Counselor's routine to ask counselors to his cabin for a pep talk, so there was nothing to fear—except fear itself. Marshall Mosgrove trembled.

Half moons of sweat darkened under Dr. Edwards' red plaid sleeves. They ate their salad, colorless slaw mined with pineapple chunks, in silence. Cook, a pyramid of woman, thick-hipped and shallow-breasted with a small head, waddled around serving sloppy joes. Dr. Edwards waited a full minute after she left.

He set his fork neatly above his sandwich. Cracked his knuckles. "Mosgrove," he said, "I wonder if you realize the responsibility of running a place like Happy Valley?"

"I certainly do, Dr. Edwards."

"Tremendous. . . . All these young boys entrusted to my care."

"Yes, sir."

"Therefore if anything comes up that's morally the least questionable, I have a definite obligation to track it down."

The girls? Marshall thought. *The girls?*

"You understand that, don't you?" Dr. Edwards was saying.

"Of course, sir."

"And if only Halvorsen were involved and another man, I would have simply done my duty. Filed a report. Sent them both home. But you. . . ."

Those bitches! Who needed it? Marshall's body tensed as he waited for the blow to fall.

" . . . you're such a fine, decent young man. No spots on your record."

Henry Lee might've been. But Stryker saved me. "None, Dr. Edwards."

"Mosgrove, it's difficult to put this into words. But the relationship isn't . . . " Dr. Edwards moved his fork a half inch.

"Isn't what, sir?"

"Straight."

Oh, God
God

Last night seemed so natural, so part of his guts, that Marshall had not considered it might be what Dr. Edwards was getting at. *Had he seen anything?* Marshall struggled desperately to put an expression of honest bewilderment on his square-hewn face. He must have succeeded. Dr. Edwards' hand left his fork.

"Stryker Halvorsen isn't normal," he said.

"Sir, I've known him for years. Years. We went to high school together, California." Marshall could hear anxiety slowing his words. "I was president of the student body and Stryker, he—"

"You'll have to take my word for it," Dr. Edwards interrupted.

"But sir, I don't understand what you—"

"I've been watching this very closely."

"I swear. There's nothing—"

"I'm not accusing *you*, Mosgrove, I want you to know that. I have the greatest respect for you," Dr. Edwards said. *He hadn't seen anything.* Marshall's heart beat a little less erratically. Dr. Edwards went on, "I've been watching this and I'm uninvolved by your personal loyalties."

Uninvolved? Marshall's still terrified brain questioned. *What does he mean uninvolved? I've obeyed all his petty rules, so as far as he's concerned I could never be the guilty one. Is that uninvolved?*

"I'm a careful man," Dr. Edwards continued. "I check. I know every move my counselors make. And Halvorsen's been visiting your cabin at night—"

"A lot of us do. Dr. Edwards, we're friends. We've been friends—"

"I respect your loyalty."

Loyalty! Why does he keep repeating that word, loyalty?

"There have been various episodes," Dr. Edwards said.

"Episodes, sir?"

"For example, Halvorsen showing off in front of you. That dive—"

"A bet, sir."

"A classic ploy," Dr. Edwards said. "And the other night you both left—"

"Sir, listen!" Marshall said frantically. Stryker might have initiated the proceedings last night, but Marshall knew with every particle of his body that it was *his* hang-up, not Stryker's. He had to prove them both innocent. "I can ex—"

"You young people tend to think that we adults are 'out of it.' That we don't know what's going on."

"No sir, but Stry—"

"I'll prove it to you tonight at Counselor's Confab." Dr. Edwards picked up his fork. "I don't care to discuss it further."

Marshall forced himself to swallow a mouthful of food. Another. Dr. Edwards discussed three missing pillows that he intended tracking down if it took all week; he had to set an example. *Queeg, pedant, small mind. Pervert. I know you. I've seen your type. You're not honest enough to admit what you are so you wait in those fleabitten nudie movies on Santa Monica Boulevard, hoping another fag'll sit near you so you can jack off at the same time.* Marshall, smiling the earnest, straight-toothed smile that had cost his grandmother eleven hundred and fifty dollars, agreed with Dr. Edwards on the matter of the pillows.

The afternoon was apples, honey, wine. The rain-purified air had an almost unbelievable sweetness. So why did Marshall's throat ache with every breath? He demonstrated square knots to ten bored, bickering Bearcats. "See?" he said. "You put the end under like this." Sixty yards away Stryker and the Cougars enjoyed an enthusiastic batting practice. Stryker never glanced at Marshall; this Marshall knew, for he watched Stryker constantly. The Bearcats tied square knots. Marshall ordered himself to get up and walk across sixty yards of uneven dirt to tell Stryker what was coming off tonight. How could you not walk sixty yards to warn your friend, your only friend? But if Stryker knew what was coming off he'd be able to play it cool, wouldn't he? A blue jay swooped. In the midday warmth Marshall shivered. *If Stryker Halvorsen didn't react, wouldn't Dr. Edwards' suspicions be diverted onto Marshall Mosgrove?*

Snake Estrada held up a tangled rope. "This right?"

"Here," Marshall said, "let me show you again."

No wonder the world loved Marshall Mosgrove not. He didn't deserve to be loved.

Dr. Edwards read the last item on his regulation list of missing items. He stood in front of the hearth, crouching into his polished boots as if he were ready to start a race.

"I won't name names," he said, "but one of the counselors, a man entrusted with the care of boys, *young* boys, has been seen entering another cabin late at night."

The earth stopped turning.

Marshall Mosgrove stopped breathing.

He stared down at his neatly filed fingernails. Then he knew he must look at Stryker. Dr. Edwards expected it of him.

Stryker—strong, handsome features stained with rushing blood, bright blue eyes glassy with shock. Stryker naked and exposed. Every man in the room must understand Stryker's expression. Dr. Edwards glanced at Stryker, then meaningfully around.

Raskin lumbered to his feet.

"Edwards, isn't that a hell of a way to make an accusation?"

"This doesn't concern you, Raskin, and it's not an accusation."

"What else?"

"I merely made an observation."

"So if a guy tries to explain he's automatically guilty?"

"An observation, that's all."

Black hairs stood out on Raskin's clenched fists. "Haven't you heard, Edwards, it's illegal in this country, trial without facing your accuser?"

"Berkeley turns out excellent attorneys."

"Bull!"

"In this case, however, there's no accusation, no punishment. I don't intend making a report. It's merely to let the person involved know that I won't stand for any more of it."

"You can't prove—"

"Raskin, if you don't mind, law school or no law school, I'd rather not make a Supreme Court case out of this."

"Stryker! You can't run." Marshall spoke in a low note of anxiety. "You can't."

Stryker didn't reply. He continued stuffing clothes into his duffel bag. Cougars slept. Outside a chill night wind swept across the mountainside, soughing through pines; a cone rattled down the steep roof.

"What did he say?" Marshall argued. "Only a guy went to another guy's cabin. Happens all the time, you know that."

Stryker looked up. His eyes were glazed, his tone thick. *"It happened."*

"Kinsey says it does to half the guys. One out of every two."

Stryker yanked at the outsize zipper; it refused to budge so he gave a rougher yank and the zip pulled off its tracks. Grunting, Stryker hoisted the open duffel to his shoulder.

"Listen, when Dr. Edwards started in"—Marshall side-stepped to the corridor made by metal screen and wall—"I was just as shook as you were."

"I don't give a shit what Edwards thinks!"

"Everyone—"

"Or what everyone thinks."

"—saw how shook I was. And Dr. Edwards wouldn't let anyone explain. Raskin said—"

"Will you get the hell out of my way!"

"You can't leave now. It'll prove him right. It'll be a black mark and—"

Shoving past him, Stryker jogged by the sleeping Cougars. There was a savage blue glint in his eyes. Marshall followed him outside.

"Stryker, don't go." Marshall caught up.

"Leave me the hell alone!"

"It's crazy—"

Marshall grabbed Stryker's arm. Stryker slapped away Marshall's hand. "Leave me alone, leave me the fuck alone!" he whispered hoarsely.

"A black mark."

"I don't give a shit about black marks!"

"You won't get in the Space Program—"

"Or the goddam space race!"

"Listen, it didn't mean a thing. We're friends—"

"Never!"

"Always."

"I despise you!"

"No."

"Yes. You've spent this whole summer sniffing around me. And now it's happened . . ." Stryker's voice broke. "Jeez, it's happened." He trotted down the path.

Marshall ran after him. "Listen—"

"Sniffing at me like I was a bitch in heat."

"You can't leave. Dr. Edwards—"

"I told you! I don't give a shit what Edwards or anyone else thinks." Stryker stopped, swiveling on Marshall. They were at the entry to the camp; three logs formed a crude arch and to the horizontal one was attached a single bulb. By its light Marshall saw the strange, harsh flickering in Stryker's eyes. "I'm not leaving because of Edwards," Stryker hissed. "I'm leaving because of *you*. I can't stand being near you! You're a lousy, stinking fag. Understand?"

Marshall finally understood.

Dr. Edwards had forced Stryker to face the reality of what had happened last night in the Bearcats' dim cabin, and *Stryker wanted to shove the full responsibility onto Marshall.*

Marshall's mind went cold and hard. He didn't see that Stryker was swallowing convulsively as if battling tears.

"You wanted it," Marshall said slowly.

"You bawled and screeched until you had me in your sack."

"You wanted it."

"NO!" Stryker denied at the top of his lungs. "I despise chickenshit fags. They make me puke. *You* make me puke!"

"You wanted it," Marshall repeated quietly.

"Do I have to kill you?"

"The pleasure was quite mutual." Marshall spoke intently into the darkness. "But. *You seduced me.*"

"You lie."

"You started it."

"Lie!"

Marshall leaned closer. "You used me," he whispered.

Stryker, dropping his duffel, aimed clenched, accurate fists at Marshall's soft stomach. The old one-two. Marshall staggered back, holding numb flesh.

"Stryker, don't," he managed to pant.

"Liar. I'm no flaming fruit. Liar!" This time Stryker's fist landed on Marshall's nose. Marshall never in his life had faced bodily battle. Instinctively he slapped out with the flats of his palms, a Jerry Lewis imitation of a fighter, no defense at all against Stryker's hard fists. "Liar," Stryker breathed, aiming at Marshall's chin. "Liar," he whispered, socking Marshall's left eye. "Liar," he sobbed again, punching Marshall's belly. Marshall grunted loudly and almost fell, and Stryker, shouting "Liar!" grabbed Marshall by the shoulders, completing the job, hurling him to uneven dirt.

He stood panting over Marshall. "YOU LIE!" he shouted. "IF I HAVE TO SPEND THE REST OF MY LIFE PROVING IT, YOU LIE!" He bent his head lower, then quickly turned, squatting for his duffel.

He sprinted down the path.

Marshall lay gasping. "All right, I lied," he called through his trembling, aching lips. "Stryker, come back. I lied, I lied."

But Stryker couldn't hear. His quick footsteps had faded into the night silence.

Sprawled on sodden pine needles Marshall lifted an unwilling hand, gingerly touching the egg-shaped mound over his left eye. Salt trickled warm from his nose into his mouth. His aching stomach twitched weakly as he thought of Stryker, whose nature was simple, decent and honest and who for the first time had acted out the strange, primeval complexities that dwell in every human being. And he couldn't accept them. Stryker, in his terrible hour, was running down a steep mountain path, running from himself, or rather from those parts of himself that he couldn't understand, much less accept. What would the sweet berserk guy do? "Stryker, it was all my fault. I lied. Come back," Marshall kept whispering. "Come back."

High above the dark-silhouetted pine branches, cold, indifferent stars glittered.

Stryker, stiff from crouching half the night on his damaged duffel, watched the two marines as they emerged from the café. The one picking his teeth was tall, big-waisted and broad-hipped. The other, short, tough, Mexican-looking. As they crossed the street the Mexican-looking one saw Stryker and poked the tall sergeant.

"We're late, Al," the Mexican said loudly. "Got us a customer."

"What brings him here so bright and early?" the sergeant wondered equally loudly.

"He wants to see what he can do for his country."

"You're right, Martinez, you're right. And this one could be corps material. If you cut his hair, that is."

"Open up before he changes his mind and goes back to his collich deferment."

"Or down the block to the Air Force boys—they got all the glamour with this space business."

The tall sergeant unlocked the narrow store that was the San Bernardino recruiting office.

"We're open for business," said the Mexican to Stryker.

5

Michele had been watching television since ten last Friday morning when her mother had shaken her awake with the news that "Someone's gone and shot the President in Dallas." Since then the two of them had been glued to the Davys' plastic-covered brown matelasse couch, Mrs. Davy's thick legs stretching on the ottoman to rest her varicose veins, with Dozer alternately snarling or sleeping in her lap, and Michele pressing the remote control to whichever channel was running the most pictures of Jackie. Now Michele pressed the button again and again.

"They're all the same," she said.

"They certainly put on an impressive funeral. . . ." Mrs. Davy sighed. "Those Catholics. . . ." She sighed again.

They watched the funeral cortege.

Lissa came in, slamming the front door behind her. She sidled over to the couch, also watching.

"I want Sheriff John," she announced.

"Lissa doll, he's not going to be on today," Michele explained. "The President's funeral."

"I want my Sheriff John!"

"All the channels're showing the same thing." Michele reached out for her daughter, feeling small bones under pink and white striped tee shirt, breathing in childish fragrances. Lissa was one month younger than John John—today was his third birthday. Michele had wept openly when the poor baby had saluted his father's coffin.

"I want my milk," Lissa demanded.

"I'll get it," Michele said.

"Now."

"Now." Michele kissed silken blonde hair.

"My chocolate chip cookies, too," Lissa added. She knew when to take advantage of the pendulum swing of her mother's moods.

Michele rose. Right now they were showing long, dull shots

down Pennsylvania Avenue; pretty soon though, hopefully, they would show Jackie, draped in her widow's weeds, following the caisson.

"Mother, call me if Jackie comes on."

Mrs. Davy nodded, absently scratching Dozer's long hair, her gaze never leaving the color screen. Michele, Lissa's hand in hers, hurried into the kitchen.

It was November, and Michele and Lissa had been living with the Davys since early June, since the night following Leigh and Ken's wedding reception.

After she had danced with Everett Sutherland she had watched, his heavy, warm arm around her, as Leigh cut the first slice of five-tier cake and fed it to Ken. The photographer had flashed away; then Everett had suggested they leave the overheated tent and retire to the Sutherlands' elegant living room. There they chatted, and Michele put away quite a few more glasses of bubbly. After showering rice on the bride and groom, when the party started to break up, Everett said, "May I see you home?"

Michele, slightly sloshed, smiled. "I'd love it." *Serve Clay right.* "I live in Parkdale. Do you know where that is?" He did, so she added, "Three oh six five Athens." It never had come up in the conversation that Michele was married, so she gave him her old address—Lissa was sleeping there tonight.

Under the reproduction carriage lamp Everett Sutherland said, "Good night, little Michele," staring down at her with those droopy eyes. He didn't try to kiss her.

The following morning, long before seven, Lissa woke Michele. Michele, queasy-stomached and dry-mouthed, saw her new pink silk dress crumpled on the floor. Immediately she remembered. What had she done? Nothing, nothing at all, but it wouldn't look that way, would it?

This might serve Clay right.

But wouldn't he kill her?

He didn't. In answer to her telephoned request that he pick up Lissa and her, he drove them home amicably, then departed for a SNAP fund raising. He didn't get home until long after Lissa slept; Michele, at the sink, stacked dishes.

"It's time for us to talk," he said. He settled on the couch, a loose spring showing under worn upholstery.

"What about?" She leaned casually on the breakfast bar, but she couldn't keep a note of defiance from her voice.

"Should be obvious."

"You mean about last night? Clay, I looked all over for you—I felt sick. Barfy. I couldn't find you. So when Leigh's cousin offered to drive me home—"

"Why make up excuses?"

"I am not!"

"You are."

"I'm not!"

"Either way, it doesn't matter. I meant, let's talk about a divorce."

"A divorce?" she cried. "Who ever thought about such a thing?"

"You have, of course," he said.

"Never."

She walked slowly, almost tripping on Lissa's Barbie doll, to a bridge chair. Of course she'd thought of a divorce. But those thoughts didn't count. Michele possessed a slender romantic streak, so sometimes she envisioned herself a pretty young blonde divorcée enjoying life with rich, attentive bachelors. However, her practical streak was fat. She rested her elbows on the table, chewing her lower lip, thinking—Melmac dishes stacked unwashed in the sink; child sleeping in the next room; pink slacks and Clay's windbreaker due home tomorrow from the cleaners and she with only twenty-nine cents in her purse; Dorot McHenry, that gossipy Dorot, invited for Tuesday lunch—all these realities crossed her mind.

"Never," she repeated, pulling on a strand of blonde hair. "The thought never crossed my mind."

"I know you haven't been happy with my kind of life." Clay sounded reasonable and less involved than if he was suggesting they change brands of toothpaste. "Let's face it. I can't give you the things you want."

"Mother buys me one dress and you—"

"I'm not criticizing that."

"You *are.*"

"Michele, I'm not."

"Yes!" she shouted.

"Be reasonable."

"You are!"

As he stared at her the shadows under his intense brown eyes seemed to darken—but then the shadows had been more pronounced since he'd grown that beard. He'd known she'd never liked it, it prickled, but he'd grown it anyway.

"If you want to know," he said, "it makes me sick, the way you ran to her. But—"

"Mother buys me one new dress and here you are, asking for a divorce!"

"It's not just a new dress," he said, taking a deep breath. "That's not the main point and you know it."

"You don't love me any more," she cried. It surprised her how the words hurt. "You don't love me."

This he neither confirmed nor denied.

"I," he pointed out, "have never been unfaithful."

"Neither have I."

"No?"

"Leigh's cousin is kind enough to drive me home and you—"

"Generally a married woman drives to her own home with her own husband."

"I felt nauseous—the champagne. Barfy. I looked and looked and I couldn't find you. Anyway, who needs a chaperone? Is this the eighteen sixties?"

"And infidelity's in?" he asked. His voice was unnaturally deep. "Your thing?"

At last she understood. Despite his enforced cool, Clay, so very idealistic, was hurt. She let her flushed cheeks rest in her palms. "Nothing happened. And that's not the point. We've both obeyed the laws of being married. But you—you've never felt married."

"By that you mean I don't buy you every dress and every new piece of furniture you've set your mind on?"

"You'll have to admit you've never been interested in making a real home."

"So feeling married means cutting off my balls as a down payment on a tract house?"

"Lissa needs a yard!" she cried hotly.

Clay said, "You've never once tried to see how I feel about living my own life."

"I did! I have! Don't I live in this cruddy apartment, scrubbing, washing, cooking for you and Lissa? Haven't I worn old dresses? Rags? I'm turning into a f-frump. . . ."

"If it's so miserable," he pointed out, his voice held so tight it shook, "I think you'd be the one who wanted to talk about a divorce."

She realized, too late, she'd fallen into a trap. Had he set it intentionally?

"Oh, you *never* loved me," she whispered and began to weep.

He half rose from the couch. For a moment she held her breath, praying he would deny her words and come across worn beige carpet to hold her. But he checked himself, sinking back on the pillows.

"Michele, we were too young," he said. "We made a mistake."

"And you've been waiting and waiting for an excuse." She barely recognized her own voice, the teary unhappiness clogged so thickly. "Just waiting! I've been drudging my life away and you've been waiting for me to give you one single excuse, it didn't matter what, so you could run off and live with those damn, dirty black, trouble-making niggers!" Only extremity could have forced this last, the unforgivable as far as Clay Gillies was concerned, from her.

His look of loathing was long and complete and total. A chill shivered through her body. *That tied it. The end.*

"Clay," she whispered, "please, Clay."

But he wasn't listening.

He was in the bedroom, turning on the light, waking Lissa. Michele stumbled around the living room, falling on the couch, clutching at the stained gray pillow, burying her face in the musty-smelling upholstery, sobbing. She cried brokenheartedly until her throat hurt. Sometimes she could see Clay out of the corner of her eye as he packed in big brown paper sacks—he didn't own a suitcase. She heard him telling Lissa three times to go back to sleep, Daddy'd see her soon. Michele's tears were genuine, as was the sorrow aching in her chest, yet she understood that, Clay being Clay, this was a hopeless situation. What was past was past. Their marriage was past. She must make her own arrangements. The realist hidden by her prettiness was already figuring out how to get rid of the furniture in this apartment, how to move as easily as possible back into her parents' house. Also, shouldn't she lose five pounds and bleach her hair? Single, you have to look your best.

As Clay opened the front door, he said, "Michele, tomorrow I'll phone—"

"Don't bother!" she sobbed.

His arms full of bags, he kicked the door shut behind himself. She cried a few more minutes, then went to wash her face. She held onto the sink, breathing deeply. What a mess her face was: swollen eyes, red nose, puffy cheeks. Tears started again. She tottered back, falling on the couch (to Goodwill tomorrow, that couch) and cried through the night.

Six A.M. she started to pack, noon the Goodwill men arrived and by five P.M. she was unpacking in her old bedroom.

As Michele poured the Extra Rich Homogenized that Mr. Davy brought home for Lissa, the phone rang.

While the first ring sounded, under her full breasts her heart ached a funny way, it was—well, almost as if a hand were squeezing, the way her heart hurt. Since the assassination she'd thought constantly of Clay. In Michele's mind Kennedy's campaign and presidency were equated with her marriage; both had lasted approximately the same time. Maybe Clay, too, was experiencing the same bittersweet memories. Maybe this was him on the phone. She pushed back her hair, now bleached to a shimmery vanilla blonde, and smoothed her new white cotton—in the months since she'd left Clay Gillies her parents had replenished her shabby wardrobe at a most gratifying rate. She picked up the wall extension.

Long Distance Operator in New York asked for a Mrs. Davy Gillies, person to person. Everett Sutherland was in New York as the finale of his stockbroker's training. She was crazy, Michele told herself, crazy, to feel so let down about getting a long-distance call from Everett, a bachelor with a big future both as a businessman and an heir, who drove a robin's-egg-blue Caddy convertible bought not on time but with *cash*.

"This is she." Michele put a hand over the speaker. "Lissa doll, run in with Grandma."

"Can't."

"Lissa—"

"Grandma says it's a no no to take milk in—"

"Tell her Mommy's talking to Uncle Everett."

Lissa liked Everett. He brought a small gift—a Golden Book, a bubble blower, a pair of miniature high heels—each time he took Michele out, so it was without animosity but with a little child's natural argumentativeness that she replied, "He's not my uncle."

"I say he is!"

"I want my chocolate chip cookies!"

"Scoot."

"I want my—"

Michele glared down at her daughter. Under clear blue eyes were pale shadows like Clay's. "Later." Michele jutted her pretty chin at the door. "Scoot!"

And Lissa, seeing her mother meant business, carefully carried her Snoopy mug with both hands into the living room. Dozer yipped. Michele pushed the swinging door shut.

She sat at the breakfast nook. She could hear the echo of the same TV announcer talking in the background as Everett spoke in somber tones of the funeral.

"I'm not a Democrat like Uncle Sidney," he said. "I belong to the half of the population who voted for Nixon. That's why it's so surprising how deeply I'm affected."

"It's affecting all us young people."

"He was the President of youth," Everett said.

"Yet he wasn't really young at all. Forty-five."

"That's not too old."

"Too young to die."

"Much too young."

"That poor baby. When he saluted...." Michele's voice broke.

Everett consoled her as if for a personal loss. His deep voice brought up the picture of his large, round body, his small red mustache. He took her to wonderful restaurants, Perino's, La Rue, Scandia, and he ordered wine by the bottleful, ones he'd learned about in France; Vouvray and Beaujolais were his favorites and the waiters poured him a little first, then waited respectfully while he took a sip. He never tried to get her in the sack; since the separation (it still hurt to think about, Clay so obviously had been lying in wait ready to pounce on any excuse), Michele had been dating a lot of guys and most expected her to put out and be grateful for the opportunity. Everett was a perfect gentleman. He kissed her good night and sometimes he held her breasts, but no more.

"It's a sad day for the country," he concluded.

"Oh, Everett ... Lissa's exactly the same age as John John, almost."

"You're way too young to have such a big girl," he said. "And you're so pretty. You must start again."

Phone clasped between her shoulder and small, soft ear, Michele wondered sadly if Jackie would start again.

In her most sincere tone, she said, "I'm still too hurt to think about that."

"It's too soon, I know," Everett said.

"I'm just not built that way."

"You're fine and sensitive," Everett said.

They talked some more about the funeral; he made a date for two weeks from Saturday, when he would be home; then they said goodbye.

Michele hurried to get Lissa two homemade chocolate chip cookies. The phone rang again. Again she smoothed her pale hair, straightened her crisp white dress, but it was only Operator making sure that the long-distance call was complete.

"Michele!" Mrs. Davy's call was urgent. *"She's* on."

Michele ran.

John Fitzgerald Kennedy, the bright, the shining, the beloved, the brave hero nonpareil, thirty-fifth president, followed by his grieving and beautiful widow, his handsome brothers, his sisters, his mother, the riderless horse Black Jack, the bareheaded dignitaries of the world, followed by we the television audience of the United States, was on his last journey. Soon he would lie under cold Virginia soil.

Clay Gillies was cold, cold, cold.

It was all over.

> *That bright shining moment*
> *That was known as Camelot.*

————————— **6** —————————

Marriage wasn't what Ken Igawa had expected.

Striding barefoot along the sandy cement walk south of POP pier toward Venice he admitted freely that marriage wasn't at all what it was cracked up to be. That firmly in mind, he couldn't ignore the idea's corollary. *What did you expect?* Gritty-eyed, his stomach raw from last night's booze, he tried to reach back through time and grasp what his expectations had been. Pondering, he started to shiver. This sudden chill, he told himself, had no bearing on his mental processes. Why shouldn't he be cold? Wasn't he shoeless, wearing only Bermudas and a dirty tee shirt on a chill, clear, late January afternoon? The horizon drew a cold purple line. A distant freighter moved so imperceptibly that it seemed frozen in the red-shadowed sea to the southwest. A gull cawed. On benches, noisy gesticulating old Jews huddled in their overcoats—quite a few of the run-down beach-front stores had signs in Hebrew, and the biggest, old and salmon-colored, which Ken was passing now, had been converted into a synagogue; a string of bare bulbs looped above a six-pointed metal star. Next door, a hot dog vendor shouted his wares—from his narrow open stand rose a far better ad, visible wisps of savory kosher steam. In this neighborhood lived a mixed bag. Old people seeking cheap rentals in order to exist on their Social Security checks. Homosexuals facing social insecurity behind the glass walls of modern "bachelor" apartments. Druggies banding together in old beach shacks. Mixed couples like the Kenneth Igawas here because they were *persona non grata* in ordinary middle class neighborhoods.

Ken hurried along. What use, he asked himself, frowning, on figuring what he'd hoped for during his nine-month banishment? The subject, current and choice, was his marriage. Now.

Last night they'd fought. Christ knows not their first fight, but certainly their worst, the sort of thing that once was called knockdown-dragout, and as the battle progressed he'd been in his usual fine fettle, cruel, very cruel, and at last his wife, face pale with hurt, had pummeled him with her small fists. Startled, he'd hit back. Hard. Then he'd slammed out of the place, dropping in on a friend to drink and brood.

Well, what had he expected, that marriage would be milk and honey, sweetness and light, roses and fucking? Did he think she was some sort of Galatea carved to order for him? He chuckled grimly. Obedience wasn't her thing. She insisted on working so he could paint all day. Once in a while Obie Dorfman, the dealer whose Patio Gallery gave Ken wall space, actually sold one of his outsize canvases and on these occasions she insisted on popping a celebratory split of California champagne. She insisted on their seeing her family all the time. She insisted on feeding Kal Kan, liver flavor, to the cadaverous cats who lurked in the sandy yard of their old frame apartment building even though she knew it zinged the hell out of him. The way a rich girl wastes money!

He jogged past a red-brick senior citizen's rooming house; over the porch, white-painted in coy old Spanish lettering, Casa de la Paz. After the assassination, blinking away her tears, she'd announced they ought to join the Peace Corps, it would be a sort of In Memoriam to JFK. Ken, naturally, had set her right on his feelings toward the idea: *Some politician gets his and you want to take the veil, O.K., but don't drag me in.* Oh, he was a prince all right.

An amber-colored mutt with a bent black tail sniffed after Ken, then jumped the low cement-block wall to squat crapping on dry sand. Ken laughed harshly. Wasn't that your universal effect of Prince Kenneth?

He was still laughing a couple of blocks later. Then he got hold of himself. He turned, slowly climbing the steep, cracking sidewalk, moving yet more slowly up his building's sagging front steps, taking his own sweet time unlocking the glass entry.

At 1A Mrs. Tindley was setting her garbage can on nicked hardwood to the left of her door. White hairs bristled from Mrs. Tindley's upper lip. Shapeless as she stooped in her wrap-around housedress, she glared up at Ken. On the day they'd moved in, Mrs. Tindley had expressed to Leigh her disapproval; the landlord, Mrs. Tindley had said, must be desperate for money, otherwise he never would run down his property by renting to the colored races.

"Hello there, Mrs. Tindley," Ken said jovially.

Her wrinkled lips moved without sound.

"How goes it with the garbage lady?" he asked.

Mrs. Tindley made a strange grunting sound as she rose. She slammed her door behind her.

Ken climbed dark stairs. The place smelled of salt, mildew and, at the first landing, of stale fried fish. He climbed very slowly, rehearsing his apologies; the impossible words jumbled together in his head and so he banged the flat of his hand twice, sharply, against his ear; a yard from his door he halted. Feminine voices. His wife and his mother-in-law. He took a deep breath, wiping his hands along his shorts before he reached for the doorknob. He struggled. In this old building the doors and locks were hampered by many coats of paint.

He jerked open the door.

On the window seat Mrs. Sutherland perched gracefully, one slender ankle wound around the other, every blonde hair in place, her pretty amethyst suit cheerfully appropriate for visiting a mismated daughter (Ken thought). On the small wicker table that Leigh'd sprayed white lay a deep, impressive bakery carton and a two-pound See's chocolate box.

Mrs. Sutherland smiled up at him. "Hello, Ken dear."

"Hello, Evelyn," he replied. He called her by her first name. She hadn't requested it, but wouldn't it be the height of something or other, his calling this blonde fashion plate *Mom?*

His wife was ironing. Ken stayed at the door, fists jammed in the pockets of his shorts, examining her through almost closed lids as if she were a canvas he'd turned upside down to see patterns of light and shade. Her hair was skinned back, throwing the boned angles of her small face into prominence. She stared at him. She was very pale.

She blinked, setting the iron on its side. "Hi," she said in a casual tone.

"Hi," he grunted.

She reached down to unplug the cord. She looked so rotten, ill almost, that even from Prince Kenneth the Proud an apology for last night seemed the simplest thing in the world.

It was a surprise to hear his own voice saying, "So we play it cool?"

"What?"

"You aren't going to ask where I was all night and day?"

Flushing, she murmured, "Ken—"

"Isn't that playing it cool?"

Mrs. Sutherland examined long, perfect pink nails; she might not have all her marbles, his mother-in-law, but one thing you had to say for her, she had manners.

"Ken, Mother brought us some coffee cake."

"Thank you."

"You're welcome, dear." Mrs. Sutherland smiled. "Apple pecan."

And Leigh said, "Why don't you try some?"

"My hat is off," Ken said to his wife, trying to master his sarcasm, failing. "I disappear a night and a day and you tell me to eat apple Danish."

"You slept at Obie's."

"My wife, the bloodhound."

"He phoned."

"You and Obie!"

"Oh, leave me alone." She sighed.

"Whatever you say."

He slammed the door, trotting along the corridor. At the stairwell he stopped himself by grabbing onto the newel post. How could he have talked like that to her in front of her mother? How? He swallowed. Tears threatened. "I am sorry. There. Is that so impossible?" *You bet your sweet ass it is,* he answered silently. Still grasping the post, mustering every ounce of will power he possessed, he forced his body to turn.

At his door he grabbed the difficult knob, twisting.

Leigh was hanging up the shirt she'd pressed. She wasn't much with the iron and a heavy crease marred the collar. Again she stared at him.

"I just got here," he said.

She nodded gravely.

"This minute," he said.

She nodded again.

"Hi," he said.

"Hi."

He went across the room to touch his lips to her forehead. As he did, both her arms went around his waist, pulling him close.

"I got drunk," he said against her earlobe. "I passed out."

"Obie said."

"He never mentioned he called you."

"I asked him not to."

"Why?"

"I don't know."

They were whispering fast and barely audibly.

"Did I hurt you?" he asked.

"I like you to."

"Hey Leigh, don't."

"But—"

"Masochism's a nasty habit. Also, like the saying goes, it hurts me worse."

"I punched you first."

"Not as hard."

"You're strong."

Evidently she'd forgotten her mother. Eyes closed, hands sliding down to his butt, she started to kiss the small sharp bones of his Adam's apple. He closed his own eyes, resting his lips on top of her head. It embarrassed him that his mother-in-law, a few feet away from them on the window seat, should be in on this. Yet at the same time a nasty little kid inside him exulted *let her see,* let her see that her daughter had the hots for boorish, inferior him.

He heard the door open quickly and discreetly. Close.

Leigh jerked away.

"I completely forgot she was here," she said, cheeks flaming. She started after her mother.

Ken held her hand.

For a half minute she poised, hand pulling his, head turned toward the door.

"I could die," she said. "Poor Mother."

He reached for the top button of her lemon sweater. She raised both hands.

"Don't," she said. And when he kept trying to unbutton, she fended him off with, "It's all better."

"Then let me see."

"It's nothing," she insisted.

"Open up."

"Later."

"Hey Leigh, I ever mention how I feel about you?"

"It's all better."

"Yeah yeah yeah. Aren't you interested?"

She smiled. "Tell me."

"Like I'm flayed. Like at the moment my skin's been taken off me. I'm all raw meat and bleeding nerve ends." He added roughly, "I despise myself for it."

Her eyes filled with tears. Her eyes always filled when she was ready to make love.

He put his arms around her again and pulled her close. "Hey Leigh, you think that's why I fought it? Not because we were different but because who needs to be so hung up? It makes for a rotten relationship."

"Love you so much."

"You're meant to," he muttered. "But a guy shouldn't be so vulnerable."

"Why?"

"S'not manly."

"S'nice."

"Nice! Hah! I feel like a stud."

"Duts." She repeated the word backward. She often said whole sentences backward to him. To tell the childish truth, he did the same with her. A private language.

"You really look like hell," he said tenderly.

"You're green around the jaw line."

"I never got drunk before," he said, reaching for her sweater. This time, eyelids lowered, arms at her sides like an obedient child submitting to an adult's care, she let him undo the small pearl buttons. He didn't take off the sweater but held soft wool apart, looking down.

A purple black oval marked the swell above her left breast, a large and ugly bruise divided by the elasticized white strap of her brassiere. He moved the strap an inch to the left. He traced the bruise with his fingertip. "Kiss and make better," she whispered, drawing down his head.

"Oh, Christ." He looked up.

"It'll go away," Leigh said.

"I figured when we got married it'd be different."

"How?"

"I'd have taken possession." He sat on the wicker chair, pulling her onto his lap. "I figured I wouldn't be such a madman."

She smiled.

"Insane?" he asked.

"Certain people, I've heard, even though married, are still attracted."

"I had it figured once we were married I'd relax. We'd belong together."

"We do."

"Nobody else thinks so. Every time we go out people stare at us like we're unmatched socks."

"No they don't."

"Mmmm. . . ." Was he paranoid? Did he imagine the too-effusive overtures of the Sutherlands? And how about his family never once asking them over or accepting invitations? And the police? Each time the Kenneth Igawas passed a cop was it purely Ken's imagination that the cop kept stern watch? He felt a dull, confused resentment, not at his enemies, but at Leigh for refusing to admit they had enemies.

"Your folks," he muttered, "keep hoping it's a platonic arrangement."

"They're embarrassed."

"Why?" he demanded. "Aren't we expected to?"

"Parents like to think of their daughters as very peeyure."

"Chaste?"

"Undefiled."

"Bull! What disturbs them is who's doing the defiling."

"Ken—"

Suddenly he grinned and raised a triangular black eyebrow. "Listen here, kid." He used his Bogey voice. "You think we do it too often?"

"Someone's got to keep up the national average."

He ran his fingers against the shaved stubble on her calf. She lifted his hand.

"Ken, it doesn't matter what other people think about us."

"Why kid yourself?"

"It doesn't to me."

"Then why did you cry the last time my mother said they were too busy to—"

"It doesn't matter!"

"Me, I'm confused and insecure all around. It matters to me." He arrived at his major point. "And every time you get a present from your father—"

"Ken," she interrupted. "You know he meant the car for both of us."

The keys her father had left with her last night while Ken was sweating at beach volleyball, the keys to a new Ford Fairlane—a belated wedding present, Mr. Sutherland called it—had triggered their fight.

"The hell he did!"

"He did!"

"O.K., O.K. He did. Listen, every time he gives us something, I gnaw inside. I start remembering that with him you didn't live in a slum clearance area. With him you never had to wipe some kid's snotty nose." (She worked at Venice Nursery School.) "With him crazy old bitches never gave you a hard time. People never stared—"

"Now you mention it, it's really rough, married life."

"He's going to pull us apart again," Ken growled.

She shook her head.

"He did before," Ken said.

"Now he doesn't want to."

"Ho ho ho."

"He knows how miserable I was without you."

"And he sees me playing bush league Marquis de Sade so he figures you're Miss Happy Toes of 1964?"

"I love you."

"I hate him!"

"That's not reasonable."

"Who's reasonable? I'm telling you how I feel." Ken raised his voice. "He can give you everything that I can't. He's loaded. He's an all-around Wasp. *I hate him.*"

"I love you."

"S'that a subliminal commercial?"

"Ken, let's not start."

"I want you to hate him, too."

"He's my father. I can't."

"S'obvious."

"Ken, listen—"

"What I'm trying to tell you in my own confused way is"—

he spoke slower, writing with a fingernail along her calf muscle—"we aren't going to make it unless we get away."

She'd been pushing back his heavy hair. Now her hand dropped. "I know we fight," she said, "but—"

"—we always fuck after," he finished bitterly.

"What's wrong with that?"

"Fight, fuck, fight, fuck. S'not marriage. S'the tag of a dirty joke. Leigh, I'm telling you the way it is. We—aren't—going—to—make it."

"We are!"

"We don't stand much of a chance, the world being what it is and me being what I am—"

"We do!"

"I'm too damn hung up on you. Dig?"

"That's insane. . . . Ken, you can't love a person so much it destroys the relationship."

"No? Bear in mind last night. There'll be one too many nights like last night and it'll be over. Phht."

"We love each other." Her jaw set stubbornly and Ken knew she was close to tears.

"Don't you understand?" he asked as gently as he could. "Whatever our generation's been sold on, love isn't the name of the game."

"Yes."

"The name of the game is adjustment. And we—I—can't adjust here."

"But—"

"No buts," he said. "We've got to get away."

"But our families live here in Los Angeles—"

"Don't you listen to a single word I say? As far as my family's concerned I've committed the worst treason. They don't want us. And as for yours! *I cannot stand one more ounce of goodness shoved down my throat by that big fat phony liberal!*"

She started to cry.

Ken closed his eyes, listening to the muffled desperation of his wife's sobs. Tension crawled in back of his neck. Never in all his life had he felt such defeat. He'd bared himself to her, heart and spleen; in this age, with God expired, Ken felt that complete honesty of motive was the sole remaining constant value. It was a shame, he admitted, that he was so petty, his motives so warped. Doubtless his honesty must come as a low blow to his wife. Still, her warmth filling his lap with uxorious

lust, he'd tried to plumb his depths with the most honest sound-
ings possible. So why the hell did she have to answer him on
an emotional level with these muffled sobs?

Fight fire with fire, he thought.

Why not fight back on an emotional level? Why not use a
little elementary psychology to clear the unadjusted waters of
their marriage? He smiled, opening his eyes. He always thrilled
to his rare practical ideas.

He drew the unbuttoned sweater off, he unhooked her white
net bra, freeing the full white breasts. How splendid it was to
act shrewdly! He unsnapped the bar from her hair and with his
fingers combed the long strands over her shoulders. "You've
got the greatest hair, you know that. Don't ever cut it. Hey
Leigh, we'll be together, just you and me, like this. Is it so
terrible?" She gave him a watery smile and he wiped the tears
from her cheeks with a strand of hair. Her fingers stroked the
back of his neck and from under her raised arms started coming,
faintly, those female scents that drove him wild. So much for
practical psychology. He forgot every rational thought. They
moved to the bed in order to have more room to do what she
called "their things." Already she was more than willing, *Please,
now, oh please?* and he, he was dying, *Oh God Leigh do that
some more no don't it'll go off,* but they waited until they were
clear out of their minds for that bone-melting moment when
she guided him into her.

Psychology can be correct, Ken had to admit it, even when
inadvertently applied.

"Where?" she asked.

"The Peace Corps."

"But you don't like it! You've told me a thousand times."

"The way they spell it, that's what I don't like."

"You have your work—"

"This'll jar you, I know it, but the world of painting will
survive two entire years without me."

"Come on, Ken. You know you're only doing it for one
reason. You can't apologize for hitting me."

"You are one hell of a man-killer."

"Darling, you don't have to say you're sorry, not to me."

"One hell of a—"

"I won't let—"

"Cut the Gift of the Magi, O.K.? Do it my way, just this
once, O.K.? Let me win, O.K.?" He rolled to the edge of the

bed, peering through darkness at the luminous dial of the GE alarm. "After eight! What *else* does a guy have to do around here before he gets dinner?"

"Babe, it's insane."

"It's something we have to do."

"I know you kids today are altruistic—"

"But?"

"I can think up thirty-seven reasons for you not to go."

"Someone has to."

Mr. Sutherland threw up his broad hands. "It's crazy. You grow up exactly the way I want you to. Yet faced with the reality . . ." His voice faded into a whisper. "I'm afraid for you."

Professor Little, hearing the news via Obie Dorfman, phoned Ken to argue him out of it. Naturally Ken told Little where to get off. Little didn't. Instead he tried another tack. Mrs. Little, the rotund heiress, was relative to a Peace Corps bigwig and Little said he wanted this man to look at the film Ken had made.

The film, while Ken was abroad, had remained in his closet at home. Since his return he'd spent innumerable hours hunched over York's Moviola, snipping, marking, taping the working print.

"The editing," he said. "I haven't finished."

"You never will," Professor Little replied. "I know you."

"There's no sound."

"You thorny bastard!" Professor Little lost academic dignity over long-distance wires. His voice rose, thick with anger. "Why must you always be so damn difficult when you think someone's out to help you? Listen, even if you won't be painting, you've got to be doing *some*thing."

"I—"

"You can't waste two years of your life reciting 'God Bless America' to worm-eaten Indians! I've put in too much time and effort."

"I appreciate what you've done," Ken said stiffly.

"You sweet, miserable bastard." The voice was calmer now. "You're the most talented student I ever had. That's why I do it."

"Which doesn't alter facts. What good is a silent movie?"

"Haven't you seen any of the other student films? A folk singer, that's all you need."

So while Leigh took the battery of Peace Corps tests and packed wedding presents into her parents' garage storeroom, Ken drove the new Fairlane north to Berkeley. He played the edited film over and over. Ruth Abby wrote suitable songs. She transferred her words and the sound of her guitar onto magnetic tape. A friend of Ken's, a grad in UCLA's Theater Arts, arranged for him to use a mixing room.

Leigh was assigned to an orphanage near Concepción. Ken was cordially invited to film the Peace Corps' Chilean endeavor.

"You'll have a chance to paint," Little said when he heard the news. "And as for the film—hell, Ken, we both know that's where art's heading."

Stryker Halvorsen was killed in Vietnam on November 10, 1964.

His platoon was wiped out as they stormed a hidden VC arsenal; Stryker, wounded in the thigh, managed to crawl close enough to pitch a grenade.

Their arsenal blazing, the VC captured him. Outside a little Catholic church they spread-eagled him on packed dirt, face up; then they drove bamboo stakes through his palms, securing him to the ground. The night, when others finally got through to him, he was dead. His long legs were burned. His big, good-natured face had so many cuts, so close, that the strips of skin were peeling. The death of a thousand cuts, the VC called it.

A grateful nation noted Sergeant First Class Stryker Halvorsen's conspicuous gallantry and awarded him a posthumous silver star. California High, too, honored his memory with an assembly, flags, orchestra, the works. Dr. Schramm gave a gravel-voiced eulogy and a marine colonel cocked a bushy, dark eyebrow on high school enlistments as he spoke quietly on the glories of the corps.

Leigh and Ken, in Chile, heard about his death and the ensuing ceremony in the same letter from Stevie Sutherland, now in tenth grade; the letter included clippings from the *Los Angeles Times* and from California High's *Battler* and ended with the words: *He was a boss guy, he was interested in Space and that summer you made the movie he showed me how to throw a curve.*

A far better epitaph for Stryker, Ken and Leigh agreed in their dirt-floored hut—both were weeping—than any medals or speeches or flags fluttering at half mast or draggy Siegfried's funeral march.

Death . . .

The darkest mystery of all.

STRYKER KEITH HALVORSEN
1943-1964

──────── · **7** · ────────

That August of 1965 was hot.

On the eleventh the mercury reached ninety-five and the humidity, unusually high for Los Angeles, kept it up there. At almost nine in the evening Clay and RG, shirtless, sat near the two open windows of the place they shared and used as SNAP headquarters, listening to the hi-fi—RG, whose nail-bitten brown fingers were clever with wires and plugs and tubes, had put it together with discarded components. Bob Dylan, silky and nasal, sang "Blowin' in the Wind." The angry words happened to be—verbatim—Clay's philosophy and so the record had lived a hard life; at the end the needle caught in a scratch. Dylan repeated himself until Clay lifted the arm. Through open windows came the sounds of a hot night: voices, laughter, kids shouting, hoses running, a car starting, Vin Scully announcing the Dodger game.

RG turned on his transistor. The battery was almost gone and RG kept clicking it on and off as the sound faded. There had been voters' registration successes in Selma. Clay and RG had spent most of this spring in Selma, and RG gave a quick, nervous smile of triumph. There was some sort of trouble across town right here in Los Angeles.

"They're really giving it to those p-police bastards."

"Where?"

"Willowbrook and Hundred and Tenth."

"That's Watts, isn't it?"

"Man, darkest Watts." RG humorously slurred his words. He'd been raised in respectability around West Adams. His mother had paid for him to go to St. Joan Catholic School, given him piano lessons, nice clothes, she still yearned after a UCLA education for him, so it was understandable that RG should feel a superiority to Watts—even though he laughed at himself for it. Watts! Where the barely literate hopeful migrated from the rural South to search for big-paying jobs and good housing but instead found termite-ridden shacks and county checks.

RG clicked off the radio, clicked it on again. An excited announcer: "... police have established a field headquarters at the intersection of Avalon and Imperial. All residents are advised to stay in their homes, all motorists should take alternate routes. Official sources are quoted as saying the violence is Black Muslim inspired...." The voice faded again. RG clicked off the radio and set it down.

"The Black Muslim bit." Clay took a swallow of Coke.

RG nodded, biting a hangnail.

"They resurrect it," Clay said, "every time they're about to go brutal."

"There'll be a hot time in the old town t-tonight."

"You think it's anything like Detroit?"

"Can't be," RG said. "Not here in Los Angeles." He frowned uncertainly. "You think I ought to go t-try stop 'em from getting their black selves killed?" He swallowed. "What d'you think?"

Honest doubt glazed his round eyes. Their battles, his and Clay's and SNAP's, had always been fought on foreign soil, so to speak, against the organized battalions of southern bigotry. No Los Angeles civil rights organization, not SNAP or Snick or CORE, yet had pitched a tent in Watts, for there the enemy was poverty and hopelessness and lack of education, and these, Odessa sighed, were far more deadly foes than your good old southern-fried bigotry. It was easier, way easier, she often said in her wry way, to go south because in the South you knew the bad guys wore white faces.

"I'll drive with you," Clay decided.

"You're not blood," RG said, looking the other way as he pulled on his tee shirt.

"So?"

"Man, you know about r-riots."

"I'll be with blood," Clay said.

He tossed his empty Coke can into the trash bag and reached

for his own shirt. Suddenly he felt eager. His stomach tensed and it was this, as always, that told him he was behaving the right way.

As the old Chevy sped through hot August night, Clay, as he often did, contemplated the past two years. He and RG Richards had shared their one-room place in Santa Monica—the most purposeful time of Clay Gillies' life, and this, as far as Clay was concerned, meant the happiest. Looking back, his marriage seemed a continuous hassle. Clay realized now that from the beginning, the first time at his father's place under crossed swords (symbolic?), Michele purposefully had set out to trap him into her ways. And he was caged until she left him. Oddly enough, she said *he*'d walked out on her. But (and even more oddly, this pained him) wasn't it proof of her adultery on the night of the Igawas' wedding, her marrying the guy the week the decree was final? She had mailed him a double-enveloped engraved announcement.

Redness and smoke clouded the night sky long before they reached the southeast section of Watts. Yet no police halted them. They drove past shabby stores, frame bungalows with parked cars where nonexistent lawns should be, vacant lots used as dumps, and once a vast wire-fenced enclosure of squat pastel cubes, government housing designed like a modern jail. Everything dark and silent. Except for the ominous red sky, the faraway howling of sirens.

RG gave quick nervous glances to either side. "It's t-too quiet here for fires on a hot night."

"Cops told everyone to stay inside."

"Guess you're right," RG said without certainty.

They were approaching a red light and RG pumped the brake. As they slowed Clay noted the sign, Palm and Oasis—suddenly
out of the darkness a voice bellowed, "Here come Whitey!"

And another, deeper, shouted, "Get 'im!"

A rock crashed against the windshield. Glass splintered. Instinctively Clay covered his face with both hands. RG hunched forward, his gnawed fingers tensing on the wheel. The car skidded into a gutter.

Out of the darkness a crowd solidified.

They seemed to have been waiting at the stop light, these shadowy men and women and children, for the sole purpose of trapping cars. Black hands took hold of the battered chassis, stopping the car before RG braked to the floor boards. Black hands shook the car. Gasoline fumes spread. Clay grunted, wondering briefly if he should fall to the floor, protecting himself with good old nonviolent techniques. But wasn't that the hysterical voice of fear speaking? He ordered reason to take over. This was a different situation. He was here to help these people. How? How could he help? What did it matter? The question at the moment was how could he help if he lay on the floor? Grunting again, Clay reached for the glass-covered dash, clutching at it to hold himself erect.

"Stop it!" he ordered through open windows.

His voice was drowned by loud shouts.

The loudest and most coherent: "Burn, baby, burn."

"We're here to help you!" Clay yelled. He grasped the dash, bawling louder, *"Here to help!"*

"Kill the white mothers."

"Hey, one be blood." This, a woman's voice.

"He pretty light." Another feminine voice, disappointed.

But the shaking stopped. Doors were yanked open. Smells of liquor, sweat, onions, pomade blasted Clay as he was dragged into the street. A fist landed on his stomach. He was aware of pain in his gut, just as he was aware of hands roughly holding his arms outspread. But everything was ignored in his efforts to shout he was here to help, damn them, here to help!

The crowd examined RG in the fuzzy light cast by a lamppost. Pale maybe, and freckled, hair not kinked properly, but blood, they decided, blood.

They released RG with a barrage of questions.

"Hey man, why you here with Whitey?"

"You an Uncle Tom?"

"You like to kiss white ass?"

And at this someone punched Clay viciously in the small of his back. Clay struggled.

"Leave him alone!" RG shouted. Redness poured from a cut on the left side of his freckled brow. "He's my buddy."

"Man, *we* your people."

Another blow aimed at Clay.

RG, free, began hitting at his friend's captors. "Let him go!" he shouted over and over. But black hands refused to relinquish their prey. A boy of seven or eight kicked Clay's shins, then scampered away. RG shouted and clawed. Clay cursed. He could feel it rising in him, that familiar, mindwiping, gut-shaking rage against injustice. *And his fury burned against these people.*

"Damn you! Let me go!" he yelled.

Down the street raced a wedge of three cops swinging indiscriminate billy clubs at men, women and children. A shot echoed. Quick darkness and the clatter of falling glass. A cop had shot out the street light. In the dark confusion the two others rescued Clay, half dragging him, half pulling him up the center of the street. Since RG had braked at the red light less than five minutes had elapsed.

"Don't you beatnik beards listen to the radio?" demanded one of the cops. "Orders was for nobody to come here." As he spoke, he opened the door of a police car, and another cop shoved Clay inside.

In the brief light before the door slammed on him, Clay saw blood dripping from his beard onto his tee shirt. He'd known glass had cut his hands, but he hadn't realized his face, too, bled. The dark car filled with the anguished sounds of his labored gulpings and he was only dimly aware of police calls coming through the radio. He turned to the rear window to see if they were bringing in RG.

His old Chevy was on fire!

Clay reached for the police car's door handle and—of course—found none.

"I've got to get my friend." He leaned urgently toward the cop in the driver's seat. "We've got to get him!"

"You the only white man there, weren't you?"

"Yes, but—"

"Don't sweat then." The cop turned. He was Negro, with a violently pitted broad nose. "He's fine."

"He's *alone!*" Clay cried.

"You're what they want, not him. White men, cops regardless of color. That's what they're after." The broad-nosed cop flicked on the car light. "You're bleeding pretty heavy," he said sympathetically.

And then Clay argued no more, for he realized he hurt all over. The glass splinters in his palms ached sharply. Dizzy, he dropped his head between his knees.

He was driven to the Georgia Street Receiving Hospital. An overworked woman doctor shot him with anti-tetanus booster, tweezed glass from his palms, wiped stinging antiseptic across his wounds. Afterward, a wiry male attendant with the avid, pinched expression of a man surreptitiously reading pornography, bandaged Clay, all the time questioning him about the trouble, finally remarking after this he was off. What was

Clay's direction? Well, a coincidence. They were headed the same way.

As they sped through dark streets, the male nurse jutted his bony jaw at the red night sky. "Got my shotgun at home," he remarked conversationally. "If one of them apes comes near, I'll blast him."

"I told you. They're burning their own places."

"Bull! Look at you."

"I went there."

The man lit a cigarette. "Want a butt?"

"No, thanks."

"The cops ain't tough enough."

"You think that's the answer?"

"You gotta defend yourself, right?"

"With shotguns? Against women and children?"

"Hell, they're rioting too, ain't they?" The male nurse tapped his cigarette into the ashtray. He made a right turn, then glanced at Clay, obviously more than eager to continue their discussion.

And Clay knew he had a chance to try, at least to try to change a man's bigotry. Clay knew he ought to tell of the incoherent rage and despair that lived in Watts, he ought to use every ounce of his conviction. Instead he sat back, closing his eyes. For some reason, neither weariness nor pain but a reason deeper than either of these—a reason Clay, who wasn't given to self-examination, couldn't understand—he felt completely unable to argue.

Bandaged hands behind his neck, Clay stretched out on his mattress, staring at the wavy red and white lines of the funk art Old Glory that covered the entire wall. Ken Igawa had painted it before that redhead of his had dragged him into the Peace Corps. The shadows under Clay's swollen eyes were dark bruises. His body ached and his head throbbed with memory of that concussion he'd gotten years ago on the Freedom Ride.

Slow hours passed.

It was almost dawn when RG returned, blood dried on one freckled cheek, weariness glazing his eyes.

Clay, sitting, demanded, "Where've you been?"

"Where you left me."

"Right there?"

"I wasn't glued to the spot, no."

"Watts?"

"Watts," RG agreed.

"Were you hurt?"

"Except for this"—RG pointed to his bloodied cheek—"no."

"The cops wouldn't let me go back after you."

"I wouldn't have left."

"The bastards," Clay said and he wasn't sure in his own mind which side he meant. "What were you doing?"

"Walking." RG sat on his mattress, his narrow shoulders hunched as he undid filthy white shoelaces.

"You were trying to stop them."

"Just walking."

"But—"

"Must've done five miles. Maybe more." RG wiggled his toes. His sweat socks were matted yellow green where his Keds had covered them, soil-caked and filthy where they had not. His left big toe stuck through. "I haven't been in Watts for years, not since my aunt died. I walked around the Watts Tower to the duplex she owned. At the end of her block is a liquor store. A Jew owns it. Or used to. They'd broken the windows, and the burglar alarms were going crazy while people rushed in and out helping themselves. A skinny little guy clutching bottles ran past me. Stopped. Asked would I like a drink? Bourbon, I said. He opened the bottle. By then ten, twelve others had gathered. One slug was all any of us got, so the skinny guy opened a half gallon of sour red wine. This time I got more. Around again. He shared his three bottles; then the bunch decided to set fire to the Mobil station around the corner." RG wiggled his toes again. "Does it sound like I was trying to stop them?"

"How could you?"

"I didn't try."

"How could you?" Clay repeated.

"I didn't want to. Anyway, someone said, 'Not the Mobil, man, that b'longs to blood.' And just then a boy passed, lugging a TV almost as big as he was. 'We done opened up Goldberg's!' he shouted. So off we went, across the railroad tracks, through vacant lots, down alleys, over fences and through yards; once we cut through a house. At Goldberg's I stood outside watching. No cops anyplace, burglar alarms ringing and black people serving themselves. A woman who couldn't handle a stereo and a radio both handed me the radio. 'Heah, brothah,' she said. I was *tempted*. You know my radio. I *needed* it. But then

I thought of Odessa and you. What'd the papers say if a SNAP worker were caught looting?"

Clay gave a small smile. "They'd say we joined with the Black Muslims to incite the riot."

"They'd say we incited solo."

"Yes."

"A SNAP-inspired looting."

"Go on."

Slowly RG unbuttoned his bloodstained shirt. "I walked some more. I came to a hot dog stand. It was closed, shuttered, but a bunch of people stood around. They were mostly older and they talked scared. A carload of cops drove by. They stopped, backed up, shone their lights. They made us put our hands over our heads and stretch against the wall. They searched us. Even this one old lady shaking with palsy. They knocked one old guy down. No reason. I said something about Police Chief Parker and his brutality squad. 'Shut up, you,' said a cop, banging me one with his stick. I got sort of nervous and without thinking I started to my pocket for some sunflower seeds. The palsied old bag next to me hissed, 'What you doin'? You reaches youah han' in youah pockets, they burns you.' All at once the cops piled in their car and took off, red lights flashing, sirens wailing. Some of us threw rocks. I threw a beer can.'"

RG, tall, naked, skinny and uncircumcised, walked into the narrow bathroom and ran the sink faucet, sloshing slow, underpressurized water on his cut face. He dried himself. He went to turn off the now-redundant light in the kitchen alcove and yawned, stretching, before he got under the thin madras spread. It took Clay this amount of time to realize that in the years he'd known RG this was the first time RG had spoken at any length without a stammer.

RG spoke again. "I walked by this shack. Through the window I could see men drinking and a naked woman pouring champagne over herself, laughing. She had huge breasts, and bubbles formed on them like lace. I walked on out of the riot area. Some guy drove by and gave me a lift to Washington and Sepulveda. I hitched home."

RG lay silent for a long time.

In a low voice Clay asked, "You sleeping?"

"Thinking."

"Oh?"

"It's funny," RG said, not moving. "I didn't beat up any

cops or any whiteys, I didn't take anything—except a few slugs of cheap liquor. I didn't throw anything, unless you count that one beer can that missed the cop car by a mile. You know me. Uncoordinated. But for the first time in my life I felt right. Like I was doing the right thing. Like I belonged. For the first time in my life I really belonged." He gnawed a thumbnail. "I never really felt part of it down south. Always above it. But tonight . . . I was them. They were me."

"No," Clay said sharply.

"Why not? I'm a black." SNAP, two months earlier, had voted *black* had more dignity and meaning than *Negro* or *colored*. Theirs the first organized insistence on the appellation.

"I'm white. Does that make me like every other white guy? Like all the rednecks?"

RG didn't answer.

"Does it?" Clay demanded.

RG burst out, "Man, I am sick of pretending! I am *not* a middle class citizen like you!"

"The hell I am."

"Listen," RG said, "you drive the car, you get no tickets. I drive the car, I've had eleven this past year. I'm not that much a worse driver, baby."

Clay shifted his spine against the plaster wall. "You're better, but—"

"I am sick of whites bossing me! The traffic cop tells me what to do, the white guy we get our gas from acts like he's doing *me* the favor, and the hag at the market, too. Any cretin who's white, that's my boss."

"I'm white."

"So I see."

"Oh, balls, RG, what is this? Haven't we lived together, shared food, chicks, the car, everything?"

RG rolled over and propped his head on his hand. "You tell me what to do, don't you?" His round eyes fixed on Clay.

"We decide together."

"The great white Moses leading his black brethren out of the desert of segregation, that's you," RG sneered. "Man, why don't you admit it? I'm your blood Joshua."

"What hit you out there?"

"The truth."

"You've gone crazy," Clay said. After a few seconds of coldly marshaling his thoughts, he added in his most compelling tones, "RG, they're burning, killing, looting. They're destroying what we've worked for all these years."

RG rolled over on his back and closed his eyes.

Clay insisted, "Is what they're doing any answer?"

RG said loudly, "You bet your sweet white ass it is!"

"It's violence."

"That's what I've been trying to tell you. For the first time in my life I know what I'm doing. *I am those people.*"

"But—"

"Save your breath. I DON'T WANT YOU TELLING ME WHAT TO DO!"

"RG—"

"Shut up, will you. I want to sleep."

And inside of three minutes he was asleep. Clay could tell by his breathing. Clay didn't lie down. He sat as he had while RG had talked, knees bent, feet flat on the mattress, back glued lightly by sweat to the cracking plaster. Outside, cars were starting up. Another hot day turned bright blue. Clay's stomach growled. He began hearing those sharp noises. He shook his head four times. He didn't want to think. *This sort of introspection got you no place*. He couldn't stop himself from thinking. He went over his brief time in Watts, the smell of fire, the heat of dark bodies pressing round him; they had smelled of lust and murder. And for a minute Clay had hated furiously.

Don't think.

I can't help it. Five years of his life had been devoted to an ideal. Black man and white emerging as brothers. Oh, he wasn't a sentimental fool. He'd known hatred ran deep on both sides. Old patterns change slowly. It wouldn't be easy. But wasn't it worth it? So he had fought as men fight for gold, for fame, for land and glory, which meant he had fought considerably harder than a man will fight for a woman. He had endured. Foul plugged-up toilets in southern jails, wormy food; he'd spent hours convincing some fat Beverly Hills renegade red writer that he (fattie) would be a second Abraham Lincoln if he'd donate a hundred bucks to SNAP; Clay'd put up with half-ass quarrels of his fellow workers, incessant bickering with his ex-wife; he rarely saw his child. He had overlooked every sort of crap because he so believed in his ultimate goal.

"Why?" he muttered. "Why d'you do it?"

Unwillingly he glanced at RG, who slept with his mouth open, snoring softly through his adenoids. When RG was balling a white girl he was cold, cruel to her, giving her no more thought than a vessel into which he could release his tensions (and hatred?). Was this what he, Clay Gillies, had done? *Can you fuck an ideal,* Clay asked himself; *can a man ball a belief?*

Clay forced himself to lie down, breathing slowly and evenly in rhythm with RG, trying to fall asleep. He couldn't.

The riot lasted that hot week.

Three weeks later, with an uneasy, National Guard induced quiet settled over the city, at eleven fifteen on a cloudy Tuesday morning, Clay Gillies found himself with nothing to do. Ab-so-lute-ly no-thing. He sat straight-legged on his mattress, taking deep drags on his hand-rolled cigarette. Windows shut tight. Behind him, Old Glory wavering. On floor boards in front of him, five unopened Pabst cans. A record had just finished; RG's soldering of hi-fi components hadn't resulted in automatic turnoff and the dull whirr annoyed Clay's ears. He didn't stop it. Instead he wiggled his hairy toes. He felt nothing. Can you be too stoned to feel your own feet? Did his feet exist? With his free hand he reached forward to pinch the knuckles of his big toe.

Brinnnnggg . . .

The phone on the ground next to him.

Brinnggg . . .

Brinnggg . . .

Three times, four, five. Ten. Clay released his toe, sitting back, inhaling rich smoke into his lungs. *Brinnnggg . . .* He killed the noise by picking up the receiver and setting it on the mattress.

"Gillies?"

Clay recognized the faint mouse squeak. RG.

"Come on, Gillies!" RG squawked impatiently through black holes.

Clay let his head loll, gazing up at the huge, funky, painted flag behind him. "Mouse." He laughed.

"Let me explain—"

Clay, laughing again, turned to place the receiver on the instrument with great care, making sure both prongs were pressed down. Who needed to hear RG's explanations? Hadn't Clay spent a full hour between eight thirty and nine thirty this morning listening to RG's explanations of why there was no room in SNAP for persons of Clay Gillies' unfortunate pallor? When, inevitably, the ringing started Clay covered his ears with his hands and flopped across the mattress.

He must've slept a long time.

When he woke the room was crowded with purple twilight. His head ached fiercely but, unfortunately, was quite clear. Therefore, still on his back, he reached for a Pabst can, yanking the key, raising the can above his head, pouring warm liquid into his mouth. Beer spilled on his beard. He had drained the second can when he heard light woman's footsteps echo along the uncarpeted hall. Maybe it was the girl from the back apartment. Viki. Viki worked as a topless waitress at a gambling club in Gardena; she had had silicones injected into her breasts to help her in her chosen profession. The breasts, though tremendous and well shaped, were unnaturally stiff. On her walls Viki proudly displayed before and after photographs.

A rapping.

"Go 'way, Viki."

"It's me. Odessa."

"Don't want any Odessa," Clay muttered.

"Come on, Clay, open up." More rapping.

"Shove off."

A key twisted in the lock. RG must've given Odessa his key. She entered, switching on the light. Clay blinked, shading his eyes with his hand, staring up at her. His objections to her visit melted. Through the years Odessa had changed not at all. She wore her hair in that proud Afro hairdo (a lot of others did now) and although Clay was too far away to sniff, his mind told him it smelled dry and sweet like his earliest memories of haystacks around Port Claibourne. Under short, cream-colored sleeves, her brown arms were as firm as ever, her breasts the same lovely shape. Clay still yearned to bare those breasts and press his face against flesh so much smoother and warmer, Clay was positive, than his ex-wife's prides, so much softer, Clay was sure, than Viki's professional marvels.

She kept staring down at him.

"Beer on beard?" he asked.

She tilted her head questioningly.

"Beer on beard?" he repeated.

She still looked perplexed. "Clay, you're stoned," she said.

"Not stoned enough."

"The place smells like Saturday night at the old hash factory."

He drew air into his nostrils. "S'been hours."

"If I were the law, know where you'd be now?"

"On the way downtown," he replied. Then he enunciated

with great care, "Is there beer foam on my beard?"

She shook her head. "May I sit down?"

"Nope."

"It's rotten, having to beg to talk to you."

"Then why beg? Why talk?"

"Because we're friends." She sighed. "I can't let it end like this."

End? Oh, God.

She took his silence as invitation. Setting down her black patent purse she lifted one of the folding chairs used at SNAP meetings and pushed the battered legs into position. He watched. She gazed back steadily. Her large eyes were bloodshot as if she'd been weeping. The great earth mother (Ge in the big Sunday *Times* crosswords that RG sweated over) weeping for the pale, underbaked child who must, it's so sad, be shoved into the abyss. She sat down.

"No need for this," he muttered. "Too much talk."

"Clay, don't make it so rough." Her lips trembled.

"RG explained."

"I know. But I'm hoping I can do a better job."

"It's wrong!" Clay burst out.

"Clay—"

"You're as rotten as any other racist bunch!"

"Listen—"

"You stink as bad as Wallace!"

Sighing, she gazed down at him. He grew calmer. And it occurred to him that although he had lusted (hopelessly) after her body and had longed (equally hopelessly) to penetrate her mind, he knew no more of either than he had at their first meeting. Oh, there was much affection, warmth and ease between them. They had spent one million hours together. Yet, it seemed to him, she had paced through the months and years of their friendship as if she dwelled in a castle, showing him only those impervious ramparts of herself that any might see. She had guarded her real self in a secret tower. Now that he thought of it, did he even know her age?

"How old're you?" he asked.

She blinked, bewildered by the conversational shift.

"S'it secret?" he asked.

"Of course not," she said. "Thirty-nine."

"Thirty-nine," he echoed. It was a lot older than he had figured, yet it in no way altered his longings for her.

"Last December eighteenth," she said. "Me and Jack Benny."

A small grin tugged at the corners of her lips. The sad little
smile emphasized her high cheekbones. Was there Indian blood?
"Don't trust anyone over thirty?" she asked.

He shook his head, lifting a beer can, trying to decide
whether he could drink another without urinating. Modesty,
God knows, wasn't his hang-up, but for some reason he couldn't
stand the thought of using the head with Odessa listening.

"Clay," she said, "let's get down to it."

"Why?"

"Because I want you to understand."

"Simple, isn't it? I'm out."

She leaned forward, crossing her slim ankles—she had very
fine legs, Odessa, long and slender. "At every meeting you
spoke and RG handed round the envelope. The kids, the black
kids, figured he was your man Friday."

"He put it another way." Clay laughed harshly. "He played,
he said, Joshua to my Moses."

"I should've seen it years ago. Maybe I did. Yes . . . I guess
I did. But I didn't want to accept it."

"Why not?"

She shrugged. "You might say I've always been afflicted
with a sort of romantic Victorian vision. I want to believe the
world can be a better place. S'the second time I've been taken
in."

Clay looked up. Despite his anguish he was interested in
her past.

She went on, "When I was little my parents had a lot of
black and white friends. Those days are a sort of mythical
paradise for me. A place of innocence. Eden. Understand what
I mean?"

He nodded.

"Well, when I hit school—let's just say I had a rude awak-
ening. And I wanted back in. But can you ever go back? Oh,
my parents and their friends had the key, or so they thought.
On the day, they said, that the workers took over, then the
separation of black and white would be abolished. Along with
other evils, like bosses."

"You belonged?"

She raised an eyebrow, shrugging.

"I never knew."

"Briefly. My parents and their friends, they were wonderful
people and they meant well. But they were naïve. I learned
my Orwell the hard way. Remember? All animals are equal

but some are more equal than others. Certain developments in my own life . . . mmm . . . let's just say I came to see the class struggle wasn't the same as the race struggle. The Party was my first mistake. The second—"

"*That* was no mistake!"

"Weren't you more equal than RG?"

"If he could've made them give"—Clay rubbed his thumb against his forefinger in a furious pantomime of folding money—"he'd have done the talking."

"You're a terrific speaker—"

"Hypnotic," Clay interrupted bitterly.

"—and what chance would RG have next to you?"

"So who cares about the lousy fund raising? S'not important to the kids. At least let me do that."

She closed her eyes a moment. "Don't you see? There it is in a nutshell. We've got to have our own."

"And burn, baby, burn; why don't you tell me that, too?"

"Listen to me. Twice I've been fooled. Well, now I'm being practical. White is white. Black is black—at least in this year of our Lord nineteen hundred and sixty-five. Won't you admit that much?"

"*Never!*"

"Please don't sound so cold."

"Cold?" Here he was begging, practically on his damn knees, for the job he loathed most, crawling after pennies, and she called him cold.

She sighed. "You've got every right to frost me."

"Why does it have to boil down to this one thing I hate, hate, hate? The color of a man's skin?"

"Because that's the way the world is." Tears glittered as she shook her head. "I'm sorry, Clay . . . sorry, sorry. Please look at me?"

He looked. She wore no make-up, not even her usual eyebrow pencil and lipstick, and this lack made her seem, strangely, older yet younger.

"I've quit snowing myself," she said. "And here's the truth. Our kids don't need token integration or even money. Pride, that's what they need. Pride. Black people they can look up to."

"And me?" Clay couldn't repress his cry of anguish.

"Maybe you could pick up the normal pieces."

"Balls!"

"I'm sorry. That was stupid."

"Yes."

"Well, there's other wrongs that need fighting."

A quixotic trip! Was that all she thought this had meant to him? The nausea inside him forced beer up to his gullet. The pressure on his bladder grew.

He rose, accidentally kicking a beer can. It rolled noisily across the silent room.

Standing above her chair he gripped the flesh of her upper arms, jerking her roughly to her feet. Her sharp, sweet odors inundated him. His fingers dug but she didn't cry out; instead she stared gravely at him. Odessa was a tall woman and her eyes were almost on a level with his own. He could hear his own harsh, uncertain breath. And he thought, hotly, of tearing the cream-colored blouse from her; he imagined the sound of tearing underclothes; he thought of a full brown body exposed, of breasts, of flagellation, of tying slender brown legs wide apart and whipping the soft secret flesh viciously before he thrust his aching self into her again and again, thus canceling the mystery of her person. Rape and more than rape. His groin ached with its dual needs. His fingers bit into her arms. She must have understood the erotic chaos of his thoughts. She gazed steadily at him, her eyes filled with compassion and sadness. And from his throat came a thin wail of shamed misery, for he realized that his thoughts were a giant combo of all the ugly lusts of white men toward black women.

He released her so abruptly she almost fell.

"I hate it as much as you do," she said softly. "Clay, don't you think I know how much you've given up for us? School. Michele and Lissa. Your chance at a career—"

The pressure on his bladder could no longer be borne.

Slamming the head door on himself, he stood urinating with an old man's humiliating slowness. He turned on the sink faucet, letting coolness wash his hands.

"Clay," she called over the running water.

"Go," he muttered.

"Clay—"

For God's sake, go now.

Footsteps came closer.

Right outside the door she said, "Clay, please listen, please. I'm sorry. Sorry . . ."

He stood there, slow rusty water from old pipes trickling over his tensed fingers. After a minute he heard the door close. He turned off the water, listening until he could no longer hear her footsteps. He went back in the other room. She had left RG's key on the table.

He dropped onto the mattress. Clay Gillies stretched out, surrounded by the heavy smell of pot and his own empty thoughts, a kite drifting, a tumbleweed, a formless nothing. If a man has no purpose, why should he take up space? Alone in the apartment he had shared with his black friend (black? RG was underdone toast), in the apartment where he had passed the happiest years of his life, Clay Gillies saw he no longer had a purpose.

None.

Pressing his face into the sheet that smelled of his own sweat, he cried.

It was more than an hour later that he rose, splashing cold water on his face. Without drying his beard or combing his hair, he pulled on his shabby windbreaker. He dropped his door key on the table next to its twin. Taking nothing with him, he left the door ajar.

A sea fog had settled over the darkness. He turned east on busy Olympic. Headlights cut blurred circles into the night. He had just lost the two people who meant the most to him in the world. He wondered, briefly, if some of their tremendous power over him came from the past, from the long-ago days in Port Claibourne, black people with their easy laughter, their soft, slurry talk, their warm comforting odors, their kindness to a half orphan who might just as well have been a full orphan. Odessa, he thought, and RG, did he love them not simply for themselves but for the echoes that they raised? He mustn't think of the past, recent or dim. It was useless.

He had no belongings. He examined the contents of his pockets: three crumpled ones, a Kennedy half dollar, a nickel and four pennies. He walked briskly, still moving east, away from his apartment. On impulse he cut in on a side residential street. Fog curtailed the lampposts' icy stations of visibility. A dog barked, rousing other dogs up and down the sleeping block. Small ugly houses lurked each alone behind a tiny square of grass. A tract unfriendly as a row of identical clenched fists. Clay visualized the inhabitants. Lower middle class. White. They would share a TV-every-night button-down-mind-*Reader's-Digest* mentality. Under every roof a dishwasher and a garbage disposal and a pile of monthly payments, in each semi-detached garage a late-model unpaid-for car. This was the sort of place his ex-wife had hammered at him for. *You could pick up the normal pieces*. . . . Odessa had said that. Oh, how he despised these neat normal pieces of stucco, the mortgaged minds dreaming of a new Chevy hardtop or how to swing the down on a color TV because the neighbor had one.

These small houses were tombs.

Another dog barked. Clay, no coward he, suddenly felt his heart lurch with fear. The hairs on his body prickled. He was alone in a dark graveyard.

Was he dead now, too?

He raced to the lights of Olympic.

Leaning against a fire hydrant he waited, panting, until his heart returned to normal, then he raised his arm, pointing his thumb east toward the continental United States.

Part Five

──────── • **1** • ────────

Michele Sutherland rested in a foam of small lace pillows propped against the rococo shell of a carved king-size headboard; the wood had been silver-antiqued to a hint of pearly green. A green coverlet curved like a huge pale water-lily leaf over blankets. It was a bright June morning, but in here the light was dappled by a stand of birches and further muted by sheer celadon curtains; the bedroom glowed with softness like an underwater grotto and Michele might have been a pretty mermaid sipping her overcreamed coffee.

At the moment she was engrossed in the color television built into the mint-green armoire opposite her bed. She was tuned to *Girl News and Views*. Mary Louise, the show's commentator, chatted about someone Michele knew or—more precisely—the father of someone Michele knew. York's father. Baron York. A still photo of the rugged movie star wearing western riding clothes filled the screen while Mary Louise's marshmallow voice described his way of thinking; Baron York, as all Hollywood knew, had never worried about his personal popularity or his career, not when it came to battling certain powerful factions in the Screen Actors Guild, and Baron York, Mary Louise said, was dedicated to speaking out against un-American activities whether in SAG or on the campuses of our state's colleges . . . Berkeley beatniks, draft card burners . . . outside communist agitators. . . . Michele finished her coffee and set the bone china cup and saucer on the low silver-green bedside table. She yawned. Always politics had bored her. But onscreen came a clip of Baron and his new wife, a tall, stunning brunette. Michele gave full attention. They looked so happy as they strolled down the beautiful terraces of their home, smiling at one another, flanked by the two pretty York girls while a young husky—by now all California knew that pup was named Niko—gamboled about them.

"Baron, please give up this nonsense that you're only an actor," Mary Louise pleaded offscreen. "Aren't our other fine actors, Ronnie and George M., proving themselves in the field of politics?" Mr. York draped an arm over his wife's shoulders and she smiled up at him. "We need strong men with strong convictions, leaders who aren't afraid to speak out against the disorders of our times. We need—"

The pale-green princess phone gave a discreet buzz.

Michele frowned. *No*body called her this early. The phone buzzed again. With a sigh she gave one last reluctant glance at the screen, then pressed the remote control; Baron York and his family faded into a glowing dot. She leaned over to pick up the phone and as she did she caught a glimpse of herself in the green depths of the shell-shaped mirror. Her pale hair was caught up on top of her head with a narrow ribbon, one full prize almost popped out of her sheer nightie. Her annoyance faded. She smiled at herself. She shopped as carefully for lingerie as for any of her clothes; after all, as Dear Abby said, a husband is your most important audience, and this nightie was especially low-cut. No wonder Everett called her his center-page bunny. As soon as she heard the voice at the other end her smile faded.

"Clay," she said.

"I'd like to see Lissa this afternoon," he said without any preliminary, just as if he hadn't absented himself a full year—well . . . eight months. In that time Lissa had received from a shop in New York called F.A.O. Schwarz for her birthday and Christmas, delivered at the same time, four *Peanuts* books! Michele had decided that Charlie Brown, Lucy, Snoopy and all the others were the biggest hoax ever put over on the American public. There had been a few colored postcards from dreary places like Chicago and Detroit. And that was all. And yet here was Clay asking matter of factly, "What time does she get out of school?"

"You can't see her today."

"Why not?"

"This afternoon's her ballet."

"What time's it over?"

"Five."

"Five!"

"And then she has homework."

"She's just a baby—"

"Five and a half!"

"—and they don't have homework."

"I wrote you. Everett's sending her to private school."

"I didn't get the letter."

"I sent it care of SNAP."

"I want to see her."

"What's the rush. Why today? You've been away a year."

"That makes a year of Sunday visits I've missed."

And Michele came right back with, "A year of child support you've missed."

"I'll make it up."

"And this isn't Sunday."

"Michele, don't lay it on."

Was that a hint of weariness in his sharp voice? Sadness? Regret? Michele leaned back in the soft little pillows. Strange itches darted down there. . . . Memories stirred . . . she felt suddenly submissive.

"I guess it won't be the end of the world if she misses one ballet," Michele said.

"I'll pick her up."

"Be here at two."

Michele considered calling Mother right away to impart the news. But it was exactly nine, time for Jack La Lanne. She turned on TV and got out of bed to follow Jack's directions. It's never too soon for a girl to start keeping in shape, she thought, lowering in a deep knee bend, listening to Jack announce that the thigh is a woman's worst trouble spot.

She got back in bed and dialed Mrs. Davy.

She and Mother dissected Clay's motives and nerve while Dozer yipped in the background. Mother tended to look on the gloomy side and kept repeating, "I hope he's not here to make more trouble," but Michele couldn't see what trouble he could make, beyond causing Lissa to miss this afternoon's ballet class at Mr. Lichine's. Clay had never gotten along well with Mother, but Mother and Everett were very close, which proved to Michele that it had been Clay who'd been lacking in that particular relationship as in all others.

This was Tuesday. Not one of her mornings to phone her mother-in-law, a stout, placid widow who cooked gourmet for herself and her crazy French housekeeper in that huge old pile in Palos Verdes. A toll call. Those could really mount up, so Michele phoned her Mondays, Wednesdays and Fridays. Religiously. Michele, fond of her mother-in-law, anxiously desired her mother-in-law to like her and overlook her drawbacks, a second marriage and not being able to have more babies.

Michele dialed Aunt Evelyn. Aunt Evelyn lived only five

blocks away. Again Michele smiled at her reflection, thinking as she listened to the dial tone that even back in California High she had envied Leigh her stunning up-to-date mother. Now she used Aunt Evelyn as her guide; Aunt Evelyn knew the best decorator, the newest beauty parlor, the most "in" restaurant, the right-size purse; Aunt Evelyn introduced her to her own special salesladies at Saks, I. Magnin and Amelia Gray (which was too expensive for Michele). Aunt Evelyn was a doll. Actually it was a two-way street, for although Aunt Evelyn never said as much, Michele knew Leigh's marriage was a low blow, and Michele was positive that it pleased her to have a pretty niece as a sort of stand-in daughter.

Aunt Evelyn picked up the phone.

"Hi, Aunt Evelyn."

"Hello, dear," Aunt Evelyn said. "How are you?"

"Fine," Michele said. "And you?"

"Fine."

"And Uncle Sidney?" Michele asked.

"Fine, too."

"Stevie?"

"His cold's better."

"Have you heard from Leigh?" Leigh and Ken, out of the Peace Corps, made their home in a ramshackle Berkeley flat.

"Not since that letter I showed you," Aunt Evelyn said. "How's Lissa?"

"Fine."

"And Everett?"

"Fine, too," Michele fibbed. She had gotten the hang of these ladylike conversations, learning it was discourtesy to mention anything unpleasant in the preliminaries; therefore she saved Everett's hives until later.

"I was just about to call you, dear," Aunt Evelyn said. "I had to change my beauty parlor appointment so I can't make it for lunch today. I'm awfully sorry—"

"Oh, don't be!" Michele cried. "I was feeling all guilty. I can't make it either." And she launched into the story of Clay's call.

The phone calls, one to her mother and the other to Aunt Evelyn, took well over an hour.

Maggie, the cleaning girl, had been here yesterday so Michele only had to stack the few breakfast dishes in the dishwasher and close the folding doors to the dining room, which was unfurnished since Michele—and Everett, too, of course—

had decided to do a good job on the living room and wait on the dining room.

At twelve she started dressing. A hot day, luckily; she could wear one of the two summer dresses she'd just bought on her I. Magnin's charge account. She stood in her mirrored dressing alcove changing from the blue linen to the pink piqué, which was A-line and more slenderizing, then back again to the blue, which was shorter, inches above the knee, and therefore way newer looking. Skirts were really up this year. Minis. Luckily she didn't have thick thighs, the usual curse of short girls. All dressed, she realized she'd forgotten her perfume, so she unzipped and lavished Jolie Madame, the world's most expensive, under her wired lace brassiere . . . how sweet to be able to squander real perfume.

Clay was driving a gorgeous Italian-looking silver sports car. Michele, wild with curiosity, hidden by celadon batiste of her bedroom drapes, watched him climb the red brick steps that divided sloping emerald dichondra. Usually Michele's throat filled with pride of ownership when she surveyed her property. But somehow in the presence of that car, her carefully landscaped garden, formal rose bushes set in circles of fertilized dirt and braced silver birches, seemed tacky and old-fashioned. Clay hadn't changed at all. He still had his beard. He wore denim work pants and a white tee shirt. She couldn't help thinking of Everett's row of plastic-covered, stockbroker-dark suits. Had Clay ever owned a suit?

Where had he gotten that car?

She waited a full two minutes after the chimes sounded to open the door. She was surrounded by Clay's familiar odors. Harsh. Acrid. Very masculine. It came to her with a shock of surprise that Clay was so much smaller than Everett. Not every place, though, and she visualized in her mind a quick comparison. Clay's was longer and fatter. Feeling her face grow hot, she moved hastily aside. She fibbed, telling Clay that Lissa should be home this minute, the car pool must be delayed. Wouldn't he like to come in and sit down? He followed her into the recently furnished living room, all muted whites and greens; *d'rectwahr,* that was the way Mr. Samson, the decorator Aunt Evelyn had recommended, pronounced the style. Clay didn't notice the elegance. He sat on the couch. Michele worried about grubby denim raping virgin off-white silk.

"Everett and I," she started, "are thinking of getting a sports car."

Clay yawned.

"We aren't sure if we ought to get an American."

Clay shrugged.

"The parts are easier to get. But the foreigns are built better, I've heard."

Another shrug.

She would have to be more obvious. "That's a beautiful one you have." She paused for a *thank you* that never came. She went on, "What is it?"

"How should I know?"

"It's yours, isn't it?"

"Nope."

"But you're driving—"

"It's York's."

"York!" Michele cried, and the car, because it belonged to York to whom such cars came naturally, faded into oblivion. "Is he back?"

"Uh huh."

"That's what I call a coincidence!"

"That he left Greece?"

"No, *no*. This morning I was watching—I mean reading in the paper, about his father. Did York say anything?"

"What about?"

"His father."

"Nope."

"Nothing?"

"Nothing."

"Not one word about Mr. York's running for office?"

Clay had risen and was looking out the bay window.

"He doesn't want to," Michele said, "but there's a move on to draft him, and everybody's wondering if—"

Clay's knuckles rapped on freshly washed glass. That was how he was, she remembered furiously. As soon as he knew she was interested in something, he would refuse to discuss it. But she noted his profile, seeing the lines carved at the corner of his eye. The shadow was a lot darker. He looked tired and much older than twenty-four.

Michele softened.

"I talked to Lissa at noon," she said. "She's really excited you're here." A kind fib.

He didn't smile.

"Clay, d'you feel all right?"

"Great."

"You look so tired."

He grunted.

"Is something wrong?" she persisted.

"If you'd told me she wouldn't get here until two thirty— or is it three?—I needn't have come until then."

His words dropped like ice cubes, bringing memories of how she'd battered and frozen herself against the chill of him.

"She's late." Michele could be frosty, too.

"Oh, sure."

"I'm getting worried."

"It's a great-looking room." He turned, pacing around. "The house is great-looking. Your hair is great-looking. Your dress is great-looking. There! That's why you wanted me here early, isn't it?"

"What you think is totally unimportant to me!"

"Hah!"

"The car pool's late," she said. "I'm worried. Clay, can't we have a small amount of dignity?"

"You play Queen Victoria in here," he said. "I'll wait out-side."

"Have her back by six!" Michele shouted as he slammed the front door. "No later. You hear! *Six!*"

She held a hand over her breast. It took several minutes for her heart to stop its furious pounding. She tiptoed, although nobody could possibly see or hear her. The empty dining room was carpeted and draped and she hid by the very edge of lined pinch pleats. Clay sprawled in the buglike silver car, head thrown back, beard raised, one hand covering his eyes. Doubt-less he was protecting himself from the sun. But for some crazy reason it popped into Michele's carefully combed head that he was hiding tears.

Clay Gillies cry?

Ridiculous.

Even during that last terrible argument had she ever once gotten through to him? She had wept buckets. He had remained cold and completely calm. So why would he cry now? Michele bit her full lower lip as she pondered the question: seeing the irrefutable evidence that Everett Sutherland had given her everything that he, Clay Gillies, could not, would that depress him so? Michele's smooth forehead puckered. It wasn't in character, but what else had upset Clay?

At last Martha Billings' black station wagon drove up. Three little maids sat in navy-checked private school uniforms. Mi-

chele peeked out the draped window. Clay opened the station
wagon door. Lissa refused to budge. Thumb to pouting lips,
she shrank from her father. He cajoled. Finally he took her
small wrist and Lissa said something that looked like *no,* shifting closer to Martha Billings, but Martha shoved her forward,
propelling her into Clay's arms. Clay tried to kiss her. Lissa,
normally very affectionate, squirmed away.

Well, after all that time, what did Clay expect?

Michele, watching from her pretty, silent house, wondered
what he had expected. She wondered, too, why she should be
crying.

It was long after six when the Yellow Cab summoned by Gillies
finally arrived.

York sprawled limp by the pool, watching the wet-haired
child followed by the tense, muscular man climb landscaped
terraces. York didn't have the energy to see them to the house;
instead he remained flat on the chaise, nerves raw—who was
sandpapering his damn nerve ends? The child raced into the
house and her cry, *Hurry up!* reached York. Shrill. York winced.
He never had been one for the kiddies and neither, so it would
seem, was Gillies; Lissa had spent the entire three hours of
their visit in the pool, alternately splashing and insisting that
she was ready to go home. Gillies—he should read Dr. Spock
in his earlier incarnation—had been totally helpless to stop the
performance.

A miserable three hours.

Not to be repeated.

York lay still on the chaise, ordering his muscles to relax.
His teeth remained clenched. His skin continued to be abraded.
After ten minutes he went twitching into the pool house.

Some time later he emerged, calmed, pulling his bad arm
through a black cable-knit sleeve, sprawling on the same chaise,
dark glasses fixed on the setting sun; it was, he decided, a
great red coin dropping into the slot machine of the Pacific and

when it sank—tilt!—three vast lemons would appear in the red sky, signifying total cataclysm. You lose, earthlings. York's open eyes could actually see the outline of those three vast lemons. He gave a short laugh. Three lemons occurred neither on earth (in one-armed bandits) nor in heaven. Yet... were they any more unbelievable than the truth, mushroom pie in the sky?

A twilight hush had settled, quieting raucous birds, stilling the moving shrubbery. Lights began to form grids on the city below, and in the house drapes closed along the glass wall of the dining room, Crowell setting the table so Baron York, the new Mrs. York and their guests could confer over vast slabs of rare beef. Every night in the three weeks York had been home there had been company, vastly different from the old guestless reign of Linda Farnahan York. York, naturally, never fed at the festive board; he couldn't, however, at all times avoid the guests—speech writers, mysterious oilmen, well-known politicians with smile lines carved deep into their tans, members of the New York advertising firm his father used for his non-campaign—but always he edged away, quickly, silently as a shadow.

York, like Garbo, wanted to be alone.

He was a loner. Sometimes, it's true, a small whisper asked if he were a loner born or bred, and this he answered truthfully: *probably both*. In Athens he'd lived alone, utterly alone, in a quiet, tree-filled suburb, Kifissia. He allowed himself no friends or acquaintances. He spoke so infrequently that on occasion he would give a grating paean into smogless Athenian air to remind himself he was not a mute. Each morning, alone, he left his third-story flat before stout Mrs. P., the concierge—her name was too polysyllabic and complicatedly Greek to use—lugged woven bags of food up the steep stairs and began to cook, clean and launder. These hours he spent silently visiting museums, digs, antiquaries, bookstores. He returned long after Mrs. P. had descended heavily to her basement rooms. Afternoons and evenings he read and made notes for a projected monograph: Athenian Drama Prior to the Roman Conquest. When desire caught up with him he visited a certain tile-roofed house in Piraeus that catered to sailors from the Near East; the girls, plump peasants plucked of their coarse black axial hair to childish nudity, were trained as passive receptacles of men's desire, and they never winced at York's arm or the pimples on his narrow back; they accepted the final convulsions of his

scrawny self with even-breathed silence—with these girls York
felt as if he were still alone. In Athens he'd had airmailed to
him the *Los Angeles Times*. A bad mistake. For this last six
months he'd been forced to follow his father's much publicized
disinclination for a political career. On this matter, as all others
pertaining to his father, the sole emotion he willed himself to
feel was a cold indifference. Yet as each pertinent news item
arrived, he found himself drawn out of his aloofness. He would
read, angered and baffled by his own fury, and when he was
finished he would tear paper into narrow strips, flushing them
down the chain-style toilet. He wanted to stop it, stop it, *stop
it*, stop this new triumph of his father's. Oh, he was aware of
his personal limitations, just as he was aware of the vast powers
that must be propelling the Great Granite Face. York, on a
rational level, knew there wasn't one damn thing he could do
to stop his father. Yet . . . each morning as he unfolded the paper
and took his first gulp of Mrs. P.'s strong black coffee, he felt
his anger rise. Inexorably, he was drawn back to Los Angeles—

He heard footsteps.

The new Mrs. York moved around the twilit pool. A white
cashmere cardigan hung loose from her wide shoulders. She
was a handsome woman, large of excellently proportioned bone,
with thick black hair. She reminded York of the caryatids, those
marble ladies who for twenty-five centuries have supported the
heavy portico of the Erechtheum on their heads.

"I've brought you something," she said.

She held a cut crystal bowl piled high with flawless purple-
black Ribiers, the kind her predecessor had called "sickroom
grapes." The new Mrs. York sat near him on a low woven-
plastic stool. With firm click of sterling shears she severed a
grape, peeling dark skin in strips. Juice wetted her busy fingers;
her broad gold wedding band glinted in the last rays of the
dying sun; there was a small wet sound and the sweet smell of
the vine. She held a naked, translucent globe in which nestled
three seeds toward him.

"No, thanks." He shook his head. His own mother, when
he'd been a small boy frightened by dark hospital rooms, had
peeled Ribiers for him in this same way.

"Open up."

It was too difficult to argue. He opened up. She popped in
the grape and for a fraction of a second too long her well-
shaped, juice-moistened fingers hovered near his lips. The feeding, the lingering fingers, were an obvious physical ploy, yet

there was a strange lack of sensuality about this woman; it surprised him that his father had chosen her. York masticated sweet, liquid flesh. Or maybe he was confusing feminine yielding with sexuality? This woman was marble strong and maybe his father, at fifty-seven (not the publicized fifty-one), had picked her for strength; maybe after all the tomcatting years he needed his broads to end up on top.

"Aren't you going to say thank you?" she asked.

"It's rude to talk with a full mouth."

"You're whispering."

"Maybe the place is bugged."

"By us?" she reproved.

"By one of those morally bankrupt Democrats Father's always talking about," York said in normal tones.

A bird began to sing in the dark trees, then fell silent.

Mrs. York peeled another grape. "It's time," she said slowly, "for us to get acquainted."

"Haven't they told you about me?" York crossed his legs. "The term is alienated."

She looked up from the grape. "Alienated?"

"Cut off from the world."

"I know the meaning," she said. "Why did you come home?"

"It's the newest kicks for us alienated types, playing prodigal son. Haven't you heard?"

"In the three weeks you've been home you haven't spoken to your father."

"One of those strong, silent, manly relationships."

"Or your sisters."

He spat tear-shaped seeds into his palm. She popped another naked grape in his mouth.

"You haven't spoken to me," she said.

"I *have* looked."

"And?"

"Daddy always did have excellent taste."

"I know about that."

He peered through the twilight at her. Her high forehead was serene; her dark eyes revealed no hidden meanings.

"Well, I suppose everyone reads *Confidential*," he said.

"I never have."

"Not even under the drier?"

"I know all about him," she said, "and you, too, Adam."

This time there was no need to search her face, the meanings were too obvious.

"I don't know about you," he said.

"That's why I'm here. So we can get to know one another."

"It's true that you're wealthy?"

"My grandfather is."

"I've read along the lines of a J. Paul Getty."

"Grandfather says more than."

York whistled.

"He's very averse to publicity," she said.

"Modest, wealthy and very, very old."

"All," she agreed.

"And love, too. Daddy hit the jackpot."

"It won't work, Adam."

"What?"

She ate a peeled grape. "The cool act."

"Genuine." He pulled at his thin, mud-colored hair. "See? Won't come out."

"A real cool doesn't play it that way."

"Oh?"

"No," she said firmly.

"How then?"

"The real cool wears a big sincere Gleem smile and uses those people who pretend to be cynics."

"Ouch."

"Well?"

"Me, I've resigned from being a user or a usee."

"No emotions?"

"Indifference *über alles*, that's the motto engraved on my manly heart."

"I don't think so."

"What then?"

"I think you hate."

"Anyone in particular?"

"Your father."

"The most elementary psychology book'll tell you that's normal."

With a half-peeled grape, she pointed at his short arm. "For that?" she asked.

"It's your idea. You figure it."

"I've been trying to," she said. "Open."

He took in another grape.

"Because of your mother?" she asked. "Everyone says you were close, very close."

"She's been cold a long time."

"That's no answer."

"It'll have to do. Helen, why this grape-feeding session?"

"Your father's political career," she said without hesitation.

"You don't believe the news?" York tossed his accumulation of seeds toward the grass. "He's not interested."

"Don't play clever games."

"He never was before."

"He cleaned up the union," she said.

"A role."

"It *was* the Screen Actors Guild," she retorted.

And it *was* funny. York peered at her again. She wasn't smiling.

"What's he got in mind?" York asked.

"Senator."

"That's all?"

"That's not all."

York couldn't help grunting. He had figured this, yet somehow, hearing her say it, he couldn't put down his surprise—it wasn't every day you heard your near and dear aspired to lead two hundred million people, was it?

"A lot of people think his chances are excellent."

"Your grandfather?"

"He has a certain interest."

"Vested?"

"Politicians are at best ephemeral," she said. "Money remains."

"And you?" York asked. "How do you rate his odds?"

She didn't answer. She glanced up the night-shrouded terraces. Headlights shone. There was the rough hiss of a heavy car braking on gravel. Guests arriving.

"That Gillies," she said, head still averted, her tone so soft that York had to look at her to make sure it was her voice, not leaves rustling, "That Gillies, the one who was here today. He's a troublemaker."

"How do you know?"

"Any person who comes to the house Jumpy checks."

Jumpy was Miss Ettiwanda Jumps, the secretary who had been hired to handle the fan mail following *Road to Damascus*. She had a long, sallow upper lip from which she tweezed dark, strong hairs and a firm conviction that working all these years for Baron York had transformed her into a modern vestal virgin, dedicated to her celluloid god and therefore above the rest of humanity.

"Did Jumpy also mention he was a high school buddy-buddy of mine?"

"Jumpy said you had no friends."

"And me voted most popular!" York grated.

"He *did* graduate from California High with you in the summer of sixty. You both attended UCLA, and in sixty-one you and he, together, went on a foray south. You both went to jail. After that Gillies dedicated himself to a civil rights organization. SNAP. Communist-backed then, possibly now. It advocates Black Power. And that, Adam, is exactly the sort of publicity we do not want."

"I suppose Jumpy told you he's not connected to SNAP now?" York closed his eyes behind his dark glasses; did she know everything, this black-haired woman his father had married?

"Yes, Jumpy did," she said. "Gillies makes trouble."

Across the sky a plane blinked red and green. The engine's roar filled the night. She spoke her next words so close to his right ear that York felt her breath as well as heard her voice.

"Don't rock the boat," she said. "There's piranhas in the water."

"Clever. Did one of Papa's speech writers make up the apt simile?"

She rose, pushing her strong, rounded arms into the sleeves of her white sweater. "Will you try to remember this? I don't joke."

"Not one hint, one snicker, not a teeny jot of humor?"

"Don't be clever."

"Comes naturally." He tugged his hair again. "Like the coolness."

"That, we agreed, isn't legitimate," she said. "Adam, I want to like you."

"Why?"

"Because," she said in her rather breathy voice, "your father's very fond of you."

"Nuts."

"He is."

"I could use a stronger term."

"Have it your way." She shrugged. "But Adam, consider this: we've been taught to believe that affection is implicit— sacred, you might say—to the relationship. But most parental love is obedience to our mores, nothing else."

York stretched his legs.

"He's not a bad father," she said, "and he'd be a better one if you let him."

"I'm not available for publicity stills."

"He's fond of you," she persisted. "But one thing you must never forget. He's an actor."

"A movie actor."

"Don't sneer," she said. "He can read every line given to him."

"Reassuring to one of the great American voting public."

"Don't see Gillies," she said.

"I've got you worried?"

"No."

"Listen, you know as well as me that presidential hopefuls have been known to lose out for divorcing the wives of their youth or having new mistresses or even for accepting minor campaign gifts of a doggy. The breath of scandal can huff and puff and blow—"

"Adam." She shook her head. "You won't be able to rock the boat."

"Then why feed me grapes and play Cassandra?"

"I've been trying to explain. Your father's fond of you, and it would sadden him"—she paused, buttoning the top of her sweater—"all right, hurt his image of himself, if you were to fall in and be eaten by his piranhas."

She walked to the pool house, flicking on the lights. Water shone cerulean, and she moved around the large oval to stand in front of him again. "Adam, we're glad you're home; both of us're glad."

"I liked it better when you were leveling."

"We are glad," she said, "very glad."

And leaving him the grapes, she hastened up terraces to greet her guests.

Alone, York chunked Ribiers one by one into heated, lighted water. The soothing drug had not clouded his brain; it had heightened rather than suppressed the weariness that extended human communications brought to him. His stepmother . . . York conjured her inside his brain, even to the dark mole, a beauty mark, on her rounded chin—this the face that launched a thousand noncampaign speeches? She was all knowing, yet . . . could she be completely aware of a small boy's terror, of a large brown horse, of a pug-nose woman's lonely death bed?

He massaged his short arm. Los Angeles nights are damp, and dampness caused bone-deep pain. He rose.

He echoed across the marble-floored hall, circling the tall, closed doors to the den. Behind, laughter and voices. As he reached the dining room, Kalpraga emerged through the swinging door to the butler's pantry. Kalpraga, moving with the light grace certain fat men possess, held a fresh drink—he drank continuously without ever passing the threshold to drunkenness. Stout and red-cheeked, he resembled Pierre Salinger and (oddly enough) also was a top-notch political speech writer. Kalpraga was his father's man. Seeing York, Kalpraga raised his glass. Ice tinkled thinly. They had not been introduced—York, in three weeks, hadn't emerged from his room long enough to meet any of his father's staff—but of course Kalpraga knew who he was.

"Hello, Adam," Kalpraga said in a voice that was deep and smooth as a cello. "Going to have dinner with us?"

"I already ate."

"Me, I drink mine." Kalpraga took a long swallow. The skin around his small dark eyes crinkled into a smile. "Tonight may prove interesting. The senator's dining *chez nous.*"

Footsteps. Baron York was starting down the curving flight of stairs. He moved well, as an actor must. Other than this ease, there was no sign he'd ever been a screen idol: he wore a black, conservatively cut suit, a dark tie, not too narrow; his sideburns were gone and his thick hair had been permitted to return to its natural gray, horn rims emphasized his cragginess and added a faint air of the scholar, his jawline sagged into maturity—was there such a thing as a face-dropping operation? York wondered.

Baron gave his lopsided grin. York averted his thin face. This was their first confrontation since his return, but neither gave a sign of it.

"Hello there, son," Baron York said as he reached the third step from the bottom. "Your company left?"

York didn't answer.

"Why don't you join us for dinner?" Baron asked.

"I already suggested," Kalpraga interpolated.

York pushed dark glasses up on his narrow nose. He wanted to bound up the steps, but his father stood guard over the bottom stair.

"You and Kal know one another, don't you, son?"

York didn't reply.

Kalpraga said, "Not formally."

"Informally, then." Baron gestured with his easy grin. "Kal, this is my boy, Adam. Son, this is Marv Kalpraga."

Kalpraga held out his hand. York took it for a second.

And two men, drinks in hand, came laughing out of the long den. Baron York faked a punch at his son's concave belly. "G'night, son," he said, as if concluding a long, humor-laden chat, then went smiling toward his guests. York took the stairs two at a time, three. Without turning on his lights he fell across his bed. Definitely he'd come out second—but hadn't he always felt this way after any encounter with Mount Rushmore?

The following morning York decided to drive up the coast, no goal in mind beyond a little over-the-legal-limits along Highway 1. Well, maybe San Simeon. He started at eleven thirty, for by then the house generally had emptied, but as he left his room, his father emerged from his, matching his pace to his son's, stride for stride. They descended the marble staircase wordlessly but undeniably together. Halfway down tall Baron draped a protective arm over his son's slight shoulders. Below, Kalpraga and another man watched; this other, gray-haired, pinch-chinned as a weasel, York sensed, was a reporter. York whirled; fatherly arm fell from him; he kangaroo-hopped upstairs. Without turning he knew his father gazed affectionately, quizzically, after the figure of his only legally begotten son— well, not exactly begotten legally, but—York's mouth stretched in a pale smile—*that* would never be brought up now.

Two days later York, passing along the upstairs hall with its new gallery of framed family snapshots, heard his father's famous flat tones boom from behind the closed door to his study. "Yes. Yes. The boy's home."

"Has he inherited your interest in politics, Mr. York?" a stranger asked.

A rustle of voices.

Press conference, what else? And York told his handmade shoes to keep moving. But for the life of him he couldn't force them to shift. He eavesdropped.

"He's exactly the same as me. A chip off the old block." You could hear the paternal fondness. "He's interested as a private citizen, only."

"Has he served his time in the service?" asked a shrill, unpleasant feminine voice.

"I'd just as soon not talk about—"

"Has he?" Again, the unpleasant female.

"If you're trying to insinuate again my boy's a draft-dodging peacenik, I don't want any!" Oh, the fatherly anger, the press-defying fatherly anger.

"I'm interested why he lived abroad so long," the ugly voice persisted. "I'm sure my readers are, too."

And Kalpraga's rich, smooth tones. "I take it you haven't met Adam, Miss Boggs?"

"No, but—"

"If you had, you wouldn't ask the question. Poor kid. . . . The arm . . . well, he's got a bad arm. Childhood horseback-riding accident."

The woman gave a small, embarrassed cough.

"Sensitive about it," Baron muttered.

"And you're always trying to protect him. . . ." The harsh female voice had melted into honey. "Of course, Mr. York. You can count on me. Not one word about your boy's service record."

His father, York noted, was no longer the Ojai oil fields' gift to Hollywood; amid the informal snaps in the upstairs rogue's gallery hung a law diploma from Colorado Collegeum. This modestly framed document was duly mentioned by the press. No denials came from the small college. Indeed, from all over the country unsolicited letters arrived, old Col graduates recalling good old Baron, as well as one spidery, well-publicized note from a Professor Emery chiding Baron for wasting his fine legal talents.

Everyone appeared to have forgotten the articles in *Confidential*.

The human mind, York reflected, is wondrously malleable.

York lay on the carpet, skinny legs propped on his desk, reading his shorthand notes on the bastardization of Euripides. Through aluminum screening came the clatter of women's heels along the stone-paved patio.

"—and the third from the left, that's Adam's." His father's new wife's breathy voice drifted up through sunlit air. "He's our eldest."

"Your husband's, you mean?" gushed a woman.

"They're my children now." His father's new wife added with a hint of maternal pride, "Adam's our brilliant one."

"Oh?"

"A serious writer."

"Any hopes for starting a new family, Mrs. York?"

"Ours is perfect now. Two girls and a boy. What more could . . . " Her voice faded down the terrace.

Adam, we're glad you're home. . . . York hurled his notes across the room.

"Yes, yes. Sure I understand what you're trying to get across, Mike. And, if you'll pardon some plain speaking, that's one more example of this generation-gap bunk. There's no such thing as a generation gap. Mike, most of our young people want a decisive victory in Vietnam. Just the other day my boy— I'm sure you've met him—he said that his friends agree the country has to fulfill our commitments. He also says he thinks the beard and bead bunch who make all the noise are less than one hundredth of one percent of the kids. Come on, Mike, you old fraud, admit I'm hearing it like it is."

Footsteps moved along the hall.

In the darkness York, fully dressed, lay on his bed, briefly a captive audience. He applauded, clapping three times. Just as once, living on another plane, he'd been forced to admit as a talent the untamable sex that the Carven Wonder projected onto a blank white screen, so now, on a different plateau, seeing his father throw another image—this time onto the minds and hearts of his countrymen—York was forced to admit another facet of the older man's talent. The Concrete Block had raw genius. But did that make him any less the enemy? York closed his eyes. He saw Linda Farnahan York, skeletal, alone, her huge eyes widening with fear at the oncoming emptiness. He opened his own eyes and stared, unblinking, at faintly luminous dark windows.

Wasn't it about time he tried, even though it was pretty hopeless, to do something?

The suitcase spread open on the unused twin bed.

"So you're leaving?" Kalpraga leaned against York's door jamb. Last night, Madison Avenue public relations people had flown in for conferencing, so the writer had stayed. Over his fat, tanned, hairy body Kalpraga wore a crimson terrycloth robe, carelessly tied. Unshaven stubble showed purple through full red cheeks. Although it was not yet nine of a cloudy morning, he held his inevitable glass. York, a week ago, had come to the reluctant conclusion that he liked Kalpraga. Isn't that a gas, York had snorted through thin nostrils, meet the kind of guy, intellectual, sardonic and honest, that you could like, and he has to be the speech writer for a tony phony baloney?

York opened a drawer.

"Heading back to Greece?" Kalpraga asked.

York removed dark wool socks rolled into neat balls.

"Taking a vacation?"

York withheld comment.

"Getting a place of your own?" Kalpraga persisted.

York placed the socks in his suitcase.

"I'm overdoing it?"

York grunted.

"Must be losing my touch."

"Must be."

"Your stepmother"—Kalpraga came in, shutting the door behind him—"you understand, has much stepmaternal concern."

"I'll say one good word for you."

"What's that?"

"Honest."

"I shouldn't be?"

"Must be a fantastic drawback"—York, gathering in his good arm a load of hanging shirts, transferred them to the bed—"in your line of work."

"You know me. Just a slob without a trust fund to my name. For hire on the glutted labor market."

York folded the arms of one of his specially tailored shirts, forming a neat rectangle with the precision of a man who lives alone.

Kalpraga watched. "You've been gone years," he said. "You've been home a month."

"Eight weeks and two days," York said. "I'm getting a place of my own, you can tell her."

"You ought to stick around."

"Give me one good reason."

"Should be interesting." Kalpraga took a swallow of his drink. "Hair of the dog," he explained. "The making of a president."

"That is funnee." York imitated a laugh. "Listen, how about situation comedy? That's where the big money's at."

"Dull," Kalpraga said. "I tried it. No challenge."

"And stringing together clichés fascinates?"

"Look at it this way. Right here"—Kalpraga gestured with

his glass, taking in the house around them—"right here I have a firsthand opportunity to examine a new phenomenon of our times. The actor in government."

"What's new? Politicians've always been actors."

"But actors haven't always turned politician, right? And there's a fantastic difference. Politicians think of themselves as leaders, policy makers, statesmen, even." Kalpraga spiraled his glass upward to denote aspiration. "Actors, especially movie actors, have been trained to think of themselves as a marketable commodity."

"As they are."

"As is a politician." Kalpraga raised up on his bare toes; his feet and ankles were surprisingly small and delicate for such a rotund waistline. He resembled a Daumier cartoon. "I'm sure you know a political candidate has to sell himself like a can of soup."

He had heard ugly rumors, York admitted sourly, that such was the case.

Kalpraga continued. "Time was when a man decided to run for office, he let the party run his campaign. Not so now. Before his hat goes in any ring, our man hires himself an advertising agency. They—first things first—need a salable package. That means they have to find out what the voting public'll buy. Polls are taken. And *that* means old ladies are hired to sit at a long table, each with her own telephone. Twenty old ladies dialing and shooting questions into twenty instruments. A horizontal Tower of Babel. Our Man's agency sifts the answers. Once they know what the public wants, they make up the package. A dash of opposition to the Big Spenders in Washington. A peck of patriotic concern, a tablespoon of quiet sincerity and a soup spoon of nonethnic humor. Your normal working politician resents the necessity, although he does it. But your actor! Another kettle of fish, your actor. This is a big boost to his ego, the big build-up for his biggest, most impressive role."

York glanced across the room. Soft stripes of morning light slanted on thick carpet. "You really think he's got a chance, don't you?"

"I wouldn't be working for him if I didn't."

"But that, too, is part of your job. The big security blanket of them all."

"Hell, Adam, don't you think I know there's risks? Even the biggest, best planned advertising campaigns fail. Did Ford put over his Edsel?" Kalpraga took a long swallow. "Don't you see? That's what makes it so damn fascinating. The risk. You work and work, but on that last day it's still a big gamble."

York, his thin face purposefully expressionless, fitted shoes in the shirred suitcase pocket.

Kalpraga said, "O.K., O.K. You resent the old man. But if I were you, I wouldn't let that stop me from being in on the biggest thing since—"

"The Edsel."

"It might turn out that way. A gamble, I said."

"Tell her no. I don't care to be used."

"I told her that's what you'd say." Kalpraga smiled. "Listen, before you leave, I want you to know one thing. I like you."

"I'm all choked up."

"God knows why. You're a cold, antagonistic son of a bitch. But I like you. It also happens I'm working my fat ass off for your old man, so if I grab you by the short hairs at some future date, understand, will you, there's nothing personal involved."

"Nothing personal at all."

"I mean it. I like you."

"That places you in a small, select, unpolled minority of one."

"And, incidentally, on the subject of fathers who call their sons *son:* it implies a forgetting of the name and a self-reminder of the relationship." Kalpraga finished his drink. "But relationships aside, this'll be interesting. Stay."

"Tell her—"

"I was asking on my own account."

"The answer is still no."

Kalpraga shrugged.

So did York.

Neither said anything more; York continued to pack, and soon Kalpraga opened the door and let himself out.

York shut his suitcase. He leaned on fine calf, his thin body shaking. For maybe two or three seconds there he'd almost succumbed. Not to the lure of his father's campaign; as far as York was concerned that could be only pure arsenic. But to friendship. Kalpraga's offered friendship, York realized, was the genuine article. Kalpraga, fat, honest, intelligent and red-cheeked, had offered friendship, and York had been lonely all his life. . . .

All?

He shut his eyes and on the closed lids saw, very clearly, the first Mrs. York.

He fumbled to lock the suitcase. Sprawling on the bed, he picked up the phone, opened the drawer and fished out a number, dialed.

"Twenty-seven," he told the motel switchboard operator. "Hello, Gillies. . . . Uh huh, me. . . . Why else? I want to talk to you."

Clay Gillies and York met at Dee's Coffee Shop on West-wood Boulevard. Lunch hour and the smells of polysaturated fat hung over office workers, housewives and giggling UCLA girls. Gillies ate a flat, butter-soaked melted-cheese sandwich while York, across from him in the narrow booth, drank black coffee and explained.

"So what I have in mind," he concluded, "is working against the draft and the war in Vietnam."

"Been thinking along those same lines myself." Gillies swallowed the last of his sandwich.

"You have the experience. I have the cash. An ideal marriage, don't you think?"

"Made in heaven."

York leaned his good elbow on the table, cupping his long, pale chin, staring at Gillies. "Where should we start?"

"Berkeley," Gillies replied without hesitation. "The networks have permanent cameras set up on campus." He shifted in his seat, taking a small brown leather notebook from the back pocket of his denim pants. He began to write swiftly. With sudden vigor and purpose.

Last summer I went to Mississippi to join the struggle there for civil rights. This fall I am engaged in another phase of the same struggle. This time in Berkeley . . . the same rights are at stake in both places—the right to participate as citizens in a democratic society.

Mario Savio said it first in 1964, about his Free Speech Movement, but Clay Gillies was to paraphrase it second and thereafter plagiarize it often and to his own purpose.

In summer a sweltering blanket of heat descends on the long valley that is the fertile gut of the state. Distant hills turn brown, the wild mustard by the highway withers, soil cracks and a hot, rasping wind comes to blow clouds of dust across Highway 99. Only irrigated crops grow. And they grow magnificently. From late spring onward, though, many travelers never see the state's huge pregnancy. They choose to avoid the worst heat by driving at night.

York and Clay Gillies were no exceptions. They drove through hot darkness, assailed by the odors of sweet alfalfa, ripening cantaloupe, yams. For miles on either side of the little town of Delano, where the grape pickers were on strike, hovered a vinous odor of rotting unplucked grapes.

York kept the speedometer of his Corvette at a steady ninety. He rarely spoke. Gillies constantly went over his plans, alert, alive. Sweating. York, for reasons best known to himself, kept the convertible's top down so the air conditioning couldn't be used. The midnight temperature in Fresno was ninety-three. Clay's piercing tones carried over the constant roar of monstrous diesels that ply their thunderous route between Los Angeles and San Francisco.

"Remember that film you made with Igawa?" Clay asked.

"Of course."

"With a little editing"—Clay shifted in his wet bucket seat— "we could use it."

York turned. For a moment oncoming headlights glinted on the dark glasses that he wore even at night.

"Stryker Halvorsen, you mean?"

"I mean."

York drove several miles. "Posthumous winner of the silver star. . . ."

"Is that what it was?" Clay asked without interest. What did medals mean to him? "Where's the film?"

"Igawa must have it."

"And where's he?"

"He got some sort of grant after they left the Peace Corps. Berkeley."

"Convenient."

"Don't count your chickens."

"Why not?"

"By Igawa integrity's not just a word. You don't know him and his work. A fanatic. He won't edit to please you." In the grating, mocking voice, a respect Clay had never heard before.

"It's not for *me*."

"You can't bug him about his work."

"But you think it's a good idea?"

"Oh, excellent."

"Igawa'll understand," Clay said. "I'll make him."

York hummed secretly as he drove.

3

Clay, after his conversation with York, worrying about blowing it with Igawa, decided to play it cool, and to this end he managed to get himself and the Igawas invited to Dorot McHenry's October Sunday night.

Dorot, an organized soul, had guests on the first Sunday of the month.

And this Sunday, Dorot decided, was as good a party as you could find anyplace, even here at Berkeley. Every available foot of her wall space was lined with white-painted boards held apart by bricks and filled with her paperbacks, serious, information-stuffed books, not a novel there. Above, hung two poster-size prints of Andy Warhol's comic strip girls. On the floor, a Kerman her parents'd stored in their garage as too old fashioned—imagine! If the setting was à la mode, her guests were more so. Graduate students and/or TAs, intellectuals all and multiracial—this up-to-date color scheme Dorot struggled hard to attain at all her parties—yet despite their differences most of her guests were as alike as cookies baked in the same mold for varying lengths of time, the men either bearded or mustached, the girls wearing short skirts and long silver (earrings and/or necklaces), everyone talking or listening with an expression of alert awareness. Dorot grasped an icy pitcher of *sangría*. She'd been setting out on a refilling foray when, in the exact center of the room, she'd been stopped by the Pakistani girl.

The Pakistani talked; Dorot nodded and smiled and didn't listen. The girl (like Dorot) was studying at Berkeley's Graduate School of Sociology. A red caste mark was above her broad aquiline nose, and she wore yards of drab figured cotton draped sari-style over a sheer nylon blouse. People kept darting interested glances, which was the main reason she'd been invited. Dorot made an effort to introduce new blood at her gatherings.

"You must be very proud," the girl was saying in her careful, somber accents.

341

"But whatever of?" Dorot asked, shifting the pitcher to her other hand. Had she missed something?

"Your friends. One finds them fascinating."

"I'm so glad you've mingled."

"Each so worldly, so urbane, so full of new ideas. One is forced to hold one's breath with admiration." The girl paused and went on in her slow, intent way, "It is difficult to find the correct word." The red dot wriggled like a living ladybug as she frowned. "Ahhh. . . . You have a salon."

She pronounced it *saloon*, and it took Dorot a full half minute to understand, but as the light dawned Dorot's attractive mouth parted in a large, pleased smile. This foreigner, in her labored English, had expressed Dorot's own opinion of her parties. She chose (privately of course) to think of herself as a miniskirted Californian successor to Madame de Staël. Forgetting to ask whether her guest took alcoholic beverages—and so many of your Pakistani students didn't—Dorot forced a paper cup on her.

"How kind of you!" Dorot cried.

And still smiling, Dorot proceeded around her crowded room, pouring *sangría* into emptying paper cups.

A tall, brown-mustached man bent over her. "Mind if I use the hi-fi? Want Mark to admit there's a distinct nineteenth-century idiom in *Eleanor Rigby*."

"Turntable's on the top shelf." Dorot tinkled the icy pitcher toward one of her board and brick bookcases, then moved on to the couch.

"But of course you've seen *MacBird!*" a thin-faced man exclaimed to Leigh Igawa. "You must have."

"We've been away," Leigh murmured apologetically.

"It is without a doubt the finest political satire since *Of Thee I Sing*."

"She's been in the Peace Corps," Dorot paused to explain.

The Beatles sang of loneliness.

Dorot stopped at the breakfast table, resting both reedy forearms on back of the broad shoulders of a short man with very dark eyes. A delta of black hair showed at the neck of his velour shirt. He sat alone.

"Having fun?" she asked, inhaling his minty aftershave.

"Me?" He turned, grinning at her. "A simple, small-town boy with your circus of intellectuals?"

"I was just told I have a salon!" cried Dorot.

"Get rid of it and I'll show you a simple, small-town good

time," he whispered against her ear. "I'm hot for your flat-chested body." And he drew back to wrinkle his nose at her.

Dorot's long legs weakened.

This was Howard Derdivanis. Dr. Howard E. Derdivanis.

For eight months Dorot McHenry had, whenever possible, shared with Howard the double bed that right now was covered with heavy Indian knit sweaters and secondhand fur coats (old furs, the older and campier the better, were currently the rage among Dorot's crowd); Howard was a resident in surgery at the University of California's hospital, which was across the Bay. Dorot, of course, never considered their relationship by any such outmoded term as "love affair," yet she often suspected this was love, this baffled fascination and great affection she felt for Howard—despite his shortness and his armoring coat of small-town humor against things intellectual.

It was unthinkable in this day for a normal girl of Dorot's age, twenty-three, to remain celibate, yet at the same time Dorot felt it a mistake to rush into matrimony before completing her education—in the mid-sixties a BA was something your everyday housewife framed in black bamboo to hang over her kitchen sink; there was not an interesting job available for a person with a simple college diploma. Therefore Dorot did as the other college women in her situation: she worked for a doctorate and slept with her boy friend. It was the thing to do. Sometimes when she and Howard stayed cuddled in bed on rainy Sunday mornings enjoying long, snug discussions, Dorot felt a little guilty, because she enjoyed these cozy talks as much as the preceding sexual activities—didn't this mean she wanted with Howard Derdivanis a permanent relationship? Marriage? It was on one of these wet Sundays that Howard pointed out to her that nowadays a spinster of twenty-three who'd slept with only four men (as had Dorot) should be classified on the same pure level as a virgin with limited necking experience would have been in Mother's pre-Enovid day. Right after that remark Howard had proposed. So both wanted marriage. But, alas, there was a big fly in the matrimonial ointment. The fly was Eureka. Howard came from Eureka. Eureka is a lumbering community in northern California near the Oregon border, a town off main highways and air routes, constantly hazed with clouds of pungent redwood sawdust. Dorot had visited Howard's family and discovered that the most recent idea in Eureka was circa 1940. Talk about conservative! Talk about *Main Street!* And it was in Eureka that Howard intended to practice.

He kept it no secret. "I like being a big frog in a small pond. Something to do with my being so damn squatty," he would explain, smiling at her with his dark eyes. There was a strong possibility that she loved Howard Derdivanis. But how could she let her brain rust? It was not only vanity that prompted her choice, but also a sense of responsibility: didn't she owe it to society to best use a brain polished at state expense? So in her straightforward way she turned Howard down, saying much as she adored his hairy body and his fine sense of humor, how dared she play Carol Kennicott in Eureka when she knew the way the plot turned out?

Now Howard was asking, "Who's the quiet, pretty redhead? The one on the couch?"

"Leigh Igawa."

"Your queer pal, Doug, seems to be giving her a rough time." Howard quirked a dark brow at Dorot.

"He's genuinely interesting."

"Maybe." Howard again looked at Leigh. "But she's not your usual type of guest."

Dorot peered through her glasses at Leigh, whose wide-apart hazel eyes sought her husband—doubtless she was hoping he'd return to hold her hand as he'd done earlier in the evening. Dorot decided that *quiet* and *pretty* and *not your usual type of guest* were Howard's genial form of criticism. And Leigh had so much to offer! Yet, exasperatingly, at even the smallest gathering she turned into a well-bred child, seen but not heard. Being truly fond of Leigh, Dorot sprang to her defense; explaining that this was no ordinary girl, Dorot pointed to where Ken Igawa leaned talking to Clay Gillies. "She's married to him."

"The Oriental or the beard?"

"Igawa," Dorot said impatiently.

"Hmmm. . . ."

"He's an artist. He's got a Ford," she said. But in this crowd that meant nothing; grantsmanship was the name of their game. So Dorot, still working hard to boost her old friend, said, "She's quiet at parties, but she used to be in the Los Angeles Blue Book. After they were married they joined the Peace Corps. They just got back from Chile."

People were forever telling Dorot that her voice carried. Evidently this was true. Ken had heard across the noisy room.

"Why not set it to music, Dorot? It's a grooving new version of *Madame Butterfly*," Ken called, then turned back to Clay. "So you're a dove," he said.

Clay had him cornered by the open front door, the coolest spot in the room. Dorot's place was full of smoke and hot air, a bunch of overeducated people talking loudly about New, it didn't matter New what, just so long as it was New. The new Leroi Jones play, the new book, *Death of a President*, the new Beatles album, the new short skirts, the new war news—Vietnam, Ken had noticed, was pronounced Vitnum. He jerked back his abundant hair. In his Peace Corps stint he'd gotten out of the habit of being hip.

Clay said, "I'm in favor of ending the mess in Vietnam, if that's what you mean."

"I told you. I don't know anything about it. In Chile we didn't get the papers," Ken said, moving outside into the cool. Clay Gillies, as usual, had put him on the bristling defensive, and Ken wished Gillies would take the hint and shove off.

It didn't work as wished. Clay followed, slamming the door with a sharp thud.

Dorot's place was in the Berkeley hills near campus. The third-floor apartments were entered from this long, well-lit veranda, and Ken moved to the end, gripping the rail, staring down. He had seen many nights in many places, and once he'd been so high in the Andes that the stars, huge there, no longer shone white but glowed with mysterious colors. Yet he still loved Berkeley at night. The surrounding daytime shabbiness was replaced by random clots of light, as if someone had spilled radioactive grains of brown and white sugar. The city stars were small, pale and blessed because they were familiar.

"Dove!" Gillies snorted. "A meaningless term. And so's hawk."

Ken sighed, stretching both arms and circling slowly like a hawk with unflapping wings. Suddenly he pounced one hand, grasping cool night air. "A hawk's a guy who says 'We' have to make a stand in Vietnam, otherwise 'They' will take over Cambodia, Laos, Thailand and all of Southeast Asia, right?"

"The domino theory!" Clay said angrily.

When Ken had left, Vietnam had been only a minor, if constant, incident in the papers; it was not a Major Issue, except, of course, to some poor guy like Stryker Halvorsen. Now it had escalated into a full-scale, if undeclared, war, with half a million American servicemen. Ken ran a finger along

the painted wood railing. His friends, and everyone else at
Berkeley, were protesting. Protest had settled like heavy gray
dust over the campus, glooming classrooms, drabbing bumper
stickers—*Hell No We Won't Go* and *Make Love Not War*—
gathering on the raw-voiced speakers on Sproul steps and in
the long hair of the sober male and female student audience;
it saddened the bearded grad pondering whether to become a
CO or to head north; its fallout grayed joyous grass smoked in
freshman dorms and weighed heavily on grades written on
postcards—if you got bounced your 2S status no longer existed
and your number was called. Thick dust descended on everything, making youth seem less desirable. And as the young
had spearheaded the civil rights movement a half decade earlier,
so they were first to ask *Why?* about Vietnam.

Evidently Clay Gillies had been studying up on the answers.

"The reasons our government's in Vietnam are all morally
indefensible," he said quietly, yet his voice carried great weight.
He raised his forefinger. Brown hair grew on the first two
knuckles. "Balance must be maintained among the great powers, that's why we're there." He held up his middle finger.
"Red China must be kept in her place, contained, that's why
we're fighting LBJ's hopeless war." He held up a third finger,
folding his little finger under his thumb, saying with heavy
irony, "We have our commitments." He lowered the hand.
"Listen, Igawa, we probably would be there if we didn't have
a single commitment. Wherever you find a movement toward
ending hunger, ending inequalities in wealth, making land re-
forms—our government's right in there, fighting it. The job,
according to them, is to support every form of totalitarianism
and thereby protect American investment." He clenched his
fists. "Vietnam is getting the works. By what right do we belong
there, killing and burning and Napalming men, women and
children, ruining rice paddies, turning the whole country into
one damned, bleeding refugee camp?"

Gillies' face had whitened above his curly beard; he spoke
in impassioned tones, the muscles of his neck tensed as if he
bore on his shoulders the full burden of every small, patient,
brown Vietnamese. It was this gift of delivery rather than his
speech's content (Ken agreed with every point raised) that Ken,
for the life of him, couldn't take.

"You know me," Ken said. "Asia for the Asiatics, that's
my bag."

"What the—"

"Something I read in a stale fortune cookie," Ken said wearily.

"I'd laugh, but war never struck me as funny." Gillies crunched his paper cup slowly in his fist, letting it drop over the railing. "We can be drafted, you and me, and die carrying out acts we're diametrically opposed to."

"Fighting wars you believe in"—who could take additional rhetoric?—"is a privilege reserved for unthinking fanatics."

"You always were a real comedian!"

"Gillies, face it. I'm not exactly hot hot hot for political debate."

"We don't belong in Vietnam."

"I agree," Ken said. "But what the shit can *I* do about it?"

As he glanced sardonically at Gillies, Ken's professional eye caught the relaxation of muscles, the slight shifting of firm flesh under blue denim. Otherwise there was no sign. Yet it came to Ken (oh, he was a genius, but always too late) that from the moment Gillies had come over with a paper cup half filled with weak punch and started to talk, first about the good old days back at California High, then about the war, he'd been waiting to hear Ken say these exact words: *What the shit can I do about it?*

"You have to help," Gillies said, quieter now. "You're an artist. An artist has a duty to society."

"Now I dig. Antiwar posters. You want me to copy those old ones with huns chopping off female Belgian hands, superimposing our GIs and little brown hands? Yeah yeah yeah. Or I'm good at sneaky Nips—"

Clay interrupted, "I don't find war funny."

"Without a sense of humor how d'you survive?"

"I manage. Listen, Igawa, remember that movie you made, the one with Lissa?"

No, Ken thought, *whatever you want with that film, the answer is no*. The film was part of a blazing summer; it was as personal as the private journal a writer might keep of a love affair, revealing the writer's most intimate reactions to every movement in the sack, his deepest relationship, a journal that was utterly private to himself and never meant to be transformed from sloppy cursive writing to cold print. *You have to be a nut to think about a film this way*, Ken told himself. *But the answer is still no*. A car in noisy gear climbed toward Strawberry Canyon.

"Remember?" Gillies persisted.

"Well?"

"Isn't it a good argument," Gillies asked slowly, "against war?"

"You mean Stryker Halvorsen?"

"Yes."

"That's pretty low."

"Why?"

"Using Stryker's death."

"Using?"

"Isn't it?"

"To prevent more guys from getting killed."

"He was a great guy."

"He was," Gillies agreed. "So are the ones we must save. Listen, I've been thinking a lot about it. How about if we put in a few subliminal war scenes like *Pawnbroker?*"

The sound of the car's struggle uphill faded.

Ken said, "You never saw the film, did you? Yet you want to crap it up for your own purposes."

"Not my purposes."

"Whose, then?"

"Stryker Halvorsen—"

"Oh, come off—"

"—and others like him."

"You can't use it."

"Listen, Igawa, *you* asked me what you could do to help." Gillies stared at Ken with burning brown eyes. "It's not for me. It's for you just as much. More."

Under Gillies' intense gaze, Ken remembered that time in his apartment, it must be five years ago, when Gillies had tried to argue him into SNAP. Clay Gillies, then as now, saw with kinglike vision. His deep-set, shadowed eyes could see only his own side and that very clearly, as if drawn by divine Hand. He was utterly sincere. Completely sure of himself. Someone like Ken Igawa, who squinted around every question until he wasn't sure if the answer were animal, vegetable or mineral, could never fight him.

"A minute ago. . . ." Ken started slowly—it might be hopeless, but shouldn't he at least try to explain his point of view to Clay? ". . . a minute ago you said an artist has a duty to society. You were right. But that duty is to show the truth. That's any artist's sole excuse for existing. The closer his instinctive grasp of reality, truth, the greater artist he is. Any artist who subverts for political ends, he, Gillies, is a plain party hack." Ken blinked, twice stepping a circle. He had dissected the heart of his work, for him an almost impossible operation. He breathed heavily and grappled the railing. "The film's sort of private. It's probably no good. I just don't want it shown."

"Keep your artistic integrity then," Clay said swiftly. "Keep your cool. But remember. We had physicists who believed their only duty was to scientific truth. They devoted themselves to it, and they built a bomb to blow two hundred thousand civilians to dust in one surprise drop."

Ken shivered.

Either wittingly or otherwise, Clay had delivered the *coup de grâce*.

Mention Hiroshima and you had Ken Igawa by the short hairs; mention Hiroshima and through him swept an icy, unreasoning blast of guilt. His grandparents might never have left the southern end of Japan's main island and he, little Kenji Igawa, might have been toddling around Hiroshima at ground level zero. *Those shadows pressed into solid brick walls, those bleeding, defecating, vomiting, stinking, mercifully dying sufferers of radiation sickness, they are me. Those gene-corrupted victims of slow leukemia, they are me; those survivors treated as lepers, they are me.* On a rational level Ken Igawa knew his oatmeal empathy not only was stupid but also meaningless to the mass sufferers. He also knew, deep, deep, that if he spent every hour of the rest of his life on the couch he could never get rid of the unfixed guilt of not being in Hiroshima on August 6, 1945.

He closed his eyes and ran his finger blind along splintery wood. Muttered, "I'll talk to Leigh and York."

"I already asked York," Gillies said. "It's all right with him."

"That still leaves my wife." Ken delayed as long as possible his inevitable capitulation. "She was as involved as me."

And at that moment Dorot leaned from her door. "We're about to eat," she called in her loud toneless voice. "Come back in."

Ken jogged along the veranda, escaping into the hot apartment. He hurried over to the couch where his wife had been sitting next to a tall, thin homosexual puffing on a joint. "She went to help Dorot," he said. "You're an artist, aren't you?" Ken shrugged, and the other started to talk, something about The Theater, in capitals. Ken found it difficult to pay attention.

• • •

On Dorot's way from the front door to the kitchen she paused, asking Leigh to assist. Leigh followed, watching Dorot remove various types of cheese from her refrigerator.

"What shall I do?" Leigh asked.

"For one thing, don't hold hands with your husband," Dorot remarked in a good-humored tone.

A blush mottled Leigh's slender neck, rising to redden her face.

"If Clay hadn't come along you'd have stayed together all night. Siamese twins," Dorot observed. "Here. Try this." She handed Leigh a sliver of gray-white Gruyère. "Big public displays of affection are famous smoke screens."

"For what?"

"For spouses who don't get along in private."

"I see." Leigh's flush had faded. She nibbled on the cheese. "Good." And said with mild, aseptic irony, "We've been out of circulation so long sometimes we forget ourselves."

"It takes time to readjust," Dorot admitted. "But you mustn't let Ken be so uxorious in public. It's protesting too much." She arranged cheeses on a wooden board. "Especially in your case. You understand?"

Leigh did. She stiffened. "Is that all you wanted me out here for?" she asked coldly.

She had never taken advice well, Dorot remembered, even when it was given from the best of motives, as Dorot's always had been.

"Bread's in there." Dorot gestured. "Cut it in cubes." Then, prudently, "Only two loaves. We can do the third if we need it." Suddenly a thought occurred to Dorot, a thought that would account for Ken's hanging over his wife so much. She smiled, saying, "You're preg, aren't you?"

Leigh shook her head.

"I know you. You won't let on until the eighth month." Dorot, still smiling broadly, removed from her immaculate cutlery drawer a bread knife. "You've always wanted one in the worst way. Congrat—"

"You want to see my Ovulen?"

"No need to snap my head off."

"I'm sorry," Leigh apologized. She got out big golden wheels of cable car bread and set one on the breadboard. "It's just I wish I were." She sighed. "I wish I were."

• • •

"Well?" Gillies asked as Ken got up from the couch.

Ken muttered he was on his way to take a piss.

When he emerged Gillies was by the door, waiting.

"Well?" Gillies asked.

Ken muttered something about a headache and getting the hell away from here, bending over Dorot's coat-piled bed, trying to remember which jacket his wife had worn.

Gillies stood right behind him. "About the movie?" he asked.

"What about it?" Ken didn't look up.

"Did you ask Leigh?"

He hadn't had a chance to. But of course Ken knew—had always known—what her answer would be. His wife clung tenaciously to good causes, especially to unpublicized, unorganized underdogs as she would doubtless consider Gillies' peace drive. She'd gladly donate the film and her own services as usherette, if needed. Ken lifted a heavy-knit, sheep-stinky beige sweater that weighed a minimum of five pounds. He didn't try to con himself; he personally loathed giving up the film to Gillies. No *noblesse oblige*.

"Well?" Gillies asked.

Ken dropped the heavy sweater. "She'll have to find it herself," he said. "She says yes."

"Good."

"No carving up, though."

"But it'd be more effective—"

"I won't let it be the hell changed," Ken growled.

"Don't you understand, Igawa? This isn't for you. Or for me."

"How great it must be, always so sure you're on the side of right."

"I don't do anything I'm not sincere about."

"Bully for you."

"What we need is something to give it punch."

"The hell we do! The crucial point is, Leigh and Stryker all shiny and beautiful and crazy about one another. They're alive, Gillies, and beautiful. Therefore it'll be enough to mention at the end that this wonderful, alive guy is now Vietnamese mud."

"But—"

Ken started out.

"Igawa—"

"Take it or leave it."

"I take it."

Howard Derdivanis poured kirschwasser into molten, rich-scented cheese for his specialty, fondue. Dorot set out paper plates, each with two cubes of bread and a fork for twirling. As her guests gathered around the chafing dish, under Dorot's handwoven Guatemalan blouse there grew a warm sense of communion. Pride. For it came to her that this generation—she and her friends—were the best that America yet had seen. They were honest and free. They weren't hung up on material success as their parents were; people like Ken and Leigh Igawa could give years out of their lives when they saw the world needed to be set right. Headstart, Vista and the nonparty political scene drew others. Some were pacifists, but that didn't mean they lacked courage, no; witness Clay Gillies' bravery. They fought hard for their beliefs. Their generation hungered after knowledge and went to school for more than a quarter of their lives. They traveled everywhere— Oh, Paris is way too expensive, try Crete. They were open-minded about grass, race, sexuality and homosexuality, international cuisine, Red China, miniskirts, nudity, four-letter words. The Beatles or Bach? Let everyone do his own thing.

They, she and her friends around this table, were the ones who counted.

· **4** ·

The first week of the fall quarter Clay Gillies organized a peace march on the Oakland Induction Center. Clay, of course, had experience in such matters. But at Berkeley, even without experience, you could always rouse a few hundred bodies.

Two hundred students, each carrying a homemade anti-Vietnam picket sign, assembled off university property across the street from Boalt Hall. Clay Gillies arrived, gave a brief, exhilarated speech—crowds always increased his pulse rate—

and as he finished he listened to gratifying cheers. Signs bobbed wildly. Clay raised both hands in the partisan V; then everyone started on the long hot hike to Oakland. Girls wearing too tight shoes dropped out first. Soon after them departed male students worrying about tomorrow's quizzes and losing 2S deferments. Clay led about a hundred chanting, sign-waving followers to within a block of their goal, the induction center; here they ran smack into sweating cordons of police. The Oakland cops set about their famed method of dealing with student demonstration, swinging night sticks with strong abandon at girls and boys both. Marchers shouted defiance, Clay's voice rising above the others. There were eight black eyes, two arrests, three bleeding skulls and York, who'd driven to meet them, got a cut lip that needed four stitches. Clay bled in his beard. In the name of peace. One strange thing, though. Clay was positive he'd seen several men with press cards pinned to their light-weight summer jackets, yet no mention of the incident appeared in newspapers or on newscasts. A grave disappointment. Publicity was exactly what Clay needed for his as yet unorganized organization.

Students for Peace.

The most ardent marchers formed its nucleus.

As Clay and RG Richards had based SNAP headquarters in their apartment, so now Clay considered the shabby dump he'd rented south of the campus less as a place to live than as home of Students for Peace. That fall, evening after evening, there were meetings of undergraduates. They preferred Students for Peace to SDS or other national organizations with the same ultimate goals—harassment of "the establishment," abolition of every warlike evil from ROTC short haircuts to nuclear testing—because Students for Peace had Clay Gillies. They looked on Clay, despite the fact he was five years older, as one of themselves; yet at the same time to them Clay was a man set apart, dedicated by virtue of his dropping out not only from school but also from the whole fucked system to devote himself selflessly to selfless causes. To Students for Peace, Clay Gillies was the power and glory, Mario Savio combined with King Arthur, Lenin and Jesus, and he was *right in the same viewless room with them*.

One of Clay's most enthusiastic disciples was Nina del Amo. Nina, large, unbeautiful, a convert to the Free Speech Movement, appeared totally bored by everything, Students for Peace included. Yet she arrived early for each meeting and was available at all times to hand out leaflets, distribute posters and pass the bucket when a Students for Peace speaker finished his oration on Sproul steps.

Clay had arranged to meet Nina del Amo at ten thirty on campus that sunny October morning. Walking along the Plaza he peeled off his faded denim jacket, shifting the heavy package under his left arm to the crook of his other elbow. It had rained the previous night, but an hour ago sun had melted the last remaining cloud shreds and now the sky was a deep, hazeless blue. Clay didn't notice. He'd never been one for the beauties of nature. He did, however, observe that the sun, its first time out in four days, had drawn the fraternity crowd (those conservatives!) from their indoor territory, the Bear's Lair, to the sunny Terrace. The Terrace belonged to intellectuals and activists, and today these talked more loudly and earnestly in the presence of lightweight interlopers. Tanned fraternity brothers paid no attention, gathering like bees around the sleeveless, flower-colored dresses of sorority girls—as far as Greeks were concerned, anyone not pinned over the heart was invisible.

Clay squinted, searching in the kaleidoscope of drab and brilliance for Nina del Amo. He found her. Alone, broad shoulders rounded over a tray, she sat near the geranium-planted ledge. Even from this distance Clay could see Nina's mournful black skirt was smeared and her shapeless brown sweater had a large tear at the elbow. Yet this squalor didn't mean poverty, not by any means. Clay hadn't undressed Nina, but he'd taken clothes off many, many girls like her, and he'd seen grimy satin labels from I. Magnin, Saks, Bullock's Wilshire hanging by a single thread from filthy neckbands.

He was almost at the round table when Nina glanced up. She smiled, stiffly, as if invoking seldom-used muscles. Sunlight emphasized her pallor. Clay, thumping his oblong package on the table, greeted her. "Hi there, Nina." She didn't answer. As he pulled his chair to the table, Clay got a whiff of underarm sweat on dirty wool, and for a moment he couldn't resist the luxury of personal speculation: why wasn't there a meeting place between the willfully dirty Ninas and the plucked and scented dead-hearts like his ex-wife? Nina's long, nicotine-stained fingers turned the package and she examined the yellow proof sheet glued to the top.

FREEFREEFREEFREEFREEFREEFREE
AN AMERICAN HERO
a york-igawa production
presented by clay gillies
Friday night at 8:30   Wheeler Hall

FREEFREEFREEFREEFREEFREEFREE

"Pretty good, eh?" Clay said.

Nino del Amo, pushing back lank brown bangs, agreed. Her left eyelid was weak muscled, and this perpetual droop over one large blue eye gave her an expression of disdainful hauteur.

Clay asked, "Can you hand them out?"

Nodding, Nina stretched. Her bosom was large, low-slung and braless.

"When?" he asked.

"I have a few hours."

"Today?"

"Right now."

"Good," he approved. "Very good."

Nina's left eye almost closed.

"You have your permit?" Clay asked. "You know the administration."

"Fuck the administration. Let them go fuck themselves." Nina had taken the Free Speech Movement to heart, and she murmured the obscenities with no break in her usual bored whisper.

"You do have one?" Clay persisted.

"Yes."

Clay smiled. He was well aware that show of white teeth in his bearded face was coin of the realm to female Students for Peace. He touched the package. "I'd help, but you know how welcome I am around here."

Her mouth tightening with faint disgust at the administration, she asked, "What's it about, the film?"

"A guy I knew. Killed in Vietnam."

"You make it?"

Clay shook his head. "Ken Igawa did. A crazy artist. He refuses to change one single frame!"

"Igawa?" she asked. "Japanese?"

"A nisei or whatever they call it."

"I never knew any." Her left eyelid twitched with her first sign of real interest. "I never had a chance to meet a Japanese man."

"I don't understand how a guy like him, who's decent, can stay uninvolved!" Clay exclaimed angrily.

"He go here?"

"Nope," Clay said without elaboration.

Nina lapsed back into boredom, crushing a red geranium petal, releasing its strong, unflowerlike odor. At a crowded table nearby a pretty sorority girl emitted a series of high-pitched laughs that rose like shrill birds in the warm air.

"Well." Clay rose. "To work."

Nina, clasping the heavy pack of papers to her full, pendulous breasts, stood. She was taller than Clay. Preceding him, she wove her leisurely way around the crowded jumble of people and outdoor furniture.

Nina del Amo had arrived at Berkeley a six-foot, seventeen-year-old, faint-voiced, convent-educated virgin. Her mother was a Woodward, her father a del Amo. From the beginning she had been too big, too pale, too indrawn. Her parents, ardent travelers, had left her to a series of nurses and governesses. Later, she'd boarded at Sacred Heart, and there, poor girl, she'd been a social disaster area, so when, against all family precedent, she'd decided to attend the University of California, her parents didn't argue but gave the ugly duckling their blessings. Who knew? Maybe at the "free school," as they called the university, she'd turn into a great big swan.

On arriving at Berkeley she kept herself apart. She didn't make any friends and she didn't accept the rush invitations of sororities (even the most impeccable wanted her; after all, despite her drawbacks, she *was* a Woodward and a del Amo); then, that December of 1964, Mario Savio and his Free Speech Movement burst on Berkeley. Nina, a freshman, found herself jammed in Sproul Plaza. She sat in, her large, hairless knees drawn to her full breasts, listening to the balding, curly-locked orator. Next to Nina sat a full-faced colored boy. He and she got into an obscenity-laden encomium of Mario. The Negro, when they stood, barely reached her wide shoulder. Jim was his first name; his last she never quite caught. He invited her to his room. There, on the hardest mattress imaginable, he proceeded energetically to deflower her. Before it was over her broad back ached and his dark knees bled. After, as he sprawled exhausted almost unto death on top of her, Nina murmured, "Yes ... oh, yes. ..." Yes, this was it. Since that December night Nina had shared with approximately fifty—she kept a loose count—students and nonstudents the pleasures of her large, full-breasted body. She preferred non-Caucasians, and RG Richards was her tenth (give or take one) black man. Afterward, she would light a Tareyton, rest one large hand under her neck, displaying an arrogant growth of brown underarm hair. "That was dee-licious," she would murmur. "If only Mother and Dad could see me now."

Often her partner would say, "Hey, girl. That's sick."

She was sick.

Very.

She dropped with a vengeance in the clinical chasm between nymphomania and the current use of promiscuous balling as a means of rebellion.

Rebellion was the word for Nina's Berkeley career. She fucked. She took her languid place in every New Left cause that might, if a del Amo or a Woodward heard of it, cause him embarrassment.

Clay sat on the rim of Ludwig's Fountain, named after a legendary dog, one of the large pack who roamed campus, watching Nina del Amo do her bit for Students for Peace. She stood to the left at Sather Gate, handing yellow sheets to passing students. The interested read, folded carefully and filed in a notebook. Others crushed paper into a trash can. She had been at her post less than five minutes when a big-bellied campus cop ambled over to her. Clay, tense, tiptoed on the fountain's ledge, trying to figure the problem, starting to step down, then remembered he was strictly unwelcome on the Berkeley campus. If he went over he would only cause an excellent worker more problems. He climbed back on the ledge. The cop held out his hand. Nina, taking her own sweet time, fished in the pocket of that dirty black skirt, extracting a slip of paper. The cop read, raised his cap to rub his bald scalp. Nina stared haughtily down. The fat cop gestured. Clay peered. But by now a quick crowd had coagulated and he could see nothing. Finally Nina and her uniformed escort emerged into the open, heading across the Plaza. Nina's pale mouth moved constantly; the cop frowned. She must be murmuring her entire FSM vo-

cabulary at him. Clay gave a brief smile; then, again sitting
on the rim of Ludwig's Fountain, he held his bearded face
between his palms.

What had gone wrong?

Later that afternoon Clay let himself into York's unlocked
apartment. York, sprawling on the unmade day bed, didn't
glance up. He continued to scan his hardcover book through
dark glasses while from his thin lips dangled a cigarette pregnant with ash. Pages ruffled. York read incredibly fast. Ash
fell onto his white shirt. Books strewed the carpet, and around
the day bed rose a barrier reef of beer cans and empty coffee
mugs. The picture window was shut and a heavy, sour odor of
masculine sleep permeated the room. Clay removed an upended
beer can from blue Naugahyde and as he sat it occurred to him
that York once had been neat; no, fastidious was a better term.
Now York—Clay glanced around the room—lived like a slob.
For the first time it occurred to Clay that York might be in
trouble. But what kind of trouble? Money was no problem,
none at all; York had every material thing he wanted. York
never sniffled, sneezed, coughed or exhibited other signs of
physical ailment. Anyway—Clay narrowed his eyes—you had
only to sit in this room with its sweat-stinky air to smell the
inner torment. There was no point going any further. Clay never
had been able to get involved with another person's inner life;
he couldn't get near enough to pry into another's pain. He
didn't want to imagine York's mental state. Clay's fists clenched
involuntarily as he wished he weren't so damn helpless; being
helpless infuriated him. But how could he stick his hand into
a snake's nest when he didn't know poisonous from non-
poisonous? He was completely, absolutely, totally helpless to
bring order to inner chaos. He couldn't help York. So . . .

Clay covered his eyes with one hand and began planning
his speech for tonight's meeting of Students for Peace.

After ten minutes York turned the last page. "McLuhan
doesn't know from shit," he announced, tossing the book toward the kitchen area where it would remain, Clay knew from
experience, fanned out, until next Wednesday morning at nine
when York's cleaning lady would waddle in and pick it up.

York thrust his deformed hand in its usual pocket. Looking
at Clay for the first time, he asked, "Well?"

"There was a mix-up. Seems Wheeler's been taken for Friday." Clay heavily underlined the words *mix-up* and *taken*.

"And you the very model of a modern protest organizer!"

"We had it all right. And for the right day."

"You arranged?"

"Nina del Amo. She's good. Very good."

"What blew?"

Clay's brows drew together. "A cop stopped her from handing out the leaflets. He sent her to Administration. Some secretary showed her a calendar, pointing out that months ago a sitar concert had been scheduled."

"Myself, I never was one for Eastern music," York commented.

"All I can figure is the administration's shaky because my name's on the film. About Mario, Stokely, RG, Hayden, Rap and me, they always sweat."

"Profusely."

"I'm serious."

"Aren't you always?" York grunted as he sat. "Well, little man, what now?"

"It'll cost."

"Easy come, easy go."

"We'll rent Sweeney's."

Sweeney, known as Ape Neck to generations of students, owned a derelict theater, the Grand, southeast of campus. Fifteen years earlier the tube had forced Sweeney out of show biz and he'd started to rent his place to organizations denied use of campus facilities; several nights a week the narrow dusty theater resounded to the earnest young offering endless arguments to those who agreed with them about abolishing capital punishment, freeing love, equalizing the races, legalizing abortion and marijuana, ending draft laws, banning the bomb. Clay, in his SNAP days, often had rented Sweeney's.

Ape Neck, as was his wont, sat in the projection room, chair tilted at a dangerous angle, booze in hand. Clay knocked on the open door.

Ape Neck's chair settled. Bleary eyes examined Clay. "Well," Sweeney said, "if it isn't my old pal, Clay Billie."

"Gillies," Clay corrected, launching immediately into business. "I'd like the place next Saturday night to show a film."

"A nudie?" Ape Neck leered.

"S'antiwar."

"You kids today! Don't you believe in having yourself any fun?"

Clay said coldly, "Is the place free?"

"Not free, fifty bucks." Ape Neck chortled.

Then, seeing the anger in Clay's eyes, to show he hadn't been poking fun at a much needed customer, Sweeney offered Clay a drink. Clay disliked liquor, he was a grass man, but Sweeney, contrite, insisted so Clay drank cheap, un-iced bourbon from a flowered glass that once held cheese spread. Cockroaches scuttled across dusty velour seats. Clay signed forms. Sweeney insisted he have another drink before he left.

Clay, lightheaded, trod down rickety steps to a clatterous basement print shop. He explained twice to the printer, a Mexican with little English, about needing new leaflets. Using a red felt-tipped pen, Clay edited the time and place. The printer, a squat man fresh from Ensenada, pleased at having more business, brought out *vino*. Since the printer was Mexican, Clay felt obligated. He drank red wine from the bottle. He was stewed as he reached his front door. Fumbling with his key, he cursed aloud when he heard his phone ring.

Ape Neck's voice was considerably less coherent than it had been an hour and a half earlier. "Looked through my c-c-cmitments . . . joint . . . the place already rented Saddy. Friday, too."

Clay sobered. "The theater was free all week."

"Took."

"You showed me the line-up—"

"Lissen beard, lissen wiseass collich kid, when I say s'taken, s'taken."

"Then we'll have to use it the week after," Clay planned. He would race back to the printer, he would—

"S'taken the week after."

"I saw—"

"Quit tryin' to ess-ess-essploit me," Sweeney whined.

"Listen, you old fart!" Clay exploded. "I'm not in this for personal gain. I'm in it to make sure your motheaten dump and your liquor-soaked skin won't be going up in a mushroom—"

But the phone already had clicked.

Clay stood absolutely still for a full minute. He silently cursed—not Sweeney, for Sweeney was a tool, a drunk, infuriating, sad old tool. Abruptly Clay slammed down the phone. He strode into the small square bathroom, splashing cold water on his face until he was breathless. He stared panting in the mirror. Droplets of water clung to his brown beard, glued his lashes into points. A permanent furrow, he noted, creased between his brown eyes. Lines radiated from his deep-set eyes. He was getting old. Old. And had he changed the world one iota? Had he? Well? Suddenly he balled his fist, shaking it at the face in the mirror. The action was filled with fury, partly at himself, partly at the huge, implacable sources that tied him to inertia. The system. If only, Clay thought, if only he had the power, oh, the good he would do! The system, the system, Christ how he hated the system!

This time York, in his strewn apartment, listened with a vinegar smile pasted across his narrow jockey's face. Clay couldn't help interpreting that smile: the grimace an airline passenger might wear if he'd bought a flight insurance policy before take-off and the pilot has just announced that there will be an unscheduled landing in this blizzard.

"Call Sweeney again," York said.

"Why?"

"To offer him a hundred a night for four nights."

"That's doubling his rates!"

"*Caveat emptor*," York said, lifting the phone, holding it toward Clay.

Clay's hand hesitated at his side before he grabbed for it.

He propositioned.

Sweeney muttered, "Have to check in the office."

Clay heard hoarse breathing on the line for the two minutes that Sweeney pretended to be gone. When Sweeney spoke he admitted he'd made a damn, dumb goofo; the place was free when Clay needed it.

"It was a holdup," Clay said as he hung up. "A holdup pure and simple. The miserable old bastard."

York smiled his pale, corrosive smile.

Two nights later, amid howls of fire engines and under a fluttering helicopter, Sweeney's Grand Theater blazed. A crowd of students and ordinary citizens gathered to watch firemen in their hopeless task of trying to save forty-year-old rotting wood. Clay jostled his way through the crowd just as the roof caved in. There was an awesome moment of complete silence. Flames stopped. A sudden crackling. Jeweled sparks shot high into thick smoke.

"Jesus H. Christ," said a boy behind Clay.

Flames rose more viciously than before. Sweeney, weeping,

covered with gray ash, was led away between two burly policemen.

"Jesus H. Christ," Clay repeated reverently.

York didn't go to the fire.

But that wasn't peculiar. He rarely left his sloppy apartment.
After the ill-fated, publicityless peace march he ventured out
only on infrequent private business of his own. However, he
listened attentively to Clay's description of the blaze. Clay said
it couldn't be coincidence; the University of California, Clay
said, evidently would stop at nothing, not even arson, to silence
the voice of truth as spoken through the lips of Clay Gillies.

"Delusions of grandeur." York shook his head. "Delusions
of grandeur."

Maybe York was right.

Nobody silenced Clay Gillies when as head of Students for
Peace he drove York's Corvette to address the San Francisco
Junior League. Nobody tried to silence him in the oak-paneled
lecture hall of the Wednesday Morning Club. Nobody quieted
him when he spoke in Marin County.

Unhampered, freely, Clay spoke his peace piece. His brown
lion's eyes blazing gold sparks, Clay dealt first with the war's
innocent sufferers, the Vietnamese women and children, starved,
burned with American Napalm (manufactured by Dow Chemical, Clay never failed to point out), mutilated by American
bombs. The audience, gloved and pearl necklaced, would listen
with expressions of abstract sadness. It distressed them to hear
of any children, even such remote ones, being mistreated. Yet
they had been inoculated by too many repetitions that no man
is an island. Virulent mass guilt no longer raised these ladies'
temperature. But as soon as Clay changed the subject to a friend
of his high school years, a tall, good-looking athlete who had
dreamed of reaching the stars but instead had died in Vietnamese mud, the ladies began to shift uncomfortably as if their
girdles were too tight. Each had a college-deferred son, grand-
son or nephew registered at a nearby draft board, a cousin,
brother, husband, even, on the inactive reserve list. They would
begin to dab handkerchiefs at eyes, seeing terrible inward vi-
sions of bleeding beloved bodies, of basket cases, corpses. . . .
They would turn beseechingly on Clay. What could they do to
stop this futile war? He let them know with emphatic thrusts
of his curly brown beard. They must let the White House and

Congress hear their disapproval; they must get their husbands to use every available source of influence; they must stand up bravely and be counted as demanding an end to hostilities. Clay Gillies, bearded, wearing the uniform of protest, faded blue denim jeans and jacket, brooding and intense. He believed. His sincerity shone. The ladies would lean toward one another, whispering that they were hearing the authentic voice of the Conscience of Young America.

Clay was not hampered more than usual in his off-campus activities with students. He organized a rally in Golden Gate Park. San Francisco State students as well as Berkeleyites watched while Clay burned a Xeroxed copy of his draft card— he was 4F by virtue of a left eardrum damaged in Collierville, Alabama. In his apartment, with Nina del Amo and three other dedicated Students for Peace, he taught various ways to avoid the draft.

He worked fourteen, fifteen hours a day, and other than routine police interference he was not stopped.

Yet . . .

An American Hero remained in large flat cans.

The ugly little woman with a felt hat squashed over her monkey face told him the truth.

"Let me clue you in, chickie," she said. "I been paid *not* to rent to you."

"I'll give you more. Double."

She glanced around the little hall; it had been gerrymandered out of a turn-of-the-century office building, a rough trapezoid with one shallow step up to the narrow stage. Sunlight came through slit windows to glint on old metal folding chairs.

"A dump, you're thinking?" she asked.

Clay shrugged.

"But mine," she said. "All mine. I want to keep it."

"Who paid you?"

"It matters?"

"Yes."

She leaned conspiratorially toward him. Her warm breath stunk of garlic. "I don't want people barbecuing hot dogs in the blaze."

"Sweeney's?"

"That film—" she started. Her eyelids flickered. She yanked her battered hat further over her ears as if she'd heard a warning.

"What about the film?" Clay demanded.

The old bag turned away. She refused to say one more word, even goodbye.

Clay Gillies walked into the bright, windy afternoon. He did up his denim jacket, scowling. *Fool,* he thought. He called himself a variety of other names, but *fool* was the one that kept recurring. "Fool, fool, fool," he muttered as he marched. Why had he never before considered York's lower-case name on the credits of that film? Wasn't York's father quoted almost daily in newspapers and on television as being in favor of escalating this war and getting it over with? Why had he never seriously questioned York's motives in backing him? Why had he put York's easy check writing on the same level as York's incomprehensible altruism on that long-ago Freedom Ride? Why hadn't he added two plus two? *Fool, fool.* "Fool!" Clay burst out as he neared York's tall building. He gazed at the huge windows that reflected cold sunlight. "Fool, fool," he repeated.

York lay on the day bed, made up, for today was Wednesday and the cleaning lady had just departed, leaving smells of ammoniated cleaning fluids behind her.

Clay remained standing as he delivered his indictment. York smoked, inhaling, letting blue wisps escape through his thin nostrils.

When Clay finished, York stubbed out his newly lit cigarette in the beanbag ashtray resting on his bony chest.

"I assumed you understood my motives from the beginning," he said.

"How could I?"

"My fault. I should've made myself clear. Had some sort of ceremony." York finger-combed stringy, mud-colored hair. "I, Adam Farnahan York, do promise to back Claibourne Gillies in sickness and in health. . . ." York falsettoed girlishly, "I do." His voice returned to normal. "And in reply I should've made you vow, on your honor, to do your damndest to get my name in public print or on the tube in order that I might harass, annoy, perturb one noncampaigner, Baron York." He stopped. "Gillies, it's your turn. Say 'I do.'"

Clay snapped, "Take your name off that film."

"Like hell!"

"This is the most important issue of our time and you— you're in it for petty personal reasons."

"In this imperfect world, don't we all act from petty, personal motives? I damn well admit *I* do."

"I'll get Igawa—"

"Sports fans, this is the York-Gillies two-man team."

"We'll never get it shown with—"

"You will. I pay, I get my way. Dig?"

Clay felt his anger rising, rising. He started to speak, then thought the better of it, silently weighing the alternatives. Without York, his work with Students for Peace would sag, weighted down with what he loathed most, fund raising.

York lit another cigarette, inhaling deeply.

"Know what I like about you?" he asked. "You're such a predictable son of a bitch. You could kill a platoon now, but you're swallowing your anger."

"There's no point trying to deal with you. You're so sick hating your father."

"Why're *you* working *your* ass off?"

"You won't understand this, York—"

"But you'll try me anyway?"

"I honestly believe a limited war like Vietnam is evil. An old-fashioned word, but the only one I can think of. Evil. Destroying small countries whose only crime is they're far enough away from us not to set off the powder keg is evil."

"I asked a question. Why give me oratory?"

"The truth," Clay said coldly.

"The truth isn't in some rice paddy across the Pacific, Gillies. The truth's in this room, inside you." York raised up on his good elbow, moving his ashtray to the floor, lying facing Clay. "Let me tell you how *I* doped you out. In the beginning there was light. When you first joined SNAP you were a man in love. Exhilarated. You honestly believed in everything you did. Blood brotherhood and all that."

"Of course I did. I still do."

"Then SNAP divorced you. I never figured why, but you *were* divorced, weren't you? I saw you. You'd deflated into an ordinary shlub like the rest of us. And you were unhappy being mortal." York exhaled, watching his smoke rings rise. "And now, once again, I have the chance, lucky me, to watch the great Clay Gillies—"

"Why don't you shut up?"

"—alive and in action again. One good Cause and you're alive and swingin', right?"

"Let's forget it, O.K.?"

"You, not I, *you* brought up the question of motives. You spoke harshly of mine. Now, give me my turn." York nodded to himself. "Give me my turn. . . . I think in SNAP you got a taste for. . . ." York fell silent, shaking his head. "I was going to say power, but power's the wrong term. You aren't power hungry, at least not in the normal sense." York snapped bony fingers. "Sainthood! That's it. You acquired a taste for saint-hood in SNAP. You acted on highest ethical standards, without frail, human self-interest. You could speak out loud and clear and therefore you were sanctified. But. Out of SNAP you became common Clay like the rest of us. Then *I* gave you another chance. Always remember, Gillies, it was *I* who raised your sad, ordinary bones back to their saintly niche. I. Once again the heavenly choir sings praises of you. Once again when you come into a room strong men fall to their knees, genu-flecting. Chicks can't wait to flip onto their backs for you. Old ladies give cash as the divine Word comes through your bearded lips. You are virtue. And you gloat in it. Yours the eternal orgasm of being on the side of the angels. And that, old high school buddy of mine, that is why you're in this." York stopped. Clay was on his feet, tense in every muscle, a vein throbbing at his temple. Then, abruptly, he sat. York smiled acidly and went on. "And that's why you will put up with my bullshit. I pay for the sanctification procedure."

"I didn't expect you to understand," Clay said in a controlled voice.

"It isn't in me to understand the higher things, right? Well, think about this. Time was when you would have called me a bummer and told me to shove my money. Not any more. Now you'll accept any support so you can remain St. Gillies. It's not the cause any more, it's the effect. On you. Gillies, face it, you've changed." And York shifted his good arm, collapsing back onto navy tweed. He took off the dark glasses, closing his bulging, almost lashless eyes. "Whether you admit it or not, you've changed. That's why I'm not worried. I know the film'll be shown, whoever suffers for the showing. Now get the hell out."

Dark gray sky hung like a sodden tent over Berkeley on that December afternoon. It had rained fifteen minutes ago, and chances were it would rain in another fifteen.

Clay, hurrying along crowded Telegraph, saw on the other side of the street a full body in a slick white raincoat, a cap of hair held high on a round neck. Odessa Norris? From the back she sure looked like Odessa. Whoever, she walked next to a short black boy, and as Clay watched she turned to smile at the boy.

It was Odessa.

Clay's first impulse was to avoid her.

His face burned as he remembered how, the last time he'd seen her, after Watts, he had pleaded, exposed himself utterly in flesh and spirit to her. *How can I face her?* Then he remembered the shape of breasts never seen except in outline under plain dresses, remembered her smile's warmth, her whimsical yet common-sense answers for every problem. And before he took his next step it occurred to Clay that personal embarrassment had no part in what he was trying to accomplish. Odessa, with her vast experience, could help Students for Peace. And he never ran away from anything. And he ached to talk to her.

"Odessa!" he shouted. "Odessa!"

She didn't hear. She kept walking along wet sidewalk toward campus, engrossed in whatever the short kid was saying.

"Odessa!" Clay started to run.

Still she didn't turn.

She was on the other side of the street and Clay knew better than to jaywalk. The last time he'd cut illegally across a street, the cop—who'd been about to let him go—recognized him; the judge, also aware of his identity, had socked Clay with a fine. Twenty-five bucks! You were forced to practice caution in small encounters in order to save yourself for big battles.

"Odessa!" he yelled.

This time she turned. Her wide mouth stretched in the familiar, warm smile. "Clay," she called.

He took her to dinner at Larry Blake's.

They descended deep wooden stairs to the Rathskeller, a sawdust-floored, pipe-encrusted basement which, as usual, was jammed. Fortunately they didn't have to share a long trestle table. Behind a narrow, crudely plastered arch they found a small one. They downed great schooners of beer and relished garlicky salad. Twice Clay's foot accidentally touched Odessa's. Twice he retreated full speed to concentrate on his romaine.

"I caught RG on the tube last week," Clay said. "He's turned into a terrific speaker." He flushed. "You were right."

Odessa leaned toward him; she wore a high-necked beige

dress and Clay caught the summery odors of her hair. "Clay, tell me the truth. How've you been?"

"Fine."

She examined him. Smiled.

"Good," she said softly. "Good."

"You?"

"The same," she said.

"Why're you up here?"

"Getting a community center started in Oakland. I don't have to ask what *you*'ve been doing."

"No?"

"Who hasn't heard of Students for Peace?"

"Who has?"

"What does that mean?"

"I'm getting no place fast."

"The way I heard it Clay Gillies is the big antiwar rallying point."

"S'news to me."

"Oh, Clay, come off it."

"On this campus maybe," Clay conceded, dipping sour-dough crust in his leftover salad dressing. "But you know as well as I you can't do one damn thing without publicity. Good or bad, publicity's what counts. And I've gotten none." He chewed on garlic-soaked bread. "I know if I show the film—"

"Film?"

"An American Hero, it's called."

Odessa tilted her head questioningly.

"Some people—friends—made it. York. Remember him?"

"Sure. The great Baron's son. He drove us to Alabama in sixty."

"And Igawa—"

"Tall and Japanese? Your friend? He came to a meeting around the same time?"

Clay nodded, asking himself how he could have forgotten Odessa's amazing memory, spool after spool of accurate fact. And instead of attending to the conversation he found his thoughts lowering from Odessa's brain to her full lips, now glossed with salad dressing. How would it feel to kiss those lips? His questioning thoughts progressed in a logical fashion and he felt his face burn. Then, thank God, great oval platters of steak and steaming French fries were set in front of them. The waiter, a sweating football player (all waiters in the Rathskeller either were football players or passing as them), asked if they wanted more beer. "No, thanks," Clay said. Odessa shook her head.

"The film?" Odessa reminded Clay.

Between bites of rare steak he filled her in. "The main thing is," he finished, "a guy called Stryker Halvorsen's in it. He is—was—great-looking. He was killed in Vietnam."

Odessa nodded slowly.

"Igawa's a real artist." Clay put down his fork. "The potential. The tremendous potential!"

"And you aren't showing it?"

Clay gave a harsh laugh.

"Why?"

"They've stopped us from hiring a hall."

"They?"

"They," he agreed. "At first I figured it's me. So the authorities were slamming doors in my face. But this was the worst! They even burned down a crappy dump I hired. I figured it was maybe coincidence." Clay gave another laugh. "Coincidence! Finally I had it out with York. He co-produced. His name's on the credits. It's *his* connections."

"Mmmmm. . . ."

"The uptight Baron, he doesn't want his son's name on a film like this." Clay stared gloomily at steak juices congealing on his empty plate.

"May I see it?" Odessa asked.

They stopped at York's. For once he was out, but anyhow Clay borrowed his equipment; laden down they hurried through light rain to Clay's apartment. The room was too small. Film blurred, projector whirred, but in spite of drawbacks, Odessa wept.

Clay switched on the lights. Odessa dried her eyes. "God, he was beautiful." She blew her nose. "You were right about Igawa. He's a real artist."

"So what? Nobody's going to see it."

"You can't find anyplace?"

Clay didn't answer. The reality of Odessa sitting on his narrow bed came as a shock. He might have been looking at her for the first time: eyebrows that she penciled into a fuller line at the center, full soft lips now slightly open, high cheekbones, full brown throat. . . . He wondered if that throat would feel as warm and smooth and firm to the lips as a sun-ripe peach, and his groin itched with the question. Odessa Norris, sitting on his bed crumpling a wet Kleenex into her purse, her oval breasts rising and falling.

"Clay, listen, you saw it properly, didn't you?"

Nodding, he forced himself to look away from her breasts. "Where?"

"Igawa's."

"So why not show it there?" she asked. "Would his wife make a thing about it?"

"Leigh? A very altruistic type. Dragged Ken into the Peace Corps. She'll be all for it."

"So?"

"She's in Los Angeles," he explained. "Been there since October."

Odessa's eyebrows went up.

"Her father's sick."

"Where's Ken?"

"Here."

Again Odessa's penciled brows rose.

Clay shrugged. "I never thought of *that* before." He shrugged again. "D'you know anyone our age who stays married?"

"I did hear about this one couple in Anaheim."

"Maybe I should try talking to Igawa again." Clay spoke doubtfully.

"You're pretty powerful."

"Not with him I'm not. Maybe someone else could convince him." Clay frowned. "At this particular point, a female someone."

Odessa's head bent as she snapped her purse shut.

Clay couldn't see her expression. He wondered, was she thinking he'd become callous, cashing in on an old friend's misery? York's words came into his head. *Whether you admit it or not, you've changed.* Maybe he had . . . yet . . . Odessa herself didn't always play it noble, did she? (Of this he was living witness.) In their particular game the playing field was mined, the rules all against them and they had to make points when and how they could. Clay went to the window, staring between slats of aluminum Venetian blinds. In the next building, new and tall, pale drawn drapes glowed. Soft rain fell.

His every nerve centered on his groin. He wanted Odessa. From the first night RG had shamed him, an idealistic, hard-studying freshman with a pregnant wife, into cutting a session at Pixwood he had wanted her. But she, by some alchemy, had always drained him of that desire. He yanked the fraying cord. Blinds closed. They were private, Clay Gillies and Odessa Norris, a man and a woman alone in a shabby apartment that smelled of gas heat from an ancient furnace. It occurred to Clay that if he'd been a different man at this moment he would have been weighing her unvarying if kind rejections, the gentle thwarting, the wordless rustle that he'd always heard inside his head when she was turning him down. If he'd been another man he would have let his hard-on disappear discreetly and as soon as she left he would have dialed one of the local chicks who were ready, willing and most able. But he wasn't another man. He was Clay Gillies. He never avoided battle, psychic or otherwise.

He turned from the window. He was sweating lightly. He went over to the bed and sank down next to her. Old springs complained. His chest ached, his throat was dry and his hand shook as he touched, ever so gently, one of her fingers. She covered his hand with her own.

"Clay," she whispered, "Clay. . . ."

This time she didn't smile her quizzical, unmanning smile. Instead, she raised her eyes so he could see the glow. He felt the warmth of her breath trembling against the hairs of his beard. Finally, he thought, finally. . . .

He lifted her hand, pressing it to his hard chest so she could feel the pounding of his heart. He touched the soft springiness of her hair, her pulsing throat; then he started to unzip her beige wool dress.

Naked, they lay in the narrow bed.

For a long time he paid gentle attentions to her breasts: he cupped the beautiful flesh, caressed and kissed the brown-red nipples; he pressed his hot cheeks against the fullness. He wanted this to be an act of love, not of lustful haste. Primal odors began to rise from her. She murmured she was ready. He whispered back that he wasn't. Her fingers touched his hardness. "Liar," she whispered, with a trace of her rich chuckle.

"No, darling. Let me," he told her. "I've waited so long."

So she let him push back the covers and rise on his knees to survey her. His lips moved down her body: her muscles were firm, her skin sleeker than oiled silk. He wanted to watch her reactions, but his eyes kept squeezing shut and it was with his lips and fingers that he explored. When he reached the furred, mounded pubis he felt a gasp go through her. His kisses lingered on the inside of her quivering thighs and it wasn't until a long

time had passed that he permitted his tongue the wet heat of
her clitoris. She moaned aloud. Her body shook urgently. *Clay,
now, now, now.* He sank into her and gasped in the wonder of
it. She might have been his first woman, his virgin bride. At
last, oh, at last he was home. "Rest," she whispered. He lay
still on her. Her body didn't move, but around him the wet,
smooth heat ebbed and flowed and caressed him suckingly until
his body melted away and he was conscious only of the soft,
pulsating pressures. Her fluttering quickened, and so did their
breathing. Then it was as if the entire world shook and broke
open and he could no longer remain still although he knew she
was coming and he ought to wait to let her again but there was
no helping it. He pounded and rushed toward the deepest,
innermost womb of his life.

Outside, December rain fell.

5

Two months earlier.

Leigh Igawa emerged from a small lemonade-color house
into bright October sun. A cheerful breeze yanked at her denim
skirt and she didn't try to hold it down; instead she executed
three dancing, heel-clicking steps, the Teaberry shuffle, then
proceeded to a tumble of large, hollow boxes, pausing to
straighten them into a train. From a window behind her drifted
a New York-flavored female voice, "S'long, Leigh hon. See
you tomorrow," and Leigh, smiling over her shoulder, answered, "Bye, Dena. Tomorrow." In the sixty-four Ford, the
belated wedding gift that had caused such upheaval in the lives
of the Kenneth Igawas, Leigh pushed down the sun visor, fitting
the key, pressing her dusty brown loafer on the accelerator.
Sharp autumn air rushed at her through open windows.

Leigh worked at Berkeley Village Nursery School.

Dena Cole, the stout, unbusinesslike child psychologist who
owned and operated Village, presented "scholarships" right and
left to disadvantaged Oakland tots—and in Oakland, what else
could a tot be? Therefore Dena Cole could only afford to give

her associate, Leigh, one thirty-five an hour. One thirty-five, Dorot repeatedly told Leigh, was wetback pay, and Leigh, just as repeatedly, pointed out that this was what she'd done in the Peace Corps and even before; she simply wasn't trained for anything higher paid. Leigh jammed the brake for a red light, smiling. Maybe she kidded Dorot. She kidded herself not. Always she'd been wild for little kids. She loved working with them. Why shouldn't she? Preschoolers were totally unable to hide their loves, hates, passions, frustrations; their breath smelled of sweet milk. And. Although Leigh never let herself dwell on the matter, each time she comforted a small, sob-throbbing body she was forced to admit, for the moment at least, that Village was sublimation. Sheer sublimation. She and Ken never had discussed a baby. That is, he'd never brought up the subject of a baby. Therefore neither had she. Tactful, tactful she. On his grant who could afford one? And the Pill, that damn Ovulen, so easy, so perfect. You couldn't even loose your normal instincts for a little biologic carelessness. She felt her face sag as she thought, miserably, of her one-time secret carelessness; then she banished the thought to its home in limbo.

Tires scraped as she parked. She checked the dashboard clock, subtracting the twenty minutes it ran fast. Fifteen to one. Time to fix lunch. Three afternoons a week Village remained open so Leigh worked, at her usual bracero pay, of course. Those days Ken invariably neglected lunch. At four he would leave his work to wolf peanut butter sandwiches, completely ruining his dinner. Dinner! The one meal she had time for.

They lunched on sliced tomatoes, melted cheese sandwiches and chocolate chip cookies home made from a mix. Ken mentioned that Clay Gillies had dropped by.

"What for?"

"Same thing he wanted last week at Dorot's. The film."

"It's for a good cause! Why act like he's—"

"Calm down—I gave him the print."

They smiled at one another.

"Well, back to work," Ken said.

Leigh sloshed through the accumulation of breakfast and lunch dishes, finger-sprinkled drops of warm water from the faucet onto her African violets, velvet-leafed and lush, successfully transplanted by her from a single white plastic pot to an overflowing window-ledge jungle growing from peanut butter jars. Ken, back at his huge canvas, muttered, "Oh, shit," without rancor. Leigh smiled.

For her, Tuesday and Thursday afternoons were a special magic place. Not time. Place. Berkeley, Oakland, San Francisco, the entire state of California bustled, raced, whirled through a weekday routine, but in the apartment, once and future place, afternoons were a slow, dreamy silence, for Ken while he worked disliked chitchat, and the small sluffs and scrapes of his brush and palette knife, rather than detracting from, intensified the continent of silence. Leigh would compose eight-page letters to her family in Los Angeles. Or mend clothes thimbleless with a too-long thread. Or she would read. Today she opted for reading. Picking up her library book she stretched out on the couch that doubled as their bed when it wasn't covered with this itchy, brilliantly striped alpaca. (For the spread they had haggled a noble two hours with an ancient Indian, ending up paying the wily old Inca his exact original asking price.) She opened to where her envelope marked page twenty-three. As she turned to twenty-five, she stretched her slim legs, arched her back and deep inside her throat a purr sounded. The thing of it was, not only Tuesday and Thursday afternoons pleased, but so did every part of their life. (Except, of course, the lack of babies.) They lived arty, intellectual, casual, sort of messy, completely unmaterialistic and poles apart from the *modus vivendi* of her parents. This last fact, for some sad, petty reason, pleased most. She let her eyelids relax, wishing Ken would lie down next to her . . . love in the afternoon, that was the best . . . unexpected joys are the best. . . . She drowsed, one cheek roughed by harsh wool, *Siddhartha* open, rising and falling on her breasts.

The ringing phone didn't waken her immediately. She struggled to the shores of consciousness through heavy rip tides of sleep. Ken answered. Groggy, she watched his triangular black brows go up and his mouth curve down. He pressed the instrument closer. So she wouldn't hear?

"What is it?" she asked, sitting. *Siddhartha* thumped to the floor.

"Yes," Ken said into the phone.

"Ken—"

He didn't look at her. "Yes. As soon as we can get a plane," he said.

"Ken!"

"I'll tell her," he said into the phone.

"What is it?" she cried.

"We'll be there," Ken said. He hung up.

"What was it?"

He came across the room. His hands came down on her shoulders, heavily, as if he feared she might leap from the open bay window through warm air to scrubby autumn grass three stories below.

"It was Everett," he said in a hoarse voice.

"What did he say?"

"Your cousin—"

"I know who he is!" She struggled to escape his hands, but he gripped tighter.

"Calm down."

"What did he say?"

"Your father—"

"Daddy!" She broke loose. Breathing heavily, she faced her husband. "What's wrong? What is wrong with him?"

"He had a heart attack," Ken said swiftly. He closed his eyes. "A pretty bad one. He's in the hospital."

It was dark when they arrived at Los Angeles International. They taxied downtown, a wildly extravagant journey during which neither glanced at the meter. At Good Samaritan, Everett met them as they hurried toward the brilliantly lit entry. Small red mustache twitching, he explained that Uncle Sidney had collapsed in his office—Dr. Bendor said heart attacks were most common in men like Uncle Sidney, strong, muscular, aggressive men with a tendency to high blood pressure. They were very lucky to have Dr. Bendor. The Dr. Caldwell Bendor. Everett glanced from Ken to Leigh, then back to Ken. Neither showed a sign of comprehension. Didn't they remember, Everett asked, Bendor and De Bakey had a big write-up in Time about their cardiovascular work—for Everett the closest current equivalent to Divine Sanction was a full page in Time. Uncle Sidney, he went on, was in excellent hands.

"I want to see him." Leigh started for the doors.

"You can't." Everett caught up. "Leigh, nobody can. The doctors're with him."

"Where's Mother?"

"Inside."

"Oh, poor Mother. . . ."

In the chapel adjacent to the lobby sat Mrs. Sutherland. Her lipstick and eye make-up were unsmeared, her shining hair in perfect order, yet she managed to give an impression of complete disarray as she twisted the large diamond on her left hand.

"I'm so glad you came." Mrs. Sutherland smiled at her daughter and son-in-law as if they were guests arriving for one of her catered parties. Then she frowned. She frowned only under gravest conditions: it's a well-known fact frowns cause furrows in pretty, aging faces. She said, "I just don't understand what's happened. Nobody will tell me. I don't know what to *do.*"

Leigh kissed her mother. "There's nothing we can do."

Mrs. Sutherland drew back. Her eyes were light blue with a dark line around the iris that intensified the color. The whites were very clear, like a small child's. She gazed at Leigh, bewildered. "I don't know how to cope. He always took charge."

The truth. Sidney Sutherland was a man to take charge. Of everything. And Leigh, trying to conquer the fear twitching down her leg muscles, saw her mother could not possibly grow up, not now. She—Leigh—would have to take charge.

"The doctor—Everett says Dr. Bendor's a wonderful man," Leigh said.

"He knows what to do," Ken agreed.

"There's nothing to manage," Leigh said.

"But I just don't under*stand.*"

"Daddy's had a heart attack."

"Yes, dear, I know that. But he never had heart trouble. Why won't someone *explain* it to me?"

"Men like Daddy are prone—"

"Yes, but *why?*"

Leigh's leg muscles weakened further. She sat on the polished pew next to her mother.

"And why won't they let me see him?" Mrs. Sutherland sighed.

"In a little while," Ken replied. His mother-in-law, obviously, questioned Leigh. Equally obvious, Leigh couldn't answer. "Everett said so."

Mrs. Sutherland twisted her ring.

Michele bustled into the chapel. Her soft, pouting lips were pulled into a line of seriousness. She refused to meet Ken's smile. The time was too grave, Michele's eye-shadowed glance rebuked, for smiling.

"Leigh." She clasped Leigh's hand. "Everett told me you arrived."

Not being able to talk, Leigh nodded. Michele's aqua suit was an almost exact replica of her mother's, but Michele was too big in the bust for a loose jacket. The style made her curvy torso seem square. Leigh closed her eyes, trying not to weep. Her father lay upstairs, *Time*-honored doctors working over his heavy-muscled, coronary-prone chest. So how was she capable of noting catty detail? She opened her eyes to the cross: *Forgive me, please. And please, please, won't You make his heart new? "If he only had a heart," like the Tin Woodsman sings. You can do that, right?*

Michele patted Leigh's shoulder. "There's nothing to do but wait." Michele sighed. She hurried back to the lobby and there in grave tones reported to her assembled in-laws that Leigh was taking it well. Ken heard her say "very well under the circumstances," as he slid into the phone booth to long-distance Dena Cole.

As Leigh entered Room 428 the first thing she saw was a green curtain drawn ominously around the bed. Refusing to let herself dwell on the implications, she tip-toed across green-flecked linoleum. Her father's face was a bloodless sulphur color. His eyes were closed, his mouth open. Above him, attached to him, a miniature television screen.

Across the screen a wiggling line moved.

He didn't.

Dead.

He was dead. Snowface Daddy, she'd called him when she was little, sitting on the lid of his john watching him shave; he'd dabbed her cheeks with his lathery shaving brush. She started to ask the seated nurse why they hadn't told her his heart was nonrepairable? Why had they let her know in this terrible, cruel way his heart had stopped?

He opened his eyes.

"Leigh." His mouth barely formed the word, the sound never came. "Babe . . . stay. . . ."

She did.

Only the immediate family, and that meant Mrs. Sutherland, Leigh and Stevie, period, were allowed in the room. Stevie drove directly from California High each day, staying less than five minutes. Mrs. Sutherland arrived at the hospital around noon, emerging often from her husband's sickroom to drink a cup of coffee or smoke a cig with one of the innumerable Van Vliet or Sutherland relatives who showed up "to take poor Ev's mind off it all."

Leigh stayed in the room.

Her father had requested she stay, and stay she did, for endless hours, sitting on the uncomfortable cane-bottomed chair where her father could see her when he opened his eyes. He wasn't allowed the effort of lifting a fork. Leigh jollied the private nurses into letting her feed him all three bland, salt-free, low-sodium and low-cholesterol meals. She sponged his face and hands. She opened the cards attached to floral offerings, books, shaving lotion that flowed into his room. She handed him the duck.

Ken hung around the overheated fourth floor hall. He remembered how grim it had been when his own father had been ill unto death, so he did what he could for his wife when she emerged; he fed her either greasy hamburgers or greasy stews from the steam tables in the basement cafeteria; he walked her around the long, hilly block so she could get a breath of Los Angeles' famed downtown smog; he put his arms around her whenever she appeared in need of such attention.

Mr. Sutherland's pain subsided, and his fever. Close members of the family were allowed brief visits. A knotty problem for Leigh: who among the numerous connections of her large, well-knit family were not close?

A week passed.

Dr. Bendor, a cautious, hunched little man, announced to the family, "Statistically, it's very optimistic."

Did Leigh diminish her attentions? No. She continued to sneak into Good Samaritan at seven with the morning shift, leaving after visiting hours when the head floor nurse would forcibly eject her.

"You don't have to be here every second," Ken would point out. "Let his specials earn their salary."

"Babe . . ." Mr. Sutherland would call hoarsely. "Babe—"

"See? He wants *me*," she would answer, triumphant, dashing in to feed her father his midafternoon Jello.

Ken's view began to distort. His Soutine-like vision, admittedly, was molded by his old jealousy—old envies never die, they just fade away into mild neurosis.

All in all, though, he might have successfully handled it if he weren't so damn edgy. See, there was the Show. Professor Little had sweated several quarts of blood to arrange that Ken be a Man in the "Three Young Men of the Bay Area Scene" at Darvas Gallery this coming January. Darvas Gallery, on Post Street near Gump's, displayed paintings and sculpture as if they were priceless apostolic relics to be worshiped rather than bought—the old soft sell. Darvas Gallery was prestige. Darvas Gallery meant you were getting there, oh, not Andrew Wyeth, but you were getting there, wherever "there" was, and if Ken hadn't talked much about the Show beyond making a few cracks about its campy title, still at the same time he knew, God help him, that this was the most important thing to come along in his so-called career. The Show ... Ken, bitten by the green-eyed monster, hanging around the fourth floor of Good Sam, didn't deny to himself that the Show mattered, mattered one hell of a lot.

Then, too, his edginess and his jealousy were worsened by frustration.

To put it in the vernacular, he was horny.

Up until now there could not have been a more genuinely talented and creative wife than his, and he (a hot from way back) was spoiled. Not many guys had it so good. Now when Leigh staggered home from the hospital she would crawl into the left canopied twin bed, and when he snuggled in with her she would murmur, "Oh, darling, I'm so tired," and promptly fall asleep. The delicate shadows under her eyes had darkened to lavender. Her breath smelled as if she had a fever. Ken, gazing at his wife with wry, aching love, would think of her most endearing qualities. She sang off key, she read dull books (they acted on her like phenobarb) in her belief that highbrow was the only polite way to live in poverty, she was scrupulously clean but reassuringly messy, her skin took light well, her nipples were tender and sensitive. He would tuck in her blankets, deciding he couldn't make things rougher for her. After all, he would reason as he switched out the lamp between the beds, her weariness and his horniness were only a matter of time. His dick didn't follow reason. It was a selfish creature instinctively standing up for its rights. About two times a week he couldn't ignore its persistent selfishness and was forced to take his wife by the hand so she could understand the facts. Of course she let him. *Let him*. God!

So here was Ken Igawa, horny, agonizing about the Show, trapped in the luxurious house of his ailing enemy, quietly freaking out. Time passed. Three smoggy, restless weeks of Daylight Saving Time.

"He's doing well," Dr. Bendor said. "Better than we hoped."
"He's out of danger?" Leigh demanded to know.
"The complications that *might* arise *should* have occurred

in the past three weeks, yes," Dr. Bendor equivocated.

Light burst for Mrs. Sutherland. "So he can come home!"

Dr. Bendor raised a thin, cautioning finger. "In one week."

"Wonderful," breathed Mrs. Sutherland, giving the doctor her most dazzling smile.

Even this cautious, deformed little genius couldn't help but respond. He stood as erect as he could, smiling back. "He'll need complete bed rest, of course."

"Of course," Mrs. Sutherland agreed brightly.

That night Ken said to Leigh, "We're off like big-ass birds."

"I can't."

"Why not?" Ken asked. "He's better."

"He isn't."

"Well enough to come home."

"Next week," she insisted.

"You won't be driving the ambulance."

"How can I leave him?"

"There's the famous hunchback, your mother, Stevie, your grandmothers, your aunts, uncles, cousins by the dozens."

"He needs *me,*" Leigh said stubbornly.

"I need you."

"Not the same way."

"You're goddam right, not the same way."

"He'll be home next week."

"Shall we go round again?"

"Ken—"

"I've got," Ken muttered his interruption, "to finish the Show."

"The show . . ."

"Even if I sweat night and day I don't think I'll make it by January."

"I'd completely forgotten about it. . . ."

He balled his fists in the pockets of his white jeans. Tried not to show his hurt. "Behind every successful man—"

"I'm sorry." She pulled one of his hands from the pocket. She kissed it. "I've kept you down here so long."

"But now we're leaving."

"You," she said.

"You."

"I'll be up as soon as he gets home."

"Next week?"

"Next week," she promised, kissing his hand again.

• • •

On his flight back to Oakland a tiny Eurasian from Macao sat herself next to him. She smelled of Miss Dior, her soft pink lips formed charming broken-English impressions of the United States and Ken listened smiling; after all he was human, but also he was a house-broken All-American husband and he kept his hands out in the open on his knees so she could see his broad gold wedding band.

Mr. Sutherland progressed well enough to ambulance home three full days earlier than Dr. Bendor had scheduled. However, once home and in his rented hospital bed, he experienced chest pains, a fever; a far milder attack than the first but frightening nonetheless.

Leigh stayed on.

"It is a known fact that large amounts of peanut butter can cause grave damage to the human male," Ken told his wife two weeks later over long-distance wires.

"Why don't you—"

"Yes. Doctors agree that an overdose of peanut butter not only can kill—"

"Idiot!"

"—but can cause permanent impotency."

"Omigod! Stop the peanut butter! Hurry. Buy a case of Swanson's frozen dinners."

"The place is filthy. Subnormal health standards prevail."

"Ken, he's still in bed."

"Bed. . . . Ahhhh, have you ever slept in a bed unmade for two weeks? An unforgettable experience. It's not the smell that gets to you, though the smell is pretty foul—"

"Nut!"

"It's the constant biting."

"Dr. Bendor says even a mild second attack—"

"Shhhh," Ken ordered. "Listen."

Leigh listened.

She said, "I don't hear anything."

"S'loud and clear."

"Huh?"

"The message."

"Message?"

"As the proud bird with the golden tail flies, Berkeley is forty-five minutes from Los Angeles."

"Ken, please try to understand. Dr. Bendor says—"

"Fuck Dr. Bendor! Fuck what he says!" Ken suddenly slammed down the receiver. "Bendor can go fuck fuck fuck himself!" Ken shouted to the unhearing walls. "You can fuck yourself, too."

She isn't stupid, he thought in his gloom-coated, unkempt apartment; *the rich white bitch isn't stupid. She understands. She knows why I call her all the time; she knows that every word means comehomecomehomecomehomecome. That stubborn redhead bitch knows I can't finish the Show without her. And she knows how I feel about him. And she knows I despise myself when I beg.*

He flicked a switch.

Bullet lights blazed in the circular window. He walked slowly over, staring at his work in progress, a tremendous, almost completed nude that was copied, loosely, from a thumbtacked, yellowing sketch he'd made two years earlier of a squat Chilean farmer. He had worked on this canvas for two full months, not counting the three missing weeks, and in it he'd intended to show all the humanity—beauty, if you prefer—inherent in this knotted little guy with big hands. This was to be The Statement of the Show. Ken squinted and took steps back. The giant midget, to Ken's almost closed eyes, lacked muscle and flesh and bones and blood and glands. Under that sepia paint there was nothing of a man, much less truth or beauty. Ken snatched his big palette knife and began to scratch viciously at still-wet paint, scraping with increasing fury until he'd ripped and shredded the huge canvas.

Seven the following morning he was at Oakland airport boarding the businessmen's special to Los Angeles. Around him men wrote on papers resting on leather brief cases. Ken stared down at dawn-shaded relief map of the Sierra Nevadas. Had any painter ever captured the vastness of earth?

He hitched a ride as far as Wilshire and Westwood. From there he walked briskly northeast in the general direction of Beverly Glen and Sunset, through the residential hush, through pools and patches of early morning sunlight that slanted through branches of the huge sycamore. Birds chirped. A Harvey school bus honked twice; a tiny girl in bright pink burst from a replica Mount Vernon. A blonde, very tanned, of undeterminable age, slid into an open crimson-red Jag, her knee socks and short skirt hinting she was on her way to a private golf course.

Here spacious houses were set back from grass-hemmed sidewalks. Here the oversize rolling lawns were magnificent emerald velvet, kept so by bone meal, Bandini steer manure, cypress chips, twenty-pound cans of chemical fertilizer, tons of Owens River water and much sweat. Ken knew this from experience. His father had tended three gardens on Wyndham, this very street, and he, Ken, from his ninth through his fifteenth summer, had assisted; it seemed to Ken, now almost trotting, that he was once again a skinny, unwilling laborer embalmed in breezeless summer, mowing grass, clipping hibiscus, hosing acres of flagstone patio. The odors of well-watered, fertilized soil brought back memories. Memories that shamed. Faceless, well-slacked housewives standing over his squatting, hard-at-work father, rich-bitch housewives uttering their orders in loud clear tones as if his father couldn't comprehend English, couldn't comprehend anything . . . his father, in pith helmet, going along with them, the dumb, hard-working peasant. At the memory Ken's face burned, and sick with marrow-deep inferiorities he wanted to slink behind a convenient hedge as that skinny kid had done. This vast salmon-colored Mediterranean was one of his father's accounts. Maybe he'd hidden behind this same dewy pittosporum hedge. Ken started to run, long legs pumping, hair flopping into his eyes. With a throat-cracking jerk, he flung back the hair. Had he been shamed by that silent peasant, his father? Or ashamed of being ashamed of being ashamed of his own father? Or shamed that the round eyes of the lady of the house doubtless could penetrate his hiding place? He still wasn't sure. Maybe it was a trinity of shames. He knew only that the old inferiorities still clung and with them—far more ancient—the sense of guilt: Ken Igawa had committed the hideous, unabsolvable crime of being born a Japanese. He raced witlessly along winding, expensive streets to the big white Colonial where his wife had grown up.

Horatio Alger Igawa.

He pressed the bell, panting. Thank God his wife answered. She wore a loose, short beige dress he'd never seen before, very I. Magnin, and as she stared at him her glossy lashes fluttered and her lipstickless mouth opened. He could hear his own crude gasping. Then, at the same moment, they fell into one another. He kissed her desperately, eyes closed, mouth open, refusing to take his lips and tongue from hers or to remove his hands from her butt even when a woman's footsteps echoed

on nearby parquet, stopped, departed. Finally Leigh managed
to break from him. "My room," she whispered urgently, and
arms around one another they hastened upstairs. She pressed
the catch by the doorknob. Neither of them yet had uttered a
greeting, voiced a suggestion, beyond her urgent *My room*,
and still wordless in the early morning cool they threw off their
clothes. He beat her to the left bed, hers, still unmade. She
lay down next to him, opening her mouth to his, fitting her
body to him.

Suddenly—

nothing.

He didn't believe it. How could this be happening? To him?
Casanova C. (for Cocksman) Igawa? But it was. It had. All
feeling gone, he rolled away. After a full two minutes of silence
Leigh lifted up on one elbow.

"Ken?"

"Mmmmm?"

"It's all right."

"Mmmmm."

"Don't cry."

"The hell I am."

"Your eyes're watering then."

This, undeniably, was true. He rolled over. She held his
face between her breasts and he dried his damp eyes on her
softness.

"A first," he muttered.

Her hand cupped the back of his neck. "I love you," she
said.

"Hey Leigh, don't say you weren't warned about what peanut butter can do to a guy."

"It happens to everyone," she consoled. "I've read that at
some time it happens to all men, especially after a long time.
Psychic impotence, it's called, and . . ." and on and on and on.
Blaa blaa blaa. *Oh, she was sweet, kind, trying to reassure,
but for God's sake did she have to sound like Dorot McHenry?*

Ken wished, prayed actually, that his wife would shut up
and let him just lie here nuzzling into the comfort and warmth.
"Want me to . . . help?" she asked. Why couldn't she shut up
and give his fears and uncertainties time to heal? He wanted
to lie naked and quiet against his wife's body—was that asking
too much? Evidently. She raised up, peering at the bedside GE
alarm.

"You have an appointment?" he inquired.

"I promised to type a letter for my father."

"In that case—"

"Really doesn't matter."

"On the other hand nothing's happening here," he said. And started to dress.

His father-in-law had settled into the long, paneled family room. There were no flowers, no humorous get-well cards, no faintly medicinal stuffiness of the sickroom. This was a well room. Propped by the hospital bed and freshly cased pillows, Mr. Sutherland sported bright racing-silk pajamas. The unshaved stubble on his broad face had grown to a youthful beard—although his receding hair was salt and pepper, the beard was an astonishing virile russet, a foxier red than Leigh's mane. His energy had returned. From his bed he spoke decisively into the phone, pausing for an aside that Leigh must write down this detail or that, he ordered lunch from Leigh— "Tell Maria no more of that sole, or spinach either"—and he had her adjust the built-in television so he could see more clearly Channel 22 with the stock market tape. The plump, useless RN knitted placidly on the curving couch.

Mrs. Sutherland, in rosy wool, descended the stairs trailing various perfumed odors. She perched on the end of the high bed.

"Sidney, dear, I'm going to lunch."

"Enjoy yourself, Ev."

"Is there anything you need before I go?"

"If there is, babe'll get it for me." He patted Leigh's hand, smiling at Ken. "The kids'll keep me company, so go enjoy yourself."

"Don't worry, Mother," Leigh said. "I'll hold down the fort."

Mrs. Sutherland, exquisite as a Gainsborough in white lace, stood by the bed. "Bette's not having a big do tonight," she said, slipping her hand into her husband's.

"Have a good time anyway." He smiled.

"I'll be home early."

"No rush."

"I'll drop in and say good night."

"As you well know, by ten babe'll have me tucked in." He

grinned at Ken. "In case you haven't guessed, your wife's an adamant woman."

The following morning. Friday. Mrs. Sutherland came down early for her, ten fifteen, a pink flowered scarf covering her blonde hair; today was her standing appointment with George Masters.

"I'm due for a bleach," she said. "I'll be a while."

"Come back beautiful," her husband replied.

"I'll phone." Mrs. Sutherland gave him her smile. "Be good."

"What else can I be?"

"Bye, dear." Mrs. Sutherland kissed the air near Leigh's cheek.

Leigh did likewise, saying, "I'll hold down the fort."

"Bye, Ken dear," said Mrs. Sutherland.

"Bye, Evelyn."

Mr. Sutherland could be most charming, and in a few minutes Ken found himself forgetting this was his mortal enemy, heard himself talking easily of Berkeley student disturbances, football, and finally, in manner casual, of that subject weighing heavily on him, the Show—he barely noticed when Leigh went to heat her father's midmorning broth. His father-in-law prompted, "So *that's* what you've been up to," and this gave Ken a perfect excuse to tell, in mocking voice of course, about the Temple of Darvas. Finally he noted his father-in-law had retreated into an abstracted silence. So Ken, deciding the older man had tired, shut up. There was only the *click click click* of the redundant nurse's steel knitting needles.

"Ken," Mr. Sutherland said abruptly, "I owe you a lot."

"Sir?" Ken, again wary, examined his antagonist's shrewd brown eyes. Saw nothing.

"For the loan of your wife."

Ken was silent. What could he say? The loan had been unwilling and made at so high an interest rate that he couldn't calculate it. He stared through the sliding glass. Across the patio dry leaves scudded; even in the slowed pulse of Southern California no gardener, as Ken well knew, could keep up with autumn, season of death and dying. He thought of the painting he'd ruined two nights ago, he listened to the click of needles, he heard the thread of sound his wife made behind the closed door to a large kitchen.

"She's been a godsend," Mr. Sutherland remarked.

I ought to say something, Ken decided, *but damned if I know what.*

"If I hadn't had her I'm pretty sure I wouldn't have made it."

Ken felt a small bubble, like champagne, form in his throat. "Sir?"

"I *am* sure. Without her I never would have made it."

In Ken's throat the bubble grew and grew, elation dispelling his autumnal gloom. Hadn't his enemy just said the magic words that freed the princess?

"But you *have* made it?"

Mr. Sutherland agreed.

"And that's the important thing." Ken's joy rose into his voice. "You have made it!"

"Of course I can't leave. Not yet. A deaf, blind infant would know that."

"Little Helen Keller Igawa, that's me."

"Ho ho ho."

"Listen, he himself, in person, told me not more than two hours ago that he's made it. *He has made it.* He knows, I know. And now you know."

"Why do you think he's still in bed?"

"The famous hunchback?"

"Dr. Bendor's very concerned about that second attack. A second attack can be . . ." Her voice trailed. "Well, you can see he's not better. Ken, if you'd stay—"

Ken growled, "There's the Show."

"You could set up an easel someplace around. The pool house, anywhere—"

"It really makes me joyous, practically manic, to know how important my work is to you."

They were in the brick-floored breakfast room, Ken eating the salami sandwich Leigh had fixed for his lunch, Leigh nibbling some cottage cheese while through the closed door to the family room came Mr. Sutherland's telephone voice, booming and assertive, the authority clearly audible if not the exact words.

"Harken to the sick man," Ken said.

"I can't leave him while he's still in bed."

"There's Mrs. Williams—" The nurse.

"He doesn't like her. She flutters."

"Get a new one, then." Ken took a bite. "And your mother."

"You saw how she rushed out. It's like that every day and night."

"If you weren't here"—he mimicked her soft, well-bred tones—"holding down the fort"—he returned to normal—"she'd stay put."

"She's just a little girl."

"Forty-six."

"Ken, when I had the body cast, he'd come home early. He was building his practice, but half the time he'd be home by noon to be with me."

"You were his daughter. Hey Leigh, she's his wife. You're mine."

"I know. I need you so much . . . I—I . . . it's terrible without you."

"You'll be less than an hour away."

"You *could* try it here."

"You know damn well Little promised Darvas I'd be around."

"There'll be other shows."

"What's that supposed to mean?"

She blinked, looking out the window.

An idea occurred. The milk Ken just had drunk formed a cold tight knot in his belly. "Did *he* tell you to say that?"

"No."

"No?"

"Yes!" she cried fiercely.

"This morning. While you fed him his broth?"

"Well?"

"Yeah yeah yeah, always fun knowing how the plotting goes," he said. "Your old man's a regular Machiavelli."

"It's not like that!"

"No?"

"Not at all. He sees how glad I am to be with you, that's all. Listen, Ken, he'll make up the show to you. He's promised."

Ken laughed.

"What's so funny?" she inquired.

"Even you'll have to admit it's a gas." Ken laughed. "First he pays me to get away from you. Now he's paying me to come with you." Ken would have laughed more except he worried he might laugh until he cried.

"That's not what he means."

"I'm sure it isn't. I'm sure he'd much rather have you to

himself. So the two of you can end up the way he wants. In bed together."

Leigh paled. She averted her eyes. Across her face a strange expression flickered, almost a frown—no, it was more as if she were a puppy trying to escape a beating. Escape, that was it. But (he inhaled) the expression was so brief it might just as easily have been anger; he hadn't had time to properly examine it.

She recovered. "What a horrible age we live in. You can't even love your parents without someone pinning a sick name on it."

"The name's the game for some."

"You're a child, you know that?"

"Also sick, freaking out, lonely."

"You'll never grow up."

"And you the clever one, picking me."

"I figured you would, but no such luck. You're still afraid to live near *your* family. Or *my* family. Afraid families'll upset your delicate balance. You're afraid to live a normal life in a normal neighborhood. So we have to keep close to our own little sandbox."

"Thank you, Madame Mature."

"You have a bad case of arrested development!"

"Doctor, tell me the truth!" he clapped a hand to his chest. "Is it fatal?"

"Grow up!"

"Artists"—he used the hated word grudgingly—"aren't supposed to. Hey Leigh, you and your old man cook up a little plot. Well, hats off. But why not face facts? Am I really such a crud because I want to live and work in my own home?"

"Under the circumstances, yes," she snapped, leaning forward, staring at him, a strange, milky-green glitter in her wide-apart hazel eyes. They often had fought, but never before had she glared at him in this precise manner. *"I have a responsibility here."*

"Ahhh, light dawns."

"Good."

"Your idea of my growing up, and stop me if I'm wrong, is for me to forget my work and move in and service you." He'd made it last night, thank God. "And you can live here with your nice white parents."

"Every time we argue," she accused bitterly, "you turn it into a two-man race riot."

"It is."

"You can't even speak the language."

"And I am sorry for it!" He felt himself slipping so he clutched the smooth, heavy glass of the breakfast table, trying to keep control, but it didn't help. "Oh, balls, balls, balls!" he shouted at the top of his lungs. "I'm through begging. Stay here. Fuck yourself! Fuck him for all I care!"

"Shhhh . . . he'll hear."

So that was all in this death struggle that mattered to her! The great white father might overhear! In reflex fury Ken drew back his hand. His palm cracked full force across her cheek. The slap rang. She gasped, pulled back. Tears filled her eyes, her lips quivered, but she didn't make a sound. They stared at one another, hardly breathing while the antique Biedermeier clock on the wall ticked away the minute that it took for slow red marks to appear on her pale cheek.

Ken leaned across the table, touching the raised bruise with fingertips that shook, shook and moved with desperate gentleness as if his light touch could halt what he knew was coming. For he had finally realized, bright Japanese boy that he was, that when an unmovable object meets an irresistible force you've got yourself a real dead marriage.

She kissed his hand.

Yearning, they stared at one another.

You're beautiful, he mouthed the words. *I love you.*

Stay, she moved her lips, *stay, darling*.

Come with me, he formed, *I need you*.

She made a wordless *please*.

Standing, he moved to the other side of the table, leaning on it. "Well, what's the decision?"

"How can I leave while he's still in bed?"

"You figure it."

"Oh, Ken—"

"But let me spell something for you. If you don't come back with me today, L-E-I-G-H, new word, T-H-I-S, new word, I-S, new word, I-T. Period."

"I can't," she said coldly. "I can't run off and leave my father in bed with a coronary."

One thing you had to say for his wife. She loved (and had almost lost) old redbeard Sutherland and in the territory of love Leigh refused to hear bugles sounding retreat . . . right now, at this very moment, her small-lobed ears were deaf to the brass notes echoing, echoing in salami-scented air.

• • •

A half hour later Leigh drove Ken to Los Angeles International. Make-up covered the raised bruise on her cheek. They were both silent. She circled the parking lots, pulling up in the red no-parking zone. There, after a quick, constrained "Bye" from both, Ken slammed the door and hastened into the PSA building. He held his head high, he wore a white tee shirt, pale jeans, Keds, the same clothes he'd arrived in, and as he walked away, Leigh thought, as she'd often thought, that his body was put together just right.

Her hands steady on the steering wheel, she curled up the freeway on ramp. Freeways unnerved her. She would have taken Sepulveda if she'd quarreled with anyone else—as far as Leigh was concerned, harsh words were terrifying. However. This argument had been with her husband, flesh of her flesh, and therefore had assumed the same quality as an interior dialogue. (Later, she knew, he'd see she'd acted in the only possible manner; later he'd admit she could never, under the circumstances, have left her father; oh, he wouldn't say any of this in so many words, but he'd let her know.) So, calm, perfectly calm, Leigh worked her way into the center lane of heavy traffic. Chill November sun bounced off car windows and metallic paint.

Time did a funny slide.

All at once Leigh realized the scenery around was strange.

Nervously she searched for familiar landmarks like the rolling back fairways of Fox Hills Country Club or Al Jolson's memorial fountain that climbed in white square marble pools down a green mortuary hill, but she could see only strange factories, some old and shabby, others new and glittery. She decided she must have made the wrong turn someplace; she would, she decided, have to get off at the next exit to find her slow way home along surface streets. She attempted to shift into the lane to the right of her. But traffic kept her trapped. Great roaring double trucks, dusty sedans and coupés might have been knotted together. She pressed a button; the window slid down; she held her arm out to signal. In the fender-dented Chevy to the right and just behind her the driver stubbornly ignored her. Leigh glanced in her rear-view mirror. A white VW behind the Chevy continued to act as if the Chevy were towing it. Leigh blinked the right-turn light. She honked. Nobody in the next lane paid any attention.

Everyone in Los Angeles travels alone; around her each

person in his upholstered steel box stared ahead, oblivious of the turning blinkers, honking, and bleeding wounds of the other human beings in *their* upholstered boxes.

She was trapped; she was going in the wrong direction, speeding in the wrong direction. And nobody cared. *Nobody.* Palms sweating on the wheel, gulping at harsh exhaust fumes racing at her from the open window, the traffic roaring in her ears like a hungry beast, she agonized that she would never get off this endless freeway that was carrying her further and further from where she wanted to go.

What would happen, she wondered, if she were to jam on the brakes?

It wasn't raining that December afternoon, but it might as well have been. The light was that bad.

Ken switched on bullet lamps in the bay window.

Gillies' dark-haired friend didn't look up. She concentrated on swishing the wooden broom handle back and forth, awkwardly, as if she'd never swept before. Yet the place, undeniably, was cleaner. On impulse Ken took his sketch pad. A few quick slashes and he had her down: awkwardness, drab turtleneck, shapeless skirt; his charcoal, too, caught perfect oval of face and deep-set eyes with the haughty, drooping left eyelid.

She happened to glance at him. He held up the sketch. Most girls swarm all over you if you choose to draw them, so when this one gazed blankly Ken assumed she was astigmatic. He moved forward, still displaying. She examined her charcoaled self with absolute disinterest, her big arms continuing to sweep.

He sneezed loudly and held his hand in front of his face to hide the snot.

"Bless you," she muttered.

"Thanks." Dropping the pad, first grabbing his paint rag, he finally located his handkerchief draped from an easel rung. He sneezed again.

"Hay fever?" she asked.

He shook his head, sneezing.

"Am I raising too much dust?"

"S'a cold."

"I have hay fever, postnasal drip, asthma."

"All the psychosomatic ailments flesh is heir to?" he asked, pushing his handkerchief in his pocket.

"Now you know the real me."

After that he was aware of her. Abrupt movements. Heavy *slap slap* of thongs—her heels were worn to the leather lining. Undeodorated female. Each time she worked near him, through his clogged nostrils came the tang of her. He dry-brushed umber onto canvas. One hour ago, give or take a few minutes, she'd trailed in after Gillies, who'd dropped by unsolicited to lend a copy of *Ramparts*. She'd glanced around and without a word started to clean up, continuing on the job after Gillies said goodbye. Ken sneezed again.

"Where's the coffee?" she asked.

He glanced up. "Want something?"

"Coffee. For you."

"I pass."

"Where is it?"

"If you want some, it's in the cabinet over the sink."

"I already looked there."

He grunted, remembering. Last night he'd carried it over here so he could fix himself a second cup to keep himself awake, the old brushwork was that dull.

He handed her the kettle and big jar of Folger's instant. She didn't take them. She was as tall as he, six foot of girl staring at him. Her message came through. And without premeditation (but when had he ever been one for plans?), still holding the coffee jar and scorched kettle, he leaned forward. They kissed. Her mouth tasted of cigarettes, her tongue raked the inside of his jaw and her pelvis pressed hard against his. The inevitable occurred. It had been a long, long time. *She's not exactly crying rape,* he thought, managing to set down the coffee as he pushed her—or was she pushing him?—toward the bed she'd recently stripped to air. They didn't bother to undress; she flung off her cotton underpants, pulling up skirt and sweater. She wore no bra. Certainly she wasn't afraid of cold germs; her mouth stayed open, covering his.

Snorting to get his breath, he rode hard, concentrating grimly on himself.

The hungry i, Ken Igawa in person.

After their breathing quieted he blew his nose. He fretted that he couldn't remember her name. Had Gillies ever told him her name? Ken Igawa, that fine gentleman of the old school, preferred knowing the name of any girl he screwed. Lying next to this large white girl, one leg still over hers, one arm pinned under her, he pondered the question of her name and at the same time deplored the question. He grew angry at his family. Without the constricting ties of family background he, like everyone else nowadays, could go around balling nameless girls as easily as saying *Hi*. Glued by mutual sweat to the girl he put all blame on his background, denying that he was also disturbed by this, his first tumble from the state of marital grace. *Forget about that*, he ordered himself. *Your guilt's caused by an overdose of parent-instilled morals.*

The girl moved, straightening her black skirt to find the pocket, fishing out a crumpled cigarette and a matchbook. "That was delicious," she said, lighting the cigarette, tucking one big hand under her neck. Her rucked-up sweater displayed overflow breasts. "If only Mother could see me."

"If only," Ken said sourly.

"Where's your wife?"

"How'd you know I have one?"

"Clay."

"Los Angeles. Her father had a heart attack."

"Oh?"

"Why oh?"

"Clay said you'd split."

"Would it have made a difference?"

"Balls on legality," she murmured. "You still hung up on her?"

"Hell no," he lied. "She's a rich girl. Poverty-stricken of the world, unite."

She gave him a small, disturbing smile.

"The trite truth is," Ken added, "she doesn't understand me."

The girl inhaled, watching him.

"She never understood my work."

"Oh?"

"This January I'm having the Show at Darvas Gallery on Post Street."

She raised her eyebrows.

"See? You're dropping dead all over the place. But she— Oh, I admit I didn't pump how important it was to me. But wouldn't you think if she'd had the least understanding she'd have known? I mean, anyone close to a painter would know it's something, being exhibited at Darvas. They sold a *Monet* last month, for Christ's sake!" He snuffed, then blew his nose. "At any rate, she never once took it seriously. She tried to keep me in Los Angeles. She even cooked up a plot with her father to pay me off not to have the Show. I mentioned he's loaded, didn't I? *I hate that rich phony bastard.*"

The girl exhaled wisps of blue smoke through thin, aquiline nostrils.

Ken shook his head from side to side. "No," he said. "The Show's not the important thing. It's a symptom. The truth is, she refused to understand how I felt about her and me." He held his arm next to the nameless girl's large, very white arm. "Look at us. See? A difference, right?"

"That's what makes it delicious."

"But different?"

"Undeniably."

"Well, she acted like I'm some sort of nut whenever I'd say, 'Look, it's a problem.' And even before, when we weren't married, she refused to admit it. And after! My parents wouldn't talk to us. And her—she's got this huge family that swallows people alive. Except me, of course. Me, they spat out. That's not all true. Her father buried us in gifts because I couldn't afford to give her stuff. Hell, anyone could see, except her, that it was impossible, living near families. So the Peace Corps. And Berkeley. Berkeley's pretty free. I mean, if a marriage won't work here, it won't work anyplace." Ken swallowed. "She thinks I'm childish. Neurotic. The thing is, maybe I am hipped on the subject, but even the most liberated will admit there might be some teensy, weensy problems involved in un-matched pairs, right?"

The girl blew smoke.

"Well, the cookie crumbled. Now she's got her excuse. So she stays in Los Angeles." Ken shut his eyes, squeezing the lids together. Black lines wriggled on a red background. "Gillies is right. She's left me. We've split." He rubbed his closed eyes. Redness intensified. "You know something? That's the first time I admitted it."

She murmured.

"We've split." Ken opened his eyes. "S'over."

"Any kids?"

"None." Ken had brooded over this lately; before the separation he'd never cared, as a matter of fact he'd sort of gone along with old W.C., a man who hates dogs and kids can't be all bad, but she—his wife—she'd always been wild about them, and now the absence of a semi-slanty infant seemed terrible, final evidence that she'd known from the beginning their marriage was doomed. He blew his nose convulsively and left the damp cloth covering his face.

"You all right?" she asked.

"Fine." He removed the handkerchief. "Well, you have to hand it to us. Very wise under the exogamous circumstances."

Ken rolled over, burying his face in striped mattress ticking. Talking about his marriage should've acted as release, shouldn't it? So why did he have a tremendous ache in back of his skull? Why should he feel like crying?

"You?" he asked, his voice muffled. "What makes you run?"

"This."

"And?"

"Straightening out our fucked society."

"You're one of Gillies' eager beavers?"

"A Student for Peace," she said, then paused, seeming to want him to question further.

But he, still distraught about her unknown name (and other matters, too), couldn't figure out what to ask.

He rose, zipping his jeans, snuffling and padding barefoot back to his easel. She house-cleaned. He barely noticed when she departed, but it must've been quite a while later, sixish, for night blackened the window.

He was still working when a single rap sounded on the door. He glanced at the wall clock. Five after eleven. Pretty late for callers, even in Berkeley.

"Who's it?" he called.

"Me." Ken recognized the girl's reedy whisper.

"Feel free," he called.

The door opened. She stooped over the knob for she was clutching two large brown paper sacks; from her left hand dangled string-tied books.

"O.K. with you, Ken?"

"What?"

"Me staying?" she asked, clumping across the big room, dropping books and paper bags on the table, sighing with relief, rubbing her big arms.

"Now wait one minute—"

"I've got no place else to go." She looked at him. "Fuckface landlady rented my room tonight."

This seemed highly unlikely, and as Ken set his mouth he realized now was the time for use of her name preceded by a firm no. *No, Whatchamacallit, go back to your own place.* That's what he must say. How could he? Cold guilt crawled along his skin. He didn't know her name.

So he said, "Make yourself at home."

She unpacked. A red toothbrush white at the roots, a box of baking soda, Scotch-taped closed—"Cheaper than toothpaste," she said—a round blue diaphragm case—"I've got an ovarian cyst so the Pill's out," she said—a dozen prescription phials containing various pills. She made several trips to the bathroom to deposit all this. Her baggage also contained a lumpy gray sweatsuit—"Warmer than pajamas," she said.

Ken, weary and shivering and hungry, opened the refrigerator, gripping cold metal. Somehow there was a certain mad humor in her being here, not from his choice, he wasn't sure he liked her even, but out of his guilts. Typical of the jokes fate played on him. *The fault lies not in our stars....* He found a piece of dry cheese and a stale French roll.

Her name, Ken discovered over the next morning's Folger's, was Nina del Amo.

Setting down her mug, she leaned forward with that small, strange, droop-lidded smile of hers. "I stayed because I like you. But I came because Clay asked me to see if I couldn't talk you into being reasonable."

"Reasonable?"

"About the film. Changing it."

Ken had three vast canvases to cover in less than a month, clogged sinuses, a queasy stomach, a temperature of one hundred and one point four, he ached for his wife, he was furious at Gillies. So what else could he do?

He said, "No problem."

He even, under Nina's prodding, designed the ad: an art nouveau woman cradling a scroll in her arms, her long hair forming the letters.

In the Berkeley *Barb* of December 5:

Thurs Fri Sat
turn south on Dwight
head the bay way
stop at 98761

Sun Mon Tue
fight for what you believe
not for the Bird Man
and his hangups

AN AMERICAN HERO
by Ken Igawa
presented by gillies and york

That first night they showed to a strictly noncapacity crowd, but the *Barb*'s reviewer came, writing in "At the Flick":

BULLY BABY YORK
First off, An American Hero *is being shown in a private pad. No hall was available. At least not after Sweeney's Grand Theater, hired for the premiere three months ago, went up in smoke. And this reviewer (hey gang, it's me, Leonor George) will stake her famed international reputation on the fact that the Birdman in Washington had something to do with the blaze.*

The reviewer again stakes her reputation, film buffs take note, that Igawa, director of An American Hero, *is the hottest thing around since Jean-Luc Godard sold out for the holy buck. Igawa. Remember that name. Igawa. Clay Gillies and Adam York are to be congratulated for their efforts in bringing this blazing new talent to public attention.*

Yes, kiddies, Adam York is the son of the uptight, strafe-those-rice-paddies-baby Baron York, the famous moom pitcher star who's given up his acting (????) career for the strange reason he doesn't want to enter politics. Ronnie, baby, move over.

Igawa's 30-minute film took a summer to shoot, almost a year to edit, and it shows a grooving day in the life of a young couple and their child. The cast is strictly amateur, but you'd never know it—or then again, maybe you would. The're that close to the reality tree. The guy is played by Stryker Halvorsen, Leigh Sutherland (Mrs. Igawa) plays his gal, and Lissa Gillies, daughter of our Clay, is the kiddie. Filmed in 16-mm Kodachrome in the Los Angeles scene, the flick peels onion rings right down to the truth of a guy and gal doing their own thing, and I do mean love. Without a hint of Hollywood schmaltz, in scene after scene Igawa resurrects the body of love.

Music, by folkie Ruth Abby Marx, grooves.

Sublimal battle-scene cuts remain inexplicable until the end of the film. Absolute silence and a still of the

*silver star. Clay Gillies' voice explains that this really
beautiful guy, Stryker Halvorsen, in real honest-to-god
life, earned it by being slaughtered in the Birdman's war.*
    Chills and more chills.
    WHEN ARE WE GETTING OUT?

The following evening, SRO.
Local papers carried a small item that another show biz son
had followed the footsteps of his famous father. Adam York
had produced an experimental film. AP and UP did not pick
up the item.

Leigh had told Ken she would stay in Los Angeles until her
father was out of bed, and now the words, because they were
spoken during an argument, took on the quality of a vow,
unbreakable, inviolable; she knew this was crazy, but she
couldn't help it. Maybe she was less pliant than other women
because of that body cast, she would decide, then would ask
herself why she'd never learned the art of gracious feminine
retreat?
    She couldn't help resenting her father and his illness. Yet
each time she entered the family room and saw him so strangely
immobile, she felt herself tangled in a blend of emotions that
took her some days to untwine. Then she realized that she not
only loved her father. She pitied him, too. And pity tyrannizes
even more than love. How could she leave him lying here like
this? He had almost died. He might die.
    She existed for Monday and Thursday nights. Right after
the rates went down she phoned her husband, reversing the
charges as part of the pretense (who was she kidding?) that
things were as they'd been. The conversations were pretty much
limited to her questions. Was the show moving along? Did he
know their film had been mentioned in the *Los Angeles Free
Press?* Did the part Persian with a sooty face—remember, she
used to feed it?—still come around? How were her African
violets? Yes, yes, she understood, she understood. He was no
gardener.
    After Leigh hung up she would sprawl across her bed,
breathing audibly as if she'd just run around the block.

By the fern stand in the front hall, Dorot repeated, "You
look thin."

"The pot's calling the kettle," Leigh said.

"You haven't been sick, have you?"

"Of course not!" Leigh, flushing, glanced at the open door to the family room where her father was playing cribbage with Stevie. Who knew what Dorot, down for Christmas, might say? "Come on. Let's wash for lunch."

Following her upstairs, Dorot said, "I'm worried about you."

"I've been looking after my father," Leigh said, shutting the door behind them, firmly getting down to brass tacks. "And Ken's been working on a show for Darvas Gallery. I think I told you about it, didn't I?"

At Ken's name Dorot sat on the orange ottoman. "When you got this room redecorated," Dorot said, "everyone at California was green with envy. Every single Rondelay wanted a pink and orange bedroom."

"That's why he stayed up in Berkeley," Leigh said.

"Precisely what I told people," Dorot said. "And when you got your own phone! That was the end. Everyone went around telling her mother that everyone at school had her own number. I remember five or six pitched battles with Mother on the subject."

Leigh went into her bathroom, placing the flat of her palms on the pink counter. "Have you seen him?" she asked, proud that the words came out so smoothly.

"Ken?"

"Who else?"

"Yes."

"How is he?"

"Looked fine."

"Where?"

"Where what?"

"Where did you see him?" Leigh asked from the bathroom.

"Larry Blake's."

"Eating?"

"Having a beer."

"Who with?"

"Clay Gillies."

"That's all?"

"Some of Clay's gang."

Leigh turned on the faucet. "Girls?"

"You know those activists. Who can tell the boys from the girls without a program?"

Leigh's laughter shrilled over running water, hanging too long, the same way an opera singer's cracked high C rises unfortunately above its orchestral accompaniment. "Then I shouldn't be worried?"

"Of course not."

"You'd tell me if he were with a girl?"

"If."

"After all, we're friends."

"I've always thought of you as my closest friend." Dorot's flat voice deepened with sincerity.

"So you'd tell me."

"If there were anything to tell."

Leigh came back in the bedroom. She was wiping her hands on a small, fringed towel. "And I was worried you were going to ask embarrassing questions."

"What about?"

"Did he say anything?"

"He was with this large group and—"

"What did he say about me?"

"You were fine."

"How did the subject come up?"

"I asked."

"Why?"

"Why not?"

"You might, being my friend, want to let *someone* know he was married."

Dorot tapped her forehead. "Sick."

"Was she Japanese?"

"Really sick."

"I am not stupid!"

"You wouldn't be my friend if you were," Dorot pointed out.

"You're a rotten liar."

"It's true. I have no patience with cretins."

"Here you are, not asking questions, not prying into our sex life, our separated sex life, Ken's and mine. I mean, I'm not stupid. *There's something going on and you're not telling me.*" Leigh flung the towel back into the bathroom. It fell on the floor.

Dorot stared at Leigh, her hurt magnified by thick lenses.

"I'm sorry," Leigh murmured. "That must sound pretty stinky."

"I never mean to pry."

"I'm sorry." Leigh's palms were sweating. "Really sorry, Dorot."

"It's intellectual curiosity. I'm no gossip."

"I didn't mean it," Leigh pleaded. "I'm sorry."

"Lu-unch ee-ees ready," Maria bawled up the stairs.

"Dorot—"

"Come on," Dorot said quietly (for her), "I'm starving."

After three rings a female voice answered.

"Is this the Igawa residence?" Leigh asked, then, conscious of her phony, formal phraseology, added, "Is this Ken Igawa's place?"

"Yes," said the thin voice. "Who is this?"

None of your damn business. "Who is this?"

"Nina."

Smashing! With a name like that you can't be a girl. You're a French poodle! "Is Ken there?"

"He's out right now. Who is this?"

You're really at home, aren't you? You poodle with your weak voice—doubtless you save your strength for better things. "Where is he?"

"With Prof—with an associate."

"Ohhh. . . ."

"Who shall I say called?"

Does he make love to you on my bed? Does he kiss your eyelids? Does he bite your neck? Does he move it so slowly that you think you're going clear out of your mind? Does he like you to—"I'll call back later," Leigh said quickly.

No further proof necessary, she thought as she hung up. Dorot's aberrational behavior had been proof enough, but if it hadn't, this reedy voice laid it right on the line; her husband had meant it when he'd said *T-H-I-S, new word, I-S, new word, I-T.* If she and her husband hadn't been so close, Leigh decided, so much closer than your average married couple, the proof of common, everyday, garden-variety infidelity would never have hit her this way. Like a bullet.

Gasping, kicking off her flats, she stretched across the bedspread staring up at that pink tester everyone in California High had been green for. Her aching chest rose and fell. Finally, unable to ignore the pain, she sat hunched over on the edge of the bed. Her face burned; her feet were icy. The clock's hour was four. Outside a car drove by, tires muffled by the rain that had started to fall in big, chill drops about a half hour ago, as Dorot had walked out the front door. Leigh's mind, up tight, would not let go of that reedy telephone voice. Through the open door to the bathroom she could see a small clear bottle containing yellow Nembutal; she'd begged that cautious man, Dr. Bendor, to prescribe them for her. A thought blossomed in Leigh's mind. She lay back on the bed, but she couldn't help staring at capsules in a stubby bottle. She forced her head to turn, ordered her eyes to catalogue the familiar room, pinch-pleat drapes, the puffy orange velvet chair and ottoman, the grouped Degas prints framed in mats of the same slubbed silk as the drapes; Mother and Mr. Samson, the decorator, had planned each detail carefully and there was no trace of her somewhat sloppy self, not a hint of her in the custom pink and orange.

She caught herself staring at the bottle.

Once, she thought, once on a warm August night we lay down in front of Station 13, and I could smell the marshy sea smells and hear rippling music like the Rhine maidens sang and salt water lapped over our feet and my muscles clenched and I stole from him a baby; but a gynecologist with a funny lumpy nose led me to his silent office and made me lie down on his towel-covered leather couch with the stirrups and the baby was canceled. *Don't look at them.*

Leigh pushed off the bed and walked pink Woolturf. Shadows crept in the room; rain lessened momentarily, then pelted harder, drowning all other sounds; through windows that opened into the vine-covered porch came damp, fecund odors. Pills were easy and painless but, alas, a dead (pun) giveaway and when the coroner did his job everyone would know you'd done a Valley-of-the-Dolls. How could you, to people who loved you?

Take me, take me.

"No, Alice, no!" she cried aloud, running into the bathroom, frantically twisting off white plastic lid, shaking yellow capsules into the john, flushing, and while they floated, swam, swirled and disappeared from the pink bowl, she remembered on the beach he'd given her a present, a poem. "If I were tickled by the rub of love," he'd said against her ear, and because he was nineteen and still almost as embarrassed at talking of love as at quoting Dylan Thomas, he'd spoken too quickly, "the world is half the devil's and my own, daft with the drug that's smoking in a girl and curling round the bud that forks her eye." I knew he meant the lovely words and oh my God help me for I truly repent having flushed your blessed Nembutal down the john.

Ken picked up the phone on the fifth ring.

"Ken, is that you?" his father-in-law asked. "This is Sidney."

"Sir?"

"Listen, Ken, I don't know what's happening between you two kids—"

"Don't you?"

"I'm not up to hostilities."

"Sir, the war's over. You've won."

"Not tonight."

"You must've noticed the spoils around the house."

As Ken spoke there was a whining, twittering sound as if a flock of black crows had settled onto the telephone lines someplace between Berkeley and Los Angeles.

"Ken . . ." Mr. Sutherland's voice was more remote. "Are you still there?"

"Uh huh."

"Look, let's come to the point."

"What point?"

"Leigh phoned you this afternoon."

"I didn't·talk to her."

"I spoke to the phone company. They say a call was completed."

"They're not notorious for—"

"From here to your number."

"Under oath, sir," Ken said. "I didn't talk to her."

"She went out tonight. She said to play bridge with Dorot. Dorot says they never had a date. And Leigh never went near the McHenrys. Incidentally, Dorot thought Leigh was acting strangely. They had lunch today. At any rate, tonight Leigh was driving in Malibu Canyon. She crashed down an embankment—"

"Is she hurt?"

"The car's wrecked—"

"Is she—?"

"She's shaken, that's all. A miracle . . . the car's a total loss."

Again the line twittered.

"So," Mr. Sutherland said slowly, "you didn't talk to her?"

"No." But by now Ken realized who had. He didn't say anything.

"Well, maybe it was an accident," Mr. Sutherland said. "She swerved, she says, to avoid a motorcycle. But what the hell was she doing in Malibu Canyon?"

"Did you ask?"

"She said it seemed like a nice night for a drive—it's pouring here. And you know Malibu Canyon—a roller coaster." On the bad connection the ripe voice faded to a hoarse whisper. "Ken, do me a favor. She's trying to hide it. But she's pretty shaken. Phone her."

"Sir, maybe *you* better talk to her. I'm not the one voted most likely to cheer."

"Try."

"It'll do more harm."

"Please."

"You don't understand—"

"Reverse the charges."

Ken's finger jammed on the clear plastic prong. He was sitting on the floor and for a minute he didn't move. There was a streak of green paint across his forehead and small globes of sweat stood up on it.

Raising his finger, he started to dial area code 213. He stopped. What was the point? For two solid weeks hadn't he phoned her every single night begging her to come home? Hadn't he spelled out his every weakness to her? Begged? Ken's toes curled tensely. He closed his eyes and fumbled a little as he dropped the receiver into the cradle. He opened his eyes. He lifted the receiver, dialed 213 again.

"Hell," he said.

And he hurled the phone. The two parts of the black instrument went as far as thick black cords, one tight coiled, the other straight, would permit. After a few seconds he heard the busy signal. He admitted it, he was a neurotic yellow bastard. A real prick. But he couldn't, he couldn't, not ever again take Leigh's soft voice coming through that phone patiently explaining that her white father, sporty old reverse-the-charges, was more important to her than he, her husband. Had he ever denied his cruel streak?

It had been an accident.

Ken closed his eyes, listening to the constant buzz. Small, oddly shaped tears squeezed between his black lashes.

Part Six

1

York lay on his bed.

December sun filtered clear lemon light through the window and he read his Bible, not because he cared as so many pretended to lately if God were dead or alive—alive He'd fucked up in the worst possible manner and dead, well, *R.I.P.*—but because the Bible was printed in Greek and he could immerse himself in the translating: *This know also that in the last day perilous times shall come. For men shall be lovers of their own selves, covetous, boasters, proud, blasphemers, disobedient to their parents, untruthful, unholy. Without natural affection.* York dabbled ashes, getting some on thin paper. Once, in a spurt of ambition, he'd taught himself Danish, French, Portuguese, Russian, plus, of course, Greek; then, as now, he'd taken no pride in his accomplishment. As a matter of fact he'd always scorned polyglots, feeling that the gift of tongues was bestowed on the excessively stupid that they might earn their living as language teachers. However, he admitted as he scanned the alien chicken tracks, now that he could no longer concentrate on reading English his self-taught fluff proved just the ticket.

The small electric box over his door came alive. York ignored the buzz. His only visitors were Gillies, who let himself in, and fat, silent Viella; she cleaned on Wednesday, which this wasn't. The doorbell buzzed, longer this time. York kept translating: *laden with diverse sins, led away with diverse sins—*

The door opened. He read until the draft carried to him the scents of French perfume, lotions, powders, silks and the distinctive aroma of well-tanned glove leather. He raised up on his elbow, turning to his stepmother. He couldn't decide whether he was surprised, but he fully accepted the implications of small chills running along his spine. She scared the hell out of him.

"Hello, Adam," his stepmother said. Shining black hair

piled in a knot, pale vicuña coat, pale shoes and gloves, she advanced on him.

"The Bible," she said. "I am surprised."

"It's loaded with unnatural vices"—York formed a smile with his mouth—"from onanism to fellatio and cunnilingus. I tell you! Bernard Geis should put out an edition in big print for the lip-reading set. He'd have himself an instant best seller."

And he let the Bible fall to the carpet. His father's wife picked it up. First smoothing the tissue pages, then raising the small book to her lipsticked mouth, she set it on the coffee table.

"God sees all?" York asked.

"One never knows."

"Does one?"

Sitting near him on the straight-backed chair, she pulled off her gloves. "Why didn't you follow my advice?" she asked.

"Nothing like coming right to the point."

"Well?"

"You warned me to stay out of the water." Relaxing into his prone position, he held up his good hand. "See? Dry."

"You're subsidizing Gillies."

"You might put it that way," he agreed.

"That movie's showing with your name on it."

"And you've been working your handsome self to the bone trying to stop us."

Her head tilted. York wondered about the antigravity powers in that seemingly casual black Psyche's knot.

"Haven't you?" he asked.

"We've spent a little effort."

"A little!"

"You don't have to be a solipsist. Admit there are other matters to occupy us."

"Arson?"

"The fire was an accident."

York clucked.

"A fortunate one," she hastened to add, "but an accident."

"The Big Director up yonder must be helping Daddy in his new role."

"Your father," she said, "does attract important friends."

"You are funny."

"Adam." With strong fingers she smoothed the soft beige kidskin of her gloves. "We want you to come home."

"I'm at—"

"Our home."

"So?" he grated. "The film's got you worried?"

"We're more worried about you."

"Me? How?"

She opened her black alligator purse and York glimpsed lace handkerchief, Gucci wallet, gold lighter, gold compact, everything immaculate except for the one crazy note of imperfection that always clung to her, in this case a half-eaten Hershey with almonds. This messy candy bar, York decided as his father's wife withdrew a small alligator memo book, made her seem almost a human woman. Almost. She closed her purse with a small click.

Half reading, half watching his reaction with those round plum eyes, she started. "Two weeks ago you were seen with a man who calls himself Argo. Argo wears a beard. He has a taste for expensive sweaters. You met him at We Sell Books on Telegraph Avenue. He gave you a small package; you gave him cash. The next Friday you met Argo by the laxatives at Popkin Drugs on Union Street. Three days later you and Argo drank coffee at adjacent stools at the Psychedelicatessen in Haight Ashbury. Do I have to go on?"

"The truth's out. I've got me a friend."

"A supplier."

York managed a casual shrug, but a cold sliver, like a knife, entered his head; soon, he knew, soon the twitching would start.

"You're an addict," she said.

"If that's your worry, set your mind at ease. And father dear's, too. Sure I'm a user. In these perilous times you'd be surprised at how many are."

"I wouldn't be."

"No. I don't suppose you would," York said. "I'm not hooked."

She sat handsome and erect in her vicuña.

"I can stop at any time," he said.

She gazed at him.

"I can."

She never blinked.

"So it's the cliché answer!"

"Why are you shouting?" she inquired.

"Because I am not hooked!"

She glanced around; noon sun showed dust and disorder. "Adam," she said, "did you know an addict's relatives can have him committed?"

"I am not—"

"My question," she interrupted, "is about the law. Do you know that an addict can be committed by a relative?"

"Yes."

"Good."

"But," he said, "I don't think one will. Mass media would have its field day. Baron York—flash—famous movie star and uptight noncandidate par excellence—flash—commits his son—flash—the junkie."

"Listen to me. Your father's not a heavy. He doesn't like the idea of shutting you away." She tapped the spine of her notebook against her teeth. Three hollow clicks. She had strong, very white teeth. "And I prefer not to."

"That sounds like a threat."

"Any remark can." She sighed. "Adam, you're not easy to reach."

"I told you the term. Alienated."

"But you are bright."

He bowed his head.

"So you can understand I've flown up here for the express purpose of heading you off before you get into serious trouble?"

"It does sound like a threat, all righty," York said.

"You've closed your mind to any good qualities your father possesses," she said. "But he's honestly disturbed."

The twitch definitely was on the way. York battled it. He would rather be dead than let his father's wife see him give one small twitch.

She opened her purse, dropping in the tiny book.

"Tell my father he can stop beating his brain," York said. "I'm not hooked."

"You're protesting a bit too much."

"What else can I do?"

"Stop," she said. "If you can."

And rising, gathering her purse and gloves in one hand, she moved to the door, raising a small draft that set dust motes whirling in the sunlight.

"Thanks for the concern," York said.

Hand on doorknob, she replied, "It's more genuine than your side of the conversation." The door closed behind her.

York, still controlling the twitch, stood by the window. A

gleaming black Rolls was parked between two lowercase cars with UC stickers plastered to rear windows. Between leafless elm trees flocked sparrows, sun whitening the upper side of their wings. After a couple of minutes his stepmother appeared, foreshortened in her loose coat. A maroon-uniformed chauffeur that York hadn't noticed jumped to open the back door for her. Even York, who after all had been gilded by the easy gloss of movie money, couldn't prevent a grimace. He was impressed. Gripping the drape he forced himself to ponder as if it were an important issue: Was this a Hertz Rent-a-Rolls-and-chauffeur? Had one of his father's "important" friends lent it? Or—just possibly this was it—did her grandfather keep a chauffeured limo in every major city in the country? In the world?

The Rolls edged smoothly into oil-stained middle of the narrow street, moving north, turning left.

York returned to his Greek Bible. That is, he opened the Bible, but the twitching could no longer be suppressed. His eyes began to water. And in less than five minutes sweat was pouring out of him.

He gave up the pretense of reading. Snapping open a drawer in the coffee table, he grabbed at a large sack of M & Ms, shoving the multicolored pellets in his mouth; then, whirling about the airless apartment, he searched for his scratch pad. Finding it on the sink under a pile of unopened letters he yanked out the attached pencil and began to write, word for word, the conversation he'd just had with his stepmother. He had a wonderful memory and he wrote and wrote and wrote and soon his uneven tracks filled five unlined sheets on both sides, but then his shakiness worsened so he could no longer write and he paced the room, up and back, back and up. It was as if raw pepper were ground into his veins and arteries, as if each capillary in his body were alive and in business for itself. He hugged his arms around his thin, quaking self and kept walking. Suddenly he gagged, making it just in time to the bathroom. Leaning over the toilet he vomited undigested chocolate until only a clear mucus came. The taste of vomit sour in his mouth and throat, he stood staring at the toothpaste-flecked mirror.

Limber-jawed, pale, twitching, at last they were face to face, Adam York and the truth.

His stepmother had spoken the truth.

He gripped the washbowl. And remembered the first time he'd tried the splendid stuff, a rainy spring afternoon toward

the end of his mother's illness. He'd done what addicts call
chipping, used only as a rare luxury, that was to say when he
could no longer bear to watch the crab enjoying its meal. Many
people, he'd learned through his research, live a perfectly normal life chipping. In Greece he'd gone without for weeks,
months even, testing himself that he was chipping. Mostly he
had used the stuff as an adjunct to sex; with it he approached
an old Arabic technique that the thin, dark madam of the Piraeus
whorehouse once had described to him as *imsak,* a prolonged
stay in the perfumed garden, and screwing those placid-hipped
whores had been like coming with Claudia Cardinale for eight
hours. Oh, he had been careful. He didn't care to be hooked.
York must be free and alone, soaring above the rest of humanity.
Free. . . . It hadn't worked out like that, had it? York couldn't
pinpoint the day of imprisonment; he knew only that after his
return to California, in his father's busy hillside mansion, his
arm had pained him beyond bearing and he had begun to drug
it more and more heavily, increasing when he arrived in Berkeley. But never once had he admitted to himself the truth. He
was no longer chipping.

"So . . ." he muttered.

He stared in the mirror at the pale, shaking creature. So that
cripple was pissing away trust fund income and inheritance at
the rate of fifty dollars per day to keep various slimy characters
in Italian knit. That poor, sad, lonely cripple needed his shot
in the worst way, which, he now admitted, was an addict's
way.

"So be it," he muttered.

He unbuttoned the left cuff, his short sleeve, rolling it high.
Ulcerated, needle-tattooed skin quivered. With a shaking hand
he managed to light the candle and hold over the yellow flame
a bent, char-bottomed spoon.

After the injection he watched his face. As the irritation in
his veins and arteries subsided, the twitching stopped. The thin
face relaxed. York tilted his head. He hadn't wanted the perfumed garden in months (*Ciao,* Claudia, baby) and the bone
still pained in the distance. But so what? He was calm. "Enjoy
it," he told himself aloud. "Things can only get worse." Re-
buttoning his cuff, he put away his kit and returned to the sunny
living room.

He replaced his glasses and picked up his Bible. *Oh, in the
last day perilous times shall come . . .*

His doorknob turned.

"Just like Grand Central," he remarked.

Gillies entered, bearded chin high, humble denims faded. *Grab yourself a robe*, York thought, *and you could try out for the part you want, the Lead in this*. He dropped the Bible again.

——————— **2** ———————

Clay let himself into York's apartment.

"Just like Grand Central," York said, dropping a black book.

Clay sat down. He was here in this airless, sour-smelling bachelor apartment to pick up York's routine subsidy for Students for Peace, and as always he experienced a certain sweatiness about the errand. Clay jangled a cash register two nights a week at Shattuck Shop'n'Save to keep himself—every cent York gave him went to Students for Peace; still, over money matters he always sweated. So since York seemed reasonable, or as reasonable as York ever was, Clay put begging off for a few minutes, instead shooting the breeze about *An American Hero*. To be frank, Clay was pretty excited about the way it had jelled and pretty annoyed with York for consistently refusing to view the improvements that his, Clay Gillies', ideas had wrought on the original print.

While Clay talked York held up his wrist, admiring his watch. Large, round, gold and reptile banded.

"You ought to see it," Clay repeated.

"I already did."

"The new editing's strengthened it fantastically."

York glanced at his watch.

"It's very powerful," Clay said.

"That's Igawa for you. Can't fuck up even when he's forced to the old artistic wall." York held his arm further from his face, squinting through glasses at his wrist. "A shame his audience is only a few college clods."

"At least they're appreciating it."

"I mean it, Gillies. That's what I call real progress. Three months and you're still showing at Igawa's place. Or is it six months? Time escapes me."

"You, of all people, know what we're up against."

"And you, of all people, know why I'm footing your bills."

Clay's fists clenched with their need to tighten around a thin neck. To forestall his instincts, he hurried into the kitchen. Opening the refrigerator he saw two lumps of cheese, one growing green hair, an unopened can of Danish ham, and a couple of six-packs of Olympia. Clay opened a can of Oly, forcing himself to take his time about it. His head tilting back, icy liquid easing down his throat, he recovered enough to return to the living room. Leaning on the wall that separated the kitchen from this room, he said, "If it's publicity you're after—"

"I ever denied it?"

"We got a review—"

"Score one for you."

"—an excellent one—"

"I can read."

"—in the *Barb*."

"The most widely circulated underground paper on all Telegraph Avenue," York said, staring at his watch.

"I'm keeping you from a big date?"

"Nope."

Clay's beer can gurgled as he pointed it at York's thin, hairless wrist. "Then why?"

"A reminder," York said.

"Reminder?"

"Time is fleeting."

"And?"

"Time, you might say, is running out."

Clay took a long swallow. "I take that to mean," he said, "you won't be underwriting Students for Peace if we don't get you what you want?"

"Bright boy."

"You're too damn inert even to go out and rouse up some bad publicity on your own!"

"And you—alas, you. . . . Back at the old grind, passing the manila envelope."

"It's your connections that're causing the tie-ups!"

"And it's my connections that'll get you the most blazing burst of publicity ever seen—that is, if you ever get your ass off the ground." York swung his legs to the floor, sitting up. "You know better than I that without televised coverage, Clay Gillies, activist par excellence, could get the entire male population of the Big U to travel north of the border to avoid the draft and still not accomplish one damn thing. You could show the film in Igawa's apartment until the year three thousand and not come any closer to ending the war."

Clay again retreated to the kitchen, hurling his empty Oly can into the trash, wiping his hand across his sweaty forehead. He took a long breath, then called, "How long?"

Silence.

"How long?" he repeated, turning the corner to face York. York faked a yawn.

"Peace," Clay said. "No more games, O.K.?"

"It's running out."

"So you said. *How long?*"

York shrugged.

"Come off it!"

"That's how life is," York said. "Cryptic." He shook his head. "I'd think you, all so nobly heated, would be far more eager than I to get the lead out."

"I am," Clay said.

"Good." And York took out his checkbook. "We understand one another," he said, writing.

Blue check stowed safe in his pocket, Clay left, taking the cement stairs. He disliked the tiny Otis elevator, which gave him a shuddering, coffin-reasoned premonition of his own death.

Christmas time. Berkeley teetered between quiet and bustle. A college town empty of college students accounted for the quiet; shoppers, arms laden with gilt-wrapped boxes and long tubes around which coiled posters, accounted for the bustle. From open windows came merciless, recorded caroling, "Hark, the Herald Angels Sing," in every form from hard rock to the velvet of an opera singer's soaring notes; someone had pasted a string of blue Jewish stars across a dorm window and in the room exactly above someone had handpainted DEAR JESUS HAPPY BIRTHDAY inside the window. Warm sun drew spicy odors from pine wreaths on front doors.

Clay walked through Christmas streets trying to rouse his brain to action with unseasonal thoughts: Dow Napalm burning living flesh, bursts of flame in a jungle landscape, the jagged light of a night-fired bullet, the vrooming roar of a flame thrower, Stryker's long body dead, brown babies with swollen bellies waiting dully for starvation to deliver them, mutilation, the jelly, the knife, the ruined rice paddy, these thoughts should remind Clay of the urgency of his work. But, walking the length of Telegraph, his guilty mind kept hurrying back to Odessa. The truth was, lately he thought of little except Odessa. Since that first night three weeks ago his emotions had been contradictory. He blazed with joy at his triumph. At the same time he was tormented that she didn't love him. Tonight . . . she had promised to come to him tonight, as soon as she was free.

Clay crossed Dwight. A car squealed to a halt. "God damn you! Watch it!" a boy yelled. Clay ignored squealing brakes and the shout. Odessa was transforming an old frame shack into a black youth center, manned by blacks, supported by blacks, to be used by SNAP youngsters, now all black. A strange collapsing pain hurt Clay's chest. Didn't an all-black center negate five years of his life?

At eleven thirty that night a small rap sounded at Clay's door. He jumped to open it. Odessa brought with her the cool freshness of night air.

"I'm so late I've forgotten the password." She smiled her apology.

"You're here," he said, "that's what counts." Then, realizing the predictability of this remark made him sound an ass, he flushed and to hide this flush he took her in his arms.

"Clay."

As was their habit they left on the unshaded overhead light. In bed her arms went around him, her lips opened under his, her thighs parted and her dark, floating flesh gave him queenly reception. Yet though they were joined he was still wondering how she felt about him. True, she was murmuring her usual word-free reassurances, true she was a warm, wonderful, attentive lover . . . and yet . . . yet, even now Clay felt a sense of separation, as if the inner core of Odessa were smiling her wry amusement at the joining of their bodies. He thrust mightily and her breathing quickened, but this seemed only to add to their *apartheid*. Balling those other chicks, black or white, even with Michele, had he ever felt this terrible apartness? Had he? The truth was he'd never before wanted closeness with a woman. He pulled Odessa's full, firm buttocks closer. He smelled their mingled sweat. He tasted the salt of her shoulders. "Odessa," he cried. And she, with small, helpless groans, flared her thighs, rising up to him, and he forgot his doubts, forgot everything, losing himself utterly in the dark catalyst of her body.

Immediately afterward, though, his heart still thudding, he again sensed their separation. He gazed down at the brownish purple of her closed eyelids. A small trickle of his saliva glistened on her cheek.

"Clay." Odessa opened her eyes, smiling, trailing a dark-fingered caress on his lips. "Clay, what's wrong?"

"Nothing."

"Then why so sad?"

"S'over."

"You like?"

"The most," he said, and this—however he might yearn after a more perfect union—was no lie.

"I'm glad."

"For you?"

She replied with a deep purr.

"Mmmm, what?"

"Mmmmm, yes."

"That's the wrong answer," he said.

"Tell the right one?"

"I love you."

"I love you," she murmured.

He put his mouth to her ear. "I mean it," he whispered.

She tugged playfully at his beard.

"I love you," he said.

"Of course," she teased. "Now."

"Now?" He heard his own pain. "Always!"

Under him her body stiffened. "Clay, hush."

"It's the truth."

"'Things are seldom what they seem, skim milk masquerades as cream—'"

"*Always*. Why make jokes about it?"

She put her hand over his mouth. "There's the difference in our ages—"

He pulled her hand away. "Big deal."

"Clay, listen." She sighed and beneath him he felt the liquid movements of her body. "I feel more for you than I ought to. But you—try to understand you. Beside age, think of how you came to know me. What I must represent to you. Don't you see? With me you're making it with all the poor, downtrodden blacks, you're making it so you can pretend we're already in the happy land where every baby's a pretty and equal beige color—"

"Shut up!" And a sudden fierceness revived him. He could feel himself stretch inside her.

He took her again, quickly. Afterward, as she started to get out of bed, he reached for her wrist, holding her.

"Stay," he pleaded.

She shook her head.

"Why?"

"I can't."

"Why?"

"I'm living at the Center."

"The hell with the Center."

She pulled her hand, trying to escape, but he held tight.

"Will it give you leprosy, staying a night in my place?"

"It'll give you landlord problems."

"I'll take the chance."

"Clay—"

"Please?"

But gently she released the fingers that held her wrist.

"It's like you're rushing home to your husband," he said, then lay back reflecting with pain that for all he knew of Odessa she might have a husband.

He watched her pull her clothes over her full brown body. Dressed in her raincoat, a blue scarf over her head, Odessa bent briefly over him. Her face was pure, free of lines and tension. Almost unworldly. *The face of a nun,* he thought, and for a moment he joined ideas; he had a gestalt if you cared to be precise. She *did* have a husband, but—like a nun—not a mortal one; instead of taking the Holy Ghost, Odessa Norris had taken a cause, and her children (like those of a teaching nun) weren't borne of her body but were all the young people she worked with. Clay's gestalt escaped him as she took her first step toward the door, for now he was thinking only of the emptiness that would come after her departure.

"Oh, I forgot." She turned. "Here's something for you." And fishing in her raincoat pocket she came up with a roughly torn square of newspaper. She handed it to him. "Sleep tight." She smiled.

After she closed the door Clay tugged the coarse muslin of the top sheet over his head to keep close as long as possible the rich, moist odors of her body. *I feel for you more than I ought to,* she'd said. He fell asleep smiling, the torn bit of newspaper unread and held loosely in his fingers.

The following morning when he aired his bed he found the clipping. He read. He took his cold shower. He reread. As he waited for his coffee to perk he read again. And again. Every word on that torn newsprint ingrained itself on his memory.

At York's he let himself in. Open drapes admitted early green light. York stirred, flinging one arm over his head. He didn't waken. Clay gripped the door jamb, staring. It was impossible to believe this was York. In sleep this wasn't the same man Clay had known for so many years. This sleeper, minus dark glasses and coldly superior expression, could have been a child, an orphan condemned to live on the cold, hard charity of strangers. Clay, looking down on the thin, lonely face, felt warmth and friendship and pity.

He closed the door sharply.

York grunted, rolled over, rubbed his eyes. Reached for the inevitable dark glasses. "So . . ." he mumbled. "The early Gillies out getting his worm."

"The President," Clay said without preliminary, "is going to be at a dinner at the Century Plaza Hotel."

"Nice for him." Fully awake, York's voice had returned to sarcasm.

Clay's bearded jaw tightened. "Los Angeles," he said tersely. "April seventh."

"And to tell me this, you wake me at—" York reached for the cluttered table behind him, came up with his watch. "For Christ's sake! Seven thirty-eight on December twenty-first!"

"You *were* worried about time."

"But not about the President."

"Your father'll be there."

York sat. He wore black pajamas; the left sleeve, as always, had been tailored for his deformity.

"Like hell he will," he said.

"Strange bedfellows," Clay commented.

"Those he's had plenty of. But never a Democrat."

"I meant politicians make—"

"I know the expression." York gave a tremendous yawn. "My father is an actor."

Clay reached in his denim pocket.

"And in this year's role," York went on, "he's not playing politician. Statesman's his role."

Clay held out Odessa's clipping, reciting from memory, "'—the proceeds will go to the Kennedy Memorial Hospital in Dublin. Financial leaders of the city as well as dignitaries of both parties will attend. Baron York will be chairman of the event.'" He extended the clipping. "Want to see?"

"I believe you. I believe you. However, any personal significance eludes me."

"It's what we've been waiting for."

"My mind's still asleep, Gillies."

"Think."

York shoved out of bed, picking his way around heaped clothes and discarded books. Clay heard him urinate and flush. He returned.

"O.K., you win," he said. "Why is the President eating dinner with my father at the Century Plaza on April seventh exactly what we've been waiting for?"

"We'll put on a peace rally."

York pushed his dark glasses up to thin brown hair. "A peace rally. . . ." He raised sparse eyebrows. "A peace rally. . . ." He nodded. "Yes, I *was* asleep." He made a deep bow in Clay's direction. "I apologize. I apologize."

"Then you see—?"

York bowed again. "I see," he said.

"Listen, the rally'll coincide with the dinner—"

"When else?"

"—and someplace near we can set up an outdoor screen. Show *An American Hero*, then march to the hotel."

York nodded.

"There's lots of ways—" Clay started.

"And you know them all." York skipped around the corner to the narrow kitchen. "Want coffee?"

"Just had mine, thanks."

York, waiting for electric coils to turn red and heat water, seemed willing to listen; Clay didn't have anything specific in mind—he never planned his actions until he was positive of his ultimate goal. What point was there in it? Under Clay's thick hair lay an orderly mind that disliked waste. Yet at the same time he was aware that there comes a tide in the affairs of men that must be taken at the flood, and if he couldn't remember which of *his* plays the quote came from, he recognized the flood. York. Rich York sitting at a littered breakfast bar, willing for once to listen. So Clay, for once, winged it.

As he talked ideas came bursting at him like exploding colors in a light show.

"Nobody wants to fight. Nobody wants this war. It's not just the Berkeley area. Listen, York, this I believe. Our generation has traveled more, seen more, has communicated more. We know there be no monsters where the ocean ends. Nowadays when the flag goes by, do you see anyone doing a Barbara Frietchie? What people want isn't patriotism but peace. They want to be left alone to live."

York was silent.

"It's true," Clay insisted.

York didn't speak.

Clay crushed an empty cigarette wrapper in his fist. "All right. I know everyone doesn't feel the same. That's why we need this peace rally. To show that a tremendous number of 'respectable' people *are* against war, this war, any war. The others'll be forced to examine their own consciences."

York twisted narrow bare feet around brass rungs of his stool. "Terrific," he said. "You're a splendid speaker."

Clay ignored this. "Sure, sure there's some who're against us. The trick is to make them work for us. Listen, remember how Bull Connor's men electrified not only their victims but also the television audience with those cattle prods?" He straightened out the cigarette wrapper he'd just crumpled. "What we want is this. The people should see protest isn't restricted. We'll show 'em that all sorts, not just hippies or flower children or activists or whatever they call us, are interested in withdrawing from Vietnam. We'll show the television audience that normal squares like themselves are against the war. Even the son of Superhawk York is against war."

York rose, spooning instant coffee into a dirty cup. "By George, I do believe you've got it!"

Clay, too excited to remain sitting, paced around the messy one-room apartment. Yes. He'd got it. This was it!

The Campanile struck in the cold green morning, and York returned to his bed, lying down, nursing his steaming mug above bony, hairless chest exposed by missing pajama buttons.

"When are you planning to start planning?" he asked.

"Now," Clay replied.

"Excellent."

"In Los Angeles," Clay added.

"Goes without saying."

"You'll drive down with me?"

"Nyet."

"No?"

"No."

"Later?" Clay asked.

"Never."

"But what about the publicity. Isn't that what you want?"

"My name's on the film." York turned to watch Clay's pacing. "You *do* mean to show it, don't you?"

Although Clay had mentioned *An American Hero* strictly on the wing, and although now, on more or less solid ground again, he was aware of vast problems involved—where do you find outdoor screens? a huge gathering point to set them up?—he answered without hesitation, "Of course."

"Good." York took a preliminary sip. "It'll be enough that my illustrious surname is on it."

"I'll need all the help I can get."

York set down the mug, reaching for clothes on the floor, pulling up dark flannel slacks.

"Never fear." He extracted his checkbook. "Help is here."

"I need people."

"You need people?"

"Haven't you listened to one word—"

"Every word," York assured. "Gillies, you and me, we're closer than Sydney Greenstreet and Peter Lorre."

"Listen, *I'*m not in this to spite a father!" The golden spokes in Clay's irises blazed. *"I believe."*

"Down, boy, down."

Clay's stomach clenched with fury. York was forever assuming that he (Clay) had a personal stake in his work—right there in that single assumption, Clay decided as he tried to get hold of himself, you had a major portion of today's ills. Today nobody could perform an act of honor, nobody could work for something he truly believed in (beside cash), without some wet Freudian trying to expose him as the worst sort of phony.

"This isn't for me," Clay said in a level voice. "It's for everyone on this earth."

"That's it, lad. Think big."

"Hell, I know one rally isn't going to stop the war," Clay said. "But it's a beginning. Someone's got to begin someplace. Maybe I'll get the right people to see that this mess could set off number three." Clay flung up his hands and let them de-

scend, describing a mushroom cloud. "All of us . . . *phhht* . . .
dead. Finished."

"No such luck," York said quietly. "Enough'll survive to
start the whole fucking mess over again—and that, son, is a
pun. Now. How much do you need for openers?"

Clay got out his plastic-bound memobook and calculated in
small, neat figures.

————————— **3** —————————

"Scotch on the rocks," ordered the fat man next to Marshall
Mosgrove.

The waiter nodded.

"Be sure it's Black Label."

Of course it'll be Black Label, Marshall thought. *At this
kind of party, what else?*

Marshall, jammed at the far end of Baron York's living
room, nursing a drink, had to give himself points for arguing
Dorot out of a Channel 28 lecture by Dr. Alan Guttmacher,
Dorot's ideal after Kinsey, so they could come here with the
Mores.

Several hundred people enjoyed themselves; through tall
doors to the dining room Marshall could see waiters presiding
over a buffet covered with huge platters of sliced turkey, glistening ham, plump curled Guaymas shrimp, various silver chafing dishes, and a crystal bowl filled with crushed ice and crowned
by a smaller bowl brim full of Beluga—Dorot, impressed, had
calculated the caviar's approximate cost in the neighborhood
of three hundred dollars. Through swirls of wit and laughter
an easy piano rippled seasonally . . . *how still we see thee lie;
above thy deep and dreamless sleep.* . . . A fifteen-foot Douglas
fir in the hall gave off a wonderful mountain odor. Outside,
late afternoon sun, but in here, with drapes drawn, a congenial
dusk in which all older women were firm-fleshed and smooth
of skin, young women universally lovely, and every man present the same age, the age of distinction—Marshall already had

ticked off eighteen very famous people as well as at least thirty
that he was reasonably sure he recognized. He'd never been
to a cocktail party like this—but how many had?

As the waiter moved away, the fat man again cautioned,
"Black Label."

This fat man was Marshall's new-found friend.

He'd attached himself to Marshall ten minutes ago, right
after Dorot and the Mores had disappeared into the crowded
foyer, the three of them answering miraculously simultaneous
calls of nature. Marshall hated to be alone in a crowd (and
who could be more alone than a nobody in the midst of the
convivial famous?) so he'd accepted the man's conversation.
The man was very drunk, and very fat, and fat people frightened
Marshall with intimations of his own obesity. The man was
short, dark, squash-nosed, with large red cheeks. He reminded
Marshall of the Kennedys' man, Pierre Salinger.

"Well, Young Republican," said the red-cheeked one, who
had gotten a pocket biography out of Marshall in three minutes
flat. "So you approve of actors in politics?"

"Why not? They're interested citizens like the rest of us,
aren't they?" Marshall rubbed a hand back over his thinning
strands of hair, longer now in accordance with current styles.
This fat man was too Hollywood, with his white turtleneck
worn with a tuxedo, his patent pumps; Marshall ached to put
him down. "I don't see why they shouldn't have the same
opportunity as the rest of us."

"You're right, Student Body Prexy, you're right. But for
the wrong reasons. Politicians always've been actors." The man
belched, spraying a mist of Scotch over Marshall. " 'Scuse,"
he said, his mouth covered with his hand. "You see, my eager
young friend, a politician always has to rouse answering echoes
in the mob, just as an actor does, and, like an actor, his success
depends on his ability to keep his audience."

"Now explain"—Marshall's tone was patient—"how that
stops a man from being a sincere, dedicated public servant?"

"Let me finish, Future Attorney. It's a McLuhan world.
Mass communications. Instant communications. The actor
function is primary, the governmental secondary. After all, isn't
a politician's first duty to get himself elec . . ."

The rich voice faded.

A blonde displaying mounded-up breasts darted around them,
calling, "Yooo-hooo, Arteeee. . . ." Her bosom jiggled. She
trailed thick perfume. "Artie!"

The red-cheeked man stared after her, watching the round rear in some sort of glittery knit swing like a pendulum. "How'd you like some of that?" he asked. Lustfully. "Available to one and all."

"I'm here with my girl," Marshall put in too hastily. "You were saying?"

"I was saying," the man said, staring after the blonde one more second before he turned back to Marshall, "I was saying, Eagle Scout, that in this age, your poor average politico has to get his message across as quick as she does. The day has passed when a candidate could chew the fat with Stephen Douglas or stay as silent as Cal. No more, no more, no more. Now there's fantastic expense—have you any idea, booby"—the fat man swayed back and forth on his small, shiny pumps—"what it costs for thirty seconds of coast to coast?"

"A hundred thousand?" Marshall guessed.

The man looked blankly at him. "I've forgotten. Well, whatever, you can see our potential nominee has to hit his chords quick. And a man like Baron York has a ready-made image. Strong. Manly. Able to take responsibility, yours and mine. Gaze on him a half a minute and you're ready to give your vote—"

"I happen to go along with what he stands for."

"You don't know *what* he stands for."

"Mr. York—"

"Rides the white horse, so he's the good guy."

"That's no way to talk, not when you're drinking his liquor."

"Pardon, Rover Boy. I'm not talking about Baron in particular. And free booze doesn't alter the way of the world. Behind every politician there's backing angels: a director, a producer, cameramen, a corps of paid hacks. An advertising agency. Should Nixon wear make-up on TV or shouldn't he? Even you will have to admit that turned out to be *the* issue of the sixty campaign, not whether he believed blacks are more equal than you or me."

The mellow, drunken voice rose above cocktail party roar, attracting attention. Marshall edged away, but the man followed, poking Marshall's fleshy stomach with his forefinger.

"From now on, take it from me, Young Eager Beaver, the man who gets himself elected will be the one with the magnetism, the one who bears grief most nobly at televised funerals and looks strongest and most reliable in time of grave crises. It's the day of the acting governor."

Marshall glanced around apprehensively. One of the famous faces had belonged to Mrs. Reagan.

The man continued in the same hectoring tone, "The world's gotten too big, too fast, too complicated for—"

The waiter had eased his way around a cluster of laughers to present a silver tray with pierced silver walls; nodding at one of the squat glasses, he murmured, "Near one's yours, Mr. Kalpraga."

"Thanks, Crowell."

The waiter nodded and moved on.

"You're a friend of the Yorks?" Marshall asked.

"You might call me that."

Above thy deep and dreamless sleep, the silent . . . Marshall felt his muscles grow less tense. For a while there he'd again been Wetpants Mosgrove, forced to hang around the fringes with the outsiders, but now, thank God, he was reinstated.

Kalpraga chuckled. "I see it impresses you, Young Republican, my being known in the seats of the mighty."

"I'm only surprised that you aren't more . . . generous . . . about your friends, that's all."

"Nice wordage." The man took a long swallow of his fresh drink. He smiled, showing small front teeth. "The Yorks let me foam at the mouth. They know I'm not rabid."

Marshall couldn't hold it another second. "I've been here before," he said.

Shaven red jowls fell with gratifying rapidity.

"Often," Marshall added. Actually it had been once only, many years ago, when Ken Igawa had brought him here. Clay Gillies' stag.

"Oh?"

"I'm a friend of Mr. York's son."

"That you didn't mention before." Kalpraga's gray eyes might be blurred and bloodshot, but they were very sharp. "You are?"

"I saw him recently. In Berkeley."

"But you aren't part of that bunch he runs with, are you?"

The thought of York "running with a bunch" made Marshall smile. "I told you," he said. "I came with Ron More."

"Who's he?"

"President of the Palo Alto Young Republicans. I was myself, last year."

"Not Adam's bunch."

"I said I *knew* him."

"You said you were his friend, but let it pass."

Marshall, scouring his brain for a suitably acid rejoinder (it would pop into his mind, he knew, but too late), sucked on the last watery dregs of Scotch and soda.

"Come with me," Kalpraga said.

"Where?"

"Don't you want to meet your hostess?" he said, shepherding Marshall through the crowd. "What did you say your name was?" he asked. His small patent leather pumps trod an uneven path, but he spoke normally; the mouth evidently sobers faster than the feet.

At the grand piano a brown-faced man, not a Negro but dark as one, rippled into easy chordings of "The First Noel." At the curve of the white Steinway, wearing a dress that glittered like ice, black hair piled high, stood a tall, well-proportioned woman. From newspapers and television Marshall recognized Mrs. York, but with a sense of surprise he realized she was tall, at least five ten, his own height. In photographs she appeared quite small, but then again she was always at the side of her tall husband. As Marshall and Kalpraga approached, the tanned, wizened man with whom she was chatting moved away. "Thank you, Lou," she called after him.

"Helen, let me present Marshall Mosgrove." Kalpraga's red cheeks rose in a grimace. "He's a Young Republican. Marshall, this is our hostess, Mrs. York."

"I'm so pleased to meet you." Marshall took her hand. "This is a won—" Laughter nearby burst sharply and Marshall's appreciations were drowned out.

"I'm very pleased to meet you, Marshall."

"He's a friend of Adam's," Kalpraga said.

Round dark eyes gave Marshall full attention. "UCLA?" she demanded. "Berkeley?"

"I'm finishing Stanford Law and—"

"Athens?"

"California High."

Her head tilted and she leaned back against the piano. "Marshall," she murmured, "haven't we met before?"

"I don't think so. I haven't been here since . . ."

"Maybe some other place?"

Marshall shook his head.

"Sure?"

"I'm positive I'd remember anyone so beautiful," Marshall said gallantly.

"Thank you." She smiled. "Well, I meet so many people."

The dark piano player swung into "White Christmas" without pausing. A masculine voice called, "Kal—" and the fat man said, "'Scuse, Helen. Bye, Young Rep." And he moved away unsteadily.

Mrs. York stared at Marshall. Sweat formed under his meaty arms. Her dark eyes never seemed to blink, and he worried that she could penetrate layers of skin, flesh, cartilage and bone; he worried she could see all "about" him.

"How's Adam?" she asked.

"Doing great," said Marshall, who'd seen York once, briefly, these past years. "Doing just great."

"Good."

"He's living in a very sharp new building near campus." Dorot had passed on this information, along with the fact that York never left the place. "He's working with some friends on a film, and—"

"I saw him two days ago."

Marshall's face burned. The sweat was pouring out now. He said, very slowly, "I should have realized that you—"

"I didn't mean to embarrass you," she said. "The truth is, I'm worried. I've known Adam only a short time, he stayed here this spring, and when I talked to him Friday, he didn't seem the same. I wanted a friend's-eye view."

"He's fine."

"You really think so?" Mrs. York probed.

"Fine."

"Well, you're his friend, so—"

"Mrs. York, I'm sailing under false colors and you might as well know it, then you can toss me out." Marshall displayed square teeth in his most straightforward smile. "We graduated in the same class, we met sometimes at mutual friends'—and still do. But he's a genius. What would he want with a slow-witted type like me?"

"You're slow-witted?"

"A regular moron." At the end of its solid gold chain a Phi Beta Kappa key burned Marshall's pocket.

"Run-of-the-mill slow-witted Stanford Law crowd?"

"Run of the mill."

"And a Young Republican?"

He peered conspiratorially around the crowded room. "They haven't made it seditious, have they?"

"Any day now."

They laughed. Marshall's laughter was sincere with relief. He'd skated across thin ice in good form.

"I really think Mr. York's on the right track," he said.

She smiled.

"We need a return to law and order," Marshall said.

"Amen."

"In this day and age when everybody important pretends he's a bleeding heart, we need honest men like Mr. York."

"I may be somewhat prejudiced"—she smiled—"but I agree."

"Is he interested in running for office?"

"He's hoping he'll be able to do enough good in private life."

"If he ever decides to, I'd like to work for him."

A waitress was standing in front of him, offering a tray of steaming hors d'oeuvres that gave off a luscious odor of cheese mingled with garlic. Marshall shook his head. Unfortunately he'd forgotten his Certs.

Mrs. York, too, shook her head. "If he does," she said, "I'm sure you could be of great help. But anyway, isn't it nice to meet someone who thinks the same way you do?"

Marshall agreed profusely. He told her how disappointed he was in the current trend to confuse lawlessness with youth; she agreed. They were on the same wave length, he and Mrs. York, which was a pleasure after fencing with that drunk Kalpraga, and if her round dark eyes were too piercing, well, maybe she wore contacts.

"Tell me your name again." She smiled.

"Marshall Mosgrove." He spelled his last name.

"Marshall Mosgrove," she repeated. "How can I get in touch?"

Marshall, pretending to fumble through his wallet for something to write on, came up with one of the small slips of paper he kept for this purpose, writing his name, the address and phone number of the apartment he shared with Stan Kielty. He handed it to her.

"Mountain View?" she asked.

"Near Palo Alto."

"But you're down here?"

"For the vacation."

"Do you have a phone?"

Marshall shook his head. He explained he was camping out, literally, using his old Boy Scout equipment in the Spanish-style bungalow that was part of Grandmother's estate; his sister Lois, now married to a dentist, had ordered the Granite phone number disconnected last month when she'd had the furniture auctioned off.

He retrieved the slip of paper, writing down Dorot's number. "My girl," he explained. "She'll let me know if you call. I'll phone you right back."

And at that moment, over the other voices, the famous flat baritone thundered as it had from a thousand, thousand screens, "Helen—"

"I'll get in touch," she said, placing her hand briefly on his sleeve. Marshall smiled.

She walked away.

And then Marshall understood.

He knew why she'd been staring at him so intently. A wild coincidence! A coincidence drawn out of a hat! They *had* met before.

He inhaled piny scents of the tall, gilt-decorated Douglas fir . . . the air emptied of cocktail chatter and filled with soughing of pines and distant music . . . "Days of Wine and Roses" . . . across dark water . . . Marshall remembered the taste of coppery terror in his mouth, a woman initiating him and Helen York writhing under Stryker Halvorsen. As always when he thought of Stryker, Marshall felt tears form under his lids, dewlike tears that however hard he blinked refused to go away. . . .

After Stryker ran, for the few days remaining in August, Marshall didn't let himself think. He kept busy. Nights he watched the Bearcats like a prison guard, checking with flashlight each hour. Days he taught square knots and slip knots, how to find your way compassless by mossy sides of pine trunks, how to differentiate various rocks in the mountain, how to set up a campsite; he taught the Bearcats, dwellers in the sunlit slums of Los Angeles, what they would never need or use. And if none of the other counselors spoke to Marshall, well, so what? He was an outcast. It was his normal state. When the big buses arrived back in the city only Dr. Edwards shook his hand. "I hope you'll be back with us next year, Mosgrove," Dr. Edwards said.

"Of course I will," Marshall lied heartily.

At home, in the two weeks before he departed for Stanford,

he kept to his room, emerging only to eat and perform bodily functions. He would lie on his bed, hands clasped under his neck. After the surfing trip with Stryker, Marshall had sought in books reassurance that he wasn't "like that," as he euphemized homosexuality. Now he didn't read. Now the ten billion gray cells of his brain clamored that he *was* "like that." The proof? He had only to compare his terror and subsequent indifference on the dock with the wealthy black-haired girl and his joyous bursting of passion with Stryker. By the end of the second week Marshall had accepted himself.

But only in the privacy of his room.

He accepted what he was on the stipulation that he didn't let the world in on it. He would stare up at the ceiling, thinking of sneers, sly titters, limp wrists, arty pretensions and (most often) of disguised cops. He would break out in large beads of sweat. One false move toward the wrong guy and years of grinding study, a Phi Beta Kappa key, club memberships, gallons of conscientiously applied spray deodorant, everything would go down the pipes. Marshall feared discovery. Marshall, physical coward that he was, preferred the stake a thousand to one over discovery.

But it's not burning vs. pariahdom—that is, not if you're discreet.

Stan Kielty was Marshall's fraternity brother.

Marshall didn't approach Stan, Stan didn't approach Marshall; it was more subtle than that, done with nerve endings rather than words. Marshall had known Stan, also pre-law, slight, blue-eyed with good coloring and a tendency toward solemn silence, for four years. Now he saw Stan with an added dimension. The two got in the habit of leaving the noisy house to study in the law library, and there one rainy night, both of them damp of foot, Stan said, "We're too old to live in that bedlam."

Marshall replied, "Listen, for what we're both putting out we could find a place where we could study in peace." They rented a one-bedroom in Mountain View, far enough from campus for privacy, close enough for comfort, a brand-new two-story built around a kidney-shaped pool.

On the first of the month they moved in.

As Marshall unpacked, his arms and legs felt strange and his joints moved like unoiled gears. Stan was quieter than ever. It was well after midnight when they had the place, as Marshall put it, "shipshape." The twin beds, freshly made with bedding bought yesterday at Penney's basement, suddenly stretched to fill the room.

"Sack time," Marshall said loudly.

Stan bent, fiddling with a drawer that refused to shut properly. "Guess so," he muttered.

"Which bed d'you want?" Marshall inquired.

The back of Stan's clipped neck reddened. "Doesn't matter."

"To me either," Marshall said.

"After you, my dear Alphonse," Stan mumbled.

"O.K., Gaston." Marshall gave a breathless laugh. "Tell you what. The left's closer to the window. Better view of the pool. Flip you for it." And from his stay-press pants he fished a coin, a quarter that he tossed with his right hand, intending to catch it on the back of his left. His hands shook. The coin slipped soundlessly onto the carpet. Both boys stared down at the gleaming head of Washington. Marshall swallowed. "Heads, you win. The left, right?"

"Right. The left."

They undressed, neither glancing at the other. First Stan used the white-tiled bathroom; then Marshall used it. When he emerged the lamp between the beds was out. On quivering thighs he groped through strange darkness until he reached the narrow space between the beds. The night swirled with impending and irrevocable actions. Marshall could hardly breathe. What if he'd been wrong about Stan? It took every ounce of his limited courage to get into the left bed. Stan lay on the far edge. Marshall's muscles tensed as he kept himself apart. *I can always pretend it's a mistake*, he thought. *Right, the left, ha-hahahahaha.*

"Marshall . . ." Stan's whisper clotted. "At Menlo, an older guy, a senior, he helped me with chemistry in return for this. I hated myself for the whole stinking deal. But I would've flunked if I didn't." He sighed. The mattress shook a little. "That's not true. I wanted it as much as he did. But I was afraid . . . to admit it. And after him there were three others."

Marshall muttered, "One . . . only one . . . only once." *Don't think of Stryker, don't.*

Marshall closed his eyes so tight that he saw translucent reds and browns like color film negative and, turning on his side wordlessly, his arms encircled Stan's slight body. The hot odors of their mingled sweat overpowered the scent of new bedding. Guilty, Marshall's whole being informed himself he was guilty, yet at the same time his lawyer's training argued that here they were, two consenting adults, and if this is as honestly a civilized time and place as we pretend, where is the guilt? Stan's sex, hard and urgent, pressed against Marshall's thigh. And Marshall rolled Stan over. He thrust silently and fast. Stan's body answered.

Atter that three nights a week Marshall climbed into the left bed. Always he was the aggressor, always they met there; much as Marshall wished to avoid the scene of their crime (?) he was unable to prevent himself from returning. The act was always hasty. And furtive.

Stan and he, both excellent students, worked long hours side by side under separate Tensor lamps; they ate together; they amicably hashed out who should do which chore and Marshall typed up a schedule, thumbtacking it to one side of the kitchen cabinet; they learned one another's dislikes in food and likes in music; they spoke of the weather, hot and dry that autumn, the Kennedy assassination, the increasing difficulty in getting pledges and which brand of toothpaste was best. They were open about everything except the tie that bound. Between them lay dark, wild minutes. And this unspoken complicity was, for both of them, too great a burden to permit friendship.

Silence might preclude friendship; however, it did allow an uncynical approach to a social life.

Stan Kielty was engaged to Amy Halacz, a sophomore at Mills. Dorot McHenry was at Cal. Every other weekend the boys drove north to double date.

So they weren't friends.

So?

In his lifetime Marshall'd had only one friend.

Stryker Halvorsen.

Marshall had flown down to Los Angeles for the afternoon of Stryker's memorial at California High. As an ex-president of the student body his being there roused no comment. And neither did his tears. Everyone in the high-arched old auditorium wept long before an offstage bugle sounded faulty taps.

Why had Stryker died?

The answer wasn't to be found in familiar argument of dove and hawk—Marshall himself, paperback *Conscience of a Conservative* in his back pocket, tended toward hawkishness; he felt we must keep our commitments to our democratically inclined friends. At the same time he admitted Stryker couldn't have cared less about either side. Stryker had never been political. Why had Stryker Halvorsen died? Why? Each time the question occurred, Marshall hastily took refuge in the fifth amendment.

Yet the question clung like enmeshing silk spun by a black widow spider. He never succeeded in getting rid of the strands, yet at the same time he refused to look squarely at the answer lurking in the center of the web. It was too ugly. Too poisonous. Too self-incriminating.

Marshall lost hair, read William Buckley and Barry Goldwater, made *Law Review*, bought a fourteen-carat gold chain for his Phi Beta Kappa key, joined one more group, the Young Republicans.

And he had a triumph.

Except for a very rare glance at Marshall or his apartment mate, and these glances all directed by people who were "that way" themselves, nobody guessed. Not a heterosexual soul guessed. Marshall Mosgrove was an ordinary, above-average law student belonging to a great many campus organizations. . . .

"Marshall," Dorot said close to his ear. "Weren't you just with Mrs. York?"

Marshall returned to the land of the living, praying his tears weren't visible.

"It's stifling in here," he muttered, blotting his forehead with a small cocktail napkin he discovered clenched in his hand.

"Was that—"

"Yes."

"She's not at all like York's mother, and psychologically speaking, a man's meant to choose the same sort of—"

"Why don't you quit speaking psychologically!" Marshall snapped, angry at her for intruding on his thoughts, considerably more afraid that during the intrusion she'd somehow read his thoughts, *the guilty flee where no man pursueth.* "You'll get a lot further. She's a contact. An excellent contact. And a young attorney starting out needs contacts."

Dorot's eyes, behind thick lenses, blinked. She opened her mouth, closed it, opened it again, staring at him with respect he'd never before evoked. Meekly she followed him to the crush around the bar.

• • •

"So you're going to live down here," Dorot said.

"S'there any other way to fly?" Marshall replied.

"Frodo lives!" Dorot exclaimed.

"What?"

It was some two hours later. He and Dorot were sitting far apart on the front seat of his Buick. Blinking red and green bulbs that looped the pine tree on the McHenrys' hilly front lawn bathed the inside of the car with spasmodic color.

Marshall was drunk.

Completely.

By his own count, admittedly inaccurate, he'd downed two Scotch and sodas before his conversation with Mrs. York, three—or was it five?—very fast shots after. Liquor's false relaxation soothed his mind and muscles.

"Frodo lives!" Dorot repeated.

"Whazzat mean?" Marshall's tongue was larger than usual. "S'it have to mean something?"

"Every little thing means something."

"Frodo's this character by Tolkien and—"

"I know, I *know!*" Marshall interrupted. "What'd *you* mean by th'remark?"

Dorot shook her head. "Don't know." She giggled. "Doesn't sound like me, does it? The words just came. *'Frodo lives!'* " This time she shouted the inane phrase.

"You're loaded."

"On big Baron's bonded bourbon," she agreed. "S'a tongue twister for you."

"How'sabout the joint you smoked in the car before we picked up the Mores?"

She giggled. "They dropped totally dead when they sniffed."

"Come off it, Dorot. Who our age's up tight about a little grass?"

"I assume you're right. But they sure sniffed— So you're going to reside down here?"

"Uh huh. I've been all over. Paris. New York. London. Seattle—"

"Seattle? There's a world cultural center for you!"

"My mother's family lives there." Marshall spoke in the ponderous, Bible-reading tones he used in any mention of his late parents. "Right on the Sound."

Dorot nodded, silent.

"And I've discovered California is where everything is happening. Losh Angeles is—"

"Where the action is," Dorot finished.

"Right. And I don't intend to spend the rest of my life on the fringes."

"Want to hear a secret?" Dorot held a white-gloved finger in front of her well-carved lips. "Neither do I. I don't intend to bury *my*self. I've got a good brain."

"Always were a smart girl."

"As one Phi Bete to another, thank you. Well, see, Howard—"

"Who?"

"You *know*. Howard Derdivanis. Dr. Howard Derdivanis. I go with—"

"Oh. . . . The Ape." *I really must be loaded,* Marshall thought, *to have the guts to say that aloud.*

"He's very intelligent," Dorot said, hurt. "Nice, too. He wants me to marry him. But. I'd be buried alive. He's going to live in Eureka."

"Eureka? Up near Oregon?"

"The very place," Dorot said. "You think I'm right not marrying him, if it means living there?"

"That's not living. That's a life sentence."

He laughed at his own joke.

In one second Dorot laughed, too.

Still laughing, she moved to the center of the seat, taking off her glasses. Without any intent or desire, Marshall found himself kissing this flat-chested girl he'd preceded by one year through the local Los Angeles school system. He'd known her practically twenty years, and as they kissed he wondered: did she remember his old nickname? The kiss was neither pleasant nor unpleasant, it lasted an undeterminable length of time, their lax tongues loosely winding around one another, their mouths smelling sour of liquor. The kiss was a wet nothing.

Dorot drew back, smiling at him in her near-sighted way. "Happy New Year," she said.

"Not even Christmas yet," Marshall pointed out, "so can it be New Year?"

"We have to pretend it is."

"You just lost me."

"Look at it this way. I've known you too long for a kiss to be casual, and you're only a year older, not yet a father figure. So . . . Happy New Year!"

"Happy New Year, Dorothy Eleanor McHenry," Marshall said, kissing her again, a dried, shorter kiss full of honest affection. After all, hadn't they known one another almost all their lives, and didn't anyone you'd known that long become part of you, not simply an intellectual snob with tiny breasts? "Happy New Year."

"So Mrs. York's going to help your career?"

Marshall's mood drunkenly veered from high to low.

"We talked. She took my address, and I gave her your phone number. I hope that was all right?"

"S'fine. Because you won't hear from her."

"Who knows?"

"I do," said Dorot, either because she was high or to get back at him. *Oh. . . . The Ape.* "And you won't see her 'cept on TV."

Marshall grunted.

"Bet you," Dorot sang.

Marshall was silent.

"C'mon," Dorot said. "Be a sport. Bet a quarter."

Marshall shrugged. "If you want." He yawned elaborately. "Very weary making, large cocktail parties." He yawned again.

"Mmmmm," Dorot agreed.

He opened the car door for her, assisted her up winding brick steps to her front door, managed to get her key in the Schlage lock. He didn't kiss her a third time.

"Glad Frodo's going to live down here," she mumbled as she shut the door.

He started back to his car, feet carefully treading for each step. It was the memory of Stryker, of course, that had reduced him to his sudden misery, just as it was the memory of Stryker that had caused his rare drunkenness. Liquor lay acid in his gullet. He belched loudly. Descending brick steps, he thought of the unfairness of it; he had used liquor to seal memory in a closed account and now the old memory bank was paying out with interest. *Stryker, Stryker . . .*

Marshall drove, letting the speedometer hover well below his usual sane thirty-five. If he were stopped, any police officer would know that this driver had alcohol (as well as misery) in his blood stream. He drove slowly through Christmas-decorated streets to a dark, unfurnished, echoing tile-roofed house.

The day after Christmas Mrs. York phoned him at the McHenrys.

Marshall and Dorot were alone, she rattling around in the kitchen fixing turkey sandwiches for lunch, Marshall in the small paneled den lying on the Hide-a-bed couch scanning *Games People Play*, his Christmas gift from Dorot—trust her! Who needed a book by a psychiatrist! He wasn't Dorot's fiancé or lover, he had no rights in this house, no duties or privileges, he was an old friend, nothing more, so when the phone rang he let Dorot answer the kitchen extension.

"Marshall, it's for you," she called. He could tell by the absence of a click that she was eavesdropping.

"Marshall?" asked a breathless female voice.

"Yes?"

"This is Helen York."

"Oh, hi, Mrs. York." Marshall sat up. "Listen, Dorot and I, we had a wonderful time at your party. Really great."

"I'm glad, I'm glad," Mrs. York said. "I hope I'm not taking you from anything?"

"You aren't, not at all, Mrs. York."

"What're your plans for tonight?"

Marshall's heart began to pound. "Not a thing on tap."

"Wonderful. Mr. York's very anxious to meet you. And I'd enjoy talking again. Will you share some leftovers with us?"

"This evening?" Marshall managed to say.

"Yes. Nothing formal," she said. "Can you make it?"

"I—thank you."

"See you at seven then."

After Marshall hung up, Dorot came in chewing a turkey wing. She tossed him a quarter. "Bet's a bet," she said. There was admiration in her loud voice.

--------- **4** ---------

"But he's very nice," Michele repeated.

Leigh, setting down her fork, gazed out the window at ghostly fog that veiled leafless birches.

"He's got a TR4, a red one," Michele continued. "He's under thirty, over six foot."

Leigh said nothing.

"He's at Rand, so he must be a genius."

Leigh sighed. "Michele, you know I'm not dating yet."

"This isn't a date. Anyway, you're legally separated."

"The law says I'm legally married."

"The law doesn't say you're dead."

A dreary March day; they lunched snugly in Michele's pretty new breakfast area, the aroma of Stouffer's shrimp creole surrounding them.

Since Mr. Sutherland had started back to his Hill Street office, two hours a day at first, now three, there was a family conspiracy to get Leigh out of the big white Colonial house. Michele, of course, had been very fond of Leigh since high school, and while Michele had considered her friend sweet and generous, at the same time she thought her . . . well, not exactly cold, but definitely aloof, certainly not the type to arouse mass love. Therefore Michele had been totally surprised to discover that the Sutherlands and Van Vliets all adored Leigh. She was the family favorite. And since she'd left Ken Igawa they had rallied to her side. It was no secret that along with the problems of a mixed marriage she'd put up with having to work, financial insolvency, miserable housing, being cut off from her family, Ken's wild idea of making it as an artist. Now it had come out that he'd beaten her. There were rumors of other girls! So while nobody said a bad word about Ken to Leigh (she wouldn't have listened, would she?), in order to take her mind off her past miseries, aunts and cousins took turns, by day inviting poor Leigh to lunch or bridge or shopping, by night to dinner; such evenings came with an eligible male to "pick you up so you don't have to drive alone at night." Michele, naturally, had kept up with the others. Leigh and she lunched together often. Michele had gone to no end of trouble to dig up this bachelor.

And yet here was Leigh, nervously lighting a cigarette, saying, "I'm just not interested in dates."

"Leigh, look, nobody could understand more than me how you feel."

Leigh sat back in her chair; she'd eaten practically none of her creole.

"I've been through it all," Michele said. "And believe you me, it's much worse where a child is concerned. I was plenty shook when I left Clay Gillies. But I knew it was the right thing. He begged me to stay. He wanted us to try counseling." These last two sentences were lies. Michele never denied to herself that Clay had left *her*, but she was not above fibbing for a good cause: Leigh must see that Ken was a beast through

and through for never once suggesting that he and Leigh try a
marriage counselor like every well-intentioned splitting couple
did nowadays. "Well"—Michele sighed—"Clay and I, we both
tried. But it was wrong, all wrong, and finally I had to admit
it was wrong. And now look at me. One thousand percent
happier." Michele gave an involuntary glance around her new
kitchen with its gorgeously expensive powder-blue Formica
cabinet doors that magnetically closed themselves. "Look at
how happy Everett and I and Lissa are. Leigh, finish your
shrimp."

"Thank you, it's delicious, but I'm full."

"You can't sit around and mope."

Leigh sighed. "I'd like to stay home and adjust, that's all."

"You have to *try*," Michele said. "Poor Uncle Sidney. Everyone knows he feels guilty all the time because it happened
during his heart att—"

Leigh sighed again. "What's this one's name?"

"Jack Potter. He'll pick you up at eight Saturday. Then you
won't have to drive yourself home. There'll be other people
here, so it isn't a date, not at all."

"Until we're alone," Leigh murmured.

"I know, I know," Michele sympathized. "Once a man knows
you're a divorcée, they all get the idea you're dying for it and
they're willing to do you the big favor. But this Jack Potter is
Mr. Clean himself."

"All right." Leigh sighed. "But he understands it's just to
pick me up?"

"Of course," Michele reassured. "Honestly, Leigh, you've
got to snap out of it. I'm worried about you."

Michele *was* worried.

Relationship and family aside, Leigh and she had been friends
ages and ages. Poor Leigh, her fingers shook as she lit her
chain of cigarettes, sometimes when you caught her unawares
her big, wide-apart eyes were watering, she'd lost weight and
her face appeared even more fragile since she'd hacked that
fabulous red hair into a Mia Farrow crew cut.

But at the same time Michele had problems of her own.

Big problems.

The Las Palomas Juniors.

Michele was dying to be in with the young married group
that supported Las Palomas Home for Unwed Mothers.

Not that Michele was the least interested in charity work.

She wanted in because the Las Palomas wore leopard coats and hand-sewn Italian shoes, they belonged to the Daisy, they gave fabulous parties. They had their retouched photographs in the Family Section of the *Times*. Michele got Aunt Evelyn, who was a Senior, to put in a good word with the Juniors' membership committee. Every night Michele prayed for a miracle. Actually, married to an impeccable, red-mustached Sutherland, Michele had a good chance at Las Palomas.

Except for Clay Gillies.

Clay was back in Los Angeles, busy stirring up trouble. His name was constantly in the newscasts. Each time Michele heard it, she would blush, remembering how naïve she'd once been to consider such publicity fame. His name, alas, was Lissa's name. Many of the Las Palomas had daughters at Miss Brown's with Lissa. Each time Clay hit the news there was a storm of polite questions. Michele, embarrassed, cursed her ex-husband, for she realized—to use a phrase of Everett's—her Las Palomas stock was slipping.

She decided to change Lissa's name to Sutherland.

But Everett, surprisingly, insisted she ask Clay's permission. "After all, she's his little girl," Everett said ponderously. Permission! The very idea! Still, Everett so rarely insisted on anything that she decided to play it his way.

Clay had no listed phone number, so she composed a paragraph explaining that she must see him, there was something terribly important about Lissa; carefully she copied the words into her embossed shocking-pink stationery, signing her name Michele (Mrs. Everett) Sutherland, mailing the heavy tissue-lined envelope c/o Students for Peace, Box 318, Los Angeles, California 90024.

Two mornings later, so early that Michele was still in bed watching *Girl Chatter*, the door chimes sounded. Pulling her white nylon peignoir over its matching gown, she opened the peep.

"Well?" Clay demanded as she unchained the door.

"You got me out of bed." Michele pulled her elbows to her sides, shivering prettily.

"How is she?"

"Come in before I freeze to death."

"How is she?"

"Fine." Michele shut the door after him. "In school, of course."

"You said she was sick—"

"I never—"

"You wrote—"

"I wrote I wanted to discuss her." And Michele led him to the family room, detouring through the new kitchen. "You know if she'd been ill I'd have managed to find you, not write." She sat on the couch, gesturing for him to sit beside her. He paced to the high-backed chair.

"It's about the child support," she said.

Clay reddened.

"It's overdue," she said.

"I know."

"Twenty-five a week."

"Right now I'm busy."

"It's not too steep," she pointed out.

"After April I'll make it up to you."

"To Lissa," Michele corrected. "Why April?"

"I can't get it before."

"You're already way over a year behind."

"Why so worried?" Clay glanced around the family room, his gaze pausing briefly at the new kitchen's entry.

"She's your daughter," Michele pointed out, "not Everett's."

"He seems fond of her."

"He's crazy about her," Michele said. "He wants her to have the best of everything."

"If he doesn't mind supporting her, and since he has plenty of plenty, why push me?" Clay asked with his infuriating logic.

"He adores children." Michele sighed. "And I can't have any more. . . . Poor Everett, so sad for him."

Clay's features stiffened. Always, she knew, he had felt guilty about her missing uterus.

"Michele, I'm working night and day. There's a demonstration planned for next month. The President'll be here. But after . . . I'll make it—"

"Well," she interrupted brightly, "if it's April, it's April. Would you like a bite to eat?"

"No, thank you."

"Toast and—"

"Nothing."

"Clay, while you're here—" Her laughter tinkled. "Everett, he says I'm a big silly even to ask. It's nothing, Everett says. But I said no, I've got to ask Clay first."

"Ask me what?"

"It would be better if Lissa called herself Sutherland, the same as me."

Clay's hands tightened over his knees.

"At school," Michele soothed, "only at school."

"She's my daughter."

"Of course she is." Michele smiled. "And not once has Everett said a word, a single word, about supporting her." Michele drew a deep breath. "It embarrasses her in front of the other girls, having a different name from her mommy."

"She never said anything to me."

You barely see her one day a year, Michele was tempted to retort. But at this point it was impractical to rouse Clay's icy temper. "She doesn't *say* much," Michele agreed. "But Clay, you know how cruel children can be."

"All right." He capitulated.

"I knew you'd understand!"

"At school only."

"Of course," she said. "Only at school."

He got up and came across the room. She could smell his masculine rankness. Everett had almost no personal odors except a slight, vinegary scent that clung to his pajamas and the sheets.

Standing over her, Clay said, "I'll take her out Sunday."

"Clay. . . ."

"What?"

She didn't know what. So she whispered, "Sunday."

The smell of him drowned her. She leaned forward and the deep-cut neckline of her peignoir and matching gown fell away. From above, her full breasts were visible all the way to bulbous, bright pink nipples. Clay glanced down. He'd always adored to play with them, and remembering she was suddenly all damp there. Her thighs fell apart.

"Sunday morning," Clay muttered.

"Fine."

"Ten or so. . . ."

"Clay. . . ."

"Uhhh?"

"Sure you don't want coffee?"

"No, thanks," he said in a strangled voice.

"We put in this new gadget, it keeps water boiling all the

time, so it'll only take . . ." She couldn't go on; she could barely breathe.

"Got an appointment," he mumbled.

"Please, Clay?"

"N'appointment."

"Coffee?" she whispered.

But already he had bolted into the hall. She heard the front door slam.

She sat, her right hand thrust into her nightgown, covering one breast. The corners of her mouth were drawn in two curves, parenthetical hints of how she might look in ten years. Her blue-green eyes gazed sightlessly, as if she were listening to very sad music coming from far away in the empty house.

Guiltily, she took her hand from her breast. Shook her blonde head sharply. She fixed instant coffee, generously sugaring and creaming it, carrying the cup to her bedroom. Before Clay's arrival she'd been planning to phone Aunt Evelyn to ask what she should wear to a Cerebral Palsy luncheon at which several Las Palomas would be present. Instead she hunched on the edge of her big bed gazing blankly at the dead television screen, holding her coffee until it was too cold to drink.

Sunday, while Lissa changed from her good Sunday school plaid, Michele had a few moments alone with Clay.

"You're sure you don't mind about the name?" she asked.

"Fine with me."

"You always were generous."

He glanced at her, saw the sincerity in her pretty face, and also her low-cut orange minidress. He quickly averted his eyes.

"So were you," he said.

"That wasn't our problem."

"No."

And Lissa burst out of her room wearing red pants and a black scowl. Usually Lissa smiled, showing new front teeth that promised to be as charming as her mother's. She very much resembled Michele as a child, both in appearance and personality. At school she was bossy and popular; at home she was affectionate and used to getting her own way. And spending this Sunday with her real father was definitely not her way. She barely remembered when they had lived together. And she loved her Uncle Everett, really loved him. She was a loyal little girl. With Clay she felt strange and uneasy. Divided.

• • •

When Clay brought Lissa home, Michele detained him at the front door for another private moment. She wore her apple-green hostess skirt with matching spaghetti-strap top.

"Did you have a nice time?" she inquired.

"Lissa was very down."

"The situation's too much for her." Michele let her soft little hand hover near Clay's jacket sleeve. "Perhaps we ought to find a counselor and get a little advice on how to manage the situation." Her hand descended ever so lightly.

His arm stiffened. Michele moved away.

"The three of us," she said. "You and I and Everett."

"The middle of April," Clay agreed.

"That's one thing about our divorce," she said. "We've both tried to do what's best for Lissa."

Dear Clay,
  I have consulted with a counselor as I mentioned I would. She feels that waiting is very, very wrong for Lissa. I'd like to discuss the matter with you as soon as possible.

                                        Michele

Two mornings later he showed up. Michele went to the door holding a robe over her shortie. Right off the bat Clay asked about Lissa's counselor. Graciously ignoring both his abruptness and the inconvenience of the hour, Michele led him to the living room, offering coffee (he refused) and explaining that upon her request the school had suggested a Stanford-trained child psychologist. A lady. Dr. Schmidt.

He sat on the couch. She on a chair, holding the loose flowered robe over her breasts.

"Everett and I met her last week."

"Oh?"

"I know how busy you are," Michele said earnestly, "so I arranged for you to meet with her . . . after you're through."

"Thanks, Miche." Clay gave one of his rare smiles. "The seventh of April."

"Changing names is always awkward. You understand why we didn't wait, don't you?"

"Uh huh."

" . . . knew you would . . ."

" . . . cooperate all I can . . ."

During the conversation their voices had grown slower and

lower. Half unconsciously Michele let go of her robe, the edges parted and inner curves of breasts were visible. Clay swallowed audibly.

"Clay . . ." she whispered. She took a deep breath and the robe fell further apart. Nipples showed dark through sheer nylon nightie. Michele's conscience rustled. What was she doing? Everett was so kind to her. *Shut up, conscience. What practical good are you?* She stood, letting the flowered robe fall to the carpet.

"Miche, don't," Clay said harshly.

The drapes were open. Tiny circles of sunshine bubbled through bare birches. Clay's fists clenched as he stared at her. Staring back at him, very slowly she pulled the narrow straps of her gown over her shoulders. Her heart thumped, part passion, part worry; *what if he refuses?* It was like that first time under the crossed swords. She knew exactly what she wanted. She wanted Clay Gillies. And sex simply happened to be the way to get him. *But why get him? I love him,* she thought in bewilderment, *I still love him,* she thought as the gown caught briefly on her rounded pink nipples, *it's crazy, but I still love him. It must be true, what they say, a girl never gets over her first. I love him.* The nightgown fell to her feet. Now she wore only her white satin slippers and the white nylon bikini underpants that matched her gown. She stepped out of the backless slippers and with trembly hands eased down the pants. Between the leg holes a soft, lemony color stained. Embarrassed, with one polished toe she overturned the panties, hiding the stain. She, naked, an appetizing picnic, was set out for Clay. But he remained on the couch, a vein in his forehead throbbing, the shadows under his eyes seeming to darken. She felt weak, as if she had a very high temperature. She shouldn't have to make all the moves, should she? Her glance rested on faded denim. The telltale bulge. And she moved toward him, no longer thinking of who should make what move, conscious only of a demanding emptiness down there. As she reached the couch he stood, his arms closing around her, like iron his chest and belly after the familiar massive softness of Everett. This was Clay. Clay's odors, Clay's fingers digging into her behind, Clay grinding her to his pelvis. He drew away a second, unzipping his pants, pulling them down, not off even. He breathed heavily. He shoved her onto her hands and knees and she whimpered, "Not yet," for she wanted him to make nice; she wanted to feel his lips on hers, feel the beard (oh, how she used to hate that beard) tickling; she wanted her breasts stroked and down there petted and to be told she was loved. But her lips, her twin marvels, her round hips Clay ignored. He wanted only one part of her and he muttered that part aloud. "Cunt." She shut out the word. She hated it. He kneed her quivering thighs apart.

"Not yet," she whimpered again.

But his hands were parting her and he was forcing himself into her. She was ready, oh, more than ready, moist and yearning, yet her vaginal muscles briefly barred him. "Come on," he muttered. "S'what you got me here for, isn't it?" He forced again. "Ohhhh," she groaned with delight. So much bigger than poor Everett's. Clay began to thrust and she got the crazy feeling he was angry at her for the impersonality—yet he was the one who hadn't wanted to make love properly, he had wanted it like this, dog style. He pressed especially hard and deep and she groaned loudly at the terrible twinge . . . was it possible to tear the neat stitchery with which Dr. Johansen had long ago sewed up the space vacated by her uterus?

"Clay, stop!" she cried.

He didn't.

And she didn't want him to. The twingeing pain and, yes, the danger drove her wild and she pressed up and back, crying aloud at each thrust; her breathing quickened and there was only the melting and oozing and her pushing back faster and faster; it had never been like this, never, and she gave a last mighty thrust, then fell, panting, sweaty faced, onto the white wool carpet. Clay, sprawling across her back, pounded and pulsed and then he, too, collapsed.

Their breathing quieted. She felt him rise. Turning, she saw him, legs astride, zip his fly. Neither spoke. As he let himself out the front door she rose, walking unsteadily to the kitchen, wetting a dish towel, returning to scrub the bubbly by the couch. She went back to bed, her face fevered, her ears glowing, sleeping naked, deep and dreamless until noon.

Waking, she remembered. Arching her body, she stretched. As she fell back, relaxed, it occurred to Michele that she'd just stamped on the seventh commandment. Oughtn't she feel a teensy guilty? But why? She snugged deeper into her comfy king-size. Why? Her heart still warmed with the same gratitude and affection toward her husband, provider of all earthly (if not fleshly) delights. Anyway, hadn't Everett in marrying a divorcée accepted the fact that a thousand times she'd done it with Clay? What difference, her pragmatic mind demanded, after a thousand could one more possibly make? Her natural self-honesty replied, *You still love him, and it's now. What Everett doesn't know won't hurt Everett,* her mind replied. *It had never been that exciting.*

Yawning aloud in the pretty green room, she smiled. Clay must be thinking about her, too.

He wasn't.

Clay's thoughts were a laser beam concentrating on the April seventh demonstration.

He rose at five thirty. He lived in a motel opposite the Mormon temple. From his room he could see the top of the central tower where, glinting in the pale new light, a huge golden angel blew a long golden horn as if to waken the city. The gilded angel inspired Clay. Didn't he, too, wish to rouse everyone?

From early morning he worked. There were innumerable details that demanded answers. Time? Location? How to show *An American Hero?* How to handle the sheer masses of people? How to best display their respectability? And how to get them?

Almost every evening he spoke. Most people's minds are unsettled; they don't know what it is they want. Clay Gillies would speak without a quaver of doubt in his intense voice. He decided, there must be no false humility in him, this was why religious leaders from Buddha to Moses to Christ had meditated on tops of mountains, in deserts, under shady tree groves; they had spent long periods alone, those prophets, discovering their own truths; then in front of their followers they were able to come on strong. Clay Gillies, at meetings of women's clubs, professional organizations, college alumni groups and at unaffiliated gatherings in the best neighborhoods, came on strong.

After the meeting but before the inevitable bitter coffee and sweet cake, Clay and Odessa jogged through heavy rain down dark ivy-covered terraces, down a stretch of dark winding Bel Air road to Odessa's battered maroon Ford. Things were not the same between them, not the same at all, but whenever he asked her to, she accompanied him to the less-demonstration-minded women's groups. Liberal ladies, menopausal Lysistratas, have a favorite tenet that women of every race are universally united against war. Clay, aware of the great influence of Odessa's calm brown presence, used it to the hilt.

Odessa pulled off her scarf, scattering raindrops.

"They really went wild over you." She chuckled. "D'you know you're not only magnificent but also you're the Best of this Wonderful New Generation?" She tossed the wet scarf in the back seat. "The word I heard most, though, was charismatic."

"A well-educated bunch!"

"You better believe it. The *best* colleges."

"Then you'd think they'd come up with better ideas than free lemonade and a puppet show." (This group, once involved, had enthusiastically supplemented Clay's plans.) "Odessa, for them life's one big fat PTA carnival."

She laughed.

Clay said, "They're housewives. So shouldn't they know you can't make an omelet without breaking eggs?"

"Oh, Clay!" The old coupé echoed with Odessa's warm rueful laugh. "You seriously believe that any of those women has ever once considered she's a mere egg?"

"One should start then."

Odessa, still smiling and shaking her head, pumped the accelerator, turned the ignition; there was a smell of gas; the motor coughed. Died. She tried again. This time the engine caught. "Thank you, Lord," Odessa murmured. As they started down the winding grade, she asked, "What did *that* mean?"

"It's all planned," he said quietly.

A sudden blast of night wind hurled water, and Odessa concentrated on driving blind.

"Well?" she asked when the wipers were again able to cope with their task.

"Well what?"

"The omelet making?"

"What about it?"

"For one thing," she said, "when are you going to let the others know?"

"Them?" He jerked his head back in the direction of the spacious hilltop house. "They'll want to apply for a police permit to start a riot."

"They *are* helping," she said mildly.

"And you know why, don't you?"

"Please, sir, let me pay my dues?"

He gave an assenting snort.

Odessa sighed. "Does there have to be an incident?"

"You of all people know there does. Without one the ten

o'clock newscasters'll sluff us off in one short sentence. Like 'While the President spoke in Los Angeles, picketers protested the Vietnam war.' Months of work'll have been for nothing."

There was a red light at Sunset, and Odessa stopped between the perpetually open iron gates of Bel Air. Car windows had fogged on the inside and she wiped with her handkerchief until they could see the stream of headlights picking out slanting bullets of rain. The steel roof echoed with rain.

"What's planned?" Odessa asked.

"Some of us're going to talk to the President."

"You won't get near the hotel."

"Watch."

"There'll be armies of police and secret police. Since Dallas—"

"Remember Nina del Amo?"

"The big white girl at Berkeley?"

"That's her."

"What can she do? Levitate?"

"Watch."

The light turned green and Odessa made a right on Sunset and a left on Veteran before she said, "Clay, listen. This'll be a far bigger crowd than you've ever handled. You know how the police behave at this sort of thing. There's women and children—"

"Who do you think it's for?" he interrupted fiercely. He opened the window a crack. A few icy drops splattered on his face and fresh smells filled the car. He inhaled deeply. "Don't worry," he said in a normal tone. "Nobody's going to get hurt. The action's inside."

"The hotel?"

"Uh huh."

"You're sure?"

"Positive."

She asked no more questions. Clay gulped at cold, damp air, wondering if she were worried about the SNAP bunch who were marching. Had she known all along that he and RG were cooking up something? Clay was filled with pain that he and Odessa were no longer close enough for him to demand an answer.

At his motel she stopped, leaving the motor running. She did not enter the parking court. Since they'd been back in Los Angeles she had consistently refused to sleep with him. For this reason he'd succumbed to Michele. Starved or not, he should've known better. In Michele's Peyton Place mind, embarking on an adultery was a voyage that smelled of passion and moonlit gardenias; an adultery was Michele's journey to the moon, her Lambaréné, her Holy Grail. She had discovered he lived in this motel and three times had phoned about "getting together so we can talk about Lissa's problems."

"Come on in," Clay said to Odessa. Despite her numerous past refusals—or maybe because of them—he kept at her. He'd never been one to give up.

She shook her head.

"Please?"

Another silent shake.

"Tell me one thing!" he burst out. "If it's O.K. in Berkeley, why is it illegal down here?" He gripped her shoulder, his fingers digging into slick raincoat. "It's the same damn state, isn't it?"

"Please, Clay."

He released her. "Odessa, Odessa...." He edged across frayed maroon plush, bringing his face near hers. "I'm so much in love with you I'm a madman."

Her hand reached up to lightly tug his beard. So he couldn't kiss her?

"Clay," she said, "Clay, it was a mistake. I never should've let it start."

"Why did you, then?"

She bit her lower lip.

"Because you loved me?" he demanded.

Silence.

"You did," he said, triumphant. "You do."

"It was a mistake," she insisted. "It still is."

"No!"

"Yes. Oh, Clay, be reasonable. You're sixteen years younger—"

"Always age!"

"—and white."

"Or color!"

"Look, for once admit the facts. You know SNAP's new motto. Black is beautiful. Beautiful is black. How can I show up with a white lover?"

"Husband?" he asked in a low tone.

This was the first time he'd suggested marriage. A truck passed, splashing water on the side of the car.

"Well?" he asked.

"I . . ."

"You do love me?"

"Yes," she whispered.

"But you won't marry me?"

The rain poured down.

After a minute she said, "I was. Once. To another white guy. He was writing a novel. I worked—you know the sort of thing. We had our own little world. But then I got ill, this stupid case of infectious hepatitis, and I had to stop working. He never sold a word he wrote. He . . . his parents found him a good job. Clay, he was a really nice, sweet boy and there aren't many really nice people. But . . ." She sighed and shifted on the car seat. "D'you want all the gory details?"

Up until this minute Clay had ached to hear about her past. Always she had locked him out. Now he shivered. He didn't want to hear her sorrows, her miseries, whatever hells she had survived to attain her present calm. He didn't want to know because he—*another white guy*—wanted to pull her through the same wringer.

He said, "This time it'll be different."

"It sure will." From her flared a brief, sharp tension, almost antagonism.

"Odessa—"

"Listen, pardon me if this sounds like the corniest renunciation scene in all grand opera. But there's no hope in marriage. We've both been there, and it's not for people like us."

"Because you had one bad experience—"

"Oh, Clay, Clay. You know there's one thing I want from life. To make things easier for the kids coming up. I guess some might call it a presumptuous goal, too big, but"—she shrugged—"black is beautiful. If I married whitey, everything I've done these past years would be canceled out."

He was silent.

"Wouldn't it?" she asked and raised her eyes to his. As he gazed into those luminous eyes he found with a sort of cold resignation that he could think of no argument. None at all.

"You understand?" she asked.

He dropped his eyes. "I love you," he said in a low, miserable tone.

"And I love you."

In lieu of a kiss she briefly touched a warm finger to his lips. He slid across the frayed upholstery and without speaking he opened the car door to run through the downpour.

He loved her more than he could ever love any other human being, he thought as he stood under his hot shower, and the next time they met he should have arguments to overcome her refusals. Try, at least he could try. He lay in the central sag of the bed, thinking about these arguments. But his mind kept wandering to his plans for the march. Tomorrow he would send a UCLA Student for Peace to pick up the posters; Igawa had mailed his design directly to Sashimoto's print shop on Olympic and Sashimoto, who was some sort of relative of Igawa's, made no bones that he didn't think much of the poster. Clay found it compelling. A black Rorschach blob that might (or might not be) a soldier sprawling dead. Above this ambiguity the single word PROTEST. All that had been left for Clay to do was grease-pencil at the bottom: RANCHO PARK—6 PM FRIDAY, APRIL 7.

So little time, Clay thought. So little time. And it must be perfect. He rolled onto his belly, realizing with a sharp jolt that if he'd believed in God or devil he would have struck a cold bargain, on his side giving up his love—Odessa—his life itself, in exchange for the promise that he would convey his message, *stop the war,* on the night of April seventh.

———————— • **5** • ————————

Nina del Amo glanced up from her Psych notes as Ken unrolled the eight-by-ten canvas on the bare floor.

"What's that for?" she murmured in that faraway voice of hers.

"Self-portrait."

"Your whole body?"

"My head."

"You've got to be joking."

Her tone contained far more anxiety than this remark warranted. Ken, examining her drawn white face, remembered the time of the month: Nina sank deep into premenstrual glooms; he'd survived three and he knew whatever he said would be wrong. He admired the coarse texture of canvas and thought of how his self-portrait should look, remembering the Rijks-museum in Amsterdam, himself stationed in front of a late Rembrandt, a self-portrait, a sad old man full of too-weighty knowledge, Igawa staring until tears poured down his cheeks, yet, too, Igawa filled with the fierce, terrible envy that any serious painter must feel for one who's totally mastered his craft.

"If it's only your face," Nina persisted, "why so big?"

"All the better to eat you with, as the dirty old wolf said."

"I mean, don't you think it's a teeny bit egotistic, such a huge self-portrait?"

He wagged a finger. "You're forgetting."

"What?"

"Criticism's a no no around here."

"You're still playing the sensitive artist?"

"Let's cut it out, huh, Nina?"

"You don't have to be sensitive. Professional critics, they raved."

"Nina—"

"'Luminous and immutable. Ken Igawa is the one man of the three to watch.'" She quoted from Ken's review in the *Chronicle*.

"Translation: I've learned technique."

"'Saved from being merely phantasmagoric by Igawa's firm mastery of technique.'"

"Will you shut up!" Ken shouted, then realized he was shouting. He shouted a lot lately. "I'm sorry," he muttered.

Nina gave him a cheerless smile. "I agree," she said. "Critics know from shit. But you should be proud of the reviews."

"Why?"

"The Show was important to you. Very. You told me that. Specifically. You left your wife, you said, to stay up here and work on it."

Ahhh, now I dig why the conversation has gone as it has, Ken thought. *To get to this exact point. My ex-marriage.* Nina, in analysis, got her kicks from dissecting and redissecting every phase of personal misery, her own as well as anyone else's, and before her period, poor girl, she revived Ken's childhood belief in witches.

"It was pretty fucking important to you," she said.

"Fuck, cunt, shit, balls," Ken said pleasantly. "See? I know them all. Without analysis and the Free Speech Movement."

"Huhhh?"

"You don't have to repeat."

Nina gave him an agonized look.

"Listen," Ken said, "I need some stretchers for the canvas."
And he hurried out of the place.

He didn't mean to hurt her. They were both in a sad way,
he and Nina del Amo, *we're poor little sheep who have gone
astray, baaa, baaa, baaa* . . . and for this reason he tried, usually unsuccessfully, to be kind.

Ken walked quickly, fists balled in pockets. He found himself on Shattuck, on the boarded sidewalk alongside the subway
excavation, BART, that subway would be called when it was
finished, which—judging from time and bond issues it was
taking—would be well into the twenty-third century. Used
white picket fencing and raw boards protected the trench.

Ken realized he was heading toward Oakland. Good good
good. He was in an Oakland mood. He passed dreary little
cafés and customerless shops, stores converted to offices by
the simple expedient of gold-lettering words like Charles Wong
Lee, Herbalist, on dark-painted glass; he passed an incredibly
ancient black lady tottering behind a wire market basket; he
passed a permanently closed movie theater with tattered posters
from *The Misfits* starring Clark and Marilyn, and he tried to
remember how long each had been cold, but he couldn't, and
this memory gap intensified his Oakland mood. He found himself staring in the window of Guild Thrift Shop. Once his ex-
wife, all excited, had dragged him here to see a two-fifty table
that was round and low and just what she wanted to refinish,
and while the saleslady had written up the order his ex-wife
had meandered over to examine a wicker cradle on wheels.
His face dark, his eyes intent, Ken peered in the dusty window.
The wicker cradle was gone. Probably long gone. That had
been ten months ago. In its place stood a narrow cheval mirror
hinged to a walnut frame, and Ken went inside and the squat,
mustached saleslady told him the mirror was a rare bargain at
three seventy-five and Ken said, "Sold," and then had to take
the bus home to get his car. His? The Ford that three years ago
he'd raised such a stink about.

"You coming with me?" Nina asked.

"Where?"

"LA."

"Los Angeles," Ken corrected.

"Same place."

"Yeah yeah yeah. But only nonresidents call it LA. For Christ's sake! S'like besmirching. Would you call San Francisco Frisco?" Ken, while he spoke, stared in the mirror. The silver backing was worn, his reflection wasn't quite true and in the dim, watery depths his already full upper lip puffed out, his eyes glittered. Fu Manchu in person. He curled his fingers toward his reflection. "Sssss . . ." he hissed.

"I'm from Santa Barbara," Nina said.

"Good old SB."

"Oh, fuck it," Nina murmured.

She lay across the bed, a stained blue quilted heating pad over her stomach. The curse had arrived and, with it, cramps. Dr. Walters, her gynecologist, explained that her pain was due to her introverted uterus and cystic ovary, and if she'd already had a child or so he would recommend a complete hysterectomy. But Dr. Marshowsky, the fuzzy-haired young analyst with a speech impediment on whose leather couch Nina spent three fifty-minute hours a week, disputed the point. Crampth, Marshowsky insisted, were thycogenic in origin, an inability to accthept the female role. Nina spent hours pondering aloud the divergent views; the battle of the father images, she called it.

"Of course you're coming," Nina said.

"Why should I?" Ken continued to stare at his reflection. He had no intention, none whatsoever, of going to Los Angeles, where dwelt his ex-wife. It was bad enough that he thought of her all the time. Why be in the same town?

"The Peace March," Nina said. "This Friday. I'm leaving tomorrow."

"You'll miss class."

"Screw that," she muttered. "You've got to be there."

"Not my bag."

"Clay's showing your film."

"S'O.K. with me."

"You designed the poster."

"You insisted."

"You're *involved*," Nina said.

Ken held a brush in front of his face, measuring. "You involved me," he said. "I am not going to Los Angeles."

"But you're *involved*."

"Nina"—he turned—"anyone ever tell you when you do that you look like Cheetah the chimp?"

She stopped scratching her clavicle. Muttering some obscenity Ken didn't quite catch, she gave him a hurt look. She didn't say another word. Silence. He'd won, won. And he hated himself. Ken Igawa, using overfamiliar weaknesses to wound those close to him.

The following morning Nina jammed her toothbrush, baking soda, a box of Super Kotex and her gray sweatsuit pajamas in a brown paper sack. She said, "Five busloads of Berkeley people're going."

"Groovy."

"There'll be fifty thousand at least."

"A regular crusade," he said.

"Oh, balls, Ken. Clay and I and everyone in Students for Peace have worked for months and you know it!" Her thin voice penetrated with an intensity that Ken had learned to recognize meant trouble. Her face was white and her lips thrust forward. She looked very young, a Brobdingnagian little girl on the verge of a temper tantrum. "You've got to drive down!"

Ken escaped into the head. There he felt guilty, guilty that Nina's female organs were in such rotten shape, guilty that she was barely twenty and so very disturbed, guilty that she was rich and hated it, guilty that he was living with her sans love and marriage, guilty that he acted so crappy with her—they rarely conversed without one or the other digging the knife, and generally the one was him.

So it was guilt that made Ken call from the head, "If it's that big, I'll drive you down."

The Los Angeles crowd at Berkeley take more pride in the speed they make it between campus and home than they do in their grades. They zip along Roman-straight stretches of Highway 99 past towns and mile-square fields and vineyards; they roar up the grade of the barren brown Ridge Route; they zoom past diesels at dizzying speed. Some cheat and call the San Fernando Valley home. The more compulsive check their car clocks as they dig out of driveways, then again as they touch home garages. Prevaricators subtract from their time. Those with worrying mothers make it a firm rule to wait an hour after arrival at the Berkeley end to call home. Four hours and fifty-four minutes (to Ken's knowledge) was the record for the approximately four-hundred-and-thirty-mile trip. A friend of Ken's from California High had killed himself in his freshman year, crashing down an embankment near Bakersfield. It was the Grand Prix, the Indianapolis 500, Le Mans. That Wednesday

Ken drove like a fiend, but the traffic was heavy. He couldn't make it in less than five hours and fifty minutes plus ten minutes for a Texaco pit stop that he subtracted.

Nina requested to be dropped off at a hillside apartment near the UCLA campus. She'd barely spoken on the trip, thank God, except to give Ken two compliments on his skill. Seemingly buoyed up by inner excitement, she completely forgot to groan. And Ken agreed with the lisping psychiatrist: psychogenic, those cramps. She got out of the car, hugging her wrinkled paper sack, leaning on the open window.

"See you Friday," she said.

"Count me absent."

"Ken—"

"Bye."

"You're going to be there," she said.

"I'm parked in the red."

"Why did you come down?"

"You pressed the point. Remember?"

"You said—"

"I said I'd drive you down, right?"

"But—"

"And I did."

"It's important," she said. *"Very important."*

"You've got thousands. What difference one more or less?"

Nina's drooping left lid almost closed. She seemed to be marshaling all her powers. "You're the only person I ever had a meaningful relationship with," she said in that intense, troubled tone. "I never related to anyone before. You know that."

He was sorrier for Nina than he'd ever been. And he liked her less. Three girls with deep tans walked by slowly, staring at Nina and him. Freaks a pair, they must be thinking, those tanned beauties. One foot on the brake, Ken revved the motor.

"And fuckwise"—Nina gave him her disturbed, disturbing smile—"you're *numero uno.*" Since the engine was roaring, she had to shout.

The girls must've heard. "Rallies aren't my thing," he said.

Nina's big body tensed and she leaned into the car. *"It's important to me!"* she cried.

"O.K.," he muttered.

"You mean you'll be there?"

"Yeah yeah yeah." Various guilts answered for him. But Ken was thinking that if it pleased her, let her think he was there; in that mob she'd never miss him.

• • •

His mother lit the low silverplate candlesticks she'd gotten with Blue Chip stamps; she prepared a company meal, potatoes stuffed with cheese and one thirty-nine a pound sirloin. Mr. Igawa, silent and dried out as ever, apparently unperturbed by life with one kidney, leaned over his plate, stashing away steak, while Ken and Mrs. Igawa talked pleasantly, as if they were not mother and son but friends.

That is until Ken, foolishly, remarked he'd come down with some people—oh, exquisite euphemism to protect his parents' sensitive Lutheran ears—who were taking part in a protest march.

"Why are they mixed up in it?" asked Mrs. Igawa.

"They're against the war."

"Our government's there." Mrs. Igawa gave Ken a quick look. "You aren't marching, are you?"

"Why not?"

"It's hippies, the people who do that sort of thing."

"My son the Japanese hippie."

"More steak?" Mrs. Igawa asked. "You shouldn't go."

"No, thanks," Ken said. "I won't."

Candles flickered and light caught on a sliver of gold in Mrs. Igawa's smile.

"You should finish school," she said.

"Hey, what brought that up?"

His mother answered so promptly that it was obvious she'd given the matter much thought. "You could be a professor and teach painting."

"I don't know how myself."

"If you went back to college you'd learn."

"Let's change the subject, huh?"

"You must finish," Mrs. Igawa said. With firm motions that jiggled her full, ivory-colored upper arms, she sawed the remaining piece of steak, placing one half on her husband's plate, the other on Ken's.

"Don't eat the fat," she warned her husband. Turning to her son, she said, "As far as I can see there's nothing wrong with having a talent if you use it to make something of yourself."

Ken almost laughed out loud. His mother's words were so typically aggravating. Yet for Ken there always was something touching about older people and their relentless stubborn clinging to a more stable age. His throat clogged as he thought of his mother's code to live by: you got educated and made something of yourself, you begot racially unpolluted children and saw to it that they were educated, then in your old age you relaxed, enjoying the spectacle of your children making it while they educated their children—your grandchildren. She may have failed with him, but she'd stuffed her code into three out of four, she'd batted seven fifty, and that was pretty good in any league. Ken blinked.

Mrs. Igawa said, "You already have two years toward a degree."

"Mom, face it. I'll never finish."

"Then you've wasted those two years."

Oh, Mother, you must know I've wasted far, far more than that. "The only thing I've ever done right," Ken teased wearily, "is grow tall for a Japanese boy."

"Finish your steak," his mother replied.

They had dessert, her luscious raisin nut loaf, Ken's favorite. His father retired to smoke in front of the television. Ken dried the dishes for his mother.

"Did you know," she asked, scouring the broiler pan, "that Shigeme Futaba has a Master's degree?"

Ken dropped stainless forks into the yellow plastic cutlery tray. He'd gone with Shigeme his freshman year at UCLA, and her memory roused strong retroactive shame; poor Shigeme had been a device to forget his future ex-wife. "I'm glad," he said.

"Shigeme's a lovely girl."

Ken agreed.

"She's teaching English at University High. She has a lot of boy friends, but she isn't married yet."

How should he reply to this one? *Mom, don't trouble yourself finding me a girl. I'm so miserable and unhappy and confused and bitter, bitter, bitter that I'm shacking up with a white girl I don't love—I don't even like her. I must be sick, very sick.*

"Ken, why are you looking at me like that?"

"The little old matchmaker."

"Shigeme's a lovely girl."

"I agree. But let's leave her out of the conversation, huh?"

Mrs. Igawa set down the squashed Brillo, which gave off a strong soapy odor, and rinsed the broiler pan, asking, "You are getting a divorce, aren't you?"

"S'in the works."

The light over the sink showed vertical wrinkles in his mother's eyelids. She couldn't resist shafting him with a brief I-told-you-so glance. Ken didn't blame her. She handed him the broiler pan and he dried it.

"You'll be going out, won't you?" she asked.

"I can find my own girls."

"What are you running away from?"

"I'm not." Ken pointed at his blue Keds. "See? Absolutely stationary."

"I'm worried about you."

"Because I don't want to date Shigeme?"

"That's only part of it. You're living on handouts—"

"A grant."

"It's money you haven't earned. You're going on twenty-five. It's time for you to settle down. First get a decent education, then make a proper living. Take on responsibility."

"Let's all stand up. That *is* your generation's national anthem, isn't it?"

"Kenneth!"

"I'm sorry—"

"I don't care for sarcasm."

"Mom, I said I was sorry."

"Your brother and sisters live properly."

Sighing, Ken squatted to put the pan back in the stove. In his mind's eye he saw what his mother wished of him: a somber expression, a haircut, a gray business suit and well-polished shoes that stepped up the slopes of success with pretty, well-educated Shigeme's thick ankles near by.

His mother said, "You're the baby. And you had such a sweet disposition, even if you did have a temper. I spoiled you—"

"It's me that's crazy, not you."

"What I want you to do, Ken, is sit down and try to understand what life is about. You can't keep running away."

"I want to paint. What's so wrong with that?"

"If you put it to use, nothing."

Ken, stung, replied, "I *do* sell."

"Sometimes."

"I'm rumored to be promising."

His mother smiled. "I know. But what do you plan to do with that promise?"

"Try to get better."

"And then?"

"Try to get better."

"And when you've mastered it?"

"I never will."

Mrs. Igawa shook her head. She poured cleanser in the sink. Blue powder rose as she scrubbed vigorously. "Shigeme's very interested in art," she said. "She belongs to the new art museum."

Ken, groaning, threw in the dish towel and joined his father in front of *Bob Hope Presents*.

That night Ken tossed in the narrow lower maple bunk bed of his childhood. He couldn't sleep. Finally he got up, padding barefoot and naked across the tiny room to stare at the shadowy yard. There was no grass; potted *bonsai* trees lined packed dirt. Of course his mother was right. Painting was Ken Igawa's way of running from the staid professional niche she wanted for him, the niche that their small, self-respecting, hard-working group were proud to occupy. But he'd never really fitted in with "his" people. And with the "others" he'd never made it either; maybe this was his prickly fault, maybe theirs, but always he'd been the outsider. Even with his ex-wife he had, on occasion, wondered if their sweats had smelled different because of their racial origins. (Fleetingly, of course—the idea was too ridiculous to pursue—still, he *had* wondered.) His choice of girls, his work, these proved his mother's thesis: Ken Igawa was running away from himself. A symptom of disorder. But so what? By now he'd noticed that everyone on this sad, lonely earth is running someplace, or hiding. Miniature trees silvered by a half moon are very lovely, he decided.

He slept late.

Unintentionally, but doubtless the old subconscious escape hatch at work. When he rose both parents were gone. He sat in his mother's small, immaculate kitchen reading the *Los Angeles Times*. Next to the Pep Boys ad was a small item:

PEACE RALLY

An antiwar movie short will be shown at Rancho Park previous to a demonstration that has been planned to coincide with President Johnson's speech at the Century Plaza Hotel tomorrow night.

Reading his parents' paper it occurred to Ken for the first time that his ex-wife might be at the demonstration. Might? Of course she would. Even if it weren't for their film, it was exactly the sort of thing to which she was drawn. He definitely shouldn't go. Pouring himself a cup of cold coffee to ease his throat, he ordered himself not to go. He was a weak, unstable character. He had made up his mind months ago never to see her again. Or at least not to see her for many years. He was wise enough to understand that the bitterness and love and almost unbearable pain churning under his father's wrinkled, far-too-short cotton robe should be allowed to settle like sediment in a keg of wine. He shouldn't see her until his emotions were calm. He also knew enough of himself, the last of the red-hot romantics, to know that having mentally decided his ex-wife would be there, nothing could keep him from Rancho Park tomorrow night at six.

Whatever you called it, you couldn't call it running away. Or could you?

6

Marshall Mosgrove and Stan Kielty shared the extra expense of having the *Los Angeles Times* delivered to their Mountain View apartment. It would have been cheaper to have a San Francisco daily, but what San Francisco paper, they agreed, was worth taking? Marshall's trust fund didn't permit many extravagances, and he wouldn't come into his share of Grandmother's medium-size estate until he was thirty, yet each morning as he enjoyed the *Times'* smooth writing, lack of printing errors, as well as Bill Buckley's fine column, he felt it well worth the cost.

This particular morning, sun came butter yellow through the big window that overlooked the pool, appetizing bacon aromas lingered and Part Two was crisp in Marshall's hand. Then he read a small item next to the Pep Boys ad:

PEACE RALLY
An antiwar movie short will be shown at Rancho Park previous to a demonstration that has been planned to coincide with President Johnson's speech at the Century Plaza Hotel tomorrow night.

Marshall gripped the paper to keep his hand from shaking. The sorrow that dwelled on the dark edges of his mind stirred, drifting . . . the people in that film . . . Marshall swept a name aside, fumbling to turn the page.

The phone rang.

Stan reached out to answer. "For you," he said, his blue eyes perplexed. He handed the receiver around the electric percolator, adding, "A woman."

An unfamiliar woman. She asked, "Mr. Mosgrove?"

"Yes."

"Will you wait a second, please. Mrs. York wishes to speak with you." *Must be the ugly secretary,* Marshall decided.

Mrs. York came right to the point. "I have a favor to ask," she said.

"Anything," Marshall replied sincerely.

"Can you come to Los Angeles this afternoon?"

Marshall clenched his teeth. He'd planned to spend this afternoon and evening boning up for tomorrow's pre-quiz on Government Contracts.

Mrs. York was saying, "There's something we want to discuss with you."

"I'll drive down."

"It won't be inconvenient?"

"I'll be there around three."

"Wonderful," Mrs. York said.

Handing Stan the humming, dead phone, Marshall explained, "I'm going down to Los Angeles. Something Mrs. York wants to talk about."

"Did she say what?"

"No. But the least I can do is go."

It was.

Since that post-Christmas dinner, the actor and his wife had befriended Marshall. They had asked him to phone them whenever he was in Los Angeles. And Marshall did—at first it had taken all his moderate store of courage, but each time the call became easier. Sometimes it happened that neither were home, they spent a good deal of time touring in their Lear Jet 24, and then Kalpraga would talk to him. Marshall learned Kalpraga was Baron York's chief writer, and while Marshall never could like a man so iconoclastic and overbearing, still, he learned respect. Regardless of who spoke on the other end of the line, the conversation routinely ended with a sincere, "Come on over," and on arriving at the sprawling hillside estate Marshall was greeted with open arms. Literally. Baron York would drape a strong arm around Marshall's meaty shoulder, booming to his assembled guests, "And this young feller's name is Marshall Mosgrove. He's a pal of my boy's."

Or Mrs. York would take his hand in hers and say, "I'd like you to meet a friend of our son's. Marshall Mosgrove."

Or Kalpraga would fake a punch at Marshall's chest, saying, "And here's direct word from the absentee heir to the manor."

Marshall understood his role.

Surrogate son.

And being used this way didn't bother him at all; in fact, he enjoyed it thoroughly.

On the strength of his ersatz relationship he had met two United States Senators, five members of the House, a Supreme Court Justice and any number of state legislators as well as almost every ex-office holder of importance. Fat Kalpraga, inevitable drink in hand, would tell Marshall which behind-the-scene power was which. The politically powerful were Marshall's gods, and he would chew prime beef thinking, *Can this really be me, Marshall Mosgrove, eating at the same table with Barry Goldwater?*

Mrs. York never again wondered out loud where they'd met, so Marshall knew that she, too, had remembered, and this, he decided, gave him a tiny advantage over her. He had another small advantage. When people spoke of Mrs. York's fabulous sense of humor they didn't know what they were talking about. She had no sense of humor. None at all. Either she kept silent or she spoke the truth. Marshall, in rare leisure time, had read an anthology and found out his patroness. Somerset Maugham had a heroine like her, and society, unused to hearing the truth, thought her hilarious.

Marshall, his brain twitching with questions, arrived at the Yorks' place at five of three. The downstairs hall was being invaded by CBS; shirt-sleeved newsmen prepared their attack with fat, snaking cables while upstairs the besieged readied themselves. Marshall greeted Baron York in the actor's long, mirror-paneled dressing room. Kalpraga ran through impromptu quips. Zonnie, Baron's make-up man since *Road to Damascus,* sponged orange pancake onto strong, craggy features.

Mrs. York said, "We better let them finish," and she led Marshall along the gallery of family photographs to the upstairs study. She closed the door.

"Now we can have our talk," she said.

Then she was silent, moving to the silver bar tray, tonging ice from a silver vacuum bucket, pouring Black Label for Marshall—no denying it, he thoroughly enjoyed the luxury around here. She poured herself ouzo, munching a handful of green pistachios. Marshall waited for her to drink before he sipped his highball. From time to time the shouts of technicians rose to beat like muffled insect squeaks against the heavy door.

Marshall's nervous curiosity peaked wildly.

His hostess spoke. "We asked you down here, Marshall, because we need your help."

"My help?"

She nodded, sitting on the black leather ottoman, holding her glass with both large, well-shaped hands.

Mystified, Marshall said, "I'll do anything."

"I knew you'd say that."

"What else could I say?"

"It's not everyone who would."

"Mrs. York, you've been wonderful to me...and, well, I—never knew my father, but...I like to think of him as, well, being sort of like Mr. York." Marshall spoke somberly, staring down at his Scotch; he'd learned that a compliment is more effective stumbled over a little and spoken without looking the recipient in the eye until immediately after delivery. He looked up. "But I don't understand," he said, "what *I* can do for people like you and Mr. York."

Leaning forward, she took from the mahogany hunt table a fresh copy of the *Times,* white string still binding it.

"Did you see the article in back of Part Two?"

Someone walked across Marshall's grave, as his grandmother used to say. Marshall shivered.

"Did you?" Mrs. York asked again.

He nodded.

"The movie is the one Adam made with his friends," she said.

Marshall agreed.

"You knew?" she asked.

"Yes."

"How? It's not mentioned."

"Dorot sees Ken Igawa, and Leigh, too. They made the film. She told me."

"So you know. And I know. But not many others do." She

tapped newsprint with a buffed fingernail. "Have you ever noticed how little actual scandal is printed about political figures?"

"Not much, is there?" Marshall replied. Wondering what she was leading up to, he stared uneasily around the room. Light slanted through dark-stained shutters onto shelves of morocco-bound books and massive furniture designed for English country living; a strong masculine room, this, smelling of pipe tobacco, leather, beeswax polish and manly companionship. It was here, Marshall had noted, that Baron York usually met with reporters.

"Have you ever wondered why?" Mrs. York asked.

Marshall fell back on his education. "I assume the laws of libel."

"More often the publisher feels a responsibility."

"Of course," he said. "That, too."

"They could sell a lot of papers, but they prefer not to print garbage. Unless, of course, the story gets too big for them to ignore."

"I imagine so."

Mrs. York again tapped the paper. "In here we have the ingredients of a so-called human interest story, a big one. An older man speaks out in favor of war. His son, of military age, is against fighting to such an extent that he's filmed an eloquent protest. The *Times,* as you've seen, has given it four lines with no mention whatsoever of Adam. I'll tell you something quite frankly, Marshall. We have gone to a lot of trouble to keep showing of this film to a minimum. The PR men as well as our advertising people feel the publicity would be very bad. And if this peace affair should erupt into trouble. . . ." She sighed. "There won't be any more silence. And that, of course, is exactly what Adam wants."

Marshall wrinkled his brow. Puzzled. Oh, what she'd just said was true—Dorot and he often agreed that York, a real loner, was in with Gillies only because the relationship might embarrass York's father. But what was Mrs. York's point in telling *him?* What could Marshall Mosgrove do about movie stars and wars and big-time politics and front-page stories? Mrs. York was staring at him. He felt he had to say something.

"Do the police expect trouble?" he asked.

She sipped her drink. "They always expect trouble in this sort of thing. Naturally, there's no problem, if it's a peaceful demonstration. There'll be no mention of the movie or Adam's part in it. But if"—she set her glass in a silver rimmed coaster—"if there's trouble, we won't be able to stop the publicity."

"You won't?"

"No. We'll have to fight it. Our people have discussed the problem at great length. They feel the only answer would be to prove that at the time Adam made the movie he'd fallen in with a group of undesirables."

"But—"

She ignored the interruption. "After all, it isn't unknown for vultures to gather around a famous person's child." A drop of ouzo fell, marking a dark oval on her beige crepe blouse.

Marshall fidgeted. "I'm not a vulture," he said, trying for a light tone. He ordered himself to stop fidgeting and also to stop sweating—he had an unfortunate tendency to sweat when nervous.

"You know all the people connected with the movie, don't you?"

"Yes."

"You were friends?"

"Pretty friendly. Yes. You could say friends. Except with Gillies."

"He's a troublemaker."

"But the others aren't." Marshall gulped at his drink. "If that's what you're trying to prove, I can't help you, Mrs. York. I can't help you at all. Honestly. They are, given the normal limitations, a decent bunch. I mean it. Nice people."

She said nothing.

"I can't tell you anything bad about any of them. Except Gillies. And he had nothing to do with making the film."

She walked heavily to a roll-top desk, an antique, but it must have been gutted and rebuilt, for she slid back an inlaid panel just below the roll top, baring a combination lock that she twisted and turned until the deep drawer slid open soundlessly on a metal track. She selected several manila files, leveling them into a neat pile. She relocked the drawer, slid back the panel, then placed the files on the end of the long, curved hunt table.

"Here's something for you to read," she said. She glanced at her watch. "Have to ready myself to face a spontaneous taping." At the door she said, "Marshall, don't leave until I get back. I want to lock those away again."

"Cloak and dagger?" Marshall's laugh came out a breathy snort.

"You'll understand," she said, "after you read."

"Why let me?"

"We trust you," she said.

"Thank you, Mrs. York."

"Trust you implicitly," she said, closing the door.

Marshall listened to her footsteps fade along the gallery before he mopped his forehead, mopped his neck under his shirt collar, took off his jacket. He walked slowly to the files.

Tabs were typed:

STRYKER HALVORSEN (deceased)

LISSA GILLIES (minor child, parents CLAIBOURNE GILLIES and MICHELE SUTHERLAND)

LEIGH IGAWA

KENNETH IGAWA

RUTH ABBY MARX

DOROTHY McHENRY

Marshall carried the files to the deep leather chair by the window, the one where Baron York customarily lounged, his long legs thrust forward.

Marshall took out his reading glasses.

A purple twilight had settled into the room and polished furniture shone dully, as if covered with slime like the inside of a sewer.

Shuddering, Marshall gulped the remainder of his Scotch. Ice had melted, diluting it. He went to the bar, pouring himself a generous slug from the cut crystal decanter with the silver Scotch label dangling from its neck. He drank neat and quick, swiped the back of his hand across his mouth, leaned on the bar table, slumping, not moving for a full five minutes. He went back to the chair, put his jacket back on, tucked his glasses in his pocket, sat. He buried his face in his hands, breathing heavily. So we're all walking wounded, he thought; we all appear whole, but inside each of us is afflicted with terrible running sores of the soul. One part of Marshall Mosgrove, a decent enough guy, felt sorry for these people, their weakness exposed in elite type on bond paper, their sad, lonely weakness. Pity, that's what he felt, and a kinship. But the other part of Marshall Mosgrove, not a nice type at all, couldn't repress a smile that was half sneer. What a bunch of phonies! They were all worse than he, weren't they? Why should they sin and never give appearances a worry while he was afraid, always so afraid, that his being "that way" would show?

He wiped both hands along the gray flannel of his slacks. Two files he'd left unread. He couldn't open those; his fingers refused, absolutely refused, to function. DOROTHY Mc-HENRY and STRYKER HALVORSEN. Stryker was his past, Dorot his future. He'd replaced their files, unseen. Say what you want, Janus had guts.

The door opened. Mrs. York touched a soundless switch and paired Corinthian pillar lamps spread light. Her orange camera make-up glowed.

"Mr. York's been detained," she said. "Those newsmen!" And shutting the door carefully behind her, she poured herself another ouzo. She pointed at the Scotch decanter.

Marshall shook his head. "No, thank you."

She munched her routine handful of pistachios. "You've read them all?" she asked.

"I didn't look at Dorot's," he replied in semi-truth.

"It doesn't matter. You won't need to."

A question occurred to Marshall. An important question that he, practically an attorney, should have considered earlier. The words were very hard to form, and he wished he could avoid them, but he couldn't, so he clenched his fingers and asked, "Do—do you have one of those . . . things on me?"

"Marshall, people in our position, like it or not, have to have information about whom we're friendly with. It's routine for those in public life. To behave otherwise would be hopelessly naïve."

"I understand." He forced his square-cut, sincere smile. "Not much to know anyway."

She returned the smile.

"I'm glad you're engaged to Dorot. That's the wisest decision you ever made."

He managed a laugh. "I think so, too. Wonderful girl. Known her all my life, practically, and then one night—Bingo." He tried to snap his fingers, failed. "Love."

"While we're on the subject, Marshall, that boy who shares your apartment."

"Stan?"

She nodded. "Naturally you couldn't know about his past. He's engaged. And he looks so very normal, but—"

"Mrs. York, I swear—"

"If I were you, I'd ask him to find someplace else to live." She spoke reassuringly, as a surgeon might tell his patient that the tumor must be removed, otherwise it will become malignant. The ouzo spot had dried on her blouse, leaving silk crepe puckered; Marshall found himself worrying compulsively that the imperfection might show up on television screens coast to coast at ten o'clock tonight when the tape was being shown.

"You understand where you fit in, of course," she said.

He shook his head.

"You knew all those people," she explained. "If any trouble comes, naturally you'd want to let everyone know the sort of influences that surrounded Adam when he made that movie."

Outside the window a bird chirped; far away, down the terraces, a boy shouted, "Tara, Tara, wait. . . ." The voice, while distinct, was considerably smaller than bird's song.

"I couldn't do that," Marshall heard himself say.

"What?"

"No," Marshall said. "I couldn't." His insides shook, but his voice came out firm, and he was amazed at his own courage. "I wouldn't." He rose, facing her.

Mrs. York's pupils were doing strange things, swelling as if thick black ink were being pumped into her eyeballs.

"How can I?" Marshall asked.

"How can't you?"

"They're my friends—"

"We're your friends."

And she stared at him with those strange, unblinking dark eyes. Lady MacBeth of Bel Air— No. She was one of those larger-than-life powers out of classical drama, Clytemnestra staring him down. *Friends?* A silly point they were picking on. Wetpants Mosgrove had no friends. However, once he had loved. He had loved well, if not wisely, and he wouldn't let this . . . this woman, destroy his dead love.

Never.

He said, "I mean, it's not that I don't appreciate your friendship; you and Mr. York have been wonderful to me." Marshall yanked at his tie. "But listen, I mean, Dorot was maid of honor at Ken and Leigh's wedding. I was an usher—"

"I admire loyalty."

People were forever confusing his other emotions with loyalty. But he snatched at the word. "Loyalty! That's it. You'd never have any more faith in me, would you, if I was a cop-out? I mean, nobody trusts a cop-out." Marshall extended both hands, pleading; lines of sweat shone in his palms. "You'd never trust me after I did it, would you? How could you trust me if I went around telling everybody stuff like that." He gestured at the files. "It'd be really disloyal, they're my friends, and—"

"I admire loyalty," she repeated firmly, "but you're misplacing yours."

"I swear to God I'll do anything for you, Mrs. York. Anything. But how can I destroy—"

"Destroy!" she burst out. "It seems to me that they've destroyed themselves. Utterly. They're a compound of what frightens us about today's young. Drugs. LSD. Miscegenation. Adultery, illegal abortions, high school dropouts, runaway hippies, wild promiscuity, communist influences. Homosexuality." She stalked to the C-shaped table, selecting a file. "Did you read about this Stryker Halvorsen? Did you see this sworn affidavit?" She shook a sheet of onionskin. "A Dr. Edwards states that he dismissed Stryker Halvorsen, the *star* of that movie, from a summer camp for making overtures to an unnamed counselor."

You know Stryker wasn't like that, you know it, you know it, you lay under him and over him both, you bitch with your wide-open thighs—

"You were at that camp, weren't you?" she asked smoothly.

Marshall's face caught fire. Trying to ignore her eyes, an impossible task, he took out his handkerchief, pretending to blow his nose so at the same time he could blot his forehead. Was that a purposeful lack of intonation? Or had it been knowing? Unnamed, she'd said.

And all at once his sweat cooled to lie like ice water on his body.

Unnamed. . . .

Why had he come on like a crazed baboon? Why hadn't he read STRYKER HALVORSEN? He reached for a monogrammed silver cigarette box, tried to open it, but his fingers shook, so he gave up quickly. *What am I doing anyway?* he thought, *I gave up smoking.* Below, the CBS news truck departed, rolling over crushed gravel, and as the sound faded, Marshall, a coward again, slumped back in the chair by the window.

"Yes," he admitted finally. "Yes. I was there. It was a Vista camp."

They stared at one another and Marshall looked away first. Unnamed maybe, but she knew, she knew.

The door opened. Baron York entered. Marshall pushed himself to a standing position.

"Well, Marshall." The famous lopsided grin settled into pancaked grooves.

"Hello, sir." Marshall managed a level tone. "How did the interview go?"

"The usual. A bunch of newsmen!" Baron shrugged. "I'm grateful, son, that you waited them out." Briefly he touched a tanned fist on Marshall's shoulder; then he strode to the silver tray, pouring himself a stiff drink. He glanced at the files his wife was locking away. "You read that garbage?" he asked.

He had, Marshall admitted.

Baron sighed. "My poor boy. He got himself in with a rotten bunch."

"A thoroughly bad crowd," Mrs. York echoed.

"Understandable, though." The actor drank somberly. Above the glass, his eyes were bruises gouged by mortal suffering. "Understandable in a way . . . right after his mother died. A long, cruel death, hard on all of us, and poor boy, he took it hard, real hard."

There was a chorus of howls. Must be six, the hour the York huskies were fed.

Baron finished his drink with a quick toss of his leonine head. "Did Mrs. York mention"—his tone of voice now turned jovial—"that she has an extra pair of tickets for that dinner tomorrow night?"

"Sir?"

"We're sort of hoping that you and your pretty little girl can be there."

"I—well . . . I just don't know what to say."

"Yes." Baron grinned.

"I can't."

"Why not?" Mrs. York asked.

And Baron's head tilted questioningly.

"It's too fantastically generous," Marshall said.

It was. The proceeds going to the John F. Kennedy Memorial Hospital in Dublin, the cost a thousand-dollar donation per couple; everybody who was anybody on both sides of California's political fence would be at the Century Plaza Hotel on Friday night.

"We have the tickets," Mrs. York murmured.

"And we'd sure like to have more people on our side there," Baron said.

"I—well, I'm overwhelmed. All I can say is thank you and—"

Baron York grinned. "We've got a selfish motive. There aren't many young fellers nowadays that are as sound politically as you. So many wild-eyed kids spouting off or destroying something they don't understand and don't know how to re-place." He glanced at his wife. "It's not time to talk about it, is it, Helen? But a lot of people have been asking about you. And we both sort of hoped later, after your navy service is behind you, you'll be willing to forget private practice. Get active in public affairs. It'd be sort of a feather in our caps if our protégé was to become a big legal man. Right, Helen?"

"Yes, dear," she said. "Marshall, be sure to tell Dorot to bring a long dress. It's formal." She was smiling at him, and in her smile was no triumph, no anger, just warm friendliness.

"If it's all right, I think I'll take you up on that drink," Marshall said.

"Come early." Baron poured for them both. "We've rented a couple of rooms at the hotel so we can have a little social get-together first."

Marshall ate dinner at the Yorks'. It was after nine when he started the long drive north on 99. Lights glittered at him, a steady, mesmerizing stream. Questions, too, came at him. Why shouldn't he go along with his friends, the Yorks? After all, was anything likely to happen at the demonstration? These things were orderly. At the same time he was asking himself how had he surrendered so easily? So quickly? The answer to these came in the form of another question: how had Marshall Mosgrove found the courage to resist at all? And what did the phrase mean, a big legal man? Judge? State Supreme Court? Hadn't another Californian, Earl Warren, a mere Boalt man and reputedly a C student at that, become Chief Justice of the United States? If the worst came to the worst, wasn't he getting far more out of this than the minimum wage? Far more than thirty pieces of silver? *Oh, Stryker, Stryker, forgive me, for I know what I do. . . .*

Marshall ordered himself to concentrate on his driving and to keep the speedometer glued to a safe, sane fifty. A guy he'd known back in California High, Dick Something-or-other, had been killed on 99, speeding near Bakersfield.

Part Seven

"What do you think?" asked Larry Marx.

"S'fine," his wife replied.

"You're sure?"

"Fine."

"Not too tiring?"

Ruth Abby, who was frying breakfast bacon on an old-fashioned high-legged stove, shook her curly head. They were discussing whether she ought to go to the Peace March tonight.

"There won't be enough toilets," Larry warned.

"My peeing's fine."

"Wasn't last week."

"The baby shifted. Or something. I can go hours—"

Larry grunted his disbelief.

"I'm a regular camel," Ruth Abby insisted.

"Every ten minutes."

"That was *last* week," Ruth Abby said, forking bacon onto a paper towel. "You didn't notice me getting up a single night this week, did you?"

Larry admitted he hadn't.

"So I'll be fine." Ruth Abby waddled heavily across the room with two pieces of bacon. As she bent to hand them to her little boy an involuntary groan came from deep within her popping diaphragm.

"Here, Dylie," she said. "One for each hand."

Dylan, a grave, red-cheeked eighteen-month-old, crushed both hands at his mouth, then sat on the floor concentrating on picking up pieces of crisp bacon that had crumbled there. He ate. His mother went back to the stove to scrape the toast that accounted for the burning smell and smoke that hazed the room. She buttered toast, set it on paper toweling with the bacon and carried it to the table where Larry sat stringing blue beads on a leather thong. This was how they earned their daily charred toast—they, like Gilgamesh and the others who lived over the Importium, made worry beads and sewed sandals to sell in the barnlike shop downstairs.

Ruth Abby pushed aside the bowl of beads. "You're hipped on work."

"That's me. Compulsive about everything," Larry said. "It's so gloriously mindless."

"Eat," she said.

He did, and so did she, pouring milk in a glass mug that they both drank from.

"Listen, Ruth Abby, you're sure—"

"We've *gotta* go."

"The baby's due in—"

"I know, I know! A couple of weeks. Larry, this is me, Ruth Abby. Remember? I'm having it."

"There'll be a huge crowd—"

"We're going."

"All right, all *right.*"

"I don't want there to be wars," Ruth Abby said, glancing at Dylan. *"They're* always harping on what we owe Dylie and the new baby! But like it's important to make sure babies grow up. That's something *they* never think about."

They were her parents and Larry's.

Parents. . . .

As she ate, Ruth Abby pondered the problem of *they.*

Up in Berkeley, the Heims and the Marxes had been vague, distant dragons that long ago had been put out of commission, if not actually slain. Then, seven months ago, Gilgamesh had heard about this place, an old store in Venice with apartments above; finances were low—nobody seemed to be getting any from home—and everyone agreed it'd be great living near the beach, making things, real things, not factory junk, to sell; they could have a business they ran, not a business that ran them. The idea, everyone agreed, was perfect. So here were Larry and Ruth Abby Marx living in Los Angeles.

And live dragon parents breathed fire over them again.

And there were four.

Larry and Ruth Abby had been married first in a ceremony at the place, later at City Hall, almost two years ago, and since Dylan's birth a few months later the in-law Heims and Marxes had become firm friends, dining out together often, driving in one or the other's Cadillacs to Palm Springs for a weekend at Ocotillo Lodge, where they sat around the pool bewailing what today's world had done to their children.

Whenever Ruth Abby and Larry took Dylan to visit one set

of grandparents, the others were always present to coo over the baby: oh, the little doll, how clever, how *brill*iant, what a little doll, here, let me change him. The sort of scene, as Larry always said, that made you feel Jewish grandparents had blood temperature a couple of degrees warmer than the rest of humanity. Ruth Abby thought it natural that the grandparents adored Dylie—who wouldn't? But did that mean they had to keep ganging up on Larry and her? All four grandparents never stopped saying that, now the "kids" were parents, they had certain obligations. The old people, it was obvious to Ruth Abby, had planned an attack. The Marxes massed against poor Larry. Larry must shave his mustache, get his hair cut, find a "proper" job with a "future," preferably in Mr. Marx's prosperous cabinet shop over in Compton. And Ruth Abby got it from Mrs. Heim. Mrs. Heim, bad complexion reddening with the effort of keeping her tone in the pleasant register, urged Ruth Abby not to take Dylan to the Venice Clinic but to a pediatrician—"I'll pay"—and to give him Poly-Vi-Sol and to wash his fruit—"Babies're so prone to diarrhea. If you don't believe me, ask Daddy, he's the doctor"—and to get him shoes, look, his poor little feet were blue, and shouldn't she stop him from doing *that?*—pointing to Dylie as he pulled his little dinglehoffer—to tell the truth, Ruth Abby herself often gave the little pink rose a tweak. Ruth Abby ate her bacon scowling. Her mother had this real rivalry complex to prove that Dylan wasn't being raised as well as Ruth Abby had been. And the thing of it was, Mother had gotten through. Clear through. Ruth Abby felt dumb. And, far worse, a bad mother.

Then, too, there was the joint campaign. All four voices raised in barrages: Larry and Ruth Abby couldn't raise babies in a dump without their own toilet yet! (Theirs wouldn't flush, so they shared Donolly's.) Both sets of parents wanted to jointly foot the bills for a little pad in the Valley with a fenced yard, a room for each baby and a color boob tube for Ruth Abby to watch while Larry was off each day soaking his brain in glue at the cabinet works.

At some time during each visit Mrs. Heim and Ruth Abby would lapse back into their old shouting sessions and Larry would get a sneezing attack, his breathing getting more and more labored until he had to inhale his plastic asthma pipe. At Berkeley he'd never needed it.

O.K., the visits were poison.

Wasn't it bad enough she and Larry felt obligated to let the parents see their only grandchild? But why should she have developed this guilt? She couldn't block *them* out. Right now she was swallowing her toast in large gobs.

"Up tight like them," she muttered. "That's what they want!"

"Huh?"

"Our parents."

Larry, making a face, said, "You want to give me an ulcer?"

"They get me. They just get me! Worrying all the time! Up tight. That's what they mean by obligations!" Ruth Abby's musical voice rose shrilly.

At the loud noise, Dylie's huge round eyes filled with water. Ruth Abby rose, hurrying across the bare room to hug him to her bulging pregnancy.

"Cool it, man," she whispered. "Cool it." And she popped her bacon in his mouth.

She pushed herself up.

"*They* make me feel stupid," she said to Larry.

"You aren't."

"Really dumb, that's how *they* make me feel."

"You're clever."

"Like I can't raise my own kids."

"And brave. Breaking away from all their bourgeois crap."

"I am," Ruth Abby said.

"What?"

"Dumb," she said. "But so?"

"You're not, but so?" Larry grinned. "You're positive you feel pre-prenatal?"

"Larry, this is me, Ruth Abby Marx. Remember? I sang for that film."

———————— **2** ————————

Salt fog rolled in early. So did the police.

Well before five that afternoon squad cars, police station wagons and two black and white striped sheriff's buses filled Rancho Park's roped-off lot. The police also had barricaded the long, narrow parking area of the adjacent golf course; police guarded each of the two entries, permitting the late golfers' cars to depart but no marcher cars to enter.

Gilgamesh cruised slowly along green-lined streets of Cheviot Hills before he spied a parking place almost big enough. Donolly, Larry Marx and a couple of others got out, releasing the brake of a red Mustang, pushing it forward into a Cape Cod's driveway and resetting the brake. The battered, flower-painted Ford wagon edged into place. Larry strapped Dylan on his back; Ruth Abby pinned the sign on the baby's jacket and picked up her guitar. The others hefted brown paper sacks of food. They became part of the crowd converging on Rancho Park. Well-dressed older couples. Mothers in fleece-lined car-coats. Children muffled in corduroy. Two high-collared ministers deep in conversation. Teen-agers flushed and loud with Friday-afternoon freedom. Suited men striding along with business expressions.

The park, a large, gently rolling meadow, was alive with picnickers, at trestle tables or relaxing against sides of the huge sandbox, or dangling on children's swings, sprawling on damp crab grass. Under an oak grove, men in white linen jackets, doctors or dentists, and nurses with caps pinned to elaborate hairdos shared huge cardboard tubs of Chicken Delight.

"It's *freezing*." Ruth Abby shivered under her poncho. "Why don't they put on their coats?"

"They want to be counted as professional people," Larry replied.

And Ruth Abby snuggled closer to her clever husband. The bunch straggled up a hill to where Donolly was saving a table.

"Look." Ruth Abby pointed across the park. "A screen. To show my film."

"And another." Larry jerked his head at canvas stretched on the pink recreation building. There, people gathered, listening to a speaker. Against the wire fencing that surrounded the Olympic-size swimming pool were propped signs, mostly hand-painted:

> BRING THEM BACK ALIVE
> MAKE LOVE, NOT WAR
> CHICKEN LITTLE WAS RIGHT
> HELL, NO, I WON'T GO.

"Hell, no, I won't go, that is what I will tell them if I am drafted." RG Richards was speaking in Churchillian cadence.

"Brother, I know where all of us blacks should draw the battle lines. If I'm drafted, I know who I will fight."

A pair of hefty black men, probably bodyguards, lounged on either side of him.

Ken listened only absently to the words. He was admiring RG in his new Afro incarnation. RG's long fragile-looking head was shaved, he wore a loose brown batik robe, and he was far more interesting, portraitwise, than during his middle-class Joe College phase.

Ken whispered to Nina, "You won't believe this. But. He used to stutter."

"Shut up," Nina murmured.

Ken gave a quick look-see to make sure his ex-wife wasn't among those present.

"I will say to the white brother"—RG raised his long arms so his robe spread like wings—"I will say to him, after four hundred years of slavery, I will say to him, I will not fight, I will not fight one more of your battles, brother."

What the hell will you do if you do see her?

A recorded voice that sounded like Joan Baez, but wasn't, sang amplified through loudspeakers:

> *Where have all the flowers gone?*
> *Long time passing.*
> *Where have all the flowers gone?*
> *Long time ago.*

Ruth Abby buttoned Dylie's jacket, and what did he do but put his hand on her stomach and ask gravely, "Baby cold?"

Blue helmets were everywhere.

A tall black-haired man brushed angrily around a policeman. For a moment Leigh held her breath. But as he turned she exhaled. It wasn't Ken. Hopeless, she was hopeless. Ken was in Berkeley. *If* he were down here, even though they were legally and uncontestedly separated, he would have called. *He's not here*, Leigh told herself; *face it, he's not here.* She tightened the belt of her trenchcoat.

She had come alone, no aim in mind, a small hope maybe, but no aim, no aim, that is, beyond demonstrating for pax Americana. And so, aimlessly, she wandered around picnickers, mostly solid citizens but a few in fantastic clothes, old army hats, toppers, serapes, thrift shop finery. At one table a bearded man in a loose-sleeved Mexican wedding shirt bent forward, smiling at a bearded man to his left. For a moment Leigh saw through eyes admittedly conditioned by a storm of magazine articles comparing hippies to early Christians; that Gallo red and food littering the long table could have been leftovers from the Last Supper.

"Leigh!" cried a girl's rich contralto.

Ruth Abby stood at the table, waving exuberantly. Her black poncho ballooned—apparently she was ready to pop. Then Gilgamesh called out and so did Larry Marx and that gentle black boy, Donolly, with his cherubic face and tumbleweed hair. They insisted Leigh share the Last Supper. Leigh hadn't seen Ruth Abby and Larry since their marriage, and thank God for it. Ruth Abby flooded out explanations and forgot to ask where was Ken. Slung papoose style on Larry's back, his son gravely chewed a drumstick. Pinned to the back of Dylan, a red-lettered sign, *BABIES AREN'T FOR BURNING*.

"They're showing our film," Ruth Abby said. "D'you know that?"

Leigh said she did. She asked, "You know any people here?"

"Just the bunch. Mostly it's old squares." Ruth Abby's laughter bubbled. "Oh, I did see someone. Mrs. Corelli. Remember? The English teacher? She had the biggest boobs and—"

"I remember, I remember." Leigh laughed, too. "She always wore tight purple."

"There's a ton of doctors here."

And Larry interjected, "Doctors're notorious conservatives, so the country *must* be ready for peace."

Leigh extended an arm to take in the entire park. "Think of all the planning."

"Unbelievable," Larry said.

"Clay Gillies did it all," Ruth Abby asserted. "There'll be more'n fifty thousand of us."

"There must be seven thousand already," Clay said.

"Twelve"—Odessa smiled, raising her leather-cased transistor—"as the news commentators count."

"If they add in our protectors"—Clay glanced at a nearby cop—"they better double it."

"People'll come. Don't worry."

"Who's worried?"

"They're pouring in," Odessa reassured.

Again Clay estimated his legions. Once (Odessa was right)

he would have shaken in the pit of his belly, fearing they wouldn't show up, the respectable, hitherto silent ones, worrying the thing wouldn't come off. But through the years he'd trained himself to forget the worrying and concentrate on his own organization. He squinted at the tennis courts, veering to the picnic area. Already he had a crowd. His bearded face broke into an involuntary smile. Oh, Clay didn't kid himself, he knew ninety-nine percent came for the wrong reasons, petty personal reasons, a mother wishing to halt the war so *her* eighteen-year-old wouldn't have to go, a lonely soul in search of companionship, bunches of high school boys hoping to meet girls and vice versa, engineers from the nearby missile plants convincing themselves that their work had nothing to do with this damn mess in Vietnam, the usual excitement seekers, hippies and Hell's Angels and taut Black Power cats, a grad student on the verge of being drafted, a fat middle-aged salesman pretending he was still a young rebel; everyone here had his own shell game, and as Clay estimated his numbers he accepted it the way it was. And wasn't disillusioned or disappointed. For at gatherings like this he occasionally (as now) sensed a real goodness in humanity, a common denominator that he must propel forward. Clay had endured the months of preparation, twittering ladies' clubs, the beehive of vendettas involved in dealing with so many organizations, a million phone calls, eighteen hours of hard labor seven days a week. His reward? In this anticipatory lull he was experiencing a strange, warm sweetness, call it love, for these thousands. They were gathered here in a chilly, hilly park, a people's army fighting for one common cause. Peace. It was reward enough. Clay wanted to share his emotions with Odessa, but as he turned to her, tears clogged his throat. He couldn't speak.

Ken, munching on a sandwich Nina had brought, saw Clay turn to Odessa Norris, saw Clay's head bow, his fingers tighten on her sleeve. The pose . . . Ken realized he'd been pretty dense not to have seen it before, their closeness. For the first time in years he felt really warm toward Clay.

Ruth Abby finished eating, licked her fingers clean, opened her guitar case and held the instrument awkwardly across her bulge. The same song was being broadcast over and over, theme music for the demonstration, and Ruth Abby's rich voice joined in, quieter, for she lullabied her son:

"Where have all the young girls gone?
Long time passing.
Where have all the young girls gone?
Long time ago.
Where have all the young girls gone?
Gone to young men everywhere.
When will they ever learn?
When will they ever learn?"

Dylan, obligingly, fell asleep, one pink cheek squashed against his father's narrow shoulder. In the misty, graying light, Ruth Abby turned to her old friend, Leigh. Leigh was more elegant than ever, slimmer, sadder around the mouth.

"Where's Ken?" Ruth Abby asked.

"Berkeley."

"And you're here?"

"My father's sick."

"Again?"

"He was never sick before."

"I mean, he's done the dirty again."

Leigh got her old snobby look.

But Ruth Abby refused to be deterred. "Pulled you apart again," she said.

"He had a heart attack." Leigh frosted.

"That's how they are. All alike. Do anything to melt you down and turn you into *them*. Take Larry's and my parents. Forever harping at us to—"

"A coronary!"

"—get a house, a mortgage, tie ourselves up in *their* knots. They say we owe it to Dylie and the new baby!" Ruth Abby inhaled deeply. "You've split?"

Leigh turned her head.

"And you're still hung up on him?"

Someone let off a firecracker; there was a sizzling sound; stars bubbled like a golden Bromo in the dusk. Ruth Abby patted Leigh's shoulder, which was thin and trembly.

"Go back to him," she advised.

Leigh looked at Ruth Abby. "You know something?" Leigh said. "You're the first person who's suggested that."

"It's so dumb?"

"No. S'right."

"So go."

"But he's making it with someone else," Leigh said quickly.

"Fight her."

"You don't understand."

Ruth Abby threw up her hands. "Come off it, Leigh. Balling someone else, it's not any more a reason for people who love one another, really love one another, to separate about."

"He thinks I did something against him when I stayed with my father."

"But—"

"Ruth Abby, do I have to spell it out? He doesn't love me. Not any more. And that's the truth. He's living with her. He couldn't live with her if he did." Leigh flushed, winced, said, "Let's not go into it, O.K.?"

What else is there to say? Leigh thought. She leaned her elbows on the damp picnic table, miserably cursing herself (the billionth time) for being so stubborn, tenacious, for flubbing the dub with her mulishness. She'd blown it. And now she could spend the rest of her life dying. The fog was cold. She wished she'd worn her heavy coat.

Ruth Abby sang:

> *"Where have all the young men gone?*
> *Gone for soldiers every one."*

The new hotel, a curve of topaz lights, was an improbable orange-slice candy above the unbuilt acreage that once had been 20th Century-Fox's back lot.

Marshall decided to let the attendant take his car. Normally he would have left the Buick in the self park, which was cheaper and you didn't have to tip. But tonight he wanted to swing. So he got in the slow line of expensive traffic moving along the Avenue of the Stars to the hotel's crescent-shaped entry. He and Dorot were going to the Yorks' cocktail party. It was early. Yet already police circled the hotel at approximately five-foot intervals.

"They been here all day," said the youthful attendant as he opened the car door. He must have noticed where Marshall was looking.

Marshall didn't encourage the boy.

But Red Jacket went on anyway, "Governor's sent in three hundred National Guard."

Dorot waited on the sidewalk. In her new long coral brocade and her mother's white mink stole, her thin brown hair professionally puffed out, in Marshall's opinion she looked as good as any of the women making their elegant way into the hotel, and a lot younger. He'd been right to tell her to cut out the Berkeley handwoven, hand-hammered look. Since their engagement he'd seen to it that she dressed like a human being.

The Rolls behind let out two couples.

Marshall knew one of the men, the gray-haired, wizened one; he was a big movie executive, Lou Cordoman. They had met at the Yorks'. It would be rudeness to ignore him. But when he spoke to Mr. Cordoman should he make it brief? Should he introduce Dorot? Wanting to behave correctly, Marshall sweated under his dinner jacket.

Cupping Dorot's cold, bare arm under Mrs. McHenry's fur, Marshall said, "Hello, Mr. Cordoman."

Lou Cordoman gave him the blank nod of a complete stranger, then turned back to his friends.

Marshall's face burned. He didn't dare glance at Dorot.

At that moment Kalpraga called from the glass doors, "Hey there, Eagle Scout! This way, you kids. And Harry and Lou, too."

A warm smile lit Lou Cordoman's shriveled, tanned face. "I didn't recognize you right away," he said, moving toward Marshall. "We met at Baron's, didn't we?"

"It was a while ago, sir." Marshall graciously offered an excuse.

"Marshall Namsour, isn't it?"

"Marshall Mosgrove."

"That's right, that's right. Never forget a name. So you're going to have a little drink with the Baron, too?" And he introduced Marshall to his wife and friends. Handsomely dressed older people showed dental miracles.

Marshall introduced his fiancée, Dorothy McHenry.

And Dorot made a small, appropriate joke about the fog as the six of them went laughing toward the lobby. Expensive cars moved slowly forward.

Where have all the soldiers gone?
Long time ago.

Leigh sat at the end of the picnic bench talking quietly to Gilgamesh. His large hands lay on the table, perfectly relaxed. He was the first person with whom she'd been able to openly discuss losing her husband, and the humiliating, sad words came and came.

When she finished Gilgamesh said, "You're sure that's how Ken feels?"

She nodded.

"You've discussed it with him?"

"No. But if he still cared at all, how could he be living with her?"

"You just told me you stayed down here when you really wanted to go back to Berkeley with him."

"It's not the same at all!" she cried. "My father was ill."

"So you stayed and stayed?"

Leigh's mouth trembled. She stared up at the dark sky.

"I'm not putting you down. But Leigh, think about it. Did you do what reason told you? Or emotion? Listen, from time to time all of us suffer from a strange, dark confusion of the heart. Maybe that's what's happening to him."

"Maybe," Leigh said. Dubiously. But she gave a faint smile.

> *Gone to graveyards everywhere.*
> *When will they ever learn?*
> *When will they ever learn?*

The sky was black. Clay Gillies opened the trunk of Odessa's car to get the two prints of *An American Hero*. RG gnawed a thumbnail while Priddy and Smith lounged nearby.

"Hey, man, you afraid?" RG asked Clay.

"I would be if I thought about it," Clay admitted. "But who's thinking?"

"I am," RG said.

"That's because you've got nothing to do." Clay thrust circular metal cases at RG. "Here. Archie's ready for these."

But it was Smith's massive hands that took the film from Clay.

On canvas stretched between two light poles, 16mm film was blown up to vast graininess. Leigh watched herself, yards of hair tossing, huge white face, mouth opening and closing, smirking, blinking, winking; oh, how that tremendous face sickened Leigh. Why wasn't everyone barfing? Yet at the same time she was examining Stryker. So alive, so beautiful . . . who could believe he was dead? A moth fluttered into the white beam, casting huge shadows on Stryker's face. Then—something. So brief she couldn't be positive she'd actually seen it.

Her own blink of tears, she decided. Yes, that was it. Ken had edited for months and Leigh knew every frame backward and forward. She had been mistaken. There—no. She must be blinking again. But—hadn't she seen a soldier?

Ken had to give credit where it was due. Clay Gillies, for his own purpose, had been right. His most masterful touch, Ken decided, was leaving the jungle silent, leaving the cries of dying men silent. York had bought the war stock shots, ten bucks a foot.

Ken sat on ragged grass, damp soaking through his jeans, his left arm almost touching Nina's, his right fingers pressing above his eyebrow. He had a headache in the making. That hot summer they had all been so young, he thought, so incredibly, unbelievably young; time had moved more slowly then, and the golden light of a more youthful star had warmed them all. York, the funny-sad Holden Caulfield cynic, defraying all costs and giving offhand advice on how not to wreck a cool ten thou of equipment. Dorot, lugging the heavy Arri camera in thin arms while she loudly intellectualized the Art of the Cinema; pretty Michele, nineteen and playing the great man's wife with one mascaraed eye on her little girl. Stryker, crowned with athlete's laurels, alive and among us, a beautiful guy and decent, if not what you'd call a genius. Himself, Ken Igawa, positive all he needed was a year at the outside and he'd out Renoir both Renoirs. Of course the film was a device; he'd never denied it. He had made love to his girl through a view finder, and she had responded with the blazing smile that right now lit canvas stretched across a stucco wall. Ken's fingers dug. His headache was no longer vague. Stryker was bleached white bones under a white-painted cross. Michele, divorced, remarried and a credit-card-carrying materialist—she might as well be fifty. Ruth Abby had sunk like a stone into tideless psychedelic seas; Dorot was about to marry that sad, pompous ass, Mosgrove. And us—well, no point going into *that*. But how have we all screwed up so badly? There had been such a hopeful light, hadn't there? Is screwing up a definition of growing up in the sixties? That well-known homespun philosopher, Will Rogers Igawa, pressing his hands flat on grass, tensing every muscle like a gymnast, raised his body and spun a hundred and eighty degrees, disturbing several people. He ignored their mutterings. He was facing away from the screen and that was what counted. His temples throbbed angrily God's blessing on headaches. Now he had something other than his film to concentrate on.

If she was here, was she crying too?

Clay slipped around silent bodies to view the larger screen, taut between two light poles. Black shadows of moths fluttered, intensifying the sense of doom, wings of death fluttering closer. A man blew his nose loudly; a woman wept aloud. Clay nodded. Demonstration and disorder were alien to most of these people. They needed huge, searing jolts of emotional electricity to rouse them.

Silence.

A young marine, face down in jungle mud. The medal, then darkness and his own taped explanation.

The crowd stirred. Rustled angrily. People rose to their feet. They were ready to avenge, ready for action, ready to form antiwar ranks.

Someone handed Clay the mike.

"Let Lyndon B. Johnson know . . . war . . . disaster . . . destroy every one of us . . . killing . . . slaughter . . . Tell him how we feel . . . fifty thousand strong. . . ." Clay's voice, distorted, magnified, eerie, echoed in the grassy hillocks, died, blared, whirled and faded again into the foggy night.

"Form your groups . . . ready . . ."

If it weren't for an amateur film made summers ago by a group of kids, Clay admitted, pausing, lowering his portable microphone, it would have been impossible to weld together a crowd of this size. If it weren't for the poignancy of the film's beginning and the tragedy of its end—despite the auspicious presence of Lyndon Johnson, the even more auspiciously long Vietnamese casualty list this week, despite his own months of intensive planning, the efforts of every Student for Peace, most of whom were now monitoring their assigned groups into position, the exhortations of notables he'd corralled for this night, the repetition of sad song—Clay was well aware that the earlier picnic ease would have continued and by now half the marchers would be departing full of food and also full of pride that they'd shown their defiance of an undeclared war. The other half, true, would be willing to amble over to the Century Plaza, but with the good-naturedness of a circus crowd leaving the three rings. If it weren't for the flickering on two homemade screens there would be none of this grim haste, none of the furious eagerness, not a single slogan like, "Hell, no, we won't go," right now being chanted angrily into the fog.

Clay, on the hill near the picnic tables, raised his battery-operated microphone and shouted an order to the medical regiment. Around him, TV station wagons ruined grass and overworked cameramen aimed busily. Hickory-smoke odors clung to brick barbecues. On Motor Avenue straggling individuals and groups were being welded into a vast, buckling line. His legions of peace. And once more on this night Clay experienced an emotion so deep that it threatened his composure. He was high on gratitude. He almost wept with gratitude to *An American Hero* and to the film's maker, Igawa. At last he understood York's mystical reverence for Igawa's talents.

On Motor Avenue the press of the crowd separated Ruth Abby and the others from Leigh.

Police, guns dangling at their hips, lined opposite one another at fifteen-foot intervals as if they'd been seeded under paved earth like Cadmus' warriors—yes, Leigh decided, they might easily have sprung from the teeth of the same dragon. Angry red faces were identically dehumanized by helmets with plexiglass shields. Shouting, they swatted people into the corridor they formed. But in terms of her own life, they had always been on her side; when she was little, her father had reiterated, "If you ever get lost, babe, remember, all policemen are your friends." And yet here they were, faceless police swinging at her with sticks. The sudden turnabout dazed her. A new, frightening world. So it wasn't until she passed Fox Studio on Pico that she recognized the man next to her, and since everything had taken on the confusion of a nightmare, it seemed normal that she should say, "Hello, Dr. Schramm."

"Hello there," replied California High's principal.

She was positive he had no idea who she was.

He asked, "Did you bring your flashlight?"

Another part of the nightmare insanity.

"Never mind," Dr. Schramm's gravelly voice reassured. "We'll share mine." And he joined his large arm under hers, switching on a flashlight, shining the yellow beam on a banner swaying ahead of them.

TEACHERS FOR PEACE

He must think she was one of his teachers.

"Keep moving," snarled a policeman. "Keep moving."

"So you're not a teacher? Well, quite a few other California alums are—"

"Dr. Schramm, do you remember Ken Igawa?"

"Igawa? Yes. Yes, of course I do. Fine boy, fine boy. American Legion winner."

"That's his brother, George. He's a doctor now. I wondered if you've seen Ken. He's my husband."

Dr. Schramm examined her. After the pause she'd come to accept as routine, he said, "It's a huge crowd. Well over fifty thousand, the newscasters say. You'll find him later."

Their feet moved slower, for as they marched along Pico the twin lines of cops were closer, narrowing the demonstrators' lane. To their left, hilly vacant lots hid the hotel. Fingers of floodlights dug into the starless dark. On top of a police car a bullhorn, four-mouthed and surely tuned to its loudest decibel, screamed, "KEEPMOVINGKEEPMOVINGKEEPMOVING-KEEPMOVING."

Clay had positioned Nina del Amo toward the head of the march.

Next to Nina was jammed Ken. Crushed to his other side, a long-haired high school girl who must be half the age of the ratty beaver coat she wore. She was paired with a tall, acned boy stuffed into a black leather jacket. They waved identical hand-painted placards, MAKE LOVE NOT WAR, and shouted constantly. With the bullhorns blaring it was impossible to hear them properly, but Ken snared certain words, the four-letter ones, which were turned louder, like commercials. Directly behind Ken a pair of well-dressed matrons marched arm in arm. Segments of their conversation were shouted directly behind his ears. Evidently one was marching for her son: ". . . for my Bobby . . . serious boy . . . doesn't feel it's right. . . . Can't be Conscientious Objector. . . . This war's the one he disapproves of. . . ." They were perfumed like the downstairs of Bullock's Wilshire.

"Shitass," the fur-coated girl bawled.

" . . . thinks you could be tried like at Nuremberg . . . taking part . . ."

"Mother fuckers," shouted the boy.

" . . . an all-A student except C in ROTC . . . "

Ahead of them, placards and banners bobbled wildly.

Ken realized Nina had been mumbling something to him. "What?" he shouted.

"I'm ready."

"Ready?"

"I told you."

"O.K. You told me."

Nina shrugged. Ken forgot her. Now they were descending the Avenue of the Stars—how campy can a street name get?— toward the hotel and he might never in this life have a chance to examine such a scene in the living flesh and not by Cecil B. deMille. He craned his neck, gazing back, then forward. Yeah yeah yeah, a solid mass moving together. Magnificent strength, solidarity. Could he ever pin such a scene onto canvas? No. The answer came promptly. No. Only a painter who truly admired humanity en masse, someone like Siqueiros, say, could get the impact of bodies straining toward a common goal (the Century Plaza? Peace?); you had to have ideals about man-the-mass-animal to paint this sort of thing.

Face it, if you had seen her, you would have turned and run.

Ruth Abby, protected by her friends, held Larry's hand. They were trapped in the Pico bottleneck. Police had narrowed the marchers, yet bullhorns kept screaming, "KEEPMOVING-KEEPMOVINGKEEPMOVING."

"Just like the fuzz!" Ruth Abby yelled in Larry's ear. "Narrow the lanes so we can't move, then tell us to."

"Crowd's ferocious. I better carry Dylie," Larry shouted. "Here. Hold this."

She managed the placards while he unstrapped the baby and hefted him to his shoulders.

"He's coming!"

"He's here!"

"LOOK!"

A helicopter whirred, descending slowly from the fog onto the hotel roof.

"We're saved," someone cried. "S'the second Coming."

And Ruth Abby, excited, cried, "Look, Dylie, it's the Man."

Marshall Mosgrove leaned back in his chair. His table stood in front of the teak screens that hid the hotel kitchens; waiters

swung out with laden trays, returning with metal dangling at
their sides. At Marshall's round table sat Baron York's West
Coast publicity man, his accountant, Eliot Goldsober—a top-
notch tax attorney with the unfortunate profile of an anteater—
two of Baron's writers, wives and Dorot.

Kalpraga enjoyed a choice location and, dizzying acres away,
at the platformed speakers' table, right next to the two empty
seats under the President's Seal, sat Mr. and Mrs. York. Baron
spoke only to his wife, refusing to fraternize with the Welfare
State Democrats around them.

Anonymous men in business suits crowded the entrance.
The band struck up a brassy "Hail to the Chief," and with a
tremendous rustle, like the breaking of a vast wave, the crowd
stood.

The President of the United States entered.

"He's not looking well since his operation," Marshall murmured to Dorot.

The fat writer overheard. "He's got plenty on his mind."

"That bunch of beatniks outside," said the thin writer, "them
he doesn't need."

Without Kalpraga's biting wit, Marshall thought, the writers're solid gray oatmeal.

"But Lady Bird's adorable," gushed the wife of the anteater.

"Way more adorable than she photographs."

Baron York sat before anyone else.

"One thing you've got to say for old Baron." The fat writer
chuckled. "He really believes the crap we grind out for him."

Kalpraga grinds out, Marshall thought, and told himself
that whatever it cost him he wasn't going to spend the rest of
his life stuck in the background with the hacks.

Dorot peered around. She bet she and Marshall were the
youngest couple in the place. Wasn't this the highwater mark
in the life of Dorothy Eleanor McHenry? She'd been right not
to marry Howard Derdivanis, MD of Eureka; she'd been right
to wait for the right man . . . but who'd ever have guessed that
the right man would turn out to be Marshall Mosgrove, whom
she'd known all her life?

She could feel beads of excitement form under her coral
brocade, and she held her thin arms slightly away from her
body so the sweat would dry without staining. Well, shouldn't
she be excited? Dorot placed the scene in historic perspective

as her education had taught her to; these were Americans, the most powerful free men the earth had ever seen, rising of their own free will to pay homage to the man they had duly elected— and whatever that mob outside pretended, this was no tyrannic Nero, no hereditary weakling Louis; they had elected him to be their leader. And she, Dorot McHenry, was proud to be in the panoply of it all. Dorot had goose bumps. This was worthwhile giving up her doctoral thesis, *The Sexual Habits of the Berkeley Female Undergraduate.* She had burned her small brown notebooks, all nine of them. Marshall had insisted— yes, insisted! Since their engagement he'd become very assertive. And he was right. Caesar's wife must be above sex research. Behind lenses Dorot's brown eyes twinkled at her own joke.

There was another tremendous clatter as everyone sat down.

Conversation broke out, but Dorot was too high to join in. Staring at her glittery diamond (Marshall's grandmother had worn it), she let her thoughts continue their pleasant way.

"Dorot!" Marshall whispered sharply. "Al asked you a question."

And Dorot obediently turned to her left to converse with the fat writer.

They dined on salad of chicory, raw spinach and chopped egg, then came filet mignon *forestière,* asparagus with soufléed hollandaise and finally lime water ice. Say what you want about the democratic process, Dorot decided, with it, alas, appetites had declined. Hers was healthy. She was still starving as she scooped the last of her water ice.

KEEPMOVINGKEEPMOVINGKEEPMOVINGKEEP-
MOVINGKEEPMOVING

They were at a dead standstill. The nearest cop thwacked Larry, shouting, "Move along there!"

"Cut that out!" Ruth Abby shrieked. "The baby! He's holding the baby!"

The cop, who was young, examined Larry and Dylie.

"Leave him alone!" Ruth Abby cried.

The young cop examined her. "You better get out of this, the three of you," he shouted and, conferring with the uniform next to him, the two moved aside. Ruth Abby, Larry and Dylan Marx were spat onto the noisy, foggy emptiness of a plowed vacant lot on Avenue of the Stars.

• • •

The sound of a crowd exhilarated Clay.

A crowd was his instrument. Even though he rarely got the opportunity to play, when he did he was the Oïstrakh, the Ravi Shankar, the Rubinstein of crowds. Tonight his instrument was in magnificent pitch. He had played the calm passages at Rancho Park; the crowd had responded in rising crescendos to the film and his speech. Here, near the hotel, the cops stood closer together, at five-foot intervals, and Clay could tell the people crowded between were taut and ready for this onslaught on the climactic finale.

"He ought to be in the banquet hall," Clay said in Nina del Amo's ear.

"Yes."

"You remember what to—"

"I remember," she said, and in the crush managed to raise her right hand as if swearing on a Bible. Her shabby black coat sleeve fell back to display a white forearm. "I remember."

"Two by two in front of the hotel," a cop shouted.

"Fuckup," growled the boy in front of them.

"Good," Clay said. "When I raise my arm."

" . . . so I felt for Bobby's sake . . ."

"We're depending on you," Clay said.

"I'm ready." Nina gave him her phantasmal, droop-lidded smile.

And Clay, with help from various muscular Students for Peace, and SNAP men, moved up a notch in the line.

"Two by two in front of the hotel!" police shouted.

"What was that about?" Ken asked.

"I told you," Nina said.

"You did?"

Blue of a police car's light shone on Nina's face. She leaned toward him. "We're going to get in the hotel. Talk to the President."

"You never said—"

"I did."

"S'insane!" Ken cried. "Who?"

"Me. Clay. And—"

"Wild! This is meant to be a peaceful demonstration."

"Shhhhh."

"They've got us penned in like the Black Hole of Calcutta. Nina, you can't—"

"Sheeyut up!"

"The hell—"

"Want the cops to hear?"

"Yeah yeah yeah! I want them to!"

"Balls, Ken."

"There's old people. Little kids. Babies, even—"

"It's for *them* we're doing it."

This Ken had heard before. "Clay Gillies! That's his line."

"He's spent his whole life trying to help people."

"Nina—"

"First civil rights, then the peace movement."

This was no time to discuss Clay Gillies' humanitarian credentials. "Listen, Nina. It's not just making it into the hotel—"

"He gets nothing out of it!"

"It's starting a riot!"

"Shut up!" she screamed.

"That's what he wants—"

"No!"

"A riot! So this'll be publicized!" Ken turned on the nearest cop. "Listen to me! She's going to—"

Nina slammed her fist in his chest. "Which side're you on?"

"She's going to make a run—"

"Which?" Nina screeched in his ear.

"Move!" the cop shouted.

"SHE'S GOING TO START A RIOT!"

The cop didn't listen. "Keep moving!" The red face contorted furiously. "Two by two in front of the hotel!"

"ARREST HER. SHE'S GOING TO—"

The cop slapped at Ken with his stick. Not a disabling blow but a sharp jab in the small of his back, painful. Kidney searing. Humiliating. Fury swept through Ken. *Police bastard*, he thought, *white police bastard*. He gave a cry of outrage and as the sound came from deep within his belly, Nina's question occurred. Which side *was* he on? Police clubbings? Manufactured riots? War? The coming terror in the name of peace? Please God, why not give another multiple-choice answer?

"KEEPMOVINGKEEPMOVINGKEEPMOVING-
KEEPMOVINGKEEPMOVING," bullhorns blared.

Clay wasn't jostled as much as the others. Massive Smith and even more massive Priddy protected him. He had reached the splashing fountains that divided the avenue in front of the hotel. He tapped the broad shoulders of Priddy, then of Smith.

They held their ground, resisting forward movement. Clay assessed the distance across the wide street and up the great, curving ramps to the doors of the Century Plaza. On the ramps were parked police cars.

And in his belly Clay felt a kind of tightening that was his personal reaction to fear. Stomach muscles coiling like a spring to cancel out any messages (*be careful, watch out, play it cool*) that his brain might try to transmit. In righteous battle Clay was a natural. He might be killed. But cop out—never! The crowd shoved forward between police lines. *An orderly bunch*, Clay thought. He must change that.

Now.

One last time he gauged the hotel. Above each window the light that gave the building its distinctive orange glow seemed redder than he recalled, the distance up the ramp greater.

Now.

He turned to signal Nina. And saw Odessa. Her eyes shone in the brilliant sodium lights. Although he'd never told her exactly what was coming off, she knew it would happen now. She called, "Good luck." He couldn't hear the words, but he saw her mouth form them.

He took a deep breath and raised his arm.

Ken, still shouting at the cop, saw Clay raise his arm.

"S'it." Nina pecked him damply on his cheek.

"Nina, for Christ's sake—" He gripped her arm.

"Let me go."

"Listen, please—"

"Ken—"

He turned to the cop. *"STOP HER!"*

Again the cop slapped at him. Nina squirmed away.

"I want to see the President!" she cried. Her voice might be thin, but—as Ken knew well—its sound could be as insistent as a crazy woman's. (The nuts always get heard.) "I want to see the President. I have a right. My husband was killed in Vietnam."

Clay saw Nina argue with Ken. Ken's mouth opened furiously; so did Nina's. She struggled. Mouths moved simultaneously. Clay turned, ready to go free Nina, but a cop slapped at Ken and then Nina was squirming toward Clay.

"I want to see the President," she cried as they'd planned.

"I want to see the President. My husband was killed in Vietnam."

"She wants to see the President, she has a right." Clay took up the chant. "She wants to see the President. She has a right."

"Her husband was killed in Vietnam." Students for Peace and SNAP members joined in.

"She has a right."

"She has a right."

Surrounding demonstrators took up the cry.

"She wants to see the President. She has a right."

"Her husband killed in Vietnam."

Police flailed energetically. A blow caught Clay on the shoulder. He felt no pain. Nina had reached him.

"NOW!" he screamed.

And Smith and Priddy, heads down, charged at the nearest cops, felling them. Clay held Nina around her loose black coat, propelling her through the gap.

He yelled. He could hear Nina and the others behind them, the long line of marchers, all taking up the cry. "SHE WANTS TO SEE THE PRESIDENT. SHE HAS A RIGHT!"

Clay's feet raced swiftly; his heart pumped elation through his body.

On the ramp, cops sprang to alertness. Clay saw them, but to him they were as unreal and shadowy as the film he'd projected onto homemade screens. How could shadows stop him?

Uniforms erupted through tall glass doors.

He saw mouths moving, bullhorns raised. He saw a cop crouch and raise his arm. Clay was aware that the outstretched blue arm ended in a hand and that hand aimed a gun. He ignored this. He ran.

"SHE HAS A RIGHT!" he yelled.

In the wall of sound he heard a faint break, almost like the sound of a dry twig snapping.

And at that exact moment the spring inside him spiraled open.

Slooooooo-ooooooow . . .

He felt all his movements slow; he felt his legs weaken; he heard himself give a cry. His feet grew heavy. Slowly, ever so slowly, their weight pulled him to the paving.

The pain started.

Icy and cruel, it grew in his brain. Liquid warmed his face;

his sphincter muscles relaxed. His body lay bound to cement. *The cop shot me,* he thought in wonder. *I've had it. . . .*

Something touched his back, as if to feel his heart's action, and from infinitely far away he heard a voice.

"Clay, oh, Clay."

His fingers clenched, his hand arching up in pain. And in that pain he trapped the truth; in that moment he held truth. On our little spinning rock, man would be changed and changed again, then die, other species would arise and wither and the earth's interior lava flows would finally freeze and for a brief eon the dead planet would continue to spin its umbilical orbit around the clutching, maternal sun until she, too, died. On his closed lids Clay saw galaxies that whirled into being, then fell away. The truth lay in flux. Everything was change and so everything remained the same. This breath he was taking lasted through eternity; the neutrons and protons that whirled in the atoms of his brain would continue in some form for ever and ever. He saw the majestic flow of time that had always existed and would exist always. *I never wanted the incomprehensible pettiness of man,* he thought. *I only desired the chill, pure beauty of right that governs the universe. And now, in this unique moment of time, I see, I understand*

thank you

His fingers unclenched. His hand flopped limp.

Odessa saw Clay and Nina del Amo break through the police line; she saw them race yelling across the wide avenue, saw them reach the sidewalk. Suddenly Clay sprawled forward. Face down, he lay still.

Very few others saw the shooting, but those who did panicked. Instantaneously the frenzy spread.

"Hold them! Hold them!" a sergeant yelled. "We don't want another goddam Dallas!"

Police shouted and cursed and swung their clubs. Momentarily they couldn't contain the mob.

Odessa ran across the divided street to the gathering crowd. "Let me through!" she cried. "Let me through!"

She shoved and pushed to Clay. One of his arms was pinned under his chest, the other stretched out at his side. In the pool of blood that widened around his head floated bits of solid matter. She knelt, resting one hand on his back. "Clay," she whispered. "Oh, Clay." With her free hand she gestured the crowd to move back. "Give him room!" she ordered sharply.

"Oh, Jesus! This ties it!" a cop cried.

"Get a doctor."

Someone blew a whistle. "A doctor!"

"I already told the ambulance to get the hell over," shouted a cop with a walkie-talkie.

All was confusion.

Sirens wailed. National Guard appeared in khaki uniforms, helmets and rifles. They began to force the crowd back toward the marching line. Priddy, with a yell, smashed his huge fist into a Guardsman's face. Three other Guardsmen were on him. Photographers and reporters jockeyed for position. A news truck came to a squealing halt. Uniforms, blue and khaki, struggled to form a ring around Clay's fallen body, and to this end a policeman blazed away into the sky with his Colt .38. The crowd fell back.

Odessa still knelt by Clay's head. Nina del Amo, sobbing hysterically, lay across his legs. RG pulled Nina's wrists, forcing her up. A Guardsman took her. "Get back in line, you!" the Guardsman shouted at RG. "The shit I will!" RG shouted back. "S'my brother." And he bent to take off Clay's shoes.

"I'm a doctor," a man called urgently.

"Let him through, let him through."

The doctor, short and slight and wearing a white cotton jacket, knelt over Clay. He felt his back.

"His heart's beating," Odessa said. Tears streamed down her face.

The doctor shook his head.

"It was a moment ago," she insisted.

"It's too late," the doctor replied gently. "It always was."

On the far side of Avenue of the Stars, police struggled. Their fear was the demonstrators might storm the hotel and attack the President. They fought viciously to hold their lines. With shouts that this was a riot and rioters can be shot, they clubbed and slapped. The terrified mob was pressed into a semblance of a line.

The demonstrators were packed too tight to move, yet move they did. Frenzied bodies, some hoping to return to safety, others attempting to reach it ahead. Despite his own fear, Ken noted detail. Stench of sweating, foul breath. Shouts. Brilliant sodium street lights showed middle-aged faces drawn into strange masks of horror, young faces petrified yet alive with gallows fever. Mouths open, eyes glazed.

The fat boy in black leather used his MAKE LOVE NOT WAR placard as a jousting weapon.

"They're shooting!" he yelled at Ken. "Get the fuck out of my way!"

The well-dressed matron, now she was ahead of Ken, struggled to turn back. "You're blocking me, you damn Chinaman, blocking me," she keened. Her face was crimson.

Ken, pressured from all sides, felt the breath being forced from his body. He was being shoved too fast. The veins behind his ears stood out in his effort to keep his equilibrium.

To Ken's left, a small boy was hidden by the mushroom of an enormous cowboy hat. Maybe it was a girl. What was it doing here in this mess? The little kid was on the edge of the demonstrators, but if it went down he (or she) would surely buy it, be crushed to death, and Ken, losing his balance, knew if he were pushed any more he would fall on the child. Back in California High he'd learned how to pivot from Coach Reo, and now—thinking, *They'll really mow me down, the cops, but what else can I do?*—he put the knowledge to use, breaking through the hefty linebackers who wore blue uniforms and blue helmets.

He heard a sharp backfiring noise.

Blong!

Simultaneous with the sound, a blow hit him across the back of his shoulders, and he thought, *This can't be happening, not to me. Why do they have to clout me so damn hard? They don't want me to mash a little kid in a black cowboy hat, do they?*

It never occurred to him that he'd been shot.

Leigh, hey Leigh, he thought as he lost consciousness.

Michele, in her new one-piece lounging pajamas, watched *Man from UNCLE.* Everett went over the day's stock market quotations—he took his work very seriously. As Michele watched, below the frenetic chase scene a ribbon of letters appeared: *While President Johnson and Baron York dine at the Century Plaza Hotel, demonstrators outside erupt into violence. FOR COMPLETE COVERAGE WATCH THE ELEVEN O'CLOCK NEWS.*

"Clay's peace demonstration," Michele said. "They're rioting."

"That's pacifists for you." Everett gave a small laugh to show he was being funny.

Although a faithful David McCallum fan, Michele switched

to Channel 5, which was local. Sure enough, they were tele-
vising the march. The camera angles were all wild and bouncing
as if the cameramen were part of the mass of twisting people.
Police flailed and the demonstrators retreated, shouting. Michele leaned forward anxiously. She remembered her first
Mother's Day almost seven years ago. She had watched televised Alabama violence. How frantic she'd been about Clay.
She was just as frantic now. That was the kind of person she
was.

When Leigh reached Avenue of the Stars, all forward movement stopped. She stood, a hard knob jabbing her spine, her
hand trapped in the incubating warmth of Dr. Schramm's arm-
pit. Bodies squashed around her. On her left were two high-
schoolers, a blonde and her boy friend.

All the time, KEEPMOVINGKEEPMOVINGKEEPMOV-
ING, yet there was no place to go.

Dr. Schramm said, "They must have us marching in a nar-
rower line up ahead."

"S'all blocked up," the high school boy agreed.

"We'll probably be here a long time," said Dr. Schramm.

"Sit down, sit down, sit down," chanted the high school
children. And they shoved their way to sit on the curb of central
shrubbery that divided the avenue.

"Get back in line!" a cop shouted.

"Sit down, sit down, sit down."

A burly blue arm raised a club over the girl's head.

Dr. Schramm stepped forward to face the policeman. "Stop
that, you," he ordered in his graveled administrative tones.

The club descended. Blood appeared on the girl's honey
hair, coursing in streams down her smooth skin. She hunched
forward, clutching her head. The demonstrators milled with
horror and curiosity, trying to see what was going on. Very
few saw, as Leigh saw, blood dripping onto the road, saw the
boy put both arms around his girl's hunched shoulders and raise
his thin face. Pale with concentration and fear, his face that of
a surfer taking a tremendous wave, he let loose a string of
obscenities at the cop.

Again the arm raised high.

"Leave them alone!" boomed Dr. Schramm, reaching for
the blue sleeve.

The policeman jerked from Dr. Schramm's veined grasp.
Sharply he rapped the balding head. *Policemen are our friends.*

... The elderly principal, smiling a baby happy smile, closed his eyes. Leigh gave a shrill cry and freed herself from the crowd to help him. As she did the swirl of reacting bodies carried her sideways into another policeman.

"You! Get back in line!"

"I can't."

"Then you're coming with me."

He pulled at her arm.

She struggled, squirming, grabbing the first idea that entered her numb horror. "I've got to find my husband."

"Disobeying an officer," the policeman said, lifting her by her elbows.

The windows of the black and white bus were netted with heavy wire. A khaki sheriff stood outside with drawn gun.

"Get inside," the policeman ordered in a tone that was neither pleasant nor unpleasant, and for precisely this lack of emotion Leigh found him terrifying. It was in his power to club murderers, burglars, children and high school principals with the same unblinking imperturbability.

The enemy, she thought as she pulled her trembling self aboard. *I'm the enemy.*

At the Athens Street Police Station the people on the bus were herded through a dark green door to be booked; then they were each permitted one phone call.

Leigh spoke to her father. She waited on a bench.

In less than thirty minutes Mr. Sutherland arrived, wearing a crimson alpaca golf sweater, his hair uncombed and standing up sparse and wiry. In February, when he'd started back to his office, he had shaved his red beard and for the first time you could see down each cheek a single, very deep vertical wrinkle. Age carved these strange lines on almost all Sutherlands. Leigh ran to him. He hugged her.

"You all right, babe?" he asked.

"Fine."

He held her away from him, examining her.

"I'm fine," she repeated.

"Sure?"

She nodded. "I'm sorry," she said.

"What about?"

She glanced around the police station. "Dragging you down here."

"I should've been there myself," he said, and strode to the desk, talking to the elderly sergeant in a low, intent voice, pulling from his wallet a plastic-cased card. It must have been printed with the right words.

He returned. "Come on," he said.

"That's all?"

"That's all."

Outside, a patrol wagon was being unloaded. A slow-moving boy was hurried along with a policeman's stick. The slap echoed in the night. Mr. Sutherland stopped, his body tensing as if he were about to throw himself into battle crying a paean to ACLU. It was totally in character, and Leigh expected he would, so she was surprised when he merely gripped her arm and walked briskly a half block to his Lincoln. He opened the door for her. She slid in. With jumpy fingers she reclaimed a pack of Pall Malls from her pocket, managing to extract one, ordering her fingers to stop that dumb twitching. Her father bent by her door, watching through the open window.

"You're *sure* you're all right?" he asked.

"A little shook, that's all," she said, lighting a match. "You used to tell me policemen were my friends. Remember?"

He didn't smile. He steadied the back of her hand so flame touched tobacco; then he leaned both forearms on rolled down window, watching her intently.

"Daddy, what's wrong?"

"Did you see any violence?"

"Plenty. They were clubbing"—she jerked the hand with cigarette in the direction of the police station—"like that. And people were bleeding all over the place. We were arrested for doing nothing."

"That's all?"

"What more do you want?"

"Shooting? Did you hear any shooting?"

"There wasn't any," she said. "At least I didn't see or hear any. But bullhorns were going full blast. And sirens."

"There was some," Mr. Sutherland said.

Her heart expanded, then contracted again. *"He's up in*

Berkeley, safe, thank God, safe and sound."

Her father walked around the car and got in. He didn't take out his keys. "It's a terrible thing," he said, as if to himself, "that they can't let people demonstrate peacefully."

"What about the shooting?"

He didn't answer. He gripped the steering wheel.

"What is it?"

His grip on the wheel tightened. Tendons stood out in his tanned hands.

"Is it the chest pains?" Leigh asked anxiously.

He shook his head.

She stubbed out her cigarette and started to slide across the seat. "I better drive."

"The shooting. They haven't announced how many, but quite a few people were hurt."

Her fingers were twitching worse now. *He's in Berkeley,* she reminded herself. She stopped her slide and at close range stared at her father.

"Babe, I didn't mean to break you two kids up. Maybe subconsciously I was glad, but I swear to God I didn't mean—"

She pulled at his arm. "Daddy!"

"Ken," he whispered hoarsely. "It's Ken."

"He's in Berkeley."

"Here."

"No," she said stubbornly. "Berkeley."

"He was in the march."

"No. He couldn't be. If he'd come down he would have phoned me— Daddy, please, please, please say he's not here."

"Right after you called, Mrs. Igawa—"

"Shot?"

"Yes."

"How badly?"

"Not very."

"How not very?"

"Calm down, babe, calm down."

"Why did she call?"

"To tell you."

"Where is he?"

"Tanglewood Hospital."

"Hospital!"

"His brother's on the staff."

"George. Yes. Take me there."

"Babe, calm down. He's all right. A few scratches they're cleaning up, that's all."

"Take me there," she ordered. "Now."

She didn't let her reflexes take over. She breathed deeply. She didn't cry. Her father talked; sometimes he was telling her he was sorry for any part he had in the separation, sometimes he was trying to reassure her. She didn't pay any attention. Her foot pressed on an imaginary accelerator as if she could move the big Lincoln faster than the illegal seventy-five her father was doing.

Tanglewood Hospital sprawled low and flat, dark oblongs wounded by slits of light. Mr. Sutherland stopped in the white Emergency zone. A gradual flight of steps led to the entry.

"You needn't come in," Leigh said.

"I want to."

"You ought to go home and rest," she said. "All this excitement, it's bad for you."

"Listen to me," her father said. "Listen to me."

"I'll stay here."

"You can't see him." Mr. Sutherland reached for her arm.

"Right now," she disagreed.

"You can't."

"The divorce isn't final. We're still married. Who's going to stop me?"

"You won't be able to."

"Why?"

The grip on her upper arm tightened. "He's in the operating room."

"Oh, God!"

"Babe—"

"He's all right," she cried. "You said he's all right."

"I lied."

"How bad?" She was shaking all over.

"His chest."

"His chest? Is he . . ." She couldn't bring herself to say the terrible, awesome, final word. "Is he . . . ?"

"No. Of course not."

"He'll be all right?"

"Mrs. Igawa, she said—they said—" He took a sharp breath. "She didn't know."

Leigh shook off her father's restraining hand. She flung open her car door, left it that way, racing across sidewalk, starting up shallow steps, tripping in the middle of the first flight, pushing herself to her feet, this time taking two at a time. Her heart thudded everywhere. Strong fluids unglued her muscles; her legs shook; it took an effort to control her bladder. Any fears she might have felt about her father dying were minor compared to this. She stumbled again; then she was at tall glass doors. Closed doors. She yanked at a massive bronze pull, one door then the other. Both refused to budge. She pushed against glass, mindless as a bird trapped indoors. A nurse appeared on the other side, pointing through glass. Leigh noticed gilt letters:

Between 9 PM and 7 AM
Please use the side entrance

She started down the steps. Her father met her.

Michele sat in her dark dining room, her face buried between her hands. Everett's engagement ring had twisted to the inside of her finger and the marquise diamond pressed into her cheek. She was cold as ice but she didn't move to get a robe. The police had phoned as she and Everett were getting ready for bed, at eleven thirty. She'd been up ever since. How could she sleep? How? She had wept for Clay, yet as she wept she had been thinking, *It's all a terrible mistake; he's not dead, he's still alive.*

Birds started chirping, but no light seeped through inner-lined drapes. Aimlessly she padded into the living room, sinking down on thick carpet near the couch, the same spot they had made love. . . . *Clay, you're alive, you have to be.* She touched the wool carpet, stroking the nap. She was shivering.

Everett must have heard her moving around. He turned on the hall light and stood there blinking in his rumpled pajamas. Clay never had worn pajamas.

"I just felt too restless to stay in bed." Michele looked up at Everett, apologizing for her too-evident grief over the death of husband number one. "It's the shock."

"Death is frightening."

"Poor little Lissa . . . she's an orphan."

"She's my little girl."

"Everett, you're so good to us."

"You're my girls." He came over, lifting her to her feet, comforting her against his large, soft body. "She's my little girl."

"Of course she is."

"And I want to adopt her. But I don't want her to forget

her own father. She must always remember him."

"Yes."

"He was idealistic."

Michele agreed.

Everett went on. "He died for what he believed in."

Michele started to sob again. She didn't want to, but she couldn't halt the tears, for Everett, without realizing it, had put his freckled, manicured finger on a sore point, the point that had tormented her through the years of her marriage to Clay and tormented her still. Clay, so elusive and impossible to understand, was willing to live (and die) for abstract beliefs that Michele's practical heart told her nobody else really believed in, no, not even while they were mouthing the fine words. And. More important, Clay never in a million years would have lived (or died) for her. It wasn't fair. She had loved him. She loved him still. She began to cry with terrible, strangling gasps. Everett patted the sheer nylon over her back. "Shhhh," he whispered over and over. "Shhhh."

Finally she managed to calm herself.

"It's the shock," she apologized again.

"I know."

"The shock."

"Come to bed," Everett said. "You need your sleep. Tomorrow there'll be a lot to do. Reporters and that sort of thing. Probably we'll have to handle the funeral."

"You're so wonderful to me, Everett."

"I love you."

She did need her sleep, otherwise she'd be all haggard, especially in black. She'd wear her new black silk, she decided, permitting her husband to lead her toward their bedroom. Her grief was the purest, most intense emotion she would ever experience (Clay gone from this world, no it couldn't be, yes it was, the emptiness opening under her), yet she couldn't help reminding herself that blonde hair, curves and black silk are a fabulous combination, and those reporters, if they came, would be sure to notice.

As they passed the closed door of Lissa's room, Everett said, "Shall I tell her?"

"I will."

Lissa was drinking her breakfast chocolate when her mother came in.

"Uncle Everett said you'd sleep late, way later'n now," Lissa accused. "He's shaving. He says I'm not going to my riding lesson."

"No," Michele agreed.

"Why?"

"Lissa—"

"And why didn't you sleep late?"

"I wasn't tired." Michele sat in one of the powder blue chairs. "Liss, come here to Mommy."

"He said I couldn't put on TV." Lissa drained her mug. Wet brown glistened on clear skin.

"That was right."

"It'd 'sturb you, he said." Lissa wriggled from her chair and came to shout next to her mother. "You're up. C'n I now?"

Michele pulled her child close. Fingering away the chocolate mustache, she gave a deep sigh.

Lissa had no inhibitions about showing affection. She hugged Michele and gave her a loud kiss. "Don't be sad, Mommy."

"Last night your daddy . . . passed away."

"Passed away?"

"He died," Michele said. "Your daddy wanted to talk to the President about Vietnam and they, the police, didn't understand. So they shot him."

"Like they shot JFK?"

Michele nodded.

"Where is he?" Lissa demanded. "C'n I see him?"

"He's getting ready for the funeral."

"I remember. Like Grandpa."

"Yes."

"C'n I watch now?"

"Not today."

"Why?"

"It's not respectful and—"

"Just Captain Kangaroo?"

"Grandma and a lot of other people'll be coming over."

"Please, Mommy!"

Everett, wearing his black suit, the new one that he wore to dinner parties and the theater, stood in the door. The lime smell of his aftershave reached Michele.

Lissa ran to hug his waist. "Mommy's up now, Uncle Everett," she cried. He stroked her fine blonde hair. "You promised if I kept quiet—"

"One program," he said in his deep voice. "Just one."

Lissa trotted away, humming. Everett fixed instant coffee with the Everboil water nozzle. In the adjacent family room an announcer shrieked, ". . . the antiwar demonstration which took the life of one man and injured thirty-four—"

Everett hurried to the connecting arch. "Change the channel, Lissa, hon. And turn it down."

He returned, handing Michele her coffee; he got her the half and half, sat next to her.

"Drink," he said.

"I don't feel like it."

"Something hot'll do you good." Shadows puffed under his pale eyes and his mouth was somber. Everett was acting the way he thought people, she in particular, expected him to act. A mourner.

Still . . .

Maybe in a strange way Everett was mourning.

For didn't this grief belong to him, as it belonged to her, to Leigh, to Ken, York, Marshall Mosgrove, Dorot McHenry, RG Richards, to everyone in their entire generation? However different Clay's goals had been, he was part of them. Despite your varying loves, hates, ways of life, the death of someone your age can't help but affect you in a much more personal way, an immediate way, than the passing of some elder, even one as well loved as Michele's father, for isn't the death of a person your age a preview of your own death? Michele sipped her well-creamed coffee, pondering the mysteries of life, death and her love for Clay. It wasn't until Everett put his arm around her shoulders that she realized tears crawled down her cheeks.

As Everett had guessed, they did have to handle the funeral. Michele couldn't think straight, so Everett made most of the decisions for burying his predecessor. It's a sign of the times, Michele decided. Everett spoke with the undertaker, he ordered a plain oak casket, which would have pleased Clay, and he bought a lot in the cemetery in Westwood. Clay would lie near Marilyn Monroe, which he wouldn't have cared about one way or another, but which pleased Michele.

"You're being just wonderful," Michele told her husband.

"I'm glad I can do it for Lissa."

A tremendous funeral. St. Albans overflowed with every type. A great many California alums, like Dorot McHenry and Marshall Mosgrove, as well as teachers and even the principal, Dr. Schramm, attended. The front pews were crowded with a

club Clay had founded; male and female members alike wore
large peace symbols dangling from their necks. And the group
of black people that Clay used to work with, Odessa Norris
sat erect and stony faced (she was looking a lot older, Michele
decided), and RG Richards slumped with his long, shaven head
between his hands. Then, too, because of Michele, it was a
society funeral. Many of her fellow Las Palomas attended, and
Michele couldn't help remembering how silly she'd been worrying they would care about Clay. All the Sutherlands were
there, including poor Leigh, ghastly pale but dry-eyed; she and
Ken had been married here and now Ken was probably dying.

Everett handled Clay's estate, as he insisted on calling old
blue denims and underwear, one pair of black shoes in need
of soles and a pair of worn Keds, lined paper with writing and
a gold pocket watch. Everett gave the shoes and clothes to the
motel maid and burned the notes—they seemed, he told Michele, to be some sort of plan for the demonstration. The watch,
Michele thought, probably had belonged to Clay's grandfather
Claibourne, and she dropped it in the manila envelope with the
ruby ring that had belonged to Clay's mother, saving both in
the bank vault for Lissa.

Since Clay's "estate" included less than two dollars, Everett
not only had to pay the funeral expenses but also had to ante
up for Clay's motel bill.

———— • 4 • ————

JOHNSON SPEAKS AS POLICE ATTEMPT TO CURB PRO-
TEST
    STUDENT AGITATOR KILLED IN ANTIWAR DEM-
ONSTRATION
    BARON YORK ADDRESSES FUND RAISING WHILE
SON'S MOVIE INCITES ANTIWAR DEMONSTRATORS TO
CLASH
    1,300 POLICE BATTLE 50,000 RIOTERS
young children and puppies played in the park, there was

folk singing and picnics on the grass, then the film and speeches started.

Pigs used their gestapo tactics on children. IS LOS ANGELES WORSE THAN OAKLAND?

1,000 police contain 75,000 rioters.

a young woman claiming to be the widow of a serviceman killed in Vietnam led a group that crashed a wall of seventy-five to a hundred police . . . name not revealed . . . later released to the custody of her family. . . .

It was a hell of a mess, wrote a veteran reporter. Those people were like animals. The police did a fine job.

Clay Gillies, student leader prominent in civil rights activities as well as founder of Students for Peace on the Berkeley campus, was shot to death in the scuffle. Unfortunate accident, the police chief is quoted as saying.

Thirty-four injured, eight seriously.

It was a chilling example of police brutality, wrote a veteran reporter. The police went around clubbing middle-aged women and young children.

Death of student agitator starts riots on California campuses.

Motion picture actor Baron York was master of ceremonies for the nonpolitical function to raise money for the John F. Kennedy Memorial Hospital in Dublin, Ireland. The President laughingly admitted to being a fan of York's, "But as an actor only," he added.

Young York's inflammatory motion picture, unofficial sources state, will be shown commercially.

York had read every paper two or three times. It was later Monday afternoon and newsprint lay thick on the carpet. The soundless television screen showed for the hundredth time, at least, a view of the fracas at the Century Plaza. An hour ago, on 2, there had been a brief clip of Clay's funeral, somber Students for Peace bearing his coffin.

York gazed out the window. Rain had started again. Across the street on fencing that protected a construction site was black-painted: *Oh Thou great flaming Prick of the universe, have mercy on all us miserable sinners*. Two girls, obviously students (and miserable sinners?) were moving into the building across the street; bright-eyed and bushy-tailed, bundled up against the rain, from a lipstick-red Corvair they lugged Samsonite suitcases, a record player, a portable TV, cartons crammed with paperbacks and LP albums, a bulbous cloth sitar case, a guitar, a six-foot cardboard blow-up of the Rolling Stones in drag. York smoked, his good elbow resting on the dusty window ledge. He'd lived here less than a year, yet it seemed to him that he'd seen generation after generation of college girls enter and depart the university . . . he thought of *Drosophila*, the short-lived fruit fly.

A rapping at his chamber door.

Quoth the silent York, nevermore.

More rapping.

York inhaled and through blue wreaths of cigarette smoke watched the girls; even from this angle, even in loose raincoats, it was obvious that both were stacked, as good as any the Great Stony Face had bedded in his heyday.

"Come on, York," shouted a masculine voice. Familiar? Maybe. Who cared? "I know you're in there. So let me in!" *Knock knock knock knock knock.*

York closed his eyes. *Go. Leave me alone. I fly over this shit. I am not part of it, I never was, I never will be.* Finally the knocking ceased and footsteps receded.

Time floated.

Marshall Mosgrove, his most honest, square-shooter grin plastered across his honest, square-shooting face, asked the manageress, a hag with wine-colored birthmarks twining down one side of her scrawny neck, if it would be possible for her to let him into Mr. York's apartment. He was a friend of Mr. York's. Here Marshall traded his smile for an expression of concern. He was pretty sure Mr. York was in, but nobody answered. Marshall needn't have worried about expressions. The old woman stood in the doorway, never veering her gaze from some old Greer Garson movie. She pulled from her wrap-around housedress pocket a key on a wooden tag. "Bring it back," she muttered, still eyeing Greer.

Cigarette smoke fogged York's apartment. Food decaying in partitioned aluminum TV-dinner trays, newspapers strewing the floor, an open door to a bathroom in equal shambles. The disorder upset Marshall—his own place, now minus Stan Kielty, he kept immaculate—but it was the rotten odor, garbage combined with sour vomit, that got to him. Marshall's sense of smell was keen.

York didn't look up. He stared through rain-drenched glass. Marshall, while disliking York for his acid tongue, at the same time had always felt a tug of kinship; York's arm he equated with his own inner lacks.

He said quietly, "Hello, York."

"So," York replied, not turning, "for every door there's a key."

"The manageress lent it to me," Marshall said. "I explained about you being my friend."

"Creative thinking."

"How long've you been like this?"

"Always."

Marshall, trying not to inhale, coughed. "It's enough to give anyone lung cancer."

"Take some and go."

"I just got here."

"And close the door behind you."

"It's not good."

York turned. The dark glasses that curved around his narrow face gave him the look of a tremendous whiskered fly. "Lung cancer isn't good? You're a genius, you know that?"

"I mean, it's not good for a person to be alone like this."

"Tell me, what's so great about the alternative?"

"It's healthier to be with people."

"Healthier?" York nodded at the window. "Out there live cheats, liars, murderers, rapists, thieves, perverts, warmongers, destroyers of little children."

"People aren't like that," Marshall said, too loud, for he was remembering Mrs. York's renovated antique desk.

"I say they are."

"They aren't," Marshall insisted.

York unbuttoned the cuffs of his blue wool shirt, pushing up sleeves that covered his good and bad arms. Marshall knew from a nonstop weekend conference in Baron York's library (at one point Kalpraga had passed out cold on the black leather couch) that York was an addict. There was a tremendous difference, however, in the intellectual knowledge and the visual proof of needle-scarred, ulcerated, deformed white flesh.

Marshall swallowed loudly.

"In here," York said, "I have my own company. A harmless junkie."

Marshall couldn't stop staring at York's arms.

York went on, "When I first realized it, I told myself, 'York, you are weak.' I hate weakness. And being an addict's the surest sign that you're weak. You don't even have charge of your own body. I hated myself for it. After a while, though, I realized something. At least it's only destroying *me*." York took off dark glasses, squinting at Marshall with contracted pupils. "Mosgrove, aren't you going to tell me it isn't healthy?"

Marshall lifted from a chair an aluminum tray that contained remnants of unknowable foods; he brushed at blue leather. Dust rose. He sat. "Your health isn't exactly why I'm here," he said, giving what he hoped was a friendly laugh.

"I'd forgotten that," York said. "What does bring you?"

Marshall glanced around him at scattered papers.

"I'd forgotten that, too," York said. "I'm getting forgetful all the way around. You're my new brother."

"I've gotten friendly with your family, yes."

"Blood brother."

"I guess you might say we have a relationship, your parents and me."

"Did our mama send you?"

"The place is stuffy. Can we open a window?"

"No."

Marshall took a Cert, crushing it between his teeth for the minty odor. "I finally got her to let me come," he said. "She certainly didn't send me."

"Oh?"

"She and your father want you to withdraw the film."

"I'll bet they do." York smirked. "Mosgrove, you know what . . ."—York pressed his thumb into coiled fingers as if shooting a needle—" . . . is like?"

"Doesn't it give you hallucinations?"

"Me, it grooves more than an eight-hour orgasm. It's better than coming eight full hours with Claudia Cardinale. Understand? But that's nothing to the jollies I get watching the news. Mosgrove, there's news at eight in the morning, at nine, noon, one, four, four thirty, five, six, seven, there's the ten o'clock news, the eleven o'clock news. The midnight news. I live for the news . . . to watch my father explaining the peace march and my part in it. That's better than *anything*! Think how it'll be when my film's on? Now, you tell me why I should give that up."

Marshall mopped his forehead. "It smells in here. Can't you open a window?" After a negative silence had stretched to the breaking point, Marshall said, "What you mentioned before, about everyone being rotten, that interested me."

"Our stepmama's been showing her goodies."

"You know about the files?"

"I suspected it—common practice among certain public figures."

"Well, you must admit that the people involved in making that film—"

"Were the scum of the earth?" York put in.

And at the same moment Marshall finished. "—were pretty indiscreet."

"Indiscreet! That is fabulous!"

"I'm serious."

"Come on, Mosgrove, admit you could make millionaire, thinking up titles for movies."

"The idea's to expose them."

"Expose?"

"That's what your father's people decided. It'll ruin their lives."

York burst out laughing. Marshall had forgotten the sound of York's laughter. Chalk on blackboard was pleasant compared to York's laugh. York threw back his thin neck and slapped his thin knees.

"Ruin their lives!" he brayed. "Jesus! Are you funnee." He turned bleak. "Listen, Halvorsen's six feet under. Gillies was planted this morning. Is there a hot line to purgatory? You figure she's got influence in hell?"

"Others are involved."

"I suppose you're aware that Ken Igawa's on the critical list?"

"I saw Leigh at the funeral today."

"So you'll have to admit we're a fine, dead issue."

"There's others."

"A very dead issue."

There was pressure on Marshall's bladder.

"Mind if I use the head?" he asked.

"Help yourself."

Marshall wished he'd waited. Gray slimed the sink; remains of cigarette butts floated in yellow water. Marshall flushed, then, with the toe of his polished black shoe, fastidiously lifted the seat.

When he returned to the living room, York asked, "Something occurred to me. Why're you so hot to save everyone from embarrassment? Are you and Dorot involved in some sort of sex scandal?"

Marshall shook his head.

"So?"

"Friends?"

"They're my friends, that's all."

"You know I used to surf with Stryker." Marshall regretted the name as he said it.

York took off his glasses, again squinting scrutiny. Marshall mopped his forehead, the back of his neck.

"Smells in here," he muttered.

"What's the reading matter," York asked slowly, "on Stryker Halvorsen?"

"He's dead."

"The grateful dead," York said sourly. "What?"

"Nothing."

"We both know, you and me, that she has something on the Holy Ghost. Now. What's the scam?"

"Nothing, I tell you."

"The invisible worm that flies in the night gnawed Stryker not?" York replaced his dark glasses.

Marshall mopped his forehead, popped another Cert in his mouth.

York said, "You and Stryker did a lot of camping together. You spent your summers camping."

"No!"

"You just said yes. Surfing, you said."

"One summer. One summer surfing—"

"How fervent you are. You were hung up on Stryker—"

"No!"

"—and he on you. Right?"

"No. No!"

"Come on. So I'm a junkie and you're a fag. We're today's swingin' youth, man."

Marshall sighed, sweated, mopped, sat back in the blue leather chair. Sighed again. "I am. Not all the way— Yes. All the way. I'm ashamed of it. I hate it. But Stryker wasn't. He was brave, honest, good, the only decent person I've ever known."

"You're bleeding all over my rug."

"He gave his summers to be with poor kids. He needed the money, but he gave his summers. Nobody ever heard him say a bad word about anyone. He was good. He was brave. One time we were surfing, a huge storm, and every last one of us chickened out. Except Stryker."

"I'm aware that the government doesn't bestow its gratitude on goose-livers."

"It's over. Buried. But I want it left clean. Listen, York, if you can understand this, Stryker was the only clean, decent, good thing in my life. I never told this to anyone."

"It's easier, isn't it, to admit you're a homo if you're talking to a junkie? Where do you fit in my stepmother's plans?"

Marshall swallowed several times, gulping like a frog. He said, "They want to discredit the film; they want to say after your mother died you were an innocent who fell in with a bad crowd. They'll sling mud at everyone connected with it."

"We've already admitted everyone's fucked," York said. "Anyway, where do you fit in?"

"I'm to go to the inquiry. Give information."

"Why you?"

"I know everyone who worked on—"

"I meant, why you? You're so in love with goodness and decency—"

"Don't."

"Why should you do it?"

"I'm . . . it's no excuse, I know, but I'm weak. A chicken." Marshall bent his head. "It stinks in here, York. She knows about me. There's been another . . . episode. But even if she knew nothing—well, I admit this. I'd do it. I'm weak. . . . You know a young lawyer has a rough time starting out . . . I—you know me. York, I have trouble with people. . . . They don't like me. Your father can be a tremendous help. I'll be somebody . . . it's the only way for me, really."

"Mosgrove, you're a fine, true-blue mother."

"I know it."

"What do I have to do?"

"After you've withdrawn the film, you'll go to a place you'll be looked after."

"That's all?"

"All."

"Can you give one good reason why I should do it?"

"I just did."

"I don't consider it a good reason, you making a career of sucking up to my father."

Marshall rose. So did York. They faced one another. Marshall had the advantage, being considerably taller, weighing almost twice as much.

"You're wrong, that's why, York. We aren't destroyed." Marshall closed his eyes. "The smell's foul." Opened his eyes. "So all of us're wounded. But who isn't? Your stepmother's files prove that. Pry into any life hard enough and you'll find something he'd rather forget." Marshall paused. "Probably Ken'll make it. I *know* he will. And Leigh's still crazy about him. I saw her at the funeral today—God, she looked terrible. But Leigh's father arranged an abortion for her while Ken was out of the country, and Dorot's guess is Ken doesn't know about it. *If* he finds out, Dorot thinks, the divorce'll go through. And whatever you think of their kind of marriage, they surely need one another now." Marshall's throat ached. He peeled off another Cert. "Michele's trying to raise Gillies' child, trying to work out a marriage. How would it be for the little girl if it were plastered all over the country that Michele had to drop out of high school to get married. And her father! God knows, Gillies' file is the fattest by far." Marshall inhaled. "How can you stand this?" He veered to the window, slid it open, leaned on the ledge gulping at fresh, damp air. "Ruth Abby's married, has one baby, almost another. Hippie or no, she's doing a good job as a wife and mother; even the investigator had to admit it. She'd probably prefer to raise her family so the world doesn't knew she slept with no less than fifty-two known partners and was booked umpteen times on narcotics charges. Dorot's a bright girl, whatever her private life. And me . . . well, I'm not a very great guy, I admit it. You might even say I'm pretty rotten. But I don't think I'm vicious or vindictive, and I have tried to overcome my tendencies. There's a lot worse lawyers— judges, even—than I'll be." Marshall, for the first time found himself loudly voicing the truth, the simple truth. The past conversations of his life, he realized, had been sad, strung-together words that he hoped would impress his listeners. Truth, he decided, breathing in sweet, rain-washed air, was a heady sensation. "We aren't whole. But what group of people ever was?"

"Bravo! Like I said, grooving California youth." York worked his thin, pale fingers—he had only eight, five and three—like a karate expert.

Marshall stepped back apprehensively. "What're you going to do?"

"As you request. Withdraw the film and hie myself to a Synanon."

"Don't joke."

"I kid you not. Your eloquence has swayed me. How can I stand by and see you cast yourself as Judas Iscariot?" And gaunt, whiskered face crumpled into the most desperate expression Marshall had ever seen. Fully expecting York to hurl himself out of the open window, Marshall moved a preventive step forward. York remained motionless. "Let's can the shit," he said. "Honesty for honesty, Mosgrove. Doesn't it occur to you that I've been guilty unto death about Gillies and Igawa? Less about Gillies—he knew what he was getting into. But Igawa. He's decent, not a user of people. And he had it in him to be one of the greats. And *I* let Gillies use him. Let? I encouraged Gillies to use him! I . . . I never mingled with people before. Never interfered. And when I did. . . ." York turned to the window. Marshall couldn't see his face. "Buddyboy, I'm seeking absolution. And the first step to shrive my soul is to get the hell out of the way and not destroy any more lives."

York ran into the bathroom. Marshall saw him ferret around the medicine cabinet, emerging with a Baggie of white powder that he untwisted and shook into the rain.

"It's not raining rain you know, it's real fifty-buck snow." His thin body started to tremble. "Oh, Jesus, Mosgrove, you don't know what it's going to be like. *You don't know.*"

"I think I do," Marshall said gently.

On their way down in the tiny elevator, York, shaking harder, said, "You'll come out of this smelling like a rose."

"I should. Wasn't I the one of us smart enough to figure you don't fight the older generation, you join 'em?"

As they stepped into the drizzle, Marshall straightened his meaty shoulders under his flannel jacket, his cheeks seemed to harden and his appearance shifted from honesty to a working politician's guarded openness, a Young Candidate coming on strong. On the fence across the street, he noticed, some college prankster had painted in black: *Oh Thou flaming Prick of the universe, have mercy on all us miserable sinners.* It was, Marshall decided, a typical sign of your Berkeley moral decay. He put his hands in his pockets and came up with the wood-tagged key to York's apartment.

"Hey!" York called after him. "Where you going?"

"I promised to give this back."

When Marshall came out again, York was wildly revving the motor of his sports car. The lights were on.

Marshall, who had flown up, said firmly, "I'll drive. It's a long, rough trip."

• • •

Ruth Abby curled in the hollow of the double mattress, tears pouring down her full face, gathering in her neck. She had cried herself to sleep the past three nights. Clay Gillies had been her friend. But even if he hadn't been, she would have wept, for she classified Clay as someone she wanted to sit in with, along with Albert Schweitzer, Buffy Ste. Marie, Pope John XXIII, Gilgamesh, Timothy Leary, Bob Dylan; Clay had been a pure, and she certainly would have gone to his funeral today except old-fashioned ritual turned her off and she didn't think Clay would have wanted it. Anyway, her mother, if Clay had been a friend, would have certainly been there. The hell with Mother. Ruth Abby's tears continued to flow.

A soft whimpering cry came from the sanded-down crate where Dylan slept. Ruth Abby tensed, but it was Larry who got out of bed. The mattress lay directly on the floor and she felt the vibration of his bare feet crossing the creaking boards.

"S'he O.K.?" she whispered.

"Fine." Larry came back, kneeling to crawl back under covers. He twined his cold feet around her warm ones.

"I've been up tight about him since the march," she said.

"S'true. Children *are* a hostage to fortune."

"What if he'd been hurt?" As she said this her stomach ached. "Turn over," she whispered. "It's hurting again." Obligingly Larry rolled over and she used his backside as a heating pad.

"I've been doing a lot of thinking," she said into the darkness.

"Me, too."

"Yeah . . ."

"Maybe we do need a nicer place."

"I guess this is pretty crummy . . . no toilets. . . ."

He said, "You can't live the same once you have children."

Ruth Abby sighed.

Larry sighed.

"But we won't stuff phoniness in them!" Ruth Abby burst out fiercely. "We won't be like our folks!"

Ken was trapped in pain.

At first he was conscious only of pain; pain was a physical presence, an iron maiden built expressly for the chest, and the vivid landscape of his mind was strewn with instruments of torture, racks, rusting thumb screws, whips, lashes knotted with iron; his nightmare took place in a world tunneled with foxholes dug by his victorious enemy, pain. The horror and detail of his nightmares might be awesome, but he kept a certain humility about the whole thing, knowing the creativeness of his vision came courtesy of those cold, blistering shots—"Roll over on your side"—of Demerol.

From his window he could see the sky, soft blue, rippling gray, darkening blue, yellow smog and an occasional jet. There must be a tree under this window, for though he rarely saw a bird, the air was alive with song. Sparrows, he guessed.

His perceptions enlarged. There was still pain, but either he was becoming immune to the drugs or they were doping him less. He was aware. Outside his door a sign, NO VISITORS, but once that sign came down he would, he knew, have to have reached certain decisions.

At first he pondered abstractions. While nurses nursed and doctors doctored his torn chest, questions came at him. He tried to understand the time in which he lived. It seemed so full of violence seen in every living room, so full of tension bared to jockstrap nakedness; there was hatred between races, sexes, generations and every sort of faction from hippies and yippies and trippies to Birchers and Black Power. On a larger scale, there warred tremendous, implacable systems, communism and capitalism. The world seemed sliding toward the brink of implosion. Yet was it the worst of times? The people he knew, the ugliness he'd so recently been part of, were they so different from the peoples and struggles of other ages? For example, were the Children's Crusades any more senseless than the war in Vietnam? Was his riot worse than other riots? Did Ken Igawa's discontent have anything to do with his unique time, the sixties? He thought of humanity intertwining and clouting since the day man had first raised his hairy hand with the first tool, which also happened to be the first weapon. And then Ken Igawa asked, *Why, when we're each God's poor moment, why are every single one of us so intent on screwing it up for ourselves and for others?*

The big Qs are the easy ones. The answers, while they concern you, never affect you.

Five days he'd been in Tanglewood. That morning they had taken out the IV and the catheter. A half hour earlier he had managed the voyage to the adjacent head and, returning, he'd climbed aboard panting and weak to stare out the window. Gray sky and a faraway helicopter.

The door opened. Creaked shut. Tentative woman's footsteps halted. She was on the far side of the bed and he couldn't see her, but light familiar scents floated on hospital odors.

The small qs.

The time has come, walrus, to think of the small qs, the personal questions with the difficult answers.

After a full minute of silence Ken said, "Hey Leigh."

"How did you know it was me?" she asked, surprised.

He, too, was surprised. The sound of her voice, soft, low-pitched, came as a genuine shocker. He'd thought he was finished with that madness, that insanity which had overtaken him in his eighteenth year. He'd figured the bitterness of the last months, the overwhelming pain of the last few days, had cured him. But inside his aching chest he felt a crazy lurch. Joy. Pure joy. *Territorial Imperative* says man hacks it for his own bit of turf. Not for love. Ken Igawa's chest told him otherwise. Well, he must be the exception that proves the rule, right, Mr. Ardrey? Ken ordered himself to conduct himself with restraint until he figured if he could take the intensity of pain that went with his way of loving.

He said, "Footsteps are more unique than fingerprints."

"Oh."

"And no nurse comes on like that. They bustle and pull and give injections. Is the sign off the door?"

"No."

"That means I'm not up to visitors."

"Me?"

"You."

"May I stay?"

"Does it look like I can toss you out?"

"Ken . . . turn around?"

"No."

"Please?"

"I'm trying to think." His hands closed, clinging to the rails which were up on his side.

She moved around the bed.

And he was forced to look at her. A girl. A nice-looking girl, true, with large hazel eyes, good bones and a skin that, if you were a painter, you could tell took the light well. He couldn't remember the world population statistics, but there must be a billion girls similar. So why did he feel his lungs wouldn't function, his glands wouldn't secrete, his heart wouldn't pump without this one? An ordinary girl trying to control the trembling of her lipstickless mouth. What was so special about her?

"Hey, you cut your hair," he said.

"Uh huh."

"Looks better long."

"Please, Ken, talk to me."

"Aren't I?"

"You're talking at me," she said. "I've been so miserable."

"You needn't worry. I'm making it back to health."

"I mean about us."

A stretcher or some other wheeled cart was pushed slowly along the hall past his door.

"You're taking a long time," he said. "Some people take longer to adjust, that's all."

"I can't."

He looked away. A bird flapped by the window, a sparrow.

"I hate her!" Leigh burst out. "I hate her!"

"Nina?"

"Yes. Nina. She hasn't been here. Not once!" Leigh spoke with a venomous satisfaction that he'd never heard from her.

"She's the girl who ran into the hotel," he said. "The girl who was quote released in a state of shock to the custody of her parents. I bet she's in a sanitarium someplace. She always was a poor risk, Nina. Three hours a week on the couch, every sort of psychosomatic ailment, big on interracial mingling. That girl, believe it or not, never has screwed a white guy—"

"Ken, please..."

"Don't tell me you haven't done a little discreet sacking down?" The words hurt, and therefore his voice came out with far more emotion than he intended to let enter the conversation.

She walked a few steps, facing the corner. After a minute or so she came back, half kneeling by the high bed so her face was on a level with his.

"I didn't," she whispered. "I couldn't."

Her skin was blotchy, her eyes red and wet. He wished he weren't so weak. He wished she looked better. If she looked better and he felt stronger he was positive he would have been able to evaluate the situation rationally. As it was, instinctively, he reached out and took her right hand, gripping fine bones as tightly as he'd gripped the metal. He held so hard that his knuckles whitened and blood left her fingers. What color was her hand? His? What difference did it make? The ugliness and pain and confusion, dark beasts, fled. Pain receded. *Hey,* he thought, *hey. Maybe I'm going to accept it. We're married. She's my wife. Why fight it? Everyone else can fight it, but why should I?*

Ken Igawa signed his armistice with the world.

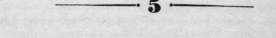

At first the Los Angeles Board of Education, divided and embittered on the busing issue, had denied permission for use of California High facilities as part of the twentieth reunion, maintaining that the program planned was too inflammatory for these troubled times. But political strings were tugged, and the Class of '60 was granted the auditorium to honor its controversial dead.

That June day, a Santa Ana wind blew desert heat across the city. On the school lawns, boys and girls in shorts licked ice cream cones. A dozen or so police officers, sweating into their uniforms, kept wary eyes on the lounging, racially integrated students as well as on network TV news trucks. Above the two main entries of the auditorium were strung banners black-printed: *In Memoriam, Clay Gillies.*

The Marxes and the Igawas, who exchanged annual dinner invitations, arrived simultaneously. Together they descended the slanting aisle, expressing surprise at the large student turnout and gratitude that someone had thought to rope off the front rows for alumni.

Ruth Abby plumped down next to Leigh. With that old, warm smile, she inquired how Nan and Janey Igawa were adjusting to Leigh's teaching full time in the inner city.

"They've been terrific," Leigh replied. "They got used to my being gone when I was at UCLA earning my credentials. How are Dylan, Buffy and Mick?"

Beaming, Ruth Abby produced Polaroids of the three children taken outside the sprawling Beverly Hills bungalow that the Marxes had recently bought. "The price of the house blew my mind, Leigh, but it's worth it for the schools."

Leigh, shuffling through the stack of photographs, couldn't quite repress her smile. Ruth Abby—*the* rebel of them all—touting the advantages of a Beverly Hills education!

Larry, who had cut his crisp, receding brown hair and gained thirty pounds since Mr. Marx's death, rambled on to Ken about cabinet designs for a tract in Orange County. "What's on your horizon?" he asked.

"Minding the girls, the cooking, the usual house-husband stuff," Ken said. At Larry's horrified expression, he added, "I've been reading scripts and books."

"With luck you'll uncover another *High Sixty,*" Larry said.

High Sixty, York's elliptically abrasive reminiscence of a decade, had received three glowing reviews and sold a few hundred copies before CBS had launched a comedy series based on it: in seven years the paperback had sold four million copies and the show had never slipped below tenth in the Nielsen ratings. The numerous times that the Igawas had visited York in his bungalow at La Jolla Park (the doctors there agreed he would never again function on the outside) he had not once mentioned *High Sixty.*

Leigh heard Larry's remark. "Ken makes films, not sit-coms," she said loudly—for her.

"What my wife means is I'm the commercial kiss of death. Larry, you know how my work's shown. At midnight in art houses."

"People respect—" Leigh started.

"Hello there, everybody," said Michele Cromie. Radiant in black, fresh from a discreet eye-job, she pushed by them into the seat next to Larry's. They were engulfed in waves of Halston perfume. She had not seen the Marxes in over a year and had to explain she was separated from Dave Cromie. "But Everett's coming today. Clay and him got to be such good friends." She curved her manicured little hand above her mouth, hissing to Leigh, "Poor Everett. You can't imagine how he's taken this thing with Lissa and Bobby! He's a wreck, an absolute wreck over it. Her first year at Stanford and she moves in with her boy friend! That's their new morality for you!"

Again Leigh had to repress a smile.

Dorot McHenry-Mosgrove emerged from the door to the left of the stage. Dorot had a tense glitter to her brown eyes, as though the years had increased her thyroid function, but otherwise she was far handsomer than she had been in the sixties: her long brown hair was blonde streaked and curled at the ends, her tinted glasses smartly framed, and cream silk set off her slenderness. Five years ago, during Marshall's first campaign, Dorot had admitted to a lesbian affair, and oddly enough this had helped rather than hindered him, her open frankness blowing the cobwebs from his conservatism. He had won a Congressional district seat.

After the greetings, Michele cried, "What an adorable outfit. Bill Blass?"

Dorot agreed it was. "The externals have a function for me. I push the ERA at gatherings where the IQ percentile is too low to grasp the issues. An attractive feminine image does the trick."

Michele wasn't listening. "There's Lissa," she cried; raising up on her toes. *"Lissa!"*

They all turned. The tall blonde with Michele's charming mouth and Clay's brooding eyes pushed through the crowded aisle toward them, and each was gripped by the realization that this stunning young woman belonged to the generation after theirs. As Michele introduced them they heard themselves babbling questions about Stanford. Lissa replied with grace, asking Dorot, "Isn't Representative Mosgrove here?"

"He's backstage," Dorot explained. "He's on the program."

"Is it true what they say, Dorot?" Ruth Abby blurted. "If Baron York finally gets the Republican nomination, Marshall will be vice president?"

"Baron depends on him too much. I can't imagine Marshall will be wasted on the vice presidency."

Her remark awed them.

The mustard-colored velvet curtains were rustling apart and they sat back.

There were eulogies by RG Richards, Dr. Schramm, the retired principal, and Odessa Norris, whose dark eyes glowed sadly. It was Marshall, though, speaking as president of California High, 1960, who got the biggest ovation.

He stood to the right of a vast blow-up of Clay's bearded face, talking without benefit of microphone, letting his politician's earnestness be carried by the faulty acoustics. He spoke of Clay's altruism, of his accomplishments, and he said, "Clay, like my fellow alumni, like myself, was part of the sixties. No. We *were* the sixties. Nowadays people mention our decade with a condescending smile. Flower children, they call us, or rabble rousers. But I have never understood the putdown. Didn't we challenge with our hearts and lives the laws that kept the races apart? Didn't we take into our own inexperienced young hands the ending of a wrongful, undeclared war? My best friend, Stryker Halvorsen, California High sixty-one, gave his life in that war." Marshall's voice momentarily faltered. "Weren't we the first to fully accept that women have the same inalienable rights as men?" He bent a measured smile at Dorot. "I say this in all humility as the husband of Doctor Dorothy McHenry-Mosgrove." He raised his head. "Didn't we put an end to the old sexual hypocrisies? Men and women need no longer submerge their sexual natures and live in fear of the police or jail. I freely admit that we didn't accomplish all that we set out to do. But this I say to you. Our failure is no discredit to us. We reached too high, we aimed too far. Our failure was the great and honorable one of trying to leave this earth better than we found it."

The crowded auditorium was utterly his.

He drew a visible, audible breath and took a step forward. "Each one of us here today has something in common with Clay Gillies. We go forth from a part of the world that looks to the future, never the past. We are the forerunners, we are the bringers of fresh ideas, we are the seekers, the triers, the doers, the movers. We are the crest of the wave. We are the California generation."

There was a moment of silence as strobes washed Clay's huge, photographed face, and then the pent-up applause broke, an avalanche of sound.

Leigh was weeping. She had barely heard Marshall's rhetoric, for she was saying goodbye to Clay as she had not let herself on the cruel April morning of his funeral. Goodbye, friend, goodbye, you walked in the paths of righteousness and now you are no more. . . . Goodbye. Wiping her eyes, sniffling the pungent, warm air, she found herself bidding farewell to all of them as they had been when these buildings were temporarily theirs, to Ruth Abby, singer of sweet, mindless song, to Michele, proudly imprinting her new initials on every available surface, to York's sourly protective sarcasm, to all of us, she thought, farewell, for haven't we departed as surely as Clay and Stryker? Only an infinitesimal fragment of what we once were survives, buried deep like a healed splinter in our conforming, mortal flesh.

"Hey Leigh, don't," Ken said, clasping her upper arm. "You

know Marshall always was full of it."

Yet Leigh saw that Ken, like everyone else, was rising to his feet. The single note striking the hour in the mission bell-tower went unheard in the stamping and clapping.